MY HEART GROWS WIDE WITHIN ME

The Story of Anah and Standing Cloud

A.K. Baumgard

MY HEART GROWS WIDE WITHIN ME
Copyright © 2024 by A.K. Baumgard

ISBN: 979-8895310809 (sc)
ISBN: 979-8895311141 (hc)
ISBN: 979-8895310816 (e)

All rights reserved. No part of this publication may be reproduced, distributed, or transmitted in any form or by any means, including photocopying, recording, or other electronic or mechanical methods, without the prior written permission of the publisher and/or the author, except in the case of brief quotations embodied in critical reviews and other noncommercial uses permitted by copyright law.

The views expressed in this book are solely those of the author and do not necessarily reflect the views of the publisher, and the publisher hereby disclaims any responsibility for them.

Writers' Branding
(877) 608-6550
www.writersbranding.com
media@writersbranding.com

Contents

Prologue xvii

I. The Great Mystery 1

    The Cottonwood Boy 2
    The Cornfield............................. 4
    Hanbleceya Time 7
    The Fourth Day 16
    The Council of The Elders 21
    The Wisdom of Spotted Owl 27
    A Small Medicine Bundle 29
    Four Scalp Locks 31
    A Mirror................................. 33
    The Mystery............................. 37
    St. Francis.............................. 40
    He Came For Her 44
    All The Pretty Horses 46
    Death Moccasins 52
    Raison D'etre 56
    Ghost Buffalo 61
    Billy Blue Eyes 65
    Swift Medicine's Story................... 69
    The Summons/Hanbleceyiya 76
    The Beaver Pond......................... 80
    His New Life 83
    Once He Prided Himself as a Great Diagnostician 85
    Horsemen of the Plains................... 88
    Circle Camp- Part II..................... 97
    Pale Calf Woman 104

II. The Widening Gyre................................108
    Destiny Manifested..................................109
    What The Years Had Wrought.....................110
    William's new boots.................................113
    The Buffalo Skull....................................115
    Waagol the Mule.....................................118
    The Spirit Dog.......................................119
    About Turn Foot the Scout........................121
    Thieves Road...123
    Nothing Lives Long..................................133
    Swift Medicine's Words To His Son..............137

III. Tout Passe, Tout Lasse Everything passes, nothing lasts................................141
    The Beginning of The Loss........................142
    Coming To, The Rape..............................144
    Those Heartless Angels............................146
    The Starry Ladder..................................149
    Coming Out of the Coma..........................150
    Darkness Ascending................................151
    The Awful News....................................157
    Laudanum Consolations...........................160
    The Cheyenne Doll.................................162
    Their Last Dance....................................163
    Attempted Revenge.................................165
    Getting Drunk.......................................172
    The Burial Scaffold.................................176
    Whirlwind Power...................................180
    Dreaming of Reburial..............................184
    Confronting Loneliness.............................187
    The Response.......................................189
    Bad Medicine?......................................190
    Digging Up The Dead..............................194

Yellow Bird 196
Running Away From Home 199
What Was Left Behind 201
Leaving 203
Why Is He In Prison? 205
Pinch of Dust, Tatanka Iyotanka's Reply 208
A New Frontier-Another Journey 210
Pickings from the Plains 213
To Winter Camp 215
Nahtona 218
The Coffee Ceremony 225
Turn Foot's Defection 226
Braids 230
Towards Winter Canyon 233
Cimarron Canyon 236
The Protective Shell 238
The Turning Season 241
The Story of Big Crow, Leavetaking 246
Arrival at Ft. Sill 251

IV. Capture 254

Gold From the Grass Roots Down 255
What Happened at Sappa River 260
The Five-Fingered Glove 265
The Ice House at Medicine Bluffs 267
Death of a Dog Man 270
Heartbeat of Darkness 274
His Shackles Fell To The Earth 282
Take, Eat! 284
Red Dancing Crane Woman 288
On The Train To Ft. Marion 295
Coup de Foudre 303
Hanblecheyabi, A Lament 310
Anah Helps 316

Basket of Aloes 319
Demon Rum. 323
Miss Mathers' Dentures 329
Pericardium 332
The Wild Calls Her 339

V. Ties That Mingled, Bind .341

Gullah Land. 342
Cloud's Awakening. 351
Welcome To Another World 360
Missing Her Commonplace Book 364
What Is Sacred? 367
What of My People? 370
To Provide and Protect 374
The Journey Into Exile 379
It Is Good – The Sorrel Mare 382
The Dig 386
A Wagon load of Dead Kiowas 388
The Fruits of Intimacy 395
The Dinner Party 397
The Recent Calamity 398
Custer's Ears 400
Kate Big Head 403
Murder of Crows. 405
A Warrior's Glyph. 407
The Bow In the Cloud 409
Burning Beauty. 410
Foreboding. 413
Chankpe Opi Wakpala Creek. 416
My Last Buffalo 420
Forty Miles To Freedom 424
Towards An Understanding 428
A Captive Returns. 431
A Woman of the Whites 435

Back There Is a Past 438

VI. Heading Back 444

Nestaevahosevoomatse 445
Matches Translates 447
The Package 450
Repatriation 452
The Ring 454
Toddler. 456
Traveling West, Thinking East 458
One Step Short of a Ceremony 460
Her First Vision 464
Overwhelming Dream 467
Kit Rabbit in the Fox's Den. .470
Sitting Bull's Red Blanket 474
Hope For Hanblecheyabi 479
The Limitless Possibilities of Silence 492
Bluebirds. 494
Quaker Kindness 497
Unshod the Mule 500
Willamette Valley 502
Chestnut Street 505
The Madman's Flea. 507
For My Son. 509
He Arrives. 512
A Breaking Dam. 515
Red Thunder Arrives 518
O'xeve'ho'e , Half-Breed 522
The International Money Order 525
Pretty Feet's Deception 528
Felicitous House 537

VII. Destiny Manifests........541

    Saiciye, The Power of Personal Adornment 542
    Saiciye, Part II............................547
    Heading Northwest......................552
    Upsetting News 557
    The Chinese Shawl 562
    At The Captain's Table 565
    The Drums 567
    Real Good Coffee 569
    Some Picnic 573
    The Old Trappers Cabin...............577
    Patience Hopes 579
    Mitakuye Oyasin, We are All Related 582
    The Palouse 585
    A Gift Returned 592
    The Old Scout 594
    A Warrior Returns 597
    The Dog Soldier and The Lady In Green 600
    My Heart Grows Wide Within Me 603

Epilogue 607
Author's Note 609
About the Author 613

Mitakuye Oyasin

We Are All Related

Tunkasila oyate nipi kta ca, le camu

That the nation will live, I pray!

" If I were an Indian, I often think I would
greatly prefer to cast my lot among
those of my people adhered to the free
open plains rather than submit
to the confined limits of a reservation, there to be the recipient
of the blessed benefits of civilization, with its vices thrown in
without stint or measure."

General George Armstrong Custer
MY LIFE ON THE PLAINS

"Storytelling; to utter and to hear... And the simple act of listening is crucial to the concept of language, more crucial even than reading and writing, and language in turn is crucial to human society. There is proof of that, I think, in all histories and prehistories of human experience."

House Made Of Dawn
M. Scott Momaday

Prologue

Ms. Orianna Illaria Stands Free PhD.

"*Nestaevahosevoomatse*", that one word seemed to burn into her as she unfolded the paper from the glassine envelope in her briefcase to place carefully on the lectern. Scrawled on yellowed foolscap dated 1878, it was barely legible now, but it gave her all the strength she felt that she would need to embark on this new path as she waited for Professor Bancroft to finish his lengthy introduction to the large audience awaiting her.

Accustomed as she was to lecturing and its attendant rigors, this presentation was a departure from her usual seminars and close-knit circles of colleagues and peers. Now she was here not as an academician, but as a writer. The faces before her were not here to learn, but to ..what, be entertained? This was all new to her.

She began to struggle then cast her eyes down to the exceedingly long Cheyenne word laid there. Her right hand went to the old German silver armband she wore as a talisman. Her lips moved in a near silent incantation.

Easing the high heels from her feet she bent to her briefcase and extracted a worn leather-bound journal of the type used in the 19th century as ledgers. She had worked so hard to gain credibility in academia, and now she would call upon another source; the blood of storytellers that ran in her veins.

"I began my sabbatical year with the intention of gathering further documentation regarding Porcupine Bear of the Cheyenne's pleas for abstinence from alcohol, as it was called in the 19th century, among various leaders, especially James Beckwourth, a mulatto trader. To that end I made plans to travel with my mother to visit relatives on tribal lands in Northern Montana. There are many stories involved in telling how I decided to abandon my research, but tonight you are here because of this."

Holding the book briefly aloft above her head she was unaware of the striking figure she struck, almost six feet tall, barefoot behind the podium, dark hair to her waist. Energized now, she was warming to her task; her audience!

"For those of you who know me professionally, I must inform you that this is a departure from my usual methods of scientific research. Though a novel, it is a fictionalized account based on the Commonplace Books of my great-great- grandmother, who lived and taught among the Northern Cheyenne in the 19th century.

The excerpt I will read for you tonight took place at Ft. Marion, St. Augustine, Fl. in 1875 where over seventy of the Plains Indians deemed hostile were held prisoner at the end of The Red River Wars. Anah Hoffman Moore is a young woman who recently lost both her child and husband out west and is now working as an interpreter at the fort."

She paused to adjust the glasses on her high-bridged nose, push her long dark hair back behind her ears. This felt so different from lecturing. She looked out into the darkness. This time she wasn't here just to impart knowledge.

"I had no idea I could write a novel; or that I would want to. Ft. Marion in St. Augustine is where my own roots in a sense began..." She began to feel herself at a loss for words, and picked up the book to read.

The Mighty Wren, *Ve'keseheso*

Fort Marion 1875

One sultry evening the Indian prisoners were confined to the fort for reasons as yet unexplained; urgent dispatches had been received from posts out West; rumors abounded. Any attempts on Anah's part to obtain information had been severely rebuffed: the atmosphere was most grim. Many of the women were seen openly weeping, and the officers were avoiding any interaction with the prisoners. Matches, who had an uncharacteristic boldness about him in dealing with these matters had drawn a small group of fellow inmates to him around a small fire and had summoned her to join them. All were somewhat withdrawn and quiet when she arrived. They were, of course, hoping that she had some news to bear upon the situation, but she had no adequate explanation.

Shortly after their incarceration in the summer of last year Lt. Pratt had made classes in English available to all those Indians that desired to learn, and Matches had been one. Tonight he asked her for a story. After she had settled herself and began to think of one that could lighten the somewhat oppressive atmosphere he simply said, "Do not tell us what you read, what you have been told, tell us what you have happened." This was a bit confusing to her. "You mean you want me to tell you a story, to make one up? Is that what you want? Not one from a book?" "No!" was his simple response, which was not much help. She was stumped, but the Indian way was one of patience so she took some time to think this through. "Do you want me to tell you something that really happened?" At this Matches' dark thin face widened into a broad, satisfied smile and he settled down expectantly. Anah, still searching for his exact meaning, pointed to herself and plodded on.

"A story about myself?" Matches nodded, saying in English, "Almost". Anah knew that this was all he was going to say. She looked around at the waiting, expectant faces so eager for distraction, and began.

"This is a story of an extraordinary thing. It was in the time of the first snowfall of the year when a young lieutenant, William Moore by name, leading his men, horse soldiers, in a cavalry charge, were closing in on the last line of defense of Cheyenne warriors down in a canyon out on the Llano Estacado, when the belly band on William's horse gave out and sent him plunging to the ground. When he scrambled to his feet and regained his mount, both unhurt, the charge was far ahead of him. He had to quirt his mount to try and catch up as it would not do to seem a laggard; it could look cowardly!"

This brought a resounding chorus of *ahos* and *hous* from her audience! Now Anah so wished that Mr. Fox, the interpreter for the Comanche were here, for he was most familiar with army terminology and Indian sign, but he had been in various parleys with the officers all day. So she would have to "soldier on" as the saying went. Commandeering Matches to her side she began asking him to interpret directly, as best he could, as she could no longer rely on her limited knowledge of their language for military terms. " We, the Army that is, think that the Cheyenne are the finest horsemen that have ever been seen." That of course met with dignified approval. She continued, "Most of you men learned to ride as soon as you could walk, while many of our soldiers never sat upon the back of a horse before they came out West." She knew to pause here till the comments died down. Finally she raised her hand, and was a bit surprised at how quickly quiet was restored.

"You," and with a wide sweeping gesture she included them all, "were almost born on the back of a horse," she went quickly on, "most rode on one in a cradle board before you could even crawl,".... She had her audience all right! But the older Comanche horse thief eyed her suspiciously from out of his blanket...."Yes, Mighty Horse Warriors of the Plains...but this soldier who had fallen from his horse was one who also had been born to ride; back East of the Big Muddy," and turning to Matches and speaking to him in English she said, "You must help me here, my friend. There is a school that trains men to be soldiers, and lead, and ride very, very well. They grow up riding the very best horses. This school is called West Point!"

Anah was at a loss to convey how the young lieutenant, fresh out of the Academy needed to save face at finding himself dismounted. How he quickly righted himself, dusted off his uniform, buffed his brass buttons, remounted and furiously raced down the canyon. Saber held aloft in one hand for full effect while whipping his mount with the other......, and for this she leaned in to Matches for a quick consultation.... pantomiming hands to her face, dropping them to the ground, then picking them up, "Saving face", saving face," she said, and William, who was a bit over six foot now stood in his stirrups. "Stirrups" she said, pointing to her foot,.. telling them also that this soldier was tall, lean, blond, noble. Oh, what was that word? Damnable English.....

Finally, a light went on in Matches eyes, his eyebrows rose up in his elegant long face, and with his hands he signaled her to wait..then he turned to the expectant crowd and in an exciting and rapid delivery he painted the picture of the lone lieutenant's dashing cavalry charge up the arroyo; hooves flashing, saber rattling....

Anah noticed that there was nothing quite like an exploit of war to keep a man's attention; all eyes were now on Matches; even that Comanche horse thief, Poppadom, seemed interested now. She entered the fray herself at this point, standing to translate once again: "As he rounded the corner of the canyon, up popped before his startled eyes a very young herd boy, right in his path. The boy had somehow escaped the initial charge of the cavalry and was now too stunned to flee. Had he hidden himself, too afraid to face the enemy, and now rose up thinking it was safe? No, it appeared, as the horse and rider continued pounding relentlessly forward, that the boy was fearlessly standing his ground"...this elicited a round of approval from all, except Poppadom, who did not approve of anyone's actions other than his own.

" There was no way that the boy could avoid being trampled now, it seemed, but a very exceptional thing happened, as often such things do at times like this. Did I mention that the herd boy also stood there before the startled soldier with his arrow nocked, aimed at the officer's heart?"

Oh, she had their attention now, and had to admit it was quite enjoyable. Quickly arranging the folds of her skirt to seat herself, indicating a deeper part of the story yet to come, she stole a glance toward the tallest Cheyenne. Yes, he was listening. Good! Lifting one arm in a slow, but elegant gesture she continued, " Just then a small dark object sped swiftly down through the sky to land on the boy's right shoulder." A collective "Aah!" went up from the group. They began to whisper speculative comments amongst themselves; this was getting to be a very good story indeed. She held up a hand to be allowed to continue. Matches, who couldn't quite contain himself, blurted out "Tell us, tell us." Ignoring him, and with the same slow, measured pace, she drew the story out; began to trace a small circle in the air with one finger. " This object, a dark blur of fiery energy, how do you say it... power, medicine..." She was egging them on, and they spoke the words, almost shouting out in their excitement, in their various tongues, the words for the sacred, *waken*..... "...it began to sing!" Rising now she took the liberty of a few small delicate dance steps; she stepped lively! "Actually, to scold this large, handsome, blond soldier, to threaten him with a loud, clear, voice that reverberated from the walls of the narrow canyon like a flute of liquid gold, melodious and clear..." They couldn't contain themselves any longer, even though they were life-long schooled in patience and politeness, for how could this white woman, this *ve'ho'e*, this *wasichu* know this...she was not a witch, no, no, they had seen her true face; she had kindness in her bones...where did she learn this story? They all wanted to shout out like children in school. The desire to give the correct answer, even though there had not been a question, was tantalizing to them. Anah correctly sensed this in the atmosphere and immediately sat down. As if in sympathy with her the firelight dimmed considerably. With a much constrained voice she continued, "Yes, yes, my friends, it was *Ve'keseheso*, Little Bird, the Mighty Wren." They seemed to know this bird of the canyons, which did not surprise her too much, as they were intimately familiar with all their brothers and sisters of the land, water and air, but she was not finished with this exceptional tale.

" Mind you, William the soldier also had his pistol drawn. The boy, his arrow nocked, the space between them closing. Then the bird flew down, but...the well-trained cavalry steed, just like your war ponies, kept charging forward at a terrific pace straight down that narrow canyon at the small boy...." Again she paused, again Matches-the-Bold, she thought of him after this night, for he actually reached out to tug on her skirt to continue. "When this Bluecoat was but a child, as we all must be, a small bird had fallen from its nest at his feet, he had put it in his pocket before the family cat could kill it, and kept it alive in an old shoe, where he kept it hidden in his closet till it could fly away. So when the *Ve'keseheso* sang, this is what happened that day in the narrow confines of the winter-locked canyon..."*Courage is never small*," the little brown wren sang out, and as she did so an indescribable color rose up, a molten gold, a burning gold, the color William was sure that a knight's armor was forged from, but sheer, and flowing, filling the entire canyon, through which he could see the boy standing absolutely unafraid as the horse charged ahead, and yet time seemed suspended. The wren sang this over and over, the notes rising in a pure lilt that filled his head, it seemed he could not quite get enough, then she flew to the boys' other shoulder, flicked her tail and said, "*You were once young.*" Now even the guards moved in closer to the fire to warm their hands, for the night seemed to have a chill. They all had just the briefest thought of their mothers. Anah continued, "William saw himself kneeling over a baby bird to feed it; there was a hole in his old left shoe that was a hand-me-down from his oldest brother, for he came from a poor family and was the youngest. The wren now flew to the boy's head and whirled in a circle, rapidly, before she shot straight up warbling, "*With dreams yet undone!*" He remembered his childhood dream, wanting more than anything to someday be called "Captain", and he knew what to do as his ears thrilled with her song. A protective gold colored shield, like the luminous lights that fall down from the winter skies in the Far North now flowed around the boy with motes of golden sun sobering through it. Time had hung suspended but now it suddenly began to fall." Anah sprang to her feet to continue, "Dirt clods were being rudely flung from the horse's hooves; what exploded in the lieutenant's mind then was something he had seen on the battlefield as practiced by the enemy, those mighty Horse Warriors of the high plains. He had so admired it when he had first seen it. He barely thought the act possible if he had not seen it with his own eyes! Today he knew he could do it. The wren had told him so! Bearing down on the defenseless child he simply reached out and scooped him up. He realized that undoubtedly the boy had a very good knife with which he could harm him, or at least slash his horse's jugular, bring them crashing to the ground at any second as they thundered forward almost neck and neck with the rest of the cavalry charge. He leaned down and shouted into the boy's ear where he had him pressed to his chest, hoping that he could hear and understand him against the thundering sound of the hooves, saying one of the few Indian words he knew, "*Kola,*" friend, and just as soon as they broke free of the enclosing arms of the canyon the lieutenant threw the boy into a bank of snow. He then lifted his saber to flash out in a salute. When I first heard this story and asked him why he rescued the Indian boy all he told me was that the boy was too young to die. Later he told me all the details of the intervention," and here she turned to Matches, making sure that he understood this word in particular, of the little bird, *Ve'keseheso, wyakin,* the boy's spirit guardian.

———

A few days later when Matches asked her how she came by this story Anah told him that William was her deceased husband. Did he understand the language of the birds, Matches asked her? That took her back at first; she was reluctant to explain how she had elaborated on what was essentially an honest experience. She satisfied herself with the privileges allotted a storyteller to elaborate on certain incidents to entertain and captivate. "Matches, my friend, he did not speak their language, but I understood the lieutenant!" More than satisfied with her response he hurried off to tell the others, especially his kola, Cloud. While the others had given Mrs. Moore, whom they fondly referred to as The Sweet Grass Woman, an accolade of handclaps that evening, something of white-man's ways they had found pleasing to imitate, all the disgraced Dog Soldier, Cloud would comment on for the fine tale to Matches was, "She doesn't think like a white-man!"

Closing the ledger the professor responded, "I'll answer one last question. As to the spellings of the various tribes and sub-tribes, well with no written languages themselves at that time...". Hands continued to shoot up in the audience. Her head hurt with trying to not respond in an academic manner, yet she had broached the personal, had she not? Removing her glasses, she placed them down on the podium; a universal signal that she was finished. Quickly gathering up her notes, she hoped to bypass those curious few intrigued or bold enough to accost her after the general question period was formally closed. Usually male, they were attracted by the resemblance to her dust jacket photo, seemingly undaunted by her cool demeanor, perhaps challenged by it. In truth, she was not really aloof, just oddly shy, carefully retiring.

As she hurried to gain the stairs that led backstage one man approached her querying as to her unusual name. "Oriannna Illaria, I could see where you might think that," she responded, "but, no, I'm not Italian." He persisted. "My surname, Stands Free, well, its a family name, a long story'" Relenting, more in response to a certain easy charm, she had paused, but then noticed him fumbling in his jacket, and thinking perhaps that he was a reporter, she threw back her waist length hair and gave out the only answer she ever gave as to that name, "My maternal great grandmother was Anah Hoffman Moore Standing Cloud of the Northern Cheyenne of Spotted Horse Creek Canyon. I don't give personal interviews," and hurried out.

I

The Great Mystery

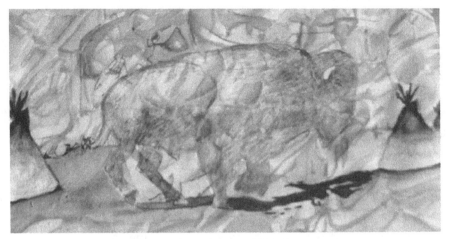

"The Ghost Buffalo"

The Cottonwood Boy

High Plains, 1851

On a sturdy branch of the old cottonwood, too high for any beast to reach, hung a fine cradle board. An elaborately quilled Morning Star design revealed it's Northern Cheyenne origins. Almost completely concealed by the thick leaves a small black-capped head peered out. Raised from birth not to omit even the least sound when danger was assessed the infant was occupied with watching a large glossy black bird that had landed on a nearby branch. All was quiet in this narrow defile where the morning's mist was just beginning to lift. A piercing ray from the sun highlighted the brightly beaded snake amulet that contained the child's birth cord. This is what had attracted the crow's attention. The baby boy solemnly watched the bird's hopping approach with fascination; that is, until it began to tug on the amulet's cord. At that the child's dark eye's glistened with a fearsome awe.

Not a bird called: the little gully lined with golden aspen and cottonwood trees was tensely still. Even the leaves appeared stunned into grim silence in the early morning cold. The only sound now came from the trill of a creek as a small band of horsemen cautiously approached, for this was the scene of a recent massacre. A cook fire still smoldered; there was the unmistakable coppery smell of blood. Unavoidable clatter of the war party mount's hooves as they carefully picked a way through the destruction alerted the crow, who glided off, abandoning the glittering object dangling from the cradle board.

"*Kangi,*" Crow! White Ferret, the lead warrior signaled to the others to halt. Bowstrings now drawn, for something untoward had drawn the keen eyes of their leader, ever on the alert, especially now, for the smallest sign of life. Dispirited all, for their raid had been unsuccessful; not only did He Who Leans lie sprawled across the back of his horse, but two others were still missing, and they were returning with no new ponies for their herd. If it had not been for the anxious eyes of White Ferret the child would not have been spotted.

Many stories were to elaborate on the significance of White Ferret's simple warning, *Kangi!*, but truly it was just the glitter of hovering tears in a hungry infant's eyes as he saw his kind again approaching. Glitter!

As strong arms reached up for the little Cottonwood Boy, for that is what they named him, *Wagachun*, for the noise the leaves make as they twist and turn on their pedicel, he let out a mighty wail.

Brought back to their encampment to be raised among the Tsitsistas, the Beautiful People, as the Northern Cheyenne were known, his origins were not quite a mystery, but much of his birth circumstances would never be known, as none of the small band in that defile where he had been found had lived through what must have been a surprise attack on their small encampment.

He had been thrust high up in the tree as a desperate act of love and hope for his survival. A Brule pipe bag was found tucked in with him along with that little amulet that contained his birth cord. In a cleverly stitched doeskin bag, clean and carefully folded, was a small white square of material, too small to be worn around one's neck and too thin to serve some other purpose. It had been elaborately embroidered with what was thought to be a letter sign of the *ve'ho'e's* possession. Much about his origins were to remain a mystery, but he was considered blessed by his adoptive tribe.

Long before he reached the age to quest for a vision he had developed a special affinity for the *Kangi*, the crow people and all their relations, especially the lovely magpies, which, of course were never far from the cottonwoods. He loved to imitate their grating calls, which to him were pleasing. He was often found in rapt attendance to their chattering discourse, seated by the banks of the creeks where the cottonwoods grew, content in their company for hours on end, eschewing the company of children his own age.

The Cornfield

Western Pennsylvania, 1851

"Thwang!" Wonderful, dry lush sound erupted from the summer grasses as she slashed through, speeding as fast as her small legs could carry her up the farm house path that led to the cornfield. "Watch out for the snakes!" She knows that she is not allowed to pause and watch that black gleaming body at rest in the sun. She'd like to give it a prod with her stick, and see what it does. She bets that it can move very fast. "He's sleek," she thinks.

    Loud, angry growls and waspish, whimpering noises are being made by her parents. She's rarely noticed when they argue, and just now the air was getting harder to breathe. She had been playing quietly, crouched under the piano, well-hidden by the Spanish shawl draped over it. No one else was around and since the grown-ups were deeply occupied she was able to escape unnoticed outdoors.

It smelled wonderful out here; like good dirt. Pale butterflies, red winged blackbirds and sparkling yellow headed dandelions here and there, but the real draw was the cornfield. Entering it was to come to a different world. A slight spin and the dark green stalks closed rank like soldiers; she knew how they stood straight and tall in formation. Turning just a bit, carefully, and then stepping back to reveal a plowed earth path, straight as an arrow, all the way back to the farm house where she didn't want to be right now. She sat down, cross legged, adjusted the fine cotton skirt of her smocked dress, then laid her stick carefully down.

Her Uncle Alex had told her when she had been brought here, that if you were very quiet, you could hear the corn grow. He was the one who helped her adjust to being away from her real home. She liked the farm, or rather, the animals. So now she waited, ears open, little heart straining for this new experience, toes a-wiggle in the dirt as fine and dry as the French talc her mother used after bathing.

Crouched down, the sun made a fluffy nimbus of the white blond plaits that encircled her crown. (She looked like a giant dandelion out here in the trackless corn.) Her heart slowed its effort and she relaxed. From her pinafore pocket she removed an embroidered handkerchief to arrange her small collection of white quartz "lucky" stones upon; three of them. Content now, she awaited the storm's approach, for she had smelled the coming rain. The sky above was still a depthless blue, silent, almost cloudless, just a few mare's tails drifting high above. But slowly gaining a delicious momentum came the signals; a coolness rising from the ground, like a hidden stream surfacing to begin flowing. The solid wall of green corn stalks enclosing her began to stir and rustle, murmuring. Pale tassels, the color of her own hair, on the unripe cobs swayed in a gentle dance. Excitement ran on her limbs, and a staccato chirring of swallows, shiny purple and amber bodies flashing in tight formation above her. Then came what her ears had been straining towards, a not so distant rumble high above.

Now it all happened quickly. Cicadas started up only to fall silent in an instant, small birds flitted here and there, and odd bits of green flashed past. A deep purple thundercloud rolled over the open sky above, darkening her world, just as a flock of crows sped overhead, seeking shelter in the nearby oaks. Lightning cracked it all open around her, wind sprang up violently, dividing the corn in rows, furrows dark and beginning to gleam wetly with the first down pelting of the rain. Fascinated by the impressions of these first drops as they spattered little bowls into the talcum soft dirt, she startled when a large black bird touched down just a few feet away.

"Oh, crow," she said delightedly under her breath, before she settled her movements and squeezed her eyes almost shut. And for an eternal second they both froze suspended in each others world! She could hear him hopping closer, and dared to open her eyes just the barest slit. So glossy black and beautiful. Forged forever in her young mind was all the simple wild beauty that had dropped effortlessly at her feet. Anah had allowed herself an attachment to a brooding hen in the chicken coop who had allowed the child easy access to her nest, to slide her tiny hand under the feathered warmth to pluck an egg, but this, this wild creature! Forget Aunt Mima's Rhode Island Reds. "I want him," she thought, and held her breath excitedly. "Don't look, don't look," she kept telling herself as the thunder rolled and the lightning crashed, bringing the full fury of the storm ever closer. "I'll grab his legs and wrap him in my pinafore," she thought, heart beating madly as the bird hopped warily closer. She wasn't the least bit afraid that he'd pluck her eyes out, as she had once been warned. Then with a rush and a flick of black feathers clacking, up, up. He was in the air. Too late she had noticed that one of her lucky stones was gone! He'd taken it. Springing to feet, "Thief!" was on her lips. Oh, she knew that word, but she felt elated, and plumped back down, laughing. "He's taken my gift, and I know just what to bring him next. One of Daddies golden stick pins." The soaking rain pelted down on her and she let it, as long as she could stand it! To her, a warm summer blessing!

Hanbleceya Time

circa 1863

As the boldfaced sun rode on its downward course towards the wide rolling plains, towering white clouds amassed on the horizon giving off a golden radiance from their high rounded edges. A lone figure rose solemnly from where he was watched in the lush grasses of the late spring, arms lifted towards the magnificence above. Silver Spotted Owl moved his pipe in the six traditional directions. Drawing the rich smoke into his old lungs he then let out a small sound of satisfaction. The turning of the seasons and the phase of the moon had finally come to a place for a young man to take his first steps on the path to an understanding of his place in the unseen, all encompassing world of the spirit.

    The time had come for Wagachun, The Cottonwood Boy, to seek and receive a vision to guide him on life's path. All the wisdom of Spotted Owl's many, many years had been focused on imparting to this one found helpless in his cradle board the wealth the unseen world had in store for him. Twelve winters had passed at the holy man's knee; now the time had come for him to be taught directly by the Great Mystery, the Everywhere Spirit, *Wakan Tanka.* Time for this *wicasa wakan* and the boy to travel to Maho Paha, Bear Mountain, the Giving Hill as the Cheyenne called it. Of what protective spirit, what power would be revealed in the four days of prayer and fasting Spotted Owl had little concern, for when Wagachun came down from the mountain's height he would have confronted a manifestation of that power, the unexplainable. Perhaps he would even be blessed by *Wakanya Wowanyanke,* The Great Vision. He would come not only to Spotted Owl for interpretation, but also seek the wisdom of the holy men, Red Feather and He Falls Down. The counsel of more than one was advised for this great undertaking; the boy's first search for a vision, power and guidance.

    Back at camp Spotted Owl set in motion all those things that must be done for the *Inipi* , the purification ceremony. The holy man's thoughts traveled back to the time when The Cottonwood Boy had first come to his attention. A small raiding party of seasoned warriors were returning from a failed strike at a marauding Pawnee band. The enemy had been driven off but no coups counted, no scalp lifted. Only the scant blood spilled from insignificant wounds, all that would be borne back to their lodges; a simple tale of the enemy routed told in a counsel gathering. Already dispirited from the failed raid when they came upon a small abandoned camp, the coals in the fire pit yet smoking. Disaster had been a visitor here also. White Ferret, the young warrior noted for his keen eyesight, discerned the slight movement high on a thickly leafed branch in the cottonwoods. There, snug in a cradle board of a Cheyenne design was a silent but woefully hungry infant. The infant was brought carefully back to camp and given to Grey Lost Bird to nurse and mother; finding him was a good omen. This boy, now at home in White Ferret's lodge, answered to Wagachun, the child of the cottonwoods, so named for the rustling sound of the tree's leaves.

One fine morning, barely first light, newly able to walk on his sturdy legs, he appeared in the doorway of Spotted Owl's lodge. Back lit by the rising sun his small form yet so dim that The Owl thought perhaps the little figure in the entrance was an apparition, one of the Little People. Of course, Spotted Owl bade welcome and the child walked resolutely all the way to the holy man, who was still in his sleeping robe. Not wanting to miss an opportunity, Spotted Owl stretched forth his gnarled hand to test the reality of the form before him. The child thrust forth his own small firm hand and with a giggle bit down lightly on a finger. "Hau", exclaimed the old man, intuiting that no offense was meant, sat swiftly up in his bedding. "My taste pleases you, not much meat left on these bones! At which the child plunked contentedly down, fixing his large, black eyes upon him. "You have come to learn?" he again addressed the seated child. Another small laugh was affirmation.

On that day this wise man, once a child himself, of a Cheyenne father and a Brule mother, became The Cottonwood Boy's beloved teacher, and Second Father. Spotted Owl understood the significance of the child bringing himself to sit at wisdom's foot, and he thus spared no effort to educate him.

Spotted Owl was sure that the foundling was of Cheyenne heritage.

Elaborately quilled and beaded cradle boards were not just handed out. There was further evidence in the beaded snake effigy that surely contained his birth cord, and which Wagachun wore now upon his person. Even before gaining his full manhood the boy stood half a head taller than most of the Lakota youths his age. There was the mystifying thin white cotton square cleverly worked with colored threads to represent flowers; this was a *ve'ho'e's* adornment. It had been securely tucked into his wrappings. At first all thought he was of intermingled blood, but his skin glowed copper, cheekbones rode high on his narrow face, and his hair grew thick, straight and black. Besides, he took to tracking and hunting skills as only a full blood could do. Spotted Owl was respectful of this assumed parentage. Assured that The Great Mystery looked well upon the boy, the wise old healer strove to see that he spoke the Cheyenne tongue, which differed greatly from the language of this camp, the language shared by the largest tribe on the Northern Plains. He had learned the Lakota at his foster mother's breast.

All too soon Wagachun would be a man. Spotted Owl, in his heart of hearts, prayed that Wagachun would return from the mountain vowing to use his gifts for healing and discernment, not for war.... to be a *pejuta wicasa,* to use the power in the green growing things for healing.

This lanky youth spent much of his time away from the other boys, preferring to go to the river early to bathe on his own. On rare occasions he entered into play, preferring at a very early age the company of four-footed beings. Blacks, bays, pinto's, chestnuts and paints.....all the colors of the wind. Of special interest was the sole gray spotted rump horse brought, at great effort from The Pierced Nose people, *Nimiipuu,* far to the northwest. White Ferret, himself a renowned Horse-catcher, brought the boy early to be with the herd boys, hoping that he would seek to follow in his adopted father's path. Eventually there was not a wild mustang brought into the camp that he could not gentle to the bridle. And he quickly learned the art of training a mount for the pursuit of the buffalo.

Spotted Owl saw that he knew which plants could be used to cure, which fats could be rendered into healing ointments; those for the people, another kind for the four-footed. Though Wagachun preferred the company of the horses he often spent time with those struggling with an illness, recovering from wounding, and those whose strength, hearing and eyesight were failing them. None who had guided him had concern for eventual outcome of the quest. His teacher hoped to make a healer of him, his foster father another skilled horse catcher, his foster mother hoped that he would accumulate enough horses and honors to have the wife of his choice. As for Wagachun he voiced no preference for the Red Road, though he listened avidly to the accounts brought back to each Victory Celebration of the warriors. And he was becoming an accomplished and intuitive marksman with both the bow, the big knife, and even the power stick. Thus Silver Spotted Owl's curiosity hummed like a stirred hornet nest for the outcome of Wagachun's quest, which path he would start on this very evening. Even as he walked out to the quietly grazing pony herd the large stones were growing hot in the fire pit by the sweat lodge.

He had come to bring Wagachun back for his *inipi*. There he was, off by himself, his superior height identifying him from the other lean, bare-chested and breech clouted boys. He let his eyes take full pleasure: a well-formed child, easily he would grow into a man that earned the appellation of handsome. Of the four great things all had to deal with, hunger in winter, defeat in battle, death of a wife, and loss of one's first born while still a child, Wagachun had had no experience. Such is youth! To endure such hard things one needed the four great virtues: to give freely of one's possessions, to show bravery in conflict, to also have fortitude in any hardship, and of course, to honor, by keeping, one's word. A rare smile came to his wrinkled face; The Cottonwood Boy sought knowledge readily, took correction humbly.

The Quest Begins
"An alertness rose in him which held him as no arms ever had"

Wagachun lived in a world where the animating force of all life was The Everywhere Spirit, *Taku Skan skan*. He was raised by example, adequate instruction, and simply by absorbing the stories told at an elder's knee he knew to acknowledge this view. But now was the time for him to actively seek a strong manifestation of what surrounded him, unseen, accountable for his every breath, and to learn of his *Wyakin*, his guardian spirit. To accomplish this he understood that all distractions, responsibilities and the composition of his daily life must be set aside so that this could be accomplished. To this end, a vision of sacred power, he would leave camp with Spotted Owl and travel north to the Giving Hill, Bear Butte. They would leave camp this evening and for four sunrises and sunsets, no food nor water would pass his lips. Oh, he knew what it was to have an empty belly, and he knew thirst, but never before had it been of his own choosing. As to isolating himself for a few days, he looked forward to that. To travel to this sacred place excited him. He did worry that hunger and thirst might come to manifest a hard-to-control need for depending on that which would satisfy. Would this not be a huge distraction?

As they rode out he talked to Spotted Owl about these concerns, and was told to expect a struggle. He was, after all, young and inexperienced in seeking visions. A warrior must first learn to overcome himself before he could conquer an enemy. Yes, hunger and thirst could be thought of as enemies, depending on the circumstances; certainly starvation was. Then with a laugh the Owl told him, "Not even the *ve'ho'e's* could stop the rain from falling!" Food and water, he went on to say, were to be thought of as gifts to all from The Great Mystery.

Riding quietly on, Wagachun thought back to his experience in the eagle pit and how he had been shown that it was not only self-control that would be tested. This time he would not try to accomplish anything without the help and authority of his elders. While he thought of himself as fearless, he also knew that he did not have much measure of his courage, and found himself thinking, Please don't let me have a visitation of The Thunder Beings, *The Waikinyans*. He could not imagine being a *heyoka*, living his life backwards, seated on his horse that way.

Excitement shot through him like the bright, brief stabs of heat lightning in distant thunderclouds. He tried not to envision what his spirit helper would be, barely realizing that his hand was clutching the sole eagle feather he had retained from the eagle pit of years ago.

A small red-headed bird was jerkily moving up the ponderosa pine he was focused on. Aware that this was the late afternoon, Wagachun knew he would have to struggle with a growing disappointment. Suddenly the little bird jumped with a half-opened flash of wings to the north side of the trunk just as the distinct shadow of a hawk circled down. The bird's coloration so blended with the rough bark of the tree that it was almost impossible to discern. Well, my eyesight is sharper today, he thought, but there had been no real significance to his stay up on the butte so far. The first day he had been buoyed along by the very excitement of the quest and what it would mean for him...an entrance into the warrior's world. He had passed that time exploring his surroundings, noting from this high vantage point how he could easily gaze down upon the plain spread below, how the greening land seemed to swell and move at the command of the wind. He felt his senses sharpening, felt the slight cooling of the air on his bare skin as a large cloud drift covered the sun. By late afternoon he could easily smell the distinct signatures of the various plants, especially the sweet aroma of the warmed ponderosa bark. And the sounds, knowing that his safety was secured in this sacred place, that he had no responsibilities guarding the herd, or trailing game, he was free just to let his ears catch the life around him. As the late afternoon wind rose the "quarks" of a soaring pair of ravens below the bluff came to him; just before sunset he heard the calling of a bevy of quail and what sounded like the bark of a dog. He roused himself from this enjoyment...a dog? There should be no dog here! He gave a quick scout down the surrounding slopes below him, satisfied that no such animal prowled he waited expectantly....but the first stars appeared in the descending darkness bringing nothing.

Neither hunger nor thirst assailed him, but with no cooking pot to watch, no fire to tend, no hissing, popping, frying sound, no delicious smells....perhaps there was some hunger. He rose from where he had been sitting on a warm rock slab, now cooling as the night chill came on, glad that he was not in a pit as many Lakota were to experience their time of vision questing. Perhaps a small fire would be good, and he set about seeking tinder.

Had he ever been so mindful of creating a fire? First, gathering just the right tinder, creating a spark, nursing the tiny blossom of flame, and now feeding the small fire. As much as he poked, prodded, dithered and dreamed over this consoling fire, nothing of the spirit world that he could discern came to him. Very slowly though, he began to be present, and stilled his mind to remain in focus. Thus passed the first night.

He woke, stiff and chilled just before a gently breaking dawn, disappointed that he had not remained awake. How many nights had he remained on guard with the horse herd, alert, mindful? But then he could go off to catch some sleep back in the camp.

Was it the lack of responsibility that caused this slackening in his discipline, that there was no one to observe him? When he stretched himself up he saw down at his feet the distinct tracks of a little wolf. So a coyote had come fearlessly to his camp circle. What if that had been his spirit guide and he had slept through it? He longed to question Spotted Owl, or anyone, then found himself beseeching *Wakan Tanka*, The Great Mystery, *Maheo, onshimala ye!*...have pity on me! His desire from earliest childhood had been to heal, not to nurture, tend or raise such as a mother does, he had no example of that, but to heal, then walk away with the satisfaction of knowing that the disruption or illness had been driven out at his behest. He stood now humbled beneath the morning stars, opening his heart, seeking his future, trying to trust in the unveiling, holding back the dispiriting feeling of his own inadequacies. Trying to bolster his confidence he recalled his naming, his good name, Wagachun, after the tree he had been found hanging from, whose leaves rustled at the slightest pass of the air. This tree had long been thought to have a connection to the higher powers, and his naming had been thought to connect him, to make him spiritually sensitive. What he hadn't been told was that this name had also been selected for how each leaf reflects the splendor of the sun, submitting to the cycle of nature as the sun moves away with a glorious burst of golden color. But so far all that had been revealed to him thus far was the strong pull of hunger and thirst, especially thirst. He had gone hungry before and knowing that there was nothing to eat up here made it much easier to forgo the slight pangs he had experienced. But the thirst; upon awakening this morning he found himself intently staring at the luminous rounded drops of dew upon a buffalo berry bush. Reaching out, just the slightest touch, caused those drops to coalesce and roll deliciously down the silver-gray leaf and drip to the dust below, which absorbed them quickly. Could he moisten his mouth, it was so dry? A small shaft of morning light illuminated the bush; had anything ever looked so inviting?

The Third Day
Glad he was to see the sun rise on this his third day. Would today be the day, he thought, lying on his back scanning the sky that was slowly lifting veil after veil of luminous rose colored strips of cloud from the emerging horizon. Small streaks of red shot though the farthest reaches. He had been awake all night, or so he thought; his mind dulled by the effort it had cost him to stay awake. But now he was content just to lie here and gaze into the heavens.

Walking the perimeter of the butte, as he had done each morning, he looked keenly for any sign. The chattering of a small animal in the underbrush spoke not to him, nor, strangely, did the high shrill keening of a hawk. Rumbles of thunder brought his attention to the Southeast where the horizon was darkening with thick thunderheads. With a small sigh he walked swiftly back to his spot and began to gather what he needed for a little wiki-up. The rain when it came had such a gentle persistence that he barely felt wet, yet small drops fell from the ends of his braids. It was a temptation to hold one, just one, over his lips. He calmly watched the bark of the pines darken with absorbed moisture. The air sweetened with fragrance, fresh and invigorating. Soon the prairie below would send up it's blanket of grasses even higher, the herds would fatten, raiding could begin, and the buffalo would come forth once again. We will all be satisfied with this gift of rain. Watching it soak into the earth he thought of how easy the earth accepted such a gentle rain. He left his little shelter to walk out into the wetness, stretching his arms, holding his face up to receive it, daring to stick his tongue out (but not to taste or swallow, just for the delicious feel.) Moving to letting his mouth fill then letting it run out over his chin, falling to his knees in a slight puddle, letting his head hang, receiving each gentle splat like a blessing as much as the land he lived on did,

This then was what the wise men had called *wacantagnaka,* gratefulness, and his heart swelled within him. So overwhelming was this feeling, Is this my vision? Am I prepared? I am, I am, bring it to me he practically shouted at the heavens, his young heart beating in anticipation, tripping away, thundering in his ears like the rapid striking hooves of the fastest pony that he had ever ridden.

Hours later doubt entered into him, swift as an enemy arrow. "How will I know? I have never done this, if only Spotted Owl was here to guide me". He was cold, wet, hungry, and very tired. Worn out with anticipating, struggling to still believe that a protective power spirit would materialize. He ached for a sign. Every oddly twitching blade of grass, each unusually shaped cloud and every call of the mainly silent birds caught his attention. The hours sped by, although to him it seemed as though the sun stood still in the occluded heavens. Surely he was in an unnatural state. In extreme frustration he began to pace the perimeters of his camp, then freed himself to run, to race, as all concern for a "vision" dropped from his tense body. Soon he was mindlessly circling the butte in a measured pace, till pleasantly exhausted he dropped down beside his little wickiup.

Darkness was coming on swiftly now. The brightest stars sparkled in the deepening colors of the sky. Here and there a gleaming arc of a star burning itself out crossed the night above him.

The Fourth Day

Circa 1863 *Noahvose*, Bear Butte

When the sun arrived to begin reclaiming the heavens on this morning of his fourth day Wagachun woke. Pushing aside the disturbing realization that he had fallen asleep, not maintained the vigilance required of him, what assailed him was that in spite of his devoted efforts no animal had announced a sacred presence to him in any way that assured him of its guidance, protection, power or blessing. As he let the knowledge encompass him that the night had passed with him asleep, instead of feeling failure he felt an odd riverine calmness flowing through him. He felt refreshed, as though he had quenched his thirst with fresh snow melt. Though he had gone without food or drink for the last three days he felt strong. Could sleep alone have done this?

Stretching to his full height his eyes took in the splendid fingers of light that were spreading across the vast grasslands below him. A fierce and unexplainable thrill sprang up in him. He began to dance, no longer knowing nor caring if he were sleeping, dreaming or moving in the spirit world, for he was experiencing an overwhelming connection, a oneness. Everything his eyes fell upon had a silvered quavering edge that seemed to move with just the slightest rhythm to his each and every respiration...as though he could breathe in, and out the world surrounding him. By pinching the tender skin of his underarm he thought to break this trance-like state, which is what he assumed was happening due to the various depredations he was putting himself through. But all the wasp-like jabs of discomfort achieved were to send small lightning like flashes through his vision. His feet seemed to move him without effort. He found his lips opening in a chant. So dancing and with song he moved through a new world where every leaf, limb, bird and wind moved in mysterious accord.

The sun burned overhead before his throat creaked dryly shut. He realized that the rapturous movements of his body were a mockery, a foolish shuffle lacking everything but the perseverance of a white-haired crippled lame deer. Sweat sheeted his limbs, stung his eyes, which were now clenched almost shut. Obviously he had been shuffling blindly around. A pall of dust surrounded him. Standing still for the first time in hours he felt the wind wrap him in an embrace as never before. He hesitated, waiting. Just seconds earlier he had been exhausted, dumbfounded, an alertness rose in him to meet this which held him as no arms ever had. Something was coming; the hair on his arms rose. Though his eyes were still closed from the glare of the mid-day sun he sensed a rapidly descending darkness. The wind abruptly released its hold and a chill fell heavily upon him causing him to drop to one knee. His eyes flew open.

Below him the tall prairie grasses were being whipped into huge concentric circles. An abnormally high thundercloud glowed from within, haloed with a crisp edging that shone like Pueblo silver. A thunderous noise bellowed from the heavens, wilder than a stampeding, trampling, snorting, bawling and bellowing herd of buffalo. He felt his youth and strength as never before, breathing deeply of the the ozone charged air that came upon him like a surging mass. Of the mightiness of the approaching storm bearing down fast from the south he had no doubt, but he was rooted to this spot with no thought of seeking shelter.

His desire for the appearance of his *sicun,* spirit guardian, was so very strong, but if his handful of winters upon the earth had taught him anything it was the rewards of patience. He did not question the validity of a world he could not readily see, of the spirit, but he knew, as all the People did, that he inhabited it. While he knew no special ceremonies to summon it's messengers he knew that a palpable sign might be given, a token that he was favored and accepted. He had done all that was required (except, with a twinge, recalling that he had allowed sleep to overtake him last night). He thought of the new warrior, his friend Limping Fox, who after his recent quest never left on a raid or hunting party without a proud and prominent display of a fox pelt draped across his back. How Spotted Owl was never without his feather fan. Every grown man carried on his person some indication of his guardian protective spirit. All the displays of power were shown in one's regalia, from the magnificent white buffalo calf robe that Roman Nose wore to the small stones worn behind the ears of the Strange One, Crazy Horse. All gave evidence that the "unseen" had been seen. A headdress of war eagle feathers, a necklace of great bear talons, numerous scalps that adorned shirts, shields, and bridles of the war ponies, even the visible battle scars spoke to all that could see them of honors won and given for personal exploits, but of what was kept secreted in a fragrant bundle, known as *sicun,* this was a gift, not earned, but given, the sacred medicine-power revealed only to others by the token of the animal or bird displayed.

As he trembled with his great need an understanding grew in him of how a humbling prayer came to a man's lips. The smaller he felt himself, the greater he felt the spirit, and yet he felt not separation, but a great draw into union.

"I am a mystery to myself," he voiced aloud. "I know not who brought me to this life. I have purified my body, my mind, but I cannot stop my thoughts. I ask for guidance. I will take all that surrounds me, the earth, the sky, the four legged beings, and those with wings. I seek that my power will come in a guise that I can recognize. I am eager to meet the helper, the strength that will bring me to my life as a man among my people. Hear those above, hear those that move through the air, through water, through me. May I receive a sign to protect me, that I may wear this upon my body, my face, my possessions. Give me a song to sing. You are my helper, show me a recognizable form, so that your supreme power may flow through me, that I may benefit my people."

Wagachun was so intent on voicing what struggled to get out of him, that he barely noticed the increasing voice of the wind, the dense lowering of the sky, the chillness of the air, but when a snapped branch from a willow bush hit his cheek his eyes flew open, and with expectant terror he knew a vision was arriving at last. Somehow he thought that he would be a mere spectator to a great display. Was he ready for the involvement that would be required of him? It was as though he were a chrysalis, that his world was a casing he had been formed in that suddenly split open, and now he gazed upon another dimension. In one incomprehensible thought he felt like he could both soar above himself on the great wings of a hawk, and simultaneously burrow down into his deepest roots like a mere worm. His eyes, his heart, his whole being now achingly open; his heart arching with a strange pain as though it would burst from the confines of his chest if he dared to free it, to let it grow..... a gnawing within!

Thus it began!

When Spotted Owl saw him come stumbling, as though in a daze, down from the butte, he knew that the boy had indeed experienced the other world, as he sometimes thought of it. In his wisdom he knew to let the evening unfold gently, as Wagachun would be both excited and exhausted, much given to incoherence. The old man greeted him with a skin of water, instructing him only to take small sips, then guided him to the small fire by his camp. Wagachun was given to small bursts of shivering, even though the night was mild. "Here, sit. I will bring you food; then you will rest. Tomorrow we will return and seek wise counsel." Wagachun's eyes burnt with the brightness of an evening star, so eager was he to tell The Owl all that had transpired in his stay upon the mountain top, but he found, much to his consternation, that hunger had spoken first at the sight of the steaming bowl the old man now extended to him. "Eat, rest, allow your thoughts to settle before you speak them. The quest was successful, was it not?" His mouth full of tasty rabbit, all he could provide was a strong nod. "It is good," Spotted Owl looked squarely at him, then went about arranging the sleeping robes for the night.

As they rode out in the early morn Wagachun began to plan how he would tell of his experience. Of these sacred things he found he lacked the right words. The ones lined up on his tongue seemed raw, lacking in beauty and unsubtle. This boy who was so graceful in all he did felt burdened now with the clumsiness of proper speech. This man, a *wicasa wakan,* my second father, would not lack words. He had such experience, could heal with plants, talk to animals, tell of things to come....

As though Spotted Owl could see into his thoughts he spoke up, "Wagachun, do not concern yourself with the telling now. Is it not a good day?" Suddenly seeing the golden yellow flash of the meadowlarks rising up from the tall grasses as they passed through them he laughed, for it was indeed a good day, the air clear and bright. His hunger and thirst were satisfied, and the feel of his pony under him a comfort.

They rode along in silence till Wagachun blurted out, "Nothing came to me on the first night, nor on the second day. Just a coyote strolling through my campsite. The next day I thought I heard buffalo approaching, but it was just distant thunder. By yesterday morning I was sure that nothing would reveal itself to me then.... "Boy," Spotted Owl said gently, "wait till we have assembled the others, they will all want to hear." Wagachun struggled with his feelings, for had they not together prepared for this quest? Many moons he had sat at The Owls feet receiving instructions carefully. Did he not want to hear of the outcome? How could he wait? And with that he spurred his pony to go faster.

The Council of The Elders

When the holy men of Spotted Owl's choosing had been assembled, and the pipe had made its rounds a respectful silence fell upon the lodge of Running Elk, a Brule *yuwipi,* known for his special power of Inyan, the rock. Directly across from him sat a *waayatan,* Cante Ista, Eye of the heart, so named for his great ability to see into the future. To his right was another *pejuta wicasa,* who like Spotted Owl found his power in rooted plants and sacred herbs. Spotted Owl leaned into The Cottonwood Boy, nudging him to stand, saying, "*Wash-ta,* good, its all right."

As he began the telling, he thought of all the stories he had heard as a child, how eagerly all gathered had listened, all the polite acceptance of both storyteller and the story and he mouthed a silent plea for his own coherence, and began....

*It was the morning of the fourth day as I woke up....*gratified to see Running Elk nod to Cante Ista as if sharing a common memory, *I had been seeking guidance, my eyes tightly closed, when a small branch slapped my cheek. H*e paused briefly, looking around the circle, but all were with eyes downcast, listening intently, so he continued. *My eyes flew open and I looked out upon a very large thundercloud, rumbling like a herd of buffalo, approaching from the south. It glowed from within in a way that I had never seen before. The edges were outlined with what looked like the spears of the hidden sun, but the sun was behind me, over my shoulder. The wind began to howl as though every wolf in the hills took voice, and my skin felt as cold as though I had fallen unexpectedly through the ice of a raging stream.* He paused to catch Spotted Owl's eye, who nodded gravely, and his confidence surged. "Yes, I am able to do this, perhaps even now my *sicun* is with me!"

When he had finished he sat weakly down, his head lowered, not at all sure of what would now transpire. Just wait, he told himself. Once again the pipe was passed.

Surprisingly, it was the *pejuta wicasa* that spoke out first. "Though

I am known for my healing powers with the plants Grandmother bares on her bosom for us, I will speak of the winged ones who appeared to you. I was told of your experience with the *wanbli,* in the eagle pit. I thought perhaps that you would be visited by this bird, as you were merciful in your treatment of the great bird family. But, you say the first that came to you was a *kangi,* a crow, not surprising since this family is sure to be the first on the scene of a kill. Also they are watchmen for all others, sure to give warning. Perhaps you will be called into a warrior society, one whose job it is to guard us. As to the piece of meat that was dropped at your feet, well, did you eat of it?"

Wagachun turned to The Owl, seeking permission to respond, a nod confirmed it.

"I left it there, on the ground at my feet. I was not to eat, and thought it perhaps a temptation," to which Running Elk went "Hau! And what of the sign upon it?" "So much was happening that I did not understand." "What do you think of the cranes with the blood red heads; they flew so close to me that I thought they would land, but then they soared up, hovered briefly above my head, then continued south, right into the storm." Cante Isa spoke up. "Cranes are one of the most difficult birds to capture, that is, to take them alive. They have free spirits and would rather die than lose their freedom, even if one is taken injured and encouraged to heal, it will perish without its mate."

Excited by the responses Wagachun queried, "What of the large-winged birds? Were they the Waikinyan, the Thunderbirds?" All laughed at this, momentarily shaming him into saying, "I don't know, I had never seen such a flying creature with such a large span to its wings." "Oh, son," Spotted Owl spoke out, "I do no think you are being called to be a *heyoka.*"

Cante Ista, the far-seeing one, spoke quietly. "Three is *wakan,* sacred, a sacred number. Three different birds came to you. Birds go easily between heaven and earth, though any creature can bear a message if we know how to receive it. The birds have chosen you." Saying thus, the holy man retreated in silence once more.

"Three times the sacred circle has been brought to you, twice in the grasses upon the plains, and in an overwhelming strength in the vision of the great circling clouds in the sky....you said it was not the pipe-like funnel that drops from the clouds and speeds across the land destroying all in its path. You said it just circled around you with an awesome noise and sense of great power. I have no name for this, but watch for it," Running Elk again spoke.

The more these bold men spoke the more questions were created than answered for him. He looked beseechingly to his own teacher, but the Owl was studiously ignoring him now. He knew he must ask about the water creature. Would they think that it was a *maiyun* or a monster? He hesitated to describe it; it seemed such a good omen. And if it was a fabled creature would this be an indication of some inherent darkness and unbalance in him? Once again he was assailed by the mystery of his own origins. Mother? Father? Lost in these thoughts he heard Spotted Owl clearing his throat. "Did I speak of the water..ah, creature?" They all sat forward at this mention. He struggled on, "Well, behind the woman, as she approached, three smooth skinned creatures leapt out of the water," Before he could continue a flurry of questions assailed him, this had certainly caught their interest. They wanted to know the size, the color, how long were the teeth? "A giant fish!" "An eel!" Running Elk, who had traveled down to the Great Water in his youth, said with authority of his years, a whale.

Maintaining a requisite respect he allowed them their say, shortly a hush fell allowing him to continue. "They did not leap and fall as a fish would, they left the water and returned with great grace and purpose. I assure you they were not monstrous, but of great beauty. Their skin had no scales." At this, Elk folded his arms and muttered with satisfaction, "like a whale." He continued, "they were no larger than a new born buffalo calf. They breathed air, not water. And," here he paused for emphasis, not caring at this point if he were to be believed, "and they were full of joy!"

....To which none of these wise elders had a response. Did they believe him? Was it not a vision? "And what of the woman?" All heads turned to him now. "Tell us again," he was encouraged.

At a loss for words to explain the fearful symmetry of his vision; the water standing up in waves colored as the blue stones from the pueblos, the happy leaping creatures, and striding towards him the beautiful woman, he remained mute. "Ah, Buffalo Calf Woman appears once again," Elk began knowingly, until Cante Isa carefully touched his forearm signaling quiet. The boy spoke once more....

All around me the world was caught up in a swirling chaos the likes of which I had never seen. Birds were screaming, trees were groaning as their limbs were being whipped by the wind. A great body of water was being lashed and beaten so that it rose up in waves above my head. I was standing on some shore fearful that the water was coming to take me away. And above all the heavens kept lowering in a great swirling mass above my head. Into the midst of this a figure came walking calmly toward me. It was easy, even at a distance, to discern that it was a woman by the grace of her movements and the elements of her garments. As she came closer confusion settled on me, for not only was she not dressed in buckskins but in such thin trade cloth that I could see the outline of her limbs. She was soaking wet as I was, but what riveted me was the color of her hair, for it was as yellow as the prairie flowers, and her skin as pale as the sand upon which I stood. In her right hand she held a small branch of cottonwood (I recognized the leaves) and in her left, strangely shaped sticks with color at their ends. She was smiling and met my gaze directly. I was too shocked to avert my gaze, as is proper. As she spoke to me..." "What did she say?" was asked eagerly, "I did not understand her language, and could not break my amazed look into her face. For not only had she great beauty, but her eyes were the pale green of the Yellow Stone in the spring when the snow melts flood it. My heart was beating so loud that I could no longer hear the roar of my surrounding. Now to my amazement she addressed me in my own language, but hesitantly. I had no fear, even though my heart filled my ears so that I could not understand her speech. She was no Mistai, ghost, but I knew, somehow, that her heart was open towards me. Did she come to warn me? There was red on her cheek. I thought it paint, but it was blood. Understanding that I did not fully comprehend her she signaled me to follow her, I thought, but then she sat and bade me to sit beside her. I liked her very much. I began to fade from myself and did not want to leave her, but I woke alone. The storm and my vision were gone."

Exhaustion overcame him then, and Spotted Owl signaled to the men to leave. After preparing some broth for them, they sat in silence. When The Owl began speaking it was near the end of the light. "Well, my son, the Great Spirit has blessed you indeed." He was ready to continue but Wagachun interrupted him, pressed by his need. "But of my *sicun*, what is to be my power animal?" Spotted Owl did not answer directly but said to him, "Did you prepare a bundle?" "Yes," he replied, and drew it from his side where he had been clutching it. Spreading it out for his teacher to see, it contained only a small light green stone and a bundle of dried yellow grasses. "There was nothing quite like her eyes, or her hair; like corn silk!"

"A man may have many visitations and manifestations of the unseen world that surrounds him, much is given to understand as the mind and heart grow in life and experience. Of what was shown to you I have confidence that, while you may come slowly to understanding, what you learn will be of great importance to you." The Owl had been thinking of the appearance of a *ve'ho'e* in Wagachun's vision and thinking of the small embroidered square of thin cloth that had been hastily tucked into his cradle board. While it was not unusual for white man's clothing to be used by the people it seemed that this scrap was not decoration, nor a charm of any kind, but a message of some import, imparted in a desperate haste.

Wagachun, his tongue eased now, spoke. "I felt that she had power of a strange sort that I did not recognize, nor had I ever heard of such. It did not threaten, overwhelm, command or even guide me. But some understanding had begun to flow from her toward me even as she was approaching. In spite of our chaotic surroundings, the clouds, the thunderous water, the horse-like water creatures that danced, and the ceaseless fury of the wind that seemed to spring from all directions at once, I felt myself open and accepting of her. And you know I am not favored of strangers and prefer my own company. How could this be, I thought."

Then excitedly he went on, "She bore no weapon, no shield of any device or design, no animal companion accompanied her, but her bearing was that of a warrior, a seasoned warrior. She had the skin of a wasichu (ve'ho'e) but," and a sense of violating this elder's patience came upon him, so eager was he to see the path his future was to take. At the same time the little cactus wren that lived inside him quietly scolded, "Shhh, can you not capture your tongue?" He then bent to examine an ant toiling at his feet. Once again he had forgotten to mention the rainbows! Were they one of the sixteen great mysteries, he so wanted to be *wicasa wakan,* a holy man someday like Silver Spotted Owl, who could speak the secret language of Hanbloglaka and could see with other eyes than the ones in his head that right now were failing him, were closing, were shutting.....

The Owl, smiling down upon him, covered him gently where he lay and went to retrieve his pipe bag.

The Wisdom of Spotted Owl

He was very proud of Wagachun, for his behavior with the elders had been most respectful; his telling of the vision humble. Now that a vision had been granted, well, that was only the beginning. Now he had to help Wagachun discern the paths that had been shown to him. He felt that much would be required of this young man, that he was indeed special. Not one but three different winged messengers had come to him, the crow, the crane and the great storm birds, but in spite of a rich and powerful vision there was much that exceeded Spotted Owl's power to interpret.

Wagachun sat patiently now that they were alone, waiting for his teacher to instruct him. What could Owl tell him? Only the truth would do because only the true telling of things would bring the absolute irrefutable beauty of balance and harmony. So he was ready for the questions and determined to keep no answer hidden. He would speak "through the pipe".

"Why did the eagle not come? Was it because I once tried to trap them?"

"No, you did what was right in your dealings with these brothers, but they did not come because they were not to be part of your medicine."

"But a *kangi,* a crow, an everywhere bird appeared..."

"Yes, the crow, who is usually first to arrive, who reports to all of approaching danger, who is clever and wise." Silver Spotted Owl sat back and gazed at Wagachun with grave satisfaction. The boy replied with a heavily furrowed brow, "But the chunk of meat, just dropped in my lap, what did that mean? Was I meant to eat it? From what animal did it come? At first I was afraid to look. I wasn't even sure what it was. I tried to be brave and when I looked the crow was still there watching. I somehow knew that I was meant to share it with others!" "So, what animal? What others?" Owl calmly queried. At that the boy hung his head in obvious confusion; he had to be hard on the boy. He reached to recharge his pipe when he saw Wagachun's shoulders sag. He had to ask him once again, though. "What kind of meat?"

" I'm not sure. There was a design on it, on the skin. I averted my eyes." Then the boy's head shot up, "It was a war pony!"

They both sat in silence for awhile. " You received no instructions at all, is that so?" "Yes," Wagachun said miserably. "Aah, I can only tell you that crows will eat anything, can eat anything, to survive." He forced himself to a laugh. "And so will we, and on many occasions it has been our sacred dogs, our horses, that have given their lives to sustain ours in times of dire need." " Then what does this mean?" Wagachun immediately queried him. "Alas only time and the great spirit can tell, my son."

"Well, what of the cranes?" "You say they flew close, but kept heading south, a pair of them. Well, I think South is an important direction. I don't understand this myself, and as to the storm birds.. there is a mystery brought to you by a great turbulence.

The water creatures? Well, Wagachun there is much in your vision that I don't understand. Are these creatures we are yet to know or do they exist somewhere? All throughout your vision there is nothing to fear, is there? You are not given any directives. You were not told to honor anything, nor to avoid any action or thing, were you?" "I was to share the meat with others...later, but I did not know where, or when."

"And the woman? Well, she is central. I think she is of the white faced people that Sweet Medicine spoke of all those years ago. You are young, much wisdom will come to you if you keep seeking it. All will be revealed in the passing of time. But for now, you have done well, your intentions have been noted and responded to. You are yet young. Look everywhere for sign, as much as though you were tracking game. Honor yourself and those around you." And with that Spotted Owl rose, patted his shoulder gently and shuffled away, then turned only to add, "Those kangi, they will assist you throughout your life."

A Small Medicine Bundle

As dusk fell a tall boy unwrapped a small doeskin bundle, feeling sure of his privacy among the cottonwoods by the stream at this time of day. Idly he handled its contents, content to hold the blue green stone in his hand, the shape of which held no significance, the color which could only partially remind him of the glowing richness of the woman's eyes. There was a bunch of dried buffalo grass almost the tint of her hair. Adding a *kangi,* crow's feather to the bundle, he re-wrapped it and tucked it away. The everywhere bird, as The Owl had named it, and in truth he saw it everywhere, was a constant reminder of his quest. He had to ask himself, for Spotted Owl hadn't provided a satisfactory answer, had his request been answered? He had expected so much and was disappointed with how little appreciation he could muster for what had been revealed of the Great Mystery. Of the presence of a spirit world he had never doubted; the Great Unseen, but he was still burdened with knowing his place in the world. Who was he really? At least a hint of his birth name... so much was shrouded in unknowing. He had hoped to have his origins explained, his purpose revealed, his guiding spirit identified. Spotted Owl did not answer much, but only reassured him that much portent resided in what he had been shown, that he must wait with great patience for further revelations.

He had not been told to do anything, nor refrain from anything, nor to treat any particular animal with reverence. Then there was that hunk of strange flesh dropped right at his feet by the *kangi.* Yes, three kinds of birds had shown themselves, but not the great eagle that he had hoped for, that he had felt a strong affinity for. He had been told that so strong a sign of the winged beings indicated that his path would involve traveling between both things of heaven and of earth. Yet it did not seem that he was being led onto the path of a *pejuta wicasa*, as Spotted Owl was. If he was not being called to use the medicine of growing things it did not seem that he was being called to be a warrior of any special repute either.

Patience was called for, but what naturally occurred in the life of a one of so few winters, his thoughts were already back with the pony herd. He meant to lay aside this search for hidden meanings, but occasionally he found his present day world being pierced by the resonant caw of a solitary crow drawing his attention up to where it had perched, head cocked, eyeing him with great interest. Was this his spirit helper come to what? Mock him, perhaps. But his solitary nature began to assert itself in pondering on the great mysteries that his mentor The Owl patiently taught him.

In those long and beautiful nights spent under the northern skies guarding the herds, he thought much on *Wakan Tanka*, who in his greatness first created himself, then all of the great mysteries of life. How this young man burned to know of them. The sun above, the elegant, changeable, ever-renewing moon that graced his night, the rivers that flowed like veins upon the earth on which all peoples trod, right down to the creation of *Hanwi*, the moon, and that great orb the sun without which all life would wither and die...it was all too much for this young man. He was never without, not one or two, indeed many questions to bring to The Owl's lodge. He tried so hard to remember all the great and mysterious manifestations of the Creator. He had so much to learn if he was to follow in the path of a *wicasa wakan*, a spiritual man. Placing his hands on his little bundle, he prayed to *Taku Skan skan*, the spirit that moves every living thing, to lead him on his path just as he caused the first breath to enter his body. Above all he asked for a *woksape wokita*, an awakening to wisdom!

Four Scalp Locks

Shadyside, Pittsburgh 1855

"You, you and that, that Count Foo-ferraw!" "My dear, he's a titled baron, please!"

What caught Anah's attention was the shrillness of her mother's voice as it rose to an edge bordering on a note of hysteria. "I want it out of here, it's an atrocity." Then came her father's deep modulating, unruffled tone replying, "Hardly, it's simply one of my valuable artifacts." At that, her innate curiosity aroused, she moved stealthily towards the front parlor to insinuate herself into the thick folds of the drapes and peer at her parents as they debated this intriguing matter. "I simply won't have it in my house, it's an abomination." Anah's eyes darted from her mother's upright rigid form to her father's amused one. Then in a huff Clare left the room.

"You can come out now. Tell me what you think of my latest acquisition to my collection, dear," and with that Dr. Frederick Chester Hoffman led his daughter into his study, covered her eyes, and turned her to the wall behind his large oak desk.

"Voila!" Spread wide upon the far wall was a Plains Indian buckskin war shirt decorated lavishly with porcupine quills inter-spaced with geometric beaded strips that ran the length of the arms and shoulders in bright pleasing colors. A breastplate of carmine beads hung with dentalium shells and four long tassels of human hair, known as scalp locks, were flanked by two elaborate turquoise beaded panels of geometric design. More than 60 black-tipped ermine tails hung as decorative fringe from the garment. Anah stood speechless before it. "Well, say something child," her father prodded her, "Has the cat got your tongue?" "Can I...?" entranced before it she stammered, "Can I?" "Can you what?" He was clearly irritated with her response. "Can I touch it?" "Of course you can." Her father, mistaking her awe for fear of human hair blurted out that those were "scalp locks", trophies, one rewarded for each enemy killed in battle. He continued that that is why they are called "Braves, "Indian Braves," that is. But his little speech went unregarded, for she was already standing on his swivel chair reverently stroking a few of the glossy ermine tails, peering closely at the minute stitches holding the bead work, trying to discern just how the quills were bent and attached, turning then to ask him of the provenance...

At that Dr. Hoffman realized finally that this child who had little or no predilection for dolls and the usual fripperies of womanhood might come to something after all, in his estimation.

A Mirror

1857

Setting the small delicate jawbone she had collected down, for she had yet to identify it as that of a shrew or a meadow mouse, Anah rose from her desk to respond to the plaintive urgent cry. Her mother needed something; she hurried to respond before the summoning voice turned shrill. The nurse must be somewhere else in the house. Anah was not used to being summoned by her mother. She was accustomed to the general neglect that allowed her freedom to pursue whatever caught her fancy.

When the time had come for the governess to be dismissed tutors were hired. Anah was actually old enough now to forgo the need for constant governance in this large house well tended by servants. If the weather allowed she roamed the countryside, specimen jar and butterfly net in hand. After pouring over the journals of the Lewis and Clark expedition she fancied herself an amateur naturalist, all too eager to add to her own growing collection. The lovely expensive dolls she was gifted with on occasions sat politely arranged on her bedroom shelf. Every other suitable surface contained "specimens", both living and dead, brought back from her wanderings. Lightning bugs crawled the sides of a mason jar, a large cocoon hung from a branch awaiting metamorphosis into an eerily elegant swallow-tailed moth, carefully labeled birds eggs resided in a dried nest, and a small tortoise ambled about, just one more reason why the maid did not frequent her room.

On days that the weather confined her she could be found in her father's study, voraciously plowing through a medical text, dictionary in one hand. Her father fostered her interest in the Natural Sciences; he made no secret of the fact that he had longed for a male heir. Anah took it all in stride, there was nothing she enjoyed more than an informative nature walk with him, both coming home with pockets laden with their finds. The good doctor never seemed to tire of fostering her education, increasing her Latin vocabulary, her knowledge of taxonomy, astronomy, whatever particular scientific morsel was currently on his mind, which was a prodigious one indeed! And now they enjoyed his ever increasing interest in the Plains Indians.

Her mother, Clare Violette, known for her great beauty, had seemingly little effect on Anah's character. Not that Anah hadn't inherited her mother's beauty, but her intellect was of such a nature that she found the latest Paris fashions of little interest. Those costly gowns by Worth she admired, but did not covet. Much to her mother's dismay Anah's toilette consisted mainly of clean clothes and braided hair. Having to dress for a special occasion was a torment not only to her, but to the maid assisting her. On the other hand the time, effort, and concern that Clare lavished on herself to enhance an already beautifully endowed person was time that wasn't spent with her daughter. This was not lost on Anah, who, when she once understood how vanity and insecurity went hand in hand, easily disavowed interest in her own appearance.

Her father, on the other hand, in spite of the demands of a busy practice, regularly scheduled time for his only child. His entertainments, grouse hunting, cards, and shooting skeet were not for young ladies, but he regularly indulged her ambitions, a new book of botany or a field guide for a current interest only had to be mentioned and it was procured for her, left casually by her desk.

As a young child Anah seethed with jealousy, not of her mother, but of the silvered object Clare Violette Rolande Hoffman held to her face and gazed into with such interest. This mirror stole her mother's time and attention; there was little that Anah could do to compete. Her mother saw that all her child's needs were adequately met by the household staff. Her Nana, Ethel, a young Scottish girl, had seen to teaching her proper manners and etiquette, and as Anah was a bright child there was nothing that was problematical with her education now that the best tutors had been hired. So this little family achieved a delicate balance: the father with his medical practice, the mother with herself, and the child with the wonders of the world around her. The Hoffman family did little entertaining.

But all this changed when her mother fell ill and began a long, tormented descent towards the grave. As Clare's strength ebbed she began to rely more and more upon reassuring evidence that the mirror still provided. The seamstress produced now, not voluminous gowns of velvet, brocade,and the Cluny laces she so favored, but ornate nightgowns and bed jackets, designed to conceal a form that was withering. The nature and progress of Clare's illness was never openly discussed in front of Anah. It was some time before she noticed a subtle change in the usual pattern of neglect. When she did, a fear crept upon her that her mother was beginning a journey where, even if Anah were welcome, she could not follow.

As Nature would have it, just when Clare's beauty was being robbed by her illness, the blossoming of young womanhood came upon her daughter. The time Anah spent outdoors pursuing her various collections, a rare trillium for her flower press, a chrysalis of a Luna Moth, brought lovely golden tones to her skin and hair. She was graceful of limb, naturally modest, and seemingly unaware of the beauty she had inherited from both parents, for her father was himself a handsome, distinguished man.

When the time came, as it must with all illnesses termed fatal, all mirrors were banished from her mother's chambers. Anah discovered with a shiver that the silver plated hand mirror had been cracked. The ornate silver frame still held intact shards covered with a film of dust. Her mother had finally acknowledged that the love of self that had sustained her all these years, that had provided her with all the acclaim, attention, and rewards that great beauty can bring, had failed her. As her health continued to decline, and medicine afforded no more promise of a cure, let alone a miracle, her husband lost himself in the bottle. She tried turning, finally, to her only child for love. Anah, so thrilled at being asked to prove her love, and eager to do so, was now blind to the inevitable. The relationship that she had hungered for since childhood was now being offered. "Come sit by me, dear," her mother would whisper. "Let me brush your hair, it is so lovely, my dear." Anah chose to ignore the weak and trembling hands that now caressed her. The dressmaker was summoned and consulted to provide a new wardrobe for Anah's changing figure. But when Anah tried to draw her mother into her own world, that of a budding lady naturalist, she failed. Clare had never learned to see much beauty outside herself and what she saw now was not her own beauty, but her daughter's. Tragically she had little or no resources with which to cling to life now that her own beauty had not just faded but disappeared. Her husband's love and devotion, the adoration of her daughter, they could not begin to erase the pain of losing the only thing she truly admired in life, her own beauty.

The mirror was banished, as it could not lie. Pain exacted a heavy toll that, no matter how much love she sought, could not fill the cavern that pain was hollowing out. She then began to doubt the veracity of those who professed love, for how could they love her when she could no longer love herself. Eventually she drove all but a nurse from her side; she saw Frederick and Anah as witnesses of what she thought of as ugliness. She entertained thoughts of taking her own life; imagined what gown she could be laid out in. Driving her personal maid to distraction, she demanded one gown after another to be displayed, then rejected summarily; tossed aside with rude and bitter comments.

She constantly dismissed the nurse, but when Clare was found lying senseless on the floor, too weak to throw herself from the open window, her dosage of laudanum, the smell like burnt flowers, mingling with her fine French perfumes, was increased. She lay supine, the pain controlled with ever increasing dosages, but her awareness of her surroundings effaced also. She had found little to live for and now the end would come quickly and without drama. Anah would come quietly to stand in the doorway, mute and helpless to understand, yet fearful to enter. Sometimes her father would find her curled asleep in the doorway, too stricken to leave. He would gather her up, carry her to her bed. He, too, had no words to ease Clare's departure from their lives!

The Mystery

Our Lady of the Woods Academy
Laurel Ridge, Pennsylvania

That a few votive lights could cast such large trembling shadows across the high arching vault of the hallways as she carefully made her way towards the winding stairway to creep into the darkened chapel, itself now lit only with such lights flickering wanly in the drafts, only added to what drew her here on these cold nights.

She sought the mystery as though it were something she could attain and thus possess. At her tender age she had no name for it as yet, only the yearning that so intrigued her. She knew it was here; she felt it. Unnameable, but real. The consequences if she were caught at this late hour would be expulsion, but that hadn't occurred to her. She kept far to the back of the chapel, crouched down in the pews. Kneeling on the cold marble by the aisle, she felt only the heat of the desire within. Totally alone as she prayed to the inanimate plaster saints for a sign, all the while keeping one eye slyly open. Eventually the cold rose through her young joints, and the dampness, thank goodness, for her greatest fear was that she might fall to sleep and be found sprawled there when the morning mass began. Who knows what they, the nuns, would do, for she was just one of two non-catholic students in residence.

Often when she crept exhausted back to her bed in the dorm, she would pause by the cell of the beautiful young novitiate Sister Benedicta, who guarded her young charges as they slept on through the night, undisturbed. A soft sobbing issued from within Benedicta's cell, the sound of constant sorrow. Anah knew it well. Sisters, Anah thought, we are sisters, sorrow binds us in secret. We will never tell. She could see it in the tall Sister's eyes when she sometimes braided Anah's hair; she was the only one who patiently worked the tangles out as she sat unmoving, enjoying just to be touched with a gentle hand.

When the sky began to lighten and the bell rang for the routines to begin once again the mystery had long dispersed and with it the longing had crept back into the darkest recess of Anah's heart. The nuns swept through the corridors, rousing the girls to quickly don their uniforms to assemble for the six o'clock mass, and the rest of the undeviating routine Anah complied with from habit. Within the folds of her clothing lay a daguerreotype of her recently deceased mother; she knew not to look at it, though.

Being an only child meant that loneliness had long resided in her very marrow, creating both an independent spirit, and unfortunately, a tendency to alienate those who who might make a small effort to befriend her. She preferred her own company. She didn't miss her father, as she simply wasn't used to seeing much of him now that she had been sent away to board here. She missed her pets considerably and saved scraps from her meals to try and tame some of the small birds and squirrels that roamed the grounds. The academy her father had chosen, apart from its excellent academic standing, was located close to his hunting lodge where he was spending more and more of his time.

She was an exceptionally good student; her ability to leave depended on her achieving academic excellence as per her father's request. While she was not required to take the catechism class she did, and found the lives of the saints fascinating. She had not found answers in any of her lessons but she hadn't formulated a question, either. Deportment, etiquette not even tolerable; the piano lessons which required infinite amounts of practice excruciating. She lived for the brief hours when she could be outdoors and easily escape the scrutiny of the upperclassman's gaze, certainly not missed while the others were playing badminton or croquet or merely aimlessly strolling the well-manicured, ample grounds. She flew down past the garden plots to the swampy marsh and often up to the small wrought-iron fenced graveyard on a knoll above the school, well hidden behind a scrim of pines and lilacs. A wonderful sanctuary for her, overlooking the bright shining coin of the marsh below, where bobolinks and red-winged blackbirds hung from cattails and called out. So peaceful among the dead. Besides, her father's uncle, a favorite one, a historian by profession, Martin, had often regaled her with tales of their family history, hints of Indian blood. When she had been sent to her room for some general naughtiness, he often appeared, respectfully requesting permission to enter, and with a finger to his lips would seat himself, and entertain her while she was sequestered from the rest of the family.

It was Uncle Martin who told her, when she had protested, practically kicking and screaming, at the very thought of being sent to this boarding school. "I'm a protestant you know, we protest after all." He found that quite charming, she could tell, he liked her!...That this school was located right on the old Warrior Trail that wound through the foothills of the Alleghenies. "The Iroquois traveled it during the French and Indian War. And I'll tell you a secret, lean close...you will have to go a roaming, there's a little graveyard behind the school. Well, there's a real Indian princess buried there!"

It was true, an unmarked, unkempt grave. She just knew, somehow! She had found it her first week, and had gotten so many demerits for being not only late for study hall, but muddy and unkempt besides that she was unable to go home that week-end, but she did not mind. Anah saw that the plot was kept groomed, and brought crow and jay feathers, lucky-stones, and marsh-marigolds to it.

Deep in the pocket of her school blazer she had secreted an ermine tail from her father's glorious treasure, the Plains Indian war shirt that was so prominently displayed above the desk in his study. The hair was beginning to shed from it, for she had been worrying it like a talisman. Now she had brought it to the Princess' grave. It had helped so much those first nights lying in that narrow iron cot on those coarse sheets in the school's dormitory, listening to the scratching of the bare branches across the tall dormer windows as the October winds began to gain in strength throughout the passing hours till dawn. Now she raised the bony remnant to her lips and began to dig it under the wet loam of the grave. Perhaps the mystery lies here, she thought.

St. Francis

When it came to the hagiography of the saints her favorite, of course, was Francis of Assisi. At first it was assumed that, due to her interest, she might be ripe for conversion, but that was not so. She daydreamed that she, too, could speak to the animals. Often she wandered from the school grounds to study in the graveyard. There, under her favorite oak, the gabardine pleats of her uniform carefully arranged beneath her, she daydreamed that a pair of delicate tufted titmice, their sweet heads with alert black eyes intent upon her every word were perched upon her outstretched hands listening as she spoke! The raucous screams of a scolding jay brought her quickly back, oh yes, the bread she had spirited out of the dining hall as promised for it in the pocket of her blazer. "Coming right up!" she announced, scrambling to her feet to scatter crumbs upon the ground, then she pulled her French grammar out. Language came easy to her now, though it wasn't long before her thoughts turned from declensions.

The exquisite warmth and smells of what is called Indian Summer brought to Anah's mind the time as a child that she spent on the farm with Alex and Mima during one of her mother's frequent declines. How clearly she recalled certain things; the huge spikes of brightly colored gladiolas, well, they would of course tower over her, for she was only six then. How strange it seemed to her now that she did not speak then, for it seems that she has a gift for languages, she barely has to study.

The teaching order here is from Germany. Undoubtedly just one of the reasons why her father chose this school. She has discovered that many of the older nuns sequestered away in the convent are from there, and she has found that she can carry on a rudimentary conversation with them, much to their delight. When Anah first did speak aloud it was in French, the language in which her mother sang lullabies to her. At first there was not much concern, they just thought she was a late developer, then shy. Then strange diets, practices, finally accusations and avoidance's, as her care was parceled out to various experts she drifted into a world of solitude. Bored with the ease of her studies, her mind drifted off.

There were some wild grapes entwined along the wrought-iron fence close to her and the droning of the bees eager to gather in the last of the harvest before the first frost set in cast Anah adrift in the past... clearly recalling how wonderful the freedom was that she experienced on the Sutherland's little farm. The feel of the air on her skin, bare feet in the soft dirt, loose hair on her cheeks, stuffing her mouth with gooseberries warm on the bush, sneaking bites from tomatoes on their vines. Who knew their juices tasted like that! And a dog to run free at her heels. Loosely supervised, but nonetheless she felt cared for, free to roam, unaware that adult eyes were indeed keeping guard over her. She loved not having to keep clean every minute, too!

One day when her father came she was hidden back under a Spanish shawl draped over the piano and heard them talking about her. She's not deaf and dumb, Mima was telling her father, she can hear. "And understand," Alex interjected. "Watch!"

Mima called her out, knowing exactly where she was. Her father watched a bit dumbfounded. "Child, bring me a spoon!" She sprang off returned with the item. "Well she read your lips." " From under the piano?" At that Mima turned her back to the child and said, "And a fork to go with it!" A fork was set down neatly then beside it. Alex chimed in, "Doc she can read, too!" "Surely not, you have somehow managed to teach her?" "No she taught herself. She's a bright one, she is. Watch!" He then rose and brought her one of the little readers they had around, handing it to Anah, who pushed it away. Alex caught her wrist gently and pulled her to him. "Please child, show us." At that she pulled and ran, only to return with a torn piece of butcher paper that they used to wrap the chickens they sold. She handed it to Alex. Stunned he handed it to her father. In neat, but slanting penciled letters it said:

I can rite two

If she expected him to be overwhelmed it didn't happen then. After a subdued dinnertime her father asked for a stroll, informed her that her mother's health had yet to improve and that she would be staying on here for a bit more. He drew on his Meerschaum pipe thoughtfully, then broached the subject ."Why didn't you tell us?" "You didn't ask?" "Why don't you talk with us?" "I don't want to?" " Why not?" "I don't need to." "For heaven's sake child," he exploded...

"I talk to my brothers and sisters!" At that he stopped in his tracks, pipe-stem in hand,

"But you have none."

"I do too!"

"Child, are you mad?" His elation at her new found powers of speech, his only child, quickly evaporated at this glimmer of possible derangement, surely a taint from his wife's side. "Stop this foolishness now, Now!" Going so far as to shake her. "Who, who are these friends?" The mother of course, he thought, imaginary, all children had those, and then feared the worst. Alex had no hired hands on the little poultry farm, and Alex was impeccable in his morals or he would never have trusted his daughter, his only child to their care. Seeing the distress on his face she took his large hand, came tugging at his jacket, pulling him. She then led him on a grand tour of her world, and introduced him to her friends. First to the little gray clapboard chicken house to meet Biddy, the bantam hen, the lovely Rhode Island Reds, where she went daily with her little wicker basket to gather an egg for her breakfast. Biddy allowed it, she told her father, laid one fresh just for her. It almost broke his heart to see the trust in the child's eyes as she demonstrated how careful one had to be reaching under a sitting hen. It was too hot in the day to find the big Indigo snake no matter how she probed the hole, she told him as she led him out to the shoulder-high corn. "Don't worry. I know all about those with wedge-shaped heads." Pointing to the big white clouds amassing on the horizon, telling him to keep an eye on them, as they were soon to change shape and color, she began to twirl, her corn silk hair a lovely nimbus as she sang in French. So like her mother, he thought. Pausing, "Don't forget to feel the wind, Papa. That's my friend too, just like the rain is Uncle Alex's, you know for the corn." So it's "Uncle" now, he thought. He felt his heart. "Oh," she said as she reached for his hand, "Listen, hear them, they are my best-est friends, the crows, Don't you just love them? They love to ride the wind. You just can't help but love them for it. Father, they will never, never, never" she sang twirling, "pluck my eyes out, you know!"

Looking down on the little face suffused with pleasure he couldn't help it, either. Once her father learned of her affinity for animals he bought her pets. Their big house was now never without them. A red-headed parrot from the Amazon that delighted Anah by croaking out a fairly intelligible "'schnapps" and was banned to the pantry for its messy seed-cracking activity. As soon as she saw how her father understood and tolerated her love for animal friends she slowly moved her wild animal menagerie into the household. Blue, a severely pecked blue jay driven from its nest came to the carriage house, then Silver, the baby raccoon was moved right up into the rose garden.

After her mother's death and because most of the household staff were let go, Anah had to find homes for her pets. The one that she managed to keep was a male canary of her mother's, Willie, a sad memento, whose high trilling song grew less and less frequent, and was finally silenced after she had been packed off to the boarding school. Often the only sound now heard in the empty house was the clink of Dr. Hoffman refilling his Waterford glass yet again with fine scotch.

He Came For Her

Classes had just ended for the day; she had planned to slip free of Sister Mary Martha's watch, ease away from the other girls at play and head down to the marsh. As long as she made it back before the downward sun touched the school's silhouette she would not be missed. Today, however, turned out differently. As she stood scraping the grass from her brogans, an angry nun descended down the cool polished hall towards her. She barely heard the jangle of the long rosary beads and glanced back to see the nun's flapping black habit approach like a giant bat when she was arrested by the sharp slap of her surname, "Miss Hoffman". Then she was swiftly delivered, not to the headmistress's office, Mother Xaveria's, as she suspected, but to the large formal drawing room reserved for visitors.

Hustled into the parlor's strict luxury, she swapped at her unruly hair and gave a pull to her uniform belt. She divined that at least she must give a semblance of propriety to whatever awaited her. The compact form of the sandy-haired man standing at the window needed no introduction. "Father!" She assaulted him, running forward. Just as he eagerly turned towards her she came to an abrupt halt. The man in front of her was not arrayed in his usual manner, an impeccably tailored frock coat and vest, gold stick pin gleaming at his throat. No, he looked as handsome as ever, but here he was, dressed down, in whipcords, and an old green Norfolk jacket. Was he just stopping by from a hunting expedition? And why was he here in the middle of a school week? His cheeks gleamed with freshly shaved jowls. Those were not Wellingtons on his feet, but some shapeless slippers of deer hide. She quickly assessed him. Something was wrong. Moccasins, as she soon learned they were named, the first sign of his new consuming interest.

While he was just brimming over with barely contained enthusiasm, she could not but fail to notice the intense agitation of the Mother Superior, her chin drawn deep into the folds of her starched wimple. Just like a box turtle, Anah thought! Agitation propelled the rosary beads deep in the folds of her habit into a disturbing clacking as one of her highly shined black shoes betrayed a restraint barely kept in check from tapping out further indignation. Expectantly Anah looked from Mother Xaveria to her father's face wreathed in a grin. Dropping to one knee, throwing open his arms, he bid her welcome. "I've come to get you!'"

And just like that her days at the academy were brought to an abrupt end. With barely a smidge of decorum Dr. Hoffman transported his daughter from the fine school he had entrusted with her education and care. Heads together, to her delight, he told her of giving up his thriving practice in the city and that they were moving up to his hunting lodge in the foothills of the Appalachians, near Fort Ligonier and The Warrior Path.

All The Pretty Horses

Moon of the First Snowfall
November 29, 1864, Sand Creek, I.T.

> *""Kill them all, big and small, nits make lice. I long to be wading in gore!'*
> *Colonel John M. Chivington*

The warriors sat their horses on the rim of the canyon above the icy waters of the creek below. Faintly back lit by the breaking dawn, they were watching helplessly, just out of firing range of the long guns. Observant, waiting, their hearts willing the escape of those that had also managed to evade the surprise attack. Having failed to fend off the Bluecoats, they had now stationed themselves here as a last defense against the soldiers skirmishing below.

Black Kettle's wife, Mo Hovato, lay sprawled on the muddy near bank, her riderless mount now scrabbling up the icy slope, fear propelling it beyond the screams and shouts of the surrounded encampment below. As the sun continued to rise, the bloodied water of the creek moved coldly on.

Those too young, too old, or too wounded to escape or fight were being rounded up and placed under guard. Silver Spotted Owl, his white braids now crimson with blood, lay slumped against a broken lance feebly trying to replace his glistening entrails, seemingly oblivious to the surrounding carnage. From the agonized movements of his mouth it could be seen he was chanting his Death Song, it could not carry above the tearing sounds of the repeating rifles and cannon booms. An old man's half-clothed body was being dragged around the perimeters of the camp by a mounted cavalryman who was waving his glistening saber in triumph.

When Colonel John M. Chivington was told that those routed by the surprise attack consisted mainly of women and children he replied, "Kill and scalp all, big and small, nits make lice!" An inventory of the spoils began once the enemy was subdued. A lieutenant approached him to inquire of the deposition of the white flag that now hung listlessly from the chief's lodge next to the prominently displayed stars and stripes. There was a gory pile of winter robes, some that had been ruthlessly pulled from beneath sprawled bodies, caches of powder and lead, and all of the villages' meager winter food supplies that had been quickly assembled. A Bluecoat was wetting a writing stick between his lips and taking note of the varied plunder, from dried meat to raw hide lariats. For what the army had no use of would be destroyed to further deprive these Indians of the least means of survival. First the officers, then some of the hated Pawnee scouts were walking among the pony herd selecting the finest mounts as their own.

White Antelope dropped his bow and staggered out into the icy waters of the creek, hands held high above his head. His death song sprang from his lips. "Nothing lives long. Only the earth and mountains." A dazed look was the only indication that his attempt at surrender was met with a fusillade of bullets. At a little cutback in the creek where some women were trying to hide with their children the sharpshooters were gamely picking them off one by one from their excellent vantage point. A child, just barely able to walk, pulled itself screaming in panic from the arms of its mother and was felled by a carefully placed shot to her midsection.

A seven hundred man force of The Colorado Territory militia had descended on this peaceful encampment of Cheyenne and Arapahoes who had left the confines of Ft. Lyon when the new Soldier Chief had told them to "Go and hunt buffalo to feed yourselves." There was no game on the reservation. Black Kettle had sent most of his warriors east towards Smoky Hill until the Army gave permission for new rations. Besides, he had been told "as long as he flew the American flag he and his people would be safe from U.S. Soldiers." Now their peaceful camp was awakened by howitzers and cavalry charges!

Each warrior on the cliff above narrowed his eyesight to try and discern just who would be led away. Every few minutes a soldier raised a looking glass to his eye and glanced nervously up at their assembly, then hurried to report . Orders were being given; supply wagons had now arrived, and those Indians not grievously wounded were being herded toward a hastily erected tent. Some bodies were dragged from the lodges before they were put to flame. Contents thought valuable were hastily carried out. Parfleches with their tasty pemmican were kept, but medicine bundles, shields, lavishly beaded scalp shirts and all weapons were to be consigned to the flames. Here and there one of the Colorado Volunteers snatched a colorful trophy to claim as a battle prize. Many were unconcernedly desecrating the dead, bowie knives flashing in the growing light of the day. Others ran, seeking those still alive, to stop their breath forevermore, even those too feeble or too young to possibly escape.

Snowfall was thin, but pitiless in how it barely obscured vision. Carbines, pistols and lances were still being brandished, although there was no further bloodshed. The four big guns the army mules had hauled here stood ominously silenced. Soldiers were being assembled to receive more ammunition from one of the well-laden supply wagons. Lodge poles were lassoed and lodges pulled abruptly down into their burning remains.

The warriors braced themselves with fear for the remaining women, children and old ones clustered in despair and shock below; would they all be slaughtered? Some men had managed to cross the shallow creek to quickly dig rifle pits and provide coverage for those still running to escape. Cooking fires smoldered and a few dogs slunk around lapping at the spilled contents from the overturned pots. One mangy yellow cur tentatively sniffed at a lifeless form sprawled in the bloody snow. Unrelenting wails and cries rose up from the few that had been spared. Yellow Wolf had gone beyond, One Eye, War Bonnet...

As one an armed detail of the militia advanced, not toward the captives, but toward the several hundred ponies backed up into the canyon. A sharp command rang clearly out, and the guns began barking again. The small war pony of White Dog's spun screaming into the midst of the herd, blood gouting from its neck. The rapid discharge of guns was deafening. The animals milled in aimless terror. Those attempting to escape the slaughter were held back by the steep surrounding walls. As the bodies dropped, writhing and kicking, screaming in confusion, the execution squad advanced. Nine hundred ponies were a lot to dispatch and there was no efficiency to this job. A captain stopping to reload had his arm swiftly broken by a crashing body: two men had to be summoned to drag him from under the horse's carcass. Another soldier running closer to get a better shot tripped over a picket pin, breaking his leg. Cordite and the coppery smell of blood rose once more from the valley's floor. A young recruit who had no stomach for the slaughter withdrew under the guise of reloading to retch into the snowbanks. Others shot carefully with a fixed grimace, as though at some competition. Eventually an order came through to begin cutting the animals throats to save ammunition. Colonel John M. Chivington's voiced desire was coming true this day when he had expressed to the new commander of Ft. Lyon, "I long to be wading in gore!"

Warriors were now screaming in outrage from the cliffs, helpless to interfere. When the neighing and pitiful nickering were finally barely perceptible a shocked silence settled in. Only a twitch of a haunch here and there rose from hundreds of animals whose blood was rapidly freezing on the newly falling snow. Ghostly wisps of steam that rose from the slight warmth of the carcasses seemed to fill the valley. The chaos that had gripped the encampment had been disciplined into an efficient rout. The army was now finished here and the order given to fire the village. One lodge after the other flared up into greedy pyres of all contents, sacred and profane. The elegant feathers of a war bonnet fluttered weakly before bursting into flame. Bare branches of the cottonwoods rose starkly against the heavens. Not a bird cry rang out. Up on the rim Cottonwood Boy watched the wealth and resources of a small nation destroyed, his blood cold, his young heart irreparably hardening.

Obscured by the smoke from Black Kettle's burning lodge the white cloth flown to signify peace hung limp in surrender next to the striped flag that had been given to the leader as a guarantee of protection for his camp and his people. The few survivors of this winter village were now successfully deprived of food, lodging and transportation; all that was precious to them destroyed except what they carried on their backs and in their hands. Something new had been given to them, a new burden to bear or to cast off, if they could. Not just loss, grief, poverty, hunger and starvation, but bitterness, defeat, and the burning coal of desire, a passion that is at times irresistible, a passion for revenge. This encampment on Sand Creek had trusted in the protection afforded them, and they were betrayed, brutally. There had been no hostiles in this camp, no Dog Soldiers. Very few warriors. The irony was that their men had been sent out to hunt, to provide food for the weaker members of the band.

The Cottonwood Boy had managed to bring a few ponies from the herd when he scrambled across Sand Creek and up the ravine to relative safety above. These ponies were now being given to the women and children that had managed to escape, and such old ones who had been helped. The bravest of the warriors fought to hold off the soldiers, allowing a few to escape. As the soldiers began a retreat the North Wind brought a screen of thick flakes to obscure the devastation below, but what ravaged the spirits of these survivors would never be blotted from their memory. Now they must attempt to survive those losses.

The question that had troubled The Cottonwood Boy's heart all these moons since his quest, "Who am I?" was answered that day as he looked down on the bloody trail left behind them in the snow. "I am a warrior!" All desire to bring healing to his people left his mind; blazing now was the vision of himself grasping a blue shirted soldier by the hair, his scalping knife already vibrating with an unquenchable thirst. Hands which he once thought would bring healing to his people now hung limp at his side as he fought back images from his mind. With each intake of the frigid air into his lungs, and with each wail and cry of loss that carried on the air as they struggled north he knew not what he would become, but whatever it was he willed it to harden, to harden, to become strong! Strength! Endurance!

That night under the cover of darkness a band of determined warriors, the boy included, left hoping to secure some of the remnant of the herd. They returned in silent triumph driving a few hundred of those ponies that had been taken during the attack. Now that they had the means to move out onto the snow-clogged and wind swept plains they would seek refuge from other bands further north. Most of them survived the bitterness of three days travel arriving at the hunting camp of Oglala warrior, *Tasunke Witco*, Crazy Horse, where food and shelter was summarily provided. When their story was told at a hastily called council a decision was made to make their way and join forces with a larger village, that of another leader known for despising the *wasichus*, Tatonka Iyotake, Sitting Bull. The survivors were most generously welcomed, not only food and lodging were shared, but robes and good pipes were bestowed as gifts, the blessings from those with good hearts. Up here, the Northern Cheyenne wrapped their braids with strips of red painted buckskin and wore feathers of the crow in their hair, but their hearts were as theirs.

Both Sitting Bull and Crazy Horse disdained the White Man's Road, and viewed coming to a reservation as something that would deprive their people of their spirits. How could they surrender the very hunting grounds that had been given to them by the spirits of the game they captured? While Crazy Horse did not lead with his oratory, Sitting Bull was able to rouse all that heard him. Both leaders understood that a massive confrontation could not be avoided. Sitting Bull spoke, "These soldiers have come shooting. They want war. We must stand together or they will kill us separately."

Death Moccasins

Anah had finished all of the Leatherstocking Tales, and with a head filled with images of Hawkeye, Uncas and Chingagook, she put the last book down and went to delve into her father's trove of Indian artifacts. He and Goethe, his barrister friend from Ligonier, had set out early that fine morning to hunt. She didn't expect them till dark, well announced by their drunken choruses and the yipping of the hounds.

Ever since the day her father had arrived unexpectedly to simply withdraw her from the academy her life had changed in so many ways. When they had arrived back in the city that day she was met by a frantic bustle of activity. Strangers were loading trunks and packing crates for storage. She found Rosamund presiding over a harried kitchen maid placing the families china into cartons. "Liebschen," she smiled, spotting her standing there dumbfounded as she set aside a porcelain gravy boat. "Come," and led her to her old room; pointed to a tall oblong package wrapped in an quilt. "This was your mother's mirror. See that it is unloaded, still wrapped, and placed immediately in the back of your closet at the lodge, behind some garments. A growing girl like you, my dear, must have a full-length mirror even in the wilderness where that father of yours insists on taking you. We have argued, and I have lost. But I chose to disobey him in this one regard on your behalf." And with that she fled the room. Today though, knowing that she had a few hours to herself, Anah intended to preen, and knew just what she would do. It had fallen to her to do what little cooking and cleaning was done for the two of them since he had given up his practice. No longer did the good doctor keep up his appearance; his Van Dyke had morphed into a full beard, his hair curled almost to his collar. His main concentration seemed to be on imbibing the most amount of alcohol that he could contain and still manage to pot a few squirrels and doves. Strange men came to sell him things, too. Indian artifacts, of which he had quite a handsome collection. Along with the trophy heads of deer and elk some new items of interest appeared. There had always been a few ornate Iroquois tomahawks hung on the walls, wonderful arrowheads resided in glass display cases, as were several beaded bags and moccasins, her favorites. But now there was, folded carefully and stored in a cedar trunk in his room, a white doeskin dress whose yoke was hung with many glistening elk teeth. This came from a tribe called The Beautiful People, way beyond the Mississippi. Today she aimed to try it on.

Often the men who brought these things scared her; dirty, unkempt, some were missing teeth, and with horrible scarring, of which they were inordinately proud. They told frightening tales, from wars beyond her comprehension as she crept close to listen. Mountain Men, her father had called them, or scouts, or guides. Some she thought might be actual Indians, but she was afraid to ask; to be noticed. She had heard the word *Metis,* but didn't know it's meaning. The french they spoke was certainly not like what she had been taught. Occasionally one would try to catch her eye, causing her to quickly slip away to the safety of her room. They often brought big brown glazed jugs her father purchased that he teased her was "Elixir of the moon's rays," but wouldn't let her have any. Clear, oily and glistening, it caused the men to lose consciousness much quicker than the darker alcohol. One night she saw her father hand over one of her mother's best cameos for a small woven blanket with a most unusual geometric design, not like the heavy woolen Hudson Bay ones he so favored. Many a night she found her father splayed out on the floor in front of a dead fire with the men, wrapped up in one of these, quite content. Asleep or just passed out, who could tell? She had grown used to this. She especially enjoyed the freedom it gave her to roam the surrounding woods unsupervised.

But today, she went quickly to the trunk. Inside were the favorite moccasins, the ones beaded all over, even to the very soles. Clutching them to her chest she took also the beautiful doeskin garment. She found that she had to undress down to her thin muslin shift to get it to sit right on her slim frame. What a delight. Heavy, but her arms could swing freely with an imagined tomahawk, and with no stays constricting her waist she could leap, twist, and turn. She assessed herself in the full-length mirror. "I need braids," she thought; nothing to do about her straw-like colored hair. Quickly she braided it. Oh, those elk teeth made such a lovely tinkly sound as she twirled, and the long fringes! Is there anything that so delights the heart of a young girl catching the edges of herself in a mirror where she sees the wings of true beauty flick past? Self love, then self consciousness; quickly she mouthed a remedy, thankfulness, "Thank you Rosamund." She felt a slight catch at missing her mother, who knew all about vanity. As she ran her hands over the silky suede of the well-tanned skin from her budding breasts down to her slim hips she leaned in closer to the glass. Is that a hole? A bullet hole? Over the heart? She ran her finger over it, mightily chastened. Then she remembered the moccasins, the beautifully colored beaded ones, as she stood there bare foot. She stooped and slipped them on, one by one, struck by the intricate handiwork. Having spent so many hours doing crewel, embroidery and cut-work that the nuns thought was so necessary a preparation for a young lady, and not liking it one bit, she couldn't imagine this. Every inch of the soles were covered. A bit large; were they men's, perhaps? They felt wonderfully soft. Who were these people? Dressed like this, feeling as lovely as she had ever felt in her life, like a woodland princess, she padded softly out into the large wood-timbered lodge to stand by the fireplace, imagining herself... A whoop of extreme displeasure cut through the air. Anah whirled to see vexation fanned across her father's red sweaty face. She hadn't seen or heard his arrival. "What are you doing?" he bellowed, standing his ground so resolutely that Goethe bumped into him, setting a good-sized brace of doves swinging madly, giving the few hounds bold enough to have followed him inside cause now to excitedly begin to bay. What had been a secret pleasure, to decorate herself with some of her favorite items from her father's collections, was secret no more. Staring now, abjectly, at her feet. The elk teeth on her dress still clinking softly, it seemed to her that all she could hear was her father's labored breathing. It sounded like Jacob Yoder's young bull that he kept in too small a pen. There was another sound, was that her heart? He barked, "Go change, then we'll talk." Raging past her, clearing a small table, he sat down heavily, reaching for his hip flask. As she scurried past Goethe his fat fingers darted out to grip her bare exposed arms. Turning her skillfully toward him and his large gut, in a liquored voice, full of spittle, he spoke into her pale face, staring as though he were a miner raising his stake to make a claim; all the while his small pig-like eyes raked her chest, pulling her closer to him. "Doc, she's developing into quite a little lady!" This was no compliment delivered by a gentleman; she felt like he had just cursed her with some vile prediction, some uncontained desire that coiled forward out of him into the air. She flashed her eyes toward her father, silently beseeching him for help, but he was lost to the monogrammed silver flask pressed tightly to his lips, his head titled heavenward!

Wrenching herself free, Goethe's roiling laughter chased after her. Once in her room she could not get changed fast enough. Then her father was upon her, roughly pulling the moccasins from her feet while drunkenly shouting, "Take them off, off!" She tried to tell him that she hadn't harmed them; that she had only walked on carpets. Then he was almost in tears, and anger was building in her. At a loss at his rage, at drunkenness and abandonment, for not protecting her, and then they were both crying and shouting. He slapped her. The first time, ever! Then she listened. Carefully. "They are for the dead, child," as he held both of her small bare feet in his hands. "Their feet will never walk upon the good earth, ever again." It felt so good, to be touched after all this time. All she could think of in her panic was his wrath at her playing dress-up with artifacts, his treasured collection, she mumbled out through her tears.

" No, No, it's sacrilegious, do you know what that means? It might bring harm on you child." "Papa," she gasped, "you haven't called me that in ages," and she threw her arms around him then, finally seeing that he was concerned. He pulled her onto his lap and was stroking her hair, soothing her. "You're superstitious, Papa?" she asked him. "No, no, but I believe in honoring, well, these customs. I don't want you to walk about in...." "Shoes that were meant for the dead," she finished speaking, and their eyes met. "I want to know more about these people, these Beautiful People. The Tsitsistas, the Cheyenne," he said. "The shyene? The sissy? Uh, tell me more. Can we study them please, can you teach me?" He stood up to leave, then paused, turned back, reached down for her hand, pulled her to her feet. "Perhaps we'll go there some day." When they came into the big room, Goethe had gone, taking the brace of doves with him.

Raison D'etre

The High Plains

It had taken three arduous days of travel through the snow covered plains to reach a safe shelter. They had been hampered along the way not only by the cold and hunger, but by the pressing needs of the helpless young, aged and wounded, not that there were many babies left alive to add their frail cries to the almost constant wail of those in mourning. Many were still in such shock from the unexpected early morning attack that the power of speech appeared to have left their bodies. Numbed into silence by cold, hunger and devastating loss. All efforts had to focus on reaching the Oglala camp, and soon, if they were not to perish. The High Plains gripped by winter were to be feared unless well-dressed and well provisioned. Weapons were not so much a concern, as this was a time that by tradition enemy raids were wisely curtailed. It was wisdom to stay by one's fire, nap fresh arrowheads, bead more moccasins, and take in the tales of honor both recent and of ages past. A time when family bonds and tribal identities were strengthened.

But now, forced out unprepared upon the plain, the survivors were indeed struggling. All but the youngest knew that they were desperate. They shared what food they had, for some had managed to escape with some pemmican that was parsed around. Most of the mothers fortunate to have their child still at the breast, and not lying sprawled and lifeless, abandoned by the hideous rout, had no milk, their breasts now as withered as their spirits. As to their leaders that had survived the attack, those able to sit a horse, they had to exert all their remaining strength, both of body as well as mind. A few fell by the wayside, a life decimated by practically inconceivable violence, spirit quenched by exhaustion and the overwhelming heaviness of despair, unable to deal with yet another betrayal.

Wagachun had watched most of the peaceful camp's destruction from his vantage point on the bluffs; he had seen the white flag that supposedly would protect them crumple, torn from the pole in front of Black Kettle's lodge, shredded by a fusillade from one of the four big guns brought to bear on the still sleeping village. Wagachun's first thought was that the *ve'ho'e's* power was not very strong if the lovely red, blue and white banner could not protect as promised. It proved as unreliable as the white-man's word.

Moons after Wagachun had reached the safety of the well-armed and well provisioned camp of the Oglalas in the Powder River country his nights were often sleepless. Lying in a thick winter robe in the Dog Soldier Red Heart's lodge, he thought he heard the pitiful cry of a hungry infant. The harsh winds that whipped through the camp at night brought him sounds like the wailings of those who had lost everything but the breath of life. Drifting off into a troubled sleep, he often startled awake at what he thought were the moans of a wounded warrior bouncing along on a travois. In fact, the wounded men that could still manage to walk had done so, so that the few sound ponies could bear the precious old ones that had been brought to safety. Generous to the end, many a precious member of the tribe, valued for his wisdom of the ages, if no longer his physical abilities, summoned the strength to roll, unnoticed into the deep snow, freeing up the space for one of his wounded people.

Night after night he envisioned the young warrior, grievously wounded, who had refused to burden anyone's mount, march resolutely forward, a stick clenched tightly between his teeth, determined not to add his pain to the collective misery. Other men moved forward singing their Death Songs. The battle was now being fought to simply stay alive. Many were warmed against the bone-crushing cold by stoking a bonfire of desire for unrelenting vengeance, vowing to live to avenge the death of a loved one.

Trodding through the late November snow they left a trail spotted by blood not only from unstaunched wounds, but from the injuries, self-inflicted, that those who had an unbearable loss of husband, wife, child.. children, as though the knife pressed into their chilled flesh could overwhelm the bleak winter that had descended so suddenly upon their hearts. A wound self-inflicted to the flesh was indeed easier to bear; distracting from the wound to one's heart! The sky hung low, dark gray clouds were thinly stretched just above the horizon to the North. The wind came in short, angry seeming blasts, whipping the dried grass and sage one way, then abruptly another, only to die down, leaving in it's wake an expectant atmosphere. As Wagachun, the Cottonwood Boy, scrambled up the sides of the butte he stayed alert for any signs that he was not alone. More than anything he wanted to be alone; alone with his confused thoughts. Even though he and the others that escaped the massacre back at Sand Creek had been so generously welcomed here, he was troubled. Troubled not only for himself and the other survivors, but a deep unease had settled on him as he watched the young children at play. How unconcerned they appeared, enjoying the games that the winter snow had provided, laughing as they did so. The women, too, accepted their daily chores, hauling water, preparing the food, sewing new moccasins. It was the old ones that disturbed him, the way they had retreated to some place in their minds, a private sadness upon their features. The sick and wounded were being given ample care; with Silver Spotted Owl passed on he made an effort to discern those men who had the powers to heal, to divine. Once again he was an orphan. He needed guidance! And while Red Heart had opened his lodge to him, the warrior was far too busy with attending council fires to do anything but go gravely to his own robes, often late at night.

This encampment had many warriors, mostly the revered Dog Soldiers, who he saw only as they went to and fro from one important council to another. The leaders here were those who steadfastly refused to take their people down the White Man's Path. Now the talk was of open hostility, many were smoking the pipe for the Red Road. There was much to avenge, much! But Wagachun had witnessed the strong medicine of the *ve'ho'e's* weapons. Did these warriors not understand the power of the big guns, the ones that sent destruction through the air to blast a huge emptiness in whatever they landed upon? He tried to banish from his mind the sight of limbs flying through clouds of dirt, blood, snow and cordite! Shaking his head, running a hand over his eyes, as though he could press those images gone, he blinked and focused on achieving the top of the bluff where he could be away from the village and his disturbing thoughts. It will snow soon. He could feel the strange tension in the errant clouds; soon they would assemble and take over the sky completely. He wished he still had his robe, the one his second mother, Grey Lost Bird, had given to him, with the thick winter hair of the buffalo. His mind still fixed on that dreadful day, he achieved the summit. He was startled to find a slim man calmly seated, back leaning against the sole pine that had established itself on the edge of the cliff. That was just where he wanted to be, there facing away from the camp, looking down and out over the wide expanse of the winter plain. Before he could decide a course of action, the man waved him forward, without turning to otherwise acknowledge him he patted a spot on the ground nearby. Wagachun approached, not quite knowing who this was and how to greet him, but assumed that his presence was to be tolerated, if not welcomed. In such a large encampment, swelled by the recent survivors, solitude was hard to come by. So they sat in a comfortable, if mysterious silence, watching the swiftly moving clouds change the landscape below them.

Wagachun covertly observed his companion. He saw no signs that this man had come seeking a vision, but then if he had, he would have brought nothing with him, no food, no water. The man was an Oglala, for he had none of the appearance of a Cheyenne, that much he discerned, taking in the unusual lightness of his skin and hair. He doubted that this man had any position of importance, as his body was completely unadorned, no discernible markings of place or honors save a lone eagle feather dangling limply down from his scalp lock. Behind one ear dangled a small gray stone. Yet even as the man sat calmly he emanated great natural power.

The longer they sat, the harder the wind blew, and the colder the day became. This man had no robe on, just a plain shirt and unadorned dark leggings. Was he real? Just as Wagachun was daring to speak to him the man began talking, still with his eyes calmly fixed on the empty plain before him.

"*This good earth was given to us to trod upon, all of us, but it is not ours to give away or sell. In respect we do not tear it open, or fence it off. We are content to gather what has been so amply provided for us; to hunt what we need to live. To do this we travel upon the face of this earth, in those places trod by our grandfathers, and fathers before them. It is not our way to stay in one place, and live in square wooden boxes. Why do the Bluecoats pursue us no matter where we go to avoid them? When we do not go near where they have chosen to settle they seek us out to fall upon, not only our warriors, but our women, children and the old ones. Their hearts are small, they do not hold much wacantognaka, generosity. With their mouth stretched up wide below their lying eyes they gather many of our leaders, shower them with beads, sugar and coffee, if only they will touch the pen to what they call a "treaty", but nothing seems to stop their greed."*

He then stopped speaking, as though he had said too much. Not once had he turned his face towards Wagachun, and yet his presence was reassuring, somehow. When the snow flurries began Wagachun came quickly back down to the shelter of the village far below, a changed, subdued spirit at rest for now in his chest. He sought no one, no food, but went right to his blankets for the night. In all that time, for now darkness was near, he realized that he had not said one word to him in response, yet his words were of strong and wise counsel. A counsel that he did not know that he was seeking.

He thought much on them over the following days. One day he woke knowing his path, the one he would begin to take to protect and defend his people, those who first sheltered him, loved him and showed him the way of life, for it was good.

Ghost Buffalo

The old man slowly distracted himself from the weasel pelt that he had been laboring on as Red Heart approached his lodge. As the young warrior waited respectfully, Swift Medicine took the time to observe the boy standing quietly at Red Heart's side, eyes lowered. It was not unusual for a younger Dog Man such as Red Heart to seek his counsel, but why was this skinny youth with the hollow eyes brought along? Setting aside his work, he gestured them to enter. The tall, gaunt boy was pleasant to look upon and had about himself the aspects of the Beautiful People, Tsitsistas, Northern Cheyenne. As they exchanged greetings he surmised that the youth was one of the survivors of the recent Sand Creek massacre. He himself was still weary and sore in spirit, though it had already been half a moon cycle since the remnants of that band had joined his camp here in their winter grounds. His own dreams and visions were yet to return back to him, and he felt an emptiness. Yes, empty, hollowed out, but heavy like a cold fire pit overfull of ashes. His heart lay with such sadness in his chest. Not good for a warrior! His attention had drifted; when it returned it was to hear Red Heart divulge the reason for bringing this one they called "The Cottonwood Boy", Wagachun, to him. There was something of obvious import to tell him as a leader. "I am hearing you," Swift Medicine spoke as he settled down upon his back rest. At that the young man began to recite:

It was the moon of the first snowfall. I was with the herd, where I usually am. Little White Bear and one I cannot now name were somewhere with me in the night's blackness. It was the time just before the sun's return when the eye can see nothing but the faint skeleton of the trees, and even the owls and coyotes keep the night's long silence still. It was the time when I would take the most care to keep alert, so that when I detected a faint milling among my pretty horses at the far end of the canyon my awareness was most keen. There appeared to be a faint glow, like the moon's light, but instead of spreading over all below it just illuminated the darkest stretch of the canyon. Now this was an area where there were no defaults, no cut banks, no way in or out. As to this strange light, it was not in the east, where one would expect the sun to rise. There began movement in the herd, but not the kind that signaled a disturbance....

At this the old warrior signaled him to halt, and reached for his pipe bag: this recounting had certain elements of a vision. He studied the boy as he carefully prepared the smoke. There was an exceeding calm about him, as though he had nothing of value to import. This constituted the makings of humility. Good, the old Dog Soldier solemnly assessed, signaling him to continue.

*The herd then parted of one mysterious accord, opening up a path down the middle. We had many, many, many ponies at this time. Our finest war horses, buffalo runners, and pack horses were amassed together in this well protected sheltered place. We were rich....*then he visibly shuddered, holding back a thought he did not want to recall, looking to Red Heart, but briefly, then continued... *The glow of light grew stronger, but it was a pale light, like the inside of a mussel shell, not golden as the sun can make... like Abalone! Down this pathway slowly trod a large white buffalo, as shining white as the clouds are that always accompany a full-bodied moon. The animal was magnificently muscled and thickly furred!*

Did he not know that this was a vision, the old man wondered? How could one of so few years recount this telling of the great white buffalo of all our People without obvious excitement. Swift Medicine began to wonder more of just who this Cottonwood Boy was, observing him closely as he nodded for him to continue. Poorly dressed, as most of the survivors of the Sand Creek Massacre were, having escaped with just the clothes on their back, though generously given, from their brothers and sisters here in the camps, what could be spared. He had no regalia of any telling significance, save a worn crow feather dangling from his scalp lock.

Of course my heart raced. Should I signal the others? Or wait and see? Was there danger? I did not think so, but I felt overcome in a way that I had never experienced before. The beast was drawing closer: the horses stood unmoving to let him past. Did I say that this was a very large bull buffalo, not a calf? Soon it would be close enough to breathe on me, but I stood rooted to the ground, barely aware that I, too, stood at attention like the horses. Did I say that the sky did not continue to lighten? This confused me. Was this a dream, a vision, or was this real, but how could it be? At that time I was too full of awe to think clearly. Oddly, I expected the great white one to come to me and stop. My heart began to race. Excuse me for thinking that I was to be chosen, but I did. Time did not move, the only movement was the buffalo as it passed by me and through the herd, working down towards the village where all still slept. As it passed, I seemed to come back to my senses and knew that I must run to awaken my guardian and tell him of the white buffalo's return, as prophesied.

But I could not move...I could not move, and as my eyes were fixed on his passage I saw each and every horse in our herd sink slowly, too slowly, to the hard, cold ground. They lay as dead, the snow beneath them seeping red. But my eyes were still fixed on the great beast who kept advancing in a measured pace towards our encampment. When he stood by the first lodge he looked towards me. I am ashamed to say that in my great fear I dropped my eyes. Shame entered my heart at my fear. Then to my horror he pushed against the hide of the lodge which gave no resistance. It did not topple, or even tear as this great white animal walked right through it!

"He knocked it over?" Red Heart blurted rudely out. Swift Medicine hand rose to stay any further interruption as the boy calmly continued.

The Great White Buffalo walked though lodge after lodge, passed right through them without knocking down even a lodge pole, nor a medicine bundle, nor waking any dogs. Not a warrior ran out. Not a dog barked. My ears burned in silence. He passed right through the hide walls of lodge after lodge, avoiding just a few and still the village slept on, unawares. That's when I realized he was a Spirit, a Ghost Buffalo. And, He hesitated again, passing a thin, long-fingered hand across his eyes; the only sign the two older men noted of a disturbance in the storyteller's demeanor. This Cheyenne was old beyond his years, it seemed. He continued.

Moving step by measured step, each white hair shimmered so brightly that I could barely keep my eye upon him. With each step the brilliance seemed to increase, as he crossed the creek and moved slowly up the steep hillside. Up, up, up into the sky!

Now fading with each further step away from our village. Great fear settled on me like a sheet of ice. I felt I must move, give warning, this was a very bad omen, even I knew this....That's when I woke to the sound of the Bluecoat's big guns tearing into our lodges, just as first light had arrived...

He sank to his feet, eyes upon the ground, spent in the retelling. I think his heart fell down once more.

Billy Blue Eyes

1858
Foothills of the Alleghenies

She loved to pit herself against them; young boys her age, to challenge them, outrun them, for she was very swift of foot, not just to take dares, but to make them up and be the first to act, her youth a leaping fish snapping at life like a succulent fly. There was no slow swim to the surface for her.

Racing through the woods behind the hunting lodge that now served as a home for just her and her father, she gloried in outfoxing her new companions, knowing just where to hide, when to spring forth in gleaming triumph, turn and run the other way. They pursued her as the hounds would, baying along. But it was all a game, and there were no leaders; she was simply privileged, a girl allowed to run with the pack.

Days passed with her father lost to the bottle. All pretense of her schooling being undertaken by him ceased, nor did the promised tutor ever materialize. She did not miss the strictures and disciplines of a boarding school. She welcomed her new freedom. As to her education, she could pursue that herself, being an avid reader with no dearth of books at hand. Meals ceased to exist as even the faintest formality; with her mother's demise there was no longer a household staff. Food was there, cooked sometimes by her, less by him. A large crock of beans baked in spice and molasses they both could feed off of for days, a crock of butter and a comb of honey along with rough loaves he brought to the table from somewhere. Her skirts had grown so bramble torn that she traded Earl ,the handyman, a jar of French preserves from the pantry for an outgrown pair of his work pants, and held them to her with a knotted rope. She took to bathing by the spring, sitting to dry her hair, watching the salamanders crawl back out from where they had hidden from her disturbed drawing of the waters. Sometimes she sat in her chemise, understanding the new sweet feel of the dappled sun on her skin, throwing back her head, letting the sun place warm red thumbs of pleasure on her closed lids.

Returning to the lodge she'd pack an old rucksack for her day, a small book perhaps to read, or her commonplace book to talk into. As the days coalesced as easily as an evening cloud her father's presence was at times only accounted for by the occasional disturbed snort of a drunken slumber. A bit of bread, cheese and a wizened apple retrieved from the bushel of the past fall's Gravensteins, her penknife and the bosun's whistle her Uncle had given her on her twelfth birthday secure in her pockets she set out with eagerness, one of the dogs at her side. Each day this summer of freedom moved towards its zenith, drawing her yet closer to an unknown but glorious revelation.

Somewhere in the woods, by the lake, up on the ridge, near the quarry, or by Koontz's bluff she would find them, or they her. It was a matter of youthful indifference; all decorum had slipped from her slim tanned limbs. She felt a new, unnameable power coming to her blood. She had shot up a full inch, as the mark on the door jamb attested; strong enough to haul two buckets of spring water along the path from the spring without pausing to rest, and when she looked into her mother's vanity mirror affixed to the back of her closet door and stood to braid her hair, she liked what she saw. Unexpected and welcome, she imagined herself a classical Diana, and reached for the small arrowhead bound by a thong around her neck. She thought of calling a "meeting", arranging a "ceremony"; she wanted a "blood brother", the child that yet prevailed in her was sullen and confused, and as yet no one face sprang to mind to bond with in brotherhood.

By Fall the cooling nights, schooling, (it was inevitable that he might send her back) and the presence of hunters hampered her loose roaming. So she was wild to be off and running through the fallen leaves, ripening apple and grape scenting the mid-day warmth, the sun hot and insistent at claiming her attention. The months spent outdoors had been schooling her in their own way. But now her father wanted her close by; afraid that her swift leaping down the game trails she knew now, by heart, could have tragic consequences. He was the most conscientious of huntsmen, but the woods were rife with those that shot at the first rustle of the undergrowth.

More and more Billy came around. Chopping and stacking wood

for them, scything back the now dead grasses in the near field, doing odd chores. He was perhaps older than her thirteen years, but seemed so much younger in his mind. He wasn't really one of her pack. He was slow, and avoided those quicksilver boys. But she had known him for years before her father had moved them up here, and he was sweet, brought her flowers.

When she and Billy first met, his large, sprawling family lived all squeezed together in a tar paper shack in a small holler close by Laurel Creek. She hadn't known at first that he was "different". Her father explained that most likely a high fever from a childhood illness had affected him, altering both brain and body, slowing him down, much like a plant that's had to recover from having some fallen log pressing it down, left with just enough light and nourishment to keep on struggling.

Well, with the splendid fall days upon them, Billy took a growth spurt, shedding baby fat and springing up lean and handsome. Those merry blue eyes danced so appealingly when they lit on her that day. Billy had just ripped his old flannel shirt over his head and flung it toward the stacked up wood when he turned toward her, the sweat he had worked up gleamed with a golden sheen on his bare chest. She forgot that she had come out to summon him in for lunch. A question passed in the air between them, these old playmates. He sunk the axe into the chopping block. With a delighted giggle she took off running. None of the other boys could beat her, but she'd never raced him before.

She flew down the trail toward the spring. She didn't have to turn to know he was crashing along close behind her. A short-cut to the footbridge across the creek, so low and lazy flowing now that she sprang from one half submerged rock to the other, wildly grasping a laurel branch to pull herself up the far bank. Where to head? Unerringly, her feet led her down towards the holler where the fallen leaves from the beech trees were thick and redolent of late summer. Once there she would have won, but where was he? Had he fallen behind? She risked turning, to see him swing thrillingly across to the other side of the leaf filled glade on a firm length of wild grapevine. Her lungs felt fit to burst, her left ankle throbbed as though twisted, and her cheek stung from where a branch had slapped her in such a fury to beat him.

Too late she saw him just tumble and roll freely down the hillside, a brilliant maneuver, she thought, then spring to his feet, multicolored leaves in his thick brown curls and clinging to his sweaty limbs. Arms spread wide in victory, white teeth a welcome glitter in his tanned face, he crowed in victorious laughter with a welcoming gaiety. Stumbling, tripping over her own feet, she allowed herself to fall onto his chest, which she then began beating at. Bitter tears burned in her eyes, and defeat was thick and dry in her throat at being bested. He was faster than her; that was maddening to her inflamed spirit, she who saw herself as a swift-footed forest creature, invincible! Men, she thought involuntarily, it's not fair, and she burned, flaming hot, to slap him. But raising her hand, she found it gripped. Struggling, they went down into the dry, crackling leaves, many inches thick beneath them. "Billy," she managed to gasp as they rolled and surfaced and began to play, cavorting like dogs. Flinging handfuls of crisp autumn leaves, the rich scent making them dizzy. Wrestling and grasping, rolling free, then grabbing hold once more, alive with the warm scented air and their youth. Suddenly he had her pinned down full length. His body was squirming to hold her there. She was trying to bite as he held both wrists pinned.

"You're hurting me! Let go!" Just as abruptly he released his grasp, then began tickling her till she again begged him to stop. When he did, they found themselves breathless, panting.

Their eyes met, and everything about her life changed in that moment, both scaring and thrilling her in a way that something newly discovered can. When Billy began to move upon her, with a slow pressure, Anah found herself confused with the feeling of response that began to flood her senses. She rolled away, and without brushing the golden leaves from her hair she ran off.

Swift Medicine's Story

Mist hung low over the camp when he went out to place his medicine bundle in the fresh sun's rays. Soon it would be time to leave the canyon, for the grass was growing higher day by day and they were all eager to move out onto the high plains again. Off in the distance on the other side of the running water he thought he saw the young Cheyenne that Red Heart had brought to him that time after the Bluecoats had sent so many of Motovato's Black Kettle people beyond the ridge on the trail to the stars.

That young herd boy, Wagachun, had not left the old Dog Soldier's mind; he felt him coming closer to him, though he rarely saw him with his eyes. What Swift Medicine knew and the boy didn't was that he had been given strong medicine. A few moons after Red Heart had brought him to share the story of the Ghost Buffalo, he had sought out Red Heart and asked him to tell him more of the one called The Cottonwood Boy. His adoptive father, Spotted Owl, a known *wicasa wakan*, had been taken from him on the day of the massacre, and though the boy had been taken into Shave Head's lodge he kept to himself now, spending as much time as he could with the herd, in all respects quietly notable as he grew into his manhood. Had the boy his time of vision seeking, he asked of Red Heart, to discover that yes, he had done so successfully under The Owl's guidance many winter counts back. But of what his power animal was no one knew, or cared, it seemed. Swift Medicine knew it was not the buffalo in spite of his story. Our first teacher is our own heart, but he was alone now. Shave Head was no one to guide him on the use of the power that the old warrior sensed was hovering about him. Was he being called to him? So many cold seasons had passed that now Swift Medicine's long bones ached at the time when the leaves began to leap from their branches and the winds blew cold from the North. True, he had won much acclaim, as one glance at his large many-skinned decorated lodge would tell. His war lance was strung with as many eagle feathers as a young tree has leaves. Great Bear had protected him well and brought much wisdom, enabling him to have many fine ponies to give away. A magnificently muscled spotted war horse from the Palouse was kept tethered outside, but it's tail had gone many seasons without being tied up; he had no need of it anymore. To sit by his fire one would think him a man of much wealth, yet to look not inside the well-tanned skins of his lodge, but inside his own weathered skin one would see how poor he really was. In spite of the snow of age that was settling on his scalp he kept two young wives happy, and three new children slept in his lodge. Long ago he had risen to the privilege of wearing the treasured Dog Rope. If Heavy Thunder had not pulled the picket pin on that day that the Bluecoats were seeking their enemies the Greycoats, near the hunting ground between Smoke Hill and the Republican River, he would have fought to a glorious death, his story told on the next Winter Count. Instead age had brought him to rest here in camp, no longer with the other Dog Men, but instead idly carving a dance stick to honor that fine war horse, Grey Blaze, who like him had grown too old to do what they once did best together.

    His first wife was a Shiheyla, a Northern Cheyenne, one of the Beautiful People, as they rightfully are called. Close to fifty of the finest ponies on the high plains he had brought to her father's herd, and would have brought a hundred more for her. She was beyond price, and aptly named for she gathered, brought to him, the finest things of his life. Things he did not know this world contained until she showed him. Much of the goodness he retained was due to her. He struggled, at times, not to water any bitter seed that her loss had brought. Inside his withered, battle-scarred hide she lived still in all the beauty of her young life. Her final gift, the son she died in birthing.

    It caused great pain to think how he may have contributed to the eventual death of that first born son. From the time he could stand on his two legs Swift Medicine placed the child before him on his finest war pony. As soon as he could pull himself onto the back of a gentle pack horse he saw that the child had a fine pony of his very own. He had his mother's blood and could sit a horse like it was an extension of his fine young body. Soon he could not be contained to play at idle games. Of course, his father saw that he had the finest trappings; his first bow was of bois d'arc. He was overly eager to be on the war trail, to capture horses of his own. A born warrior! Swift Medicine was so full of pride that the boy wanted to be like him that encouragement fell like spring showers. Due to his father's standing in the tribe the boy was often gifted and even indulged by too many others. Too late the father saw that while he embodied many fine traits, a small but powerful seed of his own importance above those of his kind was growing, nurtured by his natural abilities, his relation to his father, and his own beauty of form. Envy and a certain disregard soon formed in the boy to grow with him as a shadow, lurking, like an unseen predator, all too eager to bring him down.

Hau! Can it be since the coming of the Iron Road that he has gone beyond the ridge? Perhaps it is well that he did not live to see how those who roamed freely and hunted where they wished, were now herded like the skinny cow beasts to captivity, and if there was refusal the *wasichus* send their Bluecoats into our midst.

Last night when Swift Medicine felt, rather than heard, a great night bird pass so low over his body that a small passage of air ruffled the eagle plume on his scalp lock he did not think it as an omen of death, but, rather, remembered the very first time his *hoksila* laid his eyes on one, and it was in broad daylight!

Years ago when father and son had been walking out in the fresh snowfall, in the Moon of Snow Blindness, so that when the child clutched Swift Medicine's hand in his fierce little grip and pointed he reached naturally towards his bow. When he realized no threat, for what was looking at them, hunched on a large mound and staring intently, he was prone to laugh. Then he saw the awe upon the child's face. In all it's full feathered splendor there sat one of the great white snow owls of the farthest North lands, it's deep yellow eyes glowing like a sacred fire. Was it real, the boy asked, not what is it. That was when Swift Medicine first began to notice his child's appreciation of material beauty. The next instant the child broke from his grasp and raced, faster than it seemed his sturdy little legs could carry him, towards the bird. Knowing of the sharpness of beak and talons the owl tribe possessed his father commanded him to stop. Of course, the great bird lifted into the overcast sky leaving the child with his face upturned in wonder.

Did the boy query his father about this rare creature as they traveled on? No, he pouted most of the way back, for his desire had been only to somehow capture it, to make it his own.

The years passed swiftly, then one day his first born crawled out of the sweat lodge, a triumphant gleam rising from his lean well-formed body, so unlike his father's squat thickly muscled one. This was just the beginning of his readiness to trod the warrior path. With some concern too many heard his retelling of the successful quest for a vision, noting the swelling of pride that caused him to finally lose his balance upon the good earth. Pride, and it's kin, arrogance, impatience, conceit and a headstrong spirit that, once given full rein, carried him, full speed, to his death just a few seasons later.

Though Swift Medicine tried not to dwell on the circumstance of his death, of how his overwhelming desire to acquire the wealth of many fine ponies, to earn many feathers of the eagle, and notches for his coup stick, it remained, all these years later, too bitter to drink down. So he was grateful that the names of those gone beyond were not spoken aloud; that all his possessions had been given away, and that others built the scaffold that had lifted his remains up to the scrutiny of the heavens above. Swift Medicine knew that his story was told sometimes as a tale to caution other impulsive young men, eager to try their fate, but it was never retold in his hearing, never!

What he could not will away completely visited him more and more these seasons when his defenses were low. These days were becoming more and more brutal for the People as they tried to continue in their traditional ways. Late evenings, when darkness began to create imaginings, Swift Medicine sometimes saw once more how those young men looked that day riding into camp.

That day had opened slowly to an overcast sky. The sun appeared sullen, swollen, mostly hidden behind oddly shaped clouds of no mean import, which sent the wise ones to impotent grumblings amongst themselves, finally driving them to seek their own counsel in their favorite haunts. This alone made Swift Medicine discomfited. The raiding party was a day overdue, by his reckoning. His wives chased him from their cook fires for his aimless pestering, there seemed nothing to do but whittle away at yet another coup stick. As the day dragged on the far horizon remained devoid of riders. By late afternoon dark clouds piled seamlessly up into a heavy wall, as though they would simply sink down and snuff out the descending sun, which was pouring forth a thin vermilion line across the prairie to cast a wan red glow onto the sage. Just then riders appeared suddenly over the horizon with no triumphal calls to alert the whole village to their coming. Now the few of them who were witnessing their return stood waiting to count the cost of their failure. There was no string of new ponies accompanying them. Eagerly they searched their party for the wounded, the missing. The young warriors still wore their paint streaked and smeared upon their faces, an indication that they had fled straight back from the scene of their defeat. Swift Medicine stood rooted to the spot, eyes burning and dry as he tried to sharpen his focus in the dimming light. One, two, three, four, they came at a slow pace forward.

Struggling to count them, to look for wounds, to look for his son. Not him, not him! Then the last straggled forward, head down. A mere boy, Coyote Paw, was leading his son's horse, Arrow. Some game was slung over it's back. Was that an antelope or deer? A deer with feathers? And moccasins? No, no, what had been slaughtered was his boy, his son! His heart left him then, fell down. He could feel an ever expanding emptiness in his chest, a wild smoky fire that ate, consumed his reason in it's burning rush forward. When the flames of loss were beaten back, there was but a scorched plain as empty as a vast black sky bereft of it's stars! That fire went out, leaving only a dimming coat of ash upon his spirit, but in those final minutes of light on that day Swift Medicine stood as one without hearing. Silence surrounded him, walled him in. A dense fog rose where all sounds were distorted as he watched the young men slide from their mounts and move towards his son's body. Still he stood, hearing and feeling nothing, it seemed, just the numbing fever of loss. His fixed and yet also strangely unseeing gaze locked upon that lifeless body, as covered with blood as when he first came into this world!

They told him it was days before he spoke or took any notice of his surroundings. He felt no hunger or thirst. His personal sun had fallen from the skies, and his family respected that, even the dogs slunk quietly past him.

Then one evening when he left the lodge to relieve himself his ears finally began to work again. There in the cold night, feeling at one with the icy remove of the stars so very far above, daring to wonder if, if.. he heard the clear hoot of an owl calling. Then he did what was required. Finally aroused from where his spirit had sunk to, when he was able to speak of this with his kola, Loud Dog, he told this story:

"Shut away in my own darkness, I had kept how greatly my son's foolish death had both angered and hurt me. Though I had wives, no more sons were to come to me. Now in the owl's presence, though I could not see him, I began to concentrate on what my spirit was hearing that night. When my son and I had come upon the great white bird from the realm of the far frozen north with the glowing yellow eyes that day when he was yet a teachable child, I was ready to give him what I knew. That this bird has wondrous sight and hearing, that it can see into the darkness of a man's soul, that the light of the sun blazes alive in the owl's eyes at night so that it can go freely through the darkness. My son did not want to learn from my wisdom, not that day nor in his future. If he had come to me, or any other of the wise and experienced warriors, they would have warned him away from his foolish plan to steal the enemies' horses on a full moon night. He had the owl's medicine, the abilities granted, but I do not believe that he acknowledged them as he should have. Unlike the owl, he had not trusted what he perceived, that the moon's full light would reveal inexperienced warriors moving towards the valuable war ponies of their enemies. As the owl he should have kept silent, not tried to imitate a night bird's disturbed call that would alert those guarding the herd. That great white snowy owl is a wise, experienced hunter, and when it moves into a new territory, unlike the other owls, it does not announce its presence. It accomplishes it's aims with timing and skill. It's true strength lies in how it survives without the hot temperament of the great horned owl, an owl almost as large.

So silently I gathered the few things I needed. Going on foot, I left the village undetected. I went swiftly to where I had secreted my first wife's bones, after I had taken them down from the scaffolding all those years ago, to bury them among the rocks of Paha Sapha. I carefully unwrapped the pitifully small bundle, the skeletal remains of one who had given me, and others, much. Fifteen gatherings of the tribes for the sun ceremony had passed since I had placed her here. I did not stop but to burn some sage, and offer prayers for guidance, not fearing if this was a desecration, so great was this need upon me. Drawing out one delicate *nape,* hand, from the weathered deerskin I selected a knuckle bone, small but strong. Then I selected one from her other hand. Gently I touched the blue stone necklace that I had given her when told that she was carrying our child. I picked it up, eager, too eager, to take it with me. Then returned it to the bundle, adding back the lizard amulet she had beaded that contained his birth cord. Somehow I had removed it from his body that horrible day when he was brought to me slung across the withers of his favorite horse like a slain animal. (To this day one of her delicate bones lies in the little deerskin bag that is never removed from my old neck. The other lies secreted in the folds of our son's burial shroud.)"

Over time Swift Medicine accepted his loss, but for many, many moons he naturally anticipated his son's presence, and had to refrain from speaking his name. When he caught himself with that name that rose from his sore heart to his lips his whole being was shrouded in what seemed to be the unreality of his son's absence. At times this absence was in itself a presence, seemingly larger than life itself. Eventually the loss was contained in him like the deep, dark water at the very bottom of an abandoned well, so deep that it reflected no light. One no longer drank from it!

The Summons/Hanbleceyiya

Long after sundown, during the Last of the Cold Moons, Swift Medicine rose straight up from his warm buffalo robes. His hearing still as sharp as it had been years ago, he closed his eyes and listened. Yes, the chilling hoot came again, wending through the clear air of the winter encampment. He half expected to see a vision of *Hinhan Kara,* the old woman, "Owl Maker", who led those who had followed a good path towards the Land of Many Fine Lodges up into the heavens. For he had a peace that he would be one of those who were allowed to stay on the path, not tossed into the abyss by her. Glancing at the sleeping forms of his wives, allowing his eyes to roam the faint interior, he saw nothing to indicate that he was in the dreaming world, yet the flap to his lodge was open, as it should not have been, but nothing was amiss.

He did not hear a single sound, except the very slight soughing sound of the coals settling down into ash. Moonlight filled the doorway, so beautiful, as full of silver as the glinting of the summer sun on water, but oddly it held no glare. He found himself standing, no chill upon his bare skin, no ache in his old bones. He was entranced. Yes, this strange moonlight was beckoning him to enter its mysterious gleam. He felt nothing amiss even though this was a time of darkness for the moon. Not hesitating to explore, as though he were but a young man of but a few winters, a small pleasure filled him at the strangeness that was surrounding him now. He was still a warrior, after all.

Exiting naked from the tent: there on the other side of the icy stream stood a snow white buffalo calf, perfectly formed, its breath rising into luminous silver trails upon the night air. Once he met it's gaze, it turned north and strode along the bank, heading towards a strand of aspen around the bend by the horse herd. As he followed an excitement built in him; so long it had been since he had a vision. No matter how fast he trod, bare feet dancing on bare snow, he could not close the gap between them. At the base of a large cottonwood it knelt, and turned once more towards him. He stood transfixed, expectant, reverent, waiting for the message of great significance.

How long he stood he had no idea. The stars above revolved in their timeless gyre, or perhaps he only blinked but once before the creature nodded its pure white head, then simply disappeared....just a faint mist dissolving into the night. "Wait," he called out, desperate to know what this apparition intended. He raced to the exact spot to find that the snow held only a small declivity where warmth had melted from four hooves, only that.

He woke to a disheveled Sleeping Fox Woman looking quizzically into his face. "You shouted out in your sleep." "What?" " Wait, I believe you were calling, over and over." Disgruntled, he pulled himself up, pulling a thick winter buffalo robe around his shoulders, for a great chill had come suddenly upon him as he stepped out into the dark, moonless night. From the faint stirring of the birds he knew that the sun would soon rise, but now he could barely discern the circle of lodges spread around him. Though he could hear the running of the stream, he could not see even a glimmer of light reflecting off it's surface. Making his way swiftly through the sleeping village the dogs merely grumbled; his scent a familiar one. Which tree had it been? There, the largest of the cottonwoods raised it's skeletal arms to the still pulsing stars. Why do the stars appear at their brightest when one is alone, he mused as he searched the snow-covered grounds for tracks. Not finding any he knelt in the slight depression beneath the tree. In the middle lay a large feather, one meant for flight, with that little downy tuft at it's base to dull the sound from the wings. One pure white owl's primary!

Leaping to his feet as if arrow struck, *Hau!* He exclaimed. That swift movement and sound caused the nearby herd to stir. A soft call of alarm rose from one of the boys that were guarding them. Seizing the feather, he simultaneously called out before his presence here would be violently challenged, for running towards him, arrow nocked, was the one called The Cottonwood Boy.

As soon as the village was awake he sought out Black Cloud, another Bear Dreamer, as himself. Passing the pipe, Swift Medicine told him of his portentous night. The white buffalo calf, the owl's feather, and then of the orphaned boy, Wagachun, who had also been visited by a ghostly white animal. He favored this *wapiya wicasa,* Black Cloud, trusted his advice and felt that he needed to take it. The associations his own mind made with the ones from the spirit world were as loosely woven as a child's first attempt at creating a dreaming hoop regarding this. He knew what he had to do before the threads unraveled, or tangled hopelessly up with daily concerns. He would travel to the Center of the World, Paha Sapha, and in those black hills he would seek the meaning in a vision, a *hanbleciya* .Convinced that the weather would hold for a few days, he set out to the north, taking a strong mount and no weapons, nor provisions, for this was a sacred journey.

Coming up onto the high plains and away from the camp, his mind slowly began to assemble the signs that the spirit world had brought to his attention. Now he must begin to track these very signs. He had achieved the name of Swift Medicine due to his acute ability to know what was needed when, and to move quickly towards the telling. Too old now to ride out, his decisions for war parties were still sought, as his wisdom sped straight as an arrow. Once so strong in body that he could send an arrow from his bow right through a galloping bull buffalo, he retained his full strength of mind. This was why the confusion that surrounded him now was as troublesome as a thick hatching of flies around the eyes. Irritating! He sought a focused calm here out on the plains where the buffalo grass and sage were barely peeking through the thinning snow. Here was the place to find it, a few thin little wolves slinking by after the unwary. His old mare knew to watch for the prairie dog holes hidden by the thin snow cover; this was the time to travel in solitude, undisturbed! As he rode, he thought. Bird. Feather. Owl. North. Buffalo....White, yes, white buffalo. Two, mine, and the boy's. Bird, yes, owl. The winter owl he and his son once saw so long ago, the owl's calling, then the feather..and his mind began to drift with pain and sorrow of remembrance, till he jerked it back. Ah yes, the feather, from a large Snow Owl he was sure. Dressed warmly, the cold did not bother him, but the chaos of his mind did. Was he avoiding any portent of his own death? No, he felt awe, but no fear. What would he lose by dying, he had nothing to fear. Black Cloud had talked to him of the importance of Buffalo Calf Woman to The People, yet it was not her face he sought.

By the time he had arrived in a place he deemed good to set up a sparse camp, darkness was fast falling. Few came to this traditional place of questing for his people at this time of year; fewer still came alone. Faded, bedraggled strips of cloth, prayer flags, hung from the boughs of the trees, remnants of completed visits here. Nothing stirred. The very bleakness gave it an austere beauty, the gently rolling height rising up out of the surrounding miles and miles of high plain. As one approached, it's singular importance became fixed in one's mind. Swift Medicine was no youth embarking on his first vision, though. He knew that this questing wouldn't be in the traditional manner, but would serve more to isolate him so that he could think on this matter.

A small fire was set, with some kindling within easy reach. He sat determined to stay awake by focusing on the flames in the darkness until he knew what was being asked of him. Swift Medicine was so absorbed in his thoughts that against all his ways he had failed to notice the very real signs of an approaching squall. The air grew ominously still and quickly cooled. He merely drew his thick robe closer as the first thick, clotted flakes of snow began to fall upon him.

Neither owl, nor buffalo were his power beings, it was the Great Bear, whose claws he wore around his neck, that showed what animal spirit guided him, but he did not feel it's presence speaking to him now. Drawing a small packet out from his robe, he laid the pure white feather before him. Of the three main kinds the feathered ones have this kind was the longest, the strongest. It's purpose was to lift, to move forward, to link us to life above. He paused. Should I make a prayer stick with it? That thought passed as he focused on the downy tuft attached at the feather's base. This is where the owl gained it's stealth, for these soft feathers hushed it's approach in flight. Was there something secretive involved? Of slyness? Of wary approach? He couldn't imagine, but then he noticed the beauty of it's form, and thought of the power of healing! At this thought, his heart lurched inside his chest, the pull from those beyond to whom he was still, after all these years, so strongly connected. His breathing slowed, quieted, as the falling snow blanketed his praying form.

The Beaver Pond

A voice from above woke him: *"Open the eyes of your heart and you will be taught"*

    Looking now upon a small beaver pond in a forested glade where slanting beams of sunlight danced most pleasing to the eye, small lives scurried through the scant undergrowth. The far side grew thick with soft wooded trees that the beaver folk ignored. Here by him on this side were the neatly chiseled stumps of the aspen and poplar they preferred to harvest. He felt content at first, anticipating the appearance of the industrious creatures that lived here. But something was very wrong. How could it have escaped his immediate attention that there was no water in the pond? None that he could see. He carefully let himself down onto the dry cracked mud. Were the spillways blocked? He heard the strong gurgle of a mountain stream. Had the dam given away? Of course the wonderfully constructed lodge must be damaged, but no, it looked intact. There, towards the center he saw a dark glimmer, of water? On approach he saw a small opening, like a well, carefully protected by a stone wall.

    "Look into this," again came the voice. As he stood at the lip of this well, if that is what it was, with it's dark gleaming surface, he heard a small, but strong beat, a drumming of sorts. Before his horrified eyes a narrow band of what looked like raw flesh began growing across the water's surface. His eyes burned; felt unusually dry. The drumming filled his ears, and he knew..it was his heart. His vision began to dim. He felt weak, overcome...was he to die?

    "Listen well, what was held here quelled the thirst of many at one time. This was a place that nurtured many lives, not just those that dwelt here, but the many that came to the banks to drink of the overflow. This dry pond is your heart, shrinking. There is no overflow now ...Your tears have not stopped flowing, though they do not wet your cheeks, they have flowed instead to the deep well of your soul, where none can gain use. It has been kept even from yourself. You, warrior, understand scars very well! Scars, visible ones, show where we have been wounded, but not how, or what

caused the healing. A scar is seemingly tough, often inflexible. Tough!..... and Inflexible!"

His eyes flew open with the understanding that he, as a source that could quench thirst to his people, had been drying up. He knew the beaver as a sign of building of dreams, and admired for his industry and provision and protection of his family, but just as he was wondering what the beaver had to do with his own power animal, and how all this was linked, he heard the owl. Yes, yes, I'm ready now for the buffalo, but when he looked up, there, on the other side of the pond, stood a young woman. Dressed in plain deerskin, her long braids were unadorned, her face shining and full of generosity. Beautiful she was, but what drew his attention were her arms. Extended outwards towards him in a beseeching gesture they ended not with hands but with the large, shaggy, clawed paws of the great bear. This was Mary Standing Soldier, renowned among the Cheyenne for having fought off a bear while still a child. The People had heard many tales of her appearance on the battlefields, where those warriors felled by the Bluecoats were healed by her. Waving the great clawed paws above them, she swayed and growled in a magnificent, fearsome way as she plucked arrows from where they had been sent deep into fallen warriors bones . Bullets flew out of wounds as she chanted over them, lending the fallen brave her great spirit strength so that he could rise up and leave the battlefield. At last some understanding has come! *Mary Standing Soldier smoothed the ground around her, and in passing her hands slowly over her body in brushing motions she signaled that she had a story to narrate.*

All that she related to him that day resonated with the steady beating of a calm heart. He understood that his life had been diminished, much more by the losses of his first wife, then his willful boy, than by age. For he had lost his first love, he had not lost much love from that boy. He idolized him as he had idolized his own youth, also. His power had not been taken from him, but rather dried up. He, a fearless warrior, one of the few chosen to wear the treasured Dog Rope, had grown old with fear. Fear prevented generosity, and while he maintained outward appearances, those who dwelt within his lodge walls knew that he no longer gave freely of himself. You will be blessed, she told him.

"Follow the easiest path as the buffalo does, though you are now too old to ride out into battle, your wisdom and knowledge is vigorous and strong. Come!" She bade him follow her into a stand of cottonwood. There at the foot of a sturdy tree, encircled by a ring of blooming Bloodroot, hung an empty cradle board, one he dimly recognized. Walking up to it, she guided his hand to the small, well-worn lizard shaped pouch that once held his son's birth cord. Before his steady gaze, for now his attention was fixed, the beading loosened; the leather became tattered and worn. Then rapidly the fallen beads reassembled into a design of Cheyenne handiwork. At that he fell to his knees, and blessed with the sure knowledge of what was being required of him, "the easiest path", the wellspring of his spirit overflowed once again.

As soon as the idea of what he had to do came to him his eyes flew open, only to discover that he sat alone on the bleak plain, as blanketed with snow as the surrounding clumps of sage brush. He sprang up, almost stumbling on his cold, numbed feet, unaware of how much time had passed, the sun slanting under a low bank of thick gray clouds, broken into strong spears of golden light. Feeling a vigor that he felt would never be his again, he set off towards his camp, a song on his lips, his heart beating with the purpose and energy of a young man.

And it was an easy path, just as he had been told. He went at once that day to Shaved Head's lodge; before he could announce himself, the Cottonwood Boy emerged.

"Have you come looking?" the boy asked Swift Medicine, and even though so direct a greeting was unheard of, he stood expectantly, looking directly into his elder's face. Impulsively Swift Medicine placed both hands on Wagachun's shoulders, who smiled. The first he had seen on the boy's handsome face. He felt himself effortlessly smiling back. They knew, they both knew!

And so The Cottonwood Boy became *tiwahe,* immediate family, and by bringing the boy to his lodge with the formal ceremony of adoption, the *hunkayapi,* blessed all those who resided with Swift Medicine, and he in turn once again became a blessing to many others. As Swift Medicine found himself imparting the wisdom of the warrior's way to this new son, his heart felt good once more within him.

His New Life

Powder River Country

When the *wapiya wicasa* named him Medicine Horse he was h*u*nka, adopted into the lodge of a great man of the Tetons, Swift Medicine, a Burnt Thigh warrior of the Dog Society. In his heart he was still that rustling leaf child, Wagachun, The Cottonwood Boy, and would remain so for many moons.

A sense of being apart, different, did not depart from him on that day even as he glanced from one accepting face to another. Swift Medicine gave away much that day to show his gratitude, to honor the Great Mystery that had brought them together. Shaved Head was not unhappy to have one less mouth to feed, even though the Cottonwood Boy had approached the age of contributing to his family's meat. Though he had no rifle of his own he was quite good with a bow and frequently brought a rabbit back to the lodge. Shaved Head now stood up to say a few words about him as a *hunka*, an adopted one, telling all of his skills with the horses and dependability while on watch with the pony herd. Then an eagle plume was carefully tied to the boy's scalp lock, and the feasting began. The Cottonwood Boy sensed that this was a time not to mark his grieving for those lost during The Moon of the First Snowfall. He had been smiled upon; a great warrior had extended his wing for him to shelter under, but now he was leaving the child he had been behind. His path was now to manhood!

The next dawning, when the darkness began to lift, he woke as usual to this thin hour of returning light. A favorite time for him; with the others still lost to sleep in their robes, he could enjoy the feeling of being alone. The familiar world of the lodge began to emerge, except today it was to his eyes all new surroundings.

There was a bull buffalo shield trimmed in deep blue trade cloth. Seven eagle feathers hung from it's rim. On it's face was the deep red imprint of grizzly claws. Strong medicine! Well-kept and orderly trappings surrounded him. Extra braided horsehair ropes, feather decorated quirts, heavily marked coup sticks, exquisitely beaded pipe bags and vividly colored, full parfleches indicated that he now belonged to a lodge of much honor and respect. Every war club and rifle his eyes routinely traveled over he imagined owning. Hardly daring to look at the magnificent plumed bonnet resplendent with eagle feathers, his eyes finally came to the sleeping form it resided above, Swift Medicine, his benefactor! How could he, who had never known his own, call him *neheyo,* father?

Soon the women would stir, but he lay quietly thinking, for he much needed this time to prepare himself so that he too could bring honor to his new family. He knew that he had been chosen, and that Swift Medicine had been guided to him. " Medicine Horse", he said his new name aloud, softly, and shivered with the knowledge; rose quickly then to bathe in the icy water of the nearby stream, and went out to the herd.

Once He Prided Himself as a Great Diagnostician
Foothills of The Alleghenies

She had heard others speak of answered prayer, but what was it when you didn't remember even asking? That is what is seemed like the evening when her father sought her out down by the spring where she had gone to brood after he had gone on yet another one of his drinking bouts. Barely lifting her head from her knees, the tone of his voice alerted her to a change in his mood. His eyes sparkled. He had on one of his favorite tapestry vests, his Van Dyke was neatly trimmed as of old and a most pleasant scent of Bay Rum wafted off him, rather than spirits. Seating himself rather grandly on the sandstone outcropping next to her he proceeded to ingratiate her into his good graces once again, as only Dr. Frederick Chester Hoffman could, when he set out to do so!

Chewing smartly on a bit of sassafras root, taking care to proffer her a bit, which he knew she also loved, he announced with great flair, "I have given up Demon Rum, once and for all! Finished! Finis! Kaput! Goethe and all his friends, yes, all the others, banished! No more riff-raff, my dear. They won't be seen again!" She had many questions to ask, but he quickly raised his hand in that slight but genuinely imperious, gentle way of his. "We are going West, young lady. West, Westward Ho!" and gave out with a delectable belly laugh and a slight twist to his newly trimmed and waxed mustache. She leaned forward to examine him better in the leaf-dappled light the spring's environs provided. Was he drunk in spite of his declaration? No! He was indeed drunk with excitement. Then he began to outline for her the whole glorious seeming plan.

Within the fortnight they found themselves packed up and on their way to St. Louis and the convergence of the great river that divided the vast continent, where they would meet up with their guides and her father's old friend the Baron, and begin their "Grand Adventure" up the Missouri to witness the summer celebrations of the Northern Cheyenne. Anah's head danced with the idea of fulfilled dreams; so many wishes she could hardly count: Indians, real Indians, real mountains, real buffalo! She barely took in her father's concerns, or the incessant bustle of packing and closing up of the lodge. How could that be of any concern to a young girl? Dr. Hoffman had arranged to be taken on as a contract surgeon at an isolated outpost out west in Indian Territory, Ft. Sill to be exact. Sickened by the civil war and the effects he witnessed on those around him, the personal devastation of his family life and his response to it, he wanted nothing more than a fresh start on a new frontier. His fascination with the native culture of the Indians of the plains was reason enough for him to uproot himself and his daughter and see for himself what he knew from all reports was rapidly vanishing. Besides, he had a most pressing concern; his daughter. She was no longer a child, would no longer remain as such!

The morning that had finally brought him to his senses he had wakened painfully hung over, ran his hand over his unshaven jaw, discovered a jagged tear, cut somehow. He ambled into the main room, could not find either a clean glass or tumbler, nor any spirits to fill one, when Anah burst into the room from hauling a bucket of water up from the spring. He realized then that she was left with the chore of trying to clean up after him and his friends, many who were still sprawled shamefully across the floor and couches. She stared at him. There was water simmering on the stove; this was not her first trudge down to the spring. The front of her thin worn shift was soaked, revealing her developing form at which, with a shock, he realized he was staring. Grabbing the pail from her, he screamed at her to leave. As soon as she fled the room, Claire Violette, the child's mother, dead these few years, took up a place in his mind and began to speak. Her great beauty had mesmerized all of the fashionable society of the world, which had been his own at the time, through which she had flitted as carefree as a swallowtail butterfly wafts from one choice blossom to another. Why she chose to settle finally on him he never did quite understand; he was too delighted! Now he buried his throbbing head in his hand as he tried to prepare himself for what she would say...

Fritz, (his heart rolled over, belly up, in abject gratitude, as a dog who expects a beating does, at the use of this favored endearment of hers.) *My dear, you are known as the Great Diagnostician, your reputation was built on this, our wealth indeed came from this. No, no, my dear, don't demur, that was my dowry. Yes, a considerable one, but you built up quite the practice on your skills. Your skills alone. No, I understand about the bottle. Above all else you as a physician understand the need to medicate pain. Wait, wait..or I will go! This is about our child. You saw her today for the first time! Really saw her. Do you understand what I mean, she is becoming a woman? I want you to..*

At this Frederick leapt to his feet clutching his head, thinking that he was mad for talking with his dead wife. She wanted him to what? Take Anah back to Pittsburgh, introduce her to society, debutante, cotillions. How could he stand it? How could he? It must be the beginning of the delirium tremens.

"Doc, Doc?" It was Earl, an illiterate and itinerant woodsman that often cut wood and brought in game for him; he too was looking for some spirits with which to start the day, upending the dregs of the bottles left haphazardly around the tables and floor. At that the good doctor was out the door, and hiked at a rapid pace up to the Greenstone Ridge that abutted the old Warrior Trail. The sandstone foundation of the old Youder farm was here, destroyed by a blowdown a decade ago that leveled their apple orchard, took the roof off the barn and drove them off the land. The view over the undulating ridges was ameliorating. A good place to sober up. Soon Ruffles, a coon-hound, no good for hunting, a runt of the litter, spared by Billy himself, a runt of sort, came ambling through the goldenrod and chickweed of the gone-to-seed pasture. Billy, the doctor knew, would himself soon join them. Billy, his brain ravaged as a child by a fever that none knew then how to deal with, was a beautiful boy, doomed to remain childlike in a growing body. He plunked himself comfortably down beside "Doc", as he called him. Immediately he asked about the whereabouts of "Nana", as he called his Anah, a bunch of freshly picked wildflowers dangling wilted from his man-sized hands. Claire Violette's lovely lips whispered in his ear, *"You're The Great Diagnostician! Do something! Now, don't you SEE?"* Immediately he replied that his daughter had gone for the day into Latrobe with Earl's wife, and suggested that they hike together to the far salt lick, throwing an arm companionably around the boy, his vision beginning to clear.

Horsemen of the Plains

The Great Plains

Circle Camp- Part I

Soon they would have to stop for the night and make camp. As that involved no responsibility for Anah she was free to enjoy the ever changing territory that they were passing through. Often she felt a desire to call a halt just so that she could sketch some lavender flowers close to the ground, nestled in solitary splendor amongst all the long-stemmed, waving grasses. She had no name for it; her tongue felt the absence, was it possibly a purple Geradia? Giving a small sigh she resigned herself to looking for some after they stopped. She had heard a nightjar, and knew that soon the sun would begin it's descent. The wide blue bowl of the sky that had arched over them all day long was now beginning to gather small painted ruffles of orange, pink and salmon colored clouds in the west. As tired as she was from the long day's ride, an incendiary excitement flamed through her at the sight of small, colored strips of trade cloth tied to a low branch of a ponderosa near the trail. Then she spotted another bunch of green and blue strips tied to a high-growing white sage. These must be the "prayer flags" that the Baron had told her to be on the watch for. Ready to call out her discovery, she noted that their guide had called a halt. Explaining to them that, as they were approaching *wakan,* sacred ground, he would move the party onto a different trail that would lead them around the butte and soon place them above a huge encampment. There they would halt, awaiting welcome. He gave directions to assemble themselves in a single file when they reached the overlook, and to make no attempt to reach for anything, not even a looking glass, that could be taken for a weapon. They were to remain there, without dismounting, until he returned for them. Full trust had been placed in Blue Tongue, their Arapaho guide. Anah knew that her father and Baron Von Westenhagen were hoping to encounter a large gathering of the tribes, as this was the time for renewal ceremonies after the end of the summer buffalo hunts. At last, she thought, I will see real Indians, for the ones that they had encountered so far were disappointing to her glamorous expectations. The Baron referred to the Indians that they had seen so far as "enculturated", just another of the scientific terms that he liked to bandy about. Blue Tongue appeared disdainful of the Indians to be seen at the sutler's stores and forts, referring to them as "Loaf-abouts". Her father, hiding his own disappointment, explained that living on a reservation imposed foreign values upon them. An example being the now prevalent use of U.S. Army issued canvas to construct their tipis from. Not only were there less buffalo for the taking now that the plains were flooded with white hunters, emigrants, and troops, but the tanned hides were too readily traded away for lead, calico, and bad whiskey. With the summer buffalo hunts drawing to a close the tribes would regroup into separate bands, but before that occurred they would gather together in a great camp circle for special ceremonies, dances and socialization without the restraints that the harsh discipline of surviving a winter would impose on them. They were informed that it might be a long wait as there would be a "parley". Anah, to contain her mounting excitement thought back upon her journey.

Had it been less than a fortnight ago that they had moved out onto the actual plains? She had lost all sense of time as she had once ordered it, and she was glad of it. From the first moment that their party had departed their staterooms upon the steamboat and rose the next morning from canvas walls, Anah felt alive in a new way. The dust, the heat, the very air was an excitement in its unfamiliarity. Muscles sore from unaccustomed use, the lack of luxuries were all compensated for simply by what her eyes took in as she rode along. Nothing had prepared her for the experience of being surrounded by such vastness! No painting hung in a gallery and exclaimed for its beauty could accurately translate the reality. How could it? For she was encompassed by it, made small. She, who had free rein to roam the hundreds of acres of the Alleghenies, delight from toddler-hood into crawling under chairs, hiding in cubby-holes, crawling under bushes, seeking out limestone caves, running freely through the densest thickets and groves, now stood fearful and abashed, surrounded by miles and miles and miles of open space, to discover how infinitesimally tiny she was. The plains were indeed great, in fact they stretched beyond her imagining. And they were animated with life, both large and small. Beautiful, sleek creatures she discovered were called antelope bounded past, and when they camped there were the tiniest forms of flora and fauna to discover. And the sky! Oh, the sky; it had been a never ending panorama!

They were traveling a steady west, north-west direction toward the Powder River country, the Great Divide lay ahead, when that first afternoon storm rolled in, pulling with it two descending spouts that down twisted. Twirling and rotating in a fearful, hypnotic fashion, sucking up everything in their path. All in the little party stood mesmerized. There was no shelter on the open plain. The surrounding sky had lowered ominously and turned a very unnatural, sickly yellow-green. The temperature dropped rapidly. Hail began to pelt them. At first a novelty, but then painful, and so the tents were pulled over themselves. As quickly as the storm appeared, it moved off. Arching over all a double rainbow shimmered, going in and out of focus for close to an hour. What stirred in Anah then, as she stood with the cupped handful of large crystal hailstones melting through her icy fingers, gazing at the infinite depth of the blue sky arched over with the double shimmering bow, was the sense of majesty that had nothing to do with the hands of man. It was incomprehensible. Mysterious. And a longing reawakened in her then, as the hail melted and dripped from her fingers, and the men went about reorganizing the camp. Animals returned to grazing, prairie dogs whistled, meadowlarks called, and the little party prepared to move out once move onto the vast sea of grass before them.

"Anah, Anah, wake child." It was her father calling her back to join the others from where she had wandered off to wait. Yes, she thought, the accounts of Lewis and Clark that she'd poured over, the magnificent paintings of Alfred Jacob Miller, and Caitlin and Charles Bird King and Samuel Seymour, nothing could truly prepare her for the real experience. "Coming, father!"

The Crystal Cones

A lowering sun blazed into their eyes when they drew together atop the butte, looking down into a wide grass-covered valley, split into halves by a sparkling clear stream that wound peacefully through it. A soft breeze was delightfully cooling Anah's face. The sounds of meadowlarks and blackbirds gathering for the night, and the trill of swallows sweeping through the dancing flies above the water were joyful to her ear. But what utterly transfixed her was the sight directly below. Hundreds of buffalo hide lodges were laid out in a distinct circular pattern, enclosing fancifully painted medicine tipis in the middle. "Cheyenne", the scout whispered almost respectfully. She saw her father turn to him with a query. In turn Blue Tongue used his index finger to slash across his wrist several times, an accepted sign for this tribe, the Beautiful People, the *tsitsistas*.

She did not try to listen in, so intent was her gaze on the valley below. The tall white cones sparkled, literally sparkled in the sunlight, looking as if they were encrusted with pure crystalline powders. Which, she found out later, was quite true, as the Cheyenne coated their lodge skins with selenite when they had access to it. A special tanning process left the hides almost as white as linen, then the white clay-like substance they were painted with dried, leaving small crystals that caught the sun.

As they awaited the arrival of their scout the company settled themselves comfortably, remembering the injunction to lift nothing to their eyes that could resemble a weapon. Anah longed to have the spy glass, but contented herself with sitting cross-legged and observing.

Her gaze was charmed by a wonder she had often imagined, now sprung to life. Hundreds of varicolored ponies were grazing contentedly, almost as many, it seemed to her; as the vast herds of buffalo they had encountered. Here and there were boys, bronze-skinned, with masses of raven colored hair and little clothing, astride ponies guarding the huge herd. What were obviously women, in decorated buckskin dress, moving to and fro carrying water in buffalo bladder bags that glowed semi-transparent in the westering sun. Large racks of saplings held drying meat from a recent hunt. Fresh hides were pegged to the ground, with women crouched at work over them. A few fat puppies were waiting expectantly for scraps from the flensing knives. She was thrilled to realize that she understood some of the tranquil scene spread out below her. Outside many of the lodges were tethered ponies; these were the specially trained and favored ones. She recognized the beautifully spotted one as being from the country further west, the Palouse, she had been told. Some even had eagle feathers and colored yarns in their manes. She laughed in a special joy of understanding as she recognized exactly what the women bent over the hides were doing. She turned to the Baron. "Look, they are flensing a hide!" He countered with a query, "Why are the shields outside their homes; don't you think that they would be hanging inside?" "I don't know, maybe they are to distinguish one lodge from another," she replied. He did not answer her, and she saw that he had carefully lifted a spy glass to his eye and was more interested in observing, not talking. Any minute now and he would begin to take copious notes in his precious journal.

As the sun proceeded toward setting, cooking fires were being lit, wisps of blue smoke rising calmly up. Cradle boards were taken in. Bundles hanging from small tripods were being collected; she later learned that these were "medicine bundles" holding valuable artifacts. Quite a few children were moving slowly to their homes, undoubtedly drawn by their hunger, while others continued in their play, chasing hoops or splashing in the stream. As the ambient light dimmed, the lodges glowed from within like paper lanterns. She did not think that she had ever seen a more beautiful setting. The brush covered shelters, wikiups, seemed to almost dance as the rising breeze rustled their thick covering of leafed cottonwood branches. She wondered where the grown men were. As she was pondering this, Blue Tongue arrived with an uncustomary grin on his face. The Baron leaned over to her, "We can go down now. We have been welcomed; prepare to be very amazed when the dancing begins!"

What transpired that evening, and over the next few enchanted days, transported Anah beyond her most extravagant expectations. From Blue Tongue they had learned that there were thousands gathered here; not only northern Cheyenne, but Brule and some of his own relatives, Arapaho. Preparations were being made for ceremonies of renewal, a Sun Dance. Their guide thought they might be privileged to witness at least the bringing in to the special lodge of the dance pole, however he warned them not to expect to be able to witness the actual ceremonies.

Fort Laramie, Indian Territory:

Now that they had arrived and settled in here at the fort and her father had contentedly assumed his post as a contract surgeon, she finally had some time to reminiscence over the contents of her Commonplace Book. Before she went to sleep though, she found herself perusing her notes from that first large gathering of the tribes that she had witnessed, her first Circle Camp. Opening the pages once more she read of how she found herself that first evening, seated cross-legged around a huge bonfire, with a small, cinnamon-skinned child in her lap. With the Baron to one side of her and her father on the other she was able to learn much from their dialogue, trying to write in her own book while balancing the little girl. When the child leapt up and darted off she determined to note a complete description of at least one warrior out of the many moving through the crowds. This was a difficult task, as absolutely everything in her sight appeared to be in some colorful motion, just to catch her attention. The jangling of small bells or rattles, and even the soft swish of leather fringes competed.

The Baron had told her that a military type society, called "Dog Soldiers" were monitoring the large assembly, and by all means to give no offense. "Do I need to rebind my hair?" She queried, for with all the resplendent attire and decoration amassed by this gathering where everyone, even the littlest ones appeared to have on their very best clothing, she also wanted to do the same. However, days and weeks on the trail had left her with only one option, as her pretty frocks had been sent ahead to Ft. Laramie, along with their household goods. Anah used her best asset, her own thick reddish-blond hair, that, unbound, fell almost to her waist in waves. As she released her hair from the bun, spreading it over her shoulders, she felt that it was indeed a "crowning glory". In fact, it was this burnished halo surrounding her face that had drawn the small child to her, hesitantly desiring to touch it. The little girl's hair was itself a marvel to her, thick and black as a raven's wing, tightly bound in braids, it glistened with some aromatic oil. Reading a description of the Dog Soldier, "Bear With Feathers", from her Commonplace Book, she remembered that each warrior that rode by her fascinated eyes was more resplendent than the next. But it was this man and his horse that almost beggared her ability to describe, as both he and his mount were decked out in the most lavish regalia, that stood out even in the swirling panoply of attire that surrounded her. This warrior had even completely decorated his mount. She later learned from the Baron that each "decoration", as she called them, were actually symbols of protection, identity and power. This man, Feathered Bear, was so closely identified with his horse that he arrayed it much the same as himself. She read her hastily scribbled lines, which began:

His war horse, identifiable by it's notched ears as such. A fine buckskin. Upper torso, head and hocks painted mossy green. Same as FB's face. She had determined to get as accurate a description as possible, thus she had kept him in her sights. *red tail, braided, ears with feather tips, yellow . Red flag at chin, Hairy chin?* She amended this part later when she discovered that the small willow hoop with stretched hair upon it was actually a scalp. A horrified curiosity accompanied this and she longed to speak the language so that she could ask, Did your horse earn the scalp? How? *Notched ears = make it swift. Tail braided with strips of red. Red a favorite color.* In small print at the side she had added that most of the horses prepared for battle had their long flowing tails bound up with cloth, clubbing it was called. *Head to toe he wore red. Shirt, leggings and breech-clout were red. Left cheek only, two wide, black paint stripes, nose to ear. Hair long and braided, red cloth. Of course. A long string of silver coins hung down, attached to hair.* Later she recalled that many of the men had these silver strips with a scalp lock attached. As she continued to observe him amongst the other highly decorated men she was able to conclude that he had a strong sense of identity. For example, the upright feathered bonnet that had initially identified him as a much honored warrior, each feather having been earned by an admirable feat of bravery, she noted that his Dog Soldier headdress did not have the feathers of raven, crow or even turkey that the others wore, but that his were from eagles. Noting what was obviously a hurried notation on her part, she remembered with some small pride how intent she had been on capturing an accurate description, noting with pleasure that the Baron was bent over his own journal. It continued on for several pages. *"Beautifully quilled moccasins. Long, bone breastplate armbands, above elbows. Large silver cross with dangles."* From Blue Tongue she was told that each item was worn for power and protection. Her father later told her that the "bone" breast-plate was of carved shell. "Shell?" She had queried, "Sea Shell?" "Yes," her father replied, "many items are traded from afar, a fixed value assigned to them. The fine tanned buffalo hides have the amount assigned for their apparent quality. The large medallion was a pendant and the little objects hung from it called "najas". When she had asked what "naja" meant, he just shrugged. Bear Feather's buffalo hide shield was especially riveting, as he rode past, the colors swirled amongst many feathers hung from its rim. She had a chance to observe it closely when she found it hanging from a special tripod outside his lodge the next day. It was turned to constantly face into the sun. How interesting, she thought.

The Shield: Circled with red. Design of dragonflies(odd), two crescent moons, my favorite! The surface red, yellow and black speckles. Four large feathers, Eagle? Hung from it's side, rimmed with hairy tassels. Turkey feather mounted with sinew in center. Weapons: bow & arrow, lance. No gun? Quilled and beaded quiver and bow case. Long lance, blue paint with red flags on both ends (ferrule and butt) Feathers on it, What kind? When she had a chance to compare notes with the Count, he told her that he thought the feathers on the lance were from a swallow's tail. She told him that she thought that choosing such a delicate insect as a dragonfly to decorate something designed to protect didn't make sense to her. "Oh, but they twist, turn and change directions in an instant. Feathered Bear is an awesome horseman, I'm told," he had responded. Ah, she had so much to learn. Her assumptions had been that all the ornamentation was just for display, but sobered at the thought that each warrior assumed his *"wakan",* or sacred regalia, to guide and protect him in battle. She had even seen some mounts that had a small bundle tied around their necks; more "medicine", she learned. Each and every feather had been earned by a worthy act. Yes, she had much to learn, and she wanted to know it all.

Circle Camp- Part II

In her Commonplace Book, besides the copious notes she had taken that summer, were included some rough sketches. She had little natural artistic talent, nevertheless, she took a bit of pride in her depictions. Laughing now to herself, as when she noted that a whole precious page was devoted to a drawing of what looked like a long crooked stick with a few feathers and a strip of red trade cloth jutting from its top. Beneath this sketch it had been labeled, not in her neat print, but in the Baron's thick flourish: Cheyenne Coup Stick. She remembered how coyly she had made the assessment of "child's play" when he labeled her depiction thus and briefly gave an accounting of it's importance…to be the first to touch an enemy with one's coup stick, or even a weapon. Her quick and obviously naive judgment brought a rather severe look to the Baron's long face. He said something brusquely in his native tongue, *"Meine kliene liebschen*, turned on his heel only to return shortly bearing just such a stick. It was not quite an arm's length with a few motley feathers hanging from it. Further contributing to it's odd appearance were the number of deep notches up and down its length. It certainly appeared to her to be of no importance, not like the fearsome 7 feet tall beribboned lances lush with eagle feathers. Indicating with a flourish of his hand that she was to seat herself Anah thought, Oh yes, a little lecture from " Count One-Two-Three", for that was how she referred to him as when he acted pompously. Her father had told her that it was in his nature, having been deferred to since the moment of his birth. 'Noblesse Oblige!" my dear, the dear man is supremely humble in his bearing considering his position in Schleswing-Holstein. Once they both were seated he began, "You see this," proffering the stick towards her, "Your father traded his fine Belgian linen vest to obtain this authentic coup stick." The impish smile that played upon her lips told him how little regard she had for this trade. "Anah," he said with forbearance, wagging a beringed hand. She did not want to remain seated for some academic spiel, rather she wanted to wander around at Blue Tongue's side; there was so much to investigate. "There is a wealth of information to relate regarding this artifact," adding, "that you obviously hold in some disdain. These warriors seek to prove their valor, bravery and courage and vie to be the first to touch an enemy, dead or alive... with just a simple stick." He paused seeing the frustration upon her face. "There, there, little one, run on. I'll tell you later," offering his hand to assist her in rising. Even though she knew that he was most definitely patronizing her, she leapt up to run and find her father and Blue Tongue.

There had been so much to see that was beyond her comprehension at the time, not the least of which was a very handsome Arapaho who went around walking backwards. She had been told that he was a "Thunder Dreamer", as if that would explain everything. Having to choose between questioning and remaining to listen for an answer, always so complex coming from the Baron's well-educated lips, or simply running to and fro from one intriguing sight or sound to another, she chose to simply experience now and understand later.

Her categorization of flora and fauna she managed to hold in abeyance, as there were far more things that she couldn't grasp and some she simply intuited. She trusted that in time some form of comprehension would come, as it usually did when she applied herself to understanding a subject. And of these Indians she was fascinated!

Going through her notes now at Ft. Laramie she read some entries that were so sparse that there was little to assist in making sense. "The sacred, the ceremonial, the significance of the number four, color." Much of what she witnessed in their few days sojourn at the camp was magical to her, magic being a word she did not put much faith in. Oh, she believed in the concept all right. While she had been indulged in various rituals attributed to faeries as a child, she no more believed in their existence than she did in trolls and ghosts. The word magic was one she just did not have any use for. Anah soon found a much better word to apply, *wakan,* the sacred and mysterious. The word in her own language used commonly out here in the West was "medicine". At first it was a bit confusing in interchanges when she referred to her father as a "doctor", not a "Medicine Man". There was the impartation of a power conferred from outside oneself. A medicine man could heal, but also prophesy. And there were some men who had great knowledge of herbs and concoctions to heal, but unlike her father they disdained surgery, but knew a great deal in closing of wounds and mending bones that were broken. Anah found herself attempting to learn as much folk medicine as she could, and found little in their practices that would not recommend itself to actual healing.

Over the ensuing years, as her knowledge of the Lakota and Cheyenne tongues grew, she found herself able to answer many puzzling questions as to spiritual things. The Cheyenne tongue was quite different from most of the other languages she came in contact with around Ft. Laramie, but as her friendship with the old Cheyenne scout, Turn Foot grew, so did her fluency. She had determined that "the everywhere spirit" and "the great medicine" were interchangeable appellations for what she would simply call "God", whom, she felt, didn't really want to be named. The more she understood, the more respect she had for their practices. Not only were the Cheyenne exceptionally tall, and one of the most colorful of nations in their regalia and ceremonies, they were excellent horsemen; far superior to many of the U.S. cavalry who had never sat a horse until enlistment. Cheyenne women were held in the highest regard as to their virtue. These nomadic hunters of the buffalo were strong in the skills and abilities that made them a force to be reckoned with in war and raids. In no way were their numbers great, but they had allied themselves with the Sioux and the Arapaho.

Paging through the notes she had so hastily transcribed on that first encounter, she drifted back in her memory.

Her father, his hair still full and chestnut colored, and the Baron's hair longish and tied back, heads together arguing a point Prince Maximillian had made in 1830 about the Arikara, how their Fox Society was similar to the Lakota. Her father's voice rising in dissension "Oh, dear Baron, similar yes, but in name only." The Baron reaching for his elaborately quilled pipe case, preparing himself to listen somewhat attentively, but actually parsing together in his mind his very own defense of a contrary opinion. Arikara, Arapaho, Kiowa, Comanche, Brule, Miniconjou…the names swarmed in her mind. The quibbling of these learned men over the true meaning of a facial stripe, whether or not a tuft of hair on an elaborately decorated lance was horse or buffalo; even the varying meanings due to the placement of red paint upon the body... She had heard enough, and rather than trying to follow the very confusing indications of rank and valor in each individuals wildly variegated dress, she just gave up trying to acknowledge or understand what society each dancer belonged to, or how many coups had been struck, or why one wore stripped leggings and another didn't. She was a young girl then, just moving into womanhood, and this grand gathering of the tribes was like unto a medieval pageantry to her eyes and senses. She was completely enthralled.

Anah just shut her eyes, concentrating on ignoring, if one could, the intense discussion her father, the Baron, and now even the scout were involved in.

She began listening to the insistent beat of the drums now, having removed herself from the men's attention. She could begin to "feel" the drums in some way from the dance ground. The deep voice emanating from them was binding all the twirling and movements before her eyes into a coherency that had no name, not one she could name, anyhow. Ululations of the women, the screams, yips and whoops that came from somewhere, man, beast or child she could not point to, combined with the dense murmurings of songs in an incomprehensible language. This was a wildly exciting night. Never had she seen or heard of such a gathering, let alone been given the chance to sit so close to the dance ground that sparks from the huge bonfire could fall upon her. Cross-legged and rocking now, the smells of pinon, pine, sage and what she later learned was called "sweet grass", *Anthoxoanthum odoratum*, trailed, vaporous through the air, imparting a rich smoky scent. Experiencing this ceremony through her senses, she had soon seen fit to set her little notebook aside.

Sitting quietly, just watching, she soon felt the thud, thud, thud of moccasin feet rhythmically dancing on the face of the earth. Oh, how she longed to just join them. Even though she was half hypnotized by the flickering light from the huge bonfire in the middle of the dance ground, oddly lulled by the jangling of bells, rattles and various bones, she knew enough to not even think of joining in. Unless invited, of course!

Just then something was tossed into her lap; glancing down she saw a small rattle, shaking it gave off a sound like dried beans of some sort. The heavens moved above her unnoticed as she watched the incredible glorious assembly of the people who were called "The Beautiful Ones" by other tribes, adorned in their best robes, tasseled war shirts, feather bonnets, painted skins and furs. Why even their ponies were painted! So enthralled was she that she had totally forgotten her earlier concerns: what to eat, where to sleep.

As the stars moved in the night sky above her the hours melted into a visionary state with no cessation of the singing, drumming, and dancing. Her eyes grew heavy. She kept jerking herself awake, as this was a grand spectacle that she would remember always. Sated with images, she barely noticed when her father drew her head down to a folded blanket on his lap. She must have been carried into the lodge, for when she awoke it was to find herself bedded down on a thick pile of hides, the still sleeping forms of her father and the Baron across from a smoldering fire pit.

Breaking dawn, she savored the privacy of being the only one awake. Hearing someone coming through the entrance, she squeezed her eyes almost shut, just a mere slit to peer from to satisfy her curiosity. A young girl about her age, dressed in a fawn colored garment lavishly hung with elk teeth entered quietly and hung a small iron pot from a tripod over the fire pit. Placing more wood upon the fire and giving the pot a stir with a large buffalo horn ladle, she made to exit. A pleased gasp came from her at noticing the large white dog, Esperanza, by the Baron's side. The girl crouched down beside the Bull Terrier, who was gently thumping it's tail, and proceeded to run her hands over the taut muscled flesh of the dog. Realizing that she wasn't petting the dog, but rather examining it, Anah shocked herself in recognizing that the animal was being assessed for the stew-pot. She threw her covers off and crossed to the Baron to begin shaking him rudely awake. The girl fled without a word.

As soon as he could create some coherence from Anah's excited story he began to laugh. "Oh, my dear, no one is going to make a tasty meal of my beloved pet." Anah continued a sputtering protest to which he replied, "*Calma, Mon ami!*" speaking in an odd mix of French and Italian. "Yes, dogs are consumed, but... and he gave a dramatic pause, holding her alarmed gaze, "they prefer plump little puppies." Even so Anah made it her concern to keep a watchful eye on the dog the rest of the day.

In spite of the flamboyance exhibited in the dress and regalia of these people she felt that their true lingua franca was one that addressed all the acts and intentions into keeping a balance and harmony with each other and their surroundings. She tried to interest her father in comparing these Plains horsemen with the Transcendentalists so in fashion now. The divine, sacred, the great mystery seemed to be a guiding principle, but in no way did they seem to be unaware of the realities of their nomadic life. A disturbing exception to her was the widely held belief that a certain garment, charm, or blessing could make one impervious to bullets, lead bullets. When she cornered Blue Tongue and tried to discuss this concept he laughingly told her that the Baron's dog was *wakan* for the ridiculous reason, to her, that it was pure white, with a "sacred circle"of black surrounding it's right eye. She did manage to query both her father and the Baron regarding the warrior who was so resplendent in his attire,who had what appeared to be not one, but four skunk skins, complete with the heads, wrapped around his waist. Thus began a diatribe about the military societies of the Plains Indians, and how the man she noted was undoubtedly one of the most honored "Crazy Dogs". This was confusing to her, as she thought she grasped the concept of adorning oneself with protective regalia of one's power or medicine animal. A skunk, what possible virtues could that animal provide? The Baron quizzed her carefully, "Was his hair braided or loose? Did he wear a much decorated sash over his right arm that was so long that it trailed on the ground? Did he also have an eagle bone whistle hung from his neck?" Before she could answer, he continued, "Four, yes, four skins, four is a sacred number to them. There are four arrows and 44 leaders, and Oh yes, every year the bravest four of the "Dogs" are chosen to wear the rope." Rope? Sash? Whistle? Anah was growing more and more overwhelmed with the information he was relating; her comprehension was faltering. To buy herself some time, she threw out, as one draws birds with bits of bread, the following information: "The man was bare-chested, and, oh, yes, his entire chest was painted red. His leggings, is that what they are called? The leggings had too many stripes to count on them." The Baron, now deeply interested in this subject, also managed to notice her eyes looking a bit glazed. He was so erudite that he knew he often simply bored people with his vast wealth of knowledge on the most diverse subjects. He paused, trying to work his way back to her original query. Had he answered her? The skunks, yes, that was it. "Skunks," he began, "are fearless, and peaceful. It does not have to get out of anyone's way. It moves at it's own speed, and has the most widely recognized respect of all the animals. It teaches how to give respect, expect respect and demand it." Satisfied with his answer, he turned sharply and simply strode away, leaving Anah somewhat less baffled. She wanted to learn more about these Dog Men; her interest in skunks was more than satisfied for now.

Closing her Commonplace Book, she wrapped it once more, carefully, in it's doeskin cover, tucked it under the mattress, and thought it best to give a thought now to prepare the evening's meal.

Pale Calf Woman
1868

That a bold and beautiful young woman led indirectly to the first major incidence of Swift Medicine's displeasure with his adopted son was unlikely, or so those who gossip thought, for the tall, handsome youth of sixteen winters seemed never to have his head turned by any of the eligible maidens in the camp. His appearance at gatherings and ceremonies was always noted, and often anticipated, but unlike the other young men he kept to himself. Friends he had, the older Red Heart and Walks Lightly were often with him. He was seldom off the back of the large sorrel, Charge, and his skillful way with this captured Army horse was envied. Many now sought him out for his ability to discern what pony would be best for chasing the buffalo, and what one would respond instinctively to the challenges of becoming a war pony. He was most often found training such a one. Horse flesh turned his head; women did not!

So when he approached Pale Calf Woman, and they were seen talking, heads bent together, the old women clucked appreciatively, sensing a new development, for this maiden was also an odd one. Especially skilled as a child with both beading, and the more difficult quilling, it was assumed that she would soon be invested into one of the women's societies. However, she abandoned the traditional geometric designs that the women used to adapt those of her own design. This seemed increasingly odd, for a woman that is. Birds, flowers, even lightning signs and dragonflies, these figurative designs were the domain of the men, used on the Winter Counts, lodge covers, ponies and their own bodies. Soon she abandoned not only the traditional embellishments, but also the objects most adorned by women, the moccasins, the parfleches, belts and the like. At last summer's gathering of the tribes on the Powder River she had been rumored to have painted not only Sleeping Rabbit's face, but his kola's, Hard Shield, also. Since these two warriors returned successfully from a horse raid some thought that her designs were blessed. That her skill was of great beauty there was no doubt, but there was concern for her doing what the young warriors usually did for themselves or each other. Soon she was openly seen not only painting faces, but bodies of men and war ponies and buffalo hunters alike. It was of such concern that a small council had been called: the outcome appeared to be, if not outright approval of her doings, at least an acceptance. Not every child was born to follow the expected path. However, when the rumor of Medicine Horse's seeming interest was brought to Swift Medicine's lodge, he grew concerned. He simply did not know what to think of this possible alliance.

In the seasons that had passed since his adoption the Cottonwood Boy grew into his name of Medicine Horse. When he extended his pipe for the first time in council, proposing a raid, he was unsure of who would accept his leadership, other than his *kola,* Walks Lightly and perhaps Red Heart, but three other young warriors smoked with him. This year's grass was already quite high, lush and green. The horses themselves were well nourished by it after the hard season just past. It was the best of times for going out on a raid. Thus in the Moon of Long Days, Pale Calf Woman was seen adorning the big sorrel, Charge, Medicine Horse's war pony, with her paints. As he stood tying a white cloth to the mane she began to patiently mix the colors in her buffalo hoof bowls. Using a porcupine tail she lavished her special wolf moss mix over the haunches, transforming the hide into a bright yellow. Upon this she carefully painted a large symbol for the Morning Star in Chinese vermilion. Two turtles were then added for protection and well being. A brilliant white butterfly was painted upon it's chest to help avoid enemy arrows. When she stepped back to consider her work, Medicine Horse spoke to her, respectfully requesting that the eyes be encircled with vermilion, as he wanted his mount to have exceptional eyesight, even to seeing into the soul of an enemy. When she had done this she indicated that she would be pleased to paint his body also, this untried horse warrior. Instead, he reached for her paints. Shaking her head, she handed him an empty clam shell and three pouches of powdered paints to mix with the buffalo fat in the little pot that she was extending. "You should paint yourself as this animal to show that you are brothers on this quest." He stepped back, thanking her, but had no intention of painting himself. Touching the small medicine bundle at his neck, he excused himself back to his lodge. When Swift Medicine brusquely queried him as to why Pale Calf Woman had painted his horse, Medicine Horse politely replied, "Because I asked her to," then turned away, thinking that was all the explanation necessary. Was he not aware of breaking yet another small tradition?

Within a fortnight he and the small raiding party he had led returned whooping and yipping to alert the camp of their victory, driving 14 finely fleshed mules before them. When it was apparent that these animals were from the Bluecoats there were mixed emotions.

At the council fire that night, those men that had withdrawn from the ongoing celebration to consider this plunder of Army goods had to acknowledge that this foundling had grown into a fine young man, apparently honored by the Great Mystery to achieve such success on his very first raid. Was it a wise or foolhardy act? Brave, bold, but possibly ruinous leadership. Indeed an unwise act to have done in these troubled times with the *wasichus,* but no lives had been lost, nor had they taken any. Reprisals were uncertain, however it was decided to move camp further out onto the plains at the next dawning. Swift Medicine was at first concerned that his adopted son might come to a bad end, as his natural son had, from such haste. He was proud of him nonetheless. Would this son become one of "the bravest-of-the-brave", and some day wear The Dog Rope? Did he dare to wish for this?

In due time Medicine Horse's acquisition became a great blessing. The large, well-shod mules could carry huge slabs of bloody meat and buffalo hides back to camp without hardship, for they possessed great strength. Though mules were of a complaining nature, the young man had a way with them. Medicine Horse saw that the sick and aged had made available the gentlest of the mules for traveling long distances. As none of these fine animals went to the lodge of Pale Calf Woman's father, tongues quieted and Swift Medicine was appeased by the young warrior's seeming lack of interest.

Though Medicine Horse was to go on and earn many war honors as time passed, he only allowed himself minimal adornment, a lone feather for his scalp lock, and not a *wambli,* or eagle feather, at that.

Just a simple glossy black flight feather of a *kanji,* crow. Why not a raven? Such speculation lasted for a short time only, for the people soon recognized his desire to appear simple in his achievements. The elders approved this humility, and waited for what the seasons would bring in his life.

II

The Widening Gyre

"They turned and sped directly south."

Destiny Manifested

"Making manifest our destiny as a great nation"

By 1860 over 150,000 white settlers, that is, those who were not just passing through on their way to better things, like the gold fields, had begun the process of settling down in the I.T., as the Indian Territories were then called. Manifest Destiny: widely interpreted and much misunderstood by many to mean a way of expecting that the United States government, with their policies and troops, would reinforce laws to protect those swarming upon the land, whether they were law abiding citizens or not.

Thus the centuries long tradition of the Plains Indian's ideal of harmony was forever shattered. The circle lay broken, and unnoticed as such. Buffalo Bill, hired by the Kansas Pacific R.R. to keep the tracks clear, shot 4,000 buffalo in just eight months!

"I have seen in a vision that some day, long after I am gone, light-skinned, bearded men will arrive with sticks spitting fire. They will conquer the land and drive you before them. They will kill the animals who give you their flesh that you may live, and they will bring strange animals for you to ride and eat. They will introduce war and evil, strange sickness and death. They will try and make you forget the Creator and things I have taught you. They will impose their own alien, evil ways. They will take your land little by little until there is nothing left for you. I do not like to tell you this, but you must know. You must be strong when that bad time comes, you men, and particularly you women, because much depends on you, because you are the perpetuators of life and if you weaken, the Cheyenne will cease to be. Now I have said all there is to say."

"Sweet Medicine", Cheyenne prophet and teacher

What The Years Had Wrought

Ft. Laramie, 1872

In the noon heat the parade ground lay empty, save for the small child playing contentedly in the protective care of a muscular white dog at her side. Crouched down, she was intensely absorbed in the task of creating a lodge for her dolly, Sunflower, from old pieces of hide and some twigs. Bold rays of sun, unencumbered by any clouds, strongly backlit the child's tousled blond curls in such a way that a shining nimbus, a halo, had formed. Her mother, Anah, pausing from her pleasant task of sorting through her collection of medicinal plants and poultices, stopped to raise one hand to shade her eyes, the better to focus on this vision in the shimmering bands of heat. Fine wisps of Orianna's hair had trailed out into the breeze creating an effect akin to a dandelion-gone-to-seed. Breathtaking, the mother thought with a slight wrench to her heart, and for a mere instant it was as though the barest scrim of some otherworldly existence had been exposed, rolled back beyond her understanding, as the child felt her loving gaze upon her and looked up. Anah shivered, reached for a shawl that wasn't there; refused an understanding beyond her depths. Sitting back into the spokes of the rocker, the bundle of dried white sage at rest on her lap for the moment, she reflected on all that had come to pass, all that had brought her to this bleak army post in Indian Territory. Had seven years passed since she had crossed the great river with her father and the Baron to set eyes on her first buffalo? Bison, she thought, remembering how the Baron kept correcting her. Her glance then darted down to Esperanza, the fine English bull terrier he'd left her, dozing in the sun at Orianna's feet. What a journey, what an experience they had undertaken!

When they had arrived at the fort those many years ago she had expected it to be a stockade, as at Ft. Ligonier in the East. Well, there was much to get used to in the West, and a lack of defensive walls was the least of it. The Bozeman Trail ran right past the fort, intersecting further on with the Oregon Trail. The Big Horn mountains were to the north, as were Forts Reno, Kearney and Smith, all backed up toward the great Continental Divide. The whole Powder River region was glorious; full of game. The meadows lush. The forests were of pine, spruce and fir. Cottonwoods, willow and chokecherry abounded along the rivers that flowed down from the slopes. Her father was mightily pleased with the beautiful trout that abounded in the clear icy streams, just as she was delighted in the profusions of berries and blooms to be found out on the abundant grasslands. No wonder the Indians did not wish to cede this land!

They quickly settled into the life of the fort. Her father had seen to the task of keeping her occupied, both in the surgery as his assistant, and as his companion as they traveled to the many nearby camps and reservations. She was able to indulge in her passions for both learning the languages, Lakota, Arapaho and the more difficult Cheyenne, and the use of native plants and medicines.

There was a constant flow of immigrants moving west; with them came various complaints and concerns of a medical nature which kept them quite busy during the warm months when the passes and the trails were open. Once the cold weather arrived the fort became quite isolated and there began a different sort of social life, which included Dr. Hoffman and his daughter in the dances and activities which were held at the Bachelor Officer Quarters.

The years passed quickly, moved smoothly, then suddenly everything changed when a new adjutant arrived from the east in the person of William Bryan Moore III. When Anah raised her eyes to gaze with fond love upon her daughter, who was rocking her dolly to sleep now, she could see in the child's sweet form so much that resembled her husband. It was like a dream, a day dream, she thought. He literally danced into my life. We married, and a life I had never given thought to became mine, that of a wife and mother. In fact no one did advise her, no mother, no aunt, no sister, no female had ever schooled her in this regard. There had been no education. In fact, no engagement even. William had sought her hand in the proper manner, through her father, and once granted, came a proposal. Such procedures back East would have been shocking, but things were of such a different order out here, she understood that. They married, and within the year came the child. It seemed so natural once she fell in love with William, that is, what one did, marry and have children. At times she felt constricted with guilt, for the love she bore for Orianna was so different from what she felt for her husband. She had grown remote from her father, and he from her also, or so it seemed. Was that the way it was meant to be, she wondered? All her time and energy was spent on her child and her husband. So very many changes, but she was busy with this business of wife and motherhood and had no one to ask, not really. She was no longer assisting her father in the surgery. She had barely noticed that he had an assistant. One day he had come by and informed them that he was leaving. Leaving! Returning, not home, but back East to Philadelphia, with plans to remarry a widowed acquaintance of their families.

Not long after that she began once more to travel to the surrounding camps and nearby reservations, placing Orianna with a nursemaid for a few precious hours. William had arranged for her own "nursemaid" of sorts to accompany her on her sorties outside the environs of the fort; an old Cheyenne scout, Turn Foot. Of course she would have preferred to go alone, but the old scout was a wellspring of valuable knowledge, and a keen interpreter whom she grew to like.

A yelp from the dog alerted her that it was time to go in and begin preparations for the evening's meal, as Orianna was bored and had begun to tease unmercifully.

William's new boots

The gentle boyish grin was unmistakable; something William had been anticipating had just arrived with the re-supply wagons. Holding a brand new pair of gleaming black boots aloft, he burst into the kitchen as though he were an untried hunter and this was his prize. He didn't expect her to admire the purchase, or note the fine details, as much as he wished her to appreciate him, and his love of this new possession, for he was indeed dashing. Wiping her hands swiftly on her apron, she pulled out one of the ladder-backed chairs for his use. Anah no longer registered shock at his childish vanities; in fact, she admired the joy he took in them, even though he was the invariable focus, his adornment and his pleasure, his taste; and the position he held, that enabled him to afford such a purchase; yet another pair, of fine English leather. Knowing that her bread dough could rest a bit she pulled out another chair and settled down in it, her attention available for him. With the new boots on now he walked, gingerly at first, around the table, ear cocked for the fine creaking the new leather gave. Soon he strode the length of the room, grinning fiercely. Much as she wished to admonish him to break them in a few minutes at a wearing, she knew him well enough to know that, as he reached for his campaign hat, he'd be off for the rest of the day, arriving home with a barely concealed limp from fresh blisters.

While others might call him vain, though never to his face, she did not mind the very nature of his adornments that she herself delighted in, for he was a most handsome man. What did irk her was how self-absorbed he could become in his post, and his constant surveying of what he called "the playing field", and what he intended for his further promotion. This was not quite what she expected of a career officer, or a husband, but on the other hand his self-absorption gave her the freedom to pursue her own interests on her own time.

She had been so dazzled, no other word for it, at first by his bearing, his manners, his learning, and yes, his dress uniform. Their honeymoon, well-planned by him, a trip back East, was an overly privileged one, and a necessary component to recall upon returning to a dusty frontier fort where her elbow length bone-white calfskin gloves, purchased in a boutique off Fifth Avenue, would languish in her cedar chest ever after. (Even the fort's fanciest ball would not call for such things.)

He was devoted and loyal, and charmingly unselfconscious of his talents and beauty. Every fiber of William Byron Moore III strove to be effortlessly impressive to all who beheld him. That this was accomplished with most of his peers recognizing vanity but not applying condemnation was an attribute to what was recognizable; that at heart, he held a strong flame of decent moral character. He was what God occasionally allows, a natural born elite, begun when the stars converged at his birth. What had deposited him out here on this wind-swept frontier she had yet to question.

The Buffalo Skull

When William came to the table that night, pausing only to lift a pot lid away on the stove, before settling down he smilingly regarded his wife and child. That slight smile that played upon his lips gave Anah pause. An anticipation, for this was the look that said "I have something for you". Indeed, before she could even pour their coffee and undo her apron he led her proudly out to the porch. There, prominently displayed by the old rockers, was a bleached out skull of a buffalo. A question, ready on her lips, was stayed by his index finger lightly pressed to her mouth. "Yes, I know it is not a pair of Texas longhorns, but this is not an ordinary skull." William was referring to the discussion they had a few nights ago when a handsome pair of well-polished and brass tipped horns appeared bolted above the entrance to the BOQ; Old Bedlam, the bachelor officers quarters. William, if not his wife, had been suitably impressed. All the small, but adequate officer's housing were so similar in appearance that it was not unusual for one man's porch to be mistaken for another. To that end distinguishing types of ornamentation appeared in the most unusual forms. The camp surgeon's dwelling had an old spinning wheel adorned with a pot of Boston Ivy twining through its spokes.

"Well, what do you think?" William declared as he drew back and pointed with a sweeping gesture toward the skull. Anah knew that he was trying to please; perhaps even to make some amends for voicing his displeasure at her growing cache of native artifacts that invariably appeared after each and every foray of hers into the Indian camps surrounding the fort.

With her apron now in her hand Anah mumbled a thanks, and drawing him by the hand led him back inside. "Your meal grows cold, dear. Come," she murmured solicitously. Busying herself now with dishing up food, she bustled around, hoping that his attention would now be on the antelope stew he so favored, and not on her lack of enthusiasm for his gift. In truth she was quite troubled by the skull's appearance.

The large bleached out skull was indeed awesome, so intricately was it decorated. From red-painted orbital sockets to the trade cloth wrapped and quilled horns it radiated power in its magnificence. The gaping holes that once held lustrous black eyes of the large beast were now stuffed with sage, still green and aromatic.

After their simple meal, as she waited for the dishwater to heat, she could not disavow a most discomforting sense that the skull should not be here on her porch. She knew that it had been prominently placed on some hilltop as an acknowledgment to the mysterious powers that govern the movements of the bison across the plains. For a white man, a *ve'ho'e*, to remove it was undoubtedly a sacrilege. Here upon her porch it's decorative aspect was perhaps amusing to the inhabitants of this post, but to any native eyes it would signify not only ignorance and disregard of their customs, but sacrilege! Perhaps theft! What could she do? It was too late to reject it as a gift, for she had foolishly acknowledged it as such. To try and explain her feelings to William now would only enforce his growing intolerance for the occasional forays into a culture that increasingly fascinated her. In fact her interest was growing far beyond just gaining a knowledge of their medicinal plants and herbs, far beyond understanding their customs. At best William disparagingly patronized her as "his little heathen", at worst he merely compressed his lips into a thin tight line of disapproval, his blue eyes cooling to a glacial hardness before turning smartly on his heel to stalk away. But he had yet to forbid her pursuits. She must do everything in her power to maintain her freedom to roam at will the countryside. For now the presence of that skull stood to discredit her with the very ones she wished to gain approval from. But what to do?

Unexpectedly Esperanza, Miss Naughty(Not-Eee) came sniffing and probing to her aid. The next morning she surprised the densely muscled terrier struggling to drag the huge skull from the porch. Such a treasure, her fiercely wagging tail seemed to say, "Won't you help me Mistress?" Dogs! Anah had a possible solution, if she could enlist Turn Foot, the old Cheyenne scout, to assist her in what would be, unfortunately, a duplicitous maneuver.

If he agreed she would be placing him in a compromising position, for he could not simply walk off with it strapped to his mule, crossing boldly in front of the officer's domiciles. That he would help her she had little doubt, for she saw when he first laid eyes on the skull that he was offended. Just the slightest stiffening to his posture, but she had learned to read him well; his eyes could suddenly just "shutter" in absolute disregard to circumstances, traits that had served him so well as an army scout. Before he could turn away she boldly began....

"Turn Foot," she addressed him directly so that he had to hear her out, continuing, "This does not belong here," a small hand gesture towards the offensive object done carefully to show no particular disregard. Laughing inwardly she fancied herself a diplomat of sorts. Extending her palm now outwards towards the rolling expanse of the surrounding hills, "but back out there." He nodded in instant comprehension. With a great sense of relief she ascertained that she had lost no face with him, nor did there seem to be any need to explain how the skull had arrived here. She had no intention of compromising William, either.

So with a carefully rehearsed wording she went on, "Late at night when the parade grounds are empty and the fort is quiet I think that the dogs may drag this away." Turn Foot's face was a weathered blank. She stammered out, " Back, back where it belongs." A slight upturn at his mouth's edge, and she knew that it would be accomplished. She turned then, indicating that he should wait, then hustled to bear him out an extra large helping of the antelope stew.

Weeks passed before William even noted the luminous skull's disappearance. She postulated that the fort's disreputable dog pack that roamed so freely at night must have dragged it away. He seemed unconcerned and disinterested.

Waagol the Mule

How Waagol came to Turn Foot.

That evening, when the detail that had gone out for lumber returned to the fort, even before the creakings of the laden wagons were heard, came the irate bellowing and bawling of an injured mule. As the complaining beast was led into view, four arrows could be seen projecting from it's haunches. There was not much to be done, except to try and extract the shafts, but no one could get close once it's load was removed. It was not like they could give it a bottle of whiskey and ask it to please hold still while the surgeon tried to address the wounds. In a few days the sinews that bound the arrowhead to the shaft would grow moist and loosen inside the mule's tender flesh, but as to extracting the points, well, who would volunteer to try and dig them out of the big animal, over 16 hands tall at the withers and at least several hundred pounds? Certainly not the base surgeon! If not for the old Cheyenne scout's ministrations that mule would have perished after the inevitable infection set in. When Turn Foot asked for the animal he was teased, "It's too tough to eat," but with a wave the issue was dismissed. He just led "Waggle" away. No one expected to see that mule again, but Turn Foot knew how to pull an arrow with a deft working of a wire loop, and just what plants and poultices to treat the wounds with. Within a fortnight Waagol reappeared looking fit for further service, appropriately decked out with an old but magnificent beaded Crow horse blanket. He would let no one near him but the old scout. No recompense was required, for no soldier wanted to try and utilize it's further services as a pack animal. Both man and beast walked with a slight limp. He was not a kicker, nor biter, and had an imperturbable nature. He did not seem to mind carrying loads of up to 300 lbs for days at a time; admirable traits, in the scout's estimation. Thus the Army's beast of burden became a favored mount for the old scout; full of composure in spite of his appearance. The name was bestowed upon him for how his ears joggled when he broke into trot.

The Spirit Dog

When Anah's dear "Count One-Two-Three" came to bid adieu, before she and her father left for Ft. Laramie, the Baron told her to expect a little remembrance of him someday. How delighted she was when a wagon train pulled into the fort, to resupply before heading on, and her "remembrance" arrived. Two drovers appeared at her door one day, respectfully inquiring for "the little miss". As she stood to consider their wearied appearance, a bit concerned at why they sought her out, a flash of black and white fur flung itself upon her skirts, barking joyfully. It was the Baron's "remembrance", Esperanza, his beloved English bull terrier, nicknamed "Naughty" by her. The men simply told her that the dog had earned it's freedom to roam and therefore the "furrin" gentleman would not be taking it back across the ocean.

Cold weather would arrive soon and, as the dog was banished from the house, Anah painstakingly crafted a little coat, a dog capote, she wryly thought, for the dog's wintering. Bull Terriers have very short, thin coats of fur and William frowned on the dog being kept indoors except on the coldest nights, as this breed was notorious for shedding. William had his uniforms to consider, after all. So an old army saddle blanket was procured, along with some red flannel trade cloth, and she worked with that. Ori, bless her, wanted some flowers to be embroidered on it; otherwise how would they know that the dog was a girl, she queried, but somehow Anah never found the time.

When first the dog appeared, clad smartly in it's little capote-like garment, complete with hood, it almost disrupted that morning's bayonet practice. The drill sergeant was not at all pleased to have his tutorial interrupted thus as Esperanza sallied forth, moving smartly out across the parade ground, her ears strictly pointed up, causing a startling effect on discipline at the comic sight.

When Turn Foot first came upon the white beast rising from her nest of blankets, tail wagging, he, too, was taken back, but only momentarily. When the hood fell back he could clearly see the bold ring of black that encircled it's left eye. A Spirit Dog, he declared! This was no war paint applied as the men did to their medicine horses before riding out, but a natural marking of it's fur, he keenly discerned. The old scout kept his eye out for the animal from then on, it's pure white coat marking it also as *wakan,* a holy creature. Occasionally it was to be seen, inexplicably possessed of a mad joy, leaping and cavorting high into the air for no apparent reason. Frenzied and fearless, she raced unseen spirits, playing with the wind! Good medicine, he thought, observing how it napped with one eye a baleful slit, and fearful rumbles and growls to drive away unseen torments. A close bond developed between not only Turn Foot, but also with the mule, Waagol. To see the Cheyenne scout astride his large mule, upright and dignified, with better posture than many a young soldier, accompanied by a spirited dog clad in a capote, was to bring many a smile to those on the post.

About Turn Foot the Scout

When Anah first met Turn Foot, the first thing that she really noticed about the old Indian scout besides his amber tinted sharpshooter's glasses was that he sought and held the gaze of the many dogs that freely roamed the expansive parade grounds. Most of the creatures gave him a wide berth; never growling, never groveling. So when Esperanza sprang up from the porch, tail wagging, Anah didn't know what to expect. Then he was there, bending down, his sharpshooter's medal glinting in the last rays of the sun, gazing rather steadfastly into the face of canine acceptance, ignoring how she herself rose from the rocker to greet him.

Who was this man? Had he come for her? Where was he from? Perhaps in his 70's, long trade cloth wrapped braids, black, but mostly shot with gray. Though his garb was no more unusual than any of the regalia that the Army scouts arrayed themselves in, she noted two things. First, he was a traditional, every garment that was not Army issue was hand-made, hugely worn, and signified respect. Besides his height, taller by several inches than William, she judged his features that spoke of his tribal affiliation. A lean, high cheek-boned, narrow face with a strong Roman type nose, extremely handsome, she thought, for a man of his years. Northern Cheyenne, she would guess. There were not many of that tribal affiliation that scouted for the Army. But why was he here?

He rose from scratching Esperanza's head to finally acknowledge her presence with the slightest tick of his head. She found herself automatically returning the gesture, as though they had some previous agreement. Having caught her gaze, he now held it. Boldly returning it she relaxed, hearing now bird twitter and the clomping of a horse being led past to the stables for the night. "Mrs. Moore?" he inquired in unhurried and clear English, as he stepped up to her porch. "Please follow me." She did, quite accepting of his presence and summons. William had been vocal in his disapproval of her leaving the fort unaccompanied. She assumed that this scout was here in the guise of an interpreter; William knowing that she might accept a guardian to accompany her on those terms for her forays outside the environs of the fort. Unspoken between her and William was the knowledge that if she bridled at being accompanied on her visits to the Indian camps, it would soon follow that her visits would be curtailed. She had every reason to like this arrangement!

William had told her much about him, but quite some time passed before she knew the reason that caused Turn Foot, as the old Cheyenne was called, to follow the white man's path. He had been a U.S. Army scout for more than 30 years, and had been attached to Ft. Laramie from it's inception as an army post. She had heard that he kept a hide lodge to which he retired to, rather than any barracks, and that he would do no tracking ,in any circumstances that involved his own people or the many affiliations of the Sioux. Often he absented himself for long periods from the fort, but was eagerly returned to service as his skills were invaluable. He had command of many of the languages of the plains tribes, and had the ability to travel incognito. Often he posed as a "whiskey injun" hanging around outside a fort listening to rumors, gathering information on the sly. If necessary he traveled into enemy territory, slumped in old blankets on a skinny pony, barely drawing notice, just a blur on a far horizon. He came and went on his own accord, seeming to survive on air alone. Such was the inherent dignity of his bearing, as she was to learn by association, his character, that one barely took note of his lamed foot.

Thieves Road

July 1874

Medicine Horse sat his pony as Big Nose Matches and Walks Lightly quietly observed from their vantage point nearby. This small scouting party was up on a narrow ridge high above Castle Creek Valley in the Paha Sapha, the Black Hills, sacred hunting ground and medicine country of their people. They had been with Tasunke Witco, whom the *wasichu* call Man Who Makes Horses Crazy when he had attacked the Bluecoat, Custer, The Squaw Killer, last summer. Now this bold yellow haired warrior was entering this hallowed place in direct violation of a treaty.

Red Cloud had been given The Great White Father's word that these hills would not be entered. But what treaty that pen had touched had these white men ever kept? Once the metal that shined like The Squaw-Killer's hair had been discovered in these hills so many *wasichus* had flooded in that a trail had been deeply worn in the face of the earth by those who were now hunting gold instead of buffalo. Their desire for these shiny lumps was without measure. It was as the Blackfeet had said of the beaver...the white faces came, saw, and took with such a large hand that the pelts of the dam-makers were now a much treasured trade item, rare indeed. Medicine Horse did not want to think of what was happening to the buffalo herd due to this same sort of taking. What would stop these hairy-faced pale ones from their greedy and destructive ways?

Fast Bear rightly named the trail they were looking down on "Thieves Road". Big Nose said quietly, "Hand me your spy glass," and turned towards Medicine Horse, anger stiffening his usually soft voice. "Is it the yellow hair one at the head?" Matches asked, his hand out, as Medicine Horse reached into his war bag, also eager to get a closer look at the long column of heavily armed and laden soldiers slowly moving along below them. Through the dry clear air of the summer afternoon the jumpy, strange music of the wasichus rose to their ears.

Once Sinte-Gleska, Spotted Tail, had returned from a brief skirmish with some troops down on the Powder with a shiny tin horn, a long red braid attached to it's handle. Quite a few of the men from Black Kettle's Cheyenne and some of the men from the Brule's encampment had tried to play it pleasantly, but to no avail. Big Nose put it to his lips, but the sounds he made came out like a Prairie Hen being attacked. It's magic stayed within. After the men lost interest, some of the children brave enough to pick up a wasichu's noise maker tried, and failed. Big Nose now wore the red braid tied to his pony's mane. What had become of the shiny tin no one knew or cared.

Medicine Horse now placed the spy glass to his eye and carefully assessed the long trail of men and supplies winding so easily down the narrow defile along Hidden Wood Creek below. Matches and Big Nose turned to him when he dropped the glass from his face, looking to him for direction. Storing the scope he merely said, "Ride back to camp. Tell of what you have seen. Send scouts out to find where they will camp. I will join you before the sun sets," and dismounted, settling himself to continue his observations. As Matches, Walks Lightly, and Big Nose quietly picked their way down off the outcropping they both wondered, but did not discuss, why Medicine Horse stayed behind; after all, they respected his leading. What they never were to know was how Medicine Horse responded to the sight of Custer's advancing cavalry.

Medicine Horse watched them descend with a growing apprehension, for his heart was beating with an erratic pace. Sweat had broken out all over his body, but even as a thin trail of it ran down his bare spine he began to feel chilled. Needing to calm himself he picketed his pony and sat with his back against a lodgepole pine. He knew this feeling. It was fear, just as he had first experienced many winter counts ago. As the recall of that day swept over him he believed that he could even smell the carnage.

"He Knew If He Named It, He Might Die!"
1868 First Fear

With a glorious day upon them Medicine Horse and Walks Lightly gave their mounts, fine new ponies they were training to be Buffalo Runners, full rein. With the fresh wind in their hair and the warmth of the late sun upon their bare skin they reveled in not only their youth and vigor, but that of the horseflesh they guided so easily with just the pressure of their legs beneath them. They had headed out this way in hopes of finding a small herd of tatankas, buffalo, to initiate their horses with.

Walks Lightly was the first to notice the unusual slight darkness off on the distant plain before them. As it had been a fine cloudless day he was curious. "Ahh-h, kola, what's that?" He pointed to the dark active mass in the clear skies ahead of them. Medicine Horse had the superior eyesight, and a valuable Far-Looking Eye that he had found out by one of the ve'ho'e's trails in a busted up wagon. He drew his pony to a halt, retrieved the spy glass and focused on the apparition. "Birds," he exclaimed, "many birds. Death Birds," and laid his hand on Walks Lightly's shoulder. "Look for yourself!" "Wanbli, eagles too," as he spurred his horse forward. Heedless of what might lay ahead they raced to the top of the next ridge and abruptly halted at the gruesome sight spread out before them. As far as they could see, too numerous to count, were downed buffalo. Here and there lay a naked skinned body, but for the most part they lay whole, their thick dark hide still upon them. This was no work of a band harvesting for their winter stores. No human form walked among them, but perched on the humps, tearing at the softer skinned bellies and pecking at the eyes were hordes of vultures and crows. A rough croak of a few ravens rang out. Racing too and fro were not one, but what appeared to be several packs of wolves, coyotes and even a few foxes standing by awaiting their turn. This slaughter had not been recent, as the air was tainted with the overwhelming stench of so much rotting flesh. A few orphaned calves bawled, milling around in confusion, safe for the time being from their usual predators. No matter how many of the winged and four footed people were out feasting, there was no way they could consume what lay before Medicine Horse and Walks Lightly's horrified eyes. This was not a jubilant completion to a buffalo hunt. There were no groups of women busily handling the hides. No men were pulling arrows from a kill and claiming it theirs. No Buffalo Runners were quietly grazing, their job well done. No sturdy ponies were being hitched to travois to pull the meat that would guarantee none would starve during the winter ahead. No sounds of rejoicing in hunting skills and ample provision. The entire plain was bereft of human sound. Both young men sat their mounts, stunned. They knew of the depredations to the vast herds by the white man's greed for the lush furred hide; they had listened to tales of how tatanka's life was taken by long shooting guns stuck from the eyes of the Iron Horse, but here there was no Iron Road. What had happened here?

When Medicine Horse heard the roar of the Great Bear, spotting the huge humped beast rearing up on two legs to paw at a diving eagle, the hair on his arms rose. He felt his very breath hesitate, as though it considered not leaving his body. His eyes burned in trying to focus on all that he had never witnessed in his young life before, and no matter how hard he willed himself to turn away he could not.

He wanted to ride down there, to chase all away with war cries and a brandishing of weapons. But the real enemy had gone. He wanted to shout to his friend to flee, but now a strange numbness was entering his flesh, like something unholy. He did not know what to do; for the first time in his life he felt fear. Fear! This was an incomprehensible violation! His tongue was dry in his mouth; his limbs began to tremble. He did not even think to reach for the little bag of medicine around his neck; he felt helpless and worse, a new feeling flowed through his limbs. Weakening both his mind and body, it was depriving him of any resolve. Yet just as this weakness almost brought him to his knees and a vile blackness rose in his gut, an icy crawling sensation overcame his spirit. He knew if he named it he might die. Yet he knew if he didn't he could never face it and become a true brave. It had no shape or form. In his heart that day, for the very first time, he knew fear. And faced it as he looked out upon the gruesome sight before him. Sacred became sacrilege! Tatanka! Tatanka, the gift from the Great God above to the people lay without honor or respect!

At that the spell broke and he charged down the slope, arms raised to the heavens, screaming. Walks Lightly rode with him. These ponies not yet trained to the hunt were hard to control and skittish among the dead. When they dismounted to examine what must have been a magnificent bull in his prime they found no arrow had dispatched him, but bullets. Tracks of three wagons were found, pulled by shod oxen. So it had not been the work of the skin hunters. Why were so many of the animals left with *their hides intact? Not even the tasty livers had been cut out. As they went from one fly-botched carcass to another they determined that all had been dispatched by the long guns.*

Never had he left a successful hunting ground without gratefulness in his heart, without honor having been given to these who provided them with so very much other than just their flesh. Just then Walks Lightly called out, "The tongues, they have taken the tongues, only the tongues." That the heart and livers were left puzzled them. Was there no end to the white man's mysterious and wanton desires? Surrounded by all this waste, all they could do now was to offer up their prayers. Sadly, they took back what little unspoiled meat their ponies could carry, hearts heavy with the news they were also bringing.

Ah hau, yes, that was the first time that he had felt inadequate to what his life was. So much had happened in the intervening years; events that were but symbols on the cured hide of the tribe's winter counts, but those same events felt carved into the flesh of his heart. He recalled each recovery from yet another broken promise from the Bluecoats; another life taken, not in honorable warfare but in a massacre. He was wounded. Healed, but scarred. Tough now the muscle that beat inside him. As his body grew, so did his enmity for the depredations that had been visited upon his people. The young man who had thought he was being guided to be a *wicasa wakan*, holy man, was now a feared member of the Dog Soldier Society. Just this past moon he had earned the right to wear the coveted sash of a Dog Warrior. His spirit cried "Kill", not heal!

And now heavily armed Bluecoats were penetrating his people's sacred ground, so heavily burdened with supplies that their intentions could not be thought as honorable. They were arriving to set up an armed and well-defended camp, it appeared. So bold and sure that some arrived with noise-maker instruments, not just guns. They were boldly announcing their presence with strange, unpleasing music.

When he arrived back at camp a council would have to be called, the warriors assembled. His head as heavy as his heart felt, he sank to his knees. The sun continued on it's downward path across the heavens. A troubled young warrior, eyes closed, just as two *kangi*, crows, flew in to post guard above him.

This Was No Earthly Fear!

Thinking that he had fallen asleep, as unlikely as that would be, he crawled to the edge of the bluff. There was no sign of the army's passage. The late summer sun hung fat and swollen with last light on the far horizon. Thin layers of grayish clouds barely cloaked it's face. Smoke? Was that smoke, he did not smell it in the air, even though the light wind would have brought it in his direction. Again he felt a chill within, but of an expectancy, not fear. Still, it brought all his senses alert. How long have I been sleeping? Why was the sun just hanging there? And why am I looking out, not into the wooded hills, but onto a flat, rolling plain, the Awanka Toyala, greenness of the world? He could see now that, yes, there was indeed smoke traversing the horizon as generated by a prairie fire. A strong wind surged through the long grasses, bending them to it's passing. The flames shot higher, and higher, but did not sweep closer. They hung suspended, towering. He felt an intense heat just as his vision began blurring. This was no earthly fire!

Time stopped as the sky flared in shades of burning vermilion that danced, turned and spun in majesty, much as the Great Lights from the far north would dance in the winter sky. Down close on the incredibly expanded horizon dark shapes were struggling, or so it seemed, to emerge from the flames. Large shaggy forms broke through and surged forward. Thundering hooves struck sparks in the tall, dry grasses of the prairie. Tatonka! Tatonka, larger than life, running in numbers greater than he had ever seen, even in the abundance they had during his childhood. The buffalo milled and swirled, then merged into a grand concentric circle, driving up a great pall of dust.

Overhead luminous cloud forms were coalescing, slow as an ebbing circle of a raindrop on the water's face they darkened and began to mirror the herd below. Faster and faster swirled the heavens above; the animals spread out below kept pace. The sky beyond and above the horizon was now ominously dark. The wind wailed in strange tongues. Riding this wind came just a pair of the large, red-headed, long legged birds. Though the wind now blew with great strength the cranes, seemingly without effort, moved towards him, commanding his attention. When they were almost close enough that he could reach out to them they turned and sped directly south, to disappear from his sight, but not his mind. Light was fading; it grew harder to focus on what was happening before his amazed eyes, but as the heavens dimmed a wild howling began. Eagles, ravens, crows and death birds swooped into the revolving scene. On the ground came packs of predators: wolves, coyotes, foxes. Even a few of the solitary great humped bears ambled forward. All these four-footed brothers and winged ones now encircled the great buffalo herd. His ears hurt from the shrill keening of the wind which had risen in force, causing him to bend low, crouched with his arms protecting his sight from the accompanying dust and swirling debris. He felt a horrified awe at the animated scene before him. Just then he clearly heard a distant drumming sound, of hooves, shouts and excited cries that could only be men racing towards the kill on their Buffalo Runners. Before one arrow flew or a bullet sped towards the waiting herd the buffalo vanished. Just vanished! The hunters sped on in silence now. Lances raised, arrows nocked, powder horns at the ready..He reached for his spy glass and in drawing it to his eye saw a huge twisting spout pour down from the sky and lift up all remaining life from the plain and sky..Abruptly all was still. With horrified awe he waited. How had all this simply vanished from his sight?

 Slowly over the horizon rose a wall of dark red blood. It broke, flooding, the plain , blanketing the dry ground. Nothing moved, silence prevailed , then before his eyes the blood abruptly sank in the same way rain, in due season, is quickly absorbed, leaving only a bare plain, covered from horizon to horizon with aged white skeletons of man and beast alike. Despair welled up from his heart; he knew that what was being revealed to him now spoke an elemental truth, as even all that remained, dry bones, rose up in a whirlwind as dust upon the plain.

 The glass fell from his hand when he heard his childhood name,"Wagachun, Wagachun!" Looking up into the now dark sky he *was stunned to see the illuminated form of a man, kneeling on the edge of a low hanging thundercloud. Heat lightning flared, making it hard to discern his face. Long silver braids carefully wrapped in beaver hung down over a beautifully quilled pipe bag. Over his bare shoulder was draped a finely worked buffalo robe, pure white, of the sort that the revered warrior Waquini wore. The face was benign, wise and oddly smiling. Could it be Silver Spotted Owl? That name almost broke from his mouth before he admonished himself not to speak the name of the dead.*

Medicine Horse sprang to his feet before the sight of this holy man. Their gaze met. So much he wanted to ask right now, and yet his tongue lay silent and content. How long he gazed into the heavens he had no idea until Spotted Owl splayed his weathered hand over his heart, then extended his long fingers toward him. He could see the man's heart glowing in his chest like fire, each breath was acting as a bellows, causing a small river of fire to flow into his hands. From each extended fingertip a flame now emerged and briefly quivered there before leaping, spark-like, to race towards where Medicine Horse stood. Enthralled, Medicine Horse watched the star-like sparks twirl and spin through eons and space toward him. There was so much more he still needed to ask of the Owl. What did all this mean, and why was it being revealed to him? What was he to do? But even as these thoughts raced through his mind, his body began to respond. He threw his arms upward to the Great One Above and, as he extended his own hands skyward, the burning flames began to flutter and become a small glowing mass hurtling down towards him. As he watched these tiny stars turned into finely feathered, small blue birds upon which, as he extended his palms flat, they gently landed. An exquisite warmth flowed from their settled weight upon his hands. The little birds twitched and fluffed their feathers, quite at ease to be in his care. They chirruped softly and began to settle down. A handful of blue birds! He could feel the wetness on his cheeks. His heart burned; a fire had been generated there. This heart that had carried the painful burden of all the wasteful slaughter he had stumbled on that day, so many winters past, now began to fill with a sacred insight.

He looked heavenward, expecting to see his old guardian, needing explanations, but the night sky was silky black; empty. The horizon now closed in, forested, and he could hear the stream below once more. He felt exhausted, yet oddly contented. There was much to understand from this vision, but for now peace settled on him, bringing sleep.

Hours later he awoke, struggling with confusion. Looking around he saw Charge quietly grazing on the short grass at the top of the bluff. Had he been dreaming? Had he dreamed all that, he thought, as bits and pieces of his vision drifted across his wakening mind. Sitting up he determined that he was alone; that he needed to make his way back to camp before dawn. What had he been shown, and why? As he carefully and quietly picked his way off the outcropping he began to bring to mind what he determined had been a vision; dreams simply did not have such clarity of recall. They came from within; visions from without! Silver Spotted Owl had appeared to him. To warn him? To advise him? Confusing thoughts flitted around in his head,...like little birds, he grimaced. How had it begun? A storm with the sky in flames. Well actually, it started when he felt fear at seeing the approaching column of Bluecoats. But he, Medicine Horse, and he touched his Dog Rope just to reassure himself, had no fear of them. He winced at the painful recall... He and his kola, Walks Lightly, stumbling onto the plain of slaughtered buffaloes; that day so long ago, of The First Fear! Aaah, yes, that was just the beginning of what had been prophesied...*Motse'eo've*, Sweet Medicine, had foretold how the white hairy faces would swarm upon the land. They would come all sewed up in clothes, and would destroy everything that we depend on, and take over all the land throughout our world. The *ve'ho'e, the wasichu, white-man*! Was this not what he was fighting to protect, the land, our very way of life so dependent on our brother, tatanka? Is this not why they roamed further and further to find the buffalo, as more and more of the white-man's interference was depleting the vast herds. And now they were here in our sacred hills! And although he was one of "the bravest of the brave", Dog Man of the Hotamitaneo, unconsciously reaching for his eagle bone whistle that hung upon his chest, what he had felt looking down upon the Bluecoats was pure fear. Disturbed, he tried to focus in on the recent vision. With some alarm he realized that though the plain had been wiped clean by blood, of two and four legs alike, there had been no soldiers. And the vision progressed to where all was dark. The fires were out? Gone? No rain, no flood and he did not see himself, at first. He was alone. The cranes, two of them, his spirit guides that had arrived during his *hanbleciya*, vision quest, but they flew past him, towards the South. Oddly, this did not dismay him, he did not feel abandoned by his spirit helpers. Then darkness fell over the empty plain and he saw the Cheyenne Holy Man that had been to him as a father. Had he appeared to guide him? No, he said not a word, although when the flames had leapt from Silver Spotted Owl's extended fingertips he had expected a great pronouncement. But as the flames sped towards him and he rose in recognition of The Great One Above, arms extended expectantly, what had happened even now left him speechless. A handful of feathery winged creatures. Beautiful, but what great message for a hostile warrior did they convey! A mystery!

He rode on in troubled silence, working to derive meaning as one would gnaw on a moccasin sole for nourishment if one were starving. As he approached the camp's scouts he had just come to the unsatisfying conclusion that all his great vision had in way of portent was that in the unstoppable passage of the seasons he would have perhaps only a handful of comfort, hardly satisfying to the blood of a young warrior so troubled by the further incursions of the army into his people's sacred lands.

......just a few little birds!

Nothing Lives Long

"What is honor to them when their word is as dust in the wind?"

Having seen to the needs of his war pony, Medicine Horse sat in his lodge, listening to the crier calling for an assembly of the Hotamitaneo. He knew the concerns that would be brought forth regarding the intrusion of the soldiers where Black Kettle's band of Cheyenne, the Wutapai, were now gathered. They, along with other bands of Red Cloud's, Crazy Horse's and Tall Bull's had no intention of following The White Man's Road. Many of these warriors, termed "hostiles" by the army, had sacrificed so much to remain free, even down to the flesh upon their bodies, for many were near starvation. The "rations", as the spoiled beef and worm-filled flour was called, were not what they wanted to eat. And why should they when The Great One All Above had provided so well for them? The white-man was too lazy to walk out upon the land and search for the good roots and wait for the sweet berries in their season. The white-man dug up the earth and put seeds into it so that his food would be close to where he slept night after night. And as to his stringy-fleshed cattle, well, the beasts stood there and let you kill them. We, the People, are hunters. We hunt our food, Medicine Horse thought. Why do they not let us live ours lives as we always have? Is it because they want to live where we have always lived? Knowing that he would be called to the council to report, he tried to focus once more on his vision. Was there anything of great import to all to convey of what he had seen?

The barren plain sprang to his mind with nothing upon it, and he thought of the wisdom of White Antelope's death song, "Nothing lives long. Only the earth and mountains." A forlorn feeling of the truth of this washed over him, but then he recalled the lovely little birds! In spite of the devastation he had seen in his vision he had been left with an inexplicable feeling of peace. He could not understand it. In many ways it had reminded him of how he felt upon gazing into Silver Spotted Owl's weathered face. A small but intense sense of calm simply radiated from the man. It had nothing to do with his regalia, his bearing, nor his physical appearance. Not what it felt like when he first laid eyes on the great warrior Waquini, the one the *ve'ho'e's* call Roman Nose, because of his powerful, hooked nose. Very tall, broad shouldered and deep chested, he sat his magnificent white war horse with the feathers of his war bonnet almost touching the ground, a white buffalo calf robe carelessly draped over his broad shoulders with no less than four fine revolvers displayed at his waist. So much raw power emanated from this Crooked Lance Society member that he, Medicine Horse, was embarrassed at first to gaze directly on him. But the power of Spotted Owl's was different; it had to be slowly discovered. It was so much like what it felt like to come upon a steaming hot spring secreted under snow laden pine boughs, so hidden that once revealed, like a secret stumbled upon, one would quickly strip off wet cold sodden leggings and enter it, knowing one was safe to soak in its warmth. Spotted Owl had radiated this form of powerful medicine for him. It was comforting to know that The Owl's spirit had the strength to reach from the Land Beyond to still speak to him. The more he thought on this the less he felt that he had anything to convey to the council other than stating what he and the other scouts observed. Old muzzle loading rifles, lances, war clubs and arrows could not very well prevail against what the Bluecoats had brought into their hills. What had happened on the banks of the Sand Creek so many winters ago still raged like a fire upon the plains in his heart and the hearts of the warriors. And now the very leader who had brought about the death of Black Kettle at the Washitia was entering the sacred grounds. As a Dog Man he was more than willing to throw his life away for his people, as a brave man should, to avenge all the senseless deaths that had occurred. "Nothing lives long, only the earth and mountains" which he so loved, this refrain he now carried within as a Brave Song. There was no choice but to defend what he so loved. So he set aside the vision and the telling of it, and with his pipe bag in hand he left for the council lodge. As he laid on his robes that night he again drew the vision from his memory:

Everything had passed on. The buffalo had passed away, the hunters had thundered by, no one spoke to him, not with words, nor actions.

Fearsome occurrences; the wall of blood, the skeletons heaped upon the plain... And the disappearance. Was that not a message? All seemed to come, then go; nothing remained.

Then he remembered the birds, the cranes. Did they not fly directly toward him, but then they too passed him by. Of what was their significance? They had such balance. At times they appeared in the Sand Hills to the south in flocks of uncountable numbers, their strange calls an unlikely match to their stately appearance. How he wished Spotted Owl was here to explain such things to him. Being a warrior, he had little time for these things now, though. Come and go, come and go; his head throbbed with trying to understand, but he could get no more from this than from a desiccated piece of dried buffalo, no matter how he chewed on it.

He threw back the heavy robe and stepped out into the cool night. The birds, recall the birds... he felt a twinge of shame that no powerful winged ones had come to him, but just small, brightly feathered ones. No eagles! But they had stayed, and they had been given to him; sent to him. Though he had no brilliant insight into his vision he had a sense of peace. I do not know what is to be, but I will wait for it to unfold. Thinking thus he could live with the mystery. He had been perhaps ashamed to share this vision because instead of powerful war eagles, he had held a handful of such pretty twittering creatures; gentle, the kind that don't even bully their own kind to get at the seed, and he, one of the bravest of the brave, a Dog Man. What could this mean?

When he had glassed the valley and seen the yellow haired Woman Killer at the head of the long snaking line of Bluecoats hauling the big guns and many wagons of provisions, making their way into the People's sacred hills, the rage to ride The Red Road immediately came upon him....but when, in his vision, his hands were filled with the little blue birds, he felt such a peace. Surely this could not mean...no, a treaty made by The Great Father had yet to be honored, the fact that troops with guns were entering the hills unannounced could not mean peace. Was he meant to take off his rope? It would take much more than a vision such as this. The more he thought on this the more his head hurt. He knew that he must wait for time to unfold the mystery. A strong gust of wind came up from the south, danced around his head, full of the smell of pine resin. He looked out into the blackness of the night and felt calm. What could he do now but sleep?

Swift Medicine's Words To His Son
1870

When sleep would not come Medicine Horse quietly slipped from his robes and left to seek the solace of the stars from amongst the pony herd. As he padded by Swift Medicine's lodge a quiet but firm call came to join him. The flap was drawn back and he entered. Oddly, the sleeping robes were empty. Just a small fire burned at it's center and a lit pipe was even now being extended to him to come, sit, smoke. At once he felt a great peace envelop him; the prospect of a burden being perhaps not quite lifted, but shared.

So he found himself telling this old warrior, his friend, indeed his father, what he kept from the council, of the vision. In the dancing light from the fire that ebbed and flowed it seemed that the young man's face grew stronger, full of courage and filled with endurance as he told of it, while the old warrior seemed to age perceptibly, but with great beauty and wisdom, like granite. Like the withered trees we so admire for their ability to cleave to the crevasse in the rock face against all odds and depredation of the environment. Finally, Swift Medicine drew some broth from a small kettle over the fire for them, banked it, settled into his robes, and spoke:

My son, listen to me once more. The sun rises as it should, but each day dawns upon a different land than the one I was born to. Changes are coming faster than the first frost that turns the aspen's leaves to yellow. Since Tall Bull has gone to walk the Spirit Road, we have no leader of The Dogs. When I brought you into my lodge to sleep on my robes and eat from my pot it was for the good of all. The Great Mystery Above had confirmed in my heart that it was His will. I did not question His leading. You came to my fires a young man, and now you too wear the Rope.

Sweet Medicine foretold the coming of the ve'ho'es, that they would swarm upon our lands as many as ants upon a fresh cut hide; lay claim to it and all that roam in great herds upon it. They build iron roads to cross our plains, "forts" to keep their warriors in. No treaty that we have touched pen to has been kept! If our warriors were hard to find and battle with they satisfied their hate upon those left behind, the very young, the old and our women. When our people divided into those that chose to follow The Red Road and those that believed in peace, it was often the ones that chose to follow the white ways that suffered destruction. Some of us took heed at Sand Creek. We fled north and tried to live without conflict, but it became too hard to live without seeking vengeance for what had been taken from us, in stealth, deception and dishonor.

The more we drove them off the land, the more that arrived to replace them. With these settlers came the bare-faced, blue-coated horse warriors with their medicine guns to protect them, the long guns that could seek and quickly find the very breath of a man and cause it to depart with such ease. They did not fight as we do. They did not want our fine herds, except to destroy them. They wanted our buffalo, not to feed and clothe themselves, but to hunt just for the pleasure of shooting them. They hold the coup stick in disdain. They will not dismount to fight hand to hand unless forced to. What is honor to them, when their word is as dust in the wind? They speak of trading, but what they offer for what we need to survive is but a handful of beads and worthless paper. We had no spotted death nor coughing sickness before they came. And many a fine warrior has taken their medicine water into their mouths for it to poison their minds, and the "visions" are but fogs rising from the waters of their own drunkenness.!

Reservations are not for us. Can it ever be? We were given all that we needed to take and to use with honor, gratefulness and respect. Are we then to put down our coup sticks, our lances, unstring our bows? Let our ponies stay tethered to our lodges? Win nothing? Let our aged blunt their few remaining teeth on the stringy, worm-ridden flesh of "cows"? We are hunters no longer allowed to hunt, to live off our own land. How can we live like them when we are not them? Their ways are not our ways!

When we fled from them, they followed relentlessly, even to our winter camps. We do not fight in the cold; that has been our way. If we flee them they are sure to destroy all we leave behind, even the winter stores. They do not need it, as they bring food wagons along when they pursue us. They do not honor their word. A white flag is for peace, but we are shot down under it. They say they have a god, is it GOLD? Or is it perhaps "Land" which they spill blood to "own? Aah yes, land-hungry, wagon after wagon, till their marks in the face of the earth were as deep and as lasting as the battle scars on one's flesh. They swarmed on the Holy Road like a great buffalo herd. Their soldiers, the bluecoats...their style of dressing is so plain and unadorned. It is hard to tell how an individual warrior fared in previous encounters with their enemies. No way to tell who had conquered their fears, and who had yet to prove brave. I have learned to judge them only by their stripes, bars, patches and small medals they wear on their Look-Alike -Shirts. Their society is very divided. One would think that they had two sides to their hearts, and two sides to their faces. They have a Great Father far to the East of the Big Muddy: some of us wear their large medals upon our chests. Meaningless! They, too, admire the war eagle; the emblem is everywhere, on their trade coins. They do not like to share, but to accumulate for themselves, and can easily watch others go without food or shelter, even women and children. We came to know their war chiefs by names, but the paths of their hearts were indiscernible, at first, except to the wisest of our medicine men. They punish us for trying to live as we have always done, but, and listen closely, there are so many of them, so many. There are not enough buffalo. Who would have ever thought that could be so! Tatanka are succumbing to the greed and waste of the whites. We can no longer rely on them for hides for our lodges, and meat for our parfleches. Soon they will all move North and enter the earth once more, away from the destruction. But where can we go, those of us who will not go to the reservations? There is only one way we the People can enter the earth again, my child.

 Some of our young men have gained honor in fighting their bluecoats. True, some of these soldiers are brave, bold, and can even sit a horse well, though none can ride the winds as we do. But they have been crazed. They now will follow us into our winter camps where it is well known that we rest and do not raid until the time when the land grows green once more, and the ponies fatten. They are driven to destroy us, so much so that they bring wagons full of grain to follow them so that their mounts may keep flesh on their bones even when the snow blankets the prairies, and wagons full of food for themselves. They leave their women, children and old ones somewhere safe. These horsemen, called "Kavalree", have been sent by the

Great Eastern Father to protect those that swarm the land, more than a summer plague of locusts, looking for land, and now the miners, who tear open our mother's belly for the yellow metal. Their coming had been foretold, we had been warned. How could we who were brave flee from the assault upon our lands and people? Was it not our duty to fight and protect what has been given to us from the beginning? How many peaceful camps of our brothers have been attacked without warning? How many whose names we cannot say have gone beyond? Those that survived were left with just what was upon their bodies; no food, the lodges and ponies destroyed. I do not know why we are punished for just trying to live. I do know that, for me, I cannot lay my lance down yet!"

At this the great old warrior grew quiet, retreating into a dark world within his memory, seeing a great procession of those whose names he could not speak file past him in all their resplendent glory, eagles plumes stirring in the faint breeze of the heavens beyond, the sound of drumming resonant in his blood. He appeared to be talking, although not to Medicine Horse anymore. He seemed unaware of the young Dog Soldier's presence. He made to leave, but the old man reached out and indicated that Medicine Horse was to take the place of honor at his side. How long did he manage to stay awake? It seemed that he was both alone with him and that the lodge was peopled with many, both alive and of the spirit world. Did he sleep, or wander in that realm that bridges between the worlds? When the sun's rays strongly broke into the lodge to claim the form of Swift Medicine the next morning it was to reveal his handsome granite face stone cold dead, his message delivered!

III

Tout Passe, Tout Lasse Everything passes, nothing lasts

"Only the sky and the earth last forever!"

The Beginning of The Loss

Ft. Laramie environs

"She gratefully gave up consciousness"

The alarm rang out, piercing the evening's calm just as Little Bird finished streaking Anah's cheeks with the Chinese vermilion. The buffalo hoof container hit the robes that they had been seated on, spotting them alarmingly with great red gouts. Without hesitation Pale Calf sprang up; grabbing the nearest child as she fled the lodge. Anah looked to the others, sharp fear arming her senses. At the same time a rush of anxiety and confusion flamed up, rendering her at a loss for purpose.

All was movement: Little Bird snatching weapons with one hand, a cradleboard with the other, softly but sternly commanding orders to the older children present among them. Some primitive part of Anah's brain flared with childish excitement. "We're under attack!" no real thought of danger to herself or others intruding, not even when the northern side of the hide lodge was viciously slashed and Searches Wide, a baby just beginning to walk, was roughly pulled kicking and screaming from at her feet. Something sizzled past Anah's head, knocking an "urrgh" out of the old man rolled in blankets beyond her. Large amounts of what could only be blood was welling out now onto his belly, as he convulsed silently before her, the shaft protruding at an odd angle from below his ribs.

Time fell like a fowler's net. She stood, rooted, like one turning slowly deaf and dumb. Blindness she had not the wits to hope for! Heedless of the muffled cries and rifle reports from outside she finally managed to push aside the flap and enter the chaos outside.

Before her now was the kind of scene that she had only heard discreetly described in her presence among the officers back at the fort as "a savage attack of the enemy". "I must be in shock," she calmly thought as she watched a bullet penetrate an old woman's forehead, who then pitched down at her side. Her response to hearing the bugle call was,

"Thank God, the cavalry! But attacking us here, and why?" Feeling a pull on her, she looked down to see a blood-smeared child clinging to her doe-skin skirt. "A weapon, I need a weapon." Just as she bent for a heavy elk horn hide scraper laying next to an overturned stew pot, a wasp-like pain shot deep into her thigh, bringing her to her knees empty-handed. Now Pale Calf's ceremonial doeskin will be ruined, for blood was flowing copiously down the side of it. Just then the little boy clinging to her in his terror realized that she was not his mother and began howling in terror. Pushing him down with the thought of protecting him, she scrambled as best she could towards that scraper. No better weapon in sight, all the while searching for somewhere to drag herself and the child to hide. Lodges were burning fiercely now! Tethered horses neighed in panic and pain. Recognizing the report of the Army issued Colts, she looked to be rescued. A blue uniformed sergeant was running towards her, leaping over downed bodies. The word "slaughter" splashed like a cold wave into her consciousness, unexpected and terrifying, as she fought to deny it. Smells of cordite and blood. Why were her friends fighting the troops? Why were the big Howitzers being pulled into position, aimed at this peaceful camp? "Ori!Ori!" thank God she had left the child back at the fort for once. "William, William, help us," she tried to cry out, but her mouth was a dry vessel, tongue stuck and cottony. These were not Crows or Pawnee attacking, but soldiers, and that thought exploded into many, tiny black swarming dots before her eyes, threatening to blind her. Her head buzzed with them. The blackness was quickly approaching like a murder of crows as the sergeant grew larger, leaping over the bodies of women and children, steadily fixing his bayonet as she floated down upon those already fallen. Warm, bloodied, skin garments, shells, feathers and the eerie wisps of death songs from those not quite dead.

The child lay quietly beneath her, and as she tightened her grip on the bone scraper at last secured in her grasp, the soldier brought his hob-nailed boot down forcefully on her wrist, breaking it and causing her only weapon to arch over the hideous, incomprehensible scene. Stretching out her other hand, it closed on what only could be fresh entrails, slick with blood. She gratefully gave up consciousness.

Coming To, The Rape

She always knew that someday she would fly; it was as amazing as she had expected it to be, but something was wrong. Pain bound her, she was oddly tethered, was going to crash, so out of balance, at an odd unnatural tilt. She wasn't moving forward, she was just hovering like a prairie hawk "waiting on". Suspended above something, without movement, as though she were just hung from a stick. So strange! Yet she wouldn't look down, not yet!

A cold voice is saying, "I wouldn't do that yet," so she's not alone. A glance to her left reveals a crow also held suspended in flight. The sky is filled with dense, impenetrable clouds of reddish-orange smoke. "Where am I?" "You don't want to know," the bird responds, as a great horripilation traverses her limbs. So, I still have a body, I'm not dead, she thinks. "Fly with me" he croaks, edging slightly in front of her. "There," pointing with his obsidian beak towards the dully gleaming evening star that was flashing brightly, throwing sparks as though on fire in the gathering darkness. Each magnificent spark causes a spike-like pain to shatter her consciousness, though. Each bolt of pain brings a desire to descend. That terrifies her. She fights to stay aloft! "Just lift your arms, but once. Once, and you shall have peace...wings of peace! I will lead you," and he thrusts ahead.

A great tiredness assails her, a chorus of animal howls rise, begging her to listen. She just wants to lay down, to lay her head down..it hurts so, but the great bird has warned her not to look down. She tries to lift her arms, to fly on, but finds them pinioned, pain shooting through her left wrist. Her head drops to her chest, she then looks down on the battleground. It is a massacre, and she begins to plummet down, down, dizzyingly down.

Back to consciousness, her head was being rapped against a blood-slippery rock, rhythmically. Again, and again. Screams, cries, and the low guttural croaks of a raven are close by. Hard, pebbly ground under her bare spine, a burning pain in her thigh and a pounding screaming ache in her belly. Yes, I'd been shot, but something had her, was tearing her up, tossing her around, ripping her inside, a hard, heavy weight upon her. A load of pain. She could barely struggle, yet she was being tossed and torn like a fawn by a ravenous hound. Her body, her body! Poor, poor body! She tried to lift her head at least, felt a meaty hand clutch her jaw shut. Strong fingers dug into her jaw. She pulled herself up when the weight seemed to lift, only to be struck down, slapped into non-resistance. Quick and gone. She tried to open her eyes, not blind, please, not blind. Blood, just glued shut. Whose? Did it matter? One eye finally partially open. Look! To her left Pale Calf Woman sprawled lifeless, her braids wet with blood; one arm gripped an empty cradleboard. Then Anah's head was snapped back and she felt the cold touch of a Bowie knife to her forehead. "Got a live one here!" Recognizing that voice, she forced herself partially upright with great effort to look directly into the soldier's pale gray eyes. "Private Stubbs," she uttered weakly, and that little movement allowed enough of her blood-streaked flaxen hair to fall free.

"Mrs. Moore," he croaked, shocked that she had dazedly recognized him. Instantly he raised his rifle to deliver a well-aimed blow to her temple, all the while calling out for help to transport her back to the fort. With his other hand he hastened to button his fly. "I wasn't the only one," he thought. "Not the only one. Hell, how was I to know, her all frocked out in that squaw getup. Damn her and her injun-loving ways!"

Those Heartless Angels

Ft. Laramie, 1873

Pulling her doll along by it's ragged arm Orianna petulantly murmured to herself, "Mummy's been gone much, much longer than she promised." Mummy never told really big lies to her. All grown-ups did lie, of course, but her mother always said that she wouldn't. Orianna assumed that lying was yet another privilege allowed grown-ups!

It had been days since Anah had left for the encampment and now Ori felt her absence dramatically, for she felt sick, throw-up sick! The whole fort was upset. Dramatic comings and goings, extra hush-shushes and "Not in front of the child" when she drew near. Where was Mommy? Why were all the extra soldiers here, but not Daddy? The rush and bustle was exciting at first. She had got to traipse around, ferret things out, go places previously unexplored. She had even made her way to where some of the travelers from the big wagons had been taken for the doctor to look at. In fact she was barely attended to now. Her head hurt. It felt heavy. She wanted to wilt and droop like some flower in need of water. Cookie had tried to tempt her with some of her favorite sweet, apple pan dowdy, but she wasn't hungry. No one had time for her questions; even Hilda just shuffled her in and out of her clothes, her bath, her bed. Now in the half-empty stables she found a stall full of clean straw, golden and magical looking as dusty sunbeams fell upon it. Perhaps if she curled up here she could get warm, take what Mommy called "a good little girl's nap".

And that is where she was found. One glance told all! Sprawled, sweat drenched and smelling badly. The private that had discovered her rushed her to the infirmary, calling for the already harried surgeon. Smallpox? Cholera? Pray God not typhus! Any of these dreaded symptoms presented in an enclosed society such as Ft. Laramie was cause for alarm. No effort was spared to treat her alarming condition once she was placed in isolation, especially now with William lost and Anah in her broken condition. With Hilda in constant attendance, malaria was tentatively diagnosed. There was no quinine left on the base; no new immigrant train expected that might possibly be carrying some in their medical supplies. Still, ice was fetched regularly from the block house to cool her burning fever, and blanket after blanket was piled on when the chills came upon her little body. As she descended into delirium she called out piteously for both parents, then only weakly for her mother, who lay unconscious in a small room not far from the child. When her nanny could no longer bear witnessing her suffering a laundress was procured to sit by her. Hilda then went to Anah's side, hoping that she would miraculously awaken, but her body lay as though dead. It could not be determined if she was in a deep coma or not, due to the tremendous blow that had been dealt to her head, but it was agreed that to attempt to awaken her only to inform her of William's death, let alone the child's failing health, was too dangerous.

Daddy?" The child struggled an arm and head out of the blankets she had been cocooned in, seeing, by the dim firelight, that she was now back in the bedroom where old Hilda sat slumped in a rocker, knitting slipping from her generous lap. Hearing no reply, Ori's eyelids slid shut again. She questioned her heart, "Daddy, are you here?" Quiet abounded, except for the slight howl of the wind in the chimney and the occasional snap of a log settling down on the coals. Oh how tired she felt, so very, very tired, falling back into her own consuming fire.

She woke much later shaking with skeletal cold thinking it very late. An almost full moon was giving scant illumination to the room, for a cool, detached silver outlined the sleeping form in the rocker. The fire had gone out. "Mommy?" Oh, dear Jesus, where was she? She has to be here. Find her for me, please. The delirious child pulled the doll to her shaking chest, sunk back down under the covers, given over to the malarial encephalitis that would destroy her quickly now, as some part of her continued searching. A desperate clarity yet prevailed. She was listening for the gentle thud-thud of the heart she had known from her inception. She was given this, a final comfort. The presence so sought was here, in some way, with her. Her heart felt this as it labored on, slowly stuttering toward its incapacity to conquer and prevail.

Then there Mommy was, standing in the doorway, all golden and glowing, her bright hair massive, feathered and flowing around her just as Ori knew her when she brushed out their hair for bedtime. The child's heart pulsed erratically in response to this vision. You've come for me, as I knew you would, she thought. All yearning, all ears, she began to burn, to warm, the deathly chill loosening its grip as she relaxed into that beat, that rhythm that she had always known. One that had tapped, drum-like, the first message of love ever perceived by the child. Not strong; weak, but steady. Ori's small body relaxed for the first time in hours. She felt herself growing light… So very, very light, Oh, so light! This was heavenly. Yes, this is what her mother would call it, heavenly! Thus comforted she settled herself back into the capable, large and softly feathered arms that had come to bear her away, up into the dark heavens of the night.

When Hilda woke, cold and stiff, it was to find Orianna lying still. Rushing to her side, hoping the fever had broken to deliver the child she so loved, it was find her lifeless, the doll still clutched in her arms, and a look of restful sleep upon her pale face. Determined that Mrs. Moore should be informed, somehow, a consultation was held with Dr. Halleck. When he sadly entered the room in the clinic where still Anah lay locked in a semi-comatose state, a laundress rushed to him, shaking her head, finger to lips, fiercely ushering him out in utter disrespect of his authority. In the hallway, with a tear-streaked face, she moaned, "She knows, sir, she does! She's been as dead herself these past weeks, then she suddenly up and turns her face to the wall late last night and hasn't moved since," she righteously declared, "Ye mustn't tell her." The stoic and seemingly imperturbable surgeon looked out the window toward the low hills of the barren land beyond; and thinking of this woman's loss of both husband and child was rumored to have cursed, "Oh, these heartless angels!"

The Starry Ladder

The very novelty of it kept her on the path that first night, for it consisted of the most dazzlement she had ever experienced in her brief life on earth. The stars, they really sparkled, they really did! Everything that she had ever dreamed about them was now so apparently true, for she could see with a new clarity of vision. That was very, very good, she thought, but a longing enveloped her like a soft, thick gauze and she still gazed mostly downward at what lay increasingly beyond her grasp, but not yet out of her sight!

Deep inside her was something that she kept touching, absentmindedly, but obsessively, like a healing sore. When she lost her first tooth, it was like that for her. She simply couldn't leave that empty socket alone in spite of Mommy's assurance that a something new was on its way!

Enveloped by a mist of stars she was yet painfully conscious of looking down at what had once been her home. The empty bed where her dolly lay abandoned. The large parade ground starting to fill with soldiers to practice drills, her white dog curled mournfully on the porch, and there in a narrow infirmary bed was her dear mother, face to the wall.

Dusk was falling upon the spinning earth as the shadows of the tombstones lengthened across the burial yard. She felt confused and sleepy, and finally stopped trudging to settle down on this well-worn path.

Orianna woke to a familiar morning light, but on looking down she discovered an unfamiliar terrain spread below her. Large jagged-tooth mountains with caps of snow and a deep carpet of pines rolling up their sides were far, far below her. She sat up, then looked to the Arapaho youth striding patiently past her. "This is the Great Path we're on, right?" Without breaking his stride, but in no way unfriendly, he replied over his shoulder, "Yes, you will see the others soon," and with that he strode on. She stood up and looked around. Nothing looked familiar. She hurried to catch up.

Coming Out of the Coma

Calamitous, the word swept back and forth across her mind, like a broom being handled by an irate kitchen girl. A choking dust rising to obscure one's vision; unknown debris pinging from one object to another. Try as she might Anah found no way to control this erratic, violent and hasty movement of her mind. It dizzied her, left her faintly nauseous and most confused. Where was she? Who was she? Her head throbbed painfully with grasping at reason.

Part of her intuited that she was caught up in a struggle to understand something, to bring it back to consciousness, while another powerful force was exerting itself to block that message, and pull her back down into unknowing depths. A dangerous message! Confusion constricted her every breath. Her heart was beating faster than it should and a great panic seemed poised to overwhelm her. Trying her limbs, she found them capable of movement, yet she lay still, as though an intruder was watching.

"The minute I open my eyes, I shall leave this world and enter another." This knowledge caused a cold sweat to bloom all over her body. Like falling into a muddy river and not discerning the direction to arise and surface, all the while being propelled swiftly along. Dare she cry out? Did she even have a voice? Something terrible had happened. Why can't she remember?

The dreams and visions had been so utterly awful and persistent that she struggled to open her eyes. When she did so it was to discover that she was alone on a narrow iron cot in a bleak room smelling strongly of disinfectant. Her head, wrist and thigh were bandaged. She hurt like hell, all over, and deep, deep inside. There had to be a terrible reason for being here. Something gnawed, clawed. Where was her family? "Orri, William," she began calling. Footsteps, moving swiftly towards her bed; someone was coming to explain.

Darkness Ascending

Moon of the Yellowing Leaves 1874

Spear-like rays of the early dawn were just beginning to fill Tule Valley, one of the fabled draws of the Palo Duro Canyon, when the half-blind, aged Ponca drew up to it's rim. With skin so dried and withered that it was hard to distinguish from the tattered hide drawn close upon his bony frame, he hunched over his equally bony mount. Shuttering his eyes carefully against the rising sun's brilliance as it sparkled against the canyon's walls, the better for his rheumy eyes, he searched to find the narrow defile that would lead him down into the canyon's depths.

The Season of Tall Grasses had been anything but easy out on the plains; the great herds almost gone, and with them the roving bands of Kiowa, Comanche and Cheyenne that had dared to leave the roll calls and moldy provisions of the reservations were now heading back also, or else they stood to face slow starvation out here. But the real telling was the absence of rumbling wagons and sharp shooting thunder of the buffalo guns of the hide hunters!

The sun spoke a strong tongue, streams ran dry and springs hid beneath alkaline crusts. Only the ceaselessly roaming wind moved freely as it caressed the sockets of the buffalo skulls and rolled the rotting hooves that kept the old man company as he plodded along across the Llano. The Llano Estacado, the Staked Plains, seemingly devoid now of both Indian bands and the white hunters held only barrenness, offered nothing. But it was out here, cut deep into it's far horizon, shimmering in eye-searing bands of heat waves, that time itself had reached down to create a sanctuary, hidden deep in the form of finger-like extensions, canyons that had been used as secure winter camps for centuries. Practically invisible from the mesquite-studded horizon that stretched parched and empty for miles above, the Place of Chinaberry Trees, as it was called by the People, held all that was needed to shelter them freely through a winter: free flowing water, pure and clean, that the children could play in; streams, cool, fresh, that the women could approach safely; bubbling springs and strands of trees to sit under peacefully.

It was here that renegade bands came instead of returning to the reservations, pitched lodges and filled their bellies as their women erected drying racks for the meat and went about their old ways. Content to place their names, not on Government rolls, but on the robes of the Winter Count, seemingly ignorant of the dire consequences.

And it was to one of these encampments that this Ponca was heading in hopes of finding shelter. Pausing but a moment to consider the bleakness he was leaving behind him, the old man regretted having left the boy, but upon rising with the usual difficulty, stiff and sore, from his robes, such as they were, this morning, to find him gone, he simply broke camp and moved on.

It was perhaps best that he, a Ponca, arrive alone, without a small red-haired blue-eyed wasichu child at his side. A Ponca itself was a rarefied sight out here, almost as much as a white buffalo would be, but certainly not wakan! No, the Poncas had been hounded for generations from their lands, ever Westward, first by the fierce Iroquois, then by the equally fierce persistence of the Spotted Sickness, until just a handful were left. Then the little land they had been allotted to grow their corn on was mistakenly included in another's reservation. When the Ponca then refused to be herded off to a harsh substitute that would not only not yield the yellow ears they so favored, but kept where they were struck down once more with the Shaking Sickness until they fell like the last leaves from a winter's tree, he walked away, and kept walking. Walking, walking, year after year. It was his way.

One day not long ago in the Moon of Ripening Cherries, down on the Powder River, he was just passing by what looked like a small, abandoned wagon with a busted axle, it's ragged canvas cover fluttering weakly in the wind. It was his nature to investigate such matters, to scavenge for what he could use, or barter. The last dying rays of the sun blazed in short, choppy strokes of vermilion and gold across the water and caught a tuft of red hair sticking up from a mounded quilt. Staring mutely up at him was a pale blue-eyed child with a wild thatch of lank dark red hair that looked like it had been cut with a Bowie knife. Most obviously a boy, young, and so near death that the wild Indian leaning over him and fingering his flesh to see just how dehydrated it was provoked not the slightest alarm.

As the Ponca soon discovered no depredation, assault, wound, fever, nor pox accounted for the child's presence there. It's clothes were clean enough, if plain. No shoes, but perhaps it couldn't walk. But then if it had been abandoned to die, shoes were too valuable to also just leave behind! No grave mounds, no bodies left to fester. Nothing of value to plunder, other than the boy, so he took him. The Boy, this was as close as he ever came to naming him, was sound in all his limbs. He didn't speak, or couldn't speak, then or since. They now traveled together these past few months heading ever southward .

His instinct, at first, had been to save the child's life, but once saved he had to consider what to do with it, for he led a most solitary life, largely unencumbered, and knew deep in his soul that he was preparing to soon unencumber himself of his own.

He thought at first to trade him, for what would he do with another mouth to feed? His needs were meager, but a growing child's were not. Then he thought to sell him, but knew not how to determine another's worth. Were white children worth more, he wondered? Briefly he entertained the thought of making him his slave, he pondered all this as they rode together, back to belly on the old pony.

If the Boy couldn't talk, could he hear? And what would he do to the boy if he didn't obey him, for he couldn't imagine hitting a child. He didn't beat his horse, did he? The old man had lived so long alone that he wasn't quite sure that he still possessed a language, a sign language would do, perhaps. Well, teaching The Boy would be more work than any servant was worth, would it not? His mind grew quite tired even thinking like this and he let his gaze wander off to the distant horizon to wonder if the desiccated, fallen cholla on the far horizon were perhaps an antelope. Besides, he then brought himself back, thinking what could this runt of a boy do for him that he had not managed to do quite well for himself all these dreary seasons since She Who Gathers Berries had gone beyond? There was not much that he could take pride in, he knew that, but he did have respect for being a rare bird, a rara avis, he remembered this word well, as told to him by the very tall, strange wasichu who was so very excited to have come upon him wandering, and touched the pen for days on end following him, asking question after question till he folded his robes and left quietly in the night..well, he knew who was the rare bird indeed, the man called himself an "pologist" of some sort. A lone Ponca, a rare bird, even if he was mostly deaf, half blind! It was his way!

The old Indian and the deaf-mute boy took well to one another in their own limited fashion; in fact, each one seemed secretly delighted at the very oddness of the others presence; learning, then deferring to the others handicaps. The Boy became "eyes", and the Ponca "ears" to the other, thus they roamed, a sparse sojourning indeed, avoiding most human encounters. Mexican raiders from across the border, who would gladly sell the boy, Indian scouts, "wolves" who would redeem him at the nearest fort; Apaches who would, well...

Besides, how could he ever explain the boys presence if questioned as to how he had come to be in his possession? Was The Boy not a very danger to him? But he could not imagine harming him, that too would be troublesome!

To the old Ponca, whose life was indeed long and whose heart like the land he was now crossing, dry and hard, the Boy was like a good dog; not even a favored one, not a pet, not a companion. He had nothing to offer the boy, not really, other than to move him from one dawn to the next as safely as possible in the straightened circumstances of his own limited life. It was not right to keep him as such (other than to keep him alive). And so this morning, when he had crawled with the usual difficulty from his robes, groaning and mumbling a bit more than usual, actually, he knew that all had been decided for him. The Boy was gone!

Now as he stood at the rim of the Tule Valley, preparing to descend, with the large Conch shell clutched in his hand, ready to announce his presence to all below, he drew a grateful breath. For there he saw, gazing down with his rheumy eyes, the sparkling fall of water tumbling from a cliff across the valley below, though he could not hear it's cascading plunge into the pool below. He hadn't thought that he his heart could still swell as it once had in his youth, but even with his dimmed vision the lush greenness of the valley flowed out to surround him in a welcome blessing. Green, how overwhelming was this color alone, after the sere palette of his life, tender green like the first shoots of the corn stalks in the well tended fields of his youth. How he looked forward to what he imagined as his last winter in this canyon, sheltered with the People in the old ways, still possible here!

Thrilled to the very reaches of his old, withered soul he pushed a blast of air out into a shrill note from the Conch as he spurred his old mount fast, fast, into a trot down the narrow trail; he could not get there quickly enough.

If his hearing had been intact, if his sense of smell had not been deadened by age, if his vision were really clear, and most of all, if he had not been in such strict isolation from his fellow man....... For an ominous silence reigned, save the "roank" of glutted ravens. An odious stench from bilious waves of unimaginable mounds of rotting flesh rode the air. Horrendous destruction was blanketed by a seething, jostling, flapping, rending mass of gleaming black feathers and claws, for covering the valley floor were the bodies of a over a thousand ponies that had been driven to a righteous frenzied slaughter by the mounted troopers of Colonel Ranald Mackenzie's men. Now the beautiful Tule Valley was a graveyard of much, much more than just horseflesh.

To the old Ponca, with his dimmed senses, here lay confusion. He stood, as one does with a sense of impending doom, much as one who has long, too long, been out of touch with the spirit world, and can only wait! He knew something was wrong, and began to blow frantically on the shell while plunging forward on the narrow trail down into the dust-filled valley.

What rose up then to greet him was an inconceivable wall of darkness, so black as to obscure the very light in that narrow canyon, for these hundreds, and there were indeed an almost unimaginable hundreds, that had amassed for this feast, this bounty out here on this wasteland. Hundreds of feasting crows, vultures, and ravens, when once disturbed, the warning signal given, rose en masse, to shoot into the air as one black rolling wave of alarm, a heady portent of the dark days to come. Working in tandem to flee at the first warning, a brotherhood of scavengers,, a murder of crows. As they lifted off, the heavier buzzards flapped noisily up, stirring clouts of dust, till the air thickened, further obscuring light. Large flapping wings slapped at his face, causing him to crouch down, where more dust rose, choking and blinding him.

The good sense of his mount caused it to halt in it's tracks, though an old nag, and eager for a good graze and water, all it's innards had seized in terror. Fumbling frantically now in his bags for an old spy glass, the Ponca finally discerned what lay on the valley floor. The old man's shoulder's *sagged. As he sank to the ground in despair the dust gradually lifted and the sky cleared. Spread before him was the destruction of the pride of the People. The scavengers whirled frantically in a rising gyre above. So much waste. Buffalo. Gone! Ponies. Gone! Wife. Gone! Boy....*

He walked his mount back up the trail till he found a suitable rock to assist the hard scrabble to gain his pony's bony back once more. The morass of birds were now wheeling, cawing, diving back in and screaming above and around the canyon in a rising gyre, claiming possession with curdling cries, settling back upon the carnage once more, but he was mostly oblivious to them. He looked back up to the bleakness that waited for him, the refuge he anticipated lost. The Darkness that had ascended was but an omen of days to come, he knew. It was right that he had not brought The Boy with him.

He headed back out, not noticing that he had forgotten to fill his water flasks.

The Awful News

A fortnight had passed, so she was told. Her body was healing; just a small splint on her broken wrist. She could even bear to stand for short periods on her wounded leg. They had kept her in a small, clean room off the main infirmary, one often used for those immigrants that had need of it, as they were passing through on the trail, if they had to be quarantined. She made it through the day imagining herself encased, as in a chrysalis, protecting her mind's feeble defenses from all that she couldn't bear. The draught of laudanum got her through the nights.

She had nodded dumbly when a sober-faced Dr. Halleck explained the swift progress of the type of malaria that had overcome her child. Cerebral, he had intoned, of the brain, running a carefully manicured hand through his neat mustache, looking her in the eye, searching for comprehension. A normal response might have been a curt defense of her own medical expertise, but it was all she could do to simply dip her chin in acknowledgment. He went on to say how Hilda had thought it was just another colic, the alarming symptoms turning swiftly into the fever and chill cycle that prompted his intervention. Before any quinine bark could be obtained, and yes, they had sent a runner out to the nearest wagon train hoping to find some there, Orianna had fallen into a coma. The fatal convulsions must have occurred during the night; he hadn't observed them. The clinical details he began to espouse overwhelmed Anah into feebly responding, "Why wasn't I summoned?" "You were unconscious, my dear, in fact, in a comatose state from the, ah, blow to your head." "And her father?" Her hand flew to her mouth even as she uttered that. Yes, of course they had told her of William being lost in that skirmish that had, indeed, prompted the raid on the encampment where she had gone that awful day.

Staring at her oddly, the doctor snapped his Gladstone bag shut with a mournful expression on his face. At a loss for words he took his departure, stopping only to softly convey an order to an aide.

Was she mad with grief, for she had indeed forgotten her husband's demise? Oh William, what a distraught an unfaithful wife to your memory I've become. The shadows crawled across the bare boards of the chilly room as she lay lost. She made herself mute; feigning sleep when a meal tray was delivered. She had appetite only for the opiate!

It wasn't long, though, before she was strong enough physically to walk the perimeters of the small room, aided by gripping the wainscoting. She would not pace, no matter how strong the desire. Instead she sat in the hard little cane-backed chair, oblivious to all except her expectation and growing need for the tincture brought to her to ease her into sleep. A craving for it's bitter, smoky taste enveloped far more than her mind.

One night, as soon as the halls grew quiet, she entered the deserted hallway. Going right to the apothecary cabinet in the storage room, she pocketed one of the small brown bottles that held the tincture of opium from the back of the shelf with a wan smile of accomplishment. Now her days could be obliterated as well as her nights!

Anah's descent into a willed state of opiate dependency did not go unnoticed, nor did she seemingly care. She took to sleeping days and roaming at night, responding with an increasing incoherence to any that would accost her as to her doings. Eating little and grossly neglecting most attempts to groom herself was considered an indication of possible irreparable damage done by the assault and her terrible bereavement.

Whatever was said to her informed her altered state as much as the chatter of a magpie would; she ignored it. The noises of the base were like so much barnyard background; simply of no consequence to her. She gave herself over completely to daydreams as convolutedly patterned as a Paisley shawl. Nothing made sense to her; she thought that both apt and just. She had her panacea!

Occasionally a tall lean figure loomed in her vision, her real vision, that is. The one she had to access in order to not stumble into walls or down steps. He loomed, but never entered or threatened her presence. Always still, always silent. She grew to respect and like his composure. She knew who it was, the old Cheyenne scout with the clubbed foot. Nor did she question his appearance in her limited world. In fact, she grew to feel an odd kinship, though they had not spoken, a mutual pariahood, she ruefully imagined.

One night, an especially restless one for her, as she was beginning to ration herself the laudanum, afraid that her pilfering would be discovered, she woke to find him sitting on the little chair, looking much like a giant crane, his thin, red trade cloth wrapped braids hanging down from his weathered cheeks. The sharp-shooters medal glinted in the ambient light, his odd amber tinted glasses with the clear oval insets perched towards the end of his nose. Was he asleep? Guarding her for some strange reason? She rose, deciding to approach him. He met her gaze benignly; she immediately dropped hers, strangely thrilled that someone, anyone, would seek her out, but then she drifted back to her bed, drawn by the soft, rolling clouds of Lethe. Wrapped in an opium cloud, she felt somewhat safe, from what she could not give a name to.

Laudanum Consolations

The opiate began its sweet ministrations, offering as it did a simple acquiescence into drugged sleep and forgetting. Anah settled wearily back upon her pillow as the orderly bore the bottle and spoon away, closing the door softly behind him.

White, with a dull sheen, smooth as the cream that formed on milk, the barn owl floated silently into her mind. Settling on the back of the rocker, the wise heart-shaped head turned towards her and began to speak large, pearly words of consolation.

Try as she might, those words were incomprehensible to her, as language.

But silver running streams, small velvet-furred creatures and tufts of lush green moss unfolded in her vision. Moist, pale buds of equally pale flowers were springing up. ,She could hear a gentle flow of breezes through bending branches. Transfixed, she lay immobile as the bird continued his incomprehensible but utterly soothing utterances, shifting silently from one fawn-feathered foot to the other. The grim room of the infirmary began to darken, the only light a burnt remnant of vermilion streaks on the horizon that seeped wanly through the lank curtains. Coolness rose steadily around her ghostly bare feet which now appeared to have a remarkable semblance to alabaster. Perhaps the owl will entertain them as a perch, she thought, for I no longer have use of them, poor dead limbs!

Clad only in a thin nightgown, she nonetheless felt as though a drape of heavy, untanned hide had been slung carelessly upon her shoulders. It's weight should have been oppressive. "I will grow very, very old lying here, will I not?" she addressed herself to the owl, and shivered at that thought.

The barn owl now had it's back towards her, head tucked under it's wing.

Silence now prevailed. A deathly silence; she strained to hear anything. Was she now deaf?

There, a small steady thud, thud, thud beat its way into her consciousness. All was growing black. Her feet were increasingly chilled, and looking down she saw that they were slowly turning from the lovely sculpted alabaster to elaborate ice pedestals. Frozen in place, she tried to call out, to discover she was speechless.

The only presence her persistent heart, drumming it's message....alone...alone..alone.
I am alone, alone, alone!

The Cheyenne Doll

It wasn't until she laid her head down for the night that she discovered the doll, wrapped in a piece of faded calico, under her pillow. It was the one that had been given to Orianna by Pale Calf's mother on their first trip to the Cheyenne encampment beyond the creek. That a flaxen-haired, blue eyed child could so easily "mother" this blank-featured, doeskin clad toy, festooned with small feathers and ornate bead work, delighted her. Ori had never taken even the slightest interest in any of the other artifacts that Anah had brought back from her many trips out to the Indian camps that lay beyond the confines of the fort, but then this had been given exclusively to the child. She henceforth was not to be seen without it. "Sunflower", Orianna had named the doll, her constant companion.

Without another thought Anah pressed it to her. By morning she wondered how the doll had come to be there, although she suspected that it was the tall scout's doing. But how had he come by it?

Their Last Dance

Anah drifted on and down in the arms of the opiate, twilight coloring the walls of the room a delicate mauve. She held a tenuous contentment within, allowing only the pleasurable sound of a cricket to accompany her into a sleep she desperately needed.

As the sound of the cricket morphed into the strings of a violin she adjusted her ball gown, nervously smoothing down its folds with her little fan. And suddenly...

There he was, as she had first seen him, resplendent in full dress uniform, his saber gleaming. Thrilled by this vision, she allowed it full entry into her very soul.

Stepping lightly into his arms she rapidly assessed him. Taller by several inches than father. Lean and well-muscled, with the superb military bearing that the Academy had afforded him. He literally lifted her off her feet. Oh, this one knew how to dance...and that smell, deliciously spicy East Indian Bay Rum.

"Oh Will," she murmured, "you've come back for me." Wordlessly he pressed her head gently into his jacket, the metal buttons distressingly chill against her fevered cheek. Drawing her out onto the floor, holding her gloved hand lightly to his chest, they whirled faster and faster, moving towards one of the open doors and the velvety, star sprinkled night.

Once outside, the frosty air seized her throat. A cold crescent moon hung perilously close-seeming above them. She began to have difficulty in keeping in step with him. Stumbling, she cried out in alarm, "Wait!" but he was disengaging her from his arms. Pulling her anxiously by one hand, he headed heedlessly for the black expanse of the open prairie. The further away they moved from the dance the louder and more cacophonous the music became. A ribbon from her shoe entangled her as she stumbled, trying to keep his rapid pace. Casting a glance backwards, the lights from the ballroom seemed to be whirling uncontrollably. She struggled to keep up. Suddenly, it seemed, they flew above the frozen ground; then all was deathly still. The lights of the fort were just a dim glow on the horizon. She strained to hear anything. Was that not a cannon she heard; that smell, cordite? A slight *trembling came upon her. "Stop, oh please stop," she begged him, flinging herself upon his back. To her horror there was a smell emanating from him now, not the spicy cologne but a scent nauseatingly sweet, like decay. Fully alarmed she spun him around and wrenched her head back to look up at him. A small, neat hole glistened wetly at his left temple. As she tried to pull away he gripped her more tightly. His soft lipped smile opened on an even row of glistening, blood-caked teeth. A gush of cold liquid spilled onto her breast, freezing her heart, drenching her gown as she crashed down onto a pile of dead and mangled cavalry limbs akimbo, sabers uselessly drawn.*

Awakening, she found herself sprawled backwards from the table with a lapful of cold coffee soaking her drab black dress, her "widow's weeds", the newly risen sun burning into the stark emptiness of her strange new life.

Attempted Revenge

"Then one night she woke with a name on her lips"

Each night now Anah drew the doll, in it's smoky deer-hide dress, from beneath her pillow where it was secreted. Cradled to her chest she absently fingered it's fringes and trade beads; a talisman, she hoped, for sleep. Desperate to end another dreary, sad day, but fearful of what dark dreams could enter, she tossed and turned.

Worrying one of the toy's horsehair plaits she thought of bloody scalp locks, and touched the long thin scar on her hairline. Aches that still had her pinned so carefully to twisted sheets spoke remembered terror. She lay thus in the darkness expecting a face, twisted in triumph, to rise above her, knife gleaming. Almost afraid to draw a full breath she would grow rigid, eyes squeezed shut. Closer and closer he comes. Sweat blooms on her even though she feels an unearthly chill. Realizing sleep is futile she bolts upright, fumbles to light a lamp and read, unbelieving, a little bible, till her hands tremble and head dips to her chest in a half dazed slumber.

Most nights, though Anah simply dosed herself with more laudanum, knowing, but not caring, that she was skirting madness.

Then one night she woke with a name on her lips....Jubal Stubbs! So intense were her feelings that she carefully wrote them down as follows in her Commonplace Book:

There he was, I clearly see him splayed flat and motionless on a cindered ground...and I felt something as small and hard as a blue trade bead roll into the hollow of my heart. Deeply satisfied I fell back into a dreamless sleep, for first night since it had happened. Jubal! Private Stubbs, the striker whom we had dismissed from our service; how ironic!

Eagerness surged through me at first light. I woke refreshed. Having his name now in my possession gave me strength. From now on I will hold no terror of recollecting my attacker's face. How he had shamed me will not jelly my guts any longer! For with recollection I saw again the sharp blaze of fear that spread across his face in the instant he recognized me for who

I really was; an Officer's wife! In that half-second before his feral sense of self preservation brought his rifle stock down upon my skull I had clearly cried out his name, "Private Stubbs!" identifying him, naming my attacker!

Jubal Stubbs, that name ignites me the way a lightning bolt consumes an isolated snag. A shuddering flash of recognition and I am now ablaze with wild thoughts of revenge. As though a fire had been lit under me, I came to a sudden boil. Languor must go! I dashed the medicine bottle from my nightstand in an evil triumph of will, not caring that the tincture's smell of laudanum would permeate the room.

At first my plans and schemes rolled over me in a frenzy like an uncontained prairie fire. The sickly wraith of a woman I had drugged myself into becoming did not vanish overnight, but I steeled myself to avenge Ori's death. Yes, I blame him squarely, for had I not been so vilely used I would have been there to nurse my child back to health. And what of William? I am ashamed to say that he is well buried in my heart, so consumed am I with having, at last, a target for my pain! Someone or something to blame, other than God, for my loss, for in my isolation now I reckon no other tragedy than my own.

Dare I ask myself what I am planning to do? The truth of my ensuing actions seem to be shrouded in a cloak of hate as hot, thin and brittle as a skin of lava over a pit of uncontrollable forces. This was compulsion and I wrap myself in it, grateful for it's burning warmth and embrace.

Anah, now strengthened by a promise of revenge, was soon out of the doctor's care. After all the long drugged weeks of her recovery she was now occupied with motivation; now had a reason to come back to her senses. Within days she was back in her quarters and shed of all accouterments of the sick room. The only physical evidence of the ordeal, a splint to her wrist; the halt in her gait. What damage showed on her face she did not care to look upon, besides, the one mirror in the household had been draped in a black mourning cloth. As for the opiate she willed herself to independence, so determined was she to achieve revenge.

Free of the laudanum, her emotions became as clamorous as a murder of crows, rising to confront her still weak sensibilities. Vengeance had the loudest voice under which her conscience cowered, naming Jubal "murderer"----yet she lived! It was not his hand that had taken the lives of her family, yet dark thoughts circled above him, looking down on the carnage of life as she once knew it. Single-minded in her purpose to see Jubal Stubbs dead, she feasted on these thoughts and grew strong.

A woman who so abhorred the taking of life from any sentient creature now found the very word "murder" held tenderly in her mouth, an unholy thrill just waiting to be shouted out, bracing, obliterating in her mind the very last remains of a weakened self.

At last Anah had roused herself to a place where she could exert some control over her life again. Her wanderings would now be purposeful, for she planned to seek out the private's whereabouts. Avoiding detection was not hard as even the guards had grown instinctively to shun her wraith-like figure, her black shawl drawn close to her face. Taken for mad, she felt as though she was recovering, working frantically hard to leave the graveyard of her recent past. Boldly entering into places where her presence as the adjutant's wife once would have been questioned, her bereaved and maddened state allowed her access. Like a ghost she slunk from one darkened post to another. Dressed in her widow's weeds, and clutching the worn Indian dolly, fingering the trade beads like some rosary, she was left alone.

It was in the Smithy's where she first spied him, unharnessing a mule, clad in a buckskin jacket instead of the regulation blue tunic, with the white canvas trousers that the cavalry wore when on stable duty. Knowing he would be occupied in assisting with the reshodding of the mounts, at least for his duty hours of the day, she fled. She flitted past, head down, heart pounding, recalling that William had spoken of this enlisted man as a recalcitrant aid at any task; a disgruntled veteran of the Civil War that had torn his family into opposing camps. A Tennessee boy who had worn the union colors reluctantly, William thought, but good with farm animals, and who had a way with horses.

She gave no thought to the aftermath; all she could see and feel, as though it had already transpired, was the look upon his face, hands clutching his bleeding gut as he sank to his knees before her. There would be no imagined plea for forgiveness on his lips, for in her mind there was never any to offer.

It was important that he recognize his assailant, and that she have a determined reason to present herself at the blacksmith's shop. To this end she carefully groomed herself, setting aside the shawl, drawing her hair tightly back from her forehead. She knew the scar blazed out, slightly raised and reddened still. Smoothing her skirts, she took the walnut-handled derringer William had given her from the small brocade opera-bag, loaded it with shaking fingers, and, with the safety, off slipped it into the pocket of her riding coat.

As she strode toward the stables to get "Wind", her horse, an excuse for her presence at the farrier's, she kept one hand on the gun, dropping her head to hide the faint smile that kept coming to her face.

Excited and expectant, she rehearsed the confrontation. She would wait until he was well and truly occupied, with the animal's hoof cradled in his lap. "Well, what if the shot causes the animal to strike out?" Dismissing that she strode on with a blind confidence that she would achieve her goal; nothing could encumber her now. "In fact, why bring my pony in at all; it could confuse matters, and what if he was ordered to assist me?" No, with her left wrist still weak she needed to have both hands free. Besides, what if she ran into him beforehand? It was in the confines of the blacksmith's shop that she envisioned her revenge. The sharp ringing sounds of the sledgehammer falling on the anvil, like a Vulcan judge's gavel, flames leaping and casting the shadow of his fall. Sparks, heat, and yes, screams; screams, like the triumphant one she felt welling up, coursing throughout every part of her being, causing the very hair on her scalp to tingle.

Arriving there to discover the forge flameless, the bellows unmanned, the coals of the forge yet glowing red, moving, and settling down, the shop empty, she stepped back by the heavy bucket of water used for quenching the hot iron. Her eyes roamed wildly over the heavy tools cast around, but all was in a semblance of order. Then the doorway darkened and Jubal walked in, leading a roan mare, secured her to the rail, and turned to leave.

She felt as though she had returned to her shattered life, to only live for this moment. How swiftly could she reach the heavy tongs on the side of the forge, and strike him down as he had struck her that glancing blow? That he had forced himself upon her, thinking she was one of the native women, only made her hate him more, his death the more deserving. "Only the escaped lock of my flaxen hair had stayed his scalping knife," and her hand convulsed on the weapon in her pocket. "Yes, lead to his gut would be a the most excruciating wound," she had been told. Carefully, she stepped from the shadow, and as she cocked the gun she cried out, "Jubal, Jubal Stubbs!"

Her heart thudded loudly as he turned toward her, a look of confusion on his face. Steadying the derringer with both hands, her eyes fixed upon his groin, she advanced across the floor. "Don't look them in the eyes," came to her, an axiom from the hunt. Yet she needed him to see that it was her taking his life, as she felt that he had taken hers.

She didn't expect his swift recognition of her, and her intentions. He grabbed her wrists and pointed the muzzle of the gun towards her feet. Her eyes flew to his face to meet defeat in his knowing smirk, his black eyes dancing with the pleasure of one accustomed to the sly mastery of those weaker and less cunning than himself.

"I heard the click," he laughed, "You stupid Yankee bitch", spittle spraying from his lips, "those bloody red niggers of your'n say that if'n you wound an animal, you must do the right thing; hunt it down and end its misery." She stiffened, expecting him to discharge the gun in her face then. All power drained from her with the realization of his hatred for his imagined oppressors. Now he would pull her towards him to wrench the gun away and kill her. And yes, some part of her willed it. But with an iron grip to her shoulders he spun her roughly, shoving her as though she were a sack of grain, to fall foolishly into befouled bedding straw, dropping the small derringer, pointedly, by her head before walking calmly away.

It wasn't until after she entered the post's trader's store, stumbling in her shame and confusion, that she realized that she must have tried to break her fall by extending her arms. Now her left wrist throbbed as though freshly broken. The tears she found herself fighting back were not from pain, though. "Failure," she thought, "I have failed us all." The briefest recall of Pale Calf's body with the child beneath her caused black spots to well up before her vision, swarming all unfocused, as though before a faint. The terrifying vision of that massacre, like a ragged quilt, flapped before her eyes. An arm reached out to steady her. Instinctively, she jerked away. "Mrs. Moore, Mrs. Moore, are you all right?" The rosy plump face of one of the fort's many laundresses was before her. Feeling the dull weight of the little gun still clutched in her hand, she shoved it deep in her pocket, whirling out of the woman's grasp, hobbling off as fast as she could manage, coming back to her senses enough to press the gun's safety back on; smoothing her skirts down as she went.

In a dazed state, she kept moving. Chin up, she headed directly for the back counter of the store where an idle group of enlisted men stepped quizzically and respectfully aside. She just stood there, willing a wall around herself. No one approached her unaccustomed presence here, especially in the corner where she had found herself standing, trying desperately to compose herself. She stared holes into the oak counter and felt she could turn to stone.

"And what can I do for you today?" She met the oddly impassive gaze of Mr. Detweiler. Slowly moving her hand from her pocket, she whispered, "Whiskey." "There's none of that to be had here, Ma'am. This here's a government trading post." She raised her eyes to his, and they exchanged lives in a brief glance. Mrs. Detweiler had passed on a few months earlier, and all his good cheer had gone with her. "I can't sell that to you," he replied softly, all the while assessing the stricken form before him...the "widow's weeds" flecked with bits of straw, the loose strands of hair, her pale and distraught face. She continued to stand, meeting his gaze dumbly. He turned and left her. So she stood there, a brisk trade going on beyond.

Eventually young Jimmy, one of Mr. Detweiler's assistants, appeared at her elbow to lead her outside. He walked her slowly and silently to the door before drawing a small package discreetly from his apron and pressing it into her hand. She could not bring herself to thank him over the grateful lump that rose in her constricted throat.

Getting Drunk

Pouring herself a shot, Anah gulped it straight. A gasp left her lips, mouth open and gaping like some astonished nestling. Pulling up a chair, she divested herself of her jacket, laying the gun down carefully where it could reproach her. "Talk to me," she dared it, and a desperate laugh bubbled up. She poured herself another slug, thinking, let's get to it!

She staggered a bit when she next rose to stoke the fire; the contents of the bottle much diminished. "Perhaps its time to sleep," she thought, but instead found herself seated on the little horsehair sofa in the drawing room where it was dark and cold. She didn't want to think, but thoughts rose unbidden.

"Never look into their eyes!" This admonition floated up in her consciousness like a piece of rotten ice slides from the bank into the river during spring break-up, and she found herself in thoughtful reply. "Who are they?" to the man she had called, so long ago, "Count one-two-three", The Baron Von Westenhagen. They were in the Yellow Stone Valley, resting near the unsettling beauty of the pool he called "Morning Glory". The others in her party were still entranced, watching the large geyser faithfully spew gallons and gallons of water into the air like clockwork. "Everyone," he responded, "everyone. Unless you feel that you are somehow, by some right, god-given or otherwise, deemed superior to them, then you can look directly into their eyes; the windows of the soul, you know." He smiled graciously, continuing, "Dare to look in those eyes, if you can gaze without condescension, malice, or lust." Rising to his full height above her seated form, stroking absently his full mustache, he declared, "If you cannot rule with loving kindness then you are not royal!"

They had been discussing titled nobility. "I imagine and hope that you would learn this as you grow up!" Her heart sank a little, knowing that he saw her as a child still. "You're headed now for a new and strange frontier," pausing dramatically. He had a penchant for such gestures. "Especially as regards the fabled "wild, wild west" that now lies before you and your father." They were soon to part company. He, to travel the furthermost reaches of the Missouri then on to the Pacific, while she and her father would move to his post at Fort Laramie. His arms swept out to include the wide valley of steaming geysers before them, spewing hundreds of feet up into the jack pines that surrounded them. "If you dare to really look into another's eyes, you must be prepared to accept the consequences." And just like that the past faded from her perception. Now the growing chill of the room roused her to the realization of what had really happened when she confronted Jubal.

She walked unsteadily back to the warmth of the kitchen. Sighing, she poured herself another shot, tentatively admiring the fire in her belly as the whiskey shot through her. She felt an odd elation. "Hot damn!" passed her lips, she giggled at the phrase so often heard around the fort when men got liquored up. Yes, fiery damnation!

But as suddenly as the elation had risen she was pummeled back down into dark thoughts, the taunts of "Yankee bitch" pursuing her. He had bested her. The shame was that it never had been a contest. He was more than equal to her surprise attack, and he rebuffed her with mere scorn and shoved her aside into the fouled straw.

One could only look forward to dying by having no fear of it, or by being too naive or witless to understand the dangerous thinking involved in courting death. What strange taboos! She began to rock furiously, thinking of that defeat. Now how did she get out here on the narrow porch, wrapped in a heavy quilt? "Drunk, I'm drunk," she thought exultantly. Drunk, confused, angry, hurt, bitter and yes, burning with hate. She could handle it, but .. "Please, oh, please," she thought to demand of the hapless fate that had brought her to the brink of public scorn, "Don't let me become mournful, and an object of pity, that I could not bear."

The tall figure crossing the parade ground towards her lodging was immediately identifiable as Old Turn Foot. In the dusk the two feather head-dress and silvery braids were quite distinguishable. Even in this inebriated state she had so readily put herself into, she knew him. What squirmed in her chest with a child-like pinch was her heart, that muscle she had so hoped to drown in spirits. "The doll, he's coming for the doll. He'll take it back now that he's heard.." It was all she had left of Orianna, it seemed at this moment. Not wanting him to find it she seized it defiantly to her chest, teeth-baring, tasking him to dare taking it from her. Before her befuddled mind could direct her physical self, she heard the soft shuffle of leather and a hawk bell, and turned to find the Cheyenne scout seated well below her on the steps. The lean length of his back was to her; Esperanza already drawn up quietly at his side.

Withdrawing a pipe, which looked amazingly, in the fading light, like a genuine meerschaum, he packed, lit it and drew quietly, never turning to offer it to her, of course. It was not ceremonial. "And I'm a woman," she added to herself. But the solidity of his silhouette, a blanket now drawn to his shoulders, kept her rhythmically rocking, and a dazed tranquility stole over the now empty parade ground. A few horses were being led to the stable, and lights were being lit in the barracks. The curtains of her neighboring officers quarters remained as closed as their doors.

"The moon is filling; *ootchiachilia* in Cheyenne." He offered the translation thoughtfully, knowing her penchant for languages. "Yes, it is so," and suddenly her perspective flattened, like bales being pitched erratically from a loft, and thoughts came down upon her. "He could have shot me! Why didn't he? Am I in danger now? Will he tell? I didn't shoot. I couldn't kill him. Why? He said something to me. What was it? He hated me. His hate was stronger. Did they all know? Will they come for me? Is that why you here? Should I flee? Where? How? Now. I should just go now!" She sprang to her feet, and Turn Foot rose simultaneously.

She never had a chance to accept defeat, for it just fell upon her and pinned her to the ground she had failed to stand on. "An eye for an eye, and a tooth for a tooth." So grim, now so starkly true to her heart. An army private who mistook her for a despised enemy, and a female at that, raped and struck her unconscious, but it was a bullet and malaria that took William and Orianna.

Adapting at last to this strange new world that alcohol had provided; tipsy, then turvy. A splendor of disorder to navigate; a track growing dim, uneven, unexplored ground that unfortunately, she would have to cover.

"What do you want?" she finally moved out of her own thought to lash out at him! So rudely said; it appeared that she was born to it. No reply. She thought she spoke aloud; had she? Just as she was prepared to clutch her shawl and go inside he spoke.

"To hear the last crickets. The nights grow cold now." Yes, understanding....simply warmth and stillness. He began to speak in his native tongue. "I like to talk. Best to talk long, with stories that the people like to listen to. I like telling those." She realized that his back was still to her, as though he was ceding her a gift of privacy in her inebriation, for she did not feel ashamed in his presence for her condition. The crescent moon rode lower before he said, "I cared for your horse while you lay between two worlds. *Wanagi Tacunku,* that is what you call The Milk Way, and we call The Spirit Trail, or Star Road. I waited and watched for your return. I came to tell you that I will continue this if you need me."

"Need you?" she replied with a ragged catch in her breath, turning to enter and close the door upon even him, the unexpected kindness and understanding searing.

The Burial Scaffold

At the kitchen table Anah sat tightly clutching a mug of coffee, long cold.

False dawn revealed the grime that had accumulated on what once was sparkling glass. "How quickly does one become a slave, not a master?" she wondered as she fought herself not to refill her mug with whiskey. How many days have passed? Did I stop the laudanum only to seek oblivion in a bottle? That dream clung to her, led her to a memory of a day trip taken out into the surrounding hills, Ori firmly seated in front of her on the saddle. Lark's were calling and springing forth from the growing lushness of the spring prairie in the valley of the Platte as the horses trod smartly along, much to the child's delight.

The day was clear and sparkling with a new freshness. Ahead on the ridge loomed a structure that could only be a burial platform. The sturdy pole frames anchored by rocks held a large object wrapped in a buffalo robe. Many prayer flags and feathers dangled from the rude scaffold. Even from this distance the long pole with faded red trade cloth that signified a war party's lance was discernible. Yet the old scout, Turn Foot, seemed to be leading her party directly up the hill towards the site. Surely he did not think this sacred place suitable for the outing's picnic? She called out in alarm for the child's sensibilities, but he seemed not to have heard her.

Too fascinated to turn back, she continued on as the others held back. This funerary custom of these plains she had yet to observe first hand. As she drew near it was obvious that a horse's skull was lashed to each corner post. A much honored warrior! She longed to dismount and examine the elegant but faded designs on the buffalo bull shield. "How easily my curiosity for these artifacts overcomes my respect for the dead," she thought, and shivered. Glancing surreptitiously at the guide, she found him calmly surveying the vast rolling grasslands spread out before them.

"Mommy, Mommy," Ori was squirming to be let down; such a curious child. "Hush!" she barked at her, tightening her grip, and spurred her pony next to the scout's. "Who was he?" she queried. "We do not speak the name of those who have left us, but as you can see he was an honored warrior. We do not place our dead in the ground for the worms to eat, nor leave them under cairns for the animals to destroy. We lift the body they leave behind up to the sun and stars; we free them from this earth."

"Will he go to heaven?" asked the child. "He is walking the path you call The Milk Trail," Turn Foot replied, looking at the child most carefully. This answer pleased her, for she looked to the vast display of the stars every night that she could. "Oh yes, Mama, he's gone to heaven just like Grandmother. I like that. I want to do the same when I die. I don't want the worms to eat me, nor live in a tiny wood box under the cold ground. I, too, want to walk among the stars!"

"Hush, child!" Anah had had enough of this eerie talk and spurred Wind down the hill. There would be no end of William's chiding and remonstrances if Ori mentioned this at the table. He barely tolerated what he called "filling the child's head with Native foolishness and superstitions."

When Anah lifted her head from her arms it was to discover the flask near empty, her head throbbing, and the remains of a spare meal that she didn't even remember cooking. The sun was soon to go down and she needed to determine a path, a way out of her pain and shame. She had drowned something, akin to anger, or at least held it well enough below the surface. But forgiveness, what a foreign word!

A month had passed since Anah had rose up out of that narrow sick bed. Her body had healed as much as it could, she surmised. Just a slight hitch in her gait, and an inability to lift her dutch oven without a shooting pain in the wrist that had been broken. As to what she looked like, did she care? Besides Anah had draped the one mirror with a shawl the first time she dared to re-enter the house.

Once out of the infirmary she was still too overwhelmed by loss to deal with well-meant condolences, even from those who had once been friends. Visitors were soon turned sorrowfully away, she knew she was violating tradition to refuse succor. The covered dishes were then left on the porch when she no longer even came to the door. Her dog profited well from the unexpected bounty, though she even refused simple ministrations of the animal. Small bouquets were often left to wilt, and much food spoiled or was set upon by other dogs out roaming at night. Esperanza lay quietly by the front door, keeping vigil, impervious to the curs that stole the food.

Anah's conscience bade her to allow the chaplain entry, but as he offered his condolences bitterness rose like a miasma from a malarial swamp to blind the young widow. When he left, seemingly gratified in his mission, she mindlessly rocked on and on, long after his departure. Each beat of her heart seeming to slow and harden into a resolve that excluded everyone and everything but her bitterness and grief.

She could not bring herself to sleep in the bed once shared with William, so many a night found her curled awkwardly on the horsehair sofa with an old afghan tossed over. A few nights found her asleep in the rocker, or to wake up face down at the kitchen table. She was quickly becoming a stranger to herself.

She was forgotten, as desired. God? She no longer called on Him; what for? All that was left to her was her life, which she little valued, as diminished as it was by loss and shame. Her plan for vengeance was for nought! She sought oblivion, and sleep did not provide even a few brief hours of it, for when her eyes closed her mind opened to things that she so desired to forget: memories that had, but briefly, a shocking crystal clarity, and like a crystal simply shattered when she reached out to touch them. Little Orianna taking those bold, wobbling first steps that so delighted her father and herself, then stumbling from the safety of her arms towards William's laughter and open arms. Then came an old man, running, long gray braids flapping, clutching his prayer bundle, a sudden bright bloom of blood red on his back as he fell to one knee dragging the small child down with him. Sometimes she woke, (or was she dreaming), to the strident, frightened cry of her own departed child calling, "Momma." When she flew to the window it was only to gaze out on the empty parade ground.

One night, standing there, she thought she saw a little child walking slowly toward the gates, dragging a small blanket behind her. Her hand was on the doorknob to exit before realizing that nothing, nothing real, was out there. Had she been drinking to the point of "the tremens"? Surely not. That night Anah pulled a shawl over her head and stepped out onto the porch to discover Turn Foot seated nearby. He rose, as if to accompany her, and so they walked. At first just a quiet perambulation around the officer's quarters, but soon they easily traversed the entire grounds, saying little. How strangely comforting his silent presence was.

Thus began a nightly routine. When he spoke, it was sparsely, at first just pointing out the distant constellations, or causing Anah to note the sweet haunting call of an owl. Soon she was accustomed to the darkness. He did not try to draw her out, as others might, but rather they shared the mildest of quiet companionship.

Knowing that he liked coffee, the real kind, not ersatz, she bade him to sit on the stone step while she prepared some for them one night. That was the night he withdrew from his coat a small calico wrapped bundle. Afraid to hold it, expecting it to be some desiccated animal part she carefully withheld acceptance. He nodded, and poked it with a long, thin bony finger. Smiling, unusual for him, he said "Keep this safe." Then stood, and as he turned to leave told her solemnly. "He's gone, deserted, left with that last Mormon train, taking many fine Army mules with him."

There was so much she wanted to question the old man on, but she held her peace, knowing that he was speaking of her attacker, Private Stubbs. Again he proffered the small bundle, and many responses died on her lips as she reached for it. Some kind of Medicine, some spirit power, Anah presumed. The transaction stunned her, for in some way Turn Foot was granting her acceptance at the same time that she was denying her place in a world, that for her, had been destroyed with the deaths of her husband and child.

Whirlwind Power

One evening near Otter Creek, late Spring, close to the north Fork of the Red River, where a very motley bunch of travelers were getting ready to set up a meager camp for the evening, an apparition appeared riding towards them in the softened light that sometimes occurs at that time of year on the plains. Most definitely a person on horseback, proceeding towards them at a slow dignified pace; should they be alarmed?

Those few warriors left in the group, for most had gone to join the hostiles up North, hastened to their weapons. The women began once more to round up and shelter their remaining young. The old ones simply waited. As a strong shaft of light broke from a cloud to illuminate the approaching figure the young boy who had the boldness to crawl closer to observe leapt to his feet, turned to shout, proud and joyful in his powers of observation, "He's riding backwards!" As indeed the figure was now observed to be doing so, and skilfully. Thus the holy man, the *heyoka*, Lion Falling Backwards, arrived among them.

He brought them this word, for he had been out seeking a *wakanya wowanyake*, a Great Vision, all his days as a *wicasa wakan*, holy man, since his first quest as a youth of just twelve winters, following the difficult backward path of the sacred Thunder Beings.

Lion Falling needed help dismounting, needed food, drink, rest, but that had to wait, for he was compelled. He had been told, had he not, to go and tell the very first people he encountered, after The Great Vision had arrived, what had been revealed to him. His heart trembled inside his weary bones, for he had been out on the plains fasting, waiting, months, years, days, eons, centuries, lifetimes, it seemed. And he learned, finally, though he had had to have almost all his life stripped from his bones, to be humble, for he had imagined that when the great *wakanya wowanyake* finally came, oh did he believe that a great vision would eventually come... that WHEN it came he would deliver it before a great assembly of the people, and there would be recognition, and honors.... that it would be in the Season of Renewal. And he would be still in his prime, HIS PRIME, his powers still intact. And when he stood before all, ready to do the sacred act, he could plunge his hand into a pot of boiling water and not even flinch! Ah, yes!

Now he just briefly lifted his dust rimmed, weary eyes to these haggard travelers who were hard pressed to offer him more than a bit of wasna and water. And who were they? Just a handful of warriors with not a Dog Rope among them! Some toothless old men and grieving women. But the boy was at his feet ready to listen, his eyes upon the skin of the mountain lion draped around his old hunched shoulders, so he drew it closer to him, making sure to display its huge paws to advantage, so that they hung over his withered chest. These people had so little that such a story as his would be welcome, most welcome, indeed!

The group gathered easily; the fire giving almost the only comfort they knew, as they traveled to surrender to the unknown life that a reservation would offer them. Now they were just one more night's camp away. He stood, withdrew a small hand drum from his robes, danced a few steps around the fire, backwards, in a hypnotic, yet pleasing fashion, till both the flames dying to glowing coals and those present sat most attentive, then he turned to face them, drawing himself to his full height. In the soft, flickering glow he looked amazingly like a lean mountain lion, aged, hungry, wise. When he began to speak some said afterward his words came out almost like a growl, others like a steady purring sound!

When first the ve'ho'es appeared upon our land we laughed at them, found their pale skin and furry faces amusing. Soon there were many of them, like swarming ants, but they were not ants. They had powers, Medicine . They looked upon our Tatanka and saw it was good.

We traded for what we wanted: beads, cloth, tin, whiskey, gewgaws, but they wanted more, and more. Soon they began to just ride out and take what they wanted. Then they made Big Medicine to make a fire stick that took the buffalo's life from very far away. Then they just took the tongues, leaving the rest to rot. Did the Great Everywhere Spirit destroy them for this? No! Then they wanted to pass safely through our land? Yes, we said. Then they wanted to live on our land? Yes, if you are kind to it and us, but then they did not want to live on it with us, but without us. Then they wanted to send an iron snake across the plains. They sent their Bluecoats to herd us like animals to pens called Reservations and take from us all means we had to care for ourselves, all the ways the Great One Above had provided for us to be grateful.

We fought back, for many seasons, at great cost, and with much division among our people, our brothers, our leaders. Our blood has soaked the land. Those of much wisdom have had to decide to walk the Red Road or the White Road, and sorrow paves each path and each footfall, for the circle of harmony between brothers has been broken.

His lean and wrinkled face was contorted with dry laughter, and yet a small trace of tears ran down it's gullies as he spoke. He was indeed a most mysterious figure. Dancing backward, strange and compelling, yellow eyes full of a mysterious power, holding each and every one of the small band in rapt attention to his every word as though hypnotized.

I have flown above the clouds as the large cranes do, crawled below the clods of dirt under the feet of men as little worms do. I have felt the touch of love, the blows of hate! I thought I had seen it all until I had seen the enormity of the greed of the wasichu. If I had not seen it lifted out of his chest upon the battlefield I would not have believed that he even had a heart that beat within his chest or that it was exactly like unto ours. Exactly as to form, that is. I, who have been touched by The Great Mystery, do not comprehend what lies within the heart of the White-man. He speaks with two tongues, but his mouth holds only one. It appears as Sweet Medicine has prophesied so long ago, that the whites would prevail, and I, for one, have waited many, many winters for a great vision, for surely these whites have the most powerful Medicine yet to be seen on the face of our land. I had thought that when they fought what they called the Civil War, that they would then go back over the Big Muddy and leave us to our old ways, but now I fear they worship a devouring power that rises up out of some of their leaders like those whirlwinds that rise up suddenly from the bleakness of the plains.....sweeping, raging, touching here and there, complete and senseless in their destruction like the whirlwind!

And with that he began to spin and dance, whirling around himself, till he fell down, one large paw of the cougar hissing into the coals, a burnt smell, alerting the spellbound audience to move away, vacantly. The exception being the young boy, who reverently dragged the old heyoka to his own sleeping robes, covering him as best as he could, then kept watch, looking into the heavens. He vowed to stay awake to greet the morning star, oddly not too dispirited himself.

But when false dawn came the boy stirred to find himself carefully covered and the old heyoka gone. In his empty place lay a broken half of a Cheyenne arrow along with a heavily polished buffalo stone. The boy did not hesitate to possess them for the treasures that they were, secreted away to be passed from generation to generation.

Dreaming of Reburial

Anah knew now that she had to deal with living, that is, with picking up the remnants of her life. Just like when one wakes, still so very tired, and it's not quite light, you pull up the covers where your shoulder has chilled and you heave to your other side. Then there you are, aware, and having to deal with it, whatever bleak reality intrudes. She was never the kind that could easily slip back into sleep when awakened, though.

Turn Foot had left her last night to a cleansing of tears, the first she had truly shed. She felt somewhat released from grief. The predawn light now showed the spectral shapes of the empty parade ground out a little window. It was too early for the birds to even begin singing. Numbness held her attention; fighting it she began to list chores of the day, and alarmingly, found none. There was no routine left. A depression settled as light as a first snowfall; the kind that comes softly at first, then thicker, finally obscuring sight. What she felt most of all was not the absence of husband and child, for their presence was strong and constant before her mind. A bedevilment of grief, for they did not exist in reality any more. She did not feel like she existed either; no longer a wife, no longer a mother. She felt blasted open and wanted to howl for something, anything, that could bring healing. She had tried seeking oblivion, but the edges of this wound would not be sewn shut.

A bitter wind of memory was starting to blow. Oddly, she had no hangover. Her eyes drifted to the bottle and glass, both empty. The derringer gleamed coldly in the near darkness, but Anah was too tired and too afraid to lift it to herself, though she briefly entertained the thought. Not having been fired, it didn't need cleaning. Pushing herself up she numbly carried it back to the bedroom, knowing that she was through, spent, finished with travel down that road. How long had Turn Foot spoken to her the other night, or was it just last night? They carried on conversations now in such an odd mix of English, Lakota and, increasingly, the more difficult Cheyenne. He spoke of what his people call the soul. Was it *nagi, ma'tasooma?* He went on to talk of the soul's travel along The Road of the Departed. Was that *Seozemeo?* On the way to Se'han, The Place of The Dead. There really wasn't any hell, if she understood him correctly, but suicides did not reach this place. He spoke of The Road of The Hanged Ones, and something about spirits roaming around, but now she was very confused. Did he believe in ghosts or not? Pulling the star quilt, the *owinja*, over herself she fell into sleep as one falls down a hole.

The dream began with "Wind" being led toward her by a tall, blanketed shape. Glinting from the man's neck was what looked like one of those silver peace medallions, and thrown over the haunches lay a small wrapped bundle. It was hard to see clearly as they were moving through a mist, the kind that rises from a lake when the sun begins to shine warmly on the waters. Delicate soft tendrils rose like smoke into the air. The movement toward her was very slow; processional. But before her horse, with it's ominous burden came any closer, she shook herself.

Suddenly realizing a heaviness in her shoulders, she turned to see that she had dark feathered wings that glinted where the sun struck the long pinions. Filled with an urgent wild desire to lift off, she felt a horror that her feet were somehow secured with leather thongs. The air began filling with golden yellow flower heads; they were swirling, turning into white seed heads, and spinning off into a rising wind. A line of thin dark figures bearing shovels were descending from the cliff face before her now. Her horse was rearing back and neighing, pulling hard against it's braided hackamore. Locusts rose from the ground with a mechanical keening noise so high and thickly clustered that her vision was obscured, and so intensely loud that she heard nothing but their maddening, whirring clamor.

Suddenly they stopped, all at once, in a singularly eerie way, then a child's voice rang out, "Mommy, I want to see the sky! I can't see it. Mommy!"

She turned, enraptured at the thought of seeing Orianna once more, but to her shock she now could not see. Her eyes were bandaged. "Mommy," came the cry once more with heartbreaking finality. As she desperately tried to tear the cloth from her eyes it began to wind down her body, enveloping her, binding her as in a burial shroud. The faster she tore at these wrappings the quicker they enveloped her once again, and the greater pressure they seemed to exert upon her heart....she could feel it breaking!

She woke shivering, with a depth of cold that seemed to pinion her hips to the bed. So close, she thought, "I almost saw her face, almost," filled with the most intense yearning. Crying out to the one she felt was no longer there for her, she knew she was wounded deeply. She did not feel like she had done battle with any adversary other than fear. She felt at first empty, then bleak, flat, dull. She had survived, so far, with little or no help from anyone or anything, especially herself. There had been no response from the wire sent back East.

Confronting Loneliness

Getting ready to step up into the store, she was suddenly enveloped with what had to be a genuine feeling of loneliness. Being alone was something she grew up experiencing; in fact, she often sought it out as a comfort. But right now she felt like a naked soul, exposed to herself in a new, overwhelming and bewildering way. The evils of her recent experiences clung to her like leeches on an open wound. She did not think that she could go in, and so turned abruptly and left.

There was no more pretense of family; no longer was she a wife or mother. She held no responsibilities for anyone anymore. Nor was she needed or wanted. Ghost-like, in fact, some integral part of her had died with William and their child. She would never see them again, except in her imaginings. The daguerreotype on her dresser was but proof, not presence. Eerily, she had quit dreaming of them, and as disturbing as those laudanum induced dreams had been, she sorely missed them.

A spot between her breasts began to ache, as her throat constricted with suppressed tears. Sadness and an unbearable longing began to sweep over her in what felt like a physical wave, a drowning in grief. Now back in the privacy of the bedroom, she felt defeat sweep over her, bearing her like a riptide into the raging, muddied waters of shame. That Private Stubbs would desert, just up and leave with army supplies, rankled her. He was a thief, a deserter, but in no way branded or identified as her assailant! She had good reasons for reporting him to his superiors with her claim of brutal attack, but would she be believed? Perhaps at first, but not now, not after the laudanum and whiskey that she had taken no pains whatsoever to hide. And how many nights now had she fallen asleep, face down upon her arms, to wake cold and stiff, just groggy enough to drain the dregs of nothing but cold, black coffee.

The fire long untended, it was so quiet that she could hear the distant yowls and yips of the little wolves out beyond the confines of the fort. Anah had just enough motivation to drag herself off to an unmade bed, the clothes she had had on for many days still upon her back. She could not go on like this. Going back East was no longer a consideration. How long would it be before Paulette weaseled out her true story of degradation at the soldier's hands, and most tellingly, at her own. Her stepmother would ooze comfort of the basest sort, only to heap disdain on her behind her back. How many lives had met overwhelming defeats out on the immigrant trail that ran past the fort, and yet carried on to what they hoped was a brighter future? Could she not be one of them? She, too, could just pick up and leave!

Back at their quarters, she still thought of her post accommodations as "theirs", she realized that she should be accomplishing something; at the very least, making a pile of William's things that had been requisitioned, to return them. She reached for his steel saber; the heaviness of it matched her spirits. His plumed helmet, and that was all that she could do not to sink to the floor, overwhelmed by his absence. No, more than absence, loss. Irrevocable loss. Everything of his that she touched, or lay her hands upon, pierced her numbness with sharp remembrance. And his uniforms, how could she even lay hands on those garments that still had his scent. She found herself hefting his center-fire Colt .45, admiring it's improvements over the longer, heavier standard issue Remington. Idly she brought it up to her temple, her finger light on the trigger. The sound of a bugle alarmed her; guilt flooded through her. She dropped the pistol on the bed feeling an odd relief, also revulsion. She fled to the small kitchen and the bottle once again. How could she even contemplate dealing with this, let alone Orianna's things?

By the time taps sounded she was well adrift on waves of alcoholic fueled confusion. Standing to rise, telling herself that it was bedtime, she found herself, without remembering walking there, by the bedside, staring at the cold, metallic gleam of the pistol. A grim laugh escaped her; she didn't even know if it was loaded. Grateful somehow that it simply lay on the bed where she had dropped it, it now frightened her, proof that she had some sense left. Or did it, for she went to where the cap-lock walnut handled derringer was kept, a real Derringer that William had given her for protection. Holding it lightly in the palm of her hand, she idly traced the engraving "Derringer/Philadelph" on the lock, thinking that the protection she indeed needed was from herself, or she might find herself up taking that bend in the heavenly road to the place Turn Foot called *Hekozeemeo!*

The Response

Seated at the table, Anah prepared herself for the contents of the letter she now held. She had expected a telegraphed response to her dire straits, but could not recall how many days had passed since the news of William and Orianna's death had been wired to her father, nor what she had done in that time. Was she even now too under the influence to read this missive, penned in her father's distinct hand? She did not truly know if she was hoping for some sort of salvation, or was simply dreading being summoned back to the seemingly privileged world that she had grown up in? Pouring herself just a jigger, she threw it down and with a grimace inserted the ivory handled opener into the flap.

Dear Anah,

You have our condolences for your grievous loss. I have spoken to your stepmother and she has agreed to make room for you in our household, if necessary.

Please let us know your decision. I wish only the best for you.

Your father,
Frederick Hoffman, M.D. Esq.

How long had she been sitting here, and how drunk was she? Her one foot was numb, the other cold. The fire was out, the table top sticky. The letter, oh yes, the letter. Her deliverance! An icy strand of bitterness tightened around her like a length of that new wire with it's sharp barbs. Anah knew exactly what her father's brief letter implied. He had to speak to her stepmother, get her agreement to make, what? "Room" for his only child, as though she were a cumbersome trunk to be stored, to take up space. Her decision; it was her decision, to go where there is no heartfelt welcome!

Staggering up, shaking out the numbness in her foot, she threw more kindling on the spent coals, blew, and as a flame licked up she carefully fed her father's response to it's all consuming fire.

Bad Medicine?

"He found no way to count coup on Death!"

"Did you bring it?" flew from her lips when she saw the scout crossing the parade ground towards her in the last gloaming of twilight. "Come in, Come in!," Anah beckoned to him. " Yes, little sister, I did. This is bad medicine for you; for all of us. You know this." "Yes," holding out both hands towards him as though pleading, as the sky behind them banded into lowering strips of orange, purple and rose. The dark came on swiftly now. I will not leave you....., unspoken, but firmly acknowledged in his somber dark eyes.

Grabbing for his hands, she focused her gaze fearlessly on him, as though she meant to prove her strength for this endeavor. "You cannot bring her back." "I know that, that's not," and she broke off to rake her hands nervously through her hair. "You will come with me; I need you." It was then that he noticed the small spade leaning against her rocker.

"Anah?" "Yes." "Where are we going?" "You know, we discussed it. You know where..." Interrupting her, he said mildly, "We do not speak the name..." "Of the dead," she rudely spat out in her nervousness. "I know your ways. I wish only to visit her, where she lies. The darkness will cover my sorrow," and your friendship will blanket my heart.. she meant to add, with a respect she deeply felt, but in her agitated state had trouble mustering. She would not let him carry the spade, and surreptitiously, she hoped, took small pulls on the little bottle she slipped from her pocket. Coughing a bit, she kept plodding on towards the burial plot that lay beyond the fort's gates.

By the time they arrived only the waning moon guided their steps, but it was, of recent, a fairly well-trodden path. Her steps faltering as they approached, though she went unerringly towards the fresh mounds of dirt. Someone had placed a small wooden cross with these words, "OREANNEA, *beloved child of William and Annie Moore.*" "They misspelled her name, you know," she declared irritably, her head raised to the heavens as though she could find an answer there. She sat in a haphazard cross-legged fashion at the foot of the mound with an unusual disregard for her skirts. Turn Foot saw the glistening trails of wetness down her cheeks and took his seat, close by but not touching. He did not know what she would do, or what she actually intended.

How much time passed was only judged by the transit of the moon, the sidereal slide of the stars, the callings of the little wolves and the occasional clink of the bottle on her teeth. A nearly imperceptible moaning and rocking began. When the bottle was emptied she rose unsteadily to her feet and went to retch behind a nearby creosote bush. She returned to fumble for the spade and approached the little mound that lay right next to her husband's resting place. Still Turn Foot sat quietly, seemingly unperturbed.

As soon as the spade's metallic clink echoed in the stillness he spoke, "This is a desecration!" She whirled, hair loose and wild across her dirt and tear-streaked face. She was indignant that he even knew that word, desecration. The fiercest expression that he had ever seen on this woman's lovely face flashed out at him, and she practically screamed, baring her teeth so that she looked much like a cornered weasel to him. Extending her arms in a circle to include all of their dim, bleak surroundings, waving the spade drunkenly she screamed, "It's all a desecration!" and with that began to hack wildly at the ground, sobbing.

"Stop, Anah," he commanded. "Oh, that I could, that I could stop it, all of it, the madness, the murdering madness..." Turn Foot rose, "You cannot bring her back!"

"I want, I want," she sobbed out hysterically, fueled by the demands of the alcohol's power. "Ori, Ori, Oh, Orianna, my, mine." She flung the little shovel, narrowly missing him. Clawing at the mound, she rubbed the clay and sandy soil into her face and clothes. Now, now he reached for her, tried to contain her in his arms as she kicked, begged, alternately going limp and stiffening, pleading for madness to take her away, pulling at his garments, grasping for the large Bowie knife she knew he kept sheathed at his waist. He shook her as fiercely as a mink shakes its prey. So shocked by this her eyes flew open. She sobered, collapsing into a heap, aware of her cold limbs and the muddy drag of her skirts, heavy with earth from her daughter's grave.

"Aho! Listen to me," and he began to speak, even knowing that in her drunken state she would probably have no recall of the story he would tell her of the powerful Kiowa warrior, Santak, whose son was killed in a raid on a farmhouse on the northern Texas frontier. He carried his son's bones, wrapped in a blanket, with him wherever he went.

Whenever a camp was made Santak constructed a special lodge for his son, with food and drink available for his spirit. He was a broken man, without consolation. So grieved was the man at the death of his favorite son that he had to be roped up, at first, to prevent him from taking his own life. The horse that carried his son's remains was led along beside this chief ever after. He found no way to count coup on Death; it suffered his vengeful soul, driving him to do this strange thing.

Speaking in a sonorous voice, he hoped that she would calm, in fact, she listened intently, as a child would, responding only to say. "In our bible there was a famous warrior king, David, who was so grief stricken over a son's death that he refused food until...." and she drifted into a stuporous sleep; soft, wounded snores escaping from her parted lips now and then.

When she woke, disoriented, Turn Foot's heavy buffalo robe draped over her, she saw him squatting nearby. "Look up," he softly asked of her, and she looked up into the resplendent Milky Way that dominated the heavens now that the moon had set. Each star appeared as finely placed in the velvet darkness as a glittering jewel.

" She walks there now you know. Nor is she alone. Many will help her along, among them I'm sure. *Heammawihio*, The Wise One Above, they are going to him. Look up, Anah," and he gently took her little pointed chin in his large weathered hand. "Just like your King David, she cannot come back to you, but someday you will go to her. Is that not written in your ancestral king's book?" The scout had a very accurate and impressive command of the English language, for it was in his nature to be precise and pay very close attention to details that others would find insignificant. "That King, David, had his beloved son taken from him because he had taken another warrior's wife, and had him murdered in order to keep her," Anah responded. "Do you know that?" "Yes, yes, it's written." "No, I mean do you know if that is what caused the child's death?" Anah's jaw fell slightly open and her grasp upon the buffalo robe loosened, tears dimming the glowing spark of anger in her eyes. "I wasn't there," she began to sob in earnest. "I wasn't there to save her, to protect her. I'm as good as a murderess, am I not?" Turn Foot just stared through her, beyond her into the generous lacing of stars in the heavens above. Anah continued to mutter and sob, finally noticing that while he was right in front of her he was yet somehow gone.

This sobered her up so that she felt the cold drape of her mud-soaked mourning dress upon her ankles from where she sat sprawled on the burial mound. From the low sand hills coyotes began to yip as the false dawn gave outline to the horizon. A chill air surrounded her shivering body and she could not tell if it emanated from the ground or from her quailing spirit.

"Anah." Her vision altered to find herself gazing into the calm blackness of Turn Foot's gaze, now intently upon her. It seemed as though the stars were spiraling away slowly as the dawn broke, before he spoke. "I wasn't there either. I couldn't save my loved ones from their appointed death. I was left behind also." He extended both hands and helped her to her feet. At that, Anah hung her aching head, somehow reassured. Together they made it back to the fort before the changing of the guard. It wasn't until much later that she thought to ask where she had heard the name Santak before, and how did he know of the Book of Kings.

They never spoke of this night again though, and Anah was never seen at the graveyard, never saw that the little marker had been corrected with the proper spelling of the child's Christian name, Orianna, and her own. It was not long after this nocturnal visit that she was able to decide that she could indeed leave this place behind her and move on.

Digging Up The Dead

Anah's Commonplace Book

I had been taught that being an only child was a privilege, and not to pity myself as a child when I felt a lack of companionship, but when I came to my senses this morning I had quite the struggle not to feel just that for the emptiness of my life now.

Upon your pages I can write the truth, at least as much of it as I know. A quick assessment: I had fallen asleep in a drunken stupor on my kitchen table. I have but three friends left in the world...an old Cheyenne scout, an English Bull Terrier, and you, my journal, just a cloth bound ledger with a well-worn leather spine. If you had eyes, oh, if you could see me...my skirts heavy with mud from the grave! My hair full of little bits of leaves, and my heart..oh, let me tell you more. But first, propped before the near empty liquor flask so that I could not help but see it was a note from Turn Foot. I have pasted it here:

"Wani Wachin", a new Lakota phrase for me to learn; "I want to live"

Anah poured the last of the whiskey out with unwarranted pride, acting on a strength she hoped, rather than knew, was there. Whereas she had felt as though she had no one to turn to, she now was ready to accept the one ally that had sought her out in this desolate outpost in the Platte Valley, the old scout. Remembering the quote from Hippocrates that had hung in her father's old examination room, "Healing is a matter of time, but it is sometimes also a matter of opportunity," she now continued to record in her journal the events of the previous evening in the graveyard beyond the fort.

I now saw an opportunity in embracing a native belief, a tentative smile on my lips, to recall my little Ori's request on that day we came upon the burial platform, high on the bluff above the Laramie, when she had told me that she wanted to walk among the stars, and not be placed in a box beneath the earth. How we all laughed. Laughed! It was unimaginable that this golden-haired, irrepressible child could be taken from us.

On the evening that I had determined to disturb my child's place in the hard cold ground to rebury her, things did not go as I had planned. When one is still half-crazed and mantled by an obsession I'm not sure that such a thing as a plan, which speaks of reason, exists. Did I believe in Seano, that distant camp in the stars where the dead would reunite with family and friends and dwell near the Cheyenne's conception of their creator, Maheo? Under the influence of the alcoholic spirits I could see her sweet face imploring me, "Mommy, I want to see the sky." A reasonable request, it seemed. Looking back now I know that I could not bring myself to conceive of my golden child remaining in that graveyard's dirt. I had asked that Turn Foot would take me to her grave, for when I had brought myself to the place where I could question him about the re-appearance of the little Cheyenne doll he forthrightly told me how it had come to be in his possession. Out beyond the fort there was a refuse pile where many things were discarded, especially anything from the passing flood of wagons that were not reclaimed. When Turn Foot spotted the little doll in a pile awaiting burning he snatched it up and secreted in his robes. I had asked him why it was thrown away. Was it because it was a native craft? No, no, he had said; since they did not know the true cause of Ori's death, it was thought best to burn it with the possessions of recent cholera victims from the last of the season's trains. And you had no fear of it? I had asked him. No, was all he responded.

Yellow Bird

Looking out from her porch into the vast open skies above the empty parade ground, Anah scanned for any signs of birds. Not even a crow floated silently across the clear blue. Had the swallows gone south? Soon what she had always thought of as the bad weather would come. The snow she didn't mind, actually liked, but way out here the wind spoke in severe, frightening voices that she had never heard before. In spite of the security of the fort she had awakened many a night to draw closer to William's sturdy, sleeping form as the howling wind preached in an icy strong voice of desolation, starvation and loneliness. Sometimes on those nights she would hear the clear call of a wolf; that call, a strong force giving out solidarity and strength to the night. At those times she wished that she could be out there herself with the same prevailing fortitude!

She, too, was changing with the seasons this year, finding it somehow miraculously easier for her profoundly burdened memory to sift through it's cache to find those days that had special markings. Clutching her paisley shawl closer to her chest in the cool air, she recalled that day, could it have been just this spring, when she had heard the first chattering cheeps of the returning barn swallows? Grabbing up Ori from where she had been contentedly playing underfoot, she rushed outside to point to the dipping, swirling arcs of these birds. Not only did it spell to her the definite proof that the bad weather was past, but their seemingly effortless play in the air above all sparked pure joy in her heart. In bringing her child out to see this she had hoped to convey this promise of nature's reoccurring blessings. She was gratified then, to see a chubby little hand reach up towards them, a wide smile breaking across those blooming cheeks. Life was good, she had thought. Yes, life was good that morning. Later on in the season she had held Ori up to glimpse the lovely rose, gold and navy feathered birds with their bright dark eyes and odd gaping mouths as they swooped in to feed their own babies in the nests tucked under the eaves.

Returning to her present domain, the empty kitchen, she startled at the melodious trill that greeted her. The canary? Willi? Was he still alive? Her eyes flew to the corner where the little gilt cage was kept. A pale yellow form plopped from it's perch down to a seed cup. Looking in she saw that both the seed and water cups were filled, the cage floor itself thick with husks and droppings. She must have tended, though somewhat haphazardly, to it's needs.

Standing dumbstruck at this evidence of her absentminded pursuit of usual duties, the canary gave out with another clear burst of song, rising up and down a scale bred into it. The absurdity of the life that had maintained it's purpose in the face of her neglect caused a giggle to escape, like a bubble of air that rises from the mouth when underwater. This unabashed, unreserved sound of a quick pleasure reverberated in her kitchen, a room that had once been the center of her domestic life. One where good smells had emanated from pots and pans that in their sizzles of frying and burbles of simmering foods created a music of their own. The old copper tea kettle brought to a whistling boil never failed to cause the canary to erupt in riotous competition. She often wondered if her daughter desired tea for this reason. Tears welled up.

How could she imagine leaving here, her home? An image came to her; riding out in the long hours of the night with a little cage hung from the pommel of her saddle causing another giggle..and more tears. "Oh, you poor dear thing," she exclaimed, touching her hand to the bars of the cage door. I could give him away, she thought, but then her plans would be revealed. Her plans? Had she decided something?

She hadn't realized till right now that no matter how close she had drawn to nature and the elements; no matter how much she felt she had communed with birds, animals, and yes, even the flowers, she just missed the human connection. The one that responded in a language clearly understood. The weight of her isolation in this military community pressed down upon her.

It was then, standing at the little bird's cage that the idea blossomed fully. She WAS leaving! Willi would have his freedom too. She would release him; a small joyful feeling of beneficence flooded through her. Even if he froze or starved, as surely he would do come the first winter storm with it's freezing gales. But until then he would have the great blue bowl of the sky to traverse in unfettered flight. Most likely, a raptor would strike him down in mid-flight; he would never know what ended his life so swiftly, but he would die free, she could see to that.

Running Away From Home

Her coffee had grown cold again as she sat at the table, so engaged in ruinous thoughts that she had forgotten to bring the cup to her lips. Thinking that simple routine could somehow restore her to a life worth living, Anah had begun to rise at reveille, wash, dress and bring herself to the kitchen. Here she had expected familiar chores to lead her back into an acceptance that she had survived, and to accept that survival as a blessing. Yet here she was again, mindlessly staring into the cold black contents of her cup, aimless and thankfully numb, as though she had somehow spun a cocoon against the acid pain of remembrance. But even as she was recognizing this her heart began to beat faster; the feeling of someone unwanted coming to one's door. Abruptly she threw her gaze out the window. Winter would soon arrive, the sky would begin to surrender it's depthless clear blue of late autumn. Thin gray clouds were even now being herded across the wide expanse by the bitter North Wind. How could she possibly face the isolation of this forsaken outpost through the harsh season ahead? Barely formed scenes of post entertainment mocked her widowhood. Dinners? Dances? She could not even bear the dutiful visitations that came to her door. How to respond to the carefully scripted request of Mrs. Hoag's, slipped under her door just the other day? She did not belong here; a terrifying thought. For where did she now belong? Go back East? Go anywhere she wasn't wanted, where she didn't want to be? To face the sly gloating of her stepmother and what she perceived as an indifference by her father? There would be a widow's pension for her, but how could she stand to stay here now? It was like running away from home, the idea that all troubles resided where one lived, that those troubles could be just left behind. Anah Hoffman Moore, a runaway, at her age, a grown woman. Yes, all grown up, but with no where to go. A slight taste rose in her mouth, she felt as though she could not draw a full breath. Just a little sip of this new air filled her with what? Daring? A certain dread of wanting her life to begin again, yet knowing that she was without customary restraints, that she could do of her own choosing. Her glance fell on the beautifully embroidered cradle board Pale Calf had so generously gifted her with. Her new friends! How little thought she had given to their fate. Turn Foot had told her that the small band that had been so wrongly attacked that day had packed up and left for the winter grounds deep in the draws and canyons to the South. They were my friends, the remnant had traveled to join up with the people we call Cheyenne, Arapaho and Sioux. She envisioned riding out to join them. When that idea blossomed in her mind, to just run away, it did indeed spring forth with an unexpected beauty. In fact she felt excitement, the first twinge of this giddy emotion that she had not felt in longer than she could remember. At the same time that she thought she was being suddenly possessed of a certain madness, she was subsequently goading herself on, applauding the wildness. Here was no longer her home. Could she break her own heart, anymore than it was already, by leaving?

What Was Left Behind

Standing in front of the black cloth draped mirror Anah felt both fear and excitement, for she had not looked at herself in all these weeks. Her hands flew to her carelessly pinned up hair; as she began to loosen it remorse flooded through her. William! Oh, William! His image rose up before her as she had first laid eyes upon him. Across the crowded room he stood out; tall, lean and very composed, while all around him flowed the revelry. He looked to her like the very best of the life she had left behind. Indeed he was new to the frontier and still had an aura of private destiny hovering close that not even the dingy surroundings of this Bachelor Officers Quarters, Old Bedlam, as it was derisively called, could diminish. Brass buttons on his dress uniform gleamed, as did his cool gray eyes. His hair shined from it's meticulous grooming. And of course the tall black boots were polished to a perfection she rarely saw at this desolate outpost. She had a desire to hear his voice and began to maneuver herself across the room. He was the new Adjutant General, a West Point graduate, dashingly handsome. Her father had spoken well of him, William Byron Moore III, a bachelor, he added with a mischievous grin. The General introduced them, and his response was to extend a well-groomed hand and sweep her onto the dance floor, smiling generously down upon her. She was charmed, as he had meant her to be. Then another image rose up; one of his mild displeasure. They had been married but weeks when he confronted her while she had been scrubbing out a dark stain on one of his shirts. Capturing both of her soapy hands in his large ones, he tilted her chin up and looking directly at her in that gentle but commanding way of his. "Anah, I did not marry a laundress. Leave this!" A housekeeper, yes, she thought, for his expectations were that his domicile, as crude as the officer quarters provided were, would be spotless. The striker, a Private Stubbs, hired to cook for them, had been dismissed just a few days ago. Too much of the household silver had gone "missing".

She was more than glad not to have to deal with his uniforms. What would he think of her now, if he could see. With that thought she whipped the mourning cloth from the mirror and confronted her image. Shame and despair stared back from her face. A thin pink scar snaked unevenly across her temple, like the attempted scalping that it was, she thought. Thinking only to cut a disguising fringe she reached for the shears from her fancy sewing basket. Then in a paroxysm of despair and steely determination she began to hack away. A strange, perverse pleasure arose in her as she wielded the shears. The gleaming silver blades snapped and released randomly. She willed herself to look and, seeing the destruction being accomplished, laughed wildly. "You're gone!" she shouted at her reflection as she gave hank after hank of her tresses up to this weapon. She now gleefully attacked herself, with a savage understanding dawning on her of why the grieving Indian women hacked off their braids.

Leaving

Now that she had decided to leave a wild euphoria sprang up. She found herself practically throwing odd things into a valise. Trying to stuff a hunter's green velveteen riding habit into the already laden bag brought her to her senses. "I'm going about this all wrong, excited by this unaccustomed surge of purpose," she thought. Long accustomed to carefully considered plans and an inveterate list maker, she brought herself to the desk to record the steps that she thought she should take. But the unexpected rashness of her decision, just to leave, was intoxicating. Too many days trapped in the web of lethargy had brought her to this point. It was all she could do to prevent herself from just exiting the door unburdened by any possessions except the clothes on her back.

Allowing herself a narrow pacing calmed her. She then decided to begin her preparations by announcing them. Who should I tell, and what can I tell them exactly? That she was leaving for parts unknown, by herself? What about the dog? Her horse? A wild laugh erupted. Who would even notice she had left? Turn Foot? Well, perhaps.

These sobering thoughts brought her once again to the desk where she began to pen a note to her father. Just her father was included in the salutation, as she could not bear to even think of Polly as his wife, let alone her stepmother. Or should she send a telegram, terse and to the point, much as was his reply to the news of William and Orianna's deaths? "Am leaving the territory. Stop Thank you for your kind offer of shelter." Curt, but surely in the guise of economy a telegram suggested she could be spared sentimental greetings and salutations. She then leaned forward and crossed out "kind", in truth there had been nothing kind in his response to her loss. Not wanting them to think that she was leaving here to head back East, possibly arriving at their doorstep, she was stumped as how to word her communication. Finally she balled up the ink-splotched page thinking only, with relief, "I'll write later when I've arrived somewhere."

To think on a life enjoined once more with her father and that woman who never liked her was to enter a dense thicket where tendrils of pity and quick, sharp points of spite arose to clutch at her. The very idea of escaping those things that made her wounds bleed again shored her resolve. Knowing just how far she was straying from rational behavior in contemplating setting out on her own gave her an odd strength, like a cornered animal sensing that it's life is at stake. The thought of achieving her own freedom drove her from the desk and right to the real task at hand, packing for an adventure into her unknown future!

Why Is He In Prison?

As she was leading Wind cautiously out of the stables, Esperanza at her heels, Anah looked with surprise at the waiting buckboard, neatly stacked with bags and parcels. A tall, thin man sat with his back to her, loosely holding the reins...Turn Foot! Just when had she started to think of him as another man, rather than an Indian? This thought brought a rueful smile to her face.

Patting the seat beside him he indicated that she should tie up her little pinto to the wagon, and help the dog to clamber up. Slowly he assessed her dramatically altered appearance, from her cropped hair to the too large cavalry twill pants deeply cinched by a man's wide latigo belt. Here she was, newly shorn, in her dead husband's clothing, a tightly packed portmanteau in one hand and a small gilded cage in the other. She didn't need to ask why he was there, or how he knew. Without hesitation she lashed her pony's reins to the buckboard and, walking forward, handed her bag to the old scout who was staring straight ahead. He looked amazingly regal to her in what appeared to be some of his finer regalia. The fact that he made no comment on her radically altered appearance was a silent affirmation that he had chosen to accompany her. A grim laugh circled within her chest imagining what a strange pair they were making!

As they approached the night sentry, she spoke. "I don't know where I'm heading," looking straight ahead, the little cage balanced awkwardly on her lap. "I know," and with a few clucks moved them steadily toward the far grove of cottonwood and red willows by the creek. It didn't occur to her until much later to ponder his response. Did he mean that he understood that she had no idea of where she was going or did his response indicate that he did know, even if she didn't? As in an undreamed for consideration, the sentry did naught but nod at them as they departed the fort.

The full moon had not yet risen above the surrounding hills, but it's arrival was announced by a cold solemn light bathing the trail forward. Halting briefly, looking for the best place to ford the shallow creek, she began to open the cage's latch. Remembering with a pang the day Orianna had turned from a careful study of the canary to plaintively ask, "Mama, what did he do so bad?" "Bad?" she had replied with instant laughter, not quite understanding. But a darkening scowl came upon the child's face as she stood her ground so strongly, wanting to be understood correctly and receive the answer that would set her ever curious mind to rest. "Darling, he's done nothing bad." Clenching her little fists, her eyes narrowed, Ori queried, "Then why's he in prison?" Not knowing how to answer this Anah merely opened her arms in a mother's universal gesture of reconciliation and comfort. But Ori would have no placating, stubbornly standing her ground she declared, "Turn Foot told me that we were all born free, especially birds...so why is he in prison?"

So now as Anah sat the in buckboard, she reached into the cage, grasped the fluttering bird, held it to her soft cheek where she could feel the erratic beat of its terrified heart, quietly looked to the heavens, mouthing "Vaya con Dios!" and flung it free into the crisp air. Unerringly it flew towards the trees, the dim outlines of the fort left behind it.

Ahead rose the slabs, stones, and roughly hewn crosses of the graveyard. Without much comprehension she found herself nervously twisting her wedding band. The scene before her was especially ominous, stark shadows cast in such a spectral light. All silver and black, like an etching from a Gothic fairy tale. Stretching herself to gape at the graves, could she identify the plots where the loves of her life ended? Could she ride away, leaving them behind? A rising gorge of emotion welled up; her eyes held tears, her nostrils burned. How could she leave? As if Turn Foot discerned her struggle he lightly touched her arm and pointed to a newly risen star, flashing it's brilliance on the horizon ahead of them. A thought rose, "beauty before me..."

Her hacked off hair now clung to the cold sweat that had suddenly appeared on her face. Never one to believe in ghosts, what held her effectively barred from entering the graveyard was not fear but a chilling thought; immense to her in a newly encountered reality was that nothing lived here, natural or supernatural. It indeed was a camp of the dead.

Before she realized what she was doing her wedding ring was

wrenched from her shaking hand and flew, like an escaped bird, toward the graves. The tiny hollow clink indicated that it had struck something, perhaps a headstone. "It is finished, it's over," she sobbed. Slapping the reins, Turn Foot spurred them on. That empty hollow sound preceded her into the approaching dawn, with it's unearthly lavender and gray tints.

Neither spoke again until reaching the first true rise of the road where she asked him to halt, not being able to help herself from turning back, fearfully thinking of Lot's wife all the while. Quite sure that she was transgressing mightily, she was equally sure, in the small leaden lump of her heart, that she was doing the only thing that she could do, answering the only call that she now heard.

Pinch of Dust, Tatanka Iyotanka's Reply

Angry bolts of residual lightning fought to break through the heavy mass of departing clouds as the late afternoon storm moved off into the West. The trail up to the bluff was slick; each outcropping had a precise edge in the clarified air after the storm. On the edge looking down over the land stood a large man, his height and width emphasized by the blanket wound around him. Here stood the tribal chief, the holy man, a member of The Strong Heart Society, a Hunkpapa Lakota that the Lieutenant had traveled so far to deliver the invitation to.

As he secured his mount and left his men below, he relished the chance to collect his thoughts. Here was the warrior, yes, a warrior, not just a holy man, but a brilliant tactician of the sort he had envied while he was a student at West Point. This was the Indian who, while in his thirties, had negotiated with the U.S. Government to close the Oregon Trail, and not only that but to keep the whites out of their reservations, except for certain traders, and to keep the steamboats off the very rivers that entered them also. Why then they even burned down the forts that the army had built on their land. His was a power to reckon with. Now the lieutenant was here as an envoy to deliver a message to Sitting Bull and Crazy Horse. Those two, who had never lived on a reservation, never taken a handout from the government....

Surely the chief heard his approach. He gave no indication of it, though. As the lieutenant withdrew the document from it's pouch he read his rank and intention. Then he read the contents of the commission being assembled on September 20, 1875, on the White River, to determine the purchase of the Black Hills. He awaited a reply. Some response?

Had battle perhaps deafened him? What was protocol here? Should they have smoked a pipe? Damn, he was so new to this. He could hear the restless stirrings from below. The sun was lowering and casting a molten light around Sitting Bull, who stood like a statue, still. The chirr and chitter of the late feeding of the swallows were the only sound to be heard as they fell and swooped in the air in front of the cliff face. The sun kept falling down towards its end. Just as the lieutenant was ready to once more intone the invitation from the U.S. Government to the council, which was indeed a summons, The Bull began to speak, "I want you to go and tell the Great Father that I do not want to sell any land to the government." He then bent to the ground and slowly, tenderly, it seemed to the lieutenant, gathered something, straightened to his full height, and then released from his open palm, where the strong evening wind drove it off, just a pinch of dust.

"Not even this!" The lieutenant had his answer.

It stood forever in his mind as one of the most eloquent manners of non-compliance he'd ever come to know!

A New Frontier-Another Journey

Cold silence. Utter darkness reigned, pierced with distant, indifferent stars.

Laying back in the warm folds of the buffalo robe Anah waited patiently for the pain to diminish. While packing to flee the confines of the fort and all the memories held there she had discovered a small bottle of laudanum that she had secreted away during what she thought of as her madness. Some part of her judged that the strong desire for the drug's blessed state of oblivion was anything but madness, for it kept the demons of remembrance at bay. Tonight though, after setting up a rough camp and settling in for the night, Turn Foot somewhere guarding their perimeter, she eagerly sought the small container, and quaffed it. Her only small thought was of meeting a need. Sleep!

The laudanum began to work its seeming magic, softening her awareness that she was a lone white woman out here on the high plains just as the seasons fell towards the Solstice, her only companions an aged Cheyenne scout and a small white dog. She felt its effects this time not as a desperate attempt to medicate her losses, but as it streamed through her blood, an offer of calm determination to credit herself for abandoning the only place out here that she had called home. She began to think that it was an inherent and intuitive wisdom, this running away. What she was running from she knew all too well; what awaited her she could not begin to imagine.

As the drug continued to cocoon her mind she let a warm wave of gratefulness rush through her heart. The night's cold did not disturb her, she was free to focus on the sky above her. This winter sky seemed aloof, almost frightening in its majesty, whereas the soft nights of summer with the Milky Way glimmering like a gauzy wrap thrown across the velvet night felt close and comforting. As was her habit she began to search for the Pleiades, but there were so many, many icy sparkling points above her. Besides, her eyes were beginning to lose their focus. Recalling now how intimidated she had felt all those years ago when, with her father and the baron as they traveled across the plains, she had felt so tiny, insignificant, longing for four solid walls to encompass her. She had grown into the vastness, the endless rolling horizons, and now as she lay back and allowed herself to enter into the sparkle and brilliance displayed in the the vast bowl of the heavens she lay beneath, a thought came to her. Another journey lay ahead even if the destination was unknown.

Today they had skirted the Badlands, or Mahko-seeta, unsound lands. She had heard of this uninhabited area, covering miles and miles of the plains, but she was not prepared for its bizarre magnificence. The terrain was unique, and unlike the oddities of The Yellow Stone, with its bubbling mud pools and geysers, this land was utterly stark and seemingly devoid of life. Turn Foot proved that untrue when he returned with some plump quail to roast. But then the old scout was quite capable of calling the evening's meal to him, or so she found herself believing as she witnessed him preparing for a hunt. It wasn't magic, but a type of prayer offered up in ritual preparation, she had come to believe. She thanked God for her food only when she bit into it.

When they had paused at a promontory, she gazed in awe at the vast landscape of strange formations and colors. Hues of tan, ocher, and yellow, with bands of orange circled the many, many layers that erosion had revealed. Here and there a bright sunflower appeared, sheltered from the seasonal winds. Arid, dusty and forlorn. Swirling dust danced across expanses of land that held no river, he had told her. She wanted to camp here, anticipating the glorious hues that the rocks would be bathed in as the sun went down. The Rockies were indeed higher, not even truly barren at their peaks, but crowned with snow. This place had no lush green mantle of aspens and pines. It had an odd allure. The longer she gazed out on this land where dust dominated, the stronger a sense of morbid atmosphere came upon her. An ominous sense of foreboding, an unseen but palpable darkness. All glistened in the harsh, brilliant light. So strong! How can such a brightly lit landscape feel so dark to her? When Turn Foot snapped the reins she eagerly turned her back on the landscape, but it had haunted her mind the rest of the day. So intense was the feeling of foreboding that she wanted to ask him if he also felt this way. She had no words to broach the subject of ghosts.

After such a good meal, one she felt a bit proud to grace with a sweet, made from a precious jar of peaches in her Dutch oven, Anah relaxed, gazing into the velvet darkness. She had grown into being comforted by the vast and open spaces of which she was now a part. She could even summon a shred of hopefulness tonight, that is, if she could imagine just what to hope for. "I am not looking back, but looking up," her last thought before sleep came upon her like a breath that rose straight to the distant stars.

Pickings from the Plains

Halted by the tracks, they were awaiting the passing of the Union Pacific that was roaring past them. Turn Foot, his huge mule, Waagol, hitched to the buckboard, was composed, but Anah, at first distracted by trying to calm Wind, began to note the contents of the open, slatted cars thundering past them, for they were filled, floor to ceiling, with bones. Buffalo bones! Ghostly white for the most part, from where they had lain under the intense sun out on the desiccated prairies. Stripped clean of hide, tendon and flesh, nonetheless, they trailed an unmistakable odor.

Death, devastation and deprivation, they both knew what these rattling cattle cars represented. For Turn Foot it was proof of the strong medicine of the white ant people, whose swarming upon the plains brought the end of a way of life for the People. These cold metal tracks that at first had divided the great herds into two parts, northern and southern, now served to help transport even the last remnants of the buffalo from their ancestral grounds to the factories back East.

Huge ricks of bones sat jumbled, some as high as ten feet, waiting transport to a fertilizer plant back East. As the hide trade disappeared with the buffalo, the collection of these sad remains left scattered on the plains provided a little cash for those settlers waiting out the harvest from their first crops. These bones were the only pickings left.

"A man can never have enough ponies," Turn Foot spoke calmly. Anah could not think of a rejoinder to this aged warrior, once a Shirt Wearer among his people. Besides, she did not know exactly what to make of his dispassionate remark, as they sat waiting for the train to pass. What could she say to account for this greed and destruction? How could she get him to understand that the rewards and constraints of her culture were so vastly different from the plains dwellers. What was commerce and cash to him? She ached to tell him of her response the first time she had been served buffalo tongue at an engagement party at Old Bedlam, back at Ft. Laramie, when she had been so naive. Her revulsion at the remembered sight of the huge fly-blown humps of skinned creatures whose lives had been taken to provide only a delicacy for the table and left to rot conveyed little to a man whose taking of life was a sacrament.

Wordlessly they waited the passing of the cars, given to the endless possibilities of silence, as the bone laden freight rattled past, car after car after car, then moved silently out onto the barren plain.

To Winter Camp

"the present had stood firm once more!"

Traveling with the old scout was remarkably easy, Anah discovered. She realized that she trusted him implicitly to determine their route; when and where to stop for the night, right down to the smallest details. One of the first things that he did was to remove the horseshoes from Wind's feet, feeling no need to explain why. And she trusted him. What a relief to give up such concerns to another. So when it came time to set up their meager camp she did her best to provide small comforts. When it was discovered that, while he had brought coffee, sugar, flour and her beloved dutch oven, there was no mill with which to grind the beans. How clever she felt when she took his stone club to pound the beans to a fine texture in the cast iron skillet in which they had been roasted. Cups; he had remembered to pack two heavy white porcelain mugs. How she hated burning her lips on the army issue tin ones. The third night out she discovered, wrapped in toweling, peaches she had canned. She glowed with pleasure when Turn Foot arrived back bearing a young hare for their meal to lift the lid of her oven and release the perfume of the cobbler she had made in it with those peaches. That night when she retired to her bedroll, her appetite well satisfied, she felt a pang of guilt, for she had been enjoying herself. It was not that her lost ones were not on her mind, but rather that the painful past had, for once, taken a back seat to the events of an actual day. The present had stood firm once more!

The days were crisp and the nights cold. They were heading slowly south, but if Turn Foot had a destination in mind he had not informed her. Perhaps he meant for them to simply wander. Out here what had first seemed empty and bereft of life save for the incessant soughing of the wind through the dried grasses and the occasional spotting of the pronghorns on a rise were actually rich with diverse life forms, if one knew how to look, and Turn Foot did. It was as though he were doctoring her spirit by pointing out, to her untrained eye, the clever struggles waged by those living out here in this harsh environment.

Without a word, but by his calm presence, she felt he was teaching her something.

She had never traversed this particular terrain before, not in her short forays taken from Ft. Laramie. She understood the unspoken wisdom of avoiding any common trails where they would encounter army patrols or other parties. Almost daily she had seen old fire circles, and even horse and riders outlined up on a small ridge or swale. Turn Foot had shown no concern; she was content with this.

As they continued to ride away from the foothills and out onto the vastness of the open grasslands she had ample time to reflect on how different her experience of the plains were compared to when, so many years back, she had first been brought across them with her father in Baron Von Westenhagen's party. She remembered affectionately teasing him by calling him "Count One-Two-Three". She could not imagine nicknaming the old scout, though.

The devastation that oppressed her young self that came so unexpectedly upon her when their wagons rolled out onto the great plains and the last vestiges of familiar landscape receded behind her she could not account for. The words "vast", "infinite" and "immense" had a different meaning to her then. When she had first stood on the shores of the Great Lake Erie and looked out on the endlessly receding horizon she had been exhilarated at its apparent boundlessness. But that was water, now they were moving slowly across endless waves of grassland.

The Count, noticing her unusually quiet demeanor questioned her. "Why so glum, my little plum duff?" Blurting out, she responded, "I feel so small!" " Well, you are the smallest in our party." Testily, she snapped, "Not in stature. Be serious, I mean inside, in my soul," touching her palm lightly to her chest, a bit embarrassed by this disclosure." "Ah yes," drawing his magnificent catlinite pipe with its beads and horsehair dangles from its much decorated pipe bag. Carefully he began packing the small bowl, "Are you afraid now that we are on the plains of the natives that reside here?" "No, no, I want very much to see a real Indian, you know that." Truly, it was what had occupied her thoughts most of the time these days, for she wanted to see the regalia and artifacts that had been the inspiration for her father's abrupt decision to travel westward in actual use. "Are you afraid to die?" The Count continued, "for the Indians aren't. It's an honor to them to die in battle. They are becoming most weary of our white faces, you know?" What she had grown to adore about this titled man was that all subjects were open for discussion. Ones like "life", and "death" and even the very word "soul" were hardly common elements of speech.

So much time had passed since then. The open prairie had indeed abashed and humbled her, though it was months before she could give name to those feelings. The great bowl of the sky commanded one's attention, drawing one's thoughts heavenward in a way that she had never quite contemplated before. To her, a daughter of the foothills of Appalachia, meadows were open spaces, plowed fields, vast terrain of closely wooded hills, and carefully cultivated orchards . Out here on the Great Plains she felt insecure, not safe, not from men or animals but from the very clouds that came swiftly towards her; the infinite depth of the blue skies above, the endless rolling swales of grassland, mostly empty. Yet she had grown to love this land as no other. She was beginning to understand its timelessness as much as was within her grasp. Her very pain and grieving seemed smaller and containable.

Most night the stars were a comfort, the constellations now familiar, but sometimes those heavenly bodies seemed shatteringly cold, remote, alien and oddly cruel. They were inanimate, ever distant, and in that thought loneliness crept close.

Nahtona

Clear, crisp days and cool nights under the stars of the Moon When Blackbirds Gather had such an effect on her. As they crossed the plains to an undisclosed location she began to come alive to her thirst for discoveries of the smallest sort. In the fall of the year there was not much in the way of riotous bloom, dry as it was, so that each small cinquefoil, nestled in a seepage caught her appreciative eye. Not only did she begin to awaken to small beauties, but the unexpected brought thrills, like the exultant bugling of an elk in full rivalry for a mate.

In the excitement and audacity of just leaving, simply packing up and riding out, she hadn't given too much thought to Turn Foot's presence, of why he had chosen to accompany her. Her gratefulness for that presence increased day by day. She began to look forward to stopping for the night, to have her opinion considered in when and where to make their little camp. They worked so well as a team, and under the stars he began to slowly speak of such fascinating things; tell her stories much as she imagined had been told to the children gathered at the feet of their elders to learn by the light of small campfires such as she and Turn Foot now kindled.

She knew that in the past William had arranged for the old scout to be her guide, to see that her curiosity as to her new surrounds would be safely satisfied. As she roamed further and further afield, frequently visiting various encampments near the fort, she suspected that Turn Foot's presence was not only for her protection, but for diplomatic reasons. His presence, knowledge and guidance paved the way for, invariably, gracious social interactions with the various new groups of lodges that she chose to visit.

Occasionally he was called out on an actual scout, and she risked William's censure to go unaccompanied to the nearby Arapaho or Cheyenne camps. As her command of the language and social customs grew she found herself welcomed by the women, at times accompanying them to gather chokecherries, *monotse,* as they called them. In turn she brought them some of her preserves and bread to go with it. Many times she had brought Orianna along, that is, when she deemed it appropriate, for she wanted to instill in her daughter the same love and fascination for the things that she herself treasured.

How grateful she was that the old scout hadn't been with her that fateful day of the attack; she doubted that he would have survived. Quickly she pushed that thought away; it did no good to dwell on the past. An image of the child, strands of her red gold hair clinging to her sweat drenched face appeared, unbidden. Pale Calf Woman had gifted Ori with a child's digging stick of her own so that she could also be occupied as they dug for the deep roots of the *tipsianna,* prairie turnip. The fierce, concentrated effort the child was putting into rooting for her prize had caused her mother's heart to swell with pride that day.

Tonight there appeared a thin-horned moon, her favorite, hung like a simple jewel in the black sky sparsely studded with icy stars. Knowing that their camp for the night was secure, they had settled down by a fire, strong flames leaping brightly, with the unaccustomed strength of having been fed with the large pieces of wood they had gathered earlier from a lightening-struck cottonwood.

Turn Foot was working contentedly on a drawing with the colored pencils she had once gifted him with. He had an old ledger book propped on his knees. Anah was hoping that someday she could obtain for him some real drawing paper. He hadn't actually shown her his work, but she had glimpsed enough of it to hope that someday he would not only show the drawings to her, but explain them. Turning to a blank page in her Commonplace Book she began transcribing the events of the day, hoping to capture those things that were important to her, and her alone. Things like discovering that buffalo berries were sweeter after they have been touched by the first frost, or that the white sage which abounded here was the same as the legendary wormwood, or mugwort. She was slowly beginning to retrieve a part of herself that once she had passionately nurtured. Collecting and classifying the flora and fauna, seeking both the medicinal use and edibility of the life surrounding her. Wondering why she had ever left her Pharmacopoeia behind. *The Doctrine of Signatures,* the belief that plants have a sign or signature that indicates what ailment or part of the body they should be used for was becoming a reality to her. As her ability in Lakota and Cheyenne language grew so did her knowledge of medical botany. She had only her notes from Rafinesque's *Medicinal Flora* to go on now, but Turn Foot was eager to help her. Just today he had told her that the milky sap from spurge indicated that its use was to increase the milk flow in a nursing mother. The days and nights were being woven together into a fabric that she imagined as a sort of cocoon, a chrysalis she hoped that she would emerge from at some point, transformed.

The air was perceptively cooler. The deep fathomless blue of the overarching sky was gradually losing both depth and color as it seemed to lower down upon them. Soon they would need to find a place to shelter in for the approaching winter. She so wanted to inquire of Turn Foot if he had a destination in mind, but as she had given herself up into his care, she found it easier to simply trust him. He was a guide, she told herself with confidence. Her usual small frets and worries lifted from her; she felt as a child, secure without caring for her own safety or well-being, not needing to know how she would be provided for or how her needs would be met. As to her needs, she found them delightfully spare: food, shelter, warmth... and, she looked with affection across the golden flames to where Turn Foot was working, *companionship!*

So much had changed since the day she had plucked the orange and black butterfly from the edge of a seep where she had gone to collect water in a buffalo bladder. Lost in contemplation of its drowning she startled to find Turn Foot crouching down beside her. As he held out his hand; she carefully transferred the insect, and sat back to anticipate she knew not what. He too, sat, and held the still gorgeous creature out before him. He began to talk:

The Souls of Lost Children

When I was still a boy a group of our finest warriors returned from Commancheria, bringing not only fine mounts, but a distraught boy of my own age. He had been stolen from his own people in the south of the Rio Grande, enslaved and roughly used. Over the ensuing moons he was given much freedom, and adapted well to living with us. I surmised that perhaps he received better treatment among us than with his own family. There is no need for me to mention of how the Comanches had used him. He seemed to have a gift for languages, and soon was able to communicate so well that he eventually became a beloved Story-man. He proved to be no good as a warrior, for he had been dominated and broken in his spirit for too long. Besides, he had a most gentle nature. Seeing you rescuing this butterfly made me think of him once again. I do not use his name for he has gone on before, as so many of my people have. What I wanted to tell you, and I wish I could weave the same telling of it as he once did, was of his people's belief that these beautiful winged creatures were the souls of lost children who had died that very year....

At her sharp intake of breath he stopped and handed the small thing gently back to her. "I did not mean to pain you," and he began to rise, saying rather mournfully, "I have also brought the weight of sorrow to myself, for when I look upon the young children in our ragged camps these days, no time for the ceremonies, the lessons, the stories, but living in a constant state of being chased and attacked, I feel like I can see their souls drifting as lightly as the downy seeds of the cottonwoods, blown here and there by the winds of chance."

Anah did not see him for the rest of the evening, and turned in, bringing Esperanza to sleep at her side. Alone in their camp she did not give a thought to her safety, for if the truth be told, that night she simply did not care. Sorrow rode her swiftly into a heavy sleep.

So many years ago, when she was with her father, they had assembled in St. Louis, where they were to meet the Baron, before crossing over the mighty Mississippi, she had been full of nothing but eagerness for the trip ahead. She felt a wildness in her young spirit and a sense of destiny that perhaps she would find an entirely new life. It was the spirit of the time. Her little party were "Outlanders", moving out across the prairie and onto the plains. In the short time spent in the city on the banks of the great, coiling river, the jump-off point for those heading west, she discovered that their traveling simply for adventure made them, in the eyes of others, outrageous. This was the time and place to bid adieu, to venture into the unknown. Excitement simmered in her, like a tea kettle on to boil. Yet so much had transpired since then, and now she was traveling into the unknown once again.

When she woke the next morning it was to the bracing aroma of freshly boiled coffee. Turn Foot beckoned her over, pouring out a cup as she rose. How often she had marveled at his presence in her life. So often wondered why he was there with her. In the days of dependence on the whiskey and the laudanum she sometimes thought he was sent to her, one of those "angel unawares" the Bible mentioned. Now she simply wanted to know. Once she had assumed that it was due to some beneficence on William's part; some debt that his presence as her guide was repayment for. While Turn Foot had accompanied many forays of the army, traditionally the scouts themselves did not participate. As an adjutant, neither did William, except that fateful day! The heaviness that washed up on her at the thought, the confused assumptions accompanying William's death, caused her to abruptly find a chore to fully occupy her mind. Picking up her digging stick and hemp bag she announced that she was going foraging.

The sun hid itself behind a dull scrim of dusty looking clouds, obscuring the near horizon by the time Anah returned to camp. She was in a good mood; bearing several choice roots of soapwood. She thought to present some to Turn Foot knowing that he drank a few drams of an infusion made from them to alleviate the pains of age. In fact, he had informed her that the results of this type of draught consumed several times a day sometimes caused arthritic pain to subside for good. She had quickly noted this down. In her linen handkerchief she bore plump red rose hips; there had even been a lone valiant rose still on the bush. Much as she had wanted to pluck it, she left it there. Valery Harvard, assistant surgeon of the 7th cavalry, also a trained botanist, had informed her father that the use of just a few of these rose hips, chewed or in a tea, would prevent the dreaded scurvy. As she made her way she determined to broach the subject of Turn Foot's accompanying her. She held no satisfaction in not knowing, nor the fact that their destination was unknown to her. To wander and roam aimlessly was against her nature, pleasant as it had been so far.

Roasting on a spit was the rather large carcass of a skinned jackrabbit dripping juices into the small fire. When their evening meal was accomplished, and the dishes well scoured with sand, she brewed tea from the rose hips while he picketed Waagol and Wind. As Esperanza settled down contentedly at the scout's side she stirred a full teaspoon of their precious sugar into his cup. Tasting its sweetness he smiled up at her.

Now I will make my case, she thought. "Turn Foot," she declared emphatically. He gave her his rapt attention. "I,"...beginning to stammer on exactly how to word her query, and what words to use, in what language, she paused. He set his cup down carefully, took his hand from idly stroking the dog, "Ummn," he responded.

"Turn Foot," she began once more. He nodded encouragement. A sting of exasperation rose, "he knows that I'm trying to broach a difficult subject," she thought. Just as she was ready to give up this matter, she surprised herself by blurting, "Why are you here?" He regarded her so calmly that she felt like reaching forward to slap his face. How dare she be so tongue-tied and he so seemingly comprehending? He said not a word, regarding her, expectant in his posture. "With me?" she almost shouted in a rising fury, "Why here with me? What are we doing? Where in God's great earth are we going?" rumbling her words out, practically in frustrated tears. *"Why....?"* she began again, only to have him gently raise his hand to quiet her.

"Exahe, Nahtona! Exahe!, "a great grandchild, you would call him. It was him you sheltered with your body that day." And like a cold glass of water unexpectedly dumped on one's head she understood, but barely. The scout was referring to that horrible time that she thought of as a massacre, when she had been so cruelly attacked. He must mean the young boy she had tried to shelter with her body, but had this child not died? She was sure she had seen a fatal volley rip into him. Futilely but instinctively she had pushed him down and threw herself over him; for was he not the same age as her own child? ..who was also..... A wall of red began to rise like a mist before her as she resisted recalling the scene.

Then he was at her side, gently lowering her cup from where she had been clenching it. Seating himself next to her he was speaking slowly, sonorously, almost hypnotically, it seemed. Words swam through the mist, but was she hearing them? Was it even him speaking? His great grandson? Who had been his mother? Not Pale Calf Woman?

The beading circle that day came into focus through the red mist. The close circle of women, mothers, aunts, daughters with their severely braided black hair striped with bright vermilion down the center part, gleaming in the soft light as all quietly worked. Small children crawling around, cradle boards hung with drowsy infants, an iron pot softly bubbling over the crackling fire. The good smell of pinon smoke enveloping them all. "Anah?" She felt his bony hand on her shoulder. "Anah, *nahtona*, my daughter", he shook her gently. On recalling this later she did not know if he had spoken to her in his tongue or hers, or a mixture. She could not recall the exact wording either. Hadn't he told her that she did not think as a *wasichu*, a *ve'ho'e*, a white-man? That her heart was as red as blood, that he had been told to protect her as she had intuitively protected the child in her path? Had she not reacted from her spirit to protect little Walking Elk? How did she know his name? Surely Turn Foot had not broken tradition and pronounced the name of one dead. Did he not call her his daughter? *Nahtona!*

From that evening forward their relationship changed significantly. Now she knew. Now she knew! *Nahtona*, though he never addressed her as such again, she remained from that day forward related in the best way possible, by spirit if not by blood.

The Coffee Ceremony

When they had been traveling for a while, so that they had developed comfortable routines with one another, both in setting up and breaking camp, she began to discern an odd habit, or ceremony, that always accompanied their meals.

She observed that upon finishing his cup Turn Foot rubbed his hand quite thoroughly onto the dry ground; not necessarily a strange habit. However, he followed this with moving his extended hand over the cup four times. Always four passes over the cup; it must be a symbolic gesture in one not seemingly given to much elaborate ceremony, she thought. That evening, after a good meal of a fat Prairie Hen and a skillet of corn bread, Anah brought his sugared cup of coffee to him and watched carefully for him to finish. One, two, three, and on the forth pass of his lean weathered hand over the mug a remembrance of customs stirred in her and sprang to her lips. "Who did you kill?" She blurted abruptly out.

Before she could soften her rudeness he replied. "I've taken life from many. You know that." He rose to return calmly to a nearby rock and seated himself. But he looked, not to her, but into the now empty cup in such a manner that she proceeded with her questioning. "Murder?" she posed as a question. "Who was murdered; that was the Cleansing Ceremony," she stated emphatically, now sure of her deduction, for would that not explain why he lived apart from his people?

"Your words fly like arrows through toughened hide," said not in reproach. "I will speak of this now. I begin to see wisdom in a woman's way of opening her wounds to others. Many times it is like cleansing a wound of its...putrefaction?, is that the word?" "Putrefaction, like spoiling of meat," she quickly replied, trying to urge him with her eyes to continue.

Continue he did, telling his story in a calm manner, of how a once honored Shirt Wearer of the Northern Cheyenne, who was also a skilled member of the Mad Dogs, came to scout for the army out here on the high plains.

Turn Foot's Defection

"their hearts held more than ample tinder"

This is the story the old scout told Anah, wherein a *Wicasa Wakan,* an honored Shirt Wearer of the Tsitsistas, lost that privilege, becoming a self-imposed outcast for the act of murdering another Cheyenne.

"In the Moon of Heat Waves on Grass when I was in my prime, I was struck down and defeated by an enemy that I had yet to encounter in all my years since achieving full stature as a man. You would simply call it lust, a must-have-now response, but as a Shirt Wearer among the Northern Cheyenne there was to be no place in my heart for such a feeling. From refraining to eating any part of the first buffalo I had brought down during the feast to celebrate this important passage into adult life, to giving away most of my spoils from a successful raid, I was to demonstrate the principle that others wants and needs came before my own. These values of the prophet Sweet Medicine I had naturally accepted, having learned them as readily as I learned to pull a bow and mount a pony. They were my chosen nature."

He continued speaking quietly into the descending darkness. Shadows from the small campfire danced across his face. He told of assembling with the tribes for the annual New Life Lodge ceremonies of renewal, blessings and communion with his brothers. He had a fine string of Crow ponies; a few buffalo runners, and a spirited war horse among them, to give away. The youngest of his two wives, Sweet Grass, had just birthed a son. Another child was deemed healthy enough now to be given a first name. He raised his face to each morning's sun with pleasure and anticipation. Yet an unforeseen destiny awaited him here that would darken too many of his days.

Mid-morning on the third day of the encampment, as Turn Foot was walking back to his lodge, he paused to let a group of women bearing *wasna* cross in front of his path. Normally he would have strode on, but he was deep in thought regarding a certain pinto that he wanted his kola, Red Heart, to receive.

Was it an accident that Sly Otter, a young wife of Blue Hawk, a woman so valued that thirty ponies had been added to her father's herd for her, stumbled, spilling her basket of fine berries? Eyes riveted on the rich red carpet of fruit upon the path, he paused. The woman sunk to her knees and began to carefully pick each berry up before it would be trodden into the dirt. He had no obligation to help, but a strange inclination found him crouched beside her.

The berries flew into the basket with two pair of hands so intent on the task. When their hands accidentally touched their eyes met, and held. Seeing this great beauty, another's wife, so close before him that he could feel the richness of her waist-long hair, shiny as a raven's wing as it brushed across his bare arm. The enveloping sensation such a touch had immediately aroused in him caused him to try and abruptly stand and take his leave, not noticing the red stains across his chest. But she did! Leaning forward, she began to wipe his chest with her sleeve. Taking this as an unwanted sign of subservience he swiftly grabbed her wrist, ready to tell her that this was not necessary. They again looked into each others face, just as he mistakenly called her "Sweet Otter". At that she laughingly responded, naming him "Straight Legged". Thus their story began to unfold. That second glance was but a spark; unbeknownst to them their hearts held more than ample tinder.

An indescribable instant of recognition that travels to the stars, circles the poles then wrenchingly stops so suddenly that one gasps in recognition of what has happened...we have met a kindred spirit and stand, expectantly, holding aloft a burning brand. Such illumination!

Desire flowed from each like two streams in freshet rushing to their confluence. Her small hand on his chest described slowly descending circles as she rose to her full stature before him. Each felt as though their very breath had stopped, finally exhaling into the fascinating face before them. Just as their paths had crossed, a promise now hung in spectral air hovering above. She was slow to avert her eyes, slower yet to remove her hand from his bare chest where her touch was branding him. A most welcome fire raced through him down towards his belly.

Wordlessly he broke away, uncomfortably aware that what seemed like a small lifetime had passed in a few short moments. When he turned back to look once more upon her she was no longer standing there. It mattered little, for now her image burned like a coal within him.

As he strode along, conscious on one hand of his duties and responsibilities, he was on the other hand like an arrow nocked with great intention, seeking its aim, the woman, Sly Otter! The thought of having her was held in his mind like a rainbow trout in a frozen rill, all its great beauty held suspended; his for the taking. He began to imagine how he could bring her to his robes. Consciously aware that she was another's was too easily set aside, so great was the desire that now rode him.

Blinded, he was being led by this passion into a narrow valley surrounded by sheer granite bluffs. But what was implicit, held in his mind like a juicy slice of buffalo hump ready for the fire, was that when he summoned her she would readily come. That knowledge made him dizzier than he had ever been, even more so than when an Absaroka's wicked blade had been held inches from his throat.

So adept and composed was he externally that no one seemed to notice his passing, or that his greetings were delivered absentmindedly, no one, that is, except Blue Hawk, a jealous husband. Something had drawn his eyes to where his wife had knelt, face to face with another man, clawing in the dirt of the heavily trodden path. He hung his shield on the lodge and carefully watched. Was there some duplicity in Sly Otter's movements? This was a warrior with mustang-like jealousy, and war trained senses. Was something amiss? A late afternoon storm was plunging forward with towering, lush, purple-bellied thunderheads. The slight breeze that sprang up to scour the grand encampment swayed the securely wrapped medicine bundle on its tripod in front of his lodge. The cur that had been content to lie in its shade now slunk hurriedly off.

Blue Hawk was accustomed to his wife's great beauty, and the inevitable envy that was sent his way, but his wife's virtue was without reproach, as was required. But he knew what the raw look upon their faces had meant, and went to seek out the shirt-wearer, ready for a confrontation. Turn Foot had no right to even gaze upon her like that.

Curtains of chilling rain suddenly burst upon the encampment, obscuring vision, causing most to seek immediate shelter. Perhaps if

Blue Hawk had not sought out the older warrior and accosted him with words that stung his pride, Turn Foot's hand would not have been bloodied, nor his wisdom lost.

The body lay carelessly behind a downed cottonwood log, his neck twisted unnaturally. What had happened occurred so swiftly and in such a rush of angered passion that Turn Foot could not even account for it. It seemed ludicrous and shameful. He simply walked away, dazed, for there was no bringing that life back.

A life had been taken in the wrong way; he could not seem to divulge the truth to himself. He had no recourse but to leave; no council to seek. For a Cheyenne to take the life of another Cheyenne even accidentally merited banishment, to go outside the camp. He had wanted her so badly, and that had been revealed. But this outcome had brought an end to what both had desired to begin and meant full well to accomplish. Blue Hawk's intervention had succeeded at a great cost to all.

A holy man had said that it is in the dark where they cannot see that men get lost, and a time of great darkness began to descend on Turn Foot, who, even in his confusion, knew enough to strip his shirt, his special identity among the people, and cushion it beneath Blue Hawk's head before fleeing. He was an honored member of his tribe no more. A Dog Soldier that knows no retreat was now leaving. He was now an outcast! *He'joxones!* The Putrid One, to be shunned by all.

A lone man would have difficulty on his own. That was punishment enough.

Braids

While Turn Foot went calmly about greasing the axles of their wagon, Anah took the water bladder down to the miserly run of the creek. As she crouched, patiently waiting for it to fill, she idly glanced around at her surroundings. They were somewhere in the vicinity of the Republican River, near the Smoky Hill Trail, a country so beautiful that she easily understood why the Indians resisted moving away. The thicket of aspen, cottonwood and willow was beginning to turn golden from the frosty nights. There, in a niche of a sandstone overhang, grew a still flowering daisy. The strong, perfect yellow of its bloom had drawn her eye. With her task done now she was ready to return and begin the business of setting up their camp, but something about this small bloom caught her. Securely fastening the neck of the container she sat back down on the sandy soil of the creek bank. The sky was the unclouded deep blue of late Fall. Her immediate surroundings were so peacefully quiet that she could hear the trilling ripple of the water as it made its way over the shallow creek bed. Feeling secure, her thoughts wandered.

Anah found herself on a new footing with her traveling companion, as that is how she thought of him. This intimacy was not just due to burgeoning fluency in his language based on immersion, but due to the circumstances of their lives that found them together. She had no name for this other than love, based as it was on respect and the understanding that Turn Foot's story of how he had come to be a scout wrought in her.

Jerking herself into awareness at the clarion call of a crow she realized that she had been lost in a seemingly mindless place. She had lost track of how many days they had been traveling, realizing that obsessive thoughts of her loss had somehow lessened just in the passage of time. Idly raising a hand to her head, she fingered the wild chunks of her remaining hair as though she could somehow judge the passage of time by estimating its re-growth. No, her head was still shorn! And just like that she was transported back in time, ambushed by a recollection.

She had returned from one of her visits to the small native encampment beyond the fort. It was the first time that she had taken

Orianna with her, secure in the knowledge that no harm would befall her, for on a previous visit she had carefully observed how the small children were treated. She had envisioned little Ori stayed close to her skirts, venturing out to greet a curious mongrel, avidly absorbing all the new sights that surrounded her. One child of an indeterminate age had walked up to Ori and stuck out a buckskin clad and beaded doll, an exact replica of an adult, right down to the fringes of its garments and tightly woven braids. Without hesitation Orianna grasped the doll to her little chest at the same time extending, in exchange, her much beloved and rather tattered velveteen doll, dressed in crisply starched and pressed lacy gown and petticoat. Ori's doll had no hair left on its head, beloved to baldness by its owner. Each child was quite thrilled with its toy; the mothers equally pleased to have witnessed the generous exchange, although Anah sincerely hoped that the dark hair fringes on the buckskin clad doll were from a horse, not human!

It was later that evening when Anah had gone to fetch Ori for supper that she found her settled on the porch with the new doll, her own golden hair roughly portioned into messy braids. That alone thrilled Anah, but it was noticing that some of the canary's feathers had been carefully tucked in that gave her the realization of how much the child wished to imitate what she had seen. Orianna turned her sweet round face up at her mother for approval!

As the recollection of that day swarmed over her in its intensity, she gasped, "Oh, Orianna." The sound of the name that she had so disciplined herself not to utter out loud seemed to swell and echo around her in this shady glen. She felt her heart clutch and harden in painful remembrance as once again the child's name crossed her lips. "Oh, Ori! Ori!" The grief and loss fought its way up, wrenching out of her throat in a ragged sob! Torn between containing tears or allowing herself full grievance, she began to rock, her arms wrapped closely around herself. Empty arms! Empty! Fumbling in her pocket for a handkerchief she noticed that the Bull Terrier had come quietly up to her, and now lay prone at her side. Gratefully she began to stroke the animal as scene after scene of Ori's short life moved through her recall. She heard an animal-like moaning, realizing with a shock that it came from her.

She felt wild, confused, volatile. Leaping to her feet, astonished at how much she wanted to harm herself, to punish herself, to have real pain to deal with. Now I understand how those women grieve by slashing their arms. I could do it, and stretched out her hand even thinking that she could lop off a digit, as some had done. Physical suffering would be a blessing! Then a wild laughter ripped through her; the creek was not deep enough to drown in, her knives were back at camp. What a weak, silly woman she was, "Aren't I, Esperanza?" addressing the somewhat alarmed dog, that had risen to stand ready. Wiping at her eyes with William's shirt tail, she resolutely picked up the water bag to head back to the wagon, telling herself that she must, at the very least, learn to carry a weapon upon her person.

Towards Winter Canyon

Later that night, as Anah relaxed at the fire, drawing a blanket over her shoulders as the temperature began to drop, Turn Foot began to talk to her in the quiet fashion that let her know he had given his words much thought before speaking them.

"Once our loved ones have taken to walking the Starry Path, we keep their life on this earth in our hearts. We may tell of their honors and deeds, but we do not let the names they once owned to pass our lips." Anah knew then that he had heard her grieving down by the creek; she began to assemble the right words to defend herself, but the old man gently laid a hand on her shoulder as he tossed a small branch into the fire where it quickly flared to ash. He continued to speak as he looked, not at her, but into the fire. "A name is given to us, or earned. Some of us carry more than one name as we walk through life, but," and he paused, still not looking at her, "once we depart those left behind do not call us back. It is futile. Is that the right word? Hopeless?"

Anah, fearing to speak over the rising lump in her throat, merely nodded, then realizing that he wasn't looking at her, softly uttered, "*Hownh!*" to show her agreement. He continued in his fine English, "We do not name the dead because we are to forget them, but their name spoken once they have departed is spoken into a void." He then spoke in Cheyenne, immediately translating, "The name of the dead, when spoken, springs from our heart, like a child torn from its mother's breast." Drawing his buffalo robe tighter around him he moved to seat himself across from her. A deep silence naturally reigned. The dying fire cracked, snapped and ebbed. The wind could be heard gathering strength. Anah understood. They sat content as the stars moved above them. Turn Foot finally broke the comfortable quiet. " We will move southwest in the morning. We will go to Winter Camp in the canyons. It will be good for you, pale daughter. A small place north of the heart of the southern buffalo range, the place of the Chinaberry Trees, a small secretive place. You will like it, my *nahtona!*"

"Turn Foot, do you fear dying?" He seemed not to have heard; perhaps she had offended him, his customs so different from her own.

Just as she struggled with a properly worded retraction he began to speak. "To die is to move from one place to another. Think of the nursing child when taken from the one empty breast is dumbfounded, angered, desolate or perhaps trusting and patient..only to be moved by the one who loves it so to the fullness of the other." He pulled his blanket around him in such a fashion that she knew not to comment. "Braves", that is why they are so called, she realized with strong insight, for they did not fear death.

Knowing that the Month of First Snowfall would soon be on them, Turn Foot assiduously applied himself to heading south. Moving at a much faster pace than previously, he was gratified to note that Anah not only was able to keep the pace, but that she issued no complaint. As the temperature dropped and the north wind began to seek them with increasing determination, they crossed the Arkansas, far west of Dodge City. It had been his intention to avoid, not only enemies and military, but civilians also. From the reports he had overheard back at Laramie he opted not to cross the Canadian River and move across the Staked Plains, Llano Estacado, to enter the long and deep Palo Duro Canyon on the Prairie Dog fork of the Red River. Running forty miles in length and over 800 feet deep, it had been a shelter for many families and their allies for years, providing sufficient pasture and enough cottonwood and cedar for their needs. That is, if they arrived with good stores of dried meat, snug lodges and warm robes. He had seen to provision their departure from the fort with ample supplies, not only for themselves, but so they could share generously with others. A few others, not the hundreds that traditionally sheltered in the Palo Duro, for many of the southern Cheyenne and Kiowa stayed close to their reservations now, dependent on the government issues.

Turn Foot was leading them for a much smaller canyon on the Upper Cimarron, at the northwest border of the Commancheria. The nearest military installation was due east of them by 150 miles, Camp Supply. The old scout's presence was often ignored; the assumption being that his silvery braids and much lined face denoted an aged sensibility. Nothing was further from the truth, consequently he was privy to many plans laid out by the commanding officers under which he occasionally served. He knew that the Army was committing itself to a major change in tactics; the so-called "Winter Campaign". He had sent warnings of such southward, intending to simply avoid the Palo Duro. Colonel "Bear Coat" Miles and Colonel "Less Fingers" Mackenzie's cavalry were to be avoided.

As they left the Colorado Territory and began to traverse the rugged landscape signaling the approach to the Staked Plains, he took pains to assure Anah that he was not leading them astray. He had every intention to keep them safe. She trusted him, although the developing starkness of the terrain they were entering cast a chill upon her heart. It was a feeling akin to being too far from home, but ruefully, she had to acknowledge, no such place now existed for her.

Cimarron Canyon

In spite of leaving the northern territories behind, the beauty to which she had grown accustomed, and moving south into a more arid and desolate landscape, Anah was heartened by the prospect of being amongst a band of natives again. Recalling the richness of her first experience at entering a camp circled up for ceremonial purposes, as when her father and she had traveled with the Baron, she grew excited. She knew that the encampments that had surrounded Ft. Laramie were not ideal; too many "loaf-abouts" and the interaction with the life of the fort diminished rather than enhanced the culture she so loved. But here, where they were heading, she imagined a freer, more natural life style. Their contact with the tribes had been minimal; Anah understood that Turn Foot was moving them as inconspicuously as possible. Of course their existence was known; nothing escaped the far ranging "wolves", but their little party posed no threat. Occasionally a mounted form was seen on a far hilltop, and they often found a small haunch of antelope left by their campfire. Once they had even been blessed with a few buffalo ribs; as scarce as the roving herds had become in the last few years, this was quite a gift. So Anah knew that there was no animosity toward them. Since Turn Foot had occasion to disappear at times she imagined that he even had direct contact, as he knew when to avoid any army patrols. Not that anyone would be looking for them, an old Indian scout and an army widow!

As the terrain became more bleak, moving away from the dark green forested hillsides of the Divide, crossing the large tributaries of The Platte, Arkansas and Canadian, she found herself imagining the hide lodges glowing from the hearty fires within, some of them elaborately covered with pictographs of battle exploits. Outsides would be, to her, whimsically decorated, buffalo hump shields and the mysterious medicine bundles arranged on their tripods, their colors alive in the morning sun. And the clothing, skillfully beaded in the hues of the earth. The war bonnets! The scalp shirts! All the richness and splendor that native creativity provided.

Thus it was, on a fine sunny day, the sky a depthless blue, not a visible cloud, marred only by a constant chilling wind, when they began the approach to the canyon. Two young warriors on fine steeds had approached within a half mile of them out on the plain and Turn Foot had signed them in. A pipe was passed as Anah sat quietly apart, respectfully constraining her curiosity. When the men remounted they were to follow. What had Turn Foot told them? Who did they think she was? What of her affiliations with the military?

All these concerns swiftly left her mind as they entered a narrow defile between walls of stone that appeared to have been sculpted into place, rising straight and elegant far above the sprinkling of aspen still holding their golden leaves. A faint smell of wood smoke came to her, and though no lodges were in sight she grew ever more expectant. They began to follow the narrow trail that wound along a small brook, whose black water wasn't black at all, but crystal clear, icy cold, running over smooth round pebbles. High above the canyon walls soared a falcon. The crisp, sweet smell of dry, fallen leaves rose up as her horse trod through them. The place felt magical. Her heart loosened within her chest, for their very surroundings were a promise of shelter. No wind, there was no perceptible wind with these sheltering walls; what a perfect place to winter. As they moved along she saw that there were ample deadfalls for firewood. Firewood! She would not have to scour around for old buffalo chips. Cottonwoods arched over the streams, laced with willows, the sweet smells of ponderosa, and was that pinon? Her excitement grew as they descended.

Far up the canyon the lodges sat in chosen places along the stream. Most of them were made of the government issued canvas, but a few were still buffalo hide. There were drying racks strung with meat. There must be game, she thought, though there were few dogs. She saw no women bent over hides, flensing them, but there was a deer strung up from a cottonwood. Children were running, laughing, and women moving to and fro carrying water and wood. She had forgotten that there would be children, and a pang ran through her as she averted her eyes from a young woman most obviously pregnant.

The Protective Shell

We think of a shell, a casing of any sort, as protective of what lies within. Indeed, this is for the most part truth; consider the shell of a mollusk. Once broached its inhabitant succumbs. Why even a leather satchel is utilized to protect the contents placed inside. But consider the husk of a seed, protective yes, but exposed to the right elements it weakens only to release its contents and allow growth and fruition. We all are familiar with the thought that the mightiest oaks from little acorns grow, and I assume are not too impressed, but when this process occurs within the human heart; when the protective shell is surrendered, or broken, we stand amazed. Such is what happened to Anah, locked away in her loss as securely as a trout frozen in a too shallow pool come winter. All that she had constructed to isolate and protect herself shattered when one grieving heart looked with understanding and compassion into her eyes. Was not Turn Foot adequate? Age and gender stood between them, but another woman bereft of her child and husband? Well, let Anah tell us......

My Commonplace Book Winter 1874

We had been in the small camp less than an hour when a young woman came to stand before me. She did not speak, perhaps not knowing if I would understand her, but I later came to believe that her burning intention was simply to gaze into my eyes, thus beginning a startling chain of events in my life. Her nut brown, narrow face with the high, sculpted cheekbones and dark, slanting, almond eyes declared her as one of the beautiful people to me, a Cheyenne. I seemed to know this face, but ducked my head, for an intensely strong aversion to remembrance swept over me then. Incredible rudeness on my part, nonetheless she stood quietly in my presence. Flustered, I tried to compose myself, aware of being a stranger here. Then in a most graceful motion she stooped and laid a small wrapped bundle at my feet before moving off in a stately fashion. Not a word had been exchanged between us, yet I stood frozen, dumbstruck, lacking all comprehension. Finally ashamed at my inhospitable reaction I jerked my head up, but could not bring myself to call her back. Besides, I knew not her name. My head felt light. Dizzy, I bent down to circumvent a faint as much as to retrieve what she had left at my feet. Glancing furtively around, it seemed no one had witnessed this exchange, and I opened the package. Therein lay a small strip of buckskin beaded in pleasing colors. As I stood with it in my hand a realization crept over me, the handiwork was my own, of Iroquois design. I had begun this that fateful day back at Ft. Laramie when I had been mistakenly and brutally attacked! I had sat with the women of the Beading Society, thrilled to have been invited, proud to show off my knowledge of a native design, eager for acceptance. The half-worked strip had fallen from my lap when the first alarm rang out and we fled for our lives. But now here lay my beading efforts; the unfinished, abandoned strip had been carefully and accurately completed.

Like ice water a sudden realization drenched me! Shuddering with recall...that woman, she knew me, she remembered me, she had been there that day, had sat next to me, guided my hands in the intricate beading. She too survived! And I had driven her off, left her gift at my feet as unacceptable, and seemingly denied her presence before me. Shame flooded me, its heat preparing me to flee. Turn Foot appeared at my side as though bidden. "Grass Bending Down," he said, "she is the one we no longer name's sister."

It was imperative that I find her and make amends. I went to my Gladstone bag to search out a small gift, finding none but the cameo at my neck I began to unfasten it, but stopped, as truly I could not bear to part with it. So bearing my treasured dutch oven I sought her out! Cast iron was a much sought after trade item by the young women in the camps. This time our eyes met; it was with a mutual understanding of loss, of the subsequent pain of survival. Living when wishing to die, the flesh overriding the much diminished spirit. For as we stood, hands clasped, looking into her eyes, I saw by her hacked-off hair and the multiple scars on her forearms that her loss had indeed been great. I, too, had shorn my head. I had not attacked my flesh with a knife, but assaulted myself with the laudanum, then the alcohol. Murder had reigned in me, too. These things I had done to vent my grief-scarred soul.

Invited into the lodge of her brother-in-law, Pale Calf's bereaved husband, I saw the empty places; no elders, no children resided here. She *gave me a seat of honor and served me amply from the pot. I could feel the warm tears streaking my face; I did not understand their function then: a warm spring rain that precedes germination.*

That day, in its simplicity, had magnified a transition in my life. I had been so alone with my loss, so walled off, resisting the formal overtures of condolence from the fort's society. I received no succor from my own surviving flesh and blood. Then Turn Foot had so mysteriously and solemnly befriended me. When I dipped the carved horn spoon into the thin broth at Grass Bending Down's lodge, I partook of a family life once more, or at least a sisterhood forged by loss. She had not only lost a child, but a husband and a sister, I was to learn as Turn Foot sat with us to translate the difficult parts. The toddler, seized and roughly snatched from her feet that calamitous day had been Grass's child. Pain shared, the tragedy that had befallen us that day now served to bond us. Am I here to stay? Is this to be my home?

The Turning Season

High on the cliffs the escarpments, free of melted snow, shone golden in the afternoon light. Anah was strolling up into the canyon, following the clear Cimarron Creek. Magpies, a bird she had grown to love for more than its showy black and white plumage, darted in and out of the cottonwoods that lined the watercourse. As she slowly progressed, her presence was announced by the rattling call of a solitary kingfisher, which occasionally rewarded her with a flash of its strong blue plumage. It was unseasonably warm for mid-winter here in the shelter of the canyon walls. She benefited from the native dress she had eagerly adopted. She had even been given one of the lush winter-coated buffalo calf hides to wrap around her shoulders. Seated on a downed log in a shaft of sunlight she allowed the babble of the creek to soothe her; the rustle of the few remaining aspen leaves to add their special music as well.

"I am content," she thought. Sitting so still and feeling sheltered here down in the small winter camp among people who readily took her in, Anah allowed herself to doze. A knife in its beaded sheath hung from her waist, soft fawn moccasins, grass stuffed, and embroidered by her were on her feet. If you were to come upon her you would assume that she was a native, except here in the winter sunlight her hair blazed as the rock faces far above, a frothy nimbus of golden curls.

It had been easy for her to lose track of time, especially as she had once ordered her day at the fort where, rarely being far from a bugler's call, one knew the hours of the army way. The weeks traveling with Turn Foot had been structured by few urgencies: where to camp for the night, the next available water to be reached, the forage for the horse and mule, and these were easily met, it seemed. Here there was little routine other than what the movement of the sun provided; up at first light, to bed after darkness as one wished. These people rested, well deserved, from the rigors of the nomadic months. There would be no new forays or raids until the grass out on the high plains was lush enough with new growth to fatten and sustain the horse herd. The children played, the women beaded, the old men crafted arrows, men went out to hunt for small game, young boys stripped cottonwood bark, and stew pots always bubbled for the hungry.

At first she was utterly charmed by this opportunity to live among them. In so many ways it differed from her experience when she had been an occasional visitor to the camps surrounding Laramie. Now how proud she was when entrusted with the smallest chore; how eager to learn the proper way of doing things, from drawing water to preparing a meal from dried roots and jerked meat, for she was treated as belonging, not just a visitor.

She had fled Ft. Laramie, there was no other word for it. Indeed she had been running since what she thought of as "The Loss". Anah had been fueled by the oblivion that the tincture of opium provided, then the wild carelessness of the whiskey bottle, till she had the courage (Was it that?) to actually up and leave. But now she had arrived; had been living here for many weeks, the season had turned completely, and her birthday had passed. She was more than a bit unsure as to the exactness of the day, and it little mattered. The snows had come, and now winter, too, would pass.

If one can be blinded by love, so grief can blur the vision, distort it completely. Wanting revenge against what had happened to her, she had selected one man as its target, and failed to extract it. She had been so locked into the rage, loss, and grief that escape seemed the only solution. She now saw how self-centered she had become, and how Turn Foot had led her away from a painful world. Now she inhabited his. Had her shell cracked, or had she simply grown out of it? With what felt like new senses she observed the life of the camp. She saw that many here had experienced adversity and loss. Theirs was a poverty of possessions, not of spirit. Perseverance, dignity and adjustment were being practiced. She slowly understood this as she knew of their lives and losses. Above all there was consideration and concern, they looked after one another with no rancor. Their way of life, the trading, hunting, and raiding, the glory of the warriors path, had been impoverished. This group had not gone in to live by an agency, but the circle had been broken. What did they have to trade, with no replenishment of buffalo hides to tan; the southern plains were nearly devoid now of the huge roaming herds.

The coughing sickness, as they called both pneumonia and tuberculosis, and even starvation had come to them with regularity. Babies and old ones had frozen to death as they fled from the armies, their lodges and possessions burned, their ponies slaughtered.

Turn Foot had his own small lodge, and not of canvas, but of hide. She had assisted Black Wind Woman in erecting it, and much to her delight, she not only found herself residing in it with him, but acting as the woman of the hearth, as she thought of herself. A young girl, Sees The Berries, at first brought water and kindling, tasks that Anah now gratefully performed. Many an evening Turn Foot held forth at the fire, young and old gathered to hear him talk. What he shared at council fires with the chiefs she heard later in the women's circles, none of it alarming. These people were not hateful, vengeful or bitter, they just desired to be left alone.

Winter was a season of rest and renewal, the talk of the army's "winter campaigns" not heard here. Nor were they seeking justice; they had learned not to expect it from the *ve'ho'e's*. They would flee as necessary, they would protect, they would nurture.

Many an evening, warm and fed, seated by the fire, a buffalo robe would be brought and rolled out to reveal beautifully made and colored pictographs, a "winter count". Its history was told to eager listeners by the elder whose job it was to keep count. It was on such a night that she first heard a recounting of the Cheyenne prophet Sweet Medicine. Here, in this camp, the aging medicine men and elders performed, sang and told of the traditional way. Sadly, Anah noted, few warriors were present. Many had gone beyond protecting the old way, and a few hot bloods had gone north to add their strength to those camps of those the army called "hostiles".

The Story of Sweet Medicine, A Cheyenne Prophet

Anah wrote in her commonplace book one evening of the story of the young boy born into the Cheyennes named Sweet Medicine. The name alone had intrigued her, but more than that the story had the ring of a true prophecy. As in many stories, Grimm and Andersen that she was familiar with from her own childhood, the young hero traveled on his own. In this case to the Black Hills, the sacred Paha Sapha, and spent time underground with the Maiyun, the mysterious ones; she did not know how else to describe these supernatural beings. He was taught much and, of course, brought it back to his people. He could change himself into many things, the "trickster" that she found so prevalent in all of the tribes tales. He brought a herd of buffalo to them also, but what intrigued her was how he spoke of the future, and the values he spoke of. He asked the leaders to be men of peace, well, if she understood the language correctly, to be "peacemakers", and indeed many of the leaders were named "peace chiefs".

She was careful to consult with Turn Foot for the exact wording that she entered as a direct quote, "You chiefs are peacemakers. Though your son might be killed in front of your tepee, you should take a peace pipe and smoke. Then you would be called an honest chief." Sweet Medicine not only organized their society with councils and warrior divisions, but exhorted them to lead an honorable life. Of course, she had learned that exile was the punishment for murder. But what was riveting to her were the words that had been attributed to him on his death bed. Again, she noted these carefully, thinking, does the army know of this?

Sweet Medicine had said, "Listen to me carefully. There are all kinds of people on earth that you will meet someday. Some will have black skins, but most will be white with much hair on their faces and strange clothing on their bodies. These people do not follow the way of our great-grandfather. They follow another way. They will be people who do not get tired, but who will keep pushing forward, going, going, all the time. They will be looking for a certain stone.(she wrote in the margin, Gold?) They will travel everywhere, looking for this stone which our great-grandfather(Creator?) put on the earth in many places." She was amazed to learn that this prophet had lived before the horse arrived on the plains, and yet foretold that strangers would bring an animal with a flowing neck and tail that they could ride upon. He also told them to expect changes that would not be as wonderful as the horse, saying, "they bring something that makes a noise and sends a round killing stone, and that with it they will destroy all the great buffalo herds, but these strange men will eat another animal with white horns." He told them that these men would tear up the land, and bring strange things to move up and down the rivers and across the land. But what chilled her most were the words,.... "They will try to change you from your way of living to theirs, and they will keep at what they try to do."

Once she had heard this she tried to corroborate it, but oral traditions were so subject to amendment. She listened carefully and when she heard the retelling she wrote in her book. "The buffalo will disappear, and another animal will take its place, a slick animal with a long tail and split hoofs whose flesh you will learn to use."

This prophet had no solution to his dire prediction but to admonish his people not to forget what he taught them and to follow the laws. If they did forget his teachings he warned they would become "worse than crazy". He had also spoken of strange sickness, sticks that spit fire, a special hat and arrows. There was much she couldn't quite comprehend, but this much was very clear ....the coming of the white man had been predicted, but, interestingly, there had been no call to war, but a resistance of the spirit, a clinging to the old ways...which she could see was becoming harder and harder to do.

The Story of Big Crow, Leavetaking

As Anah walked back from the creek with fresh water for the evening, drawing her robe closer against the descending chill, she heard a distinct wavering cry and looked up in the rose colored sky to see a skein of migrating geese heading north. "Winter is loosing its grip," she thought, the days lengthening quite perceptibly. Most telling of all was the coloring up of the willow bushes along the draws, vigorous red with a deep yellow shooting up their stems. She had even found some yellow-green spear-like leaves thrusting right through the rotting snow under the southern cliff faces. They looked a lot like what she had called skunk cabbage, the first plant to come to life after the winter snows in the foothills of the Appalachians.

Walking slowly back to the lodge, she once more contemplated what the new season might bring for her. Once the grasses thickened enough out on the plains so that their horse herd could be sustained, this small band would begin to move back north themselves. She counted herself a member, though no formal overtures to adopt her had taken place. From all that she had learned while residing with them she had no desire to return to a life out here as an army widow, nor as a frontier person of any standing. She had grown quite comfortable with the children, and felt she could be of use with teaching them English, at least, if they so desired. Her coloring; the pale golden skin, flecked now with freckles across her nose, the sea green eyes with the orange flecks, combined with hair not only golden and rosy, almost like a sunset, but wondrously curled, had make her an object of fascination to the young children. At first she was uncomfortable being stared at, let alone having her hair plucked to see the springiness of a loose curl. Now, though, she was no longer a curiosity, but "A-Nah" as much as they had become Sits In The Night, Yellow Nose, and Little Coyote Fox to her. She kept herself busy, trying to live neither in the past, nor in the future, but now with the sign's of spring's imminent burgeoning she started to look ahead to the disbanding of the winter camp, and to speculate on her future.

It was in this gentle, mulling mood that Turn Foot found her, seated at a small fire, working on her beading. He had been gone the last few days scouting, she assumed. Being a Wolf, for that is what they called it when it was for their own tribe. She sensed that his leaving Ft. Laramie with her was concurrent with a decision to end his service to the U.S. Army, though they had never discussed it. Once he had reclined upon his back rest, she served him from the pot she had learned to keep full of something and simmering. Setting it aside he reached for his pipe bag, a concerned look upon his face. Anah knew to wait quietly while he made the tobacco offering; she also knew that he would smoke a while before speaking.

"Anah, my daughter," he began to speak so abruptly that she startled, half rising to her feet as though an intruder was at the doorway. "General Sheridan may yet bring his winter campaign to us. We must leave." Yes, he had been back across the plains to the forts, it seemed, or had information from another scouting party. "Yes, *ate,* father," she addressed him thus, without thinking it unnatural, "We will be leaving soon; the willows are coloring up, the geese flying to their nests." He held up his hand rudely, for he wished to halt her attempts at normalcy and get on with his unpleasant news. Seeing that he had startled her by his unusual abrupt delivery he settled back, indicating for her to do likewise from where she had risen. Once she had settled down on the sleeping robes he made to continue.

"I have a story to tell you. I know you understand that we do not leave our winter camps and are safe from war and raiding parties during the months of snow. But the Great Father, as he is called back east, has made many changes in our lives by his ways, even if we chose not to follow them. To the white-man we Indians are as hard to discern one from the other as blades of grass. Listen to me now.

Ten winters ago, at Ft. Laramie, the soldiers hanged a Burnt Thigh by the name of Big Crow." She knew not to interrupt his telling, though he paused now to refill the pipe. "This peaceful Indian had been accused by a white woman who had been captured previously by some other "Indians". After she was ransomed, on her return she passed through the fort and pointed out this peaceful Indian as the one who had killed her husband. He was dragged, unprotesting, wrapped in chains, and hung on a newly erected scaffold outside the fort. Before a large crowd this was done. There had been no trial, but Big Crow had never left the fort. He could not have been the man who had abducted her and murdered her husband, but he was an Indian!" Where was he leading with this? Anah searched her memory for such a story, for she, as the adjutant's wife, had been privy to much gossip passed on as history, of the fort in its previous incarnations. "Just a moon later, two more Indians were also hung, members of the Spleen band of the Oglala."

She was trying hard to connect the parts of this story, assuming that what bands they were from was important. "These Indians were accused of mistreating a white woman, but the post trader told the authorities that these men had actually paid to rescue her from the Indians who had actually captured her" " Did he mean ransom?" she wondered, or was she sold as a slave, a question she did not know how to tactfully ask. "Two Face and Blackfoot, for that was their names, brought her into the fort themselves. The words of the trader meant nothing and these two Oglala went to the second erected scaffold singing their death songs. The Commander ordered that the bodies be left to rot as an example of "all Indians of like character". Anah was very confused by this story and was horrified when Turn Foot was finally able to explain that the woman who had been captured mistakenly identified Big Crow, who was subsequently hung.

"Why are you telling me this?", she blurted out, alarmed and confused. What did this mean to her? Her mind did not comprehend, but her pulse was racing and her chest felt constricted. "Tell me, father," she practically begged him to be uncharacteristically direct.

Turn Foot said, "We must leave, at first dawn. The word is out among the forts that we are holding a white woman captive in our camp. The adjutant's widow from Ft. Laramie has gone missing, and it is believed that you are that captive. They will ride out to rescue you." "Oh," Anah gave out a soft expulsion of a sigh of relief, "Don't worry, when they come I will simply tell them that I am here of my very own free will, and not a captive at all. Besides, I have no connection to their army any more." She was greatly relieved; she thought there might have been a genuine concern, and rose to put water on for tea. "Daughter," the rebuke sprang from his lips. She froze, her back to him, to listen, the water bladder leaking a bit on her moccasins as she stood rooted in place, such was the authority in his soft voice.

"Yes, they will come to rescue you, but over our dead bodies. You think that they will ride into our camp at daybreak while we sleep in our robes and politely request an audience with our "prisoner"? It is their way, shoot first, kill all that moves, burn the lodges, slaughter the ponies, empty out our dried provisions, and then ask questions. Big Crow, Two Face and Blackfoot are only names to you, unknown men, but listen now to the story of Lean Bear, a prominent chief of our Southern Cheyenne who had pledged to keep peace with the *wasichus*. In the hunting ground near the Smoky Hill River where many Cheyenne and Black Kettle's Lakota were gathered to hunt for much needed buffalo meat, for it was past the Moon of First Thunder and our parfleches were near empty, a party came across a large column of Blue Coats, a Lieutenant Early in charge. Lean Bear rode boldly forward to declare the peaceful intentions of his men, his large flashing silver Peace Medal in prominent display upon his chest and in his hand a paper signed by Father Lincoln verifying his peaceful status. Just a few days earlier a band of Cheyennes had been victims of an unprovoked attack because they were suspected of rustling horses and cattle, so Lean Bear rode forward to present his credentials. Before he could, he and his kola were shot from their ponies. Wolf Chief, who had stood witness to this unprovoked attack said that "the soldiers rode forward and shot them again." Of course, this brought about an immediate confrontation and more lives were lost senselessly on both sides. No food was procured that day, bitter animosity the only drink. Seeking vengeance is an almost unquenchable thirst."

Anah slumped to her robes. The loud coarse chuckle of an owl seemed to mock her. She wished to be left alone to reason this out, but she knew Turn Foot was right. She must leave; there was no way she could be responsible for jeopardizing these people. To appear whole and unscathed at Ft. Sill would protect not only them, but other bands in their winter camps, she assumed.

Turn Foot, who had sat quietly, now spoke. "We will leave with the first light." Not being able to bring herself to speak for the lump in her throat, she only nodded, not able to meet his gaze.

Arrival at Ft. Sill

Following Turn Foot in single file out of what had become, for her, a beloved sanctuary, she looked back into the canyon whose narrow walls were yet to be touched with sunlight. A surreal blue light prevailed, heralding dawn, but giving her a feeling of unreality, as though waking up, but into a dream.

The few lodges still in sight glowed softly from the fire lit within, luminous like golden candles. A picture of serenity, the only sound the burbling of the icy water flowing over the pebbles in the stream. The early morning chatter of the black and white magpies flitting from branch to branch had yet to begin and the nightly chorus of the little wolves had long lapsed into silence. Night was preparing to relinquish the earth to day, a natural acceptance that Anah found herself still struggling mightily with. Her departure not only was sudden and unexpected, but it felt forced. Here she was preparing to ride into the arms of what she had begun to think of as a foe, returning to an army base. Her escaping breath rose wraith-like in the dim light.

Remembrances of those previous winters spent at Laramie assailed her. As the snows would come and the high mountain passes close, a halt came that brought an end to the constant stream of emigrant traffic through the fort. The days grew cool, the air clear and crisp. While some of the Indians left for winter camps, others arrived at the agency once the fall hunts were over and their renewal ceremonies concluded. Inter-tribal warfare and raiding ceased till the prairies greened up again in the spring, giving a needed respite to the troops at the post. It was a good time for Anah to go on her visits to the nearby encampments. How she had loved that.

Then the deep cold descended, holding her a prisoner of sorts. An unholy cold sometimes descended, one she had no familiarity with. Those long nights in the depths of winter she lay curled next to William with the child between them, hearing the distant snap and pop of trees exploding from their sap freezing in the depth of the coldest nights. How did the animals survive, she would wonder? When each long western winter on the plains finally released its iron grip she had looked forward, with the eagerness of a child, to the first tender blossoming and greening signs of spring. What joy had sprung forth in her to see the renewing of this vast land.

She was now on the journey she had once so imagined, traveling once again out of the canyon onto the open prairie, but this small band that she had been accepted by and grown to love, she must now leave. Trying to understand that it was herself that posed the threat to these people she had begun to love and live with so agreeably left her taut with a rigid sense of isolation. To return to the governance of the U.S. Army was not just painful, but distasteful.

Regretfully she had folded her winter robe, moccasins and dress to leave behind. It would not do to give any indication that she had actually lived among these people, for she could not be questioned as to their whereabouts. The thought that she had to leave without a good-bye, to disappear, was required, for it would not do for them to have any knowledge of her whereabouts, either. She rode along in a stupor, barely noticing their arrival on the plains that stretched out in a barren winter's desolation toward their destination in the south, Ft. Sill, Indian Territory. When Turn Foot drew them to a halt the sky in the east was painted in the soft, muted colors of the dawn. The land rolled away from her on all sides, matching the vast openness of the sky above.

Nothing, nothing disturbed the singular horizon stretched out before her….no shelter, no tree, no signs of life, no black roaming clouds of buffalo, not even a solitary antelope buck, just dry, withered grasses tossed indolently by an indifferent wind. "This landscape," she thought," matches the desolation of my heart!"

Yet she moved along, a new type of brokenness invading her, for she had only to look to see that this land was fiercely beautiful. Empty! Empty of what had been dear to her these past months. It had an everlasting glory to it, the slight rolling hills now bathed with the light of a breaking dawn. The unending barrenness had power and magnificence that was totally independent of her, of any life, really. The beauty of it, the stripped quality, the vastness, that emptiness was filling her heart in a most unwanted way. Not just her heart, but her whole being, her mind emptying of a certain consciousness of who she was and what she meant in face of this impersonal beauty. Truly as it was said, only the earth and sky last forever! A small, sharp thought pierced her; if only Orianna and William could see this. Deep in her breast she felt her heart lay small and cold; what had she to feed it with but memories?

IV

Capture

Take! Eat!"

Gold From the Grass Roots Down

"One could say that the advantage was all theirs!"

Rising prominently out of the rolling vastness of the Great Plains loomed a large black land mass. It would appear, to one approaching it from east of the Rockies for the first time, like an island in the midst of the ocean. The Black Hills, Paha Sapha to the Lakota, Mo'ohta-vo'hona'aeva to the Cheyenne; so named because of the thick blanket of trees covering its hills. It's the axis mundi to the nomadic nations that dwell on these lands, or as they say, the sacred center of the world and is revered in legends and myths told by firesides generation after generation. By treaty carefully forged in 1868 at Ft. Laramie, whites were to be kept from settling here "as long as the grass grows green", and so pen was touched to that piece of paper!

But there is something that breeds unquenchable desires and lust in those men described by the Cheyenne prophet Sweet Medicine as "having hair on their faces that even grows down over their lips". Gold! That glittery stuff, even the slightest rumors of which brought miners invading these hills in open defiance of the treaty. The Indians, of course, did not tolerate it. Sherman proclaimed that any whites found in the hills would be driven out at gunpoint by the army, but it was like trying to dam a flood, one that only increased in volume and fury!

Just two seasons had passed since the Moon of Red Cherries when Custer, the Long-Haired Woman Killer, had violated the treaty and entered the Black Hills with more Blue coats than ants upon a honeycomb, 1,000 soldiers to be exact. As their encampment on Hidden Wood Creek was watched it became apparent that they did not come to destroy any lodges, in spite of the Big Guns that the mules were dragging, but they brought another kind of harm, men who came to dig into Mother Earth and find the yellow stone, the soft kind, too soft for proper use by the People. When Custer reported that these hills were filled with gold "from the grass roots down", that report was subsequently published on August 12,1875 to a nation barely recovered from economic depression. It meant the death of the 1868 treaty that was to have kept these hills inviolate "as long as grass shall grow". But then gold, though a soft metal, has always been stronger than words! A Professor Jenney, geologist, headed another expedition to verify that the hills were a veritable mountain of gold. California Joe, a Western scout, agreed, and the rush was on! So much so that the Great Father back east immediately made plans to try to purchase the hills that held such stones.

    Now problems began; how can one buy what cannot be sold? That did not prevent the white men from wanting what they couldn't have; the Black Hills! What did ever stop them? Spotted Tail took himself off to the Hills to see for himself. He found Colonel Dodge and a Professor Penny sent by the U.S. Government, making sure that the reports of the gold assayed there were correct. Indeed they were, but the People were in no mood to sell their sacred medicine ground. Over seven thousand Indians agreed to this in council and were quite adamant about it. There were, of course, so-called Peace Indians, like Young-Man-Afraid-Of-His-Horses, who advocated a calm response even as weapons were being brandished about. Spotted Tail was no fool, though gold was worthless for arrowheads and spears, he knew it was valuable. "This hill is our safe. We want seventy million dollars for the Black Hills." Red Cloud thought that cattle should be provided for many, many generations into the future. Little Big Man rattled his lance, full of hatred at any thought of compromise. It was known that Crazy Horse, who wouldn't attend, was staunch in his belief that one does not sell the ground that one walks upon. No agreement was reached, and many divisions were formed among the People at this time. The whites were crazed for the gold, and the Army was maddened with trying to protect them from the wrath of the Indians. There was a general failure at protecting what every side thought was of value. Those four letters, g-o-l-d, caused men to swarm upon the land, hell-bent to seek and make their fortune, no matter what the cost.

    In just a few months eleven thousand fortune seekers had invaded the Paha Sapha, the sacred Black Hills. A rough town named Deadwood sprang up almost overnight. The Indians preyed upon those fortune hunters when they could. A clamor went up for army protection even though they were in violation of the treaty. Finally a grand meeting was called to take place on September 20, 1875 on the White River, near the Spotted Tail and

Red Cloud Agencies. Military, traders, Cheyenne, Arapaho, Sioux, all the leaders, even missionaries, non agency as well as agency Indians were invited.

Ready to parley, the commission was assembled under a flapping tarpaulin strung to a wizened cottonwood, the lone tree on the open plain. The 120 cavalry were most welcome on their white horses when they arrived from Ft. Robinson, as there already were throngs of Indians; thousands. They had been assembling for days and pitching camp. They came from the Missouri country, from the Bighorn, and they brought their family and their friends; a mighty show of strength. They milled around, many warriors, dressed in regalia, painted, with feathers and weapons, too. Some rode in fiercely brandishing lances, war whoops just to create some drama. A few fired rifles into the air, some ululations from the women. They moved restlessly behind the neat rows of the cavalry and kept moving restlessly. Spotted Tail rode up in a buckboard. Red Cloud never arrived. Sitting Bull had sent his answer on the wind. No one expected Crazy Horse, but just when the whites' nerves were really aquiver a war cry burst out and in rode Little Big Man, Crazy Horse's envoy, two Army Colts stuck in his breech clout, dancing his mottled gray war pony in front of all as he shouted out through gritted teeth, "I will kill the first chief who speaks for selling the Black Hills!" then he was gone. Nothing good did come of that assembly once calm was established!

In December of that year the Interior Dept. of the U.S. sent word that all Indians, mostly those in the Powder River environs, were to come in to the reservations by January or be considered hostile. It was a very severe winter; why should they leave the comforts of their buffalo robes? Why come when there were still buffalo to hunt; to struggle down to an agency, with its paltry provisions, where everyone knew food was scarce? "We want to sit in our lodges with the laces drawn tight while the winds howl and blow enough wind from the parched brittle grasses so that our herds have little to eat besides peeled cottonwood bark. Why expose our frail newborn and weak elders to the brutal cold that even mocks those already upon their burial platforms? We will come when the snow melts, at The Moon When the Green Grass Comes Up," was the reply. "We want to have peace with you. We are not full of cunning like the little wolves. My words are straight, my heart is single. We have no where else to go. We will not flee."

The chief had spoken, and they settled in for the long, snow-bound winter in the hills, draws and sheltered canyons where the piercing fingers of cold probed incessantly for them, as was their custom.

Back in 1871 General Sheridan had issued orders forbidding Indians west of the Mississippi to leave their reservations without permission. Gradually this came to mean, "stay on the land we wish to keep you on! Do not leave to follow the game as you have traditionally done, not even when there is none to hunt on the land in which you now reside!" But how were they to replace their lodge poles when they came only from a place far to the north by the Rocky Mountains, and when the buffalo herds migrate to the north as they do every summer? They needed to replenish their clothing, the skins for their moccasins, the food in their parfleches, and to trap new ponies. It soon became a matter of staying on the reservations or disobeying to meet these needs. Those that left were to be considered "hostiles".

If those that left the reserves could have done so quietly, as many did, and simply gone on their way unaccosted, all might have been well, even though the great herds had been so vastly decimated, as well as the minor game depleted by the many thousands of migrant trains passing through the land. It had been decided back in Washington, and orders passed on to the various Army posts and agencies, not to give any errant Indian off reservation a rest, but to pursue him, or them, relentlessly. No more could they retreat to their traditional winter camps in secluded arroyos to prepare caches of dried food, repair clothing and lodges, sit around council fires and recount tales passed from generation to generation, and just rest themselves until they, and their herds emerged again in the spring when the grass grew high enough to feed their ponies. No, they would be pursued by an army that was well clothed in long coats of buffalo hide against the winter cold, with ample food and ammunition brought along in supply trains. Of course, these soldiers had no encumbrances such as women, children, and aged folk to protect or concern themselves with. A large body of Crow scouts, the traditional enemies of the People, were brought along to hunt them down. One could say that the advantage was all theirs! The pursuit was unrelenting; total harassment, and by March 1875 the last important group still at large of the so-called hostiles on the southern plains, those avoiding coming in to the reservations, those desperately trying to live as they had always lived, struggled in under Stone Calf to the agency at Darlington. The agent there said of them, "A community more wretched and poverty-stricken than these people presented, after they were placed in the prison camp, would be difficult to imagine.

What Happened at Sappa River

A long hard winter of shattering events that broke the expected cycle yet again brought the young Dog Soldier, Medicine Horse, to this position. Defeated, he had suffered this in battle before in confronting the *wasichus*. Wounded, his body bore a multitude of scars that befitted his position as a leader of men. Bereft of property, in this he was like his fellow warriors that shared among one another what little they had freely, but held captive, that was never borne before. Not only captive, but "ironed", hands and feet bound in shackles with lengths of chains. Now he lay on the cold stone floor of an unfinished ice house, open to the elements, along with 103 other warriors. They were at Ft. Sill, Indian Territory, what the People called the Soldier House at Medicine Bluffs. It was the Time of First Thunder, 1875.

Pain woke him; by long practice he forced it away, though it continued to whine, "Feed me, now!" Quiet. "Warm me!" He ignored it, trying to draw his body into a curl, though a sharp jab below the ribs said, "Not that way." Forcing his eyes tightly shut he felt the weight of his shackles increase a hundred fold, as though he might be dragged beneath the ground. Trying then to sit up, the chains upon his wrists mocked in grating laughter, while the leg irons burned ever colder. "I am going mad." It seemed he could still hear the agonized screams of the dying as they were being clubbed to the ground at Sappa River. The ululations of pride of the women when he rode in from leading his first war party, the dull thud of the howitzers, and now the drums, yes drums and taunts..the women screaming of their cowardice...he tried to lift his arms to cover his ears, but fell back to begin a meaningless chant, a prayer for oblivion. He would not open his eyes. He could not be here. He was no longer who he had once been. He would not speak the name of the dead! He had died back there; that Dog Soldier known as Medicine Horse was no more! He quickly thrust his fingers once more into the wound in his side. The flash of pain as it washed over him sent him down, down, down into the blackness that he so desired.

Coming to he had no idea how long he had been out. Now it was night and quiet. His wound throbbed in such a manner that it obliterated all other concerns. Probing, he found it wrapped with, of all things, the remnants of his sacred Dog Rope. There, curled nearby, lay Walks Lightly. In the faint light he saw no visible injury upon him, but that he, too, had the heavy shackles upon his thin bony wrists and ankles. A thin snow fell from the dark sky above. How had they come to be held here?

Just a short while ago they had been traveling south of the Platte River in northwestern Kansas, a place where there were hardly any buffalo left roaming. Not that they were hunting. They certainly hadn't expected to run into hide hunters with their dreaded long ranging guns. They had been most careful to skirt the ranches and farms, and to avoid any areas where the Bluecoats were most like to be on patrol. They kept well clear of the agencies and reservations, of which there were many between their usual rendezvous with Red Dancing Crane Woman's informants and the safety of the Powder River camps. They were on their way back north, bringing valuable information regarding the planned campaigns and forays that would affect their People. A simple sighting could send a message on the magic string, the "telegraph" that ran on the tall lodge poles that followed the Iron Horses to pinpoint their movements. Now any Indian seen off reservation was deemed a "hostile" and could be shot on sight.

They had run into a small band of fugitive Cheyenne on the banks of the Sappa River and decided to camp for the night with them, enjoying the company. There were but a few warriors, mostly women and children, and a *wicasa wakan*, Lost Heart Wolf, who wore his long gray hair unbraided, and whose lean weathered face, with his eyes yellowed by age, had indeed a wolfish appearance. After a simple meal, to which the Dog Soldiers were pleased to offer some coffee they had been bringing back from the Kiowa Agency, Heart Wolf began his stories. All were hunkered down by a small fire intent on the well loved tale of "White Bull's Scout" when Lieutenant Austin Henley, with a detachment of the 6th Cavalry and 13 hide hunters, burst into the peaceful camp, pistols blazing. No warning had been given; any attempt at surrender was immediately met by instant annihilation. The few warriors tried to allow the women to scramble to the soft mud banks of the creek to dig in with the children. Most were yanked out and clubbed to the ground before their eyes. No attempt was made to take prisoners. No declaration was tended as to why the presence of the army was in their midst. It happened so fast, as all surprise attacks do, but when Medicine Horse had a chance to examine it he realized that there was no reason for the unprovoked attack. There were no white captives in the camp, nor had they any stolen cattle. He saw no evidence of any stolen rifles. Their crime was that they were "off reservation", thus "hostile", and could be "shot on sight". It was a small scale Sand Creek massacre all over again.

 He and Lightly were on their ponies in a trice, lances in hand. Within minutes Horse saw that the Bluecoats were simply gunning every warrior down, accepting no one's surrender. As the women and children began to flee toward the creek banks, Lt. Henley raised his white gloved hand and gave the order to charge after them. Wheeling his horse to cut them off, he slipped easily to the flank, cutting across the line of the charge. It was then that a fusillade from one of the hide-hunters long guns ripped into Charge's belly, and down she went. Medicine Horse sprang easily from her, knowing she was lost now to him, taking but a second to cut the war eagle plume from her mane and mutter a quick prayer of thankfulness for all she had been to him. He wished that he had time to slit her throat, and send her quickly off; her going now would be agonizing, but he would soon be with her. That thought gave him added strength as he began his Death Song, and with that drove his Dog Rope into the hardened ground with all his strength. Amazingly calm and clear-headed, he felt the accumulated power of his warrior society and all those who had gone beyond. He had always assumed that he would go down fighting for his People; had thought that the field would be glorious, not this little creek, but it was not his to choose. His vision was clear, his voice strong. He did not fight alone; his *kola* out there, also ready to fight to the death. He would not just walk the path, they would ride free, ride the wind along the stars.

Then he was on his feet, his eight foot lance firmly staking his Dog Rope into the ground with a powerful thrust, his Death Song upon his lips, he faced the onslaught.

That he would die there was no doubt; a lone man, with only a large skinning knife and war club in hand. Those hide hunters almost upon him. But his story would be told around Council Fires forever, would it not?

Women clutching babies to their chest ran screaming past, blood running down their faces. Young children scrambled, running as fast as they could. Camp dogs circled, most gut shot, for sport, by the hide hunters who just like to shoot. Of Lost Heart Wolf it pains to tell, that once shot while trying to surrender, his scalp was taken. That fine head of white hair, so fine, what a trophy it was for those hide hunters!

A fine red mist descended from Medicine Horse's brain, a hot boiling energy rose from his gut, strength welled in his arms, tautness rose in his spine. A chant drummed in his ears, in the air, protecting him now. All he wanted, all he ever needed, all he ever knew.... what he was born for was to kill, kill, kill!

The huge skinning knife flew from one hand to the other with a life of its own, it flashed in the sunlight, giving a fierce message. *Come, taste, see how good. Come, taste of me, I hunger for your blood.* He crouched, ready to spring. His wonderful, brave horse, gut-shot, screaming in agony behind him, but he couldn't hear. The filthy, fur-faced hide hunters, buffalo killers raced toward him... "I will gut you, eat your liver." He slashed the air, screaming like a war eagle. "Come die without pride upon my blade. Taste my hate! I will skin you, and leave your body for the wolves to feast upon!" Hate rode him. A bullet ripped through him; he barely felt it.

What of Walks Lightly, a Dog Soldier too, did he stake himself? Only four of this great society are the "bravest of the brave" and Medicine Horse is one, but no Dog Soldier ever lived who knew or showed fear. Lightly had been fighting like ten grizzlies once he saw the first girl pulled screaming by her braids from her mother, and then clubbed with a carbine. He swung down from his mount, lanced that corporal through his throat and pinned him to the ground. That was a satisfying start. He saw Medicine Horse's favorite war horse get shot out from under him and was ready to sweep him up, then he saw him pin his Dog Rope, the indication that he would fight to the death. "Brother," he thought, "you may hate me, but we must get back to Sitting Bull and Crazy Horse with the news of the recent campaigns; I cannot make it by myself. This is not a worthy enemy!" He turned his horse and began to fight his way toward him, then he saw Lt. Austin raise his Peacemaker and shoot. Medicine Horse staggered, blood shot out from under his ribs, but he remained standing, and Walks Lightly flew on, "Horse, Horse, your medicine is strong today, my brother!"

Then he was upon him, his knife out, slashing at the Dog Rope, pulling up the picket pin, his arms extended, they grasped forearms, he lifted him up, and off they flew amid a fusillade of bullets. A wild despair swept over them as they looked back on the dead and dying. Burned forever in Medicine Horse's mind, as he tried to capture the wildly flapping loose ends of his Dog Rope so that it wouldn't trip up the horse and cause them to crash to the ground, was the sight of his long, many feathered lance lying trampled in the bloody dust.

They rode on trying to evade the Crow scouts looking for them, their trails easily discernible by the extra weight of two on one mount. Desperate, by nightfall they approached a small rickety barn that looked unattended in the moonlight. They entered cautiously, but their presence was betrayed by a recruit on leave, out heaving up his overindulgence behind it. An alarm was raised, and in short order a swarm of men with guns and pitchforks had Medicine Horse and Walks Lightly trussed up. Only the presence of the womenfolk, who had also come rushing out, saved their lives. They were duly delivered to Ft. Kearney and thence on to Ft. Sill.

The Five-Fingered Glove
1874

In The Moon of The Yellow Leaves, when the People would be most most happy to be quietly filling their drying racks for winter, mending their lodge covers, and preparing paints to make the new Winter Count rather than keeping to a reservation, for they were hunters, not farmers, General William Tecumseh Sherman, Commander of the U.S. Army, stretched forth his hand and sent his Bluecoats out upon the land.

The reservations were located close to the military installations for purposes of control, but the Indians wished mainly to evade trouble and be left alone; not engage in hostilities with the Bluecoats, as they called them. Many quietly left those reservations to seek adequate game, hoping for buffalo further north, where they were still free to roam. There were those who had no wish, ever, for reservation life! It was deemed that all Indians were to come in off the land to live now, permanently, on these reservations, or be considered "hostile". Surrender or be pursued relentlessly! Thus all Indians off reservations were deemed hostile.

A military campaign to forcibly relocate those tribes still hidden in the deep recesses of the Llano Estacado, The Staked Plains, was formed. Five columns, a total of 3,000 troops, went out in the time of the year when the tribes were usually in their Winter camps. Bear Coat Miles from Ft. Dodge, Bad Hand Mackenzie from Ft. Concho, Major Prince from Ft. Bascom, and Colonels Davidson and Buell from Ft. Sill rode out with big, barking guns and much meat to supply them for many, many days. The army, of course, had limitless supplies and was fully equipped.

General Sherman had ordered them to converge on the Texas panhandle in the upper tributaries of the Red River. Only those Indians that had avoided capture kept their freedom, with nothing but the clothes on their backs. The pursuit was such that they were routed with scarce means to survive, fleeing for their lives. What goods were left behind were destroyed. Those fleeing were never given the chance to replenish their supplies, always hampered by their care of women, children, infants and elderly, never given a chance to regroup or care for their wounded. Hunted and hounded relentlessly, group after group came into various agencies and forts. This round-up became known as The Five-Fingered-Glove.

On the morning of September 26th, the U.S. Army entered the peaceful defiles of the Palo Duro Canyon, where a few hundred Kiowa, Cheyenne and Arapaho men, women and children had set up Winter Camp, as was their tradition. They were routed; those captured returned to the agency at Ft. Sill. Those that escaped to survive the harsh winter, one of the worst in recent memory, deprived of mounts, lodges and provisions, somehow managed to straggle in to surrender at Ft. Sill on Feb 25th, 1875.

At his headquarters in Ft. Sill, in December of 1874, 1st Lt. R. H. Pratt of the 10th Cavalry received a special notification in connection with his assignment to Indian Affairs. He was to make a list of all the Indians being held for various crimes at the Agency, including the Comanches at the Wichita Agency, and those for whom no crime had been charged, but had been agitators, disobedient, or otherwise troublesome. He was to be discreet in this task. Several hundred Indians at this time were being held prisoners at the fort. He enlisted the aid of several chiefs and sub-chiefs in the selection.

Several weeks later Government orders arrived. It had been determined that those hostiles and ringleaders should be removed from the territories, for they could in no way receive a fair trial for their crimes here in the west, so they were to be shipped to Ft. Marion in St. Augustine, Florida, there to be held indefinitely as prisoners of war. Seventy-three of the worst offenders from Ft. Sill and from the Cheyenne and Arapaho Agency, seventy miles to the north, were then sent in chains to Florida under the supervision of Lt. Pratt. Included on the list were two Cheyenne Dog Men captured in the attack at Sappa River.

The Ice House at Medicine Bluffs
Ft. Sill, April 1875

It was the time of first thunder, when the sun rises high enough to bring a certain warmth to the land, but the nights still keep ice closed upon the mouths of the creeks. Here at the fort that the People call the Soldier House, near to the Medicine Bluffs, a most sorry assembly of a once proud people have been arriving day by sorry day. Some under guarded escort arrived, clinging, half-starved, onto equally starved ponies. Others came, heads held high, bellies scrunched up under their ribs, walking sure-footed with their last surge of will, knowing that to surrender to the "protection" of the Great Eastern Father was all that would save their kind from annihilation. The old sunk down on travois, hearts grieving for those lost; some gone beyond. So few warriors were left, most rode off north to join forces with those leaders still holding out, like Crazy Horse and Sitting Bull.

What little possessions they had managed to keep were soon taken from them, weapons especially. Those leaders left among them were sent to the guardhouse and locked away. Would there be rations for them now that they had come in, as they were promised? This is what the Great Father wanted, was it not? The huddled and starving stood grouped in the light drifts of snow and waited to be herded to a place for safe keeping. The Bluecoats marched around smartly, efficiently dealing with their prisoners. Light and sound from the foundry filled the air, where the ones deemed most "hostile" were being "ironed".

The piercingly bright and distant blue of the April sky disappeared quickly, as it was wont to do, by the sudden appearance of low-riding, dense laden clouds bearing hail. All those out and about that had any shelter began to move swiftly toward it. Horses were stabled. Officers disappeared to orders transmitted as if by magic, it seemed. Orderlies were scurrying here and there. A certain frenzy of activity belied the adage of "a calm before a storm", as small dust devils swirled across the now empty parade ground and the wind began to howl. At the forge those prisoners not yet ironed were remanded back to the guardhouse and the fires dampened down.

An eerie quiet now settled upon the area as the darkened sky took on a sickly green cast. This was the time of year when twisters could literally spring up unannounced to tear through the land, creating massive amounts of destruction. While the Army seemed to be busy with certain preparations, the scattered bands of Indians, both prisoners and those accompanying them, appeared to have a stoic indifference.

Now an incessant moaning and whispering of the ever present wind increased and raced around the hunched and sprawled groups. Despair and defeat hung as heavily laden as the skies above them. Most were close to starving, few had enough clothing left to keep out the chill that the wind insisted on penetrating. Many had moccasins with ragged soles, if they had footwear other than rags at all. Of course none possessed anything that could be used as a weapon, or a comfort, like a medicine bundle, or even a doll for a child. All remnants of rank and standing as warriors, healers, leaders or wise men among the people had been stripped from them and burned in the large pyres that were kept stoked at the entrances by Medicine Creek, fed by the various bands as they came in to surrender, or were brought in by the soldiers.

A few hundred of their very best ponies had been spared and given as rewards to the Crow scouts who had helped to track them down. Some of the elaborately decorated parfleches had also been spared, not because of their beauty but because someone had taken a liking to the pemmican that was held inside. Later the bag would be carelessly tossed onto the flames. Occasionally an ornately quilled pipe bag was taken as a souvenir; those made from a mountain lion skin were popular. It was too disheartening to listen to the women recount these things. It was not just the soldiers that held them prisoner, not the irons upon their legs, nor the shackles on their wrists.

Down from the bluff sat a small building, the stockade. It was unfinished. Just 150 x 40 ft. It lay uncompleted. Its walls and floors were of rough hewn dark gray stone, exceedingly cold and damp to the touch at this time of the year. One hundred thirty men were crammed in here, all the prisoners that the army considered to be most deserving of these accommodations. A bit of straw had been scattered on the rough stone for bedding and a few army pup tents set up for the most grievously wounded. A horse trough had been shoved up against the wall for water. It stood open to the elements, as it had no roof. This was called The Ice House.

Death of a Dog Man

The earth is heavy; a dark load upon the lowly worm whose life is lived below the light, to burrow down and bring but small mouthfuls to the surface. Never to soar above the earth on powerful wings, nor thunder across its surface, mane flying in the wind. He lay inert. Blind. Captive. Fettered. A worm. Not even that, for a worm could crawl away. He had given up trying to block out the wails and taunts rising from the women in the prison camp over by Cache Creek. He knew all too well the poverty and destitute conditions that existed there. His heart had fallen down at Sappa River. What lived now in the hollow of his chest he did not want to know. All the years since he had earned the right to wear the Dog Rope, he had fought to earn that right. Now he watched with horror as a part of his mind saw the unarmed, aged Lost Heart Wolf struggle to his feet from where he had been recounting a Cheyenne war story, his back bent with age, to extend his arms upward in an universal gesture of surrender to the Bluecoats, calling out "We surrender," and even though the little band was obviously peaceably camped on the banks of the Sappa, with no white prisoners, no farmer's or rancher's cattle being butchered and eaten at their miserable little fire, Lost Heart was immediately gunned down in a fusillade of bullets. Even then, as a few able-bodied warriors also tried to make the signs of surrender rather than fight back, they, too, were shot down.

Well he, Medicine Horse, wearer of the Dog Rope, Bravest of the Brave, Cheyenne Dog Soldier, died there too. He had staked himself out with his many feathered lance, began his Death Song, ready to go beyond, his *tasoom* would then leave his body to travel by The Hanging Road, the Milky Way, to join *Heammawihio*. True, his kola, Walks Lightly, had then cut his sash, pulled his pin, dragged his body onto the back of the war pony and bore them out of the fray. They escaped, only to be ignominiously captured a few days later. His own gallant war pony, Charge, left behind, gut shot, upon his war shield. His long lance lay trampled and broken under the cavalry charge. Lost Heart Wolf was scalped, the unarmed warriors all dead. The women and their children were pulled, like wolf cubs, from their dens along the river banks and clubbed to death. His heart had fallen down! What is a warrior without a heart?

The worm turned in that hollow where his heart once dwelt. It was quiet without that constant beating. With the fever came a rustling, a soft susurration, like the sound of many leaves twisting on their stems. In fact, it was the exact sound a grove of cottonwoods would make when a sudden spring storm was upon them. Wagachun, Wagachun, they called. A most pleasant sound. He was never to know the birth name given him, nor the one who gave it. Wagachun, Cottonwood Boy, the name they gave him sufficed for awhile. Medicine Horse was the name given for his excellence with the herd, but now he would take a new one. So he renamed himself... Standing Cloud!

For everything in his life hovered over him now, as a cloud stands over the land below it. He did not assign it a deeper meaning such as rain, or dark, or even thunder. In some sense it simply implied that he was waiting for an uncertain future to unfold.

Captured. Ironed. Held in a square cell. It was horribly clear that, like with so many of the People, there was now only one place to go. Those reservations where the land was not to be stripped or stolen out from under them, worthless as it was, on these worthless lands his soul would wither and die, apart from all that had nurtured and made him who he was, out on the vastness of the plains. The young Dog Soldier who now called himself Standing Cloud lay curled on the cold stone floor of this Ice House at Ft. Sill and despaired of how he, who once pledged himself to fight to the death for his people, could help them now.

When a Cheyenne travels The Hanging Road, what we call The Milky Way, suspended between Earth and Heaven, he knows that soon he will be in the camps of those who have gone before him. There is no burden of guilt beyond, he travels to those passed on before him, who reside with the Great Wise One. A peaceful place, but not for those who have taken their lives. Sometimes those who hover on the brink of death are sent back to earth by those above, the Spirit People. It is hard to talk of these things, they are better felt, better experienced. One just knows. Thus it was that this warrior on the cold icy floor with the great despairing hollow in his chest lay in great danger, for his tasoom, what we would call the essence of his spirit, had been set free by his despair at what he had not only witnessed at Sappa Creek, but what he had seen and lived through all these hard, debilitating years since that horrible attack at Sand Creek. His lance that lay now under four inches of hard packed snow and ice bore no less than fourteen eagle feathers on it. His chest and back bore further evidence of the ceremonial scars he had endured for his People. He had no wife nor children, because the tribe came first. In fact, almost every war prize he had ever taken he had given to those in need, and had done so with gladness, and yet he had lost..lost. His heart had fallen down. He thought that he could have at least gone down in honor, with his Death Song on his lips. A new feeling came to him now; he curled his lips at its taste, bitterness.

He was indeed a worm! The cries and taunts of the women carried all too well from across the prison camp at Cache Creek to where the prisoners lay crowded together like sheep in their defeat. Many men had surrendered so that their families would not starve, but for many women pride was just too hard to swallow. He remained numb. Let the cold come, let it take him. He had served his purpose, and it was not enough to turn the tide. But the spirit people turned him back; his destiny was not yet fulfilled. Wagachun, Wagachun, the soft rustling began again. A golden spin-drift of leaves come down in the early autumn sifting through the white stippling of the aspen groves on the banks of a small mountain stream as it runs quickly over the rounded stones. A cooling breeze ruffles the soft down of his cap of hair. A soft voice nearby is singing as she approaches him. How very peaceful. His limbs are tightly bound. He has no desire, nor need, to move them. Wood smoke hangs in the air, and he hears the clatter of approaching horses. Soon he will see her face. Oh, how he longs to see her face. His tasoom rises straight above his head when a clear strong voice resounds.

He sat bolt upright to find the heavy oak doors were being unbolted, and the guards were leading in even more prisoners, shoving them rudely down amongst the others. Walks Lightly dragged himself with his heavy irons next to Cloud, and wordlessly sat close. He appeared to be uninjured. He, too, was naked except for the long red breechcloth. A thin army blanket had been issued to them and they wrapped themselves up in it for the night. Before Lightly could say a word he felt the need to explain to him that he was no longer the warrior known as Medicine Horse, and he felt no gratefulness for being rescued. He had no energy to speak. They stared dully at one another. Lightly still had an eagle bone whistle around his neck. Cloud's was gone. Just as well, he thought, just as well.

    He wished above all else that he could wander off into the hills, perhaps into the Malpais, the Badlands, to fast, pray, and seek a vision, but here he was in chains. So here he would become this other person, this "Cloud-That-Stands-And-Waits".

    He still saw that broken lance, heard the agonized groans of his gut shot horse, saw the dirty, bearded face of the hide man brandishing the blood soaked, long, white haired scalp of Lost Heart Wolf, the agonized weeping of the women as they lay dying with their children. Yes, he had escaped, his life had been saved, but what of his honor? What of his People?

Heartbeat of Darkness

"They feed us like lions..."

A hard bright disk of noonday sun hung with grand indifference above the fort, but as the air grew ever cooler it seemed to glaze over, move slowly as the hours passed, till it was finally enveloped in an encircling haze of filmy, greenish light that held it above the far horizon, where steel gray clouds rushed to capture and drag it down. Darkness abruptly fell. Winds rose, howling, bearing great clouds of choking dust to further torment all those still without adequate shelter from the approaching storm. Small, swirling flakes of snow began to drift down, idly at first, then swept away by the savagery of the wind. Familiar shapes on the parade ground soon became obscured as the snowfall intensified; sounds became muffled.

    This unseasonal cold only added to the great desolation of spirit that moved through the darkness of the surrendered bands at the detention camps out on the flats of Cache Creek, east of the Army post. The keening of the wind wove into the wails of the women along with the intermittent bugle of tattoos and the final sound of the retreat over at the Fort proper. Wagons that had delivered their meager provisions to the captives and prisoners in the cells and Ice House had long ago returned through the slowly accumulating snowfall. A few small, but inadequate fires, for wood was dear, glowed out on the flats. In the cold, damp confines of the Ice House, open to the elements, Standing Cloud moved in and out of a fever induced by his suppurating wound. He was young, yet strong, as malnourished as the hundred some other prisoners packed in with him, fighting now a battle for his *kola*, Walks Lightly. Every time Cloud struggled forth from his own delirium it was to find Walks Lightly even further removed from him; harder to reach.

    Then one day the wagon was delivering raw chunks of meat to them, which were simply tossed over the walls, and a certain bloody haunch landed at Walks feet, one that bore an unmistakable marking, the war paint of his very own beloved war pony. Well, that was the day, the turning point for Walks Lightly, who had born up so well under all the atrocities of The Red River War.

Each day as the sun began to warm the air, the undeniable stench reached them from the slaughter of the Indian's pony herds, a common practice of the Bluecoats. Cloud had to admit this was cunning enough to weaken their heartstrings to the breaking point, but when the wagon began to deliver their very own mounts, drawn and quartered, raw chunks thrown over the wall for them to feed upon, it was merely evil.

Yes, in times of starvation they had, with gratefulness and blessing, thanked their brothers for the gift of sustaining their lives with their own flesh, but this was sacrilege. Some of the men now ate of this flesh, but with shame, and only in darkness. Many a night he heard the sound of stomachs being violently emptied.

But Walks Lightly took that haunch of his very own war pony into into his hands and, lifting it to the sky, vowed to let no food nor water cross his lips, ever again. On that day Gotebo had risen to his feet to shout out, "They feed us like lions!"

Walks Lightly, his kola, the one who cut his buffalo sash, his Dog Rope, who pulled his pin to free him from where he had driven the lance into the ground to take his stance, and spared the life he had staked, then stood and faced the huddled, starving, miserable, defeated men and spoke, "If my body cannot leave here," and he rattled the heavy rusted irons around his thin wrists, "then my spirit must!" He sank down at Cloud's feet. Those were to be the last words he spoke aloud to the men he was imprisoned with in the Ice House.

Days passed; Cloud could not even get water past Lightly's lips, though he tried. Moving in and out of consciousness himself, Cloud did not know how many days that they had been there, but Walks Lightly had arrived swiftly at the last stages of starvation, for he was already malnourished when they had arrived. They had been fighting and moving with inadequate supplies and no women to care for them for months. Walks Lightly was barely aware of his surroundings, his breath was at times irregular, as was his heartbeat. He was so weak now that neither hunger nor thirst called to him for its satisfaction. His stomach had shrunk months ago, also his muscles, so that movement itself was painful. Cloud sensed this and kept him cradled upon his lap, tried to keep his lips moistened with snow. His breath now had an odd smell, almost sweet, from his fasting.

It had been assumed, when they had been brought here, that they would eventually be hung, and if so that their soul, *nagi,* would not be able to walk the Sky Path beyond. He and Cloud had once discussed this. Walks even jokingly had said that well before they choked off his last breath, he would die knowing that his irons would be left in this shameful place. Cloud daily now tested those irons, thinking, perhaps, that Walks' flesh had wasted to the point that he could slip his friend free from them at last.

When they had first been shackled and brought here the moon had been white as an antelope belly, casting a cold light so that Standing Cloud could identify most of the warriors held hostage within, but now he only had eyes for his kola. Gripping the heavy links of the chain that shackled their feet, he tried to make him comfortable. How many days had passed since that vow had been spoken he no longer knew for certain.

White Horse, Big Tree, Woman's Heart and others he did not know were confined elsewhere on the grounds of the fort, and in separate cells in the guardhouse, but here in the Ice House over a hundred languished, with many more tossed in day by day. The stone walls and floor seized the cold air and held it as captive as they were. With no roof above, the scant moonlight revealed too much; little clothing and less hope. Standing Cloud had spent much of the last days clinging to his own hope and coherency, continuing to search for words that he hoped would cause his friend to hunger for life yet again. Had Lightly even heard his beseeching pleas? In the defeated warriors weakened condition they were not fighting only the Bluecoats but many battles of the spirit, not the least of which came to them from the strong odor of rotting horse flesh beyond Cache Creek. Many men here were wounded in body as well as spirit. Outside the fort large pyres smoldered still with the remains of their shields, war bonnets, medicine bundles, pipe bags; anything of value. What indeed remained other than the breath in their lungs?

For the first night since they had been caged here the little wolves began to yip and howl, their tremolos at times sounding almost as exultant as the full throated cries their women gave when they rode into camp victoriously. Walks Lightly, who had distanced himself from all, now seemed to rouse himself somewhat at the sound. His dark eyes caught the moonlight; a wan smile seemed to grace his thin lips. He looked truly skeletal. Ribs stood outlined on his narrow chest, high cheekbones cast deep shadows on his already gaunt face. His eye sockets would have appeared almost hollow, but within those sockets gleamed a mysterious light. Oddly, he appeared at ease.

One dry hand searched for his friend's to try to grip it. They both knew what he was trying to communicate. *I am here with you now, still, in this place, for a little while, yet....* It was sufficient. Cloud knew not what to say, knowing the last hours were approaching. He gave a silent thanks to the spirit of the wild that had risen up with the moon, and as the song dogs quieted, he heard the faint drumming of his kola's heartbeat and he gave in to sleep. Not yet, not yet, not tonight, but soon.

How much time had passed he could not tell. Walks Lightly lay limp in his arms, night was thick around them, and a fire began to burn once more in his blood. As a fine sweat poured out, obscuring his vision, he struggled to drag them both to a far corner by a north wall where they would be as much out of the wind as possible. His eyes closed and his head drooped as he give in to the next bout of fever. How he wished for a robe, a thick winter robe to cover with, for once the fever broke then the wracking chills would begin.

It was to be one of those nights of exceptional cold that distinguishes the High Plains in early spring. As it grew ever colder out on the hills sap froze in the trees, causing branches to pop. Small animals burrowed ever deeper into the earth, and ice quickly spanned the banks of the creeks, freezing right down to the pebbled bottoms. Unbeknownst to him, deep in the remnants of his buffalo hide rope that had been cut to release him from his defensive stance on the battlefield, ice crystals were starting to form in the blood that had seeped into it. They would remain there throughout the next day, their own secret; cold, hard, devoid of any warmth and of any meaning. The sparse amount of firewood that was delivered to the prisoners crammed in here provided little more than a faint light, almost no warmth. Now just eerie, flickering shadows danced along the cold stone walls where the moisture had frozen into tear shaped ice drops.

When you wake, seemingly alone, those who may be at your side asleep or unmoving, darkness has a heartbeat; a pulse like the one beating in your throat! Once you listen, carefully, you may become aware that it is not your own.

The night sounds that floated into the air after the fort quieted down and the temperature began to fall, began with the yips of the little wolves heard from afar off, but never the howls of the true ones; never the presence revealed of the real pack. I knew why the scavengers were out there, but did not want to think on why, the "why" sickened me, that "why" filled the meat wagon of the army and emptied my soul, thought Cloud in his fevered, near dreaming state.

My soul! My head was clear. My fever had broken. I looked down at Walks Lightly, he looked amazingly at peace as his chest rose and fell, but slowly. For so long I had been a respected Dog Soldier. I had felt strong in that, I rode out in my powers knowing that my strength lay in the swiftness of my war pony, the keenness of my spirit; but tonight I wanted something more. I, too, wanted to leave this flesh. Not as Walks Lightly vowed, but to inhabit as that of another, as a brother, one with the night, one with a different cunning, one whose weapons could not be taken from him, thrown on a burning pyre. One with claws, fangs, different skills, and yes, blood lust that I did not ordinarily possess; the ability to track down and hunt those who had brought such heartless destruction upon my people!

Now, with a clear head, I felt the stab of pain from my wound and the chill that the heavy irons lay upon my wrists and ankles. When my flesh cannot escape, how can I keep my heart from not touching the ground? How I envied those shape-shifters, and I regretted in that moment a vision of myself as a child by the banks of the Crazyhead Springs, crouched at

Spotted Owl's side, learning the difference between Black Sage, a stringy withered dried mass in his left hand, and an equally indistinguishable plant in his right he called Man Sage. For I was to learn what plant is best to heal with, then what feathers are best for fletching arrows, and then every trick I taught myself to tame the wildest mustang. Such dark arts as where one ought to walk the ridge at night in the shape of another, I knew not, nor cared.

Standing Cloud moved his hand to the folds of his severed Dog Rope, where he had wound it around his waist to serve as a makeshift bandage. Probing there, he was surprised to find, when he withdrew his hand, that it was yet bloody. A red mist was rising once more into his vision. He held his hand before his face and slowly turned down two of his fingers. A bloody hand, Bad Hand, one called Bad Hand, Lt. Ranald MacKenzie, who led the Bluecoats down one of the trails into the Palo Duro, at Cita Blanca Canyon, so steep that his soldiers had to dismount and go in single file. The people were able to flee, but every possession, all goods amassed to see them through the winters, were destroyed. Once a few select mounts were given to the traitorous scouts that had led them to the winter camp, every horse, pony, and mule that had sheltered in this deep canyon with lush grass was ordered slaughtered, all 1,046, and left to rot. Thinking thus and still holding his bloody hand aloft, he let the fever take him down again.

This time it was the drumming that awoke him. Or was it? The sky was overcast, the moon hidden, a deep quiet except for that sound prevailed. What was it? Thud-thud! A heartbeat. A very strong and loud, preternaturally loud heartbeat. From his own chest? No, it was ..Walks Lightly's. He had not heard his heart beating this strong and regular for days; in fact it had been somewhat irregular and faded in and out. It was then, as he went to prop Lightly up, that the drums began. Deep, insistent, big skin drums, the sound being sent from across Cache Creek, out on the flats by the Detention Camp. But this was not possible. All such drums had been seized and burned. Perhaps a small hand drum had been secreted in the folds of some clothing, or a small one had been fashioned from a poorly cured rabbit skin (that is, if the skin itself hadn't been consumed). It was not unheard of, for bands coming in to surrender, to bury a secret cache of weapons out in the Sand Hills, but drums? These were the ceremonial ones, deep-throated, speaking out into the awesomely cold night air. Was he dreaming; was this a vision? His head felt too clear. Was this all brought on by too little food; did it matter? He glanced down at Walks Lightly, who appeared to be sleeping. With each throbbing beat of the drum, it seemed that his own heart followed in response. The air seemed warmer and had achieved a life of its own within the confines of the Ice House, now throbbing and pulsing with each drumbeat. Snow that had lain gently on the stone floor now rose up and began to move in a rhythmic swirling dance, circling around the perimeters of the square, walled cell, lending it a harmonious circular appearance.

It was so late that only small embers still lived in the meager fire, but suddenly, as though summoned, a thin flame came to life and rose waist high to cast illumination upon the walls. It was then that Cloud first saw them in the far reaches of the shadows, pacing, loping, each footfall matching the drums incessant beat just as Lightly's heart beat against Cloud's chest. Through the rising and falling of the silvery snow the wind again began to howl, the drums pounded, his heart beat faster, and the wolves, for that is what they were, appeared and disappeared. Eyes glowing like red coals, nose to tail, large padded footfall to large padded footfall. A strength of purpose, a pride, as though they had been doing this forever and always would, around and around they went. None paused to lift their head, to give voice. No ululation came from the camp. Yet deep echoing tremolos of the wild pack carried from out past east of Cache Creek.

Suddenly he was aware that he was not alone, of course he was not alone, crammed in here with a hundred other Kiowas, Comanches, and Cheyennes. But sitting erect, one in each corner, were Medicine Water, Howling Wolf, Wolf Marrow and a *wicasa wakan* whose name he did not know. They all nodded to him simultaneously. At that the tall flame in the fire pit began to fall. The sound of the drums slowed as a heartbeat would, naturally at rest after exertion. Each lupine form then gracefully leapt the shadows into the faltering flame, to twist and turn into a plume of gray and silver smoke, to rise into the open sky above.

Into a stunning silence the faintest sound now rose from Walks Lightly's lips. Cloud almost felt like covering his ears, as though he could stay the end. He recognized the Death Song on this starving man's cracked lips. "Could he feel the beat of my heart through my veins, as I now feel his weak pulse?" Cloud wondered? Then he finally relented and opened his heart to what Walks Lightly had so strongly and so fearlessly willed for himself.

"You saved my life, friend, kola! You set me free!" He went to bow his head, a most natural inclination, and as he did so he saw that Lightly's eyes were now open, lifted up. There above them the sky had cleared to reveal, only momentarily, the merest sliver of a crescent moon just risen above the rim of the Ice House, and moving to rise above it was one of the most glittering stars in the heavens, which nothing can outshine, the Morning Star. Abruptly the distant howls, yips and wails of the little wolves ceased and the moon slid behind a wall of heavy cloud cover. A silence fell upon the land, and in that quiet suspense of sound what came to the Dog Soldier's ears was what he feared he would never forget, the last breath of his dying brother.

Before dawn Walks Lightly's *nagi* surely would follow.

His Shackles Fell To The Earth

The Ice House

For Walks Lightly now there was no future; he had lived, really lived in the past! There would be no more life for him as a warrior in any future day. No buffalo to hunt, no buffalo runner to ride, no war pony to mount. With the last of his strength he worked his eagle bone whistle from his neck, a gift for his kola. Weak, nauseated, chilled, lying on his back as his vision dimmed, the stars above began to console him, their pathways coalesced. What felt in those first days of captivity like a heavy rotten stone in his belly, both bitter and rancid, began to lighten. His hearing began to dim, and when the late snow came he welcomed it with an open spirit. The first flakes that fell upon the Sun Dance scars on his chest felt warm, his hands open and accepting. He thought he could smell drifting sage and cedar burning and the clear piercing cry of an eagle. Someone would come soon to cut his rope; he was getting lighter. How very white his surroundings were. Was he growing blind? He could feel the warmth from his kola's hand, but could barely discern his song. The whiter his surrounding became, the more he seemed to notice a colorful, milling throng of ponies on the far horizon. A large sorrel stallion reared and whinnied, its call moving across the heavens. How had he missed hearing the unmistakable sound of hooves crunching over a crust of icy snow? He lay surrounded, yes, lost in a frigid black of endless night, until the moist, sweet breath fell upon his face.

The time had come to leave. He tried to open his dry, split lips to utter his Death Song, but found his tongue too swollen from the fasting. Was he blind also? No, he would know his faithful war horse anywhere. She had come for him, but how could he mount her when he had no strength left in his limbs? With a gentle movement of her loose tail, no longer bound for war, he understood. He was to grasp it. Surely he could manage to do that! A remnant of joy rose in his starved flesh at the thought of a once proud Dog Soldier being dragged into the heavens that way. How long did it take for him to struggle forward over the cold stones to claim a firm grip upon that tail? Hau, he thought, we must hasten now to join the others, and as horse and rider rose into the deep blackness of the sky, Walks Lightly's shackles fell from him to strike the earth far below with a peal of thunder and a clap of lightning.

Small pinpricks of light appeared. The environs of the fort lay spread out dimly below. His hands, he could feel them once more and see the deep ebony haunches of Red Robe, his war pony, running hard now. With each stride he could feel the medicine she was delivering unto him; the strength that was flowing from her tail down into his limbs. Oh, he could hardly wait to arrive at the camp. What a story he would have to tell the others and with that he simply vaulted up onto her broad back as an exultant shout escaped his new, fully fleshed body!

Take, Eat!

"All is sacred if we make it so"

Fog rose with the coming light, just enough to reveal the husk of the Dog Soldier's frail body lying stretched out on the frozen ground. A deathly silence prevailed within the Ice House. Just dark, huddled, sleeping forms, the fire burned down to ash when Cloud woke. Bitter cold ate at his bones, without opening his eyes he knew that his kola lay stiff beside him. There would be no ceremony, no burial platform to raise him to the heavens. The Bluecoats would come, drag this husk to the long trench where all the others had been thrown.

His heart fell down. An image began to rise in his spirit, a dark one. He both feared that he had not the strength to fight it off any longer and that he might welcome its arrival; it was pointed, sharp, probing at his wakening consciousness. An Arrow! A broken arrow. A specter of doubt swirled, like a puff of black ash from the fire pit, obscuring his vision. Was last night real? He was so feverish. His hand probed his side, only to withdraw at its tenderness. The wolves, the medicine men; again ash rose from the pit to swirl where they where hunkered over, backs to him, when, with a whoosh and a hoarse, strident *caw*, a glossy crow landed on the wall directly above him. The bird flapped its wings with such a power that Cloud's vision instantly cleared, and he knew that this was the *kangi* from his vision quest, his spirit helper! When the bird began to speak Cloud understood, in that place of his spirit where words are not necessary,

"I have flown through the night, down from Bear Butte, past the many flowing rivers, to come to you. Did you not learn last night that what perishes here on earth, what fire eats, what pox takes, what the stalking lion kills, what the flood destroys, while real, is not meant to last forever? Did you not see, did you not hear the drums call you? Did not the one within your own flesh answer? Did you not feel the power, the manifestation of the everlasting spirit?" And with that he heard, quite clearly, the wind howling, *"Taku, skan,skan."*

Rustling those feathers, snap, snap, snap, so as to focus Cloud's attention; hopping down from the wall, the crow paced a bit before him, then continued, *"As a warrior you were a leader, but never meant to be a chief, did you know that? Well, never mind"* and hopped, bent down to pick at an attractive pebble, as though he hadn't meant to reveal that, *"Now you are worried that many will follow "He-who-has-just-gone-beyond's" example, and take no nourishment into their bodies, and thus leave the confines of this prison in this same manner. You think that you have been defeated, and on a certain battlefield you have."*

At this he sprang up, almost leaping in Cloud's face, who defensively threw up his arm, fearful for his eyes, only to then see the bird upon the wall, his wings spread to the fullest extent, like a ceremonial fan. Its obsidian eyes glittered, each feather on the underside of its spread wings mysteriously darkening into the depths of a starless night into which Cloud felt himself falling, falling.

There lay a naked body on a bed of white sage. He could smell it, the aromatic goodness of it. Flames, like small tender hands, were running the unblemished length. So very, very bright, but he was helpless to avert his eyes from this vision. At points the head, the hands, the heart seemed to flare up, at other times the flames seemed to move back and forth as in a caress. Then there would be a great flare, an outburst of brilliant blue or greenish color almost lifting the form up from its place. Then a bloody hand shot up as flames rose up to cover it. His heart was sore watching this. As the flames slowly died back, a medicine lodge was revealed on a far hill. From the pictographs on it he knew it to be Silver Spotted Owl's, which had been burned at Sand Creek, of course. The hand, when he looked again at it closely, now resided next to the body, unharmed and unbloodied, just spotted with old age.

He heard the voice of his old teacher, Silver Spotted Owl, to him, "Allow yourself the courage to accept defeat, take the robe of humbleness within. You will find warmth." These words reverberated within his cage of ribs, his lungs expanding with an air not quite his own. Strong words lined up on his tongue, pushing to be loosened. He saw, but not with his eyes, all the beauty of the herds, the pintos, sorrels, paints, the *wakan shunka,* holy herd, hides gleaming, manes streaming, racing free across the prairie once more.

Thunk! His eyes flew open! There at his feet lay a glistening, raw chunk of horse flesh. *Take! Eat! The bird now screamed defiantly at him, challenging him to pick up the gauntlet!* "The blessing of much power has been conferred on you, little man, you have been purified by fire. You have come through. Not for yourself. Not for him!*

Hopping irreverently upon Lightly's cast off body, still laying there stiff and cold.

"But for them, for them, for the People!"

The great black bird seemed to shrink down in size, and walked in an ungainly fashion, crow-hop a few steps, then quickly he rose to circle the confines of the room in a very unnaturally slow fashion to gain the wall. As the black bird slowly ascended, a large flock of crows appeared overhead screaming what sounded most like, "Eat, Eat, eat eat eat!

The morning fog was rapidly burning off, the men stirred in their rags of bedding to a confused wakefulness, rubbing their eyes and looking towards Cloud, who appeared to be conversing with a crow of rather unusual appearance. With each shake of its ebony feathers blackness fell in such tiny flakes as to obscure the vision, until all the birds appeared to blend into the light blue of the morning sky and simply disappeared.

The fog had indeed lifted from Cloud's mind, as well as the sky. Turning to those awake he addressed them, holding the bloody chunk of horse meat in both hands, as though it were the proffered liver of the first kill of the first bull of the Buffalo hunt.

"This is something holy. For this I give thanks," and he raised it to his lips and bit into it, tasting that it was indeed sweet. "We must eat. We are still here. This is a different battle! We will now fight on a different battleground."

Before he continued he could feel four pairs of eyes upon him, intensely watching, and turned to Medicine Water, Howling Wolf, Wolf Marrow and the other holy man. Holding the meat towards the men he indicated, "They have served us well in life, taken us into battle, on the hunt; now they will yet serve us again. Let us honor them by taking their flesh into our bodies. All is sacred if we make it so!"

Out of the corner of his eye he saw that Matches had risen to start a cooking fire. He continued, encouraged. "Survival is our only defense. These are the only weapons they have left us," and he placed a hand upon his head, then his heart. "We must feed our spirits and our bodies."

All eyes were now upon him as he began to chant, raising his voice as it had not been heard, in full vigor, since the defeat, standing with the hunk of bloodied horse flesh still in his hands. "This, too, is *wakan;* something holy." Offering it then up to the four directions, anticipating the strength, courage, and energy that would soon flow into their bodies from partaking. His heart swelled when Minimic produced, from somewhere where it had been secreted, a sparse branch of sage, and offered it to the fire to smoke the room.

Red Dancing Crane Woman

On the Eastern Seaboard

Night had fallen, filling the coach swiftly with a dark and vague comfort. Shuffling, rustling sounds of the passengers settling in for the long night finally quieted in the train's compartment. Anah felt no need for sleep, but instead let her mind wander back to the very strange chain of events that brought her here, hurtling through the darkness toward an unknown future.

On the tiresome journey down from the plains to these lowlands on the the country's east coast, where the ancient Spanish fortress of Castillo de San Marco at St. Augustine, Florida was located, Anah found that she had much time to spend in contemplation. She was traveling unescorted, and thus maintained a demeanor that harbored no intrusions, friendly or otherwise. She had much to consider. As strongly as she felt that her decision to hire on as an interpreter, a contract she had skillfully negotiated to her advantage, being knowledgeable that the pay rate was the right one, she still had no vision for her future. She was truly alone now, and although she did not feel helpless or abandoned, she did feel a bit reckless. One glance at her wrist, where Turn Foot's arm band gave off a dull glint, was enough to fill her with the determination to feel purposeful. Reckless perhaps, but not foolish!

What she had once assumed would be a time of moving from one Indian camp to another till the northern hunting grounds by the Powder River were reached, sharing, to her, a unique richness of the community of women, became an abrupt and unexpected rupture; a hurried exodus out of the winter camp across the Llano Estacado, barely surviving a late blizzard, to arrive exhausted and heartbroken at Ft. Sill. She could barely believe that she had been torn from that peaceful village to find herself amidst the headquarters, BOQ, stables, barracks, and commissary of an active army establishment once more . As she rode in at Turn Foot's side, past the officer's quarters, she hung her head, not bearing to look. All thoughts of somehow blending in evaporated. She was distinctly white, distinctly female, horribly estranged from what had once been her world. Numb, cold, hungry, full of self-pity; knowing that she was losing what had been, to her, a salvation, the world of Turn Foot and the winter camp, she now let herself be led like a pack animal right from freedom in through those heavily guarded gates.

The army is nothing if not an efficient organization that can function well without probing or asking for emotions, thus Anah was settled in temporarily, her presence given only enough explanation to be accounted for. These forts and agencies out on the frontier in the Indian Territory had a constant flux of humanity; few were regulars! Strays, misfits, Dukes and missionaries mingled freely with the commissioned soldiers. Anah could not say how many days she had been there when Turn Foot again appeared. Her heart leapt; she foolishly thought that he had come to take her away, but she immediately discerned, by his stern expression, that he had no such intention. She noted that he was dressed for travel as he summoned her, saying only ,"There is someone I want you to meet." They rode out to the Kiowa-Comanche agency in the Eureka Valley, near old Ft. Cobb. As they rode, he spoke of an old friend, a Burnt Thigh woman, a Sicangu, Red Dancing Crane Woman, who had been married to a courier, one who rode between Laramie and Sill. " Her English is perhaps better than mine," he told her, "she has a mixed-blood son. Her other son is with Sitting Bull, I think." Anah began to ask him questions, but he only responded that the woman would speak for herself. Why was he taking her there, she wondered? A small excitement grew; perhaps I can find a residence with these people. I would like that, she thought. I am not ready to go back East, not yet. Nor do I want to stay on at this fort. Her hopes were up.

When she stepped into the woman's presence, she was immediately impressed. There was no particular beauty to her, in fact she was rather thin, her plain calico dress circled by a thick latigo belt studded with many silver conchos. The woman was chestnut skinned and rather stern looking. Her hair, strictly parted, hung in two neat braids laced with gray framing her narrow face, and when she stood, extending her hand as a man would, her unusual height was immediately apparent. As she stepped forward to further close the space between them and enclose Anah's small hand in her own large one the movements of her gait had an awkward grace, accented by the swinging fringe from her arms. A large bird indeed! In one hand she held a newspaper. "She could read?" Anah pondered. Bidding them to be seated, with no further formalities, she began to speak.

Holding out the paper, headline prominent, she asked, "Have you seen this?" As it was proffered to her, Anah took the paper, and read, Cheyenne Daily Leader, April 3, 1875 "14,200 Indians on the agencies depended on the 350 beef cattle issued to them three times this month." Dancing Crane exploded, "Astonishing!" as she snatched the paper back from Anah's startled grasp, causing Turn Foot to utter a muttered sound of amusement. Before Anah could comment, the Lakota woman bounded to her feet and began to expostulate, the fringes of her garments dancing in agitation, like ruffled feathers, as she hopped about. "Do you have any idea how much work, hard physical labor it takes, to turn a buffalo skin into a robe? And just how many robes are demanded by those unscrupulous sutlers for that poisoned rotgut that it sold as "whiskey"? While a man's wife and children go without? How many of our buffalo are now slaughtered just for their tongues, their tongues, and left to rot...to rot. While we are given cloth, cloth, not hides for our lodges!"

At the start of this impassioned outburst Anah turned a frantic glance towards Turn Foot; why had he brought her here? Just as she brought her heel under her hips to rise she felt a gentle squeeze from the old scout, and turning once again to him she saw that nod. That nod! The one that said patience. Observe! Learn!

Dancing Crane was hopping, her arms flapping in her impassioned delivery, as Anah settled back, determined to hear her out, for surely she had been brought here for some reason, not just to be exposed to a diatribe of this sort. She struggled to keep her indignation at bay. Who was this woman? The Indians here were so different from what she thought of fondly as her little band, thinking of that Kiowa leader, Kicking Bird, wheeling around in his high sprung wagon pulled so ostentatiously by not one, but two white mules!

"All We Had To Eat Was Defeat!"

Noting a pause, had her wandering attention been noticed? Anah managed to interject, "Was that at this agency?" Without missing a beat, the woman responded, "No, that was at Red Cloud's. But it is typical and," "Yes, I'm somewhat familiar with the problems with contract supplies, often," her further response was rudely waved away as Dancing Crane simply said, "Do the math; that many people could not be sustained on that little meat even if the full amount was delivered. Besides, the women do not know how to use the flour, so on and so....."

Again Anah tuned her out, but not before noting that indeed her command of the language was extraordinary. What was this woman doing living here on this god-forsaken reservation? Thinking that, "God-forsaken", she began to listen. The tenor of the speech had changed, less impassioned, less preaching, or were Anah's defenses less?

"Turn Foot has told me much about you," she said, fixing Anah with a piercing gaze. Piercing, but not withering. "What does she see in me?" Anah wondered. Red Dancing Crane Woman continued as she seated herself, reclining comfortably against a willow backrest, summoning a young woman to bring them tea.

"This summer on the Southern Plains we had severe drought. The heat made the mercury go up above the mark of 110. Water was hard to find in the usual places, and often alkaline. Then the skies were darkened by the locusts. This was hard on everyone. But here the Kiowas, Comanches and Cheyennes were running from the army. Bear Coat Miles, Price, and perhaps you know of Capt. Chafee." At this, Anah gave slight acknowledgment, wondering where this intense woman was leading, and why. "All across the Staked Plains battles were waged. When the dryness ended it gave with so much rain, cloudbursts, it turned the ground to mud, and yet the fighting raged on. So much rain that we call this time "The Wrinkled Hand Chase". And in saying this she gave a slight smile. "Who is this woman?" Anah again thought. "As a young woman I was wife to a white man, who, before he cast me away, saw that I was well schooled in the White Road at the Spotted Tail Agency. I have learned much of the white man's ways, though I do not agree with much of it now. A wasichu's attitude toward the good earth is to alter it, own it, fence it, build on it, and not share it or give it away. The Indian's attitude is to use and respect what the land has to offer, to revere it and to share it. However, trying to share our hunting grounds and the Black Hills has brought destruction upon us, and as to the buffalo, well," here she looked deep into her cup and grew silent.

Thinking that she had something of import to respond with, Anah drew into herself to prepare, but no words came. Red Crane Woman continued to speak of the ravages of the Red River War, and Anah's thoughts were only of how secure she had been in the beautiful sheltered confines of Cimarron Canyon . She could almost hear the rill of the icy brook and the clear call of a startled magpie.

" Last Fall there were soldiers everywhere. Our people, due to the consistent and constant policy of punishing raids, suffered damaging losses of their stored food, their lodges, (and how could they replace them, the buffalo hides, the poles from the Black Hills) their ponies, and all their possessions, but most importantly their lives. They were kept constantly on the move for fear of attack. The rain, cold and hunger of fall turned to the horror of one of the worst winters. Winter, a time when traditionally we do not travel. A time of renewal, when there is no raiding, nor warfare, and yet the army relentlessly pursued us. Rain, sleet, snow. If we were not plodding through snow up to our knees we were tearing our moccasins on shards of slick, crusted ice. Bitter winds, dead ponies, subzero temperatures...and the relentless pursuit of Bear Coat Miles. When there was no game to shoot, no buffalo to track, no parfleches with pemmican, no robes to keep us from freezing, no ponies to slaughter for food, then all we had to eat was defeat. We began to come into the agencies. Here to Ft. Sill and Darlington. Some struggled up north to Sitting Bull and Crazy Horse rather than admit defeat; rather than be fed like a dog at the mercy of an enemy. For if they have been hunted by the army, are they not then an enemy?" Her shoulders sagged, and she hung her head. Quiet reigned. The fire crackled as it fell upon its ashes. Anah did not know what to say, nor did she look to Turn Foot. She thought, "Should I tell her that I know of these conditions and the unjust treatment? What does she want of me, if anything? What do I have to defend other than the color of my skin?" And an odd, disturbing thought flashed through her, "In any way did William have anything do with any atrocity? No, surely not. But what can I do; I have no influence, no funds?" Anah sat lost in the prevailing silence; eventually Red Dancing Crane Woman broke it. "Here at this agency I have my ear to many drums. One of my sons is up north; he fights for his people. He will never come in, he says. He will never touch the pen, nor eat agency food. I wait here for him. Perhaps he will send his wife and children, if they still live. I have been told that you have a heart for my people."

She gestured, "Here, come, sit closer to me." Anah did as asked, and Crane Woman placed her hands upon her cheeks, turning her face up towards hers, looking into her eyes. It was a most pleasant experience, and though nothing was said, they broke their gaze with satisfaction and moved back to where they had been seated previously. "Now we can talk," she announced with great solemnity.

"There is an Army man here who is not two-faced; he has been seen in a vision. He apparently does not think like a white man. He sees beyond the color of one's skin. He has the Buffalo Soldiers. You have head of him perhaps, Lt. Pratt?"

On The Train To Ft. Marion

"there was a child..."

Turning in her seat, trying to settle, perhaps sleep, instead lulled by the incessant clacking of the train speeding southward, she let her mind drift back to the recent events at the Kiowa Agency.

What occurred after that first meeting between her and Red Dancing Crane Woman had not created a friendship or a bond, but instead a trust; one carefully forged, crafted of an unique pattern. One that was entered into with great sincerity due to the character of its participants. Anah was given a privilege, entrusted, commissioned in a sense, to serve in whatever way she could these unfortunate Cheyenne warriors that, in defending their traditional way of life, came up against the harsh consequences of Manifest Destiny, the push westward that had been prophesied by Sweet Medicine himself. Of influence she had none, of means she had barely enough for herself, but of compassion and comprehension she carried a brilliant torch to illuminate darkness, that of translation, for she could aid and abet understanding between the army and their captives. But that had to be shown to her as a valuable and necessary contribution. To this end Dancing Crane applied not only herself but the obvious plight of the people surrounding her on the agency. The poverty and deprivation were all too obvious, and in stark contrast to the orderly routines of the fort.

Anah had been free to wander the agency established outside the confines of Ft. Sill. She did not have to sit at anyone's fire to feel the heaviness of the atmosphere. No one wanted to be there, even the few dogs slunk by, tails tucked. There were no meat racks, no hides being flensed. She saw no children raucously running and playing. No wondrously decorated shields displayed on tripods to the sun, no industry that the buffalo hides had always provided, moccasins, shirts, or even bones being carved for spoons, but especially nothing that dealt with weaponry of any sort. Not even the smallest child wielded a tiny bow and arrow! All guns and weapons had been confiscated! The people were now totally dependent on army rations, or what could be trapped or caught; lizards, ground squirrels, small birds. Certainly no way to feed the hundreds that had been forced onto this reservation. And this white dust, this "flour", with no taste, ugh! The worms in it were better, some thought! Misery did not need to be spoken outright. Anah had seen the pride; the glory that once was. After her first visit she did not want to return, but return she did.

Worst of all was the pervasive smell emanating from where the captured horse herds had been slaughtered. Most days that odor did not carry, for which she was thankful, but at night there was no escaping the yips and howls of those scavengers assembled for the banquet the army had spread. Perhaps it had been a blessing that many thousands had been slaughtered and left to rot out in the deep recesses of the Palo Duro, as she had heard.

A series of meetings were arranged between Anah and Dancing Crane till she understood the exact circumstances of how over 72 Kiowa, Comanche, Arapaho, and Cheyenne were to be transported as prisoners of war to an old fort on the east coast of Florida. General Sheridan had wanted a military trial for all those he called "criminals". These meetings between the two women often had others in solemn attendance. Nothing was secret about them, which was encouraging to Anah, but there was much concern for the prisoners who were thought to be sent off to be hung. As conditions for survival worsened out on the plains and the military patrolled relentlessly, more and more leaders brought their people in to the agencies in a desperate bid for survival. Just last month over 800 Cheyenne had straggled in, starving, to lay down their arms, peacefully, here at the fort. Many warriors, though, would not submit, and headed north to join forces with Sitting Bull and Crazy Horse. Without these men to hunt for the increasingly rare game, survival outside the dependence on government rations was almost impossible.

Anah came daily now to listen to a forum of complaints and concerns from the people who lived at this agency as well as to hear the impassioned advocacy of Dancing Crane. She no longer thought that she was being harangued, and could at times sit back and admire the tall woman's eloquence, as others did, for she commanded great respect. Dancing Crane said that the Army did not understand the Indian way of fighting, to gain honor by counting coup. "They did understand killing," and she paused for emphasis, the fringes of her garments swaying on her tall gaunt frame, "our ponies, our women, our children, our way of life."

Anah ate nightly now at Crane's fire, and when the coals settled, and the others had drifted back to their lodges, Dancing Crane spoke earnestly of this man, Lt. Pratt, the one who led the Buffalo Soldiers, the one who would be taking the prisoners away, all the long way down South. "He has a heart. He, unlike Long Hair, has ears, he can listen, I am told."

When Dancing Crane finally outlined what she wished of her, Anah blurted, "Well, why don't you go with them? Your English is excellent. If Lt. Pratt is color blind then it will not matter that you are not white, will it?" Crane looked at her sadly and responded only, "I am an old woman. I am needed here. Perhaps my son will come in." Anah felt that something was being withheld from her. Dancing Crane rose. "You must decide soon, as they will leave in just a week, but I must tell you this. In the vision, the one where Lt. Pratt was seen, there was a woman." Anah sighed, not knowing what to say, feeling somewhat coerced, until Crane added her final words, "There was a child." Anah tried futilely to get her to say more, but she would not respond, so she left in a huff, feeling hugely manipulated. Of course there was a child, there is always a child. "She knows of my loss, there's always children, I'm a woman, a mother, or I was, Ooh!"

Anger flamed through her. Galloping her horse fiercely back to the fort, she enjoyed the piercing cold as the wind whipped her shawl away from her head and lashed the hair into her eyes. Yellow Nose, a Cheyenne from the north, escorted her as always, silent at her side. The pace was steady, the stars especially brilliant, angry tears so blinding she called a halt to slash at her face, pausing briefly to gaze upward. Yellow Nose placed a steadying hand on her bridle as he, too, turned his face into the great panoply of stars coursing overhead. Extending his long arm he pointed directly overhead, exhaling with such a vigorous sound at first she thought it was the horse, and almost gave in to laughter. The beauty of the universe had exerted its power to stun!

Anah avoided going out to the agency after this, and on the third day Turn Foot appeared. "I know you have come to upbraid me." "No, I have come to tell you a story. May I sit?" Anah then learned how Red Dancing Crane woman had come to her fierce commitment to her people.

She had married early to a white courier, Jacques DuBois, and was quite content to live in one camp or the other outside whatever fort her husband pursued his life, and to raise her family there. She liked the easy life that living close to a fort provided her and her children, for she seemingly had the best of both worlds. One fine day, in the Moon of the first Snowfall, 1864 to be exact, when her youngest daughter was just old enough to seat a pony, she went to visit an Uncle and Aunt at Sand Creek, having heard that they had arrived there under the protection of the army. Anah gasped when she heard November 1864, for this was the time of the scandalous Chivington's massacre, so highly condemned by most of the officers at Laramie. A dark silence fell whenever a woman entered a room where it was in discussion, so she had never learned any details. William refused to allow her to even mention it in his hearing, and forbade her to make any inquiries, saying only that it was "prurient" and unfit for a woman's ears. She had gathered that more women and children were slain than warriors, though. Now she was being told the story of a survivor. By the time Turn Foot finished the story Anah felt gutted, not sure of what response she could offer. But Turn Foot continued, saying that for those that escaped there was more yet to deal with.

Dancing Crane and her daughter had survived. They had only the garments on their backs, escaping on foot. By nightfall it had begun to snow. The few ponies that also escaped destruction were needed for the very old and the wounded. Some of the old ones threw themselves away to help others escape. There were few robes against the cold, no lodges to erect for shelter as temperatures dropped. The soldiers had come to the camp as it still slept, then put the village to torch, so of course they had no food. The journey north to the safety and protection of another camp took over two weeks in bitter cold over rough country with little game. Soon the few ponies remaining were slaughtered for provisions. Forced to travel through hardened icy crusts, their moccasins were soon worn to tatters. Slim Face Girl, Dancing Crane's youngest, had no pony to ride, her small legs wore out and her stomach shrank, so her mother carried her. Soon they had no tears left. One morning the child did not wake up but Dancing Crane still carried her. And all the next day. Two days later they reached the safety of Crazy Horse's band, who were camped on Beaver Creek, east of the Tongue. They had to pry the dead child from her arms. Turn Foot finished speaking, turned to leave, touched Anah's arm gently saying only, "There is a child, my dear," and left.

Anah sat in silence, letting it descend on her, cloak her in the savage, bitter comfort that only a mother's heart that has known hurt and healing knows. Let herself enter another world, not the world she was born to, but the world she had somehow been brought to, a world she had found herself welcoming and gaining an acceptance to. A world where the God she had been taught to revere reigned, not high above in a heaven inaccessible outside of departure from this earth, but where He was an Everywhere Spirit inhabiting the world that she herself inhabited. Visions? A child? What did it mean? She did not quite understand, but was beginning to believe that certain forces she did not understand were shaping not only her life, but all life surrounding hers, and that she would try to be responsive to them. She dressed warmly and, as she rode out into the fading light, back out toward the Kiowa agency and the lodge of the tall Lakota woman, she thought she saw hunched and tattered figures drifting wraith like through snow, their limbs stiffening, crystallizing, snapping and popping like the aspens did in the depths of winter, and the searing voice of a lost child crying for its equally lost mother.

A crying child woke her, and the odd ratcheting noise of the train on its tracks. She had been dreaming; a child had awakened her, but there were no children in her compartment. She must have dozed off. With such bold illumination to the sky now that the trees flashed by in stark silhouette, tall, skinny, and so evenly spaced that they appeared as though planted in rows, as indeed they had been, for these were turpentine pines of the coastal lowlands. Thinking it was dawn, she bestirred herself, only to discover that a brilliant full moon dogged their progress, glimmering, throwing cold spikes of silver down onto a landscape alien to her. Pressing her forehead to the cool pane of the window she watched this new terrain as they rattled by. Many undernourished but tall trees on a flat unvarying land, little fencing, few roads, no habitation that she saw. A barrenness with no apparent horizon, not a rock or stream in sight, no bluff or escarpment. How could it seem so barren when it was covered with a thick mat of undergrowth that looked like sharp, scruffy green bayonets? Bored with watching it she turned once more inward, back to the plains that she had left behind. Reaching into her portmanteau she withdrew a small, carefully wrapped doeskin bundle tied with red thread. Dancing Crane Woman had given this to her on the eve of her departure, saying that it had been brought from Ft. Laramie expressly for her. She called it "The White Ghost" and told her that it mustn't be unwrapped. When Anah demurred, saying that she simply did not believe in ghosts, Dancing Crane pressed it into her hand, laughing. "No, No, it's not like that at all." That it was "Medicine", or what was holy or *wakan,* holding spiritual power. Afraid that it had bones she probed it carefully before accepting it, finding that it was not only pliable, but had a pleasing scent. Anah realized that more of an explanation would not be forthcoming, so she thanked Dancing Crane, embarrassed to realize belatedly that she had not thought to bring her a gift. Seeming to comprehend the situation Dancing Crane drew herself up, crossing her arms across her body as though she were holding a baby, she gave the sign for love, and smiled. A bold wolfish grin crossed her face, as though she knew that nothing could unnerve Anah more, then she laughed. What a strange woman, Anah thought, compelled, of course, to return the same sign to her, but with a tightly composed face!

Aah! Would she find such friends where she was going? Anah thought. How naive she had been upon her arrival at Ft. Laramie, how little she had understood "The Indian Problem", and how much there was yet to learn. How important it was to try and see both sides. She remembered with poignancy her young self arguing so vehemently with her father and an army surgeon, whose name she couldn't recall, but remembering him, tall, corpulent, and resplendent in his green silk sash that indicated his office. She did not understand why, if the country actually went to civil war, our people fighting one another over the emancipation of a dark-skinned people for their rights to live freely, well then, why are we trying to move the red-skinned ones off the land they already inhabit? Then these well-educated men turned to one another in a well-rehearsed, oft-practiced ritual, cut and lit one another's Havanas, sharply inhaled, and in a rich, choking cloud of aromatic smoke laughingly dismissed her.

"*Tunkashila, Tunkashila*, now why did that name for grandfather come into my mind just now," she mused, remembering how little Orianna loved to clamber up on old Turn Foot's lap with no hesitancy at hugging and kissing his dark wrinkled skin. She sorely missed the old Cheyenne scout, wondered where he was now; how he was. She must get word to him, stay in contact. Her hand moved automatically to the German silver armband he had given her that she wore as a memento. She continued to stroke the White Ghost and felt a comfort, a soothing, This is medicine, she thought as she let herself drift, she was tired. Soon she would arrive. She slept.

"Mother, Mother, come help." She jerked awake. Wasn't that a child's cry? The compartment was stirring. "Won't someone help that child?" but wait, there was no child in Anah's compartment. She had been asleep. She had been dreaming, perhaps. Where was she? She was sure she had heard a child. Dismissing the porter, who had come to her cries, she reached again into her belongings and withdrew a list of the prisoners and began reciting the names in the dawn light, hoping to memorize some. Perhaps she could even capture the most difficult pronunciation before arrival. She would start with the Cheyenne , there were 33. Her favorite name was Heap of Birds, Mo-e-yau-hay-ist; she was dying to meet him and find out how he had acquired his name. Both he and Eagle's Head, or Minimic, were older and known ringleaders, or "hostiles", as the Army had decreed them. She had been told that some of the men had been pulled at random from the captives, but they had all been warriors, that is, they had all fought defensively. Many were just in their twenties, and one, Star, had been ironed and brought along, though not charged with any offense. Ah, here's another Roman Nose; a popular name, obviously this name is given by us...Wo-uh-hun-hih. Since their heights and weights were listed, she couldn't help but note that these men were quite tall and quite thin, emaciated was a polite way to put it. Starved! Her eyes closed. She saw the strong features of Dancing Crane Woman prodding her cooking fire. Gaunt but elegant, she did resemble one of the tall cranes that called The Platte home, dancing around as she spoke, "They know me. You must tell them I sent you to give them a *h'gun*, a brave word, what a warrior uses when he wishes to keep up his courage." With both hands now on the little ghost bundle, Anah hoped that Crane would say a few such words for her, also.

Coup de Foudre

Ft. Marion, Florida, Spring 1875

"The prisoners were arriving today, please be available to interpret. An orderly will be sent to fetch you when needed." She folded the message into her pocket, prepared to await the summons.

Anah barely had time to settle herself and her meager belongings into her new accommodations since her arrival just a few days ago. St. Augustine, which was first settled in 1565, looked quite civilized and she was dying to explore the town, but that would have to wait. Moist, overwhelming heat and the worst of the weather was just beginning, her landlady had told her. How the women with their elaborate hoops and petticoats could stand it she did not know, let alone fashioning their hair in elaborate curls, only to confine the results into such constricting bonnets. No woman here ventured out into the sun without a dainty parasol, and here she was with her cropped head of curls and a complexion golden from exposure to the elements. Well, she had not only grown accustomed to the styles of the West, she had enjoyed the freedom from corsets and such. She was quite content to wear a simple dress of modest calico. Once dressed, Anah had fastened the worn German silver armband Turn Foot had given her to her wrist; her only jewelry. Sitting on her narrow bedstead, content to await her summons, she gave herself over to pondering the events that had brought her to this large peninsula on the Atlantic coast.

Anah and Turn Foot had only been at Ft. Sill and the Kiowa Agency a few weeks, yet so many changes had occurred. The full compliment of the year's seasons had yet to pass, all Anah had to do was run her hands across her scalp to judge how many months had gone by. Her hair was almost down to her shoulders in an unruly cap of curls and ringlets. Soon enough, though, a year would mark her great loss, and glancing down at her dull dress she thought that if she had properly donned "widow's weeds", soon it would be the occasion to shed them. She had left many of these traditions of her gender and class behind in these past months while traveling and living with Turn Foot out on the

Plains and in the little narrow canyon she thought of as magical. The sojourn there at Fort Sill had shown her that she was not willing to step back into the role of an officer's widow, though she had discovered that accepting a pension could be advantageous. She could benefit Dancing Crane and Turn Foot by it, also.

When they had first arrived at Ft. Sill in Indian Territory, almost frozen from the late blizzard, hungry and in need of decent shelter, Turn Foot made arrangements. She was in such a daze that it wasn't until she had been summoned to the adjutant's office that she had even given a serious thought to her future. Then came her introduction to Red Crane Dancing Woman, and the meeting with the commander of Davidson's Indian Scouts stationed there; Lt. Richard H. Pratt, of the 10th Cavalry, of the fabled Buffalo Soldiers. The idea that she, who had once been so filled with despair and hopelessness, could somehow be of aid to the seventy-two Kiowa, Comanche and Cheyenne prisoners that were held here at this far-flung fort appealed to her. Oddly, she had no struggle with judging if they deserved her help or not. These past few months in which she had experienced her own brokenness had healed her of many, many things, the least of which was a certain judgmental attitude toward others. Once herself a prisoner to bitterness and unforgiveness she understood all too well what it meant to be in chains!

When the old scout saw that she was taken care of at Ft. Sill, and ready to travel down south as an interpreter for the Cheyenne prisoners, he came to her, as she knew he would, informing her of his intentions to travel back above the Arrowhead, up to the hunting grounds by the Tongue and Powder River, to be with his people. She sensed that he was now through with his service for the Army. Esperanza was to be his, a gesture that pleased them both mightily. He made light of it, though, for he knew it pained her to leave the dog. Anah could not imagine restricting the animal's freedom; she could not imagine that anyplace back East would have the roaming qualities that Turn Foot could provide. Seeing the tears in her eyes he assured her that if he were starving he would even eat his mule first, then the dog! As he saw her to the train that would eventually deposit her in northern Florida she unclasped the delicate cameo brooch that had been her grandmother Rolande's and pressed it into his dry gnarled hand. A broad smile broke across his face, so pleased was he. Pinning it onto his old military blouse and patting it he thanked her; the raised silhouette of the goddess Diana that had been so carefully incised into its surface he had thought was her portrait. It was then that he plucked the wide arm band of German silver, with its worn inscription of the Cheyenne symbol for the Morning Star, from his arm and placed it in her hands. They exchanged no further words. There are no words for goodbye in his tongue. She could not bring herself to speak the ones she knew, over the very large lump in her throat, though her heart beat madly, "Goodbye Old Friend" with each pulsing beat. With every movement of her wrist the arm band dully gleamed, not just a fond remembrance of a man, but also of a people and place that she had grown to love.

Now, as she followed her escort down to the fortress, she noted that no horizon existed that was not strictly limited by a wall of lush green growth. Gnarled oak trees hung with gray Spanish moss overshadowed the narrow bricked streets, lovely homes stood well back, surrounded by green lawns and tidy, painted fences. No expansive horizon loomed as out on the plains, that is, except when one had a view towards the rolling swells of the gray blue Atlantic, breaking right on the shores of the old Spanish garrison, now occupied by the U.S. Army, under the name of Ft. Marion.

She could not imagine what the captives would make of these surrounds, and where would they put them, surely not into the dank dungeon-like cells of the old fort, the Castillo de San Marcos, built by the Spanish at the turn of the 17th century and used by the army to hold prisoners from the Indian wars, transported from the High Plains down to these coastal lowlands.

The fort itself was quite impressive, she thought, surrounded in part by a moat and facing the sea, with an actual drawbridge. She had been told to meet the others up on the large courtyard overlooking the bay, the terreplein. The lieutenant had sent for her to help in taking the roll. She simply had to match the prisoner to the name on a list which was supplied phonetically, and with an English equivalent when possible.

George Fox, who was skilled in Comanche, used a sort of inter-tribal language. She would assist him.

As the shackled line of malnourished men moved forward under light guard, past her and the other interpreters, she tried to quickly assess those who by appearance were most likely to be Cheyenne. Running her finger down the list she queried them. Height made some an obvious choice, all were lean. She had hoped to say something encouraging to them but it was so obvious that, after more than three weeks of travel to arrive here, that there was not much that she could say to reassure them of anything. Most were beyond responding to her, deep in the throes of hopelessness, oblivious to their surroundings though the sky was a deep blue and the ocean spread out right before them, exceedingly bright and sparkling. Most of them wore impenetrable masks of resignation. She knew that many of them had left wives and children behind. Perhaps the fact that there was not a gallows being built was an encouragement! Or perhaps they were looking forward to it. She gave a furtive glance to the narrow little cells called casements where they were to be confined; they had no windows. She continued trying to match names and pronounce them correctly, all the while realizing the abject futility of any welcoming phrase. Welcome to what, imprisonment?

For the most part she kept her eyes respectfully averted from these travel-weary, defeated warriors. Each shuffle, as they moved steadily forward, brought the dull heavy clank of the irons, a sad resonance to the bright, sunshine filled day. They, too, kept their heads down; shame weighed heavily on them. Most of these men, if not all, had been honored warriors all their adult lives, so firmly committed to keeping their lands and the freedom that they put their lives and the lives of their people at constant risk. And it had come to this!

She turned back to scrutinizing the list. The names! Heap of Birds, Long Back, Shave Head...most did not respond to the translation of their names as she struggled to correctly pronounce them. She tried to acknowledge them when they gave out with more than a nod of affirmation or a grunt. None responded in English, although some must have known a few words. "Sock-oh-yo-uh, Bear Shield," she called out his name phonetically and paused. A middle-aged Cheyenne of medium height leaned forward to touch a long finger to where she had placed a check mark, and awarded her a hostile glare before shuffling along. "Chi-i-tie-dud-oh". She liked the sound and meaning of this name, he was quite young and quite tall; Matches, his name meant Matches. She noted that he was listed as a ringleader.

Suddenly her wrist was strongly seized, jerked forward, so that she flew off the small camp stool that she had been perched on, and brought into an upright position, pulled halfway across the table and brought face to face, to find herself looking into the blackest eyes she had ever had to encounter at such close range. A very tall warrior was elevating her arm, drawing her forward to get even a better look at the design inscribed in the silver armband, at the same time hoarsely shouting in Cheyenne, "The Morning Star, *Tah-me-la-pash-me,* how did you get this?" The eyes that now bored into hers were flashing with the most intense passion and heat. Anah could not believe that this was coming from a man brought here shackled, in abject defeat. She felt as though the armband was beginning to burn upon her wrist. An unknown fire began to travel up her veins. Speechless, she stood there held in that gaze then.....

A shout rang out as a sentry sprinted across the terreplein toward them, the barrel of his rifle raised menacingly. "It's all right!" she finally managed to gasp out, as though she were returning back from some other world, her arms flung out as though to block the impending blow. The soldier paused, but did not lower his weapon, nor did the Cheyenne loosen his grip from her upraised arm. Their eyes were still locked as though in mortal combat. Time seemed suspended at that moment, that precise moment when a lump of precious metal meets its exact melting point, then suddenly, magically, just yields! (It had not gone unnoticed that she had flung her arms up to ward off the soldier's blow from the Cheyenne, not herself. Nor did the Indian react to the guard's threat!)

Turning fully toward the man now, she saw at once that in spite of his abject condition he was beyond a doubt a Tsitsistas, one of The Beautiful People, a Northern Cheyenne of exceeding natural beauty of form and face in spite of his malnourished condition. She began to speak to him in his own language. Whatever imprisonment, near starvation, defeat and irreparable loss had wreaked upon him, nothing could hide that he was still a man in the prime of youth. Handsome, in fact, with a certain appeal, in her eyes. She had long been a student of this sort, envisioning an ideal fostered by James Fennimore Cooper's Longstocking tales, Karl Bodmer and George Caitlin's romantic renditions of native beauty. Well, he had matched it, even in his soiled skins and bedraggled braids. The entire line had, of course, frozen during this proceeding.

"*Washte yelo,*" It's all right." Impulsively she gently placed her other hand on his forearm above his shackle. Then turning to the guard, "It is quite all right, I will take just a minute here to calm the prisoner." As she continued to speak, she drew a quite small circle on his forearm, a gesture that in no way could be mistaken as anything but comforting, little as it was. To her amazement he allowed this. "My armband," she told him, "was a parting gift when I left Ft. Sill, from my *nameseme*. I miss both him, the people and the plains." Then slowly removing her hand, she gently placed a closed fist to her heart. At no time, as she spoke, did his gaze leave hers.

So startled was Standing Cloud, a defeated Dog Soldier, by this interaction that at no time did he seem to notice that an enemy and a woman, a white woman, a *ve'ho'e,* was speaking to him coherently in his own language. Nor did he take much account of her beauty; he was ravished only by the "sign", the appearance of the Morning Star inscribed in the bracelet upon her wrist.

A palpable tension left the air in the same way that a large owl departs, as he removed his hand with just the slightest bow of his head to her, and turned away. It was then that she noticed his well worn, bloody Dog Rope wrapped tightly around his lean waist. Then, of necessity, the line moved on.

He was much taller than the others. Realizing that she was willing him to turn around and glance backward toward her caused a surge of unexpected feeling that she tried hard to suppress. She bent down and fiddled with the laces of her boot, and yet caught herself glancing from between the spindly legs of the camp table at the retreating line of the prisoner's legs, trying to identify his. The thought that she might never see his face again seemed almost unbearable. She wanted to leap up and run toward the retreating line yelling, "No, don't leave me." This thought, brief as it was, seared her with its unexpected heat, for it was a passionate feeling the likes of which she was unaccustomed to. It altered her in a way that she could not understand. It felt like a loss, and yet it was an anticipation, a yearning, for the impression he had made on her was indelible, and it had occurred in that great unseen realm of the spirit.

He was a fabled Dog Soldier, one of those who would die for his people. Now he was here before her, in shackles, naked to the waist, bloodied. She knew she wanted to know, she had to know this person who was not selfish, who did not put his life before others! Who was he? That great entity, Time, had moved on, had surrounded her, with him, and when she looked down at the list she had no indication of his name. She had not checked his name. It had seemed to her as though time had stopped, or stood still, or somehow parted, and she had entered into some other place. Her wrist still felt warm. Yet he had not looked at her kindly, had he?

Hanblecheyabi, A Lament

The moon had waxed from half of its fullness to a round orbed beauty, and they had yet to know their fate. The Dog Man once known as Medicine Horse, who now called himself Standing Cloud, stood looking out over the wide sea wall beyond the dry moat below, out towards the ocean, which roiled ceaselessly on to the shoreline of Mantanzas Inlet, where the old prison had been built in the 1700's. That the harbor held not just one, but two lighthouses was of little interest to the prisoners after the grueling experiences that twenty four days of travel by wagon, several trains, steamboat, and finally, horse-drawn carts had taken.

Several times a day they were herded in their clanking irons out of the confining pen that had been built for them, open only to the sky, out onto the terreplein where they could walk around under the watchful eyes of a heavy guard. Rumors as to their fate abounded. Some thought perhaps they would be taken to those two oddly striped, tall, black and white towers that stood as sentinels across the bay. Who could understand the ways of the Whites; could they not conceal gallows inside?

This was the hottest time of the year in Florida. Damp, humid weather devastated their health and sat upon their already depressed spirits. Their holding cells were damp and black with mold. Quite a few were ill, and there were several deaths in spite of the humane treatment that they were receiving. Cloud wondered if they were to be transported to the Great Father in Washington, but no one seemed to know how far away that was, even though some of them had been brought there, on occasion, for the peace treaties. Lone Wolf, a chief of the Kiowas, was one who had made that journey once, but he kept silent since he had been transported, nor did he wish to take the white man's food into his body. He was not the only one who refused to eat.

The white woman who wore the Cheyenne arm band appeared on several occasions to "doctor" the worst abrasions that some carried from the shackles, for in the heat the sores they caused festered. The army doctor just saw to major wounds and emergencies. Cloud found her beauty exotic in much the same way that he had found the young women from the far off Pueblos when he had traveled with his uncle Bear Stands In Shade, years back, to trade for feathers, shells and pots. They had crossed the plains, gone up the Cimarron, down across the Sangre de Christos, and followed the Rio Grande, visiting many of the pueblos along the way. In one called the Sky City, the young girls wore snow white, tanned antelope boots wound thick around their legs, and one-shouldered, woven dresses. Their thick black hair gleamed like raven wings and was wound into huge horns, like mountain rams, on each side of their round, brown, lovely young faces. He was so entranced that he could barely look at them, and when he did they just giggled into their many strands of silver and turquoise necklaces. Not that this white woman looked anything like that! It was just that she also looked so very different from the Lakota and Cheyenne he had grown up with. Not that he was interested in her. Curious, though; she was not a Mission Mary, nor a Quaker, nor an agent. She was hired as translator, but she did much more, and that made him suspicious. How did she know the old Cheyenne scout, and why had he given her the arm band? When he realized that he was dwelling on such things, he understood how very different his life was now from what it had been just a few moons ago. What now dwelled in his chest? He was not sure who among them were holy men that he could consult, or if he wanted to. They were all cast down, dispirited. Bitter Woman, a contrary known to have lost his powers had told him once, in confidence, after a successful raid, when he returned from the confluence of the Yellow Stone and the Missouri, that "Nothing with a spirit lives to the East of the Big Muddy," and not to ever cross that river; that was what explained why the *wasichus* had no heart, he said.

He let his gaze focus on the surface of the undulating blue waves out in the bay. A smooth, dark form arced up and roiled out and down in a half crescent out of the water, followed by another one just like it, then another right next to it. It was the scaleless water animal from his vision. Excited, as he hadn't been since capture, he watched the surface of the water till his eyes burned from keeping focus, but there was no further reappearance of the sleek water creatures. Monsters they were not. Imagined they were not. The sky was a clear blue above in which no birds flew. No other portents abounded, except the small lizards that raced to and fro along the crumbling casement walls in their ceaseless search for sustenance. The sun blazed upon his skin; the tide grew slack.

Once the prisoners were herded back into their damp casements there was nothing for them to do. Narrow slot openings ten feet above the floor, with iron bars, were too high to provide much ventilation. Most had damp sand floors, but several had plank floors to make them more sanitary, for that is where they slept. Cloud spent the night coated in sweat, feasted on by the hungry mosquitoes, dreaming of his homeland in the high portion of the Great Plains, a vast grassland with few trees and a magnificent open horizon, where one could see the huge thunderclouds riding towards one in their purple and black terrifying and thrilling majesty. Sunsets cast a glow of such ripeness upon everything they touched that the very thought that "gold" is some metal that must be dug for in the earth sounded crazy.

Scant rainfall occurred out on those great plains with the wide open vistas, where one could see the approach of an oncoming storm. What rain did come arrived in the summer in such thunderstorms that one understood why lightning was to be revered! Grass grew quickly, and with its luxurious growth the ponies fattened rapidly in the spring. Soon the buffalo arrived and the People left their Winter Camps and the good life of the nomads began once more. It was a cycle that had never been broken, that is, until....

As the sweat bathed his body, he tossed and turned, remembering the wind. His friend, the wind! In no place does the wind blow as it does on the Great Plains! It has been known to drive many a settler's wife mad, but then she was not born to it, as the People were. The eyes dry out, the lips crack, anything that isn't tied down rattles incessantly, and anything one wishes kept moist dries out.

But to be on one's pony and face into the wind upon your skin, to kick your heels and race off with it. Holler into it! Feel one with creation, to raise your feathered lance in joy crying out to *Taku skan skan!* Bare thighs upon one's horse. Racing the wind! The thunderheads above moving with them, the waves of grass flowing... Wind, wind embracing all that surrounded him, and above all, filled with the wind, the very spirit of life within and around, surrounding him, lifting his spirit, *mitakuye oyasin!*

Sweat poured down his brow, tears down his cheeks, and he knew then, Bitter Woman had been wrong, for as Cloud lay shackled, bathed in his own sweat on the damp, gritty, sand floor thousands of miles from the high plains he so loved, what he recognized as the Everywhere Spirit flowed through him once more; the hot, damp night air held a sweetness. The strident, grating noise of what he was yet to learn were the insects that clung to the trees called cicadas had a rhythm that lulled him to the first restful night's sleep that he had had since his capture.

To the Lakota there is a time, a rite of sorts that they call *Hanblecheyabi*, a lament, a period of expressing grief, where one waits to receive a new vision of life to enable one to continue living. Beauty stored in the heart is such an ointment that heals, no one can take it from us. On the other hand, bitterness is such that it eats away what little heart you may have left.

Cloud knew when the tide turned, as he had learned this by the sound the waves made from the shells on the strand. It was the hottest part of the night and there wasn't a breath of air, nor was there any water jug in his cell to relieve his thirst. That would have to wait until morning. He could wait. Now he chose to think of the times of first snowfall, long nights, and much story telling, especially those times when the weather changed with incredible speed. A large, black cloud would appear on the horizon, the wind whipping up an accompanying, swirling, almost blinding mass of dust and sand as the temperature dropped so fast that one could barely get the lodge liners up and stuffed thickly with grasses, then the winds would blow the snow, and all the world would turn white. Anyone caught outside would not only be in danger of freezing to death, but could become hopelessly lost just a few steps from one's lodge.

Soon, instead of feeling hopelessly sad over what was left behind, he found himself drifting off, seeing once again the lovely face, framed by her long black braids, of Fire Crow, a Cheyenne maiden that he had once thought it possible he could call to his blanket for courting; that, of course, was before the incessant warring with the whites began, and then there was no time for such things. She no longer trod the earth; that saddened him. He forced his mind from thoughts of who now trod the sky path. Through the iron bars in the cell high in the wall above him a star shone dimly, he was not sure, but perhaps it was the Morning Star; eternal.

Shortly after dawn the guards led them out onto the terreplein. All of the Comanches, nine of them, with the exception of Pe-ah-in and her daughter Ah-kes, who were not really prisoners, were separated out and led off under guard.

Spotted Elk drew the Cheyennes to him, along with a group of Kiowas. They began to discuss the situation. Matches, always outspoken, said that they were not to be hung, as he had not heard any sound of gallows being made. Bear Killer, grimly laughing, countered that of course, they would just shoot them. Wolf's Marrow, one of the oldest of the warriors, speculated that they might be taken to Washington. But Making Medicine walked away, saying only, "We were not brought all this way just to die like dogs!" Standing Cloud, along with the others, dispersed, each to his own thoughts and speculations. "Die like dogs! He who was no longer an honorable "Bravest of the Brave". Dogs! He dragged himself to the parapet and let himself be practically hypnotized by watching the endless rise and fall of the slack tide, trying to discipline his mind. His body, it was true, was held captive, but he could set his mind free...

As the warm air rose over the land and met the water, large white clouds rose to sail out over the vast horizon, very much like the appearance of those that graced the vast open sky of the Great Plains. Soon he was lost in recall of the first great ceremony of his People that he had attended, the Arrow Renewal ceremony. It was held when the sun was at its highest in the summer sky, when the glories of Spring had run their course, and the strength of the sun shone for its longest time in the day. Every Cheyenne that could manage assembled in the chosen place where there was enough water and good green grass for the wealth of over a thousand lodges, which were pitched in a great crescent shape, like the arms of a new moon. Their door flaps were positioned to open to the rays of the rising sun in the east. Each lodge displayed medicine bundles and decorated shields to catch those rays. Lodges were grouped by bands, and down in the nearby cottonwoods and streams there were children and young men and women, visiting, courting, playing games. Wonderful smells coming from cooking fires, and people dressed in their ceremonial finest. Horses being groomed and painted. Drums and singing, and nighttime brought dancing, and stories, and even if you were but a child and barely understood the significance of the Sacred Arrow Lodge in the great inner circle, and there were times when you absolutely had to go into your lodge and not even a dog could sulk about, you would be thrilled above all to be a Tsitsistas, one of the People.

"Cloud, Cloud." It was Matches. "It is time for us. They are taking the Cheyenne now." "Taking us where?" He was ready. He had fought well. It had been a good life.

The large white clouds had moved in now, bearing the afternoon's rains, increasing the burden of humidity. He gazed up at them and found them full of beauty.

Anah Helps

Those first weeks that followed the prisoners incarceration at the fort were ones of adjustment for all involved. Heavy rains brought an increase in the oppressive humidity to those men used to the much drier environs of the high plains. Illness and a few subsequent deaths made it tragically apparent that the climate, which could not be altered, had to be accommodated for in some manner.

Lt. Pratt became their advocate, and soon saw to it that permission was granted to have the heavy iron shackles struck from their hands and feet. Anah then was quick to offer her services to care for the sores and abrasions that those irons had caused. Of course there were the services of an army doctor, but as she assured the lieutenant, the doctor would be more concerned with broken bones than blisters and such. At first the lieutenant seemed adverse to allowing her access to the men, until she assured him that she had no fear whatsoever of them. They were not savages to her. Had she not lived among them? Had not her father served as a frontier contract surgeon at Laramie? As he well knew Indians were comfortable in the presence of women. In fact, did not Black Horse have his own wife here with him in the barracks?

Then rising dramatically to her feet she won him over as she deposited a worn Gladstone bag at his feet, and crouched to open it. The interior displayed a varied collection: bundles of dried herbs, small brown bottles containing tinctures, tins with ointments and unguents, and small cloth pouches, largely provided by Red Dancing Crane Woman and others from the Kiowa agency at Ft. Sill. Anah declared her knowledge, training and skill not only of Indian medicinal cures, but of all she had learned while assisting at her father's side over the years. Lt. Pratt looked at her thoughtfully as she continued so earnestly, launching into her own theory on how she felt that an application of a bit of the healing properties of both worlds might foster an understanding that would be advantageous to these men. Pratt felt it would be most wise to hold his tongue.

"You sir, have been in the field eight years. You have worked in a position of leadership with colored soldiers and Indian scouts. You obviously have a deep sympathy for minorities." Feeling perhaps she may have gone too far she faltered, glanced at his face, and soldiered on, "When the train stopped in Indianapolis with that crowd of gawking, curious onlookers, you brought your very own six year old daughter to walk among the prisoners.....a six year old child!" Dropping her eyes, that's it, what had been in her heart, that this man had trusted his small girl with these men accused of heinous killings; to let a mere child walk in their presence...well.... A most hearty laugh broke from Richard H. Pratt. "Well, I can see that I certainly got more than just an interpreter when I hired you on, Mrs. Moore, did I not?"

Anah left his presence with a *carte blanche* to come and go at her leisure among the prisoners. Anah also found that she was to become welcome at the Pratt's table on those evenings when the household was open to informal gatherings.

The depression and hopelessness of the prisoners slowly lifted, due largely to a dawning comprehension that they had not been transported thousands of miles across the country to be hung; a most ignoble death, in their belief. Lt. Pratt continued in his appeals for more liberty for those prisoners in his care. He was not a warden, nor acting like an agent. He understood that they needed fresh air and provided bed ticks filled with grass laid on rough board beds. Soon an entire new dormitory was to be built, and by the prisoners themselves.

He had so easily taken Anah into his confidence; it seemed that they both thought these prisoners capable of much in the way of redemption. "Why not have them construct their own barracks?" Anah had asked casually at the Pratt's one night at dinner. Second Lieutenant Stuyvesant, a recent West Point graduate, who was also dining with them, thoughtfully concealed his smirk by patting his mustache. "After all," she continued eagerly, "they are so incredibly skilled at crafting their own tools." "And let us not forget how skillful they are at crafting such fearsome weapons!" Stuyvesant quickly interjected. She paused to forcefully stare the rude lieutenant down. His gesture had not gone unnoticed by her. "It will keep them from pining away with idleness, and give them something to take pride in." "Ha, Mrs. Moore, a capital idea, I shall entertain it, indeed," Lt. Pratt said in a manner intended to end the discussion. "More chicken?" Mrs. Pratt hastily interjected, being sensitive to a developing hostility between the two.

In the parlor before dinner there had been a contretemps over Harriet Beecher Stowe's merits as an authoress. She noted that both this determined young woman translator and her husband, when in one another's presence, referred to the Indian prisoners as men without fail. They constantly had their heads together, trying to make arrangements to better their imprisonment. The wild ideas of that woman; she wanted to use the scrap wood from the construction to make a small bonfire up on the terreplein so she and Mr. Fox, the Comanche interpreter, could tell American folktales to entertain the prisoners by its light....as though they were guests, not prisoners, of the U.S. Army!

Within the week construction was started on a large, one room shed, mainly by Indian labor, that covered the entire space of the terreplein on the north side, and thus the prisoners were able to move up out of the dank casements and enjoy better health. During this time Anah had been busy with projects of her own devising. She had received parcels of dried sage and braided Sweet Grass from Red Dancing Crane Woman. Already she knew that any objections to the dispensing of this could be overcome simply by pointing out how these plants were used to perfume the air; the casements the men now resided in being most moldy and dank. Through her correspondence with Dancing Crane she could help to keep the men in touch with their families and to convey the news of their well being here. It was with great sadness that she wrote at length of Grey Beard's suicide and Lean Bear's death. She tried to convey just how very much Lt. Pratt was trying to do to encourage the men and give them reason to hope. She could not bring herself to formulate what that hope was to be, though. She did mention that the townspeople here were not only quite tolerant of the army, who had, after all, defeated them not too long ago in the Civil War, but were also civil toward the prisoners; not at all fearful and hostile, as many were out West.

Basket of Aloes

Anah had seen to the gathering of a goodly supply of fresh aloe spears from local sources, and had brought them up to the men on the terreplein in the early evening when they were free from their duties and chores. After explaining their use as a natural relief, not only from sunburn, but specifically to ease and heal the sores inflicted from the wearing of the irons, she then sat back in a shady spot against the wall to just observe. Of special interest to her was the tallest Cheyenne. She had begun to identify many of them by name and personality, agreeing with Lt. Pratt that they were exceedingly well disciplined and adjusting well to their captivity here in this climate. Lt. Pratt was even looking into providing excursions out to Anastasia Island. Many were now attending the language classes taught by Miss Mather, who was a friend of Harriet Beecher Stowe, a known abolitionist. Many diversions were being provided; even opportunities to earn money to send back west to their families. The spirits of the men were lifting. Good reports were appearing in official documents and local newspapers, but nothing was yet known as to their fate.

In conversations around Lt. Pratt's dining table it had been argued that self-discipline was a natural trait imposed upon these Indians almost from birth by the harsh conditions of their environment, and in order to survive what benefited the group must come before the good of the individual. Many interesting conversations centered around such topics. How often Anah bit her tongue to avoid speaking out in regards to the policy of Manifest Destiny, with which she strongly disagreed. The implied destruction of another's society was not a subject for dinner table conversation. Though she longed to retire with the men to the parlor when fresh news of skirmishes and battles regarding the Indian Wars were being discussed, it simply wasn't her place. She had to remember that she was not an adjutant's wife anymore, and privy to such news. Now she had no such authority, whatsoever. She had to rely on what news reached her from Ft. Sill from Dancing Crane Woman. She longed for news of Turn Foot and Esperanza; were they well? She dreaded carrying some of the unfortunate news that she had to bear to some of the prisoners here, though. Occasionally Crane enclosed a memento. Once came a very small pair of moccasins wrapped in red trade cloth. Anah kept them on her dresser for a week before she worked up the courage to bring them to the man, dignified in his confinement. Before she could even break the news he gently took the small parcel, as though he knew what the contents foretold, and turned away, head lowered.

Realizing that she had been aimlessly twisting the silver bracelet, she let her attention drift back to the present and the wicker basket of aloe spears which she had set down by the wall. It was almost empty now. Good! Noting that there had been no grabbing for the largest pieces of the plant; in fact when it appeared that there wasn't enough to go around, parts of the thick fleshy leaves had been broken off, and quietly shared. Now she observed that Matches and the tall one called Cloud sat looking out to sea, talking. Once they glanced towards her, then quickly away. It was not just that he was so handsome, there was something else; she had seen it that day that she had brought him the bundles of white sage, the Sweet Grass from Dancing Crane Woman, to distribute.

At times, in persons of great sorrow, there resides a reservoir of odd strength, a reserve that is never called upon. One can sometimes catch it if one looks carefully into their eyes. It resides there as a deep calm, an impenetrable pool that can leave you wondering, as it did her......late at night, days, weeks later, what is the source of its mystery; do they even know? At the same time one is forced to acknowledge its inviolable privacy. It's never spoken of. Turn Foot held this in his great eyes; it was what gained her immediate trust, she realized. In that brief instant on that first day, when the prisoners had arrived at Ft. Marion, and the tallest Cheyenne had grabbed for the silver bracelet upon her wrist and their eyes met, she had seen that strength. That, and that alone is what had told her to stay the guard when he came rushing forward to her aid; that she was in no way in danger! She found herself not being able to forget him. Her wrist burned where he had held her; upon examination she found not a mark, even though she felt as though she had been branded with a hot iron! And those eyes; such hate. Was it hate? She had tried to discover his name from the rolls. Thought him to be Medicine Horse, the Cheyenne Dog Soldier, but there was none that would answer to that name. Yet he wore a bloodied Dog Rope, of the kind only worn by the Bravest of the Brave. As Anah pulled her straw boater down upon her brow to shade herself from the fierce rays of the descending sun, and to dwell upon her thoughts, Matches and Cloud began their own discussion regarding her.

"That woman is a strange one!" Cloud noted to his friend as he carefully split the aloe leaf and rubbed it over his ankles. "First she brings us the white sage and Sweet Grass, even telling us to use it for purification, as if we didn't know its use from the cradle board. She speaks our language, a good Lakota dialect, too." Matches silently went about peeling his leaf carefully, then laughed before saying, "Of course she speaks well, she was hired as an interpreter." Cloud continued rubbing his other ankle now, clearly not satisfied with the conversation. "She comes most every evening." "Yes," Matches said, "I like her stories." "How does she know about our ways?" "Why do you care, Cloud?"

He stood, looking out over the bay where the evening clouds were beginning to amass, the air growing heavy and sullen, bringing rain and more humidity and the-can't-be-seen-biting-flies. " What is to become of us? Don't you wonder, or care, my kola? Did you ever think about her connection with Dancing Crane Woman, the very one we would go to, to relay messages for our brothers up North? For all her good-mouth-stories, her skin is white, white, white," and he sat abruptly down and put his head to his knees, flicking small stones at the wall.

Matches did not know what to say. He remained silent till he felt her gaze upon him from across the terreplein. She knows we are discussing her, but he said nothing, just concentrated on her, as Cloud mumbled into the dust. Slowly Matches raised his eyes to hers. Matches had the wild courage of a fool, often the bravest kind, so he returned her gaze. She did not drop her eyes, very unlike the modest behavior of a Cheyenne maiden, yet it implied nothing immodest in it. Matches was thrilled, knowing that this was a contest of sorts; words like arrogance held no sway, phrases like "meeting of minds" could not be put into a common language, but in the spirit world of which he was born, and to which she had but a brief introduction, an agreement was passed between them. They each then gently smiled. Anah walked to her now empty basket and proceeded home.

Cloud began on a new tact as the wind picked up, lashing the nearby palms, spreading small swirls of sand across the bricks. "That arm band she is never without, the one inscribed with the Morning Star. It belonged to Turn Foot, the old Cheyenne Scout, from Ft. Sill. He's *He'joxones*, a putrid one, he committed murder, he polluted his whole tribe, what was she doing with him?" He was not about to give up, she was getting under his skin, he preferred to remain "dead", did he not? "Cloud, Cloud, that was many, many years ago, I believe. He has been forgiven; it is our way. He has made the proper amends. Besides, he is an important part of the way we bring news to our brothers fighting off the reservations. Cloud, I believe that she does not think like a white-man! Remember, too, that she is a friend of Lt. Pratt. Yes, he is our jailer, but he is the one who had our irons struck from us, brought us up from the dark below, allows us to work, be like men again." As Cloud reached to yank at his braids, which were no longer there, Matches caught his friend's wrist. "Yes, kola, I know. Do not let that bitter root grow down into your soul."

Cloud stared moodily out at the black clouds that had begun to amass on the horizon and remained silent, lost in his conflicted thoughts, as one more night darkened and fell upon them.

Demon Rum

Ft. Marion, Summer 1875

When Anah returned to her lodgings that evening, she spent some time pondering a story Lt. Pratt had told following that evening's repast. He had introduced it as "The most desperate experience of my military service". When she heard that, she was ready to grab her shawl and excuse herself, fearing a story along the lines of The Sand Creek Massacre, or worse, especially since Lt. Stuyvesant made a point of catching her eye and smirking; a challenge of sorts. However, Mrs. Pratt did not suggest that the ladies adjourn, and as Anah trusted those sensibilities, she settled in to listen.

What followed was a most interesting tale of fortitude and persistence that had occurred during a "Norther" in the winter of '73, at Ft. Sill. He said that the cavalry had headed out as the temperature began steadily dropping, finally registering fourteen below zero. They were hoping to find, capture, and arrest the corrupt whiskey dealers who had been supplying, illegally, the Indians on the reservations. They accomplished their aim under the most adverse conditions imaginable, and saw them brought to trial. Just as Anah was ready to deliver praise, she felt Lt. Stuyvesant's eye upon her, his pale glittering eyes expectant. Now what, she thought! She held her tongue. Lt. Pratt concluded his tale with all eyes upon him. "Yes, we brought these corrupt men to justice, but only to see them receive just ten dollar fines, and a one month imprisonment!"

The evening was spoiled for her now. She had seen first hand the "Hang-about-the fort-Indians", knew how they traded what little they had in order to receive that adulterated whiskey to poison themselves and thus impoverish their families, in spite of the efforts of their own leaders, BIA agents, or the best efforts of the army to keep it off the reservations. A great sadness settled upon her spirit at the futility of it all.

Walking out onto the terreplein just as the sun was going down, Anah was struck by how orderly in appearance the prison yard was. Neatly stacked in the area used for the fire circle were scraps brought back from the lumber yard where some of the prisoners were employed. Pe-ah-in and her little daughter were seated on a length of palmetto log, weaving some kind of marsh grass into small baskets. At the sight of her a few men began to gather by the fire pit, which they had constructed themselves from salvaged bricks, for they expected storytelling time to begin.

Lt. Pratt's tale of his ordeal had not left her heart, and she did not feel like entertaining them tonight. It would have been better if she had stayed away. As she looked around, she couldn't help but wonder how much alcohol had been a factor in some of the outrageous crimes they had been accused of. She had read the list of the offenses of which they had been accused; stealing horses, which was second nature to them, was the least of it. A few of them had been chosen at random and were innocent, but quite a few were notorious, "carried the pipe", that is, they had been leaders of a war party. Some had abducted citizens, not just soldiers. Some had murdered, not just defended. It made her head swim, and she had tried not to identify a man by name with his alleged crime as listed, but to judge the man, if at all, by his actions towards her and the others.

Those who had worn the Dog Rope, the Bravest of the Brave, as they were called, well, they had too.... Just then Matches came up to her and most politely began, "Miss, will you story us?" His command of English was improving day by day. There were quite a few women from the town who graciously volunteered now to teach daily in the classrooms provided. He was one who eagerly attended. Now he led her to the fire pit, where a small fire had just been set. Directly across from where Matches indicated her to sit was the tallest Cheyenne.

Sighing deeply she began, " I am going to tell you a story about a common spirit of the ve'ho'es, the White-man." A discernible ripple of discomfort spread among them. She didn't seem to care, other than to say, "You do not have to listen, but it would be good if you did." They all stayed. "In The Moon When Birds Return," she began, "I had just arrived at Ft. Sill from Cimarron Canyon, crossing the Llano with my companion, an old Northern Cheyenne scout known as Turn Foot." A ripple of muttered comments flowed through the assembled, which she chose to ignore. Let them wonder and speculate what they would regarding her; she was no more the average *ve'ho'e* than they were storefront wooden Indians!

"Upon arrival we were cold, hungry, and very tired. I was given lodgings at the fort and quickly fell into deep slumber. Upon awakening, I discovered that the Indian Bureau had again decreased the Indian's insufficient supply of allotted foodstuffs for the month. You may wonder at my concern; I will explain someday, but for now just allow me to continue." They were not used to her being like this with them, and turned to Double Vision, a Kiowa, one of the oldest among them who simply nodded, as if to say, continue, and she did. "Hostilities ran high, discontent and empty bellies prevailed, and when the Indians were not given ammunition with which to hunt, nor weapons, nor allowed off the reservations to even trap game, well, air did not fill bellies, nor did heated words suffice. It was then that a bootlegged influx of whiskey from one of the ranches south of the Kansas line along the Northern border of the reservation arrived. I wondered at the time if these cut-throat, heartless, snake-bellied, thieves," she stopped herself just short, then continued, "waited for just this time of near starvation to descend upon their "clients", as they called these pinched-bellied, starving souled people!"

Reminding herself not to get overwrought, she sat down and arranged her skirts studiously before continuing. "Once the running of the buffalo brought celebration, high spirits, dancing, and a different sort of excess. When morning came the bodies sprawled upon the ground came from a different sort of excess. A spiritual exhaustion directed to the proper source for the proper reasons. Medicine Men were there to guide, vows existed to be kept. Honor was a shield, chastity was a crown. Ponies were wealth to be given generously, buffalo to renew life never-ending. The rivers, the plains, the sky!" This brought a chorus of *ahos*! "Then everything changed with the coming of the *ve'ho'e's*." An intense murmuring began; where was she taking this story they wondered? Many looked to Double Vision again, but he seemed fixed upon her.

"But what is a man without hope of a future or a link to his past?"

Does he want to forget yesterday? Does he want to remember that tomorrow is coming?" This brought a chorus of "ahos!" "Whiskey, though, was now what many on the reservation traded their souls for, what they hoped to drown their shame, their sorrow in, and it did indeed provide a dark entrance to an even darker cave, but the spirits they encountered there were unlike any they had ever been told of at any wise man's knee.

These were white man's spirits. Strange, cunning, powerful. Many thought that they were but just another manifestation of old Wiley Coyote, the Trickster-Changer. Iktomi." At this Cloud leaned into Matches, "How does she know these things?" "Now listen carefully Cloud, a lot of the whites don't tell us these secrets."

"First came Lethe, who brings the sought for supposed blessing of oblivion, I say supposed," and she leaned in to Mr. Fox, telling him how important an exact translation was here, "for we yearn to remember, not forget, what blesses us, is this not so? But when Lethe takes us in her mighty teeth we feel powerful, like Gods, some of us, women especially feel more beautiful, men, stronger. We destroy, we murder, we rage, and then we forget. But under the spell from the little brown jug we think, "Oh, how wonderful, we will give anything, trade anything. Empty! Can't be! Here, take my finest winter robe! Take it! The one covering *Tunkashila*, grandfather, well, pull it from the old man, there. My wife, well take her, too, now give me that jug! Share! We! You? No!"

Out of the corner of her eye she saw Matches lean in toward Mr. Fox, undoubtedly trying to clarify a word, such was his thirst for understanding. It was so hard to bridge the gap between these cultures at times, she often ran ahead of her own understanding. Perhaps it was the concept of "Lethe".

"Lethe," she began, looking to Mr. Fox for assistance," is a river in a place called Hades, that a people of long ago believed that, once dead, your soul drank from and forgot all you suffered while you were alive, and," this she paused to emphasize, "all that you had accomplished, that is, all your coups," and here a collective sigh erupted from them. " We white people now call it The River of Forgetfulness, and use a word, lethargic," oh, she was so given to these rambling over-explanations, but Matches was looking up at her with a rapt expression on his face; he was following this. She plunged ahead. "Back to Demon Rum, the whiskey, that is!"

"I cannot begin to understand all that you have lost, but I can understand why you would want to forget those losses. There is more to drinking whiskey, though, than just the Spirit of Forgetting." She went on, since they sat so quiet, "Then feeling sated, another spirit might come slyly forth to place a hand in seeming compassion on your shoulder, guide you to a quiet corner, away from all others, saying soothingly, "Now tell me, take a good look at yourself. You fool, you failure. Go ahead, have a good cry. Lay down right here. Go ahead. Sleep now. It's okay. Nothing matters, now does it?"

Now her audience was not liking this very much; the honor and dignity of these most successful warriors, that they had lost by being captured and submitted to shackles, was being once again pricked, but by a different sort of remembrance. The tall Cheyenne was giving her a strange, piercing look, making her uncomfortable. She forged quickly ahead. As for Matches, he was hoping for an opportunity to question her about this god, Demon Rum, of the whites; was it one of their lesser god's?

"When you wake in your own vomit, well, you think it's your own, but it might be others, too, the last spirit arrives. There is no mistaking this one. She is very tall and very wise. You feel so small before her. There no longer exists any pleasant effects of the alcohol in your body, in fact your head hurts, your stomach feels as though you have eaten an unskinned porcupine, and you do not want to look at the bright light that is morning, or listen to the voice that is in your head saying, "Look at what you have done."

"You are barefoot. Where are the new moccasins your wife just made for you? You are way beyond Cache Creek. There is vomit all down your chest. One of your braids is completely undone. And there is a woman, a white woman. Why is she following you? Everywhere you go, you move so gingerly and slowly. Such a cruel spirit, she mockingly says, "Pull yourself together, man, what you need is a good stiff drink!"

One of the guards had hold of a prisoner now, by the arm, who had threatened to kill an innkeeper in 75', he was on his feet, yelling in Spanish at her. Pe-ah-in had drawn her daughter away from the circle. Mr Fox leaned towards her, "Best you leave quietly. I'll have one of the guards see you home." Gathering up her belongings, she left quickly, rather confused as to how she had disturbed them so.

Miss Mathers' Dentures

Ft. Marion

Anah returned from tea at Miss Mather's filled with a great, abiding sense of loneliness and a drifting aimless feeling throughout her limbs, like a slack tide. She had been so excited at the prospect at meeting Mrs. Stowe, the famous authoress and abolitionist, that she had spent an inordinate amount of time sorting through her meager wardrobe, even knowing that proper garments would not impress the great lady. Oh, and her unruly, sun-bleached hair! She had even thought of trying to borrow a bonnet from her landlady, but finally recognized the hypocrisy involved. Finally, as a signal act of who she truly had become, she selected a lovely pair of beaded moccasins to complete her outfit and set out, bearing a bouquet picked from gardens along her way.

Her worries were unfounded; Miss Mathers was a charming hostess and gave her a gracious introduction. Soon Mrs. Stowe and she were on a first name basis. Harriet was eager to learn of her first hand experiences among the Cheyenne; Anah also eager to recount them in an academic fashion. Accompanying Mrs. Stowe was a lovely young woman, introduced as her companion, to be fully educated at Mrs. Stowe's expense at one of the women's colleges up north, a privilege now extended to certain ex-slaves since the Emancipation. Having an intellectual conversation was so stimulating that Anah could barely recall what they had discussed at such great lengths.

Mrs. Stowe kept a small cottage on St. John's River, and was here in St. Augustine to sit in on Miss Mather's classes, of which she was quite impressed. Miss Mather had them in uproarious laughter in retelling how she had difficulty teaching her Indian students to pronounce the "th" sound. She simply removed her full set of dentures and enunciated more clearly. White Horse, Isa-Tah, a Kiowa chief, was unduly shocked, covering his eyes and pronouncing her evil. This was big medicine to him! She redeemed the day by declaring her dentures an example of the white's progress in the medical field and how the body can be repaired. Anah was also impressed by this unladylike side of this

Victorian spinster, and subsequently developed a new respect for her teaching methods.

Returning to her little room, Anah drew forth her Commonplace Book, noting how she missed academic stimulation, recalling how she felt when she had first read *Uncle Tom's Cabin*. Noting her descent into a dark mood, she closed the book, changed her clothes into more comfortable ones, brooded a bit on her place here on the southern tip of the continent, so far from where she had grown up.

"I could stay here, perhaps, carve out a place for myself, a little cottage; it's a lovely town," she thought as she eschewed going to the fort, and instead headed down to the harbor. "Lilacs don't grow but there are camellias, and azaleas and crepe myrtle," and thus she strolled along looking through wrought-iron gates into lush gardens and over white picket fences, imagining a life in this gracious old city. She saw the colonnaded porches and large balconies, the charming cottages tucked into the cobblestone lanes. She did not see the couples strolling arm in arm, the children rolling hoops, the young men carrying fishing poles, the handsome lawyer looking her direction as she ambled past, nor did she want to.

By the time she reached the waterfront the sky had turned a molten orange. She had this display to content herself with. Like most people who have experienced great loss and witnessed indescribable horrors, such as war, massacres, violation and starvation, they go to great lengths to avoid speaking about it. For to retell of it is to recall it, and what they want most is to forget. They go to great lengths to try to forget.

Now as Anah looked out to the horizon, the very pleasant thought of settling here and having these sunsets to enjoy ended abruptly with a small but sharp shiver a remorse. For out on that far horizon she saw, not endless ocean, but an endless rolling prairie, and a catch rose in her throat, one that she realized she had held in her heart the entire time since she had left Miss Mathers'. She recognized it as the feeling when one is torn between filial responsibility, marrying the fiancee one doesn't love, or running away with the gardener's son; how did she know this? She had never been in this position. She began sobbing, bending herself to her knee to conceal it, for it was the custom of many to take an evening stroll down here to watch the sunset, but she didn't care. She loved the West, she loved the wildness, the escarpments, the freedom; even the wind that howled so madly at times it drove her to a frenzy, the antelope that danced away at the slightest movement, but that could be lured close by their curiosity....her mind began to recall so much that she loved there. She sat up, wiping her face on her sleeve, laughing now at her foolishness. She had shut away her good memories for fear of the bad!

Pericardium

"Our first teacher is our own heart"

Summer 1875, Ft. Marion

The coals of the small fire snapped, flared up into a thin translucent flame through which the gaunt form of Heap-of-Birds could be seen as he leaned forward to add a small scrap of lumber. Anah, seated comfortably across from him, craned her head upward to the vast bowl of the open sky above the terreplein. There was just the faintest drift of cloud cover through which a much diminished Milky Way shone. She sorely missed the magnificent display that it gave out as it shone over the vast western plains. Feeling eyes upon her she looked down to see the handsome Cheyenne, who now called himself Standing Cloud, gazing impassively across the fire at her. As she met his gaze, he then dropped his eyes. A strange one, she thought, so self-contained, keeping to himself, but not aloof. She was prone to observe him, for he fascinated her. She found him listed on the rolls as Medicine Horse, a renowned Dog Soldier, about 24 years old. But ever since that first day when he was so taken by Turn Foot's arm band, it seemed to her that he had studiously avoided her, but then again she had not sought him out, either. In fact, when she was doctoring the prisoner's rough abrasions from being ironed, she noted that he alone seemed to avoid her ministrations.

Later, when the shipment of sage and sweetgrass arrived from the territories, Anah planned to take it to this young Dog Soldier to distribute as he saw fit. She had hopes of fostering good relations with these men. Already plans were in effect for classrooms and teachers to school them in the English language, but she wanted to create a bridge, an entryway that didn't depend on dress, speech and mannerisms alone, though she wasn't quite sure of how to do it. She sat down with her Commonplace Book; looked for the notes that she had taken on the Dog Soldiers. She remembered that each tribe that had those societies where only four, the "Bravest of the Brave", carried the rope. Could he be one of those at such a young age? So, if he was a leader, it would be right for her to submit to his judgment about the distribution of this gift; it was a gift, wasn't it? Now, should she tell him that it was her idea? Anah thought about this for just a minute. No, not yet, I want them to accept these "gifts". They will accept it from Red Dancing Crane, they may not take it from me, even if I was the one to arrange it. So Anah, in her growing wisdom of not injuring bruised pride, made light of handing off the fragrant bundles that spoke so eloquently of their homes and ceremonies, and simply walked away.

Standing Cloud, his long black braids now shorn, his thin limbs jutting from an ill fitting army uniform, though dressed as all the other prisoners, stood out uniquely in her vision. She struggled not to pity them. She failed daily. In her mind's eye she saw them, still thundering across the endless plains, dressed in their magnificent regalia, songs upon their lips, in full pursuit of a roiling herd of snorting buffalo. But this evening the air was sweet, the breeze caressing. Just a few men remained at the fire: Zotom, a Kiowa, Good Talk, Flat Nose, and Pile-of-Rocks, an older Comanche horse thief. Most nights, if there was a fire, Black Horse, Po-ka-do-ah's wife and child, Pe-ah-in, and Ah-kes, a girl of just nine years, would come out and sit quietly, absorbed by it. They never spoke. His wife had mutely refused to leave his side when he was arrested, and somehow managed to be brought here. A most unorthodox arrangement, but just one of many, she was learning.

Last night Anah had been recounting the old Appalachian folktale of Johnny Appleseed, the American hero of the frontier, John Chapman. Mr. Fox graciously translated into Comanche as some Winesap apples were passed around. She commented on their spherical shape, which was as much appreciated as their taste. Tonight, hoping that Black Horse's wife and daughter would be there, she had brought several wizened old apples that had been fashioned into "grandmother" faces by leaving them in a cool dry place for several months. Night after night Anah had so easily been able to recount small tales from her own childhood, fairy tales from The Brothers Grimm, that held a certain fascination for their commonly held belief in magic, power, and wisdom in the spirit world. They were well received. Rumpelstiltskin was accorded the status of a trickster-changer, and soon the men were eager to regale her with tales of their own. When she produced her copy of <u>The Last of The Mohicans</u> and read parts of it to them there was a small interest in learning how to decipher the markings upon the page. Indeed something unexpected was happening, not just at these campfires, but in the hearts and minds of the authorities who were governing these prisoners, as they were receiving unprecedented privileges, thanks to the interventions of Lt. Pratt. They were to receive schooling, allowed to form their own governance, go about the town unchaperoned by day, and to obtain small, menial jobs among the merchants willing to hire them. There were even plans to mount camping expeditions to Anastasia Island by boat. Unheard of privileges, ones that these men were not abusing!

Arriving back at her lodgings that evening, Anah was in an elevated and agitated frame of mind, certain that she must in some way capture her feelings, if indeed they could be put in words. On one hand she felt that words alone were inadequate; she who seemed to have a word for just about anything seemed to be quite at a loss to describe what she was now feeling. Nonetheless, she hauled out her well-worn Commonplace Book and began to write:

St. Augustine, Florida June 1875

I must transcribe this while it is yet fresh in my head, or is it my heart from which I am speaking? I am here, at the U.S. Army's behest, Ft. Marion, as an interpreter for the Cheyenne hostiles transported from Indian Territory, Ft. Sill, Oklahoma. Translate now I must from my heart to my head to my hand to this page: am I making any sense at all? Outside, darkness reigns, yet I am in the light. I fear that I have been traveling between two worlds, perhaps more all my life, and have not become lost, but have been, at last, found. I know that this can only sound as though I have taken leave of my considerable sense, but in writing this I am trying to explain (But of what and to whom, you may ask. Why to myself, of course, for this is for my eyes only. And, alas, it is only myself to whom I am accountable)

The hour is late, just hours before dawn. Mr. George Fox, the Comanche interpreter here at the fort, accompanied me home to my lodging. I have imbibed no spirits, and yet I feel in a strange state of alteration, quite unlike that which I experienced when I partook of spirits or laudanum. I feel a clarity, such a clarity. Let me try to explain: When I returned from seeing Pe-ah-in and her daughter to their lodging, Mr. Fox was deep in conversation with Black Horse and a Comanche I know as Tail Feathers. As I usually waited upon Mr. Fox to escort me home through the darkened narrow streets of the old town, I knew to settle in for the duration. There were only a small group of men remaining at his hour, Cheyenne, it appeared, and the lone Caddo. I decided to sit with them, the young Matches, Heap-of-Birds, Making Medicine, and the handsome Dog Soldier now known as Standing Cloud. Seating myself, I remained quiet, and the talk continued. With a bit of concentration I was able to discern that they were discussing those incredible headdresses of the Plains Indians we call warbonnets. My heart sank a bit, surely some sort of insurrection was not being planned, or were they simply indulging in some late night nostalgia for glory days? As a past resident of an army post, I was more than familiar with the rambling talk of bygone glories of battles won and lost! The immediate image of these incredibly magnificent emblems of the prowess and status of a warrior, where each golden eagle feather indicated an attained honor, rose in my mind, and I saw each one of these men gathered now around the fire in my imagination, bare chested, with an eagle bone whistle, mounted on a painted war pony, lance in hand, silhouetted on a ridge, the feathers of their bonnets gently rising in the wind, the thick richness of a milling buffalo herd rolling towards them. Then my heart sank, knowing that never again would this be! I also knew that this nostalgic talk was not good for them, and was readying myself to intervene in someway, when I realized that they were actually discussing the method of attaching the feathers to the bonnet itself, that is, it's construction. The feathers had to be attached in such a way that they flexed in the wind and moved in a manner so that they maintained proper alignment. I never thought of how that was possible. The material required would have to be both extremely durable and incredibly flexible, strong, and capable of enduring exposure to the elements. Right away I assumed it had to come from the buffalo, their General Store. I crept closer when I realized that the exact membrane of which they were speaking came from the animal's heart.

Embarrassing myself, and alarming them, I leapt forward, shouting out, "the pericardium, the pericardium, of course. Brilliant! It's both flexible, durable, one of the toughest, membranes, in the body," I must have even danced around. I think they thought I had gone a bit mad. Unfortunately I could not revert to a proper ladylike demeanor, nor control my excitement, and rambled, "There are two portions to this membrane. The serous, and the epicardium." At this point, Mr. Fox's interest had been piqued, but he had no translation for these medical terms and stood at a loss. I continued, now beginning to wave my arms, but Standing Cloud had slowly risen and signed for me to sit and look at the men surrounding me, who were half-raised up now in confusion and alarm. I then, and only then, realized that not only was I excited but speaking fast, too fast, in English and in medical terminology. Realizing that I badly needed to explain myself and wishing that we could pass a pipe, I now looked to the tall Cheyenne as though he would somehow understand. To this hour I'm not quite sure what he said, but somehow a quiet attentiveness was then guided toward me, and I felt a strong compulsion descend on me to speak, and not about war bonnets either, nor the pericardium, though it did involve the heart.

The hearts of men. Nature seemed to set a stage as an odd chill, most unusual for this climate, fell upon us. A dense fog came rolling in off the ocean, blanketing the stars, obscuring the usual landmarks, causing us all to draw closer in an intimate circle around the small, glowing fire of red coals which seemed to almost throb with the rhythm of a steadily beating heart, matched in a most uncanny way by the pulse of the oncoming tide as it broke on the beach below us. It was quite strange, but not in the least frightening. Emboldened by some encouragement of the spirit I began, "You may know me as Mrs. Moore. My given name is Anah, some of you call me The Sweetgrass Woman, I know. I am here to interpret your speech to those in charge of you, and their words back to you. I hope to learn more of your speech and your ways, and I hope that you will want to learn more of mine." This more or less was what I tried to convey. I had no title, I told them. I was not an army person. I could not harm them. Perhaps I could help them. I suspected that they knew of my connections through Red Dancing Crane Woman to the Kiowa Agency at Ft. Sill, but I did not wish to make a public announcement. Then all changed, as though a sudden breeze swept in from an unopened window in my heart, my soul perhaps, the moment when the lecturer tears up his notes and speaks wildly, and I began again, now seating myself, my back pointedly to Mr. Fox, as if to disassociate myself from any official connection with the army.

"There is the lance, the bow, the club, the knife; warriors wield these, and wield them well, but there is a much more dangerous weapon that we all possess, male and female, young and old, white and red...our tongue. My tongue is my weapon." I spoke slowly, sticking it out just a bit for emphasis, and touching it with my forefinger. I felt deadly serious in my intent, but at the same time feeling slightly possessed; of what? "It is what I use to capture what is in my heart," and I placed my hand there, again, for emphasis. Out of the corner of my eye I saw Matches, who had let his blanket slip in spite of the chill, give a slight, approving nod, "and take words like hobbles, so that when I speak, certain words do not escape my mouth; harmful words. So that the words I let loose are ones that do not kill, but capture." I saw now that Matches, dear Matches, had come to my aid by cutting sign for me; perhaps I was speaking too fast. I was getting excited! Now that I had made a slightly clever remark, what was I going to say? I had in no way rehearsed this. Standing Cloud came to my aid too, guiding me closer yet to the fire with one hand, while adding more fuel, and summoning Mr. Fox and the Comanches to move closer, also. I knew that Mr. Fox had a tolerable regard for me, but what could he possibly think of what I was now conveying? The young Dog Soldier remained standing protectively, slightly to the left of me, all eyes were on me now as I continued. "When I first came west I was a young, unmarried woman. My father came to serve as a contract surgeon at Ft. Laramie in the North." There was a grunt of approval at that. Then I simply cut to the chase. Mr. Fox kindly began to interpret that particular expression as I went on to describe my familiarity with the human heart as a physical specimen, seen in the operating theater and on the battlefield; its physiology and anatomy. I was quite impressed with Mr. Fox's command of medical terminology! I had underestimated him, of course; he had seen much in the way of warfare, also. (The Civil War gave us such an education. I did not mention that to them, of course. They had much of their own sufferings to deal with.) I went on to say that there was no difference in the heart of a

Lakota from a Crow, nor a Blackfoot from an Apache, nor a Negro from an Arapaho, no difference in their blood, no difference based on gender or tribe. Yes, skin color varied widely, even among themselves; hair quite a bit. I cited the now decimated Mandans as having such amongst themselves. Health mattered, age mattered, but there was no way, no way to tell if the heart belonged to a wise man, a kind man, an evil man, a chief, a murderer, a thief, a general, a foot soldier, a maiden, a mother or even a Dog Soldier, and I braved a glance at the tallest Cheyenne; the little crowd grew increasingly still, the fire sank and hissed upon its coals. I really did not have more to say and wondered why, indeed, I had chosen this subject, or if it had somehow chosen me. Then Standing Cloud again spoke, "It is as though you speak through the pipe, though we have no pipe. It is said among my people that our first teacher is our heart." Having spoken, he moved his arms heavenward in an encompassing circle that drew our eyes upward to where the fog had lifted, to reveal the star flecked depths of the night sky where momentarily we felt, I thought, a simple comradeship, of one heart, of a late night spent by a small fire by a booming ocean on the ramparts of an old Spanish fort.

Mr. Fox and I went home in a comfortable silence, lost in our thoughts, I presumed, as the low, rhythmic chants rose from the men, a pleasant fading background to our footfalls on the damp, cobbled, paving stones.

Almost dawn, I feel as though I am straddling two worlds, or would it be more apt to say two roads? What the Indians call the White Man's Road, and the Red Road, or is it just really the road, one road which all life travels? One that, in becoming unified, becomes more real to me as I am beginning to perceive it? For surely tonight I felt men's spirits coming together in harmony!

The Wild Calls Her

Towering, white cumulus clouds marched in seemingly endless progression across the morning sky. Anah lay in bed, content to just watch them drift slowly by as they appeared to change shape and darken, become a deep purple mass of thundering buffalo. "Thunderstorm," she thought as she drew herself up out of her tangled sheets to gaze out onto the tops of the palmettos now being lashed about by a strengthening wind. It would be but a brief storm, so she turned her pillow to its cool side and decided to wait it out. As the sounds of the storm approached she realized that she could not drift back to sleep and ignore what had transpired last night, no more than she could ignore the fact that she had looked out her window and imagined those clouds as a charging herd of buffalo!

What she had been attempting, what Red Dancing Crane Woman had intended, had in some way been achieved, had it not? She had fairly interpreted the men's needs and the army's wants; had drawn the men out into real discussions...but of what? Fairy tales? She knew the military codes and formal language, had she not heard this talk at her own table as the adjutant's wife, alliances and allies, parley's and accords? She was searching for a less formal word for what had been achieved between them. In their language they had words like *kola*, for close friend and *tiopayse* for other forms of close relations, but she was at a loss for adequately describing what had drawn them together last night, though she knew they had all felt it. *What had occurred wasn't a bonding exactly, nor a friendship, but an acknowledgment of a commonality of their humanity, and it sounded so...* Scholars would have some very fancy word to encompass it. All she knew was that they had started out discussing how to best tie golden eagle feathers to war bonnets with the pericardium membrane from a buffalo heart and ended up talking into the wee hours of the night about what each one harbored deep in the recesses of their own hearts. She was not sure if she had ever spoken in such depth with anyone like this, other than Turn Foot, from the depths of her misery. Was this a trait common to them, she now wondered? Did the very vastness of their lands and the intense struggle to survive place a sharpness in their vision; a depth to their souls? Did their nomadic way of life cause them to treasure less material possessions and more what is carried in the heart?

Anah lay on her bed as the brief storm thundered through, pondering all this, knowing something had drawn her and her father out west. She now recognized a response in herself. The Wild had called to her; she had responded. It was out there, had always been there, surrounding all of them always, and these men had been born knowing of nothing else, and might may be the last generation to experience it.

She had tapped into a different sort of wildness in bringing Grimm's fairy tales to the fire circles in the evening, thinking that she was showing them the sophistication of European heritage, but actually it was opening another doorway into that other world, that other realm. And here she was acting as an advocate between these worlds that Red Dancing Crane Woman and Lt. Pratt represented.

The strong, throaty warble of a male cardinal alerted her; brilliant sunshine now flooded the worn oak boards of her little room. With eagerness she dressed for her day, not quite realizing that she was a woman whose life had slowly been infused, by others, with new meaning.

V

Ties That Mingled, Bind

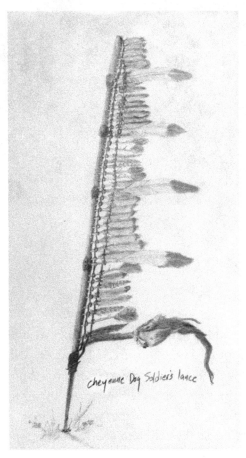

"and what of my people?"

Gullah Land

Sea Isles, Georgia 1875

When Salifu heaved his aging bones from the worn and ragged quilts before the soft light of dawn appeared he knew that finally the storm had moved on. He didn't need to prop the storm shutters open to scan the heavens, for the sweet susurration of the incoming tide as it rose off the beach spoke of a gentle return to its normal ways. Besides the gnawing, hungry beast that chewed at his old joints without pity told him that the pressures that had brought the hurricane onto the land had passed by. Last night the whole village had throbbed with drums, chants, call and response, those prayers to ward off disaster. Today he would rise, check his nets and traps, and leave Mariama to her troubled sleep. She worried too much. For all her fretting and fussing, and festooning of *wagnas* tied around her person, he could not see that it did her much good. Himself, he was a believer; had put the beliefs from the Old World behind him, though he never ceased from fond and sad remembrances of its ways and charms of a different sort.

He sang softly, as was his custom, heading slowly for his pirogue in the small sheltered bay on this side of the island. The water glittered so fiercely in the bright morning sun that it was hard to discern the many objects that the night's fierce storm had scattered on the shore line. Salifu adjusted his worn palmetto frond hat and scanned the heavens where a few frigate birds had been blown to riding the now fierce updrafts like the kites he flew as a boy. The skies were extraordinarily clear, a lucid aquamarine, startling in clarity. Cleansed! He breathed deeply!

It had been a good while since The Emancipation arrived here on the lowlands. Working the rice fields had been hard, especially with the malaria and the breakbone fever that swept through during the rainy seasons, and with Mariama working in the Big House, and him feared for her of the Master's attentions. But the Civil War had been a blessing in disguise. Y'am, not for Adah Buckram de white man, but for the slaves. Then the hurricanes took the rice crops and the indigo and we free to go, and we come to these islands. Um-mm, he thought, rowing on, oars dipping and rising, dipping and rising.

Lost in these simple thoughts of gratitude this big black man, whose ancestors probably hailed from Sierra Leone, but himself born into slavery on an indigo plantation in Georgia, automatically went about putting his little fishing craft into the bay, and headed out of the harbor as he had done day after day, year after year, content to be a free man living off the land; his land now.

A small bump brought him to and he turned, aghast to see that he had struck a spar, a crude raft of sorts. Flung across it was what appeared to be two bodies wrapped in a loose netting of some sort. Instinctively he crossed himself, then lunged to grasp for a secure hold, at the same time scanning the immediate horizon for evidence of a shipwreck. Their little village was not close to any shipping channels. It had been chosen especially for its seclusion and privacy, but a hurricane has its own priorities and anything of consequence can and does occur. Salifu was not without courage; his Christian faith was his best asset, in that he held no fear of the dead, in fact, held respect and knew that the right thing to do would be to bring these poor lost souls back to shore. All God's children deserved that! After all, his traps and nets could wait, could they not? His brother Bala or Colombo might be coerced to gather them and check the catch for him later on. Old Salifu was indeed old, but still strong, unless the arthritis was wicked in his bones during the cold, wet weather, but the day was warm and sunny and he felt the urgency to haul the bodies into the boat before the crabs and fishes had their way.

A man and a woman he noted, young, well made. Out of an innate decency he averted his eyes as he went to haul the woman aboard; it was then he noted that the two were roped together. It brought a lump to his throat. What dark skin the man had. Not black as his, though! Was he a Seminole, perhaps? Not an African. Look at that hair. Not a kink in it, he thought. He was mortally afraid to give as much as a glance at the woman, for he could see that, even bound and limp, her half naked form held great beauty, and her skin was as white as a pearl! This would take effort. He stood and took a strong stance, knowing that he would have to haul in both at once. Bending from his old knees, steeling himself, with a half whispered incantation, "Mary, Mother of God, give me strength," he cut the knots that bound them to the improvised raft, drawing them towards one another in an even tighter embrace, and asking forgiveness of the dead for the intimacies he was taking of them hauled them aboard as though they were a prize catch! Prize catch indeed, for as he hauled and heaved them over the gunwales face down, they began to sputter, cough, spew, vomit, cry weakly in Cheyenne, Lakota and English. "Holy Mother of God, Jesus, Mary, and Joseph, help us!" he thought. There was life in them yet!

Rose and lavender golden-tinged clouds rose high against the horizon now as Salifu pulled with all his might, stroke by laborious stroke toward the shore, muttering exultant praises under his breath, for he knew the dire importance of life that was most fragile and yet clings against all odds. Surely what lay slouched against his gunwales was such.

As the expectant crowd upon the shore edged closer, the sense built in them that this was no ordinary catch that he was hauling in. Hurricanes had a way of delivering the oddest, and often most macabre flotsam and jetsam. There was much jostling to be the first to examine what the old man had found in his nets. The small crowd stood expectant, some ghoulishly eager, hands raised to their brow, peering to obtain an even better focus against the hard, golden glitter of the rising sun, scattering itself like a handful of pirate coins across the surface of the bay.

As the old man leapt out into the shallows, his brother Bala grabbed the frayed painter to assist. When Salifu lifted the golden skinned, nearly naked young woman into his arms, Mariama's hand flew to her mouth to contain a gasp. Nodding to his brother Coloumbo, a much younger giant of a man with well-developed muscles from years of baling cotton, who then hefted the limp, copper-skinned man over his shoulder, they proceeded up the path. The crowd as one stepped back.

These ex-slaves had gone through much to carve out an existence here. They did not welcome strangers. Mariama, by nature a bold woman, met her husband's eyes unflinchingly. She understood his commitment, otherwise he would not have arrived on shore with this burden. He turned from her with no acknowledgment. Nor was any needed. As was their custom, they would discuss it later. At the top of the gentle slope he turned to address the crowd. *"Uh gwihe he'p dem'!* The village of Pojoh, Heron Bay on Cootuh Isle was a true community forged by adversity.

They all strove to help these castaways hauled miraculously from the storm-troubled waters. In their Meeting House that Sunday they had ample encouragement to assist these two apt symbols of what they themselves had passed through and been delivered from in the strife of the recent war years. From the very first hour of dawn's light, when they were brought ashore to an old cabin, there were those who cleaned and those who fetched water, those who heated that water to bathe them, and those who dug through their own meager clothes to supply their needs. Young girls appeared to tend their many cuts and bruises. Old women, wise in the way of doctoring, brought their very best balms and salves. Their intentions were not just to heal the flesh but the spirit, for these were a people who had a long history of grievous wounds. Here on this little isle, far from any governing authority or any overseeing white master, just the vagrant forces of nature itself, they were free to govern themselves. At the mercy of man's intent for good or evil, they mostly intended good. They meant but to reap the good they sowed; rice, beans, some cotton, no more dat indigo!

So the women gently settled these beautiful castaways, male and female, onto clean old quilts over a corn shuck mattress, where they lay muttering deliriously for days. Small children brought a steady supply of various herbal teas, patiently held to blistered lips at various hours of the day and moonlit nights, often just keeping incredulous and curious watch by their sides, hoping to be the first to report their awakening. Watching and waiting, they amused themselves with fireflies caught in the night, now held in luminous jars tucked beneath their small bare feet.

When Hawa appeared as if by magic out of the cane brakes just at dusk, she had said not to separate them, so they now lay entwined in one narrow bed, just as they had been found bound together on the improvised raft. Hawa had drawn her ample self up, further amplified by the many layers of cloaks and colorful skirts, to declare "Just as they had been delivered from the jaws of the mighty storm bound to one another on the vast waters," pausing and waving her hands ominously for effect before she continued; the small children a rapt and somewhat frightened audience, "So let them remain," and here she gave a tiny, but very impressive leap forward, practically shrieking, "BOUND on land!"

Hawa's appearance was as impressive as her reputation. Strung around her neck, wrist, ankle and waist hung a multitude of *wagnas*, or charms to make, break or fend off various evils that lurked behind every bush, the children were quite sure of it. They knew several of these took up nightly residence under their beds! Hawa was to be obeyed!

Not heard! Or avoided! To some she embodied the lure of enchantment itself in the colors, the layers of her clothing, the jangle that preceded her approach, haunting and elusive smells that rose from the folds of her person. Others noticed the dried lizard chained to her ankle, or the pelt of a small animal she consistently stroked while staring into your eyes fixedly and smiling at you, all the while running her very pink tongue over her golden eye tooth. Oh she was one to fascinate all right!

At that pronouncement she had absolutely no need to tell the few children that still remained to heed her in any way. Indeed, a few had instantly scuttled off, for Hawa was known to be a practitioner of the dark arts, though none spoke openly of it. She then drew from her large basket of *wagnas* various items as she casually lit a thin cheroot, waved it carelessly towards the remaining children, and dismissed them. But Sorie, a boy of almost twelve summers, only drew deeper into the shadows, watching with great curiosity as she went about filling small saucers with dried herbs from little applique pouches hung from her waist. Satisfied with the arrangement, she lit them, then sat back on her heels, rocking for some time, talking in what sounded to him like Creole. He almost liked the sound of it. Then, taking quite a long thin strand of bright red silk of some sort, she approached the sleeping pair.

Were they sleeping, Sorie wondered? Apparently Hawa wondered this herself, for she then drew a pin from somewhere within her voluminous skirts, gently drew off the man's coverings and gazed down upon his form for the longest time, it seemed. Sorie found himself holding his breath. Did Hawa prick the man? He missed it if she had, for now she was winding the thread carefully around the copper-skinned man's wrist, now attaching it to the woman's. Again Sorie found himself holding his breath, anticipating that Hawa would also uncover the nakedness of the white woman's body, for he had never seen such a thing, nor had he ever hoped to. Yet all she did was gently ease the woman's wrist from out of its covering. Before he had even a small chance to mourn his loss a great fear rolled over him, as Hawa burst into laughter, not cackling or moaning, but making an indescribable noise so low, so eerie, that the hair on his arms stood and he truly feared that he would reveal his presence in some way. Whatever had compelled him to stay and witness what Hawa had in mind, he now felt riveted to the spot. That string, or thread, was quite long; how would it not be noticed he wondered? They would know that she had been here and up to her juju, surely.

Hawa was not well liked. Her magic was not condoned, though some sought her out for various potions and love charms, but even condemnation from the Meeting House didn't keep some away. Like him, he thought.

Mesmerized, he watched as she withdrew a small candle stub from her multicolored turban and lit it with her cheroot. Her eyes glowed fierce and glittered strangely. The room had quite filled by now with an aromatic smoke of some sort. He was beginning to feel even more uncomfortable, wanting to leave, almost afraid. He prided himself on being fearless in front of others, but here he was alone. Well, almost, just with her. Setting back fully on her heels now, she turned to Sorie. She knew he was here, didn't she? She fixed him with a most beatific smile. She looked so young, so different. She must have been a most beautiful woman when younger. Was she speaking to him? Was she motioning him to come by her side?

The room seemed to dissolve before his eyes. Before him lay a naked man, perfectly formed in all his limbs. That he was quite tall was apparent, taller than any of them. He was an Indian, he thought. In his arms lay a woman of equally exquisite form. A white woman, with hair like the rising sun. Binding them together at their wrists was a thick scarlet cord. He could not avert his eyes from them. Is this what Adam and Eve looked like in the Garden? He tried to shut his eyes, but she was so beautiful, so very...he had kept his eyes on her face only by a supreme effort. He heard a voice, but was too frightened to seek its source, saying " *Whatever is bound in heaven,*" so badly he wanted to look at the woman's naked body, so badly. Would he be struck dead? Where was Hawa? Was that her voice? Could she do that with her voice? Was that her hand on his shoulder? He turned just as her silken turban began to unwind, filling the room with light and sound and color, blood red, crimson, vermilion, bleeding, her hair thick, moving, alive like a whip snake, many snakes all writhing over him, over his eyes, blinding him, holding him down as he struggled to pull free of them. "Look at me!"

He heard that command, but squeezed his eyes so tightly shut that his forehead froze in pain. He feared eternal blindness while still seeing white creamy thighs, begging God's forgiveness, not quite sure for what sin. Then that smell, not a goodness, was it burning flesh? Oh God, hell's fire, surely. He must flee. A candle. His flesh? Did he set the cabin on fire? The castaways? They're innocent! He had to move. He was paralyzed. The darkness, the smoke descended, thickening. He forced his foot to move, and kicked out. A jar shattered, and sparks rose up; glittering, sparkling fire? No, oh no, the fireflies. Little lights! Thank God!

He forced his eyes open once more, now saw the string, it was only a string, but it was crawling, moving upon the bodies, binding them like a thick, pulsing, blood-filled, throbbing vein, wrapping the naked bodies, while above them the fireflies were assembling into beautiful constellations like the Milky Way. Spellbound, he was being spellbound; screaming, he fled, to Hawa's delighted, full-throated laughter. Reaching into her pocket for a little sewing shears, she snipped the red string. The pair were already bound by a force far greater than hers, one she could never best, but it never hurt to reinforce her status in the black arts in the village among the susceptible, like the young, and Sorie would be her messenger.

On the morning of the third day the woman sighed, turned, and moved closer onto the man's chest. He placed his arms around her protectively. A fast paced, rhythmic hand clapping that resounded across the square from the village's Praise House easily penetrated the awakening consciousness of Anah. Carefully noting her immediate surroundings in the dim light of the cabin, she was more than overjoyed to be in Standing Cloud's arms. We have come through! It was enough for her at this moment. She fell back into a grateful sleep, not knowing or caring at that moment where they were or how they came to be there.

When she next awoke it was almost dark. That they weren't on any army base was most certain; they were in the same narrow bed. That brought a wry smile to her lips. A well-worn but clean cotton quilt covered them. His head was bandaged, but not still bleeding. She gently rolled back the quilt to see that his ribs were tightly bound. They appeared to be alone in a small cabin. Unguarded? But why would they be guarded? Her lips were blistered and cracked. Where were they? As Anah went to rise, she discovered that she could not put full weight on her one leg, the one that had been damaged in the attack back at Laramie. A very nasty cut ran the full length of her right arm. How long had they lain here? And where indeed was here? As she tried once more to put weight on her leg, a flicker of movement caught her eye, and a small form rose from a rocker in a darkened corner of the room and melted into the night before she could call out.

She must have drifted seamlessly back to sleep then, only to wake when a young woman, bearing a small bowl of deliciously aromatic soup wafting up into her broad, dark skinned, smiling face, spoke to her in what sounded like jumbled Creole, "Mange, Mange," gesturing encouragingly with lovely hands as she proffered it towards her.

Cloud's Awakening

Late summer, Sea Isles 1875

As the hurricane that blew across the Atlantic finally spent its force and began moving up the eastern seaboard, the defeated Plains horseman now known as Standing Cloud roamed a rugged interior fraught with storms of his own. Those caring for him feared for his recovery in spite of that miraculous rescue at sea, for it was apparent that he was in a great inner turmoil, alternately sunk in a coma-like state or briefly thrashing in heated fever.

He was, indeed, reliving the greatest display of power, or "medicine", that he had ever witnessed; a tropical storm known as a hurricane that had both awed and terrified him. Born on the high plains, he was quite familiar with frightful extremes of weather; tornadoes, twisters and blizzards were commonplace, but to have ridden out a hurricane, well, he was still in its grasp and struggling to fashion questions before he could even dare to seek answers. He knew that before he could travel the path back to full consciousness that he would have to find some of those answers and that he was ill equipped to do so for it was a world that was uncommonly new to him!

As a youth when he went off to fast on the sacred mountain, *Noahvose,* Bear Butte, with no water, weapon, fire, nor food, he had been provisioned with the wisdom and prayers of a holy man and all the prayers of his people. But was he not on his own now? What of the spirit world resided here with him? This was one of the questions that begged an answer. He was weak, was he not? His medicine bundle had long been destroyed and any symbols of protection, or amulets were gone, and yet, was he totally bereft? For what had brought him through the storm? His body ached in strange places. It hurt to breathe, yet he knew that hands had bound his wounds. Hands that could have harmed him. Whose hands?

He struggled to rise from where he lay out of the darkness into a warm red layer. Then a jumbled, rushing murmur of voices washed over him. Women's voices, their language indecipherable. Children's voices, perhaps. They left abruptly.

He fell back, but he was not alone. Growing rigid, alert, he froze. The redness that enveloped his spirit then became as the melting rose of dawn, for there was a warm presence next to him. Breathing. He matched his breath to its. Finally, he felt no danger, no alarm, and fell back, down, down, to sink into a yet lower consciousness, a healing immobility, his breathing slowed like a gentle wave as he sunk into a warm recall: There is a question here and a confusion of weak struggling for an answer. He settled gratefully down...

Those last days of August confined to the fort had been so hot, then Mr. Fox had gotten permission for a small group of the prisoners to go oystering out to Matanzas Inlet. He, Matches and Minimic were all too eager to escape the heat and camp out unchaperoned. Wandering the strand, searching for hardwood from shipwrecks, he finally sought a place to rest in the shade. Sinking down in the shelter of an old abandoned brick building, Cloud stripped off his boots, much enjoying the cool feel of the sand upon his bare feet. He had left the others, saying he wanted to look for driftwood for carving bows and such. In truth he savored just being alone. Mister Fox would not miss him, nor would his kolas.

At the time that they had been sent into exile they were the most elite fierce fighting warriors the plains had ever known. The Dog Soldiers had in essence been disbanded and defeated, the remnants driven far north along with scattered groups of poverty-stricken, ill-equipped bands, many without proper weapons, lodges, clothing, horses, or provisions. The great buffalo herds, which were once the inexhaustible wealth of the Nations, were finally decimated, never to recover. It was only a matter of time before even the great Tasunke Witco would come in to save his people. He could hardly bear to think this!

Cloud was again fighting discouragement, even though by now it had become quite apparent that the prisoners were not to be hung or dealt with harshly. In fact, the men had been given unheard of opportunities to tread the white man's path, to earn some money, to learn English, and to read and write. Still, he often felt his heart and spirit contract, pull in as tight as the hard-shelled creatures that lived down on the plains of the Llano

Estacado. He had seemingly recovered from his defeat, even missing his homeland. He no longer grieved openly for the plains and his old way of life, for he knew that those old ways were mostly gone.

He had found new things, new ways, but in his spirit there was a hollowness, like a wind cave through which a breeze occasionally blew. Oftentimes he heard just a still small voice. It bothered him more and more that the sound had grown faint and hard to decipher, and yet he heard it still. Strained so to listen, for it was most precious, most precious, and he knew not how to preserve it. A sadness washed over him. He missed Silver Spotted Owl! He missed his kola, he missed his war horse, and his buffalo runner, and a large red wave of fever rose up, washed over him and tumbled him, back and forth, back and forth.

The women kept bathing him, and finally brought the fever down. It appeared he was sleeping calmly once more. Little Nola asked, "Will he live?" and was told, God willing. That answer was good enough for her, and she resumed her vigil at his side, ready to go running for an adult if he began the thrashing and crying out once again. The white woman slept calmly, occasionally reaching out a small hand to touch some part of him, as if to reassure herself that he was indeed alive, still breathing, still there. At her touch he grew still, and set sail once more on his healing journey...

For several days before they had ventured forth into the waters of the Mantanzas Inlet there had been no bird cries. Birds had been oddly silent. Dogs turned restlessly in their sleep, and the sea birds that flocked around the fort and down at the docks had been steadily flying inland. The men had discussed this, for they knew it was a bad omen. Down at the inlet no boats had put out, but this did not deter Mr. Fox's plans. There was a light overcast, not too unusual, and of no bother to them, just a bit of wind with foam capped swell. They were hunters not of the sea!

For Cloud, out by himself, he welcomed the change to the moody, overcast, windy weather, for it mirrored his inner turmoil. The barometer kept dropping, which meant nothing to him, and the ocean swell was obscured by the wind-driven waves. There was no rain on the first night, but in the morning the winds began to pick up. Streaks of foam began to ride over the surface of the waves and coalesce into a large gray mass as they headed toward the shore. As the skies lowered, turned solid, then deepened to purple, the waves rose and mounted upon the beach, charging like enraged fighting mustangs. He thought perhaps he should head back to join the others, but became fascinated by the way the feathery tops of the palm trees began swaying and bending towards the sand. He didn't know they could do that. Branches were breaking off, to sail at great heights through the air. Perhaps a great tornado was approaching. He should seek some shelter. So much sand was in the air that it was difficult to see clearly. Salt stung his eyes. The wind was so strong now that standing upright was hard.

When he woke the air was saturated with spray. He was so soaked that he had trouble discerning objects around him; all was a haze. Heavy winds drove waves with such force upon the stretch of sand that each crashing wave stunned him with the power that was being exhibited. His head felt too large for his body, full to bursting with a throbbing pain.

Wind, no winds, more than one, thousands, were shrieking, howling. He could not stand the noise, and in trying to cover his ears, found he could barely move his hands, so strong was the force of the wind. What was happening? What had happened to him? There was a large lump above his ear as though he had been brought down by an enemy's war club! He must have been stunned by some flying object. Palm trees were lashing the ground. Impossible! He tried to stop shivering long enough to focus his thoughts. He felt like he had been thrust into a new world borne by raging waters. Had he called this down upon himself? It had all happened so fast, and yet he had no conception of how long he had actually lain here since the storm had begun. Where was he, where were the others, the boat? Trying now to rise again, he found his leg pinned by a small timber. As he dragged himself free of it, he felt a warm rivulet of blood down his cheek. Small matter.

With darkness beginning to surround him, trembling in both body and spirit, he saw overhead the sky begin to mysteriously open into an area comprising a circle in the heavens above; pale, flat and strangely devoid of life. Small, sheer, somewhat translucent clouds like the puffy, white seeds of the cottonwood drifted from horizon to horizon on the periphery of the unusual opening like an eye. Into his sight, effortlessly afloat, not a wing in motion, sailed a storm bird.

Instantly Cloud was alert. Was this not a sign from his vision quest? Now, in an even greater state of alertness, he surveyed his immediate surroundings, in awe of the force that he was in the midst of, for suddenly the fierce howling winds had stopped. Just stopped. After hours of raging, they had just stopped. The air now was warm and humid, just like that!

A huge wall of thick, impenetrable clouds were whirling around above him in a vast circle that opened to reveal a dark blue sky, pierced through with stars glittering like the penetrating eyes of hungry wolves. The rain had stopped; the sea calmed. He was alone. Absolutely. Absolutely alone. His ears ached, not with what had been the seemingly ever present roar of the wind, but with a silence so profound that he felt a growing apprehension, in spite of the apparent calm. He had to ask himself, do I live?

This was the very fabled Eye of the Storm, the very heart of the hurricane......

"Oh, Great Spirit," he spoke from his heart, "I am listening, struck alive, not dead, by the very wonder, by..." and he had no more words that his tongue could form, and finally understood why birds sing and wolves howl. He ached with the wild urge, a storm born, wild passion, that he had the strength and the ability and the spirit power to throw back his head and to do so at that moment, to use his last bit of energy and strength to join this celestial power!

It was then, as his gaze was heavenward, that a moon sailed out into the circular patch of night above, to spangle the water below and provide just enough light for Cloud to note the silver furling of becalmed waters as the two sleek water beasts of his vision arced forward towards him, heralding the approach of what, at first, appeared to be a solitary palm, silvered in the moonlight, gliding now towards him.

Oh the Great Mystery and wonder of it all, for as this apparition approached, it became a human form, a woman, the thin, water drenched garments revealed it so!

The pale, smooth skin of a ve'ho'e, a white woman of unparalleled beauty, smiling, calling out to him. Dumbstruck! At last his spirit helper had come. He was dumbstruck!

Cloud fell back into a deep healing unconsciousness to be tended by the caring folk of Cootuh Bay as Anah slept peacefully on by his side.

Days later awareness finally came in the form of a tight stricture across his chest, a binding that caused a searing pain with every small intake of breath. Caution stilled his limbs and kept his lids closed tight. Drawing air through his nostrils he found it dry, not damp, nor foul. He appeared to be alone, unguarded. Slowly he tried his wrists; amazingly unbound, as were his ankles. Then a nauseating wave of pain washed over him; his head throbbed, his stomach sickened. Feeling his forehead, he found it well bandaged, as were his ribs. Opening his eyes, the light coming through thin calico curtains stabbed him back down; he was way too weak to resist. Pain! He grew up schooled in it, along with his brothers. They all had held out their wrists: eager, willing to let sunflower seeds be set balanced upon them to burn, determined not to be the first to flinch and jump to their feet. The first of many small trials to steel them to fortitude, to be a man among The People one must be able to bear pain. How else to properly provide, and protect those weaker than oneself: the women, children and aged! Physical pain had become something he had learned early on in his training not to seek out or glory in, but to tolerate as it presented itself, and he had seen and experienced many kinds. The wounds and scars upon his body bore witness to that. But there was a pain that resided, not in the flesh, but in the spirit, that required a true warrior to face.

For now, Cloud had to recover from the vicissitudes of the storm. As he drifted down into a place of healing, dreams began once again to lull him, and he walked once more the wind torn and wave pounded inlet where Anah appeared to him out of the eye of the storm, as in a dream, on the shore of Anastasia Island so many days ago. He had not recognized her then; even now, as the fever still ruled him, he gave in to recall.

That woman, that face! Pale, slicked with salt spray, her whole being as she approached him radiating an odd triumph, but one his own soul now instantly met, survivors! Her long hair hung in golden strands, plastered to thin shoulders, with sea wrack strewn over her arms and chest. Eyes flashed recognition; eyes the color of the blue-green silt-laden glacial melt of the spring runoff of the Yellow Stone. How odd! And that hair as light, thick and curly as a new born buffalo calf. A small, straight nose and teeth like a kit fox. He stood transfixed. His vision, a ve'ho'e. Here, after all these years, his spirit helper. That she was white and a woman, caused no little concern, but her great beauty, well, that was another matter. Had she finally arrived on the whirlwind, the most awesome display of power he had yet to experience, only for him to die? Well, yes, in spite of all his failures, his defeat at the hands of the wasichus as Sweet Medicine had foretold, yes, today he could die a good death, a good day. His hands, which had, to this point, hung limply at his side, he now flung up to the circular opening in the star-studded sky above, thinking, this would be a glorious day to die. He was being called home. At last he would be released from what had imprisoned him here, and another exultant cry burst forth from him.

Anah, thinking now that he was no longer in a state of shock, but indeed recognized her from the fort and was also glad at not being stranded here alone, picked up her pace, her face sweetened with added relief. Then she was upon him, her thin arms wrapped around his chest, squeezing him. What was this she was babbling, over and over? He struggled to understand the language, English. She was attacking him, screaming, "We're alive, alive!" Shocked! Mortified! Instantly transported back into the bedraggled, storm-beaten body of a prisoner of the U.S. Army, he roughly pulled from her embrace to hold her at arms length as she looked openly into his face, somewhat bewildered, rebuffed.

Like that his world had changed! Iktomi, The Trickster, it must be... This was not a vision, but just a white woman, one of the "lady teachers" from the prison fort. Not knowing how else to respond, he shook her, as though to make her disappear. He was startled beyond comprehension when she threw back her head and spoke to him in his own language. "We are alive," she had been saying, Cheyenne and English, and again. "We will drown," she was now shouting, screaming at him, yes, screaming.

The wind was picking up again. "The Eye of the Storm," raising her lovely white arm towards the great white eye opening in a circle above their heads, "The Eye," she is shouting. Who is this being? What does she require of him? "The other half of the hurricane will be upon us and we will surely drown. The storm surge will come and sweep us away. We will not be so lucky a second time. We must make a raft. Help me, please!" but she is the enemy, a ve'ho'e!

"Cloud," she reached out to place both small hands on each side of his face, and in the instant that their eyes met he remembered her; the Sweet Grass Woman, Anah.

Mesmerized by her eyes. They glowed with little flecks of orange, cast randomly in the greenish pupils. Bits of gold sand clung to her cheeks among the scattering of freckles. He had never seen a creature quite like her, and yet he had seen her almost every day at the fort. Such a small mouth and nose; teeth like a young fox cub. "Cloud, do you hear me?" She grabbed at him rudely. He just stood there, transfixed. Maybe it was the blow to the head. She struggled to gain his understanding. Maybe it was the thinness of her drenched chemise, all torn and muddy. The sky above was beginning to swirl with angry clouds as two dolphins leapt back and forth in a playful way, plying the still, becalmed waters. A pair of the tall red headed cranes paced the sands. "I must be dreaming. This is a vision within a vision. This woman he knew as the Sweet Grass Woman, who spoke his language so well, the Go-Between Woman who wore the Morning Star upon her person now stood before him; how could it be? And yet he could do nothing but let it be, let his eyes but look upon her. So look he did, as she continued, voice raised. "We will drown. Do you not understand?" She began to resort to rudimentary sign language, trying to indicate that a large wave of water would come over them. As she lifted her arms to show how the water would roll over them he thought how nicely they were formed, and as white as the new moon. He watched the fire ignite in her eyes, glowing hot like a coal. "We must make a raft. Do You hear me?" Now she was stamping her foot. Like a scolding wren, he thought, making those small, perfectly round breasts dance. She is cold, he observed. These white women are not so strong, but spirited. As Anah's hand flashed out to strike him, thinking his strange, fascinated demeanor was due to shock, a stray beam of light flashed from her German silver bracelet into Cloud's eyes.

Pulling her to him, he realized that, though seemingly fierce, she was *frightened, for he could feel her heart beating. He had no medicine bundle, only the remnant of the Dog Rope still securely wound round his waist. With one hand upon it he pledged, "I will help you," touching that hair that was much finer than any horses. Quelling now the slight spinning in his head, he felt loathe to give voice to his Death Song, and so remained quiet, thinking. He slowly grew in awareness that her arms were soft, her hands rested quietly on his chest, and that she had quit talking. How nice! They now breathed in unison. The rising voice of the wind could be clearly heard.*

A door that many cultures had formed to keep closed, the forces of nature had opened, and these two were entering it. As the dark heartbeat of the approaching storm sent its gradually accelerating pulse into the slowly intensifying atmosphere, Standing Cloud and Anah began to enter a place that neither knew existed, revealing a place where they came as equals, momentarily trusting and hopeful. Everything that now surrounded them had a destructive ferocity, the potential to claim lives, and everything within them was being compelled with such a primitive desire to burn, to forge a link with the tiniest shred of that which might give them an edge towards survival. This eagerness seemed the most natural thing in the world at this moment, and vibrated with the desperation of those who knew that they were alone in their struggle.

Together they had to build a raft with what they could find...quickly... as the barometer began to fall, rapidly, once more.

The far bank of the luminous cloud wall that surrounded them now began to move forward. Towering magnificently, illuminated by the diminishing moonlight, an eerie, ominous setting as the winds began to pick up and howl the wall began to slowly, but inexorably revolve around these two. The Eye's journey could also not be delayed!

(Cloud, sunk deep in the recesses of his healing sleep, once again lashed the two of them to the raft and journeyed on, far, far beyond Anastasia Island, not realizing that he now lay safely in Gullah land, the woman of his vision safely at his side.)

Welcome To Another World

"...that woman has no shame!"

A delicious honeyed drone of cicadas thrummed thru the canebrakes here at the edge of the small meadow where they had come to be alone at the end of another full day. Anah, lulled to near satisfaction after a days labor, drooped her head like a day old morning glory onto Cloud's bare chest, still lightly bandaged from the broken ribs he had suffered during the hurricane's passage. Alert as ever by habit, he scanned the edges of the brake, knowing that as the day cooled the deer would rise from their beds and head for the fresh water, cautiously picking a path along the faint game trail where he and Anah where now resting.

Since Cloud had regained enough strength during this idle time of recuperation among the Gullah to fashion quite an adequate weapon, he was now wanting to bring fresh game to those who had so generously sheltered them. Besides, he was eager to show them how delicious venison could be. These gentle folk were not really hunters, having the bounty of the sea and land to eat. Shrimp, crab, oysters, and strange nut-like things they called "goobers", and fish. Fish were always available.

Songs filled the air. These people sang, all day. No wonder those awful birds, roosters, crowed such fierce war songs, trying to outdo one another. Drums all night from the woods, the ring shouts from the Praise House, the children's chants as they jumped their ropes, the men hauling nets, the women's thunk and rattle from their looms, where such wondrous colored cloths rose, it all blended into a riotous hum of life that reassured both Anah and Standing Cloud that yes, yes, yes, they were alive and bound together miraculously. They had no words for it, but each touch said so.

After the initial shock and wonderment of the arrival on the shore of this island, where their presence was accepted by most as a miracle of God's grace, who had brought Jonah forth from the belly of a whale and could certainly bring these two forth from a mere hurricane, they were simply accepted. A few harbored dark thoughts as they sat on the far shore mending cast nets, palmetto needles flashing, sneaking sideways glances at the strange healed scarifications on the tall dark one's back and chest, as such markings had not been seen before. One hand was kept busy with mending the nets while the other fingered the charms deep in their pockets, just in case. Her they did not pay much mind. But his scars; they weren't from a master's whip, now were they?

The lazy days of summer rolled on, as those days will. By now Standing Cloud was assured that Anah was the woman from his vision quest, but knew that she was unaware that this held any significance. He was at a loss at how to explain, and was so wrapped up in the simple creature comfort and companionship of her presence that he simply forgot to explain.

As for Anah, what had been a fascination with the tall Cheyenne now had become the reality of his physical presence in her life. They had weathered a true storm together. All the childhood fantasies embodied in her conception of "the noble savage" had seemingly come true in an almost fairy tale manner. Being literally thrown together in the throes of a fierce storm and surviving, followed by the foundation for healing, was now being laid in their lives respectively.

They resided together in the little palmetto log cabin where they had been tended. He was astounded when he came out of the being awakened and found out where he was and how long he had lain there and who he was with, but most of all he recalled just how his awakening came about, for he was quite certain that it was Iktomi's doing, that great trickster!

Here is how it happened: On the very morning that it was decreed that Standing Cloud was to return to full consciousness, at dawn's first light, the biggest and brightest and most pompous of the island's cock roosters decided to investigate just exactly what was demanding so much attention in that little cabin. So much scurrying in and out, and every time he went to investigate, he was swept out of the way. Did they not know that he was Le Rouge Royale, that all the hens gave way before him, unless summoned? Did he not cause the golden orb to rise up in the sky every morning? Not a day did he fail to crow it mightily forth upon its path upward into the sky. Well, today they would not keep him out; he knew they were bearing gifts of tasty things into the cabin. Even now, instead of announcing his regal and royal presence from the railings, he was slinking along the hollyhocks. Clever he was, ah! Just barely light, like a newly hatched chick, he would gain entrance when the first girl came. There!

Cloud recalled waking that morning to a vicious attack. A sudden attack. The enemy always struck then for the obvious advantage. Suddenly appearing, back-lit in full magnificence in a mottled beam of light leapt a red wattled strutting pompous cockerel, poised but briefly in a shaft of full sunlight that now filled the door of the cabin. Then with an incredible outburst of ascending peals of throaty cries, known as triumphant glory only to a rooster, this feathered creature with dagger-like spurs landed hard upon the half-awakened Dog Soldier, digging those talons in deeply for purchase.

No Crow or Pawnee's war cry ever uttered upon the vast plain had ever resonated with such power as this upon Cloud's unsuspecting ears. Totally unprepared, having no idea where he was, he flung himself buck naked from the quilts, seeking his lance, his hatchet, his bow and case, they were not to be found. His teeth bared, a fierce cry upon his lips, ready for a battle to the death!

The rooster sprang directly into his face, a blazing feathered fury, talons up, as a fighting cock does, flapping those wings in his astonished face. What demon is this? Cloud thought, for out of the corner of his eye he hears and sees a woman, a ve'ho'e, a white woman. God, she's naked too! He looks down, but briefly. Has he passed over? The woman is spasmodic, hiccuping in helpless laughter, clutching at her ribs, tears streaming down her face, trying to utter some word..... Fool's crow! Coyote's half-breed daughter! What is this? What is she now saying?

*...KOKOHEAXA....chicken, no, no.. Now she was on the floor, tangled up in a sheet, and laughing at him, at him, a*nd saying now, HETANANEKOKOHEAXA..the chicken's husband, *as he stands there with the bird subdued, hanging helplessly from his hand, wings flapping violently in an attempt to escape his grip. Metallic green and red feathers flashing, and the golden skinned woman laughing...at him! Her hair shining, blazing in the soft rays of sunshine, looking at him, looking at him, shooting him with her gaze, filling his heart with her laughter, filling*

his ears with golden peals...as the bird beats and flaps helplessly against his thighs, leaving him feeling...

"My hero!" she's now trying to say, "You're my hero." That woman has no shame, he thinks, then he to begins to laugh too, also helpless, helplessly in love......

Missing Her Commonplace Book

Anah was truly grateful for having come through the hurricane with her life and Standing Cloud's, both of them of sound limb. How generously they had been sheltered and cared for here on this little island. She sorely missed the comfort that confiding, writing in the pages of her Commonplace Book, brought to her. Paper of any sort was at a premium here, and she didn't know how to obtain any. About the only source were the precious bibles and cookbooks. So Anah kept her considerations in her mind these days.

She began a review, week by week of their time spent here. Their first week, to her, was a blur, relieved by a rosy haze of gratefulness just to be alive, and to see him breathing at her side. That gratefulness only expanded as she recognized that they had been rescued and brought into a safe harbor where they were accepted as a couple, tended, fed, and lovingly healed, with no judgments. To this day she was not sure if anyone knew that Standing Cloud was a prisoner from Ft. Marion, to the south. She was ambulatory before he was, not suffering any broken ribs, and thus was able to assist the women with the chores. This was a farming community of ex-slaves, with the loosely regulated chores built around the seasonal necessities of crops and livestock. She was more than glad to give a hand, even occasionally helping to midwife. As soon as Cloud could he, too, pitched in, though he was reluctant to go out with the fishing boats. Anah could understand that. No man had less fear, she knew, but the power of the great water was a spirit of which he had no liking; nor did she. Instead he picked up the bow he had fashioned and went into the woods. He didn't like joining the men and women in the fields, either. No one seemed to expect much of them, though, and they often just wondered off, exploring the great swathes of beach front, dragging driftwood back for bonfires. Sometimes they brought a muskrat, gator, or snapping turtle for the communal pot. Occasionally wild honey was located. If truth be told, neither of them gave much thought to anything other than the intense joy of another day of life that had been, they thought, so miraculously granted to them. They felt obligated, privileged indeed, to celebrate it in the manner that the surrounding world provided. The burgeoning, upthrusting shoots of swamp grass pushing up through the dark rich loam of the soil, the croak, the thrum and hum, the purr and shriek of the toad, frog, cicada, locust, blackbird, and gull. All nature was call and response; burgeoning, reproducing, blossoming, blooming, opening, responding to the forward arc of the sun. Half-way down a sandy path among the dunes, strewn with lemon-yellow and tiger-bright day lilies, she accidentally brushes his hip, he reaches out to steady her, his long copper fingers glance her warm, bare shoulder, and then they are upon one another. Want. Desire. Thirst. Need. Hope. Joy. Laughter. But is it love? She wonders this now. Did they ever say the words? Do the words matter? She tried to tell him, touching her heart lightly, saying once that many years ago she had dreamed...but he interrupted, "You dreamed of me?" "No, Cloud, not you exactly, someone like you," further complicating the matter with difficulties of language. How could he possibly understand a young girl's wildly romantic notion when reading the Leatherstocking tales? He just turned away with no further interest, it seemed.

What are words? In the beginning.....Oh, yes, WORDS...they must matter more than anything. She realizes that she doesn't even know the words for love in Cheyenne, nor in Lakota. When did William tell her he loved her? "Oh, William!" and she almost doubles in grief, remembering when she first saw the young officer as he came across the ballroom floor, striding tall in dress blues, the newly issued sky blue cavalry twill pants crisply pressed. Who the hell cared when he said what, she loved him at first sight, did she not? "Oh," pressing a hand to her eyes as though she could keep out the thought, " No, no, no," then, "She's here.... My darling.....Orianna!" Anah bowed her head and just let the memory of her daughter fill her completely. So long she had suppressed it. So fearful was she of overwhelming grief. So fearful of feeling guilt at feeling love once more, and then she just let the memory arrive. And here the child was! Even with her eyes squeezed tight shut, even with her brain screaming in high falsetto that there are no ghosts, no ghosts! Even with a voice of reason, Turn Foot's, so sagely telling her that we do not speak of those who have gone beyond, she cannot keep the memory out, cannot keep out what once was so beautiful, smiling, laughing, always a child, turning, fading, leaving, "Oh... Don't go, my darling, don't, please...."

How long had she been sitting here in the cabin, wishing she had her little book in which to organize her thoughts. Her tears had dried. She felt better. She had recalled both William and Orianna and survived. Well, well! Now what to do? She had no one to advise her but herself. The story of Ruth and Naomi from the Bible came to her. She never could remember how it went exactly; who was to follow whom and why, but the idea was to be loyal, and Standing Cloud was loyal, and she could be, too. She had no idea what the future held for her, or for him. Or for the both of them. Well, that was knowing something, was it not? No idea, but that was the point of blind faith, was it not?

What Is Sacred?

Their time with the Gullah passed quickly in one sense, and in another was timeless in the way that an endless summer feels to young children free of the responsibilities and concerns of a distraught childhood. Anah and Standing Cloud were indeed given shelter from the storm here on this little isle off the lowland coast among these gentle people. The dark interests of Hawa and her like had been turned aside by the simple luminosity that radiated from their presence, but such is the simple grace of a pure love. Having nothing left but their lives to lose in a storm of a magnitude of proportions that neither had ever experienced, they each expected to surrender that life as the hurricane swept back upon them, but before doing so they reached out to experience in an almost violent paroxysm of affirmation that they were yet alive, the joining together in another's flesh, and in some miracle that lay beyond their understanding, beyond their culture, came love...

Bound together in the flesh, by rough, salt-drenched ropes that abraded their limbs, tied to salt-soaked timbers that filled them with splinters and gouged wounds, yet buoyed them up through the seas, they were propelled, thrown, tosseled; more than half-drowned and delirious, till they finally arrived in Salifu's bay. They were bound now, not just in the flesh; salvation at hand, what mortal can explain?

The rhythm of the days had a seeming intent, like the little plovers working the tidal rhythms, up, then back. Communal, as when Anah was helping the women winnowing the rice, or later, in the heat, when all the hazy blue of the afternoon sky would offer was the lone drift of a vagabond gull, and all had retired to hammocks and cabins to rest, and the two lovers would gently pursue their growing knowledge of one another. Consider: One day Old Salifu had brought Standing Cloud to help him mend nets, and spoke to him at length regarding the slave ships that had brought his people to this land. Cloud was a good listener, as any Indian raised at a storyteller's knee would be, and he craved tales of another's strife, hardships and overcoming at the white-man's hand, for these people had overcome severe hardship. Perhaps there was reason in breaking the Mother's skin to plant and harvest, he thought, as he looked beyond Salifu's dark shoulder to the rippling green shoots of rice in the paddies. Later, when the cicadas began their concert and he drew nigh to Anah and placed his head in her lap, as she liked, he looked up and asked, " Did your father own slaves?" He was glad to be rewarded with a peal of laughter. He sought, but he did not find any solace for what still lived in him untamed; he envied the wind, indeed!

These afternoons were times for learning of one another's past; evenings they spoke with their bodies, and there was solace in that, as there was meant to be. Mornings they rose renewed, at least for the concerns of the day, and the concerns of an island summer day were so easily borne, when love was so well mingled with desire.

Cloud had conceived an eagerness to learn more of her language; she was already quite fluent in his. Love has a way of increasing reciprocation in others. So one day he found her quietly at work cleaning some turnips. He took her hand, and said that he had a surprise. Just using that word in English, he knew, would delight her. He loved the way her bright reddish blonde curls danced above her eyebrows when delighted! They walked quietly into the small grove of pitch pines beyond the little white clapboard Praise House, down the winding road shaded with the very old, gnarled live oaks festooned with Spanish moss. Proud to practice his growing command of English, he paused in the deep shade of the oaks and pointed upward, "I like this, reminds of tassels upon leggings, yes?" Anah embraced him, "Yes, it is much like the fringe upon your leggings." " Fringe," he thought to himself, filing it away, "fringe, not tassels. What is a horse's mane, I wonder?" After they had gone a quarter-mile he veered into the palmetto scrub and she followed. They soon came upon an open meadow, thick with deep green ferns. It was noticeably cooler here.

"Salifu told me of this old spring, an artesian well, coming up from deep, deep in the ground. Limestone." He was speaking slowly, carefully now. She was trying not to beam. Digging around behind a rock, he came up with a battered, dented tin cap.

He drew himself up; his hair, grown since they had been here, gleamed black. She admired his height and posture, aware now that something ceremonious was to occur, for he had a certain air about him. It was very, very important that she stifle the urge to giggle. He certainly would not understand. Instead she threw down her gaze upon the little spring, for it was indeed beautiful. Crystal clear, with a sand bottom, not much wider than a basin, quite shallow. As a child, up in the foothills of the Alleghenies, she liked nothing better than to overturn rocks in such a spring as this looking for the hellbenders that lived underneath; catching them, with their little fringed gills and oddly spotted orange and black skins. She knew now to pay attention. She could see a gentle, bubbling upwelling off center in the spring. It drew a thirst to her mouth. He bent on one knee, and she admired the rippling of his back muscles as he rose and handed her the cup. It was delightfully cool in her hands. Cold, actually, perhaps the coldest thing that she had felt since their arrival on Cootuh Isle. Still, she had not raised her eyes to his; now why was that? The urge to laugh had passed. In fact, as the refreshing coolness of the tin cup passed from the cup into her clasped palms, she felt quite collected. As she went to raise it to her lips, she thought to look to him at last, but the grave look on his face stayed her. "Oh yes!" she thought, "the lesson, the ceremony."

"The Holy Man, the one they call Deacon, gave me this word," and he paused. This was her clue. They were learning to work together. "What word, Cloud?" "Blessed. This water is sacred, *wakan!*"

As he drew her in, she lifted the dented cup to her smiling lips, and her hand flew up to light upon his cheek in the same fashion as a bird settles on a chosen branch. "Sacred, yes, this is indeed blessed!"

What of My People?

By the time they had arrived back at the little cabin the full moon just risen; the light it dispersed behind dark, bunched clouds cast thin, starved shadows about. Anah pulled an old shawl from the little rocker as soon as they entered, even though the night had yet to grow chill, for a certain coolness had indeed entered the atmosphere.

This was not the glorious time of Fall's riotous russets, golds and browns of celebratory harvest, but one of sere, bleached tones, of dry and withered plants whose fruitfulness had been long spent. Once the "flesh" had been harvested the skeleton was revealed. Fields lay fallow, shores scoured by wind blown spin-drift, and here and there a solitary Great Blue Heron stood immobile, like a sentinel of some unutterable longing. Huge, messy nests of the ospreys in the snags stood empty now, and as the evening wind picked up, the dune grass whipped the sand into concentric circles that by morning lay undisturbed by tracks. A silence and sadness prevailed, where once was riotous bird call.

In the village they all drew closer to the evening fires as days grew shorter, chillier. Seas grew choppier, turning deep, murky blue. The men heeded the weather and the running of tides with greater caution, spending more time mending nets. The old men were all too eager now to recount tales of lives lost at sea, draw on their pipes, sit back and gaze silently into their own limited days. The old women simply busied themselves with making more and more elderberry preserves. Some took to finishing up quilts before the days grew short and too cold to work out under the spreading oaks. The children, well they played on the strand now that the waters had cooled and the breakers rolled in higher. A few bold ones dared the waves no matter how high or cold, and went beyond the eyes of the old women who would tell on them. The griots gazed into their hearths and thought of the new tale they would try out this winter when the first big gale blew in, of the strange man and beautiful white woman caught up in old Salifu's net... and how they would spin it out, unsure yet of the ending. Thus they kept careful eyes upon those two.

But for now, before Cloud could even unstring his bow, Anah

had stripped off her shift and clambered beneath the quilt, and was taken by sleep, it seemed, one hand tucked, like a child, under her small, pointed chin. He moved close to stand by her, looking down. Her beauty amazed him now as much as it did when he had seen her appear in that last day of his vision quest, up on the sacred mountain. She lay before him so vulnerable, so trusting, so human. It was not his to question why he was to be bound with a white, was it?

Was it only a few months ago when the immense power rose and stirred the heavens into the storm, to thrill his being to its heights and depths, as it had never happened to him before? Truly he had no fear. Was he not one of the four, the Bravest of the Brave, a Dog Soldier of the Cheyenne!

He felt, then, a charge run through him that he had experienced only a few times before: when he had felt the first charge of a marauding mustang herd come raging, unchecked, undaunted, over a bluff towards him and his brothers, and when he was just nine summers old, and experienced the great northern spring movement of the Buffalo Nation commencing above the Powder River, causing the earth to tremble so, well before he even saw the rich, black, moving carpet of the beasts. Ah, the Thunder Beings, as their great talons blazed forth upon the peaks, splitting ancient rocks, shattering great pines, rending the heavens with jagged forces and blazing streaks of light, setting the sage on a fire that surrounded him. He was not yet a man when he had experienced these great unfoldings of the spirit world!

But truly, as he watched the heavens coalesce in the storm that he had since learned to call a hurricane, as the waves rose in the normally calm waters of the bay that they had sailed into just hours before, and the palms bent so before the fury of the winds that they bowed to the sand; he had no idea what great medicine was to be visited upon him once more.....

He was simply thrilled to witness the awesome power that was being manifested in the wind, waves and sky, even knowing that it would be a good day to die. The thought came to him as he began his Death Song, for he was indeed willing to once again lay down his life, as in the day he staked his Dog Rope...then the winds abated, the waves calmed. Then he saw her rounding the little spit of land. Walking towards him, as on water, back-lit by a few spears of moonlight that had so valiantly pierced the eye of this violent storm; it was the Sweet Grass Woman, Anah; she had been with his group, as she often accompanied the camping trips. But it wasn't her, was it? It just looked like her. This woman was haloed in an aurora of golden light, her hair was a nimbus of reddish gold water. A beaded net crowned her head and shoulders. This was the ve'ho'e from his vision quest! The hair rose on his arms, he would die now, surely! He knew not what to do! He simply stood in awe! This was sacred ground!

Plowing closely alongside the waves beside her came two of the sleek, furless, scaleless, leaping water dogs. Her cotton shift was plastered to her golden limbs, seaweed was strewn around her neck and in her hair, and what looked like streaks of vermilion face paint, but were actually small cuts. A wide smile played upon her small mouth. This woman had been sent to him from the spirit world as he had prayed and fasted up on Bear Butte all those long years ago. As she moved toward him the wan moon threw glints, from the German silver armband she wore on her wrist, into his eyes, almost blinding him...

And now here they were, on this little Gullah Island, having ridden out the storm; bound together. Was this the promised land that the holy Black Book the Deacon talked to him of? He did not look to a little book for signs and portents, but every time Anah and he had gone out from the village he had kept his eyes cut for sign. He did not expect to see a white buffalo calf kneeling down, half hidden in some leafy swale, or a coyote to rise unbidden from a cook fire, to lead him to an answer. He did not know what powers were at work in this land. It had been said that the Great Spirit had left the land east of the Mississippi! But now he had much to think about, much to resolve, and little to work with. He had no holy men to advise him. No medicine bundle. No special places where the powers could be felt and contacted, and yet, could this earth be somehow devoid of power? He thought not. The Everywhere Spirit, *Taku,skan skan* was what it was, beyond mysterious, beyond comprehension, the great mystery, and he turned and looked at the woman in the bed!

He let his mind drift back to the most beautiful river, the Yellow Stone, in spring melt from the glacial run off. Turquoise waters, milky, tumbling waters, the rushing sound, the brave little wren-like water birds that dipped and ran right under the cascading water. They built their nest right at the edge of a waterfall, so that the spray would keep the ferns they lined their nest with lush and green. There were dark green, towering Lodge-pole pines that the people traveled so far to gather for their lodges, and the coolness of the air. The beauty of the place! He missed those mountains. And yet, was it not beautiful here? " Yes, yes, Everywhere Spirit, I feel you," he thought.

Heavy feelings, like ancient yellow river stones deposited ages past upon the river's heart, that had been worn away, not by persistent raging of spring floods or torrential downpours, but by a woman's consistent love. He felt his heart rising, rising once more to the surface. Is this what is meant to be? She was the woman from his vision, but what does it mean? How could he ever explain this to her, his world and her part in it, if she does not even understand it? And what of my people, he thought? Of Matches? Of Heap of Birds? Kotom? The others? "What of this?" as he looked down at his copper-colored limbs, and stretched out a forearm to lay across her as she lay sleeping. What of my People?

To Provide and Protect

As the late afternoon tidal bore slowly rose up through the channels and into the creeks that meandered through the cord grass of the salt marsh down from the village at Pajo Bay, Standing Cloud could be observed respectfully pardoning himself from those men he had been in company with. As of late he would rarely be seen gathering at the fires come evening, nor would his presence be much noted or missed.

At first his tales, so similar to theirs, of the wily Coyote and strange Iktomi, were compared, discussed endlessly, marveled at, and even to some degree assimilated by their own storytellers, the griots. Eventually though, tradition won out, and a clamor arose for Brer Rabbit and Brer Fox, told as of old. The griots, who swaggered in the firelight, swung their limbs wide to once again cast their voices into the night shadows, lunging ever closer to the child whose attentions seemed to wander. For competition seemed to rear its head, an element that Standing Cloud had no consideration of in his telling of his stories. He had a difficult time describing Coyote, let alone the majesty of a bull buffalo! In fact Old Man Lomboi did not seem to take too kindly to his suggestion that the large herds of buffalo that roamed the plains were better than the cattle here. Cloud had tried to find the words to explain how the Tatanka's hair was so similar to the hair on Lomboi's head, except that there was much, much more of it, both thick and dark! He made matters worse by a reference to Lt. Pratt's "Buffalo Soldiers", which Anah did not know how to translate. No matter how he tried, he did not have the natural ability with languages that she did. With his own people one could sit down with the pipe to reconcile such matters; here they wished to take such matters to the holy man they called a deacon for what was called a reconciliation. A pipe was so much easier! Such complex ways were not that of his people; he feared never to understand! And so, though he felt no offense, he was not sure that he had not given some, so he rarely came these evenings to the fires, as he once had.

Besides, the seasons were changing and sending an age old message of their own. One that was read differently by Cloud than by these people who were rejoicing to see their harvest being brought in, and another hurricane season coming to a close. Cloud read the skeins of geese threading their way across the skies day and night, heading south, ever south; honking, penetrating wild cries that thrilled his blood differently than the man putting away his plow for the season. The amassing of the ducks on the marshes and ponds, fattened and now freed from their burdens of raising a brood, free to migrate, were largely unnoticed by those winnowing the rice and bundling the corn into shooks. The lengthening of the days and the warmth of the sun had brought a great fruition, but now the nights grew noticeably cooler and the beaches became devoid of the turtle kraals. The woods grew silent of the mating call of the birds and little foxes. Prosperity dwelt in the hearts of the residents of the village, but Standing Cloud's heart was not at rest. He tried to imagine himself raising a hoe above his head, turning what is called a furrow in his mother the earth, or on his knees patiently plucking a worm from a plant's stalk, watching the sky, anxiously hoping for rain. Nothing to chase, nothing to hunt, nothing to track, to elude, to test his skills, and where was the brotherhood in that? The bravery? Horses? No, just sway-backed mules and dumb oxen! He had listened to a few of his brothers who had spoken of the travesty of "hunting" the white man's buffalo, the cow, how they rode after them in a corral, shot them with arrows, fell upon them with skinning knives. The meat was tough and stringy. Did it poison you? he had asked. No, but one old man, Lame Wolf Woman, a half-blind Kiowa, had jokingly said, "It poisoned my soul, little brother!" and he knew just what he had meant. When the days of thunder came here, he had to leave the company of others to find a quiet place and let the sound roll through him, the glorious thunderous sound, like buffalo, like horse warriors, like his nation on the move!

As Cloud wandered past a small lagoon, through the woodlands, over pine needle carpets that muffled his footsteps, he was all too well aware that no enemy lurked. There was no need to ever have a weapon at hand. The island was secure and, as such, was desirable to those that harbored here. Such safety was unnatural to him. From the very first breath he drew began a life-long training that involved an element of survival and protection, and not just of himself, but for his people. He had been raised to protect and provide, not just for himself, but for those smaller and more helpless than himself. It was the age old way of life for his people.

Here he wandered aimlessly, responding to the windswept dunes that rimmed the wild ocean, for it was rarely calm. Now it was turning, with the seasons, ever darker, churning restlessly with ever larger swells, foam racing to the shore on their crests. He watched, transfixed, as large ospreys sailed off to the snags that held their messy nests. Herons, egrets, and even an occasional gator would surface in a slough along the way. Any path he trod away from the village and its fields and plots brought his eye to coot, and fox, and mallow, and milkweed. None of the wild beauty escaped him. But it was only in the isolation of the shore where he could gaze out on the far horizon and imagine that it was not endless rolling waves, but the endless rolling prairie of his heartland. As the clouds amassed on the horizon and darkened into velvety purples, deep rose and burning, blazing crimsons, the wind would whip the spume to the tops of the incoming, rising surf to a mounting frenzy. The wind, in intensity howling, so that he could imagine the steady bucking of the mounted onslaught of the surf charging, riding forward like a herd of his beloved mustangs, and he would lay there till the light left the sky, his heart trammeled!

And what of his Sweet Grass Woman, as she learned to brown a roux or separate the chaff from the hull as she expertly tossed the rice in a flat basket of her own making, content in rising each morning from the arms of love. Was she aware that the seasons were turning? Of course, for oft times, when the sun began to dip down and turn blood red, it had been a time for them to draw apart from the others, to seek their own company. True, her bed was never left empty once dark had fallen, nor had he taken to rising from it in the dark of night when odd creatures called out; what the Gullah here called haints and haunts. And his need of her had not lessened, but at times he took possession of her as though her flesh were an escape that he needed desperately, that he could somehow mount her and ride away, not that he was rough with her, but that, well, as it was, it left her somehow not connected with him. She was missing the sweetness of their union, that was it!

More and more she found him with his back to her, his back to the others, gazing out towards an empty horizon, lost within himself. Once she came upon him seated in the pitch pines, cross-legged, utterly composed, shafts of golden light thrown down all around him. He looks like a fairy-tale prince, she thought, and could not bear to advance another step across the thick carpeting of soft needles and disturb his reverie, so she left as quietly as she had come. Later that evening she asked him, "Did you know I was there?" Laughing a bit, as he rarely did, "Of course I did." "But why did you…" "I wanted to know what you would do." He took her wrist ever so lightly and brought it to his lips; bit it. "Is this what gentlemen do?" He answered. " No, no, like this, let me show YOU!" She knew something was creating a wall between them, and he was purposely distracting her, and she let him. She did not wish to discuss it, either.

Then another day she found him absently stroking the old spavined mule Sunny. He was stroking the ears, over and over. "Cloud, Cloud," she called to him, as he seemed to be almost in a trance. He turned to her with a look a profound sadness. "Salifu told me that they no longer have any horses here. That they cannot afford them. Besides, mules will do, he said. Mules will do!"

He turned and walked off. Came home later and threw a brace of rabbits on the small table in their cabin, knowing that she could skin them quite adequately. As she reached for them, he stayed her hand. "Anah, I am to protect and provide.." and he splayed his hand over the two small furred bodies. He quietly laid his bow and sheath of arrows down next to the game and went out into the darkness.

Anah knew. It was time. They would have to be moving on. But to where? She knew that undoubtedly they were both reckoned as lost back at Ft. Marion, and thus were free to make a life for themselves, but how? And where? She could no longer collect a widow's pension if she were thought deceased. They would have to talk. They had been sheltered here, but the storm was long past. To protect and provide…that was a declaration, but she did not really comprehend his meaning.

It was near dawn when he came for her. She had been dressed, seated and expectant, on the small rocker, her face drawn in the pale light of the morning's mist. She followed silently behind him as he led her out beyond a small tidal marsh, where the breaking dawn colored the tidal pools like handfuls of golden coins, down to a shoreline where small flocks of shorebirds raced in and out of the lacy tide. Normally she would have taken great joy in just watching the skittering antics of their search, but she sensed a great heaviness in Cloud's bearing, a weightiness that implied his carrying some decision of import. Indicating that they should seat themselves on the crest of a dune overlooking the ocean, he turned to her and fixed her with his great, dark, commanding eyes. He looked very tired. Had he been up the night? She arranged her skirts as he remained standing, looking out to sea.

There was so much he wanted to tell her, how he had been watching Hawa gather the burnt wood from the tree struck by lightning, her drying of the red-winged blackbird tongues, and the small effigies she was preparing. One did not have to understand the complexities of her exact auguries to know that she wished them harm, and wanted them to leave. Well, it was his desire to leave also. The day he came upon that juju woman with those little dolls clutched in her bony hand, peering into their cabin, he notched an arrow and felt malice twinge his own heart, and knew that they must leave as he returned the arrow to its case. Hawa was not their real enemy!

The rising sun broke through the mist to cast a golden sheen upon Anah's face. Did she realize how beautiful she was? She truly was the woman from his vision. What the future held for them he could not imagine. He could stand here looking at her forever, and it caused him great pain, for he felt he was in some way betraying his people, and he did not understand his heart. The sun continued to set her ablaze, to consume her in liquid fire so severe that he felt as though he must snatch her up from it somehow. Sorrow seemed to suffuse the planes of her face, as though she knew the weight upon his heart and soul. How could he have her and not betray his people? Just then a fine, dark scrim of just hatched may flies rose up between them, and a dark cloud wiped the light away!

The Journey Into Exile

"Here I can only ride the wind!"

"Have I spoken to you of our bitter journey into exile?" She made to reply, noting that he was using a formal form of Cheyenne, then realized that he wasn't soliciting a response from her.

" It was the Moon of First Thunder, when 72 of us looked upon our people for what we thought might be the last time, and were placed in heavy irons to be guarded by troops, taken by wagon and iron rail from Ft. Sill to Ft. Marion. Did I speak to you of the Ice House, where they fed us like lions, with meat from our own horses?"

Anah dropped her head to her hands. Oh, where could this be leading? This could not be good. From between her fingers, she dared a glance, but he was gazing steadfastly outward towards the horizon. She could not think of anything to do with her hands, and began to pluck nervously at the folds of her skirt. Besides, the winds were not yet up, and the gnats were viciously attacking her fine skin.

"We expected to be executed, of course. We were curious as to why we had been brought so far. But Lt. Pratt was a white man like no other in our experience. Many among us were Kiowa's. Many elite *Onde*, principal dogs, or Crazy Dogs as I was, the bravest of the brave warriors, fought against this man, and he against them, and yet now, when he had these men in his power, he stayed his hand and did not destroy them.

The lieutenant removed our chains, lifted us up out of the damp, dank cells. We had no air, no windows, and showed us how to build a new place to live. But not all of the captives were war leaders like myself, some were selected at random, and some were just Mexican captives from raids. Innocents of sorts! I will speak later, at length, of the part Kicking Bird played in this, and of his death, as Mamanti predicted. We traveled in a wagon, chained in one long line, we who had earned many, many honors, then we were forced to sleep on the cold, bare ground while shackled together. Our hearts fell down each night. And riding in the wooden cars, square, Anah, you know how disturbing a square confinement is to me, with no opening, screeching, moving, rattling, smelling so strange, and at every stop, crowds of whites came to gawk, is that the right word? Laugh, jeer, and the little children turned their faces in fear. Many of us who still had blankets pulled them over our heads. One of us threw his life away, and one of us was shot. On arrival many of us sickened, and one of our great men chose not to take food into his body and thus passed from this earth. I tell you only the bare surface of this story." He sighed deeply, and turned toward her, reached for her hands and drew her up. "Anah, I must leave here." She heard this. She didn't want to hear this. He did not say "We must leave." She expected this, and yet she did not know how to respond. She blurted out. "Yes, yes, we'll go," desperately wanting to insert herself into his future, assuming that she naturally belonged. How could it be otherwise; were they not together now? What had she assumed? She forged ahead. "We can go to Savannah, ah, Philadelphia perhaps, you'd like, well, maybe, upstate New York, the woods there. Maine, Canada, I know, the foothills of the Alleghenies where I grew up, you'd like it, the mountains aren't so high, but there's plenty of game and.." then seeing his face, she stopped mid-sentence.

"Anah, I'm going back." Perhaps she hadn't hear him correctly. Going back. Back where? Back west? They would hunt him down, surely. "Back to Ft. Marion," he answered her. "You're mad!" She raged at him, "You're a prisoner, they think you're lost in the storm, and now you have a chance at freedom. A chance with me, Cloud! I can get us some money," and even as she said this she knew it was not a possibility, and the words died on her lips, seeing the resolve form as he spoke these words, "I cannot leave them there! They are my people. Matches. Tail Feathers, Pe-ah-in and Ah-kes, Heap of Birds and Making Medicine, Wolf's Marrow, and Big Nose, Bear's Heart and Squint Eyes. She held up her hand; she had no doubt that he could name each and every one of the prisoners by heart. "I cannot leave them there. They are my people. Here I can only ride the wind. I fear the waves, for not even Salifu can master the water, and yet I will find a way to travel back to them."

And what am I, her heart cried out? What am I to you? By a great dint of self control she prevented herself from accusing him, but she could not stay the tears from flowing down her cheeks unchecked. She did not wipe her face; he did not notice them.

A murder of crows rose at this moment, in silent formation, from the pine woods behind them, and as they began to fly out in a wavering formation over the water they called out one by one, passing overhead. Each squawk, each caw sounded like a verdict of some sort, but both the distraught man and woman held still in the silence of their decision, as the sun disappeared like an idly tossed coin in the pale autumn sky.

It Is Good – The Sorrel Mare

Ft. Marion, St. Augustine, Fl

Anah arrived at the barracks while it was still dark enough to see the morning star shining brilliantly in the arriving dawn. She had exercised all her powers of organization to plan this. When Standing Cloud appeared, still buttoning his tunic, she briskly had him follow her out onto the terreplein through the confines of the fort, explaining just how Miss Mather had arranged a meeting with a Professor Baird of The Smithsonian Institute in Washington, D.C.

She knew that this would not carry much import to him until she explained what it meant to them, that this man who visited here recently was interested in some Indians who had lived many, many years ago, not very far from where Ft. Marion was, right here in St. Augustine. Professor Baird and his colleagues had begun to dig up some artifacts. "Artifacts?" Cloud"s expression darkened. Anah brushed this aside, not knowing how to answer, exactly. "Well, I've arranged for us, just the two of us, to be his assistants. We'll meet him out at the dig," as she continued to propel them on toward the stables and then out toward the paddocks. "These ancient Indian mounds need excavating." "Ex... Cave.?" He tried to question her, but she was talking rapidly, "and the contents labeled, cataloged, and shipped back up to the museum. Certain drawings need to be made. Your friends, like Kotom, and some of the others, who have been working in the ledger books would be good at this." She was talking rapidly. From the perplexed look on his face she finally understood that he didn't see the importance of her arrangement; that no amount of explaining would do. The sky was continuing to lighten. She was so very excited; a fine rosy flush to her cheeks, a gleam in her eyes. Cloud understood her propensity for surprises, and was assuming that this mysterious "dig" was yet another one, but he was also absorbed in this new assignment. "Dig, what's a dig?"

As per her elaborate arrangements, there was just one horse out in the paddock at this hour, a fine sorrel mare, grazing with her head down. Now Standing Cloud had been around the army horses since incarceration. But these prisoners, some of the finest horsemen ever seen, were now not only without mounts, but the soldiers here were not cavalry. There were horses around, but not for the prisoners, of course. As they stood at the fence, light wisps of mist rose from the ground. A male cardinal was calling from a hidden spot in the trees. Anah knew to remain quiet at his side. Just a few clouds rode white above the horizon; it would be a fine clear day. The sky lightened to pale lilac, and one could actually hear the sound of the grass being rasped by the mare's teeth.

Anah leaned into Cloud, "We will be riding horses out to the excavation site. Then carefully, she spoke into his ear, "This is your horse!" and she stepped decidedly back from the railing. It was as though she had left Cloud and the mare in their own world. He stood transfixed. At first she was not sure that he had even heard her. It looked as though he was not even drawing breath, so calm and serene did he appear.

Then she watched, fascinated, as he slowly drew himself up to his full six foot, four inch height. Slowly, carefully, he removed the shiny, dark blue, worn army tunic with the too-short sleeves, to reveal the remnant of the Dog Rope that he kept always on his person. That, and his glowing copper skin with its many battle wounds, and scarification from The Sun Dance ceremonies formed his real uniform. Draping the jacket carefully over the paddock fence, he entered the field and began to approach the mare. All the while she realized that some sort of song, or words, indecipherable to her, were emerging from his lips. At no time did he acknowledge her presence, and she began to struggle with that; of course she did! She had gone to so much trouble to arrange this, this gift!

The mare stopped her grazing, raised her head, and looked him full on as he approached. Then he did what seemed to Anah an odd thing; he reached out for her without any hesitation. Cloud had secured the mare's head, and began to breathe into her nostrils. She thought horses hated that sort of thing. Dogs did, she knew that. But Cloud stood for the longest time head to head with the mare like that. Then he began to run his hands all over her, as though he were checking for soundness, she thought at first. With an odd stir, she dropped her eyes, as she realized that the very intimacy of the gesture was the way his hands roamed her own body. When the mare let out a soft whinny of acceptance, Cloud vaulted upon her without the slightest effort, it seemed. In fact, Anah wasn't even sure that she had seen him mount up.

Then he was off, circling the paddock, bareback, no reins, no halter! A lump rose in her throat, for she fully imagined him soaring over the railings and disappearing! But no, he circled carefully, fully in control, slowing, until after a few laps he came up to her, dismounted, only to say, "It is good!" A shy, but rare full smile glowed upon his handsome face. Her elaborate efforts were well rewarded, if only to see this. "Yes, It's good, isn't it?" well pleased that her plan to reunite this fallen horse warrior of the plains with a mount for his use after all this time was working so well. "No, no," he continued, "I'm naming her "Isgood," as he led her toward the stables where they would saddle up and head out to the dig.

Once they were well clear of the outskirts of the town, Cloud removed his boots and placed them in his saddlebags. Anah thought his tunic might follow, but he seemed content to just liberate his feet from the hard leather. Good, she thought, but I will wait a bit to spring my next little surprise on him, for nestled in her saddlebags, along with their picnic lunch, was the simple pair of beaded moccasins she had arranged to have sent to her from Ft. Sill. Riding slightly behind him on her quarter horse, she was lost in reverie of the first time she had come upon the Cheyenne encampment on the Wind river, when she was such a young woman. Looking down on that milling herd of hundreds of horses with those copper skinned boys clad only in loin cloths so easily herding them, then riding into that camp where men, women and children bedecked in skins, feathers, paints, and animal headdresses and ornaments of bones and stones beyond her wildest imaginings and fantasies. Well, nothing, but nothing, could compare with the reality of the figure now seated on the sorrel mare in front of her, for she was now looking upon him through the lens of love and its magnification, as he rode down this simple dusty road toward the site of the dig, the Indian mounds. This was real to her, no longer pages in a book. Her youthful fancy of James Fennimore Cooper's *The Last Of The Mohicans'* Hawkeye, striding through the woodlands, buckskin fringes swaying, had been replaced, when she had first laid eyes on the sparkling lodges of the Cheyennes, with their milling herds surrounding them. This man with her was flesh and blood!

The Dig

Anah's plan for them to assist the workers at the dig was working out wonderfully. Not only had it provided a way for Standing Cloud to have a horse once more, but it gave them the time traveling to and from the site unchaperoned. They both knew that once back from the Gullah's that their relationship could not be openly acknowledged. Among the prisoners it was soon widely accepted, as both were well liked, and The Sweet Grass Woman was seen as an advocate on their behalf. Anah was sure that there was speculation on the part of the Lt. and Mrs. Pratt, and that there was a subtle form of tolerance, if not acceptance on their part, for they had not been hindered in the least in their comings and goings around the fort and town's environs.

That first day that Anah had taken such pains to arrange for the sorrel mare was well worth all the intricate planning, right down to the pair of beaded moccasins that she had tucked in her saddle bags. When they had called a halt in a well-shaded glen, under an old live oak, well off the road on their way back, and she had spread out their little picnic, she waited till Cloud lay back, looking well satisfied, his feet still bare. She rose and drew a package wrapped in butcher paper from her saddle bags. "Oh," Cloud disclaimed, "Not hungry." She tossed it toward him and an interested look crossed his face as he caught it; one that turned to amazed delight when he discovered the gift within. "Anah," was all he said, or all he had to, as he pulled her into his arms, pausing to unbutton his tunic and spread it upon the grass for them. Later she had to explain to him how Dancing Crane Woman had provided the footwear once she had sent the size. Anah went on to tell Cloud of the developing relationship between her and Crane; of how each received news from their respective forts and passed it on. "As you know this is how I have been able to get such a good supply of sage and sweet grass, and in return I see that foodstuffs arrive at Ft. Sill," she told him. "We are working to see that families are kept in touch also; she can serve as a go-between, and has certain connections with the military there."

As the weeks passed, Cloud's expertise with horses did not go unnoticed, not only with the military, who were well versed with the

Cheyenne reputation as some of the most accomplished horsemen the West had ever seen, but with the local gentry. Soon Cloud's services were in demand, for much of the rolling countryside surrounding St. Augustine was given over to pristine horse farms of the landed gentry, many who, while rich, had little or no talent in animal husbandry, and less in equestrian pursuits, but who were eager for their children, wives, or themselves to accomplish a graceful seat upon the back of an equine mount. So there were frequent forays out to these horse farms, for not only Cloud, but Anah also. Although his language skills improved daily, it was assumed that a translator would be necessary. Quite frequently Matches accompanied them in this capacity. Anah soon began to envision a future for them here once his imprisonment ended, but she did not discuss it!

A.K. BAUMGARD

A Wagon load of Dead Kiowas

O sun, you remain forever but we Kaitsenko must die
O earth, you remain forever but we Kaitsenko must die

Spring

Bright veins of heat lightning streaked soundlessly through the night sky, each random flash illuminating huge thunderclouds stalled far out on the horizon over the flat, molten surface of the calm ocean. In this season the heat and the humidity drove the prisoners out onto the terreplein late in the evening, hoping to catch the least little breeze that would occasionally spring up as the earth cooled.

Cloud was often the last, though, to return back to his bunk, for he so treasured the silence; the feeling of being alone and unguarded with his thoughts. It was so quiet that he could hear the turning of the shells upon the strand far below, sometimes even the sound of an oarlock from a fisherman coming in could be heard. On nights when the moon waxed full he sat late into the night, straining to see the sleek-bodied animals, not fish, he had been corrected, that were called what sounded like *dolt-fins,* that danced and sometimes leapt through the waves. He never tired of watching their play.

But tonight Matches was in a rare mood, and eager to reveal all that he knew of the recent Kiowa uprising to him and Ah-ke-ah, recalling all the incredible events involved in the foiled escape plan that occurred during the past full moon. Matches had a never-ending fascination for the Big Medicine of the *ve'ho'es.* With his growing proficiency in the English language, he had managed to become an aid to the steward in the army hospital. Thus he had learned the details of the "Big Medicine" that had stunned all the prisoners last month. They had never seen anything like it. A mystery that had captivated them all. Once witness to how Miss Mathers, a schoolteacher of theirs, had removed her full set of teeth, they were eager to see more of the white's "medicine". They had even seen a glass eye taken from a white man's head, and returned. Lt. Pratt and a visiting Major dueled with sabers when the man's leg came off in his hand, only to be shown that it was "replaceable". Such big magic! But that night, at the last full moon, when Lone Wolf, White Horse and Wyako of the Kiowa were sent to the "land of the dead", then brought before all of them, laid out like cord wood, arms stiff at their side in a wagon, rolled away, not to be seen ever again.... only to reappear among them weeks later, walking and talking. White man's big Magic, *adah*! Raised from the dead!

"Tell us, tell us, Matches," they all begged him. Of course, he delayed the moment...

"Of that very night," he began the tale now, certain of a captive audience, "of the planned escape, if you remember. The first sign that anything was wrong was that all visitors to our fort were kept out, and the massive doors were closed. We were all locked in. All Indians were herded into the dining hall." "Yes, yes," they told him, eager for him to get on with it, they wanted to know how the living had been brought back from the dead. Was it a Christian trick? "Wait," Matches told them, "You are acting like impatient white-men yourselves. Let me talk." At this they felt humbled and sat quietly, and let the tale unfold.

"We did not know why we were being put under guard, but those Kiowa planning an escape did. By now Death Songs could be heard rising softly and eerily during the long night hours, especially from the Kaitsenko, the warrior society of the Kiowa, who were sure that they would be found out, for they had secretly prepared bows and arrows for their flight. The entire command from the St. Francis Barracks was posted outside our own gates. We were told our casemates were to be searched for a missing bottle of poison from the pharmacy. Don't you remember? They began with us, then the Arapahoes, Comanches and, as nothing was found, we were dismissed to our quarters. But the Kiowas were detained until the ringleaders White Horse, Lone Wolf and Wyako were led away. Would any of you deny that Lt. Pratt was not an ordinary Bluecoat, not an ordinary white man?" And he held his hand to stay a response, continuing, "this is not to say that we, the prisoners, completely trusted him. One thing was for sure; we held no trust in the Army, nor the Government, nor the Big Father in Washington anymore. But we had to concede that we were being treated well. Certainly eating more than we had in months; well, years! But who knew how very clever he is, a real trickster! Now listen well to what plan the Lieutenant had conceived to trick the ringleaders of that plot." And of course they were apt listeners at this point! What they all knew was that White Horse had led a rebellion against Lt. Pratt, the one who held his fate here within these walls, and yet lived. They had seen him with their own eyes, back from the dead, how can that be? Tell us, Matches! How had he had been brought back miraculously from the dead? To be restored to Lt. Pratt's good graces and again trusted? Come now, the story, tell us, and he began once again....

And as the three Cheyenne settled themselves against the cooling, damp stones of the terreplein floor, each held in their mind the eerie scene that greeted them when, under last month's full moon, they had been called from their beds to stand at full assembly. Then a small cart came creaking forward in the very bright moonlight. Now they knew already of the Kiowa's foiled escape plan, that they had been taken away to the St. Francis barracks, but they were quite unprepared for this.

Laid out side by side in the empty cart, as though they were just cords of wood, were the bodies of Lone Wolf, White Horse and Way-a-Ko. Not a word was spoken as the cart with their stiff bodies rolled slowly past. Then the rest of the prisoners were herded swiftly and silently back to their barracks that night. None could sleep, imagining their own fate, for it had yet to be determined. Each and every warrior there had been raised to imagine a worthy death. They feared that the Kiowa's bodies might be taken out in the dead of the night, dumped unceremoniously over the ramparts, to fall down into the dark, murky depths of the ocean; not laid upon a burial scaffold with the infinite sky rising above.

Matches, realizing his own importance as a storyteller, knowing that this information would be carried around to the other men not present now, now began slowly to explain:

Sleep would not come to me that night, though I had no involvement with the plot. I was afraid that we all would be punished; we all were Indians, were we not? The next morning at assembly we were all told that not only were there U.S. soldiers surrounding us, but civilians from the town who would shoot to kill any escapees. You see, I thought, nothing had changed. But then Lt. Pratt said that the Army and the Government might think that if our "good behavior" continued, that "sooner or later" we would be allowed to return to our people. I'm not sure how many moons this "sooner or later" is, though, and good behavior is more than just manners, I think. He also said that many people did not like him treating us "kindly", as kolas, as brothers, that is, as people."

"Remember at the last time of the moon's fullness, when all visitors were excluded, and hurried out of the fort, even Sweet Grass Woman? Then the big doors to the fort's entrance were barred and we were all assembled in the dining room and locked inside, along with Mr. Fox and the hospital steward? Do you recall the steward holding up a bottle with a skull and crossbones painted on it, claiming a bottle such as it was missing from the doctor's dispensary in the hospital? What was actually being set in motion was an elaborate plan by Lt. Pratt to foil the scheme of those Kiowas who were attempting to escape. The three ringleaders," Cloud queried him, "Ring leaders?" "The war chiefs that would lead the escape party, they were Lone Wolf, White Horse, and Way-a-Ko." Cloud, still unsatisfied, continued to question him, "How did he know of this, did he have a vision?" Matches was a bit disgruntled at being interrupted again, but Cloud was his kola and his elder, so he patiently explained, " *You know the weak one, Ah-ke-ah, who is always hanging about the interpreter; he listened well, he heard plans."* Aho!

Not giving them any time to speculate further, he continued, "*So the lieutenant now knew who the leaders were, the three Kiowas. He had them taken to the big guardhouse, and had the post blacksmith iron them. Then he called the entire command from the big barracks and had the entire fort surrounded from the outside.*"

This bit of telling especially pleased Matches, as he didn't think that the men knew about this, and if they had, it would had concerned them. If they could see the look on their faces right now!

"*It was on orders from the big General Dent that the men from St.*

Francis Barracks came to surround the fort. The townspeople were quite alarmed too, at the thought of us wild Indians getting loose and scalping, and such," (well, maybe he was going a little too far here, he thought, but he was enjoying his audience)

He quickly righted things, and continued, *"The lieutenant, being a right hearted man, did not want to upset the townspeople, so he dismissed the command, sent those men back to their barracks and said that he would take over. So with the help of our great chief Manimic, who agreed to enlist the Cheyennes in case there was a general revolt, those Kiowas planning an escape were routed. The search of the barracks for the poison let all know that a plan to escape would be futile and would endanger any future benefits. However, the ringleaders were given special treatment.*

Very, very, special indeed, as you will see, my friends!" Matches' eyebrows arched up in his eloquent face as he leaned back against the parapet; he had a bit of the Trickster-Changer in his natural storyteller abilities, letting those listening lead themselves somewhat astray in speculation. He crossed his lean, long arms and legs, waiting for them to urge him on. This was the most enjoyment he had had in some time, short of pulling "water buffalo" from the waters of the gulf.

"Well," he continued, " *Lone Wolf, White Horse and Wy-a-ko had been briefly paraded before us men in irons, then taken away to dark cells under heavy guard. Remember! Nothing was conveyed to us then of their fate. Remember waiting on the terreplein as the evening grew dark and the full moon sailed into the sky, casting long silvery fingers across the water. We knew not to talk amongst ourselves, did we not? A few owls called feebly out, but an ominous quiet reigned, except for an unfamiliar voice as the guard was challenged and changed."* It was then that I was summoned to aid the Post Surgeon Major John H. Janeway, so I can tell you what happened next. No one else knew of this. Most strange. Most strange. No one asked me not to convey these deeds, although I have debated taking this to my grave, since I do not fully understand this Big Medicine. I leave it to you, my brothers, who you tell. It was very late when I was called to these dark cells where the captives where now held. I had no fear, as I had done no wrong. Two very large and well-muscled soldiers brought out Wy-a-ko from his cell first and told him to remain standing, and not to speak. They *also instructed me to assist the post surgeon, whom I recognized, but at no time to speak, even when spoken to. Lt. Pratt appeared to tightly blindfold the Kiowa's eyes. I assumed Wy-a-ko was to be shot or hanged. I did not want to witness this. He was then led away to an open courtyard. Imagine my surprise when I could hear the shuffle and clank of his irons returning, then proceed, backwards and forwards, backwards and forwards, until he was so exhausted that he hung limply upon their arms. White-men have no end to their strange ways, I thought at this time This same exact procedure was carried out upon Lone Wolf; again not a word was spoken. When this was instituted to White Horse, a Kiowa war chief, a notorious murderer and raider, he insisted on marching with his head held high throughout the lengthy treatment, back erect, showing no fear, though his fate was unknown and his eyes completely covered.*

I imagined that I was there simply as a witness. I thought it most strange, but it became stranger still when Dr. Janeway, a tall, thin, very pale, ghostly looking man entered their dark cells with a large needle in one hand; nothing else that I could see. Way-a-Ko's arm was extended and the doctor touched it with the large needle in one place only. It made no noise. It drew no blood. It had no smell, no smoke. The exact same procedure was done by the doctor to the very exhausted Lone Wolf, who uttered not a word, but sank to the floor within minutes as asleep, or dead.

All was deathly quiet in this room. My tongue lay as in its grave, then the Dr. came to White Horse, who had never felt such restraints in his life. One of the first to count the coup, to rob the dead, to kidnap white children, he now spoke boldly to Mr. Fox, who in turn inquired of Lt. Pratt that White Horse wanted to know what was being done to them. Imagine my surprise when the reply came with such calm wisdom, for Lt. Pratt said that he knew that we Indians have some very strong medicine, and do wonderful things with it, but that the white man has even stronger, and can do more wonderful things, and that he was having the doctor give the men a dose of the white man's medicine! White Horse took no time to think this over, but replied, "Will it make me good?" Lt. Pratt told him, "I hope so. That is the object." He then submitted to the needle and fell asleep like the others.

They sat deep in their thoughts, waiting for Matches to go on. Surely there was more to this strange tale.

"The cart we all saw was then brought, and four strong soldiers carried the Kiowas out. By now I knew they were not dead, but I was told that they were in a place called "unconscious", a long dreaming. The cart took these men, in the full moonlight where, later that night you, and all the others witnessed them lying side by side as dead, moving slowly, so that they could be observed fully and carefully by all. You know the rest, my friends. For the full turn of the moon these three were kept from our sight, imprisoned, out of our sight, with no word that they were indeed alive. Then they were brought back to us! I was sworn to secrecy. I could tell no one. Now you know the full truth of the white's Big Medicine!" *"Unconscious! He caused them to cross over, did he not? And return?"*

Matches was finished. They gathered around him and Cloud saw this as an opportunity to wander off. That evening of the uprising and attempted escape of the Kiowas was profoundly disturbing to Cloud. All of his grown years he had been a warrior, fighting for the freedom of his people. These last seasons he had been a captive, and did not know what he was, or was to become. He moved to the far corner of the terreplein and gazed out onto the watery horizon to once again recall that time of the last moon's fullness. Unconscious, that was the white-man's word. Could they really cause one to cross over, and bring them back? He could not bear to think of this as deception.

The Fruits of Intimacy

The time now afforded to Anah and Standing Cloud, as they traveled to work at both the dig outside the environs of the town proper, and on those occasions when they traveled for Cloud to train horses for the gentry out in the surrounding countryside, provided them with ample opportunity to be alone. Much of that time was spent in the companionable exchange of information, for they had settled into a phase of their relationship in which they drifted around one another as relaxed and free as two butterflies afloat around a ripe stalk of milkweed. There was little or no urgency, no concern or discussion of future plans. Indeed, said future was a great unknown. Any attempt on Anah's part to discern how long the men would remain imprisoned, and if they were to be kept incarcerated indefinitely, was simply ignored to the point that it had become more than embarrassing for all involved to even broach the subject. So, of late, she was more than happy to ignore it.

Lt. Pratt's care and concern for the prisoners under his command was well respected, if his methods were somewhat questionable. It was thought by quite a few that he was more interested in education than incarceration. Several had the temerity to openly accuse him of outwardly seeking amusing pursuits. There were camping excursions, picnics, fishing expeditions, and Indian Dances, and even a simulated bullfight staged, of which Anah heartily approved. She took every occasion that presented itself to point out that she thought Lt. Pratt's unorthodox methods had much to do with the excellent discipline of the camp. For the most part the townspeople were very accepting of the Indian population, and many of the prisoners were able to obtain paid employment outside the fort. Some worked in the orange groves, some as baggage handlers for the northern visitors, a few in the sawmills. They proved to be such disciplined and responsible help that their presence was accepted in the town when they went about in twos and threes, unaccompanied before curfew. They formed their own guards and no untoward incidents ever occurred. Thus Standing Cloud and Anah's presence together did not seem unusual, as long as they maintained a certain decorum, which of course they did, in public.

Late one afternoon, when their assistance at the dig was not needed, they left early and found themselves settled under their favorite live oak. The sky was clouding up in a pleasant way, and Anah had drifted off into the sort of nap she had so grown to favor when they had finished making love and she felt completely secure. A Carolina wren was calling from somewhere up above them; insistent, hopping from branch to branch. Cicadas were rising up in sudden chorus, then just as abruptly coming to a full stop. Cloud was half asleep himself, but by habit kept himself alert. As much as he missed his plains, these little meadows had much beauty, especially at this time of day, when the lowering sun blazed golden upon the tangled, rough, twisted limbs of the oaks, making them look as though the little meadow was a bowl of amber honey.

He found himself in full recall of that morning when he awakened in the near dark, wakened from the most awesome power that he had ever experienced, knowing immediately that the slight form curled next to him on the bed was the Sweet Grass Woman, now his woman.

Each breath brought a sharp pain, his ribs he surmised, feeling across his chest with his hand, he felt that they had been expertly bound with soft cloth, though he had no recall of that being done. He head ached so.

Well, they had survived, both of them. This woman, white woman, his spirit guide then? But where where they? He was for now content to lie here and just watch the gentle rise and fall of her breasts as the sky continued to lighten outside the window. What had become of the rest of the men from the fort? As his thoughts began to drift back towards his captivity she sighed, turned on her hip to face him. A small beam of sunlight raced down her cheek where a bright abrasion looked like a streak of vermilion face paint, and his heart was pinioned to an unknowable future, and a yearning for her to wake just so that they could begin to talk began to flood through him.

It was then that the brilliantly feathered and spurred creature named a rooster sprang upon him! His laughter woke her. "Cloud, Cloud, what? What are you laughing at, dear?"

"Do you remember the bird that attacked me that first morning in Gullah land?" "Oh, how could I forget."

The Dinner Party

Early July, 1876

They were finishing up a grand repast, including fresh oysters the men had brought back in the yawl from Mantanzas Inlet that very morning, when the adjutant arrived, looking terribly grim. Without pause, he broached the gathering, summoning Lieutenant Pratt to him. The obvious dire import caused all table talk to cease and focus on them as they conferred quietly in the archway of the dining room. When Lieutenant Pratt returned to the table, pale as the linen napkin tightly clenched fiercely in his hand, he declared, "I must beg your pardon. Excuse me, I've been summoned."

As Mrs. Pratt began to rise from her seat, he placed a hand to stay her, and in a grave voice told them, *"General George Armstrong Custer is dead, and all of the Seventh Cavalry with him!"* Turning smartly on his heel, he left.

Dumbfounded, the dinner guests looked to one another, but there was no further information to exchange. Second Lieutenant Stuyvesant practically overturned his chair in his haste to exit; to follow, then realizing that he wasn't commanded as such, sat abruptly down to profusely apologize to his hostess, his gloves left neatly folded by his plate. Mr. Dawes reached rudely for the sherry decanter, overfilling his glass, gulping it down, but taking his leave with great care, as one by one the table emptied. Mrs. Hayes began sobbing, great gulping sobs, barely capable of achieving a breathe in between, as her younger sister helped her to her feet and quickly gathered their shawls, the egret plume on the elder one's head erratically bobbing as she was helped out. Soon only Anah and Mrs. Pratt remained at the table, as their veal chops slowly congealed in Madeira sauce. The kitchen was ominously quiet; the help that had been hired expressly for the party had discreetly left.

The two women found one another's hand across the spotless white linen and sat there quietly as the candles slowly burned down. The only noise in the room the mournful sound of the guttering flames.

A.K. BAUMGARD

The Recent Calamity

Ft. Marion, July 1876

Lieutenant Pratt referred to Custer's horrendous defeat as "the recent calamity in the northwest". The terrible news of his annihilation, and part of the Seventh Cavalry, at the Battle of the Little Bighorn on June 25th, did not reach Ft. Marion at St. Augustine until well after the grand celebration of the nation's first centennial on the Fourth of July. The timing could not have been more disheartening!

The reports, and the subsequent exaggerations, when received, prompted much fear and outrage among the residents of the town. There was a general call to rescind the prisoner's access to the streets; to suspend all their privileges, especially after the sun was down, when the narrow, twisting cobblestone alleys looked particularly sinister. Some were even calling to have them returned to their cells once more.

No women were out and about, nor could the joyful sound of children at play be heard. Lt. Pratt immediately came to their defense, noting that in their previous fourteen months of incarceration there had not been one incident, and that they had displayed exceptionally good behavior. Nonetheless it was determined, for their safety, as well as for the well-being of the townspeople, that they would be confined to the fort for an indefinite period. After much heated discussion, it was thought best not to reveal the actual news of Custer's defeat to the prisoners at this time, though. Most of these prisoners were deemed "hostiles" by the U.S. Army; many of them had been fierce warriors, and had actually fought side by side with the very Indians that had brought about Custer's defeat.

The Battle of The Little Big Horn in Montana entered into history books, known to the People as the victory in the Valley of the Greasy Grass. At the time of this occurrence almost all of the Comanche, Kiowa, Southern Cheyenne, and Arapaho were on reservations. The strength of the mighty Sioux nation was scattered and in disarray. Great herds of buffalo no longer roamed free, and neither did the Horse Warriors of the Great Plains. But that summer solstice of 1876 saw a herd of twenty thousand strong grazing on the Greasy Grass, known as The Little Big Horn to the whites, where those Indians still free responded to the call of Sitting Bull to assemble and celebrate in their time-honored fashion. It was one of the largest gathering of the tribes; many even came from their reservations. Among those gathered were the great war chiefs Crazy Horse and Gall. It was to have terrible consequences.

Custer's Ears

The Valley of the Greasy Grass
Montana, June 25, 1876

The two women had left their camp early that morning when all was still quiet. Here on the rolling prairie above the Little Bighorn, meandering and looping like an undisturbed snake of gleaming silver below them, they hoped to find the tubers of tipsinna that they had staked out earlier in the spring when it was still in bloom. Under the blessing of this summer's sun those tubers would have grown to the size of a crane's egg. The young women were already imagining how, when cleaned, cut and dried, strings of these turnips could be traded for corn and other desirables.

As yet unmarried, Pte-sau-waste-win, a cousin of Sitting Bull and Strong Right Hand, had no pressing duties back at the villages where more lodges than they had ever seen in their young lives were now pitched. Last night they had wandered freely, entranced by the majesty of their own people. Yes, the winter had been hard, but all winters recently were becoming such, and this gathering for the renewal ceremonies had been propitious. They had seen with their own eyes the great war chiefs of their people. Two Moon, Little Horse and White Bull. With the Oglalas was the fabled Tasunke Witco, and the San Arc leader's Spotted Eagle and Fast Bear, Hump and Lame Deer. Fast Bull too, was present. All the great leaders who refused to walk the White Man's Road were present, including the Hunkpapa's Sitting Bull and his war chiefs, Gall, Crow King and Black Moon. As they wandered through the tribal circles last night and saw just who were gathered there, faces luminous in the dancing flames, their regalia spectacular, each bonnet, plume, feather and lance a tale in itself, of war honors, the girls had grown dizzy with awe.

Here above the camp in the clear, dry air scented with abundant sage, they were quiet, introspective; each one thinking of their own future as young, unmarried women were prone to do. The burble of meadowlarks, and occasional scree of a hawk were all that disturbed them as they dug among the small stakes that they had planted earlier, to disclose the whereabouts of the turnips once the grasses had grown taller. Soon the wind would pick up and the thrashing of the grasses would bear the gentle sounds coming from the huge encampment on the streams below them.

But when cries of alarm rang out, carried up to them, they knew what to expect. The dust cloud from gunpowder and hundreds of hooves alerted them. From their vantage point they could see women and children fleeing towards the deep ravines in the cliffs; war parties being quickly assembled and heading away to the north. The older of them, Strong Right Hand, cautioned, "We'll stay here little sister," and pushed her down into the grass to wait. "Do not rise up, keep your curiosity bound. Hidden here, we are safe." And they were, although hot and parched. By late afternoon when they heard cries of jubilation, the clear sounds of victory over the enemy, they cautiously rose. The camps below looked rerouted, though there was much activity to indicate that many bands were in serious preparations to move out, now that the conflict seemed resolved. They agreed to head back, scouting a safe path as they traveled. Pte-sau-waste-win was the first to notice the green strips of paper blowing and scudding across the land towards them. "Soldiers," she called out. Of course, they knew it had to be the Bluecoats, no Pawnee or Crow would be so foolish as to interrupt their People's gathering of strength; their time of renewal.

Late in arriving on the Greasy Grass ridge, there was little left in the way of spoils for them to gather. Horses and men lay strewn about. Many bodies lay stripped, scalped and mutilated as was the custom, to hinder enemies in case they decided to remain in pursuit in the afterlife. Any curiosity they had harbored as to how the whites differed from the People were resolved with a glance. Their blood was as red and as eagerly drunk by the abundant flies swarming over the rent flesh.

Eager to find and rejoin their families, they hurried on among the jammed carbines, broken knives and worthless remains, when Strong Right Hand drew herself up with a gasp at the foot of a pale white body, totally naked, seemingly unscathed, with the exception of a small black hole at his left temple and breast. She pulled on Pte-sau-waste-win's tunic to halt her, and dropped to her knees to examine the man closer. He had a long gash in his right thigh, thus marked as an enemy. His unseeing eyes matched the color of the skies, open now to infinity. The deep, ugly cut exposing the strong muscle in his thigh was the only sign of acknowledgment. The lack of mutilation was in respect of his courage, they assumed. He lay unscalped, the hair, well-bloodied, was the color of ripened wheat.

The grass of the prairie had been set to burning earlier, and the thick, gray pall of smoke was just now beginning to lift, allowing spears of the lowering sun to illuminate the battlefield. A wounded horse stood outlined above a soldier, whose foot was still held in its stirrup. No other enemy remained up here on the ridge. A general exodus of the camp was in an orderly motion below; the severely wounded were being loaded on travois. Ululations, shrills and whoops told the story of unprecedented victory. Pte-sau-waste-win was anxious to rejoin her family; there would be riotous celebration. But Strong Right Hand had sunk down beside this ve'ho'e, holding his curly head on her lap while rooting in her pouch.

"This is Squaw Killer, I know. Medicine Arrow had warned him, many, many years ago when I was still a child. His name is Custard! He was at times brave, but he could not listen. Medicine Arrow told him, "You and your whole command will be killed if you pursue war against us again." She drew a sharp awl out her bag, and turned his head on her lap. "What are you doing?" screamed Pte, for she herself could not bear the thought of touching that white skin. But Strong Right Hand now had his bloodied head cradled firmly in her lap. "Remember, Sister, It was Rock Forehead who dumped the ashes from the pipe on this officer's fine boots, and he did not even notice the offense."

Strongly plunging the instrument into Custer's ear she exclaimed, "He would not listen in life; perhaps this will help," and with that she deftly flipped the lax head to its other side and pierced that ear, too. Dropping his head to the bloody dust, she rose. "No more wax in his ear holes!" Dusting her hands in the universal gesture that signals dismissal, she turned to her friend. "Let's hurry, we have much to celebrate!" As they headed back, the younger woman turned on her heel, then quickly stooped and cut a wavy, blond lock to tuck in with her bag of turnips.

In the years to come all such "artifacts", anything at all that would indicate a presence on this famous battleground, had to be secreted away for fear of reprisal, that is, if you were Indian. On the other hand such "artifacts" were prominently traded, collected and displayed in museums.

Kate Big Head

July 1876

The slight breeze was enough to luff the curtains that draped the small door that led out onto her porch. She could not sleep, and saw this an an invitation to go out and search the sky for a consoling star, but an obscuring mist had risen from the gulf. Her hair, which she had plaited for the night, clung damply to her neck. The air was close; heavy with moisture. Returning to her stuffy room she lit a small candle at her desk and opened her Commonplace Book to seek some consolation there. Lighting just a small candle at the escritoire, she began once again to write.

"It's been so long since I have "touched pen" to you, as the Indians say. I write as though you are my friend, as though you are alive. Well, you are my truest confidante. Who else can I tell of these disturbing thoughts when I am feeling sorrows for myself. It is not myself that I sorrow for these days.

Today I received a letter from Red Dancing Crane that broke my heart. I have read and re-read it. I can barely digest the pain it contains, but I must in order to pass on the information as she has requested of me. It has been sent in the utmost confidence that I will keep. It must be done discreetly so that no harm can come to the informants, nor can any repercussions ensue from this information. The letter contained a first-hand account of the battle at the Greasy Grass as witnessed by a southern Cheyenne woman, Kate Big Hand, who rode there to look for her nephew, Noisy Walking. She was able to safely observe the whole battle and record the aftermath.

Before I destroyed the letter, as requested, I made a list of names to deliver to the prisoners here of their relatives who were killed, of how they died, and in what manner. Apparently the manner in which they die is of great importance. The women after the battle brought their travois to carry away their dead and wounded. None were left on the battlefield. This would bring them a great comfort. Many were buried in the traditional manner, Kate Big Head said . Many in nearby caves. Some on scaffolds. The Sioux even left some of their dead warriors in burial lodges, set up as they had been when living. Chief Lame White Man was the only married man of the six Cheyenne that died; that comforted me.

It took the Army three days to retrieve their dead. I have not the heart to ask, or speculate why. Dancing Crane said that Taku Skan skan, what they call The Everywhere Spirit, caused the panicked soldiers of Custer's Seventh to go crazy and turn their guns upon one another and themselves. This grieves me sorely. Sorely!

I will be sure to tell the men the story of the brave Scabby, who stripped naked, wrapped a flag around his body, mounted his pony and raced back and forth five times in front of the soldiers without being hit by any bullets. This show of strong medicine will cheer them greatly! Also, Kate said that the Northern Cheyenne were considered the special fighters along with the Oglala Sioux. The fighting was so fierce and day so hot and dry that at one point the dust rose so thick that it was impossible to see the men and horses through it.

Be sure to tell them that Calf Trail Woman went into the fray with her six-shooter on; that she followed her husband Black Coyote. She wanted to give her pony to a Cheyenne who had his shot out from under him, but instead she simply snatched him up and rode him to safety. Oh, could I ever be so fearsome and brave as these women?

I know that my conveying this information is so valuable to these men who are imprisoned here. Red Crane told me that many of their relatives are fearful of recounting the events of the battle for fear of reprisals, as they are desperate to keep any information of their involvement in the demise of Custer from the Army.

Crazy Horse still lives, as does Sitting Bull. Gall survives, but he lost his wife and children. I can write no more tonight. There is much crazy talk and rumors going around!

Murder of Crows

After what had seemed to be an awkward, painful foray into discussing their respective upbringings, both Anah and Cloud began to freely and openly exchange stories and anecdotes, not giving too much concern to whether they were being completely understood or not, as long as they each kept pent up the various hurts and private joys that they wished to avoid.

Cloud spoke of his desires for the open prairie, the wild abandon and fierceness of the wind, as though it were an entity. Anah thought now of how she felt when seeing the opening of newly blossoming buds on the branches of an apple tree; of being the first to find them. They rambled on, speaking of childhoods that neither could experience of the other, and yet sometimes they could concur. It didn't much matter, for they simply enjoyed one another's presence.

Late one afternoon, returning early from the dig, as a storm was threatening, a huge flock of crows began to float overhead, silently at first, as they rode back toward the forest. Cloud was the first to notice them. As the rising dihedral stirred the air, the crows began to sport and play, and soon the number of birds returning to roost began to darken the sky. They pulled their mounts up to watch. Anah rose in her saddle, delighted, calling out, "A murder of crows!" He turned toward her. "Yes, it's an old expression, like a gaggle of geese." He shook his head, "these birds do not murder. I will never understand your people. You cannot read the signs before you. Yellow Hair, Custer, that man who led an attack on a peaceful gathering of many, many thousands gathered to celebrate a traditional gathering at the end of summer. Those Indians were not there to kill soldiers, did not know they were coming, even. They were there to celebrate, to dance, to feast; not to kill, but this man, this Yellow Hair, this Custer, he is remembered for his attack as a victim of a massacre!

Anah had no words to defend herself against the policies of her government. The crows swirled, clamored, cawed exaltedly overhead, screeching. She wanted to cover her ears, to not hear his reproach. To argue, to say that she was not who she was, that her skin did not make her an enemy, but then.... The purple mass of the approaching thunderstorm could now be felt as well as heard in the rumblings of not so distant thunder. Abruptly the crows fled, swift and silent. She raised her head. She had hung it in shame. He held out the reins, "Anah, Anah," gathering her into his arms, "is there not the saying that the pot calls the teapot black also? I have had much white blood on my hands. Now I have you in my arms!" Was this an attempt at humor?

A Warrior's Glyph

June 27, 1876

In the Moon of Long Days, in the Year that Long Hair was Rubbed Out, two men rode quietly out into the soft, gray mist rising on the open ground, where yesterday's battle had been fought. In that hour before the sun rose there was still enough dew so that their passing left dark slashes behind them through the high grasses of the open plain. It was as though the very earth agreed in solemnity to mark their passage. Having no need to speak the tall Northern Cheyenne, Braided Locks, kept pace with his shorter companion. Grotesque shapes of dead and bloated horses seemed to rise up out of the mist, as though some spirit was still left to animate them. The army had yet to bury their dead, so neither warrior looked to the bodies of those slain as they picked their way through. The various tribes and bands had already departed with their own honored warriors long before the sun had set yesterday. Though there was a great victory over the Bluecoats to celebrate it had been decided to make great haste heading north. There would be repercussions; there always were. Ghostly forms of feeding predators slunk away into the mist; what appeared to be an uncommon boulder out on this barren plain was but a slumbering, well-sated grizzly.

A disturbing silence prevailed. None of the sibilant stirrings and susurrations of the birds that usually heralded the coming dawn were to be heard. Instead the hoarse hollow "cronk" of a solitary raven gave but slight warning before it rose up with such a great, fierce slapping of wings, an indication that it was weighted down with heavy feeding. Beast after beast slithered, flapped and slunk away at their approach in the obscuring mist, as the rising sun created a merciful blindness to the carnage that they were passing through. The abundance of spoils had guaranteed a gruesome truce among the scavengers, and nary a yip or growl among the foxes, coyotes, and lesser little brothers was to be heard as the feasting continued. Here and there lay objects to plunder; swords, guns, saddles; but the men did not even look down, so intent were they on their journey.

Even though they had but one lance, one pistol and a quiver of well-made arrows between them, today of all days they had no intention to fight. By mid-day the sun burned above them, baking the sky into a dull blue, as they reached the place known to the whites as Inscription Rock. The smaller man circled the rock, occasionally pausing to touch a glyph he recognized. Braided Locks was surprised to find the symbol of the Morning Star that he had inscribed in the year he joined the Kit Fox society. While he was lost in his thoughts, the one called Tasunke Witco dropped from his pony, pulled a knife from its sheaf, and began to make a few deeply incised markings, his sole intent in this journey.

A horse, a snake and a large bolt of lightning, his warrior glyph!

Satisfaction then settled on him, this man who wore little or nothing in his regalia that indicated that he had earned the most honors to lead his people in war, and in peace. Only two others had been recognized as such, Sitting Bull and Touch the Clouds.

Making his mark on stone, which lives forever, as is said, was in fulfillment of what had been shown to him when he was yet too small to pull a re-curved bow. This was all the acknowledgment that he needed of his role in the grand defeat of the Bluecoats on the Greasy Grass, this great warrior who both led and fought for his people. This great warrior the whites so mistakenly would forever misname Crazy Horse, who once possessed a buckskin shirt honored with more tassels on it than any other man in the whole Lakota nation, and who had to take it from his body for the broken-arrow love of the wrong woman, yet he rode quietly back to camp with his kola that evening, content with only this simple mark incised upon the stone.

Books recorded much that was known of him as facts; there was no image of him ever taken. Long after he passed from the earth hearts have kept his spirit.

Tasunke Witco, June 26, 1876
Pehin Hanska Kasota Waniyetu

The Bow In the Cloud

Bruised purple thunderclouds flowed like a sheet from the far horizon across the bay towards the parapet where Cloud had come to be alone. The first cooling drops of the approaching rain welcome on his bare chest, the cooling breeze excited him. He could almost consider being here bearable, in spite of the differences from the world he once knew. As his gaze looked outwards, the colors of the waters deepened; the movement of the wind across the bay's surface mesmerized him. A glowing seam of light opened along the horizon where the storm had lifted, parting like the lips of a wound that had not quite healed, and it was into that most tender region that an overwhelming desire to return home engulfed him. Slipping over the parapet he could leave this world of the white-man behind...

Then he felt her. No need to turn and look to know she was close by. A picture formed, complete. Her hair a nimbus in any light, changing from gold to red. Eyes through which light could travel and come back, that mouth which spoke no lie and whose truth remained sweet. The others knew. They all knew, and those that didn't did not care. In no way could Cloud and Anah acknowledge that they were lovers, though they exuded an air of utmost, tender respect of a sort not even merited for the closest of kin. At her entrance the gathering soon reflected this air of regard: not to suggest that solemnity reigned, nor favoritism, not at all. Many evenings when Anah regaled them with stories around the fire, a few would pull back to darkness along the parapet to talk in quiet groupings and to gaze out upon the bay. Cloud and Anah would often have a chance to talk then, head to head, hands touching, thigh to thigh. That would be enough, as the warm breeze blew wisps of their mingled hair across their lips. Cloud did not know how he could ever bring her to share the difficult life that would await him upon his return to the west. He had no one to counsel him now, and sorely missed Silver Spotted Owl. His own heart said both that he loved her too much to expose her to the hardship, and that he couldn't bear to leave her behind.

A light touch on his shoulder, hers, then she pointed to the faint rainbow now in the sky.

A.K. BAUMGARD

Burning Beauty

November 25, 1876
Powder River region

Box Elder, a much respected holy man of Dull Knife's band, had withdrawn to the furthest edge of the camp's site of destruction, where over two hundred fine lodges were still smoldering in the rising light of dawn. He was not bitter, though he felt vindicated, for had he not informed the camp's leaders of his vision that many Bluecoats were on the way? He was known for his strong Medicine powers. Many in the camp took heed and had struck their lodge poles and packed their ponies to leave. But the hunting had been good that day, and fine elk and deer had been taken. The Kit Fox society wished to celebrate that evening. Soon dissension broke out, and the Foxes intervened and placed the camp under their control, even to the point of cutting the saddles and bridles from those who were attempting to leave. In the end the edict was obeyed in spite of the dire warning. This is where the soldiers stumbled upon them. As the morning's chill wind rose, a lick of flame sprang to life from the side of an elaborately painted buffalo hide lodge, the skillfully depicted images of horse and rider seemed to race around its side as though moving into battle. "H'gun", escaped from his lips, "keep up my strength!" A plea to the heavens to stand vigil, for he felt that it was all he could do, as the beautiful beaded and quilled handiwork of his people passed away into the flames, and left the earth in thick greasy vapors of smoke. The shields that were sacred to the warriors now could no longer protect them. War shirts that once told of the many honors hard won, now gone up in smoke. The eagle-plumed war-bonnets...he longed to turn his head from this destruction. He knew that never again would his people be able to amass such wealth of spirit, and pride of achievement; the very word reservation, well, he had to banish it from his mind.

One needed a special Death Song for this burial ground that lay before him now; he could not bring it up from his stunned heart. Such splendor! Such burning beauty before him on this bitter cold day in the Big Horns. He turned to leave, wrapping his blanket tighter against the cold when he saw her. Had she been here all through the night? The soldiers had rounded up and seen to the orderly departure of all, he thought, amassing their goods to the pyres. He called out to her; received no response, and so he sat quietly observing, thinking, praying.

Running Quail sat with her long spindly legs pulled up to her knees, the grease-spotted shawl tucked over them as much to hide their scabbed and bony appearance as to try and keep the chill out. She sat morosely, propped on those knees and gave the appearance of keeping watch, but all that spread before her were the scattered remains, the still burning pyres of the band. Hidden in the folds of her clothing was a half-burned eagle plume that she had snatched from the flames. The ash and soot upon her tear-streaked face, for the most part, covered the welt that had risen from the lash she had received when driven off by the sergeant, who had caught her pilfering from the burning remains. They let her be, for no one really wanted to deal with an angry, grief struck Cheyenne child whose intent to harm was made clear as she slashed the air with a large skinning knife. So it appeared that the holy man and the girl had paid their respects. Now Box Elder debated as to when and how to approach her. How to encourage her to depart with him, now that the Bluecoats had left. Some of the people had managed to escape to the hills; few women, fewer children. This young woman's womb was most necessary to bring new life to his people someday, but was of no worth if her mind had departed. So he waited, and prayed. He trusted her young wisdom, too. He called upon his wayakin, spirit guide, to show him what, in her, had been so wounded as to keep her on the brink of madness. Then she stood, cramped from the night, and the fire-ravaged eagle plume protruded from her tight grasp. It had been wrapped in red trade cloth and elaborately beaded so that it could be attached to a warrior's scalp lock...now ruined! Quail turned to him; when their eyes met she began to speak with a wisdom beyond her years. "They have burned our beauty and what they have not thrown to the flames they have carried away, given to our enemies, to those who have no idea of its meaning or value. They have burned beauty!" Her dark eyes held tears that did not spill. She did not have to say more. He was looking into those eyes and knew that it was imperative that he bring her back from a trail of utter destruction. He was a holy man. He had seen years of destruction, of beautiful men, women, children, not just ceremonial shields, parfleches and embroideries.

He knew where the People were going, The Beautiful People, the Tsitsistas; to the reservation..to dire lands, controlled by the government, treated like prisoners of a war they never wanted to fight, watched over by an agency, dependent on others not their kind, forbidden to follow their old ways or even to hunt. Beauty, he must speak to her of beauty. She was beautiful; a pitiful little, crushed thing. He sought his wayakin, felt it, spoke boldly as he approached her. He held both hands toward her, palms open. This was so crucial. Would she place her palms upon his? Did she know who he was, would she accept him as such? She just stood and allowed his approach, never breaking their gaze. "Oh, she has a strong spirit," he thought. Then she willingly placed her small hands upon his palms. She had obeyed. "We are Cheyenne. Our beauty is inside. Our strength comes from within. We are spirit within the flesh. Everything that you see, that was destroyed, was made by us with these hands," and he lightly gave her hands a squeeze, "All this," and his hands swept out and over the burned remnants scattered and smoking before Running Quail, came from our hearts, our heads, our spirits; from above. Fashioned by our hands, yes, but the beauty! Do you understand, my child?" He stole a look towards her before he continued. "Spirit cannot die. It can be quenched like flame, it can be smothered, but feed it and, like the smallest, carefully tended ember, can grow once more. Spirit is always." He saw that her upraised face was now wet with tears, looking to him. "Come with me now. I will take you to the others who have escaped."

Foreboding

Ft. Marion, May 1877
The Moon of Shedding Ponies

Each day the sun rose into the pale sky to eventually lose itself as a colorless but bright disk. He felt that something bad would soon happen. He searched the four directions and the earth around him for sign, yet all remained free, calm, clear. In fact, the waters of the bay were exceptionally smooth, welcoming and transparent. He could not shake this feeling. He looked to the elders amongst them, Minimic and Chase-yun-nuh. They kept their own counsel, but they too, looked troubled. There was nothing untoward from the Army or the town, nor from Matches, who had access to the newspapers. Nothing seemed amiss. Finally, reluctantly, when evening came he spoke to Anah, inquiring of what news she had received from Red Dancing Crane Woman and the agencies. He knew she had a tendency to try and shield him from what she determined as bad news. She told him that Indian scalps were going for $150.00 in the Black Hills, and of course, that the Army was trying to put a stop to that. She hesitated to tell him this sort of news. He made no reply, and made to leave. She drew out her hand to detain him, "Wait, there's more, Sitting Bull," as he rose to walk away, she went on to say how some of Sitting Bull's warrior's were reported to have come back across the border from Canada to fight the Nez Perce as scouts on behalf of the army. Disgusted, he abruptly left.

The time of feeling content with being here was past, no matter that he was no longer starving. Being brought here in chains, then having them struck from his limbs only restored a feeling of freedom to his body. He had given up his name Medicine Horse and taken a new one, Standing Cloud, but did it change who he really was?

Walking out to one of the far reaches of the oddly shaped corners of the terreplein, he hunkered down to be one with the oncoming darkness, knowing that all the others would grant him solitude. Ragged bolts of heat lightning danced along the water's horizon, barely illuminating the tall thunderheads amassed there. Hurricane season would be upon them once again, he knew. The humid air oppressed him. There was not a breath of moving air. "I need to see with the eye of my spirit," he thought; he had such an overwhelming need to understand what was pressing down upon him. Something portentous was happening, but not here. Not here, that was all he knew! Thinking, perhaps, to be closer to the powers, he fell to dreaming as *Hanhepi Wi*, the night sun, rose to silver the bay below his sleeping form.

A beautiful, welcome sound of many voices; triumphant voices, trilling, ululations rose up to him. A warm spring breeze drew the scalp hairs of his feathered lance across his bare chest from where he sat his war horse high on the bluffs that rose above White Earth River, overlooking the wide valley spread out below. A great cloud of obscuring dust and much obvious sound gave indication that a wealth of people and their herds were moving forward and shortly would draw into sight. Cloud strained to see just who would appear, but as he did so a chill ran up his spine. He slipped from his mount to stand rigidly at attention.

Spread out in a straight line four warriors rode ahead, dressed in full regalia, but the one who commanded his attention was, as usual, unadorned. No warbonnet, no face paint, just a simple buckskin shirt and leggings, and with only one eagle feather in his light brown hair, flanked by his headmen, He Dog, Big Road, Little Big Man, and Little Hawk. Tasunke Witco, one of the very last to come in, is coming in now.....with what is left of the People's wealth! One thousand seven hundred ponies...

Cloud stood at attention to count them, his heart trembled, he saw Touch The Sky's pinto mare buffalo runner, he rode her once, his heart quailed at the thought of the Crow scout who would get first pick, he saw wild feral stallions, unbroken, and an Appaloosa that made his desire quicken.

He watched till his eyes and his mind blurred and his memory fell down. Did he dream, or sleep, or only awaken into another dream? To once again hear singing, but it was coming from his throat. It was the Peace Song of the Lakota. And he saw them, his kolas, could he bear this? This surrender? No, no THE STRANGE MAN OF THE LAKOTA, THE MAN WHOSE HORSE WAS CRAZY, *the one the whites call crazy, he would never be a loaf around the forts; a coffee cooler. He saw the people. His people, the ones who took him, The Cottonwood Boy, just a grub, just a grub.*

He hung his head. So! It was over. Not just for him. Not just The Army's Red River War, the fighting. But for him, for Tasunke, his kola.

Then his eyes filled with color, flooded with the beading, the parfleches, the robes, the saddlebags, the lodge covers, the war shirts, the vests, and the shields. Then he saw them, it seemed to be a triumphal entry, not a surrender to reservation life. They would get a place in the Powder River country! They would! The white-man's magic medicine would heal Black Shawl, would it not? They were 145 lodges strong, with 217 grown men, all Warriors! Eight hundred and 89 people all together. Give up the guns! Give up the horses! Like a drumbeat slowly in his blood he heard this, the army's demands, and rising triumphantly above it The One who led his People in a Strong Heart spirit!

*As he watched Crazy Horse ride so calmly, his face staunchly set into what would, in essence, be captivity for a warrior who had always known a nomadic life, Cloud looked out onto the horizon where a lone golden eagle assailed the clear sky, lazily riding the dihedrals. A few dust devils rose and fell. A solitary grey cloud rose up out of the horizon. How odd! It seemed to hover in an insignificant way, small, but then it moved forward to shadow the great one's path as he rode into the fort. At that sign, Cloud grabbed his quirt, urged his mount forward to the others...*and woke chilled, shivering, his face wet with the morning dew.

A.K. BAUMGARD

Chankpe Opi Wakpala Creek

September 1877

> *"It's a good day to die. It's a good day to fight.
> Cowards to the rear. Strong men follow me."*
> Crazy Horse's rally

Brooding low on the horizon, the sun cast a dim orange presence as the tide crept towards Anah's bare feet. The summer passed uneventfully it seemed, though Cloud kept more and more to himself as unfavorable reports came in from the West. She had not even seen him these last few days, and had gladly accepted the occasion to leave the environs of the fort. Soon she would have to rejoin the small party that had rowed out to Anastasia Island to celebrate the engagement of the Chatwood's eldest daughter, Fredericka. It had been all that she could do to honor the invitation that she had accepted previous to hearing the horrible news that had arrived from Camp Robinson. She badly needed to be alone today. Rumors abounded. An air of mourning hung heavy over the fort among the prisoners. Even Lt. And Mrs. Pratt had a respectful air about their persons concerning the news. Dead! That he was dead, yes, she expected it would eventually come to that, all the great war chiefs were brought down, hunted down. Great campaigns mounted at great expense, but murdered! That is, if the rumors were indeed true. And what stories abounded! The great Crazy Horse! Tasunke Witco, His Horse Is Crazy! Cloud had ridden with him, that much she knew. Even in this humid heat of late summer an icy dread began to uncurl deep within her bowels. Nameless and unthinkable, one of those minute fears that can fester and grow towards the heart. She picked up her book and shawl and began heading back toward the others.

She had heard so many stories of how the great warrior had brought his people into Camp Robinson in May, heads held high in full regalia on their wasted bodies they rode in, He Dog, Little Big Man, Iron

Crow, Touch The Clouds, warriors still, brandishing their empty rifles, knowing they would be roughly disarmed upon arrival, singing nonetheless, following, as always, their leader, the slight lean figure almost unadorned, just a lone eagle feather in his light brown hair hanging unbraided down his lean torso. Tasunke Witco, the last of the great Lakota war chiefs to come in from the north. The last of the "hostiles", as the army called those trying to keep their way of life sacrosanct, leading his warriors and the women and children, nine hundred, weak, not strong any longer, for they were all starving. No game left, no ammunition left to hunt with anyway.

Red Cloud had brought a 'promise', she had been told, from Three Star Crook, of a reservation for them if they would come in, a reserve on the beloved Powder River that Tasunke loved so well. He wanted to save his people more than he wanted to keep his freedom, so he gave the order to pull the lodge pole pins and move! That's exactly how Cloud had worded it to her. *That he loved his people more than his freedom!* The last of the free, the bravest of the brave; never defeated in battle, a master tactician.

And now Anah thought, and now he lies dead! Murdered? Did he believe a "promise" ? When was a promise made by the whites not broken? But they rode in, surrendered, like Dull Knife, Little Wolf, and others before them. His wife, Black Shawl Woman had the lung sickness; perhaps the Big Medicine of the whites could save her, perhaps! They would go to the beloved Powder River country, would they not? It was as yet unceded. For four months their village of nine hundred souls near the Red Cloud and Spotted Tail Agency waited to go north to that promised land. It was not given as promised. She thought of all the table talk she had heard, all the late night discussions at the Pratt's, how the internal troubles began on the agency. Jealousies. Rivalries. Competitions. She knew now to keep her opinions to herself, for she was way too sympathetic to the Indian cause to voice her concerns at an officer's table these days!

Then just this month the Nez Perce fled their reservation in the far west to make a bid for the freedom of Canada. This could not be tolerated by the Army. All accounts of what occurred were terribly confusing, but a devil's bargain was purportedly offered to Crazy Horse. "Lead your warriors to head off Joseph and the Powder River will be yours!" Touch-the-Clouds, his seven foot Miniconjou cousin, was to accompany him. Something was lost in translation, something added, twisted, conjured, rose up like an unknown deadly spirit, and it was thought that Crazy Horse had " threatened to kill". All the jealousies, rivalries, competitions rose and condensed. Oh, Anah knew all about those dividing factions that swarmed around an army post! But as she swept the damp grains of sand from her skirt to return to the polite society of the Chatwood's celebration, her troubled heart worried over the reaction of the small band of Cheyenne prisoners here, who had lost yet another; perhaps the finest of them all. A most humble man had died. Murdered. Held in the arms of his kola, his friend, Little Big Man, who fought at his side in many a battle, and had now led him into a trap. Had he? Had he held his arms while Pvt. Gentles ran a bayonet into the mighty Horse Warrior of Plains, an Ogle Tanka Un, a Shirt Wearer, delivering a mortal wound? Why?

The story that would be brought back over the mountains, plains, rivers, fields, down over the marshes, cities, through the wires, hands, hearts, gossips, translations, interpretations, mouths, imaginations, prejudices, to arrive at St. Augustine was one story, and at the officer's mess was another. Among the prisoners was yet another, and in the pictographs sent to their relatives from various agencies out west to Ft. Marion, still other versions. How could this happen to one whose medicine was so strong? Some even said that it was by his own hand, for there had been talk of sending him to the Iron House in the Far Tortugas. But what is truth, after all?

Crazy Horse's aged father, Wagula, and mother, were brought by wagon to the guard house to be with him. Touch-the-Clouds was there also. They spent the night in the little guard house as he lay dying on the floor. When he passed that night and rose to the stars, his body was taken to the Spotted Tail Agency and placed on a well guarded scaffold. His band never received that reservation in the Powder River country, a most beautiful place.

It is said that his heart and bones are buried somewhere near a creek called Chankpe Opi Wakpala, Wounded Knee.

My Last Buffalo

(The buffalo population was reduced from about 15 million to a few thousand by the end of the 19th century)

Near sundown the man appeared over the slight rise and looked down into the wide-spread valley below. He was trailing a lone bull buffalo, had been following it closely. They were equals in this dance of escape and pursuit. The beast had been wounded in the rump from a long gun that flashed forth from a passing train. At first the bull had been able to keep up with the small herd, but as the day lengthened his strength had waned. As for the hunter, he had been weakened by the passage of years. His mount, too, was near the end of its strength, having been goaded incessantly into the pursuit. The ribs that protruded from both man and horse indicated they were near starvation.

He had been trailing the buffalo for many sundowns. All the provisions he had managed to bring with him when he left the reservation were now gone. This country he was tracking through was devoid of game. Of course, he could have stationed himself by a small creature's hole, but he was as lacking in patience now as he was in teeth with which to chew the stringy flesh of a mouse or vole. Once he was capable of sustaining himself on moccasin leather, but nowadays even his footwear was inadequate, full of holes, for he had no woman to prepare him new ones. His two surviving children had been taken away years ago; they had yet to return. He carried the few "letters" he could not read in his medicine bundle.

The strong insistence of his empty stomach brought to mind the deliciousness of well-prepared pemmican. Once, every time he left camp, it was with a full parfleche of the dried meat and sarvis berries, his favorite. The disease ridden cattle the agency provided as rations barely gave enough flesh for their pots, let alone a surplus to dry. Give it up old man, he told himself, you have no wife to care for your needs anymore, and you couldn't even gum the meat. Aaah, but, he thought, right out there is my last buffalo! He smacked his dry tongue to the roof of his mouth, recalling the taste of a fresh slice of liver juicily sprinkled with bile!

Once Blue Rabbit Woman had gone beyond, taken by the wet lung sickness, as so many of the very old and young had done on this unblessed harsh southern lowland, he had no will to stay. He had only come in in hopes that the wasichu's white medicine could cure her. Besides, he was ashamed to admit that he could not mount up and ride to war as he once had. It was up to the young men to protect them now, and dragging the travois laden with the young and old hindered the escape of all. Besides, so much had been destroyed, lodges, ponies, the thick robes. There was less game, and few buffalo. The wisdom of the elders cautioned them to submit, to come in, go to where the Bluecoats would not pursue and destroy them, but even he knew that while the flesh may be spared the spirit was withering. He had watched the white-man's Medicine Water make all who drank it crazy, as crazed as the men who roamed the Paha Sapha, digging for the gold metal. Metal so soft that one could not even use it for arrows!

When the provisions the Great Father back East promised them came, there was never enough to drive away hunger from their bellies, yet they were not allowed to leave the reservation to hunt for themselves. And the white flour came with bad worms and weevils. Like several of the others he had not surrendered all his weapons. One old breech loader that had not been confiscated he had wrapped well in oiled elk skin. It was this he had dug up one moonless night when he had determined to go hunting. Hunting as he once had. With his age crippled hands and waning sight he cleaned the weapon as well as he could and blessed the small amount of ammunition he had been able to hide with it.

There was no one to miss him; none to notice his absence. He would not have left if his old wife had not been taken by the wet lung sickness. He had been careful to picket the horse away from the camp. As there was no more horse raiding, nor buffalo hunts, let alone war parties, no one much cared about the pony herd; they survived as well as they could. A mangy white dog was at his heels for the first leg of his journey, but soon returned to camp, he assumed, when not even a rabbit had been scared up in this over-hunted area.

He knew to avoid the settled areas, forts and reservations, and soon found himself north of the Arkansas river. Any Indian "off reservation" was considered a "hostile"; chances of being shot on sight were great. With overwhelming gratefulness he set up a dry camp and rolled into his thin blanket. He had traded his last winter robe for medicine for Blue Rabbit Woman, now he had neither a good buffalo robe nor woman to warm his bones. Overhead the stars roamed the night sky freely and the smell of sage filled him with restful sleep.

He woke to the quiet chatter of a few horned larks, and lay back in his bedroll just to enjoy the warmth of the rising sun. He had left with the idea of filling his much depleted spirit with just one more sunrise, one more sunset; he meant to die a free man. But stronger laughter than he thought he still possessed rumbled out of him, as the hunger pains he felt let him know just how greedy an old, half blind warrior could be. Um mm, buffalo liver, he would have some if the Great One Above willed it.

It was later that morning, shortly after he had crossed over the Iron Road, that he had spied the lone, wounded buffalo. On this, the third day of the tracking, he realized that they, he and the great shaggy beast, were traveling steadily north, crossing one river after the other, skirting the face of the great mountain range. They were out of the reach of the long guns now!

MY HEART GROWS WIDE WITHIN ME

As he rode along he thought about his life on these great plains. It pleased him to do so. The pain of many losses dropped away the further behind he left the shame of the reservation. He felt joy. The buffalo was leading him home. Yes, today was a good day to cross over!

Forty Miles To Freedom

Haydn 's No. 2 Concerto in C for Trumpet, yes, that was the piece! Anah was desperate to recall a pleasant memory, one that had provoked humor between them, as now as they were settling themselves down in the shade of their usual trysting spot beneath the huge live oak on Moccasin Hollow Road, after returning from their chores at the dig. This was the first time she had the opportunity to be alone with Cloud in close to a week, since the news of Crazy Horse's death had reached the fort.

As Cloud busied himself with the horses, she thought back to that concert on the green. They had arrived late. Just as they had settled themselves discreetly on the quilt she had brought, a picnic basket decorously placed between them, the sounds of the concerto broke out. Cloud listened so attentively that Anah impulsively leaned toward him, fascinated, eager to know what he thought of this classical music. "It's hundreds of years old, you know!" "I could dance to that!" was his hearty reply. She had to stifle her laughter by riffling in the picnic basket at the image of him, in full regalia, moving swiftly to the trumpets' sound. Oh, how she loved this man! He leaned into her to softly whisper, "My people's music is hundred's of years old too, you know." That happy time seemed so long ago, now it seemed as though he had been avoiding her at every turn, ever since the news of the great war leader's murder had reached the fort. "Crazy Horse," she began. "Anah, you know we don't speak the names of the dead." "Yes, but we do. I do." He said nothing in reply. "Cloud," she placed a hand on his forearm, trying to placate him, "please do not shut me out. I mean no disrespect, my ways are not your ways, but I wish you to know more of this matter of his death. In fact, I do know more about the circumstance, and I want to..."

At this, he turned toward her with a most sorrowful gaze, then looked upwards into the branches of the widespread arms of the oak, just now beginning to turn with the season. The sky above held an infinite depth of blue. She was afraid that he was going to seal himself away in silence, but finally he began to speak. "We have lost so many. He was the last, and perhaps the greatest among us. His woman, Black

Shawl had the lung sickness. There is hope for her that the white-man's medicine may save her."

Anah realized just how much ground was lost between them when he reverted to speaking in such terms as "white men", but she said nothing. "He did not believe in what you call boundaries, in ownership. Yet he came in, traded his freedom so those he loved could live. Little Big Man, they say he held him by the arms while he was thrust through. I do not understand..." "Nor do I," she interrupted, "I was told that he was denied the Powder River Reservation unless," and Cloud waved his hand to silence her, "I rode with them, Anah, sat with them in ambush as cavalry picked their way up narrow defiles. Have you ever seen what a Gatling gun does? Have you?" She had no choice but to sit and listen as he recounted the battles, the skirmishes, the ambushes, what the army called The Red River War and what, to Cloud, was the People's fight for a continued existence on their own lands.

She had never heard him speak like this. The bitterness, hurt, pain and loss seemed to have no end as it flowed out in words, coldly. Calmly, her only response was the feel of the wetness upon her cheeks. Finally she moved forward, laid a hand gently across his mouth. "Please, I cannot bear it." He rose from her side, mounted up, and left her with these last words. "There will be no more young men trained as warriors among the People!" How long she sat there stunned she did not know. Finally it was the noise and chatter of the squirrels running upon the oak branches above her that brought her back into the present. What she had experienced that awful day when she had been attacked at the camp outside Ft. Laramie had been a way of life for Cloud and his people. How could she think that they could somehow make a life together? They had love, a passionate love; it had seemed to her an overwhelming blessing after the loss of her child and husband. But did they have a life?

Each successive day to her had been a delight; she had not looked to the future. She had no one to account for. Now she saw the selfishness of her lack of concern. They had returned to Fort Marion expressly because he could not leave behind the other prisoners. He was here because he was a warrior, a leader. How foolish she was to forget that.

All this time, while the others had learned a trade; to bake, carpentry, to read and write, Cloud had shown little or no interest. The fact that his English was so fluent was due solely to his involvement with her. But what could she offer him? What was to become of them?

That evening, after dining with the Pratt's and hearing more of the details surrounding Crazy Horse's demise, she determined to say nothing to Cloud of his abrupt departure that afternoon. She waited until most of the prisoners retired, knowing that he would go to the darkest corner of the parapet overlooking the water. There he was, a lean silhouette, gazing out to sea.

"When Crazy Horse was denied the Powder River reservation that General Cook had promised him," she began. He stood as though he hadn't heard her. "He was told that if he and his cousin Touch-the-Sky," "Clouds, It's Touch-the-Clouds, not Sky," he corrected her, not unkindly. "So," she went on, "Crazy Horse was told that if they were to lead a party of war scouts, Wolves, I think you call them, against the Nez Perce, that had left their reservation out in Oregon and were trying to head for asylum in Canada with Sitting Bull's people, that then he could have the reservation in the Powder River country that he wanted. Did you know that Cloud?" Cloud said nothing, but the stiffening of his body spoke volumes. She went on. "He and Touch-the-Cloud began to speak out against this involvement of the Sioux, that no Sioux should scout for the army against the Nez Perce, but some did go."

This was too much for Cloud, and he broke away from her without a word. Anah debated following him, as there were few to observe her doing so, until she noted a small pile of wood shavings where he had been standing, aimlessly whittling.

Days passed, and Anah avoided him. Slowly Cloud seemed to return to a more amiable presence. Mid-week Matches approached her with a small, woven reed basket of apples, saying that Cloud wished her to have these; then she knew that he was welcoming her company again. There was to be no more talk of the departed.

Anah, though, had a keen interest in the continued flight of the far western band of the Nez Perce, and their increasingly desperate bid for freedom. In fact, for once, it seemed public opinion was on their side.

Reporters were eager to give an account of their progress; their Chief, Joseph, while not a war leader, was a great leader of his people. Cloud did not want to hear the news that Anah was privy to from the Captain's table, though. She knew that the army was in full military pursuit of the Nez Perce, with Gatling gun, Howitzers, muskets and the like, while the Indians were finally reduced to stripping bark from trees to eat. By late September they had struggled across the Bitterroot Mountains of Montana, and were poised to enter the great plains, hopefully to ally themselves with the Crow Nation. Col. Miles, however, had left Ft. Keogh to intercept them there, with seven companies of infantry and a troop of cavalry.

Anah could contain her composure no longer; as they rode out to the dig she began to tell this to Cloud. "Anah," was all he said, "the Crow will not shelter them." "But they are allies." "They were, but too long have they scouted for the army, they cannot serve two masters. My heart is too cold. I will hear no more," and he rode ahead.

By October the snows came down from the north and fell upon the struggling Nez Perce people. The very sad saga of the flight from their reservation was drawing to a close. They had traveled over 1,600 miles; just 40 miles short of freedom. Their trusted leader, Joseph, when he saw the mounted bluecoats of the cavalry sweeping into his camp, thrust his 12 yr old daughter onto his best horse and sent her racing, shouting to the warriors, "Horses, Horses, save the Horses!" His wife appeared at the door of the lodge, gun in hand, "Take, fight." Six of the bravest of the brave headed out into the storm of driving sleet and bitter cold to make for the border and Sitting Bull, hoping to come to their aid, only forty miles away. A desperate bid for freedom.

Their blood stained the snow, cut down by Assiniboine treachery. At this their chief declared that he would fight no more forever!

Towards An Understanding

The Baroness' Advice

When Anah arrived home at her boarding house that evening it was as though a veil had been stripped from her eyes; not her heart, for in many, many ways she felt her love for Cloud strengthened. In an odd daze, a kind of incomprehension, she dragged a spindle-backed chair out to her small balcony and just sat there, watching the arcs and swoops of the returning swallows until the last of the light faded from the sky. To all appearances she looked calm and composed, a beautiful woman at rest in last warm rays of the sun. In her very fine mind though, she was holding a balance pan, and on those scales rested these things: love, and what she had been struggling with for the last few hours, something that she hadn't a name for as yet, something the society she grew up in didn't take into account, when matches were made. As for those who lived out on the great plains, well, when they found one another with irreconcilable differences, moccasins were left outside the lodge! Not that hearts weren't shattered, tossed aside or scorned! Exhausted, she began to unpin her hair, and glancing in the mirror on the wall she caught a glimpse that brought to mind her Great Aunt on her father's side, the Baroness Von Eisenbach. "Tante Scribel Drivel," as she had thought of her; tall, whip-thin, elegant woman who had used a silver-headed cane for dramatic effect, smoked thin cheroots, affected black lace mantillas, and was the person of whom the word eccentric was applied, sending Anah rushing to the Oxford dictionary to discover what that word meant. The first distant adult relative for whom Anah, as a child, came out of her self-imposed shell to observe closely.

The Baroness was simply fascinating. Her father appeared to both despise and yet tolerate her. Her peers desired her company and approval, both of which were hard to obtain, as the Baroness was most selective and discriminating. It soon became apparent that she didn't tolerate children well, but then Anah was not the ordinary child. Approval was given on the day the Baroness found her pouring over the gruesome illustrations in her father's anatomy books, tucked away in his library, a favorite spot of Anah's, chosen for its seclusion; cool, dark and rich with the smell of leather bindings. Instead of shock, scorn or dismissal, the Baroness produced a silver lorgnette from her slim bosom, sat down on the floor beside her, and they spent a delicious time pouring over the various graphics. Her aunt most graciously corrected her pronunciation on the difficult Latin. From then on an alliance was formed. Tante loved to talk of her adventures, of which she had many. Anah was a rapt audience. A new audience; not easily bored.

As Anah grew into a lovely young woman she pondered why the Baroness had never married. Her mother, when questioned, then brought out a daguerreotype of a strikingly beautiful young beauty with dark flashing eyes, creamy bare shoulders, hair piled high to spill in thick lush curls over one smooth shoulder, full lips in an enticing smile. "Her?" is all Anah could manage, "but why?" "Well, she had three excellent proposals; a minor prince among them even, but why don't you ask her yourself," is all her mother would mysteriously reply.

When Anah could bring herself to question the regal old lady she drew herself up, then found a seat, placed her thin-skinned, blue-veined hands, that glittered with too many ornate, showy rings, upon her equally showy cane handle, cleared her wattled throat, beneath its Belgian lace jabot, and motioned for Anah to seat herself on a tussock across from her. Expecting a customary long discourse on each and every aspect of how the suitors failed to meet her high standards, Anah suppressed a sigh. It would be a long haul and Anah was hungry already!

Tante looked off into some distance, a far distance into the past, that in a way draws ever closer to us as we age, drew herself up to her most regal height, the silver, marcelled waves of her hair riding above those chiseled, aged features like a crown, and said only, "My dearest, this is my only advice for you, remember this: There are many men that you can love, but not many that you can live with! Above all, you must dismiss one thing from your mind, from your thoughts, from your heart," and she paused, most dramatically, and she knew just how to strike a most dramatic pose, her hands resting on her cane, waiting expectantly for Anah to respond." "Yes?" Then, and only then, she delivered the answer, "Fear! You must not give in to fear," and with as much dignity as her advanced age could muster, and with no more explanation, she hauled herself up, and slowly, head up, left the room. Anah tried very, very hard not to feel sorry for her.

How long had she been dragging the brush though her hair? It was now just a nimbus of static. Yes, love is not all, nor passion. That is, can I, could I live with him? That's it. The enervation was gone. Just like that! Her mind raced. She grabbed for her Commonplace Book and began to record her thoughts. In Gullah Land they had lived together, it had worked, but that could not work indefinitely, so they came back here. Why? Yes, for the others, and now? Her thoughts raced on. Well, did she want him? Did she want a life with him? Cross-legged on the bed, she wrote on into the night. What about the plans for the school up in Pennsylvania? Would her father help? Hope unfurled its fragile wings!

A Captive Returns

Agwrondougwas of the Iroquois

Scheherazade. Anah kept softly repeating that name to herself as they rode along in tandem, returning from the dig, the soft afternoon light casting random shadows across their faces. The time had come to put her plan into effect. Much as she despised feminine wiles and artifice, she had great respect for intelligence and literature. So the story of the Persian princess who wove tales to prolong her existence came to Anah's aid; not that Anah's life was in any way at stake, but her heart's desire was, for she knew not how to bend Cloud to her will. Her plan was to tell him of her own commitment to his "People" as he called them, of how she had come to be out west. Could she then convince him that this new Indian school up in Carlisle was an excellent plan that held a key for their future? And how to begin? On their way back from Findley's farm she would institute her plan. Toward this end she had packed an especially nice basket that held crisply fried chicken and the pickles he had developed such fondness for. After she was sure he had eaten his fill she began. "I want to tell you some of my family's history, Cloud." He was lying back idly, observing the sky. "My father's people came to these shores hundreds of years ago," covertly she observed him picking at his teeth with a pine needle. She then thought it best to skip over how the land had been granted to them in Western Pennsylvania, and how a small fort was built and given the family name. "One day my great grandfather, who was just a boy of eight summers, was helping his family to bring in the hay with his father, mother and older brother, Gaspar, before the late summer storms could come to ruin it, when a band of marauding Senecas came. They took Philip. That was his name, Philip Hoffman." She did not need to say what happened to the others. Cloud was raised slightly on his elbows now, interested. "This is how I heard the story from my father's Uncle Thomas. I was just a child myself when he told me this story. You remember that I was an only child. Well, Thomas was a historian, like a record keeper, and he wanted me to know of my family history. He was a good storyteller, Cloud. I will try to remember how he told it.

Agwrondougwas of the Iroquois

Night had fallen hours ago in the old hunting lodge nestled deep in the foothills of the Alleghenies, close to the Warriors Trail, as we called it, on a well-traveled foot path down from the Great Lakes, with much deep woods surrounding us. The first snows of winter were brewing up and I and my cousins had been called in from our raucous play, as early dark was falling. Cold was quickly rising up from the thick fallen leaves that carpeted the now barren ground. A scrim of frost fast appeared on the rocks in the waning light, as we hurried toward the shelter and warmth of the cabin. A good fire was going, and we needed no urging to shed our wet boots and gather close, knees to chest. Aunt Hilda silently handed us heavy crockery mugs of cider to warm our hands on. The snapping and pop of the coals were only interrupted by our uncle's rocker, as he leaned forward to begin:

"Thirty-eight years had passed since that day in the hay field of Western Pennsylvania, when mother, father and my aunt were struck down. My brothers, Gaspar and Philip, had been taken to avenge the loss of their own kin by the Seneca of the Iroquois Nation. Gaspar, a strong, resourceful boy, managed to escape early on. Philip was mourned, along with the others. He was not struck down with the heavy tomahawk like the others, but taken, never to be seen or heard of again. Yet, years later, he stood before his birth family, and proved who he was by taking us to the exact field where he had been abducted. Imagine! Eight years old at the time of his abduction; remembering! Surviving the gauntlet, too! But we are good German stock. A Hoffman, after all. How could he forget! But to live with them. Five children! A wife too! Could this really be the boy taken from the hay field thirty-eight years ago by the blood-thirsty Iroquois, those Seneca raiders? How could it be?

The lamplight shone on the shaved, domed head, bald except for a dark blond scalp lock. Many shining ornaments dangled from his earlobes. An elaborate, delicate tracery, like a South Sea native tattoo, around his neck and throat. His blue eyes shone peacefully. His countenance radiated an unearthly nobility as he told us, in King's English, that he had returned to receive his share of his father's estate. "Returned?" they gasped, "from where?" Why, from his farm on the Canadian shores of Lake Erie, where he lives with his family. I was just busy creeping as close as I could, to examine his intricate tattoos. Over his shoulder was a finely woven shawl, a garment that appeared to designate a rank of some sort. Later we were to discover that he was a Sachem, a chief, the first white sachem of the Iroquois, known as Good Peter or Agwrondougwas of the Iroquois." (She stole a look at Cloud. Yes, he was listening.) Peter went on to tell his astounded relatives how he had been taken, made to run the gauntlet, and since he had survived, adopted, and then, by learning the true ways that led to becoming a member of the Iroquois Nation, he rose to being a Sachem." By now they sat as rapt as rabbits in front of a fox.

He did not want to remain with his people, The Hoffmans though, and that is when the trouble began. Many did not understand how he could live and marry into the very people who had murdered his family. Of course they did not understand how he could return to claim his share of the inheritance and expect to take it away. Calmly he addressed his brother Gaspar, requesting a private audience, then explaining to him simply, "Does not the bible itself tell us to cleave to our wife, to practice forgiveness, and to love one another?" Then he awaited his brother's response. "If you can fault me for taking what is rightfully mine, then do so. You are most welcome to visit. It makes my heart glad to see you well and prosperous, brother dear." Gaspar saw that Peter returned to his family with many fine provisions, of which his well-tended farms were noted, cheese, barley, hops and wonderful Gravenstein apples.

Turning to me, my uncle said, "Your father followed him every minute that he was with us, until he departed for the north woods again. I think that is where he began his interest in collecting regalia. Good Peter went on to become a well known statesman of sorts, an advocate for peace, but that's another story." "You see Cloud," Anah sighed contentedly, for she had gained his attention. The sun had moved well down on the horizon. "Good Peter had earned his name in spite of his white skin. He was a wise leader and a peaceful man." She just couldn't help but add, "and his blood runs in my veins!" At that she felt embarrassed , and not being able to read his expression, she busied herself with packing up the picnic basket to leave. On the ride back Cloud moodily kept his own counsel.

A Woman of the Whites

"Have you ever killed a man?"

That evening by the parapet, all Cloud had to say regarding her tale of Good Peter, Agwrondougwas of the Iroquois, was to ask if she knew what clan he had been adopted into. His decided lack of interest was confusing to her. Turtle Clan was her abashed response. It seemed as if, by some mutual agreement, they then spoke of other things.

Undaunted, Anah intended to carry on with her plans that next afternoon, and as she laid out their small repast on the quilt she was surprised to hear him say, "I wish now to speak to you of certain matters. Stay your hand!" He motioned her to sit back and listen. She did not think that she was going to like what he was going to say, though she tried her best to keep her features arranged in a neutral fashion.

" You are a woman of the whites," he began, "what do you know of the ways of war?" In a not unkindly fashion, but as much as she hated to ascribe such a mannerism to him, it was most definitely inscrutable, yes, inscrutable! Oh, what had she unleashed with her attempt at feminine wiles? She immediately interjected. "Oh Cloud, my father was an Army surgeon, my husband, a cavalry officer, I did not follow the great buffalo hunts as your women did, but I know how to skin and gut..." "Anah, sit here by me, I mean you no disrespect. Listen to me. Listen. You have seen flesh and blood when it was laid open, yes?" She nodded quickly. "Your father was a man of white medicine, a surgeon, and he, like yourself, may have turned living creatures into food upon one's table, is that not so?" "Yes Cloud," she answered a bit hesitantly, not at all sure where he was trying to lead her; not at all sure she wanted to follow.

He then knelt in front of her and took her hands into one of his, tilting her chin up toward him, his large black eyes focusing down on hers, not at all unkindly, but in disconcerting directness as he asked, "Have you ever killed a man?"

She watched his perfectly formed generous lips, forming words, saying more, much more. She caught such words as "intention", watched his dark, well-shaped thin brows move eloquently as he spoke. Releasing his grasp on her chin, judging it too tight, knowing now that he had her full attention, as a young hare would feel when trapped. But she didn't feel such, did she? He had such beautiful eyes. She focused on the clear part in his hairline, the high forehead, his calm demeanor as he spoke, anything, anything but what he was saying. She tried very, very hard not to hear what that was, and yet it filtered through, washed through on dark waves of gore. Have I ever killed a...Oh God!

She nodded dumbly, yes I understand, he'll think I know what he's talking about, won't he? Then the name floated up before her eyes. Sand Creek, the others would follow, she could not allow that! So very, very important not to remember! Why was her head starting to pound? Her thigh to hurt, and that smell, like cordite! His voice was so sonorous, he would not name the dead, nor would she, so something perverse in her sought the safety of numbers, his hair, black as a raven, shiny too, its growing long once more, she noted. 20,000, she thought, they said fell for the Union at Gettysburg. Over 750,000 in the war called Civil, of course we know war. "We?" Yes, we know war. She tried to remember the dead from the Revolutionary War. Did she ever know? Was there ever a count? The Napoleonic War! Wasn't there always war? Weren't men always fighting? Count, count Anah, force yourself to count. Safety in numbers; no blood, no gore, no limbs being trucked past in rickety wheelbarrows, past the open door of the surgery, your father's bloody apron, she helped in those times, too! Stop! She wanted to throw her hands up to her ears, to not listen. Stop! Stop listening; count, count instead, back to how many pinion's in the tertiaries of a falcon's wings, anything. Primaries, secondaries, tertiaries. Think of horses, not men, not bloody men. Comanche, the only thing left standing at the Greasy Grass. If he didn't stop soon. She realized then that her eyes were shut. Was it Traveler? Spelled with one "l"? I'm sure of it. "Anah, Anah, who is Traveler? You were crying and calling out that name, and Sin-sin-at-ty!" Opening her eyes to a concerned Cloud, whose quizzical look slowly reconciled into an understanding of how very little attention she had granted to him. "Who is Traveler?" she began to explain, then airily dismissed him with a wave of her hand.

She felt that they would never be able to bridge their differences. Her eyes began to brim with unwanted tears. What she wanted most was for him to just say those words, I love you, just once, just once. Instead she angrily blurted out in a patronizing manner that Traveler was Robert E. Lee's horse, and let him figure out just what Cincinnati was or who General Lee was, for that matter.

But then he drew her to his chest and began to speak softly to her, in Cheyenne, what was most certainly an apology. For what she had no certain idea, but it sufficed.

Finally, to break the uncomfortable and unusual silence that enveloped them on the ride back to the fort, she spoke of Myles Keogh's horse Comanche being the sole survivor of General Custer's last stand, and how the wounded horse was tenderly cared for, its wounds dressed so that it could be transported back to civilization, along with the other wounded soldiers, on the steamboat. She regaled him with tales of what a fine horseman President Ulysses S. Grant was, and how he was once arrested on the streets of the nation's capitol for speeding in a carriage; of his bravery, that he never, ever flinched at a bullet. It was said that there was not a horse born that he could not master. Soon there flowed between them a fine thread once again. What had frayed had not broken, though neither understood why!

Back There Is a Past

"Life and Death were mingled in the spillway of her soul"

In the Spring of 78, after three years of interment, it was determined that the men who had been imprisoned at Ft. Marion could be set free. The War Department then released these prisoners to the care of the Indian Bureau.

Lieutenant Pratt's petitions to have the prisoners released were granted, based upon their excellent examples of good citizenship, behavior, and the fact that twenty-two of them had learned to read and write. The atmosphere around the fort became jubilant, as most of them were returning to their families back west. They were to return in care of their respective agencies, many with a small nest egg that they had earned while a prisoner. The Cheyenne and the Arapaho were to return to the Darlington Agency and their families there.

They had once been the terror of the whites out west, now about thirty of them desired to remain back east to receive further education from any place that would receive them, to learn such skills as farming and blacksmithing. Provisions had been made for seventeen to attend The Hampton Technical Institute to further their education. Some already knew carpentry and baking. Some would go on to become ministers of the protestant faith, like Okuhatum, Making Medicine, once a ringleader among the Cheyenne. Others would train as teachers and return as such to instruct their own people. Unfortunately some, like Eagle's Head, Minimic, one of the oldest Cheyenne, came home only to succumb to malaria just a year later on the reservation.

Matches, Chisiseduh, just twenty-one at the time of his capture and listed as a ringleader, was one of the twenty two prisoners who, during their time at Ft. Marion, had learned not only to read English, but to write it as well. After the incident of the Kiowa's foiled escape attempt, their being drugged and thought dead, Matches became enamored with western medicine. He had decided, along with about thirty of the others, not to return west, but to travel the White-man's Road. Anah had little or no idea what Cloud thought of this. She had been hopeful that Matches would influence Cloud to stay on in the east also, but apparently not. Once the government had given Mr. Pratt permission for the prisoners to return to their respective agencies, or for some to seek employment in the new trades that they had been taught, many were hoping for nothing better than a swift repatriation back west. Talk brewing regarding Carlisle, the school for Indians up in Pennsylvania, was Anah's dearest hope for a future for the two of them. And of course Cloud had never been a reservation Indian. He had never "gone in", never been a "friendly", or even a hang-about. He had been a "hostile" at the time of his incarceration. Anah was assisting in recruitment and general plans for the Indian school in Carlisle, for which she still held out hopes that Cloud would show some interest. Since he was not on any agency roll, it was not known where he would be required to report. He had not spoken of his plans to her until today. "I have spent three years, as you call the passing of the seasons, in the white man's camp. Plenty of time to think about my release from this captivity. Lieutenant Pratt offered me to stay if I wish, or to return to where Black Kettle's people have been settled." Anah knew that there was a serious issue for Standing Cloud to address at this time of day, for she hadn't seen him in their usual meeting places for the last few days. Soon it would be dusk and they had stopped to watch the sun begin its gentle descent. Pulling her knees up to her chest she settled down to give him her complete attention as he spoke. "Once I was a warrior, and a hunter. My part in the life was to protect and provide; I earned much merit. But I sang my death song and my kola, whose name I do not bring to my lips, pulled my pin and rode me out of the battle where I had staked myself to defend or die trying. That was the day I became Standing Cloud. You know that story." (She didn't, not really, but how could she interrupt him now?) Of the *ve'ho'e*, the white men, I have learned many hard lessons." Watching him struggle to select just the right words in her language, she nodded to show him that she was listening. She felt her heart fluttering like a trapped sparrow, her breathing stilted. "Yes, go on," she afforded him. "They want us to be like them. To eat what they put into their mouths. To dress like them. To speak in their tongue and forget the words that first gave us life.

To honor the great above, the mystery, in their way, and to honor life as they would. I have heard that they are taking our children away to schools to learn to read and write, as some of us have been learning here. This is good, I believe, but I have also heard that these same children are forbidden, and punished, if they dare to speak with the tongue that they were born to. So many of the bluecoats have come to this country with another language on their lips, yet it is not forbidden them to speak their tongues, nor are they forced to learn English."

Her concern was growing; this was not leading where she hoped. More and more he was using idiom, like bluecoats for soldiers. "They have captured us, rounded us up like their cattle, put some of us in chains, yet they have not made us their slaves. If we had been made slaves then we could have been emancipated, set free. True? They try to provide for those on the bad lands, those reservations they have driven us to by starvation. But the lack of meat for our pots is due to their greed. Our lodges are now made of thin army cloth and our mouths are filled with stringy cow. They want us to dig up the face of our land and work hard to grow the plants that we do not like, when once we could walk out upon the land and simply gather what we had been blessed with. We are not allowed to hunt game beyond the reservations. We are not allowed to leave, not even for our yearly gatherings. Those living on the reservations are imprisoned without walls, without chains. Much sickness, and sorrow," at this he hung his head, and made to sit, not facing her but staring out across the sullen, molten face of the turning tide moving in the last rays of the sun.

Soon it would be dark, but she knew there was no interruption possible, as his heart opened to her, yes, but to her as a white woman, she feared, not as his friend and lover. There was no seeming anger in his voice, and she could discern no palpable pain, in spite of his distressing judgments. As he continued, she set aside her hopes and just tried very hard to listen. "They do not want to adopt us, nor our ways. To marry us or bear our children. They do not want us to live in their homes, though they want us to live in their kind of dwellings. They treat us, at times, like we are the little six-legged creatures that live off of ones' blood. When we imitate them as they like us to, they then send us back to a place not of our choosing, from which we are not allowed to roam. These places they have reserved for us are, to be sure, lands that they do not want themselves, that is, unless gold is discovered. No chains, no walls, not a prison, not exactly a zoo, since no one wants to visit us there!" Oh, Anah thought, he has kept such bitterness inside. "They have killed many of us, and by many means, not just with guns. Are they not our enemies? They appear to be through with fighting us, now that they have what they want, yet they do not wipe us from the land. We are allowed to multiply as we can. We have no more buffalo robes to trade for their pretty "baubles", is that the word?" But not waiting for her answer he went on, "To poison some of our dispirited ones with whiskey of the sort that not one of them would drink. Yes, they no longer kill our bodies, but they roll upon our spirits as the great dust storms rolled across the plains. We cannot see well to walk through, we try to breathe and choke on, what is that word? Yes, atmosphere. I was brought here with my brothers, in chains, because I fought for the life of my people. You had a great war that you call civil, where you fought one another, but now all is forgiven. There is no Johnny Reb reservation," and he laughed, somewhat bitterly. She thought to rise and go to him then, to offer some paltry comfort, but he stood abruptly and began to rhythmically pace. " My first teacher, whose name I may no longer speak, in his wisdom once gave me a large bow that had been made from a lightning struck ash tree. You know ash is one of the best woods for this. At the time I was just past the winter count of eleven robes, and my intention was to work with plants and ceremonies for healing for my people. Yes, of course, I already had my own bow. He told me that the tree the wood had come from was still standing, still growing when the wood had been cut from it. When he saw the lack of understanding on my face he merely said, "A great life force produces great strength." Of course I thought he meant the tree the weapon was made from, but now I understand that the struggles I have gone through just to survive have made me strong and bendable. Where now, do I point the arrow of my remaining years? There is no future here for me, little one, but back there is a past. I cannot stay here!"

"Yes" was all she managed to speak, a furious mingling of hope and despair flowing in her thoughts like flood waters at the brink of a dam. Life and death were now mingled in the spillway of her soul as she realized just what he was telling her, what it meant. "The one who taught my spirit would bring me out on those clear nights when the heavens could be easily read. Though we roamed over the vast plains and even into the foothills of the great rocky mountains, he pointed out the stars as an example of constancy. He no longer walks the earth, but the heavens remain."

"Yes," she numbly assented, "the same stars we are looking at now." "Hoa, the same when they can be seen, but the lights from these towns obscure them. At times I dream the thunderous approach of the buffalo herd and a keenness springs up in me. I want to leap from my bedding and run to pull the picket pin from my best buffalo runner, but it is only a distant rumble of a speeding train, and all the pretty horses are gone. Then my heart fills with sadness as easily as one fills a bladder with water. I do not know how to empty it. My spirit broods like a red hawk in full molt, when there is no possibility of rising up. So many have gone on the long walk; I close my eyes and see them still. How can a boy grow to manhood today? Achieve honors? There are no ceremonies, and without the buffalo robes we have not made a winter count as of old. Some of us, like Zotom and Making Medicine, make a record in those ledger books; it is but paper. I overhear one of the agents saying that our nations are "backward", that's the word he used, because we have never developed the use of the wheel to our advantage, and the only metal we value is the tin we now sometimes fashion our arrowheads with. I think they wished that we had decorated our garments with gold thread instead of porcupine quills. Progress, part of the white man's trinity! Hau," he laughed softly, "Progress, ownership and wealth! I've seen the progress of as many wagon wheels as the leaves in an aspen grove; the earth lies scarred season after season after their passing. Iron roads run from one ocean to another, I'm told , and miners have brought very bad ways into our sacred hills as fast as they can dig the gold out. Is it noble to kill for what does not sustain life? To leave our buffalo to rot on the plains and call it sport?"

Anah placed her hand on his forearm, hoping he would look at her, and for a fleeting moment he did, before continuing, "I try not to dwell in this dark place of bloodied memories. My future I cannot see. No life can avoid sadness, and yet it seems that every white foot that crossed the plains brought more than we could bear. Our prophet Sweet Medicine spoke of this. I have watched men brave enough to attack a great humped bear with only a knife lose courage when surrounded by the four square walls of a prison cell. Those that counted many, many coup on the fiercest warrior threw themselves away when there was no enemy to fight. I must go back and bring what strength I still have to what remains, and if all the strength I have is only to lift my eyes to the mountains," he faltered, looking down at the now despondent woman at his feet. He could not read her posture. "I do not expect you to understand!" But she did. Fighting to keep the tears from her eyes, she nodded up at him, dumbstruck with perception.

He had not included her in this speech. He was leaving, leaving her. She, too, had not thought of a future, had been content for the day to day unfolding of their life together. The specter of loss began to rise in her like a miasma from one of the nearby swamps, dampening her spirit. She could formulate no response other than to rise quietly, "I must go now," her nature bidding her that she must deal with pain privately. She left without any mention of the Carlisle School!

VI

Heading Back

"I miss you, I miss you, I miss you!"

Nestaevahosevoomatse

Muggy, gray skies didn't help to keep the damp calico of her skirts from clinging to each calf as she paced the narrow circular path trod between the small writing desk and her yet unmade bed. Punching the helpless pillow didn't do much either, nor did sweeping the accumulation of unwashed linens to the floor. Yanking open the screened door to the balcony and flinging her only Staffordshire china cup as far as her impotent rage would carry it helped but a little, only a little! What was she to do? At least the souls in Hades had the waters of Lethe to drink, to quench their suffering!

He had been gone just a few days. Gone! Gone! Without a word, without a leave-taking, unless this counted, as she leapt to her feet once more to pace, from where she had collapsed on the bed in a helpless heap, holding aloft a mere scrap of paper, shaking it fully extended at the leaden, indifferent seeming heavens.

"This! This! What is this inexplicable nonsense...a billet doux from a mad man? He can't write, this is not even his handwriting."

NESTA..EVAH...OH..SEE..VOOH..MAT..SEE!

"I can't even pronounce it. It's Cheyenne alright! I can speak it. Hah!" as she spat out each syllable of the nearly unpronounceable word of twenty letters, "but read it? Maddening! Goodbye. It must mean that. But there are no words for that in their language....Ooh!"

Stamping her foot in frustration and incomprehension, desperate both to understand, and not give in to a mounting feeling of abandonment and loss, she turned the paper over and over in her hands, growing ever more distraught. Speaking out loud, not to try and calm herself, but hoping to invoke whatever sympathetic furies may be lingering in the turbulent atmosphere, where the purple thunderheads amassed to boil on the near horizon, and receive small shards of heat lightning in ever increasing jabs.

Determined not to give in to tears, she began to kick at scattered clothing on the floor from one wild heap to another, mumbling to herself, "what to do, what to do, I brought this on myself, a common harlot, to think that he loved me! What does that word mean? Calm yourself, think, think," but of course she could not, she was caught in the talons of intense frustration, pulled now high, high above the jagged cliffs of despair and far, far below her a faint glint of the flowing river of their history together, which of course she wished to return, to float up in recall.

Ask, is there hope? Always hope, well not always, but then she felt that scrap of paper and the word intruded. She smoothed the crumbled paper out and once again tried to make sense of it. So difficult, looks a bit like: let's go ride horses, and then again like, I'm eating berries, *nesta..evah...oh..see..vooh..mat..see,* like a falling autumn leaf drifting past her understanding! She ran a wetted finger over it, smoothing out the paper. Perhaps it was written in blood, an oath.

Exhausted, she collapsed in angry tears; wet, sweaty tendrils clinging to her neck, head thrown back into the pillows upon the bed one minute, then up and pacing. Then collapsed in despair, legs spread out akimbo on the naked floorboards, where she had kicked the scatter rugs aside in frustration.

Cloud's message lay crumpled up into a wad now. It eluded Anah's attempts to decipher it. Cheyenne was ever so much more difficult a written language than Lakota. Her brain hurt from all her attempts to parse some meaning from it; she fell into an exhausted sleep, which came to release her finger's grip, and let the small ball of paper roll slowly beneath the bed .

Matches Translates

With the crumpled slip of paper in her hand Anah approached him; one look at her face told him all he needed to know. In spite of his youth and wit, if Matches had been born into another culture, he would have made an excellent diplomat. The orderly at the clinic had come looking for him, only to say that he was needed to translate. Matches led the distraught woman to a quiet linen closet, unused at this time of day, and motioned for them to seat themselves on bundles of fresh sheets. He then began to patiently and respectfully explain much, very much to her, bridging his vast understanding that his knowledge of the English language, both written and spoken, had provided for him of both cultures.

The first thing he did was hand her a clean serviette, knowing that a strong white woman, when her defenses are finally broached, lets loose tears like a beaver dam during spring freshet. Then he gently called her Sweet Grass Woman, to remove formalities, watching her face and shoulders for softening all the while. Placing one hand most carefully, high upon her shoulder, he eased her slightly back upon the large mound of sheets so that she could relax. He had a lot to say. Then continuing, "You are like my mother's child, an older sister to me." He noticed that her foot was beginning to fidget; he knew from Cloud that she had a legendary, what the whites called "temper," like one of those little lava pots at the big Yellow Stone, and that she was crumpling and uncrumpling the paper rapidly in her hand.

"Anah," he cleared his throat nervously. She was formidable, a medicine woman after all, even if she didn't know it, "You know our language, but you do not understand our ways!"

Eeeh! Immediately she launched a counterattack. How Cloud had regaled her, yes, that was the word she used, for hours, about warfare, massacres, scalping, the French, Custer; he finally inserted a word, gently, "No Anah, I mean, our ways of marriage."

She screeched, he could see the roots of her beautiful hair burning with the blood that rose up to it; blushing! Oh, how interesting, does it rise all over? Why is she looking at me like that? Oh. Tact, that's the word, small, sharp things, hurts to step on. Now what is she saying? I think she is going to cry. These white women, why do they do this? A very clever tactic, because it weakens the men. Well not me! Married? I must pay attention. Now she is grabbing me. Eeeh! A wildcat!

"No, no, he's not married, never, no." Amazing, such control, immediate calm. All I said to her was that she should consider herself betrothed. Betrothed, yes that's the word. She actually sat upright, pushed the tendrils of that flame-like hair behind her ears and smiled cat-like at me, then laughed, hands in lap to say coyly, I think that's the word. So many words I need to verify after this. "But I have no proof," she said to me with amazing calm. "Proof?" I said, "I wrote down his vow, the vow of a Dog Man of the Northern Cheyenne, undoubtedly the last of the fighting horse warriors of the plains, the bravest of the brave, pledging himself. Do you not know what *nestaevahosevoomatse* means?" "Oh my God, no!" she practically screamed, grabbing at the front of my shirt. I couldn't help myself as I yelped out, the meaning, "I will see you again later," and then her nearly hysterical response as she repeated it over and over, crying, that inexplicable white woman response of tears once again. Tears when happy, tears when angry, tears when sad; as unreliable as rain on the prairie, both of us in a call and response of English and Cheyenne. I felt like I had trapped a wildcat in a poke. I repeated the word again in English and Cheyenne, just to be absolutely sure she understood. N*estaevahosevoomatse,* I will see you again later (I must admit I was intrigued by the response), until quite a few orderlies and other staff came running to what sounded like some obvious distress to them, only to find nothing really amiss.

Later that evening Anah had many more questions to ask of Matches. He carefully explained to her how dangerous it would have been for her and Cloud to travel together out west. She interjected that they could have married. She began to voice the question of prejudice but Matches simply said, "Anah, surely you're aware that Cloud wishes to establish himself first." She then became quite irrational, Matches noticed, a tendency of white women regardless of their intelligence or breeding. It appeared to him that Cloud was most wise in his method of departure, although he, Matches was becoming more and more uncomfortable with having to explain the situation.

"Oh, I don't care."Anah was quick to respond to every objection. "But he does, Anah, so you have to, for his sake." "But where is he, where has he gone, how will he survive?" "Anah, how did he survive so far? Do you not understand what it meant to have worn the Dog Rope? What do you know of this elite society?" At the moment she was much more interested in finding him, feeling bitter and betrayed. "How can we stay in touch, smoke signals?" "Anah, please! Did Cloud ever tell you of the significance of a vision quest? Did he tell you of his quest? Do you think that *Taku skan skan, the Everywhere spirit,* can lose sight of you, of the both of you?"

Then he stood to leave. He was, just like that, finished with talking to her. She was like the woman in the story from the black book perhaps, a woman of little faith. "Did you find the package?" he called out over his shoulder as he walked away.

The Package

A very contrite but joy-filled woman rowed out through the early morning mists to a small cove off Manzanitas Bay. One could tell by the way she now sprang carelessly to the shore, disregarding the incoming tide's lunge at her skirts, that buoyancy inhabited her spirit as well as her step. With a generous arc she flung an old quilt under the sparse shade of some Eleutheran pines set above the high tide line, and prepared to settle herself in with the simple needs that she had brought for an afternoon's contemplation: a soft pillow, a mason jar of sun tea, apples, cheese, and of course, her Commonplace Book. The strand was deserted except for a few sanderlings coursing along its length, undisturbed by her presence. Taking but a few moments to assure herself that her privacy and the boats anchorage were secured, she opened her journal and, turning to a fresh page wrote in bold script:

NESTAEVAHOSEOOMATSE –
I WILL SEE YOU AGAIN LATER!

Then drawing the book to her breast, she bowed her head to it in silent contemplation, sending out her heartfelt message, asking forgiveness for doubting him, their love; saying out loud a barely audible, "There are no words for goodbye in Cheyenne, or Lakota." As the dear image of old Turn Foot rose and brought tears to her eyes, one dropped to blur the ink upon the page, which she quickly blotted, laughing. Nothing, nothing could spoil this day, and noticing a rather large gull warily sidling up towards her wicker lunch basket she gaily called out, "Wait, just wait, I may feel generous later!" Then she fell eagerly to the task of recording what had transpired when she sought out Matches and he had translated that word which had caused her so much turmoil.

The Commonplace Book

Faint light illuminated the shambles of my room which I had hastily straightened up before going out in search of Matches earlier in the day, not noticing any package. Upon my return a quick scan of my dresser and small writing desk availed nothing. As I searched among the folded piles, I noticed something far back under the dresser and crawled flat to drag it out, discovering it to be a soft tanned deerskin bundle. Trembling, I hesitated to open it. Redolent of white sage, I clutched it to my breast. Afraid to question why. How long I sat there, I don't recall. There was a gibbous moon rising, and the late call of a mockingbird. So very quiet, just a passing carriage could be heard on the old bricks of the far street, and the soft, falling water from a small Cupid's fountain in the garden under the large Magnolia. My head hurt and I desired sleep, knowing that Cloud, or perhaps Matches had an intended message for me in this bundle. Could it not wait till the morning? I must have dozed off then. I woke with a start. I don't believe I can do justice in words to what I then experienced. Oh, I wish I were a musician or an artist, or a poet, or that I had captured my tears in a vial of the finest Venetian glass. I heard his voice, or I felt his voice. Is that even possible? Telling me to open the deerskin, and it seemed to simply unfold on my lap, I swear it, emitting the most wondrous fragrance. Even as I now write this I think I must have dreamt it, for it moved as a dream sequence.

Within the bundle lay the blood-stained Dog Rope of Medicine Horse, Dog Soldier, one of the chosen four, bravest of the brave, Cheyenne warrior, who I knew as Standing Cloud, imprisoned these last three years as a "hostile" at Ft. Marion. I carefully lifted the long, tanned elk sash, only to discover that it had been cut in half. That was when I broke, to sit weeping, convinced of my betrothal with a scrap of paper in one hand and a length of Dog Rope in the other. There must have been several feet of the tanned elk skin sash in my lap, the same rope that he had pinned himself to the ground with to fight to the death when his kola Walks Lightly had pulled the pin, releasing him from his vow, and now in my lap was the half from which a red painted picket pin dangled!

He had staked his life to mine!

Repatriation

April 1878

With spring came the release of the prisoners from the war department to entrust them to the care of the Indian bureau once they were remanded to their respective reservations. None of them would return to a life as they once knew it; the buffalo and the way of life it once provided for them was gone forever more!

Some chose, like Matches, to remain east of the Mississippi. Many to further their education. Some to join families that had taken them in. The winter visitors saw the turning of the season as a sign to also make preparations for leaving. Many departures, leave takings and goodbyes were to occur, and Anah, who determined to stay at Ft. Marion in hopes of hearing more from Cloud, made good use of her time in long, fruitful conversations with Matches. A subject that she could not seem to work out was why Cloud had simply not asked her to accompany him, or at least explain the situation to her face. After all, she reasoned, if he was such a brave man, well then could he not face up to her ire? "What is "ire?" Matches asked. Or disappointment? " Anah, he did not ask you directly, for you would have said yes. Is that not so? He did not tell you when he was leaving because you would have stowed away. Is that not the right phrase?" He looked at her for confirmation; one look told him that, indeed, she would have insisted on accompanying him. Go on, she waved irritably for him to go on. This was of dire importance to her, this conversation. "He did not stand face to face with you, you are not the enemy after all, for his heart would have fallen down. Do you know that expression we have?" She nodded, getting more and more anxious for him to make some sense; to come to his point. "He brought that package to your room as you slept." She gasped at that! "'He brought the message and the Dog Rope, his most precious possession. The only remaining thing he owned of his old glory, I might add. All that he had left, and he gave you half. He could not reach into his chest," With a strangled cry she reached up to place a hand to his lips. Matches, uncharacteristically reached out for her hands, capturing both of hers in his long thin ones, drew them to his chest, looking to her eyes, called her a sister of his mother. "Did he leave you the half with the picket pin?" She could only nod over the lump in her throat, her head tilted up to keep her tears from spilling. "I thought so!"

The Ring

As the weeks passed the daily routines of the fort changed. The prisoners, who were no longer so, but once again free, left. Zotom, once known as the Biter, and Making Medicine, both who had developed their considerable artistic skills while imprisoned, had earned money producing drawings. They had sold sketchbooks, some ceramics, and even decorated fans for the winter tourist trade. All in all twenty-two of the men had decided to stay and continue their education.

The terreplein, once a lively scene at night, where Anah looked forward to meeting not only Cloud, but so many of the men she had grown to know, now seemed somewhat forlorn. She envied them their talk of home and family, and dearly hoped that they would be able to assimilate. Of course there was much busy work to be done to keep her occupied, and she was expecting to hear from Cloud, or to receive some form of summons any day now. Several weeks had passed since his departure. As discreetly as possible she kept a keen ear tuned to his possible whereabouts, and was ready to write to Red Crane Woman regarding this matter so very dear to her heart when Matches appeared, smiling, at the stables where she had gone to groom the horses. Cloud had left his horse, at first a complete bafflement to her, but as Matches explained so simply, "They shoot us for horse thieves; who would believe that it had been a gift?" Slowly and painfully she was beginning to understand the wisdom of Cloud's silent leave taking.

"Here," Matches said, extending a small butcher wrapped package, "for you," suppressing a grin. "From him?" No, it was in a packet from the Kiowa Reservation, directed to you, from Red Crane." Crestfallen, she pocketed it and sullenly went on grooming with a needlessly strong stroke. Matches did not leave like she wanted him to, though. Continuing to ignore him, stroke after stroke, he sat himself comfortably on a bale. In the afternoon sun the flies droned in the warm manure, and droplets of sweat formed on her brow. Neither said a word. What was he waiting for? The swish, swish of the tail began to aggravate her; what did he want? Finally she turned on him, dropping her brush. "Do you know what's in that ?" "Of course not," calmly said, "I'm waiting for you to open it." "Matches," summoning a grace she did not know she possessed, "I will let you know. LATER!" "You're not going to open it now? If I was't here it would be open then?" Matches did not think that he would ever understand these white women; very tricky. How can she be hiding what she doesn't yet know? Hmmn, perhaps this is indeed a cunning move. If he wanted to find out he thought it best now to leave, and with that he mentioned that low tide was at sunset, asked if he would he see her on the terreplein, and took his leave.

As soon as his back was turned, she sank down with her back against the hay bale and extracted the packet, ripping it open unceremoniously. Out tumbled a note, thank God, with Crane's familiar handwriting. Barely taking the time to scan it she read nothing to indicate Cloud's whereabouts. Had there even been time for her letter to reach there, she wondered? Wrapped in a muslin cloth was a small, carefully wrapped parcel. Strange. She set that aside to open later. Something stopped her from unwrapping it further, and she went back to the letter. The words jumped from the page in Dancing Crane's clear hand, *"This is from the Kingman mine. He left it for you to wear until he returns."*

The lowering rays of the setting sun cast heavy motes among the floating specks of hay, and still Anah sat admiring the beautiful large, oval, turquoise and silver ring that sat upon her hand, from where she reclined upon the hay bale, no diamond of any large carat had ever earned higher praise than this ring did in her heart that day.

(Later she discovered that he had inscribed the symbol of the morning star, *wohehiv*, on the inside surface.)

Toddler

1878, At the confluence of the Mississippi and the Missouri

Bullboats, pirogues, canoes, two chimneyed steamboats, stern wheeled paddlers, ferryboats, even an occasional log raft; all manner of craft were being plied up, down and across this mighty flow of waters. It wasn't until he himself stepped off onto the firm far banks of the other side of the Mississippi, as the *ve'ho'es* called it, that he felt his lungs fully expand with the air of freedom for the first time in his three years of incarceration. Oddly, he even felt taller, or was it that he stood taller? This was the fabled jumping off point for those heading "West", as they called it. Home to him. It would not be found, he knew, but he would seek what did remain. Surely they could not destroy the mountains; he turned back to take in a reassuring glance at that mighty, muddy river that rolled past, seemingly heedless of the commerce that lined its banks and plied its path to the sea. Surely they could not dam and alter this mighty flow! He turned his back on it and headed west.

He had made his way slowly, diligently and with great care. He could not disguise the copper color of his skin, nor the hawk-like shape of his nose and high mounded cheekbones. Raven black hair now hung to his collarbone; he intended to let it grow . That and his towering height and military bearing, well above six feet; for that there was no disguise. Facial scars invited inquiries, but as he bore no visible weapons and his clothing was clean and respectable, his feet well shod, he thus remained an enigma. One that bore a cautious approach. And when he gave out with a respectful greeting, in such good English, offering his services in exchange for his simple needs, he was often accommodated. That, and his proficiency with horses, helped him in his travels as he moved ever westward. His skills with blacksmithing helped, also. Anah had schooled him in rudimentary table manners so that when in those homes where he was asked to the table he did not embarrass himself, and would have done even Mrs. Pratt proud. Cloud preferred sleeping in the barns, or haymow though, and longed to be where he could gather sage and sweet grass once more, and have a fire. Oh yes, fire, fire! But in the orderly fields and farms he passed through he knew not to raise a suspicious chant or prayer, let alone a wisp of smoke.

Just before he crossed over the Mississippi, at that last homestead, he came to learn that there were good people that had themselves been driven to the lands they now farmed, not for gold or cattle, but just to raise their family. They had wanted him to stay on as a hired hand. He couldn't bear to stay much longer, their very kindness hurt. He didn't understand why. The littlest child was a "toddler", another new word he learned, that meant when the bones were not yet hard and would wobble when they walked. He liked that word on his tongue. If they were nice and fat like a puppy, they were a "waddler", he believed. Well, the toddler, Josie, had wisps of hair on her head, like the yellow flowers that go to seed and drift to heaven, so that the sun shone through like a sun dog. When she would see him come in from the fields at the end of a day she would break from her mother's skirts and run so very fast on those short, plump legs that she would fall, unless he would drop his hoe to hasten his pace, throw out his long arms and run to grasp her up, toss her in the air, and together they'd swing around, and find themselves laughing, laughing. It felt so very, very good. Amazing, for the mother let him. She let him!

It had been at the end of what the *ve'ho'es* called May, and the great red star that rose in the heavens at dusk called Antares made him so long to be on his way out on to the high prairies he knew as home. He left that farm with a sack of provisions, and a good mule bought for a fair price. He rued leaving the sorrel mare Anah had gifted him with back at Ft. Marion, but there would have been no chance to explain how he came by it honestly once he crossed the big river, besides no one would risk stealing this old mule.

Traveling West, Thinking East

With each flick of the mule's tail the flies rose, only to settle once more upon its flank. Cloud felt the same trapped restlessness as he supposed the animal felt as they plodded along. Traveling by himself gave him much time to keep his own counsel, whether he liked it or not, and like the inevitable pesky insects certain thoughts just settled on him.

He would never understand what led men to destroy thousands of horses. To deprive his people of their livelihood, yes, but why not just drive the horses away, give them their freedom? It had taken him quite a while before he began to understand that it was not cruelty, nor cunning, but a tactic, a necessity of warfare. The army simply had no way of providing for such large herds. Thousands! Then he reasoned that they could have kept the herd boys, or sold the horses for profit. Well, they did sell some, gave the finest as rewards to their enemies, the Crow and Arikara scouts who had tracked them down. It pained his heart to see them destroyed. Was that the purpose?

So many of the ways of these whites involved destruction, at least for his people. The strange diseases they had brought: coughing sickness, typhoid, spotted death, pox, and malaria. He had no objection to growing food, but it seemed that all the land given to his people to do so was not good. Why did they not give them good earth? It seemed that the land that was good for growing and rich with game also had the yellow metal that the whites so coveted, and thus it was just this land that they took away. He regretted nothing but sorrowed that he had been prevented from traveling back north to rejoin Tasunke Witco and the others, but then....he knew not to follow that chain of thought. How wise it is that we do not let the name of those who have gone beyond cross our lips. He found himself avoiding many of the places they had camped and fought together, though it added miles to his journey. Many prayer flags danced in the wind, and here and there a lone burial platform still rose on the horizon. He had been told that many of the old ways were not only not practiced, but forbidden, and punished by the agencies. But he had seen women with their hair hacked off unevenly, as of old, their forearms heavily covered to disguise the traditional mutilations for mourning the departed. The pain and despair of being a conquered people held them in such invisible chains that he made detours around most reservations, stopping only for the most necessary supplies and information.

He met up with a distant nephew of Two Moon's, who had been at the Battle of the Little Big Horn. He did not want to talk of that encounter at all for fear of reprisal, much to Cloud's chagrin, but rather to complain incessantly of reservation woes. "The shoes they send us, brogans, have soles that come apart when wet, like the blankets. Flour grows bugs like magic, and it is pure white, like their skin! Stretchy things called garters they send to hold up things called socks that none of my people wear on our feet. These are not "good" or "goods", as they call them to us." He went on to tell Cloud that he had heard talk of a bounty on Indian scalps, as though they were lowly vermin! "The white man is land hungry, land crazy! What was civil about the war they fought with one another; they are the same tribe are they not?"

It had been so long since Cloud had held council with another that he found himself talking into the night. He spoke simply of how the US Army sent thousands of the people to reservations as the outcome of what they called The Red River War. He had been one of those seventy four warriors, sentenced without a trial, convicted of murder, rebellion and an infinite number of hostilities, and sent to a far off place, the very tip of the country, far, far to the east, where the sun first rose over the ocean. Two Moon had little comment to make, for he, too, felt imprisoned on this reservation.

Before Cloud left at dawn he told him that there were good white people, that many of the men imprisoned with him were now returning to their families, and that he still carried a vision. To his people, he realized sadly, he was still Medicine Horse, the famous Dog Soldier, if he chose to acknowledge himself as such, what the whites would call a hero. Yet he had been imprisoned as a hostile ringleader, a villain of the worst sort. He thought it best to move on as Standing Cloud, to move, to drift as *vo'e*, as the cloud does!

One Step Short of a Ceremony

Fourteen hands high at the withers, intractable, with a smooth easy gait, stalwart and with an easy composure, the sorrel mule he'd been riding had been a good choice for his journey. Not much of a companion, but he didn't want to dwell on that, hadn't even given the beast a name, though it certainly deserved one. He reckoned it might be close in age to him. He certainly didn't want to travel with a mount that others would consider worth stealing! This was a good one though, and such ones had at least twenty-five years of usable service. He knew he'd chosen well; Mr. Miller had seen to that.

Cloud realized, as he moved ever westward, that he was traversing much of the same routes that the settlers, the pioneers, those whites that had so disrupted the ways of his people had. How his heart moved within his chest as the familiar sights and smells, the sharp poignant tang of sage crushed underfoot, the smell of burning pinon, the sweet smell of ponderosa bark. But above all he was once again enthralled by the way he exalted in the vast display of the sky as it moved from dawn to dusk on the seemingly endless horizon that the prairie provided. What caused certain strictures in his heart, like being too short of breath when you've run too hard for too long on too steep a grade, came from seeing miles and miles of the sharp twisted barbs of wire that can tear and rend flesh, clothing and hide, strung from fence-post to fence-post, enclosing over-grazed, empty-seeming land, with nary a gate or cattle-crossing. Soon hoo-doos, arroyos, and caliche signified the approaching Badlands. He'd head for the Shell River with its many thin threads, crossing lands where battles had been fought bravely, and lost. Now much of the land had been turned by the plow. Not a buffalo was to be seen, not a lodge glowed softly within as the last light fell, with no fine pony herd feeding near by.

He slept once more, gratefully, on the face of his mother earth. Withstood storms. Stood in the elements and felt once again, but in a new way, that he would never again be the man Medicine Horse, Dog Soldier, yet he was once again a Cheyenne.

At the Standing Rock Agency he witnessed a farce of a hunt, where scrawny cattle were turned loose to be lassoed and wrestled to the ground, dispatched with a hatchet and knife. He discovered, to his souls' sorrow, that Sun Dances, giveaways, and many other traditional ceremonies were now prohibited and enforced by a Court of Indian Offenses. He left without hearing more.

Once he dreamed of being an Eagle Catcher, then a man of herbal medicine, a *pejuta wicasa,* like Slow Bull of the Oglalas. Now he heard tell of a good white man, they were calling him a *wicasa wakan,* Holy Medicine Man, U.S. Army Surgeon Valentine T. Gillicuddy, because he worked so very, very hard to try and bring back Crazy Horse's *nagi,* soul, when he was bayoneted. So, Cloud thought, there are a few good men! He remembered Anah telling him of the governor of a land far to the eastern edge of the lands, Roads it was called, Road Island on the ocean , many years far back, whose colony did not believe in taking land from the Indians who lived there. Roger Williams was his name; he would always remember that good man's name.

Soon he would be approaching what they called the Continental Divide, the backbone of the world where they had once gone to get the best lodge poles. He ached for the moment when the first faint blue rise of the big mountains, the Rockies, would appear. He knew he would have to cross those passes before the big blue star of midsummer rose in the night sky, the one Anah told him was called Rigel, in her language. Regal! Yes, regal, so beautiful as it rode the heavens. He liked other names too, like Antares, Aldebaran, and Spica! Tonight there was a horned moon, a crescent, she called it. So much of him had been invaded by her speech, like the confluence of the many tributaries of the Platte. He missed her so badly, he was just one step short of a ceremony, from turning away from the vision he was pursuing with such a saving intent. So close to abandoning his grand vision and turning back to seek her out!

Desolation, reservation after reservation! He had skirted them carefully, observing what he could, like a "wolf" of old. Now they all have the *"cesca mazas,* metal breasts, the tribal policemen. And on one where he observed the "hunt" of skinny cattle in a pen, there were more and more "hang-abouts" trading what they could for *mni wakan,* whiskey. Indian whiskey, a poisonous blend of black tobacco, red pepper, grain alcohol, some molasses and lots of water.

He thought back to when Red Crane Woman had come out to his little camp. He hoped that by now Anah had the ring. It was the finest one he could afford from the Navajo trader's; not one from the sutler's store, not one that had been traded for whiskey. Crane would have written a letter for him, but he had too many things that swelled up in his heart and his thoughts could not capture them correctly. He was afraid of how they might twist into the English language. He could only trust his arms around her, he told Crane. "Shall I tell her that?" Crane cackled, slapping her thighs as she crouched at his fire that night, sipping at the tea she had thoughtfully brought, along with some fine jerky. Cloud thought not, and responded that the ring alone would do. "Men, hmph! It is a fine gifting, the best stone from the Kingman mines."

Now in the quiet of the night he allowed himself to fully miss her. Ironic, the fact that he even knew what this word meant was due to her influence, her ways, the blending of their ways. Well, Sweet Medicine, the prophet, had predicted this coming. There had been no way to prevent it. He and others of the Hotamitaneo, Dog Soldiers, had fought and lost. No way to stop the blending, no more than how he and Anah had blended their limbs in the blankets; far better than their blood on the battlefield. Far better!

Mitakuye Oyasin- Let it be! Ironic. He tested that word again on his lips, pulling a piece of the red willow bark from its pouch, to smoke before he settled down in his bed roll, adding "bittersweet" as he leaned forward to poke at the embers of the very small fire, thinking of her again, as he held that word in his mouth; bittersweet.

Missing her, yes the nights were chilly here, and dry, so unlike down South. He allowed himself to briefly miss her warmth, then it all flooded in, the feel of her skin, smooth as the breast of an eider duck. Her smell, which he could not describe. His hands almost ached to clasp the fat of her small hips, to lift her up. He loved to hold her small chin in his hands. He even liked to hear her language fall from her lips, not listening to its meaning, just to watch her mouth shape the words, like the lulling babble of a nearby stream. He had to be careful, though, for if she suspected him of not listening, she turned like a jay that had caught a crow at its nest! Ah, to give in now to these memories, however sweet, for what had passed and cannot ever, ever be reclaimed. Well, if they were to have a life together he had to succeed, had to believe in his plan, thus he reached into the pouch at his waist and lifted the small, most delicate and downy feather of an owl to the palm of his hand, brought it to his lips, and with a good strong breath, and every desire in his heart, he sent it arching heavenward! *Wakan tanka kici un*!

Her First Vision

St. Augustine

Captain Pratt had been negotiating with those in Washington, making arrangements for his dream of an Indian School. The old Carlisle Barracks had been practically abandoned for use by the cavalry recruits and he had petitioned the War Department for the use of them. Well, it was all very complicated, as Mrs. Pratt had tried to explain to Anah, but the Captain was a master at these things, a genius of sorts. Mrs. Pratt told her how he went from Secretary McCrary to the Adjutant General E.D. Townsend, and that in the end a special act of Congress would even have to be called to have the old, unused barracks transferred and released to the Interior Department for an Indian School. At this point Anah's head began to swim; she began to feel rather faint from all the intricacies that seemed to be required. A law actually needed to be written, passed upon by the House and Senate, and on it hung their hopes! Or what she thought of then as their hopes, hers and Cloud's. That was back when she imagined them moving up to Pennsylvania to help with developing Carlisle. How perfect they would have been as a team. But then he just up and left! Four months had now passed. The barracks had been secured for a school, and she was to be a teacher there. Capt. Pratt firmly believed that the only way now to keep the Indian race from complete extinction was by removing the young people into schools and educating them into what he considered was a proper form of civilization. It had worked so well with the prisoners he had under his control for the past three years that he had finally been given the go-ahead to proceed with his plans.

The Pratts, along with Miss Mathers, had then departed for the Dakotas to secure future pupils from the Kiowas, Cheyennes, Arapahoes, and Sioux. Etahdleuh and Okahaton would return, along with the English Quaker, a Mr. Alfred Standing, who had been at the agency school at Ft. Sill. As much as she was trying to stifle her bitter disappointment over Cloud's decision to leave, she was finding herself looking forward to these developments at Carlisle. There was so much to be done in preparation, and she had been feeling so poorly lately.

She had conquered her initial wild impulses when she felt betrayed and abandoned by Cloud. How would she have ever been able to explain her response if she hacked off her hair, or her gashed arms and thighs, as an Indian woman would, sometimes? Well she could have covered the cuts to her body, but not the loss of her tresses. She so understood the intense expression of grief that such extreme acts signified; so much more that a black wreath on one's door, or the wearing of black clothing, but then Cloud wasn't dead, was he? Slowly she came to understand just how much her sympathies aligned with his people. Yet when she had lost both husband and child her only solace had been the laudanum and alcohol. She had shut all others completely out. Except Turn Foot, dear Turn Foot! Slowly she accepted the idea that she had developed an inner core of some strength, and that she hadn't been abandoned by Cloud. Even as her preparations advanced for teaching at Carlisle, she knew in her heart that she would, in an instant, leave at any summons to join him, no matter where he was. She thought of herself like Penelope at the loom, well, that wasn't really right, she had no other suitors, nor was she doing any unraveling. Hmmn, Ruth, yes, Naomi's Ruth. She went to fetch her worn King James Bible from the drawing room table, quickly perused it, only to blanch at at what she read in Ruth, Chapter 1:17 *Where thou diest I will die, and there will I be buried.* She quickly put it down, her romantic notions quenched, as an image of a sparse burial platform, half obscured by driving, icy winds rose up before her, alone and unattended but by a mongrel dog! Well, such morbid thoughts; it would not do to think like this. Best to keep busy, so she set off to help in the kitchen, where an extra hand would be most welcome, now that most of the staff was gone.

Potato water slopped heavily from the pot as she staggered and sat down. Nausea overwhelmed her. Why hadn't she thought of this before? When her first child came along she would often pause, sure that what she was feeling were those first palpable stirrings. When Orianna had announced her presence, the nearest that she could come to describe it was " like a newly shucked pea rolling across the inside of your cheek", except the sensation was most definitely not in her mouth! Four months had passed, she knew, four months since he had left!

She would not think of the one and she dare not think of the other! The pattern on her apron began to blur. Almost dusk, or was her vision fading, her mind clouding? *She could not be...* Thoughts were spinning into a gathering vortex; a storm from which she saw no possible shelter. A buzzing, was it the insistent call to shrillness of the cicada's chorus starting up? Was she going to faint? No, no, she sat down quickly, leaning back against one of the shaggy poles of the grape arbor, each hand splayed firmly down in the gritty loam. Then, suddenly, she was.....

Lying on the frozen earth next to she who must now remain nameless, coppery blood steaming in the cold air. Dead arms rose up from the bloodied, torn elk robe, reaching towards her.

"The sun falls upon you today. You have been given one of His children to be brought forth on this earth. Live for this, Sweet Grass Woman! Stand tall. We do not praise the tree just for its height, nor straightness of its limbs. Stand and provide shelter! Once again you have been chosen to share your body for a brief time with another, to give shelter to another life. In every generation there are those who are chosen to bear new life, so that life can go forward, and the circle remain unbroken!"

As her vision began to clear, she found herself sprawled on the ground, the water from the potatoes soaking her skirt, and the face of Pale Calf Woman dimly receding in benediction before her. Echoing in her ear was the commanding, husky voice of Red Dancing Crane Woman, *"There will be a child.....a child ..a child,"* until it echoed and blended with the cicadas calling her back to consciousness.

Overwhelming Dream

Ignoring the concern in the cook's voice to just come sit and rest awhile, Anah gathered her few belongings and rushed back to the boarding house in absolute confusion, bordering on panic, barely able to mumble a polite acknowledgment to those that greeted her in passing. Of course she must be coming down with some fever from the nearby swamps; it could not be otherwise. " Oh dear God, it is not possible, How could it be, after all these years," she thought. She hastily counted the months. Yes, it had been four since he left, but she thought she had been so badly damaged from the attack back at Laramie that it wasn't possible. "Oh Cloud, where are you? What am I to do now?" She was so distraught that it barely registered that she had had a vision, not a dream or hallucination. She had been given a prophetic confirmation, but had far greater concerns, for she was a gentle bred, unmarried white woman, now carrying an Indian's child. A child that would be forever marked in an indelible way by his skin alone. No amount of education or wealth could protect it from the odious label of "half-breed". Nor could there be any shield to protect her from the shame accrued from its bearing.

At one point Anah had planned to seek out Cloud, if he had not returned for her, by traveling back west to the various agencies; after all, she was proficient in several of the languages, was familiar with their customs, and had lived among what the U.S. Army had termed the most violent offenders. But if she were with child, how could she travel under rough conditions, where would she shelter, give birth, raise the child? Oooh, her head began to hurt; a great cloud of worry began to rise up like a monstrous dust storm out of the plains. Her heart seemed to twist within her chest. First at the thought of Cloud not knowing of this, then, *wrench*, of his leaving. Such emotions battered her that she felt like the storm itself, wanting to rise up and rage, rage and blow and travel across miles and miles to scour the very earth. Howl and weep ,cold, hard, bitter, copious tears upon the unfeeling breast of the earth, of Cloud. Oh Cloud, where, oh where are you tonight? This could not be good for the child. Oh, I have so forgotten how to be a mother, I have not given one thought to anyone but myself, have I little one. I must rest, she thought, and lay back exhausted on the fully made bed, just pulling an old shawl over herself, brogans still on her feet, a vague sense of nausea roiling in the pit of her stomach, fighting for her attention. Outside her window the late call of a solitary mockingbird halted mid-stutter, then began, irritatingly, once more. Why does one never see them in pairs, she thought? And the irritating call bored into her brain as she drifted into an exhausted, troubled sleep.

Every object before her eyes gleamed in a silvery haze, but the moon had yet to rise. Mist hovered close to the ground. The sky far above to the west was hung with just a few strong stars. Uncommonly large buffalo skulls gleamed wickedly in a huge pile on the bleak plain before her. A small child was busy plucking a bouquet of cone flowers and phlox growing among those bones, stopping to arrange a few in her loosely plaited, blonde hair. Finally satisfied, she turns to smile at Anah. It is Orianna. Overjoyed, she tries to call out to her, but only a deep groan escapes her body, which, to her horror, is immobile. When she looks up, the child has vanished and the mist has risen. Totally helpless now she sees, protruding from just beyond the edge of the eerily bleached buffalo skulls, now glowing pure white in the risen moon's strong rays, a pair of feet, obviously a woman's; one lightly covered with a fine winter buffalo robe. Cries are heard. They echo and re-echo across the prairie. The woman is in labor, but then comes a cry, not from the woman but from the child! An eerie silence penetrates Anah's heart. How could that be, can you hear your heart beat? Then she heard it again, so faint, was it...she felt something, something rise in her, then the cries began once more, as though the whole prairie erupted with the gentle sounds of night; the chorus of the little wolves, the hoot of an owl ..and could it be, no, no, a newborn, but it was, crawling on all fours, copper-skinned and still slick with after-birth. Dark hair, black eyes glowing with recognition, he drags what looks like a beaded amulet through the sand towards her.

She wanted to cry, to scream, to run, there's thorns and....

And she woke, terrified, shaking with a reality that so overwhelmed her that she leaned right over to throw up onto the bare floorboards.

Rose, her pulse drumming wildly in her throat, her heart beating hard. She hastily retrieved the ewer to clean the mess, gagging as she did so, then on trembling limbs went to her closet, and far back on the highest shelf retrieved the small package where she had hastily stored the severed Dog Rope.

Kit Rabbit in the Fox's Den

"o'xeve'ho'e, it is not a hateful word!"

Anah hurriedly dressed and set out for the fort where she found Matches deep in conversation with one of the Minorcans that often supplied the Pratt's household with the choice seafood they so favored. He was holding a fine specimen of sawfish, which they were examining closely. Quo-yo-oh, one of the Comanches, had then appeared with a board sufficiently large enough to carry it and support its large, toothed bill, for it was about sixteen feet in length. That she was able to divert Matches' attention from such a strange example of the sea's bounty was evidence of her distraught appearance, and his sensitive nature, so at once he excused himself to hurry to her side. The strong smell from the fish and the nets, combined with the intensifying sun began to overwhelm her; she pleaded to seek out shade. He guided her to the deep shadow of nearby oaks.

"Anah, you are troubled." With just a quick furtive glance around she reached for his hand. "Can we go somewhere quiet to talk?" With that he quickly led her up onto the terreplein and into the deep recesses of one of the brick casements that were once used to shelter the big guns, now abandoned. The area was cool and deserted at this time of day. Once seated, he assessed her pale, damp face, the rigid posture, her clenched hands, and remained silent. "May I speak freely?"

Inwardly he sighed deeply, so very formal these white women. Oh Cloud, you have entrusted me with Little Sister, yet she acts like a kit rabbit in a fox's den; she continued to twist and torment that scrap of useless cloth called a hank-e. He waited. Twist, twist! Patience. I can wait. She should be happy, should she not, to have this child, to be chosen? Women, white women, so strange, perhaps I should encourage her, lean forward. Oh, but to touch her is more dangerous than putting one's hand in a rattlesnake's den, I've been told. No, she was truly distraught, dis-raught, was that the word? "Matches!" His head jerked up, "Matches!" "Yes?" How those splendid eyes of hers flash, more like a cougar's on the cliff above one..."Are you even listening to me, or are you trying to discover the secret meaning of the English language?" Oh, he snapped to. Alert. Yes, yes. "What is a vision?" " A vision?" " Yes, a vision, I had one, that is, I think I had one, just yesterday." He began to explain, but just as quickly she overrode him, as fast, as adroitly as one overrides a bull buffalo on one's fastest pony. He could not get a word in edgewise, so excited was she to tell him. She was practically trembling, and that tortured little scrap of linen was now being dabbed here and there at her forehead, and then at her eyes, as she blurted out the story. He had never seen her like this. But he knew. Yes, Cloud was right. She was the one. He felt the hair rise on his arms; the word rose to his lips, softly, a beautiful English word that he always wanted to use but could never imagine using, until now, that is; horripilation!

The sun was high overhead now, and poking into their casement, sweat causing Anah's pale skin to gleam, her golden eyes to look as though they were pouring forth silver, not tears as she sobbed out, "a child, a child." She looked so frightened, so vulnerable, dare he try to calm her? He rose to place both hands upon her shoulders. "*Nesene*, my friend," and with a shudder, like a balloon expelled of all air, she quieted to slowly recount the whole story in a more rational manner.

Matches, filling and refilling his small clay pipe, proceeded to ask a few questions. "You were at the encampment outside Ft. Laramie when you were mistakenly attacked by the army, is that not so? And you were beading with the women, that is why you had on the elk skin dress?" Anah simply nodded in affirmation. He smoked quietly and knocked another dottle out. The cool breezes emanating from the bay had drawn them down there, where she began to tell him of the dream. Anyone seeing these two from afar would have taken them as old friends, which indeed they had become, thrown together in such strange circumstances that the enforced confines of Ft. Marion had provided. The urgency had left Anah, a relaxed mood now prevailed.

"Anah," the younger man began, "you know the roles Cloud and I played with Red Dancing Crane Woman at the agency at Ft. Sill when we were still fighting to preserve the way of life for our people." Seeing the scrim of tears that rose in her golden eyes he continued, "Well, Crane was much, much, more than just a go-between, I think that is the right word, she could see into..." Anah, rising up, understood that he was struggling to supply just the right word, so she interjected, "the future; a visionary, perhaps." "Yes, that sounds right. A visionary, not a prophet, exactly." He wanted to ask how that differed, but knew that this wasn't the right time, so he just went on. It was so quiet here in the heat of the day. The fishing boats were pulled up on the strand below the walls of the fort, the dogs and fishermen gone. He wanted to prompt her to continue. "So, the child?" "Yes," she sighed softly, and seemed to fold inward, but momentarily, as though steeling herself. This woman has great reserves, he thought, even though she looks so frail. Calling them palefaces is a misnomer, proud of himself for this correct usage. He found that the awareness once so necessary to life on the prairie he now employed; such trivia as noticing that that scrap of cloth now lay in her lap, indicating that she was now relaxed, unwary. As to Anah, she too noticed his alertness, but had no intention of discussing her intimate female matters with him; the fact that she might be with child, but she desperately needed to discuss the import of dreams and visions. As she turned to watch the idle rise of the tide creep up the strand below their feet, a wretched feeling of impeding nausea rose within her once again. Oh how she did not wish to entertain this truth, if indeed it were true!

"Matches!" she practically shouted at him now, "tell me the difference between a vision and a dream." Ah, he thought, she's like a newly caught mare, all over the place, but he carefully replied, "A dream arises within oneself. A vision comes from without." He was really tired of this. Could she tell? Why can't she just tell him what she already knows, is instinct dead in her? Then, amazingly, he saw understanding transform her: she began to tell him the dream. It poured out of her in such a way that he felt the great Thunder Beings begin to move in to surround them, to shelter the two of them as she spoke, to shield them from all interruption. The sky grew dark, the air cooled quickly, as it often does in this part of the world, and just as quickly the storm passed on; a very faint rainbow, like a calling card, left on the horizon.

She was spent now, and looked to him to interpret. He began to speak. "Ah, *o'xeve'ho'e*, a half-breed. Remember this word in our language. Savor it on your tongue. Yearn for the day when you will hear it come from Cloud's mouth. Tell your heart it is not a hateful word, though you will hear it spoken in hate. Your child's blood has been mingled in love, never forget that." He could not help but notice that she did, indeed, look as stricken now, as helpless prey would look in the predator's clutch. "You will be a *nahkoa,* mother, that's a badge of honor." He could not help adding, "Cloud a *nehyo,* father. You could say he counted coup on you!" At that she flashed him a look that told him all he ever needed to know about the killing instincts of white women. He quickly grew serious once more. "You will have a son. It is why Red Crane told you that there would be a child." "If Cloud knew all this, how could he, how could he just leave me, how could he? I have no way. Does he know what it means to be in my condition?" 'He doesn't know," Matches answered, "I learned from Red Crane. It was foretold." "You knew?" He could see the blood rising to her cheeks; it made him nervous. "You let him leave me?" How was he to deal with this? Then she just jumped up and ran. White women, ugh!

Sitting Bull's Red Blanket

Powder River Country

Cloud stood erect, facing the advancing sun, free to pray as he wished once more. He looked down upon what his people had called The Holy Road and her people called the Oregon Trail, and as he began to try to see with the eyes of his spirit his thoughts flew north to the land called Grandmother's, Canada, where Tatanka Iyotanka, Sitting Bull, had taken his people to Wood Mountain after the battle of the Little Big Horn. From the time of the unexpected massacre at Sand Creek to the unrelenting assault upon the sacred Black Hills, the *ve'ho'es* had not given ground except for the few forts they had ceded here. True, he thought, the defeat of Long Hair's entire Seventh Cavalry at the Greasy Grass caused them to lose what they called face, but that had only caused a pause, at which they then redoubled their efforts to see that all Indians were to be confined to reservations! But I am free now, he thought, but free to do what?

When he had first come near to the Standing Rock reservation he sent word to Dancing Crane. She rode out to meet him at his modest campsite, bringing supplies and much news. He was saddened to hear that her son had gone on to walk the Starry Trail, along with so many other brave warriors, but in her stoical fashion she went on to speak of the living; told him that Bear Who Walks the Ridge of the Kit Foxes survived the Little Bighorn, and the Cheyenne headmen, Sits In the Night, Red Cherries, Brave Wolf, Two Moons, American Horse, Buffalo Hump, Spotted Wolf, also Old Wolf, and…finally he stopped her. "Crane, for all those not named, it's too painful, we cannot bring their names to our lips; they must live on in our hearts."

During the time he spent with her she told him of so many feats of bravery that his heart swelled near to bursting with pride, yet felt tight, as though bound with old, dry antelope sinews, for he knew that he would no longer ride out in battle. A small, but very deep, hidden wound opened in him with the realization that he was one of the very last of the men to ever wear the Dog Rope, just as fated to die out as the buffalo. Seeing the descending dark burden come across his handsome face, Dancing Crane had leaned across the small fire, risking singeing her fringe to shake his shoulder, "Cloud, wake!"

He had jumped to his feet, untangling his long lean legs, until she forced him back to his seat. "Did I tell you of Sitting Bull's prophecy at the Rosebud, before the battle? You know until the very last he had still hoped for peace to settle upon the hearts of the bluecoats as they rode up the draw at the Little Bighorn. He rode out to meet them on his favorite pony, you know the one, the big gray, but it was shot down immediately." Cloud hung his head as he knew all too well; losing one's favorite mount was tantamount to losing a best friend. He remembered Tasunke Witco talking and singing to his favorite war pony before battles. "Sitting Bull told his warriors," she went on, "My best horse is shot," and turning to those with him he then gave permission to attack, for it was as though he himself had been shot. I don't believe he wanted fighting, but let me tell you of his vision," and she began:

The Story of Tatonka Iyotanka's Red Blanket

Well, as you know in The Moon of Making Fat our people come together to camp and make our pledge for spiritual renewal, and there had never been greater need than this past year, with Three Star Crook hot on our tails. Our Wolves had been out on the trails, bringing in news of all the Bluecoats swarming like ants, coming to destroy our peace again. Sitting Bull, in his 45th summer, had fasted and danced for two days. One night he made a pledge to Wakan Tanka of a "scarlet blanket." He had done this many times before. I know you've seen his many scars, Cloud. He is our wicasa wakan, is he not? Many of us had again slipped away from the reservations to come to these ceremonies on the Rosebud. It was to be one of the last great assemblies of our people. Oh Cloud, if only you could have been there! Well, let me go on. Stripped to the waist, all those close by could see his great composure. Such beautiful livid scars on his back and chest, from previous sun dance ordeals, spoke of his love for us! He sat with his back to the dance pole, the sacred cottonwood. It was dry and hot. The air throbbed with drumbeats. Holy men who gathered round him, Hunkpapas like him, painted his hands and feet in bright vermillion, drew slashes of indigo across his broad shoulders.

His adopted brother Jumping Bull walked before him, then knelt, produced a sharpened awl in one hand and a bone handled skinning knife in the other. Taking the Bull's wrist in one hand he sliced a hunk of flesh off; as he did so Sitting Bull continued his prayers, evidencing not a single hint of pain or disturbance. Jumping Bull moved in this fashion all the way to his shoulder until 50 gouges were done and his entire arm was a river of red blood. Jumping Bull then turned to the other arm and proceeded in the same fashion, making another 50 cuts. Once more Tatanka Iyotanka was making a sacrificial altar of his body for his people. We sat filled with pride and gratefulness to the Great Spirit that held us together. All those warriors who had earned the right to wear the eagle bone whistle bore it to their lips now, and the high-pitched, exultant shrill of the lords of the air filled the sky as the steady throb of hands beat upon the drums, and hearts beat in our chests in unison.

At last blood was flowing in rivers from each shoulder to Sitting Bull's wrists. Then and only then did the great holy man, whose face was suffused with beauty and whose hands were steady, hold out this scarlet blanket to the sky as an offering. He rose to face the sun, Wi, and began to dance in its blinding honor as he continued praying; as his feet moved upon Maka, our earth, our good, red earth. Oh Cloud, I felt Taku Skan skan moving, I felt the spirit that moves everything move among us, all of us gathered there together on the land of the Indian Nation that day, and he danced and prayed as his blood flowed down to meet that red earth for us, his people. "I give you these," he said before he fell into a trance, "because they have no ears." He saw the soldiers falling headfirst down into our camps, dropping from the sky like grasshoppers they came, their hats falling off, because white-men have no ears and will not listen!" Wakan tanka gave them to us to be killed. Cloud, that vision of the army soldiers falling into our camp and their defeat at our hands, it was predicted. It was! And it happened just as he saw it!"

"Crane, I must pray and fast after hearing this. I think I must go to Saskatchewan to join Tatanka Iyotanka and his people, how could

I not? I'm free," Cloud said, his face suffused with joy. "They have me on no government roles. I'm not enrolled at any reservation. I can easily cross the border."

The tall woman drew a burning stick from the fire, lit her pipe, slowly drew on it, smoking quietly, then knocked the dottle out before speaking. "What about Anah?" Cloud looked startled; had he not assured her of his eventual return for her? Had he not told Crane of how Anah was the woman in his vision. What more was needed, he wondered? He thought it best to allow this wise woman to respond with her counsel, and thus remained quiet. "If you go to Grandmother's land, how will you support her?" Cloud thought the same plan would perhaps work there, but kept his peace. "Crane, I will look for a sign" "Good," was all she had said before she abruptly threw the remains of her coffee on the small fire and began to gather her things, indicating that she was planning to saddle up and leave. She wanted to tell him that Turn Foot had been seen in the Powder River area, but thought it best to not mention it. He had enough to think about as he prepared to seek wisdom for his path.

As Cloud settled in that night, he wished that he had thought to ask Crane to send a letter to Anah, although he wasn't quite sure where to send it. Matches, he had hoped, would keep track of her for him. Sometimes he wished that he had learned to touch the pen to paper, most of the time, though, he didn't care. He wished that they could talk of Sitting Bull's Red Blanket; Anah would like that, for she thought much of the white man who hung on the cross for his people, though it was very hard for him to understand that prophet. Winter counts were no more; there were no more buffalo robes to write upon, no elders to mark the counts. He began to understand the wisdom of writing. Storytelling and storytellers were dying out with the old men, along with the skins upon which the tales were recorded. In fact, those "tales" were not being made. Who wishes to recall only our losses, our defeat, our constant record of shame. Where is the hope? Then he thought of Zotom and Making Medicine, and the ledger books they had worked in so diligently at Ft. Marion. How they told the story of their captivity, and their survival. Wasn't that a good story? Yes, perhaps that was good. He knew that between those covers some of their story may survive. He also knew that the story of Sitting Bull's Red Blanket would someday be told everywhere, and his heart felt warm within him.

Hope For Hanblecheyabi

As darkness began to descend over the valley Cloud found himself preparing, in the best way he could, to seek a vision or a sign. He knew that such a thing comes from without, not within. Within himself he had plenty of dreams, of what the whites call aspirations. They do not rely on counsel outside themselves, it seems. He had a plan, but now he was in doubt. To go, to join up with Tatanka's people across the border, or to continue west on his own? When Dancing Crane Woman had ridden down the trail that had led off the bluff, and he had watched her tall figure diminish until it had fully receded, he had thought of catching up to her and asking her to pen a letter to Anah. He had even thought of how to word it, "May the sun that shines on me warm you also." Anah would like that. But he felt a great artificiality in the construction of a letter, and simply thought again of Sitting Bull's prophecy. He remembered the shimmering hope that Custer's Last Stand, as the Army called The Greasy Grass, generated in the People that summer of 76'. It was replaced with the utmost despair over Crazy Horse's death just a year later.

There was no way to have an inipi, a sweat, as he had no way to properly prepare one. He had but the remnants of his dog rope, some good white sage, and his newly accumulated medicine bundle. The good sky was above him, the good earth below. Soon *Hanwi,* the moon would rise, and the ever present *Wani,* wind was here. He would welcome all those spirits who would come to bring him a word, a guide, a message. A *pejuta wicasa* who had been at the Greasy Grass had told him that Sitting Bull told the warriors not to mutilate the dead, that it would make *wakan tanka* unhappy; that if they did so they would find themselves hungry at the wasichu's door, hungry for his food, and jealous for his goods evermore.

Cloud meditated on what he had seen that seemed true on the reservations as he had traveled here. The "goods" they now received from the government as allotments were far inferior to those the Indians had been able to make themselves from the buffalo and antelope, and as to the food, well, the sugar rotted their teeth and the whiskey made them mean, poor and crazed! A Brule, Red Looking Horse, who had given him a small amount of his treasured *chanshasha* to smoke said dryly of reservation life, "They want us to cut our hair short, wear tight, dull colored clothing, live in square boxes that have no life and no beauty. I drink to forget I have no way to earn honor anymore!" Cloud felt his spirit lift when he rode off the reservation lands, left with a burden of sadness for those left behind.

Oh how his heart had sung when first the land and the sky had once more opened up to him, as he remembered it, like a large hand to welcome his return back to the lands of his birth. He knew not to look for *tatanka*, not even a bone, for he had been told of the bone-pickers that gleaned the prairies. Here and there he saw a weathered skull nailed to a barn door; that grieved his spirit, for once his people would decorate such skulls and leave them upon a prominent hill in thanksgiving for the generosity of such blessing of abundance. Changes were everywhere; the wheel of life revolves. He was taught not to fear that, but now he must seek a vision. No longer was it as simple as to choose either the Red Road or the other. He looked down upon the road below him where one could still so easily see the wagon ruts embedded by the thousands of immigrants that had traversed it.

He felt himself of a divided mind now about seeking a vision. It was not that he had turned his back on the old ways, not at all, but in a more chilling fashion he thought that perhaps those very powers had somehow become less accessible. After all, the very plight of his people gave testimony, did it not? He was a warrior, or had been. That was when he heard the shrill scree of the eagle, but faint and far off. He turned to the east where the Black Hills lay. Yes, once he thought he would be an Eagle Catcher, and the thought crossed his mind of how those who live on these plains must confront the winds.

Carving a wide dihedral above him a war eagle pierced the dry clear air with one sharp scream of frustration before it swept up higher into the cirrus sky above where Standing Cloud had come to be alone. Being back in the ancestral hunting grounds of his people was both a torture and a pleasure, for it was no longer theirs to freely roam. But the vastness of the sky that rose above as he lay stretched out on the escarpment above the old trail called The Holy Road filled his heart with gladness, and the mountains, those could not be taken away, surely not! Much as he wanted to stay here, to linger, he could not let himself. He had seen how life was now for those who were living on the reserves. He could not bring Anah to this.

The young men had an enemy to fight, for which they did not know how to prepare. They had no wise men to guide them. No visions to seek. There were no ceremonies, no lodges to even repair. With no animals to hunt, why make weapons? Why learn skills? The few ponies in their herds were but skinny nags; no wonder hearts had fallen so low! As he began to sink deeper into an interior of despair for the future of his people, heavy purple storm clouds began to amass on the far horizon, rolling in over the Sand Hills toward the North Fork of the Platte. As the air chilled, Cloud's thoughts turned to the time of his capture, when his heart fell down and he died as the leader, the wearer of the Dog Rope, Medicine Horse. He then took the name Standing Cloud upon himself as the irons were placed upon his body, "He Who Waits Beneath The Heavens", and as the first cold drops of the rainstorm fell upon him he lay there, recalling that ignominious surrender just a few fateful years ago.

April,1875 Just south of The Platte, On the banks of the Sappa River

Walks Lightly had pulled his pin from where he had staked himself to fight to the death, dragged him onto his horse behind him, that starved, rib-thin, over-burdened pony, as tired of running as they were. Do they kill it to have something to eat so that they can go on? No! Surrender? No! Go on foot, weak, both wounded as they were. The unbelievable shame, two Bravest of the Brave, Dog Soldiers of The Cheyenne! One War Pony, our brother, that they couldn't bring themselves to sacrifice, they abandoned the horse so it could live. Stealing into the haymow to hide, discovered, surrounded by soldiers, too weak to fight or die. Defeat!

Yes, he was one who waits beneath the heavens! Slight rumblings of distant thunder indicated that the storm had passed on. Cloud stirred himself, thinking of how he had come here to consider his direction in life. This was the turning point if he was indeed to continue westward beyond the Rockies, now that he was released from his imprisonment. He was free to start a new life, discovering that there was nothing of the old life left for him to regain.

The land below him was not so much traveled now, though once thousands upon thousands of emigrants had traveled it, more white faces than buffalo. Hard to imagine! As the buffalo and game diminished the white faces grew, the herds moved further off, and we moved after them. They brought their cattle that cropped the grass to the roots, then the railroads that divided the great herds came, and divided our people too. Forts sprang up, towns, and problems, big problems. Retaliations, peace treaties that never worked, allotments, reservations, the army way of control, when all we wanted was to preserve our way of life, our ever diminishing way of life. The buffalo soon vanished, the game, like the beaver, then gold was discovered, but what was impossible to preserve was our freedom. Roads, railroads, forts.....but he tried to encourage himself...and he felt the sun on his back as it emerged from the clouds and he lifted his eyes to the skies once more.

There rode the eagle, again on the hunt. He thought of his beginnings, how he wanted to be a *wicasa wakan* like Silver Spotted Owl. The great bird was circling the fenced fields where often coyote and wolf pelts were nailed to rot, rising up on the dihedrals, searching for unwary prey to amble out amidst the clumps of silver sage. "Give me a sign," he thought, letting his mind drift back to the time when, as a young man, he tried so hard to impress his mentor with his daring and abilities. He idly kept his eyes upon the gyre of the bird, which flew in a seemingly effortless search that Cloud knew could and would go on for long hours, propelled as it was by a need to survive.

Medicine Horse, he was no longer that Dog Soldier, the name of the dead was not to be spoken, and he was as one dead indeed to that man, that warrior, though at times it rose in his blood like the bold, shrill cry of the war eagle circling above, when it shrieks in frustration at missing its intended victim, its very nature denied! Squeezing his eyes tight against all the past glory of the hunt, the battles fought and valiantly won, he realized how the recall could flare and ravage his memory with unrequited desire, like the smallest spark from an unguarded fire could set the whole prairie aflame. Fire, fire, just the thought of it, his blood hot throughout his entire body, his kolas readying themselves to ride out, as he raced to leap his pony, feathered lance in hand, war cry opening his throat to the sky....

With a great effort of long practiced discipline he pushed past, and before him rose the face of Silver Spotted Owl with his finely hooked nose, high cheekbones of the Northern Cheyenne, and the deep crevasses and ravines of age. His silver braids, carefully wrapped with fine, plush otter pelts, hung over his withered chest. He eschewed most ornamentation, a trait he shared with his nephew, the strange one of the Oglalas. Knowledge and wisdom were adornment enough for this *wicasa wakan*, he could not bring the name of the dead to his lips, but upon his heart, aah, taken from him that bitter morning at Sand Creek, and his memory rode him effortlessly back to a time when life rested but nine seasons upon him and he was known as The Cottonwood Boy, the foundling of the Cheyenne.

The Eagle Catcher, Desire Is Not Always Right

Bear Butte 1860

The loose thatch of branches above him let in air and glimpses of the sky above. Tethered to this flimsy roof was a dead fawn; Cottonwood Boy did not raise his eyes to it, though, for he was deep in prayer, his ears alert to the slightest noise from above. He did not know how long he had been crouched in this pit below the eagle's nest high on the bluff above, so concentrated was he on the task he had appointed himself to.

When Blue Runs Water did not recover from the coughing sickness that came upon him this past winter, the tribe deeply mourned him, for they lost not only a seasoned warrior, but he alone had held the special ability to trap the large war eagles so valued for their plumage. Moons passed and no one had been given a dream of eagles. At nine winters his blood ran bold, traditions had little hold on him yet. Cottonwood Boy felt in his spirit that he could take upon himself this special privilege. Though he was young, his strength and endurance had proven strong. He felt the need and undertook on his own to meet it. Besides, he had accompanied Runs Water the last nesting season of these birds. His need to prove himself to his clan was strong. He would become the new Eagle Catcher, providing the strong flight feathers for those whose bravery and accomplishments merited it. He prayed that he would succeed.

The shrill cries of the eagle's nestlings announced their hunger, dependent still on their parents for food. Soon, though, they would leave the nest, no longer ugly chicks, but sprouting those feathers that would lead to their fledgling. This was the right time to bait one of the parents, as this was the hardest time to keep them fed. The sight of the limp fawn on the rocks below the cliff would be sorely tempting to them. One of the nesting pair had returned with nothing to feed them just a short while ago. They would be driven to come closer to where he lay in wait. Once he grabbed a bird, it would have to be tethered onto the roof where its beseeching cries of alarm would bring down its mate.

He intended to somehow pluck some feathers from the large birds and then release them to tend to their nest. This was not the usual practice, but he could not imagine taking the life from one who soars so high, just to secure some feathers. Runs Water's practice was to secure a bird as a lure to bring down it's mate. He then ritually took the life of just the one; a few feathers plucked from the other before releasing it. With one bird captured and slain, the remaining bird was without its mate and heavily burdened to feed the eaglets.

Cottonwood Boy was beseeching the powers to strengthen him for this task when with a great thump the bird landed. He reacted instinctively, shooting both hands up to grasp it by its strong feathered legs. His grip was secure, the bird stunned into silence, at first. Then the struggle began, its strength was amazing, pulling him up so that he had to maintain his hold from a contorted position within the pit. He began invoking its spirit, asking for forgiveness, intending blessing for its gift of feathers. Feathers that would soon be given to honor brave deeds and accomplishments. What Cottonwood Boy hadn't reckoned on was the effect that the eagle's cries would have on him. The great bird was sorely angered, screaming outrage to the heavens. The shrill harshness of its cry tore through his own spirit; he found himself not just pitting his strength against the eagle's, but what, in himself, cried out for the sacredness of freedom. He did not recognize what he was fighting against in himself, for he had never encountered it so directly before. Confused, trying to confront this feeling, he fumbled his grasp. As he repositioned his fingers to maintain a secure hold, the eagle sank his great talons into the web between Cottonwood Boy's thumb and the forefinger of his left hand. Caught! Now he was in the great bird's grasp, and knew that there was but one way to obtain release, for a bird of prey will not release its grip until its catch ceases moving, not a twitch of life left. Positioning himself as comfortably as he could, he settled in, to remain motionless, trying to block out the incessant screams from the outraged bird.

When a great silence fell he looked up through the network of branches above him. The eagle was also looking upward into the clear depthless blue of the sky. There came a slight piercing trill. With it he felt a great yearning surge through him. Now both boy and eagle had their eyes riveted on the heavens above from which a small black form was beginning to resolve. High above, magnificent wings holding its flight path, circling the trapped bird, was its mate. The lone eagle circled, the trapped bird held still, the boy clutched its legs fiercely, not feeling any pain in his impaled hand yet.

How long had this struggle been going on; how could he resolve it? With a thrust of his knife he could end it. With a sense of pure thrill flowing through him he knew what to do. Releasing his grip, he gave himself up utterly to the great Everywhere Spirit, Taku Skan skan! Knowledge flooded through him that he had just been taught a great lesson, that he could not take from any living thing its freedom in this way, by deception and subsequent capture. He did not even realize that the eagle had simultaneously released him as he threw both hands up in praise to the very glory of the life which surrounded him, and to the acknowledgment of his part in it "I am one who will take no man's freedom from him, Hau! As the once trapped bird hauled itself up into the sky to meet its mate with exultant cries, the boy scrambled up out of the confining pit. He watched the pair come together, talons clasped, then swiftly circle higher, shrilling cries of triumph. He watched till he could see them no more, then bent to pull apart the trap, filling in the pit. Knowing that these great birds return to the same nest year after year, he worked carefully to obliterate any sign of a trapping site. As he unbound the dead fawn and prepared to haul it back to where his pony was tethered, he felt led to leave it as an offering for the eagle family. There at his feet lay not one, but two elegant feathers. Bending down to them, he felt failure in the task he had set for himself, but his heart lay warm and comforted in his chest as he placed the primaries carefully in his shirt.

Three days had passed since Wagachun, the Cottonwood Boy's return from the eagle's nest. He now sat quietly before Spotted Owl, the wicasa wakan, who was as a father to him. All the while the holy man had been filling his pipe and quietly smoking, his attention rapt, Wagachun had told him of his failed adventure. "Why have you come to me?" Spotted Owl finally spoke into the uncomfortable silence. "Do you feel that you have done something to offend?" "I'm not sure, Father, I just know that I failed in what I had intended." "You do not need me to affirm a failure, it is your own heart that will convict you." "But you have great understanding, better than mine. I come to you to learn." As Spotted Owl set down his pipe and with some small effort stood, he gestured to the door of his lodge, indicating that they would leave, saying "Our first teacher is our own heart. Come!" They walked together to the shade of a small wikiup on the edge of the camp. where at midday it was quiet and cool. "Let me ask you some things. How did you prepare yourself, did you fast or sweat?" Wagachun shook his head, not daring to say more. "Pray, then?" "Oh yes, I felt as though I was constantly lifting up my desire to the heavens." "Hmmn," was all Spotted Owl had to say. Wagachun could hear the rhythmic chirring of the tree insects start up, then abruptly fall silent. Still Spotted Owl said not a word. Was he waiting for the boy to say more?

"The war eagle, is this my power spirit then?" Wagachun blurted out, his heart thudding so loud with hope that he thought that certainly Spotted Owl could hear it. But still the old man kept his silence. Finally reaching into a small skin bag, held by a braided cord under his left arm, he withdrew something small, a stone perhaps, which he rolled around in his closed hand. The holy man grew even more still, with the exception of the slight rolling motion of his hand, which rested on his crossed legs. His eyes were now closed as he began to speak. "You did not obtain a vision, nor were you dreaming. In truth you were not seeking such." Wagachun knew to keep a respectful silence as Spotted Owl continued. "When one invokes the spirits perhaps they will come, but my son, the eagle did not come to you freely. You tricked it, then trapped it. You meant it grave harm, to take its life. Yes, I know you intended good, that its feathers would be gifted to our braves. You meant to fill a need because our Eagle Catcher has gone beyond. Did you not think that the Great Spirit would give us another? Were you called to this, or did you run ahead?" Tapping his head, he continued, "There is the truth of the mind," and thumping his heart, "And the truth of what resides here. They are not always in agreement. You are wise when you know what to listen to. Desire is not always right."

At this Wagachun was heavily humbled. No man would think of going ahead of the buffalo hunt, yet here he was thinking independently, without the wisdom of counsel.

Extending his punctured hand, which still throbbed with slight pain, "Look." "Ahau, yes, you think as a child; that this was the eagle's vengeance for your trying to capture it. You did capture it. This small wound, your first battle wound will scar; that scar will be a reminder forever of your first coup. Understand my son, the bird was not the enemy, but something that resided in yourself, that part of you that, in trying to do good, was seeking mainly recognition for doing good. This was an example of Taku Skan skan, you touched the everywhere spirit, the universal power that flows through all life. You connected. Blessed you were. You were in many ways foolishly brave, as young as you are, without invoking the usual precautions, but the "brave" counts. You counted coup on a sky warrior, the mightiest of birds. The power of the eagle lies in his great talons, his powerful vision. Unci, grandmother earth, and Tunkashila, Grandfather sky, were watching you when your heart spoke; all living things knew you then. Your few years on this earth did not matter, for you came to know the need that governs all of us, freedom. Do not despair because the great eagle will not be your spirit guide as you go on with your life. Remember you released him, but you connected with Taku Skan skan, and power is shared now. And my son, who is to say that the eagle will not come to you at some time, for you did show him mercy." With this Spotted Owl opened his great, dark, glistening eyes, brimming with pride and approval of this orphan boy that the clan had taken in many years ago. *From within his robe he withdrew two perfect flight feathers from the eagle that Wagachun had given him before he told his tale.* "Take one, it can be your *wotawe*, war charm. Tie it to your shield or on your person. The eagle is first among the creatures of the air."

A loud crack and roll of thunder and lightning from the receding storm caused Cloud to whip his head upright. Large purple cumulus clouds, backlit with rays of emerging sun, were now striking the fields below. Startled into the present he saw, emerging from far across the valley, a small herd of wild mustang, and leading them a spotted stallion. Leaping to his feet, he fumbled for his small spyglass. He hadn't known there were any wild herds here, let alone any appaloosas, the strange spotted ones of the Pierced Nose people. Was this a sign? By the time he had glassed the area he saw no sign of them, but at his feet lay an eagle's primary. He simply bent, saying *pilamaya,* returned once more to beseeching all powers of the heavens and earth, streams and winged creatures and four legged beings to hear his cry, his heart-felt cry for guidance, and so he passed the night, until his voice left his body and joined the eternal speech of the ever coursing wind. His body, if one were to have come upon it, would have been seen as graceful, handsome and in repose, at one with its surroundings; one would not disturb him.

"Wolf-With-Plenty-Of-Hair"

Towards evening of the second day of his fast he saw the apparition, not too far in the west, out on a small butte, but the sky lowered towards sundown and dust devils were spiraling up into the dry air. It appeared to be a tall, thin figure with arms uplifted in the universal posture of prayer. When a spear of light broke through a cloud it was apparent that he wore the *hotam'tsit*, Dog Rope of the Cheyenne, and from the profile now revealed Cloud could have sworn that it was Wolf-With-Plenty-of-Hair. How could that be, for he had staked himself and fought to his death many years ago. A strong wind then blew the long black braids across the warriors face, and like that he was gone.

A true Hanblecheyabi, or Lakota rite of lament, to give oneself up to a period of expressing grief and hope for a new vision to enable you to continue on with your life, should be undertaken with the help and encouragement of wise and holy men. But what did Cloud have? He could fast and pray, one always has that. The remnant of his Dog Rope, some chanshasha, some sage, determination, dreams, hopes, and now he was going to head out to where he saw Wolf-with-Plenty-of-Hair. It was quite dark when he got there. Was it the right place, he even wondered? He found himself not only missing all those who had gone before, to walk the Starry Ladder, but he found himself missing the brothers he had been imprisoned with. Matches! Anah wanted me to stay back east with them; my soul would not let me. Was I right? He started to climb up the rock face in the dark, expecting to find it bare, as bare as he felt his very being to be. The moon had yet to rise, and not one little wolf had yet to give voice. Why was it so quiet?

Then he was on top and a good smell of burnt pinon perfumed the air. He sat until the small horned moon rose over the land and the yip and resounding howls began of the night animals. He realized that there was no hurry. After three years of army life he could once again settle into the cycle of the seasons. Off to his left he saw a small fire circle that exuded the spent ashes he had smelled, next to it sat four mussel-shells with fresh paint. Red, green, black and yellow, the colors of the Dog Men's face paint. Cloud did not hesitate, but crouched down, raised them to the sky in blessing, and began to cover his face in the traditional manner, knowing that the answer he would seek would soon come. Nothing did, that is, until morning brought the unmistakable sound of a thunderous approach of a herd of mustangs galloping up out of the bottom land below him, such a mighty, free herd as he had yet to see, their hooves tossing up small chunks of chert and granite that caught the morning sunlight. They came splashing through small puddles, sending bursts of spray aloft, neighing with joy at their unbridled freedom. Here and there a spring-born colt kept up with its mare, and some late colts, scarred stallions, pintos, sorrels, and at the head the large stallion, what his tribe called the Pelousies, was running like the wind; like the wind. Cloud was on his feet, shouting, screaming his war cry. He felt alive once more. Oh, Wakan *tanka, wakan tanka kici un,* bless me! He felt he could fly from this cliff, that he could fly like the *Wanbli,* the eagle. He closed his eyes and felt his blood racing freely once more. "Oh, if only," he felt the tears of unmitigated joy upon his face. "Oh, run free my brother, my kola, run free, *Shukan waka,* Sacred Dog of my people," and when he thought his heart could bear no more he saw the mare, golden yellow with a mane and tail the color of the foam from a waterfall, racing up to join her mate, a yearling colt by her side. Oh Anah, oh Anah! And he knew! He knew! So with the light heart that comes of having one's purpose confirmed, he struck camp and headed west toward the Wallowas, feeling the strong winds that poured unfettered down from Canada, to sweep him ever closer to the huge upwelling of the Rockies, a welcome goal.

Pot-shot

When he settled down that night by his sparse fire, his thoughts turned to the first time he laid eyes on her, "The Woman of the Whites", as he thought of her at first. Actually, it was not at all her beauty that struck him, not the "coup de foudre", that fancy French phrase Anah had tried to explain as how she felt on seeing him. Of course she had a way with languages, and was given to using odd turns of speech. He did not have the heart to tell her that it was the large German silver armband she wore prominently displayed upon her arm, inscribed with the Cheyenne sign for the Morning Star, that drew him to her with such passion! He smiled to himself, lost in thought, as the night darkened around him and the horizon melted into rich shades of pink, purple and orange.

There had been no mistaking his profile for anything other than what it was as he sat there poking at the embers. Once the shock wore off, he was grateful that they had just taken a passing shot, winged him, and rode on.

He had cleaned it as best he could. It had passed cleanly through the muscle of his upper arm. Later, when it began to ache, and hindered his movements in the chilling night, his resurgent pride as a freed man reacted to the realization that he had been as casually shot by those passing drovers as any farm boy would knock a tin can off a fence. He wished he had some whiskey to sterilize it now. Instead, he rose with a little effort to fumble in the saddlebag on the mule and withdraw the beginnings of the *sicun,* the medicine bundle where he kept a lock of her red-gold hair and the eagle feather, then lay down for the rest of the night.

The Limitless Possibilities of Silence

First dawn had yet to arrive, but the oddly rhythmic cawing and clacking sound of the crows amassing in the nearby grove of the cottonwoods assured Cloud of his relative safety. He had only to reach out and poke at the resting bed of ashy coals for them to burst into sufficient flame for his morning's needs. He was dry, warm and fed enough. The bullet had been a clean shot, too. Apparently all the satisfaction those drovers wanted had been taken. The ache in his flesh wasn't what bothered him as he lay there, waiting for the sky to lighten, listening for the crows to settle their petty differences before they flew off to forage for the day.

Ever alert and preternaturally cautious, traits that three years of incarceration had not dimmed; he just hadn't expected a potshot taken at a lone man, unarmed at a campfire, for meanness sake. He reckoned he'd just rest up a bit here, then move on as he'd been doing, skirting the small towns, most occupied areas, and the large ranches. He'd been picking up odd jobs here and there, trying his best to judge where he would be welcome, relying on outlying camps from the reservations as he headed ever west by northwest. He was savoring the change in climate, altitude, the dryness in the air, the familiar smells!

When the last of the crows had silently lifted off and the soft, warm wind began to rustle the leaves of the large cottonwoods, the small song birds began their morning chorus to the rising sun. What was troubling him so? He rotated his shoulder gingerly. Yes, sore, to be expected; probed it a bit, not too hot. It would heal, given time.

Mist lay so thick that he could not see those chirruping creatures that were hopping and twittering so. Fussing so busily around, so full of life, so unconcerned. Then he saw one, a flash of blue, then another, and he held his breath! Bluebirds!

And it fell upon him then like a thunderbolt from ages past, like a lightning strike, but it was neither, of course. His tongue had no words, his brain formed no thought, his heart swelled, and tried vainly to connect and make a meaning that he could understand, and be as grounded as the tree that does experience the bolt of heaven-sent power from above, so that he could understand what was being shown to him at this moment. Oh, he thought, if Turn Foot, that old Scout, if my old teacher Silver Spotted Owl especially, my kola Walks Lightly, Red Crane Woman, she'd know, even Matches, the Captain...

Yet, as the mist began to lift, and the gentle, sweet beauty of the feeding flock of mountain bluebirds revealed themselves to Standing Cloud's amazed eyes, he felt with an unutterable and almost unbearable, bittersweet pleasure the sensation of missing Anah so much so that he found himself saying out loud to the universe, as a few softly feathered blue beauties nestled on his outstretched, wanting hands, "I miss you, I miss you, I miss you!"

Bluebirds

The child woke with two longish strands of her fine, black hair stuck to her rosy cheeks. Assured that the others slept on in the cool mist of the early dawn, she quietly drew her worn brogans to her little feet and headed confidently down towards the slight run of the creek, where they had set up camp the night before. An enchanting source of mystery was now all hers, to explore on her own.

Just on the other bank lay a small meadow; the rising sun creating a haloed nimbus from the mist through which rose random heads of wild bergamot, spikes of mullein, pink mallow, rose and phlox. Here and there a morning glory twined idly around a yellow daisy-like flower that she had no name for. A veritable bouquet was hers for easy picking, the likes of which she had yet to see in such abundance along the dusty alkali trail her family had been following for days.

Just as she made to enter the meadow a crow, left as a sentinel perched high in the top of a lone lodge pole pine, rose ramrod straight to sound out an alarm. What is it that causes us to freeze in the face of beauty, should we not melt in our core and flow towards it? But freeze the child did, for suddenly her mind was no longer so terribly, greedily intent on picking every single one of the flowers that she could get her chubby little hands upon, for she heard twittering. An intriguing sound to such a curious child, a riotous twittering! Such a susurration, an immense sound, and yet so intriguingly soft, and so very busy. Oh, she had heard the terrible sound of hundreds, no thousands of locusts, a frightening sound, in the harrowed fields they had left, stricken by drought, behind them. But this was not a bad sound, not a scary sound, how did she know? Children know! Some children know, that is, for she had that trust; she was raised under its roof, took her first breath in its atmosphere, and now that her beloved father had passed on she would rely heavily, innately on this sense. So though the child immediately knew, and cleverly identified this as a feeding sound, it was not to be feared. That rustling, that twittering, that softness, yes, it was wings, but not the dreaded wings of the devouring locusts. Feathers! What's to fear? Then she saw them, far to the left of her, in the greening up bluestem grasses hanging, then dropping to the ground. Swooping. Flying back up, clinging to harvest more seeds. Arcs of glorious, riotous color. Why, there must have been more than forty or fifty of them, a flock!

Bluebirds; blue, as blue as the sky, bluer perhaps, the bluest she had ever seen. They were real, the Bluebirds of Happiness her dear, departed Pa used to sing to her about; here they were. She began to run toward them. The wildflowers dropped from her hands and her mind as she ran. She would catch a bluebird and their troubles would be over. They were a riot of glorious azure, cerulean, indigo; blue as her lovely eyes! Mountain bluebirds in full plumage. Such sweet twitters, oh she loved them so much. She pursed her little rosebud mouth, kissing the air as she expectantly knew, to deliver that first kiss to their soft, feathered breast. She knew just how sweet their feathered lightness would feel in her hands, and how she would cup them to her breast. Her happiness was lifting her above the ground, she felt like a cloud, as though she could fly herself; she ran as fast as her little legs would carry her, she was almost there, just a slight mound in front of her to navigate. She could crouch behind it, then run out and, with so many of them swooping and darting and milling about, surely she could scoop at least one up into her pinafore.

There! Throwing herself down to launch her attack, if only she had brought a biscuit to lure them, that was her last thought before the mound rose up and up and became a blanket wrapped man, not only a man at all but, to her further distress, an Indian, and not only an Indian, but a large, bloody one, who bent far over her with one large finger to his lips and signaled her to be quiet! Utterly unnecessary, as she was rendered totally speechless!

Much to her relief she kept her scalp and was even offered a seat at his side. She was proud of her accomplished understanding of sign language when he patted the ground next to him and smiled. She did so, being careful not to sully her pinafore with what looked to her like fresh blood seeping from a bullet wound on his shoulder. His blood looked red just like hers did, too. Hmm!

As the flock continued to feed, she noticed that the dun colored birds amongst the brilliant blue ones must be the lady birds. He seemed to be content to watch the birds. She relaxed, assuming that he wasn't hunting them. The continuous twittering had a melodious sound. She felt somewhat sleepy, and slowly, carefully let her thumb rise to her mouth, from where she now sat comfortably at his side. As the mist lifted, the earth warmed, bestowing peace upon those two so calmly watching.

This is where her older brother Caleb found them, side by side. When he poked a rifle, rather gently, in wounded man's ribs, he was Quaker after all, he was astounded to hear the tall Cheyenne address him in rather perfect English. Mercy woke to chime in, "Mother will fix your hurt. We'll pray for you, too." Thus Standing Cloud joined the small family of Quakers who had recently lost their father to typhoid, and were now on their way to the Willamette Valley in Oregon.

Quaker Kindness

Carefully handing him the steaming tin cup of heavily sugared coffee, the woman addressed him with mild curiosity, "You were pot shot by the drovers we heard coming through last night, I suspect. They make it their business to eliminate as many of you as they can, against all God's intentions." Cloud made no reply, and she seated herself calmly nearby. The fire crackled against the coolness of the rising wind. Finally he spoke. "I am quite amazed at your doctoring skills; you had little trouble dealing. I thank you for it." Again she made little response, was comfortable in the ensuing silence, during which the child crept closer to him to settle by his feet, dragging her bed roll with her.

Rising, the woman retrieved the blue marbled enamel-ware pot from the coals to extend it towards his cup, indicating he was welcome to a refill, for which he accepted, being sure to thank her. He had grown quite attached to the sweet drink. Seating herself, she spoke softly, "Don't thank me, thank God!" At this little Mercy, who seemed to embody the ebullience of all the other family members combined, including the dog, leapt to her feet from where she had ensconced herself in a worn Star quilt, gave herself a twirl, received an admonishing glance from her mother, then sank back down, but not before she aimed a bright twinkle of a blue eye toward Cloud, where he could see it spark out, gleaming, from her hidey-hole in the covers, as she nestled in for the night.

As the woman spoke, he learned that they were a Quaker family who had come west to an agency just north of Ft. Sill, where her husband had come to help teach the Indians there to farm. We left our homes on the call of the Church, she said, and the Peace Policy of the President. When she came west to join her husband with the children, they had passed no habitation for over 400 miles, except those of mud-baked brick, the adobe dwellings. It was an unaccustomed desolation to those who where used to city life, she said. He remained silent, sensing her need to just talk.

Their mission on the reservation was to teach the Indians to farm; they themselves had a very prosperous farm back east. It looked to him as though a glint of tears were pooling in her large, blue, weary eyes. It was hard work, she indicated. He nodded; he understood that much, yes. The melons that the Indian women grew, the men ate while they were still green. The men left the reservation to hunt; they were hunters, not farmers. We understood that she said. The government didn't. Her shoulders slumped with a weariness of an impossible burden. They both sat silent for a spell. Their eyes met uncomfortably, then she gave a shrug, and what sounded to him like a small animal's last expiring cry, "TB grew very well." He wanted to ask what that was, but she then said with a most bitter sound, "the lung sickness, the wet lung sickness."

    He looked at her face in the firelight. It was smooth and without malice. He looked at her posture, and her rough-hands. She worked hard, he could tell. Her soul was still alive in her. Her heart still beat in her chest, but it lived there like a caged bird. Two of her children were in the ground, her husband was dead also. Now the family was going to live with a brother-in-law in Oregon. The fire grew small. She must be tired, but a brave spirit, like a bird on its seasonal journey. Now she had to bring her children west without her mate. He looked to her. Looked to the wood pile. She nodded assent, and the talk continued. She spoke no ill. They had tried to keep the Indians on the reservation. They tried to keep the alcohol off. They tried to keep the killings from happening. There were never enough rations. The numbers never matched the ration cards. Every penny spent had to be accounted for to the Commissioner of Indian Affairs. The promised quinine never came in time, but the malaria did. She spoke of President Grant and the Peace Policy; did he know of this? Abolition? She was surprised he knew. Yet she had bandaged his wounded body, and thus knew much just from seeing his scars. He said nothing, though, and in doing so he was saying all that she needed to hear.

    Soon the boy came back, announced by the dog, and they, too, sat by him. They all watched the flames die down and settle into coals. When the last tendrils of color whisked from the horizon she rose, settled her skirts, and pulled a few crisp, jacketed potatoes from the embers where they had been roasting and broke out tin plates, forks and salt. Bed rolls were laid out. Before Cloud drifted gratefully off to sleep he remembered the decoration on the cover of Anah's precious journal, her Commonplace Book, what she called the equivalent of a winter count; she had drawn a fine rendition of a mountain bluebird!

The sheep dog, for that's what she was, rolled to her side, heaved a sigh, a small snort, and began to lightly snore, her head on the boy's thigh. The coals dimmed, then sputtered when the woman rose to pour the the last of the coffee grounds out on them. Far out on the sand hills the little wolves gave a few desolate yips, oddly comforting to this cobbled together family. As heaven spread its fine blanket above them they all slept, knowing that for another night their needs had been met.

Unshod the Mule

Caleb stood too close to him as he lifted his head from the left rear hoof and told the boy, "This mule needs new shoes, but I'm no farrier. It's best to unshod him. It will correct that uneven gait." That the pack mule had trod too long on the old ones went unsaid. That money was the object also went unsaid. That the mule trusted Cloud knew of what he spoke was evidenced in the gentle acceptance of Jack's soft flicks of his large grey ears as Cloud picked him over fore and aft, and continued his assessment. "They don't really need shoes, just good trimming. Ride them over here, too. The saddle must be away from the animal's shoulder blades. Their strength is here," and to illustrate his point he reached down and hoisted up Mercy, who had been giggling and crowding in, hanging on to Cloud's leg as he worked. Plonking her down well back on Jack's posterior set off a delighted rill of laughter from her. Ignoring her now, "Oh, and don't curry him, let him roll in the dust; it's good for his coat in the cold of winter." Caleb, wanting to show his knowledge interjected, "It's the hind legs, then, that are stronger?" "Yes, good observation." Cloud saw that the young man was sorely missing his father.

Shooing little Mercy off to be with her mother, the two of them proceeded to break camp. It had naturally been determined, to everyone's benefit, that Cloud would accompany them on their journey west into the Willamette Valley. The family gained a good guide in taking on Cloud, one who could cut trail, provide small game, and in turn their presence guaranteed a protection of sorts from those who thought the best way to deal with any influx of Indians into what they thought of as their land was to put a nice bounty on their scalps, or, as an outspoken editor of an Idaho newspaper felt free to advocate in print, "distribute blankets full of smallpox."

Cloud had studied the calm, sun-burnt contours of the gentlewoman's face as she told him of these hate-filled westerner's that she was bringing the remnants of her family to live with. Why? She had no fear? And the oldest child could barely handle a gun, and would not kill a man even if his life, or another's were threatened. "God is our protector," she had told him in her calm unruffled manner. Cloud, too, lived with hope, much, much hope, but had given up on talismans of any sort, noticing that, unlike the Black Robes, these Quakers did not seem to carry any charms about their persons, though they both quoted from that black book.

As they traveled on though, Caleb and he exchanged many thoughts, many agreements on the spirit that surrounded them and that they held in respect and trusted to see to the continuous workings of their world. Out of Caleb's mouth came "Vengeance is mine, saith the Lord," and Cloud would ponder this the rest of the day, riding off a ways, returning to agree in kind that *Taku Skan Skan*, the Everywhere Spirit of Cloud's and Yahweh were most similar, and that they both held their peace until they were moved by the spirit to speak. He did convince Caleb that he should at least carry ammunition in his gun. A gun that was loaded could shoot rabbit, could it not, faster than the one he had to stop and load. He had no words to tell the boy how brave he thought him to be for turning that unloaded arm upon him in the meadow that day, when he sat wild and bloody, with one arm wrapped upon his baby sister as she rested against him in the morning's mist!

They found one another's company enjoyable. Cloud taught Caleb certain Lakota phrases that were easier for him to pronounce and remember than the Cheyenne. Caleb especially liked trying, then, to instruct little Mercy in the Cheyenne though, just to hear her stumble over the words, like the phrase, *Wounspe gluha blihihunkioiyapi*, we strengthen ourselves with knowledge. But when Portia came upon Caleb practically rolling around the ground at his sister's expense at this lesson she chided him, saying, "We do not use teaching others as a means to amuse ourselves," and sent him off on a chore he found detestable. Cloud found her ways of dealing with the boy quite skillful at times, and quite baffling at others. But like his people, she never raised her hands toward them, or her voice.

Willamette Valley

A certain heaviness weighed upon his heart upon leaving his Quaker friends. The Willamette Valley was even more beautiful than they had described it, and the erstwhile families settling there were doing their very best to tame it, though he suspected that it did not have a spirit of wildness that inhabited the prairies of his homeland. He had been initially encouraged to stay on with Portia and the children, Caleb and Mercy. He even had taken it into consideration. The vast green fields here in this valley would provide for the large herd of his dreams. But Aaron, Portia's brother-in-law, while outwardly very polite to him, had a deepening coldness, and couldn't seem to help but treat him like a hired hand. Of course, he was not an actual relative. His ability with horses could not be ignored though, but matters came to an unfortunate head when it appeared that he was to be "hired out" to some of the surrounding farms. He would have gone there willingly, of course, and in exchange for the slight amount of room and board that he felt he was already earning. Portia tried to ease things by explaining that actual money was what was needed, but Cloud didn't understand why he wasn't consulted directly. He went to Aaron and simply said, "You must treat me like a man," and went back to his room off the stable.

Later that evening Caleb came to him, looking quite forlorn. "Uncle Aaron said it might be best if you found work elsewhere." Cloud said nothing initially, but rose to enter the house to say his goodbyes and Caleb stopped him, almost in tears. "What is it boy?" "You're not to enter the house again. Ever!" Cloud reached for the knife at his belt and the boy stood transfixed. "Here, I want you to have this, and the sheath, too. Wait a minute. I have to undo the belt. There. Hold on. Got to give something for little Mercy, right? Sit a minute." He left to go fumble in his slight belongings, and returned with a beaded armband. "Don't let your uncle see this, okay? Remember what we've talked about. To fear not, that the spirit is everywhere, surrounding us. *Mitakuye Oyasin*, that means we're all related. Now go in there and have your dinner. I'll be gone when you're done. Thank your uncle for me. And especially your mother. Especially her."

It was time to move on. He had taken this opportunity to move out here to the Pacific Northwest, closer to his goal, the Wallowas of the Nez Perce, the ancestral home of those spotted rump horses. Ever since he had seen the first one flash across the plains his heart was set ablaze with a fire whose ember had never dimmed. The Appaloosa, with its mottled skin, narrow shoulders and hindquarters, some with white stripes in their hooves. The pierced nose people say these lean runners have such attitude that they merely "allow" one to ride them. And he knew. Oh he knew! The last horse he rode into battle as Medicine Horse was such a one.

The Nez Perce lived in such excellent horse breeding country, the Wallowas, relatively safe from raids of other tribes, not like on the Plains. They didn't hesitate to cut their inferior males rather than let them breed and weaken the stock. They traded those away, all to keep improving the herd. He was going to learn all the tricks. He felt remorse that the so called recent war of 1877 had ended badly for them. That is, if one could call it that; trying to flee with elders, women, children, babies and just a few warriors over some of the most rugged territory this country had to offer, with 2,000 U.S. Army soldiers in hot pursuit, to end up surrendering hungry, frostbitten, and heartbroken just 40 miles from freedom at the Canadian border, to be shipped off in shackles to the Indian Territory in Oklahoma. Cloud knew all too well! Captain Bear Coat Miles again. At least he recognized good horse flesh, Cloud thought, for when Joseph surrendered, Miles sold over 1,000 of those fine horses for what he could get, but unfortunately, shot the rest. Now Cloud was going to try and recover and breed a herd from those that had been left behind. Pregnant mares, foals, ones too old, too lame to travel; the ones that had been abandoned on the long arduous march toward what they had hoped would bring them freedom. The saddest thing, to Cloud, was that the army did allow the 400 of Chief Joseph's survivor's that were taken to bring some horses with them, but they were eventually required by the Army to crossbreed them with draft horses to attempt to create stock suitable for farming. Cloud tried not to think of how, when the farmers in the Willamette Valley wanted to purchase an Appaloosa from the Nez Perce before the revolt, they were frequently turned down; even offers of hundreds and hundreds of dollars for one, though an ordinary horse went for just fifteen bucks.

As he rode back out of the valley he thought, "Well, they have pursued and fought us from one big ocean to the other," then let his mind go mercifully blank, adjusting to the rhythmically plodding gait of the mule.

Chestnut Street

Philadelphia, Spring 1879

A fine lace curtain luffed in and out the tall window, imparting a sense of languor to the woman reclining on the chaise lounge. The book was slipping through her fingers to the carpeted floor. Through the branches of the blossoming linden trees she could see the strolling figures by the far pond as her thoughts idly drifted back to that morning in St. Augustine, it now seemed ages ago, when her landlady summoned her downstairs with an urgent message. There was a young man downstairs, then whispering, *sotto vocce,* he's an Indian! How her heart leapt! Without pausing, except to pat her hair into place, she flew down those stairs, barely able to conceal her disappointment at seeing Matches standing there, instead of her Cloud. It was all she could do not to burst into tears. He skillfully guided her out onto the porch, where they sat quietly until she gained control. Then he withdrew from his pocket an object that changed the direction of her life.

When she had run away from Matches the day before in such confusion and fear, well panic, she had no way to understand what was happening to her, other than what her body was certainly telling her, that she was going to be a mother. An unwed mother, one of the most reviled creatures, perhaps even lower than what good, upright citizens thought of Indians! She had little direct contact with them, but knew of their plight from what Dickens had written and, of course, Jane Eyre. Employers turned them out as soon as their condition became apparent. There was the workhouse, or perhaps her relatives? They barely responded when she had lost both husband and child; her heart quailed at the very idea of turning to her stepmother for any aid. She would gloat. Anah carrying an illegitimate child of a man who was both an Indian and an enemy of the U.S. Army, and an ex-federal prisoner! After the child's birth, who would think of employing an unwed mother with a child to feed and lodge; a child with a nurse cost money. Begging on the streets, infanticide, prostitution. Her mind reeled. Her conscience howled.

Anah's social class and widowhood contributed to her dilemma. Queen

Victoria, the role model of much valued marital and social behavior of the times, bore nine children, called pregnancy "the occupational hazard of being a wife". Thus Anah's position was unjustified in so many, many ways to society, and unbearable.

As to the father, Cloud, no one knew where he could be found. The care of illegitimate offspring were usually considered to be born by the sinful woman, the expectant mother, that is. Society would wash their hands of her, as once they assumed she had washed her hands of it!

Anah had not slept well! And now here was this young Cheyenne again, holding out something to her that she could barely see through the tears in her eyes. Oh, what was wrong with her lately; she felt so out of control. He smiled, his teeth so white in his handsome copper face. Oh, she thought, I miss Cloud so, and suddenly she's sobbing, and this dignified, reserved young man is holding her on the porch swing where anyone passing by could see them, and she's pregnant. Oh yes she is, and he's talking into her ear. He set her back away from him a bit and told her to listen carefully, saying, (She remembers it so well) "Keep your eyes shut. Listen with your heart. Open your hands. There. Feel this. Yes, its beaded. Yes, its the amulet, the one you saw in your dream, a lizard. For a boy; its for the umbilical cord. No, there, there, no more sobbing. For girls a turtle is beaded. It's the people's way. We place this on the child for protection. It is yours now. Cloud did not know when he left. I had a dream. I do not know if he had one. The Great Spirit knows. He knows all. The amulet was sent to me from Red Dancing Crane months ago and I was told to keep it, and I am patient.

Now you know. Mitakuye oyasin, do you understand Little Sister?" Laughing, he removed his hands from her shoulder and sat further back. "Open those eyes! "Oh, it's what the baby was dragging." He stood, "I arranged for a boat, let's take a sail. Are you up for it? I have much to tell you."

A sharp knock on the door brought her back to the present. "Anah, the doctor will be here in an hour or so to examine you. The time is getting close now, you know, how are you feeling? "Lucinda, I would be untruthful if I said I was without fear, but I am also eager to meet my son." "Your son, you are so sure?" As her hands closed upon the amulet in her pocket, she only nodded.

The Madman's Flea

Philadelphia

After the doctor left, leaving Anah assured that her precious cargo was doing well, if she was not, she still felt like an overburdened mule. She chose to plop back on to the chaise and allow herself the luxury of yet another reminiscence. She understood that once the child arrived, her time would not be her own; she remembered the day that Matches and she sailed out into Mantanzas Inlet. A momentous occasion for them both, for it caused a deepening in their understanding, not just of one another, but of their respective cultures. Even now it brought a smile to her lips as she envisioned the small painting by William Blake, "The Ghost of a Flea". There they were, settling themselves comfortably above the tide line in the shade, eager to begin discussing visions and dreams. Matches thought the white man's world was stunningly bereft of the spirit world; the exception being Christians. As soon as he mentioned the conquistadors, who had come ashore here in Florida, Anah desperately sought to change the subject.

"A flea!" she interjected. A small sand crab scuttled by their feet, that caught his attention. He snapped forward, dug in the damp sand and proffered for her benefit, a sand crab. "Yes, listen to this story," and of course he did, reclining on the soft quilt, reaching for the plate of ham biscuits she had thoughtfully brought for them.

"In London there's a man who they say talks to spirits daily. He told his mother, when he was just a boy, that he saw an apple tree full of them, just hanging there, glittering like little stars." "Is this true?" " Shh, let me tell you, and yes it's true. Well, he grew up to be a poet, a writer, an artist. He had a young friend who was a student of astrology, that's the relationship between the celestial," and seeing the look on his face she threw her hand heavenward in an encompassing gesture, "and the terrestrial," to which he nodded in quick comprehension. "He also studied physiognomy, that's the interpretation of one's character by judging their outer appearance, especially their face."

At this Matches threw back his head and outright laughed,"We've been doing that for hundred's of years, hau!" She sighed, decided not to be peeved, and continued, "This man, John Varley, was a watercolorist," Matches decided to not ask what this was; if a man wanted to paint water, well let him! "He believed in spirits like Blake, but to his great, undying frustration he couldn't see them. Valery was writing a book and commissioned Blake to create small portraits based on visions that Blake would have. One night, when Varley arrived at Blake's studio, he was peering deeply into a dark corner. Blake ignored his entrance, but said in a passion, "I see him. I see him before me now," and told him to fetch his paints, explaining that it was very small, and he did not want to take his eyes off of it. The flea he was seeing, or rather the ghost of the flea, had burning eyes and a face worthy of a murderer, and was gorging on a bowl of blood!"

"Oh, you're good, you're a good storyteller, you are. More, tell me more!"

"Well," she continued, "in one hand he had an acorn and in the other a thorn. He had a long, slithering tongue" "Slithering?" "Like a serpents" "Oh, yes, I see, I see it!" "With which to slurp up the blood in the bowl!" Matches, who was caught up in the description, quickly added, "because fleas crave moisture and feed on blood, they are bloodthirsty," and he sat back, popping another ham biscuit in his lovely, round, copper skinned face, both of them laughing.

Anah unlaced her boots, hiked up her skirts for wading, walked out a bit into the surf and, turning over her shoulder, called back to him, "Visionaries in our cultures are called mad. Madmen. Often locked in asylums. Driven out of towns." Under his breath Matches mumbled, "hung on crosses, burned on stakes." He rolled up his pant legs to wade out and join her, shouting a bit to be heard over her splashing, "While we revere them as holy men and prophets!" and thought best how to tell her of White Buffalo Woman, or the Thunder Beings. What tales had Cloud already told her, what would best prepare her for the hard path ahead? But for now the gentle surge of the blue water beckoned....

And thus they continued a dialogue and an exchange that went on until it was time for them to go their separate ways. Matches to his further training in the medical field, and Anah to the Felicitous House up north in Philadelphia, to await the birth of her child.

For My Son

Philadelphia, The Felicitous House

"There is a child!"

After the doctor left Anah she hurried to gather her things and head out to the small, private grove of elm trees on the grounds, where she so loved to go. She felt this strange surge of exhilaration coming on, an exorbitant welling up of health and well-being of the sort she had experienced right before Orianna's birth, which she had expended in washing all the contents of her rather sparse trunk, and folding and refolding the baby's layette. This time the burst of energy that she knew, full-well, would be followed by the exhaustion of a hard labor and the days and nights of seemingly endless child care, she intended to use to compose a letter to the child. An unwelcome tremor went through her that she could not quite suppress, after all, there was a chance that she might not survive the birthing, though she felt as healthy as a horse, and the maternal care provided here was excellent. Excellent!

She slipped out through the kitchen; it was frowned upon that the mothers here in such an advanced stage go out alone upon the grounds. The concern was not that they would be seen, for the gracious house, actually a mansion, that had been so generously donated for this purpose, sat many miles from the city, on over thirty landscaped acres. Most of the women here were gentlewomen; it was assumed that they would panic should labor begin, if they were unaccompanied. Anah, in so many ways, wished she were back on the plains in the good care of the native women there, with herbal teas and a birthing pole. Night after night she prayed that Cloud would at least come to her dreams. Oh, she could conjure him up, all right! She only had to open her bluebird fronted Commonplace Book to see the sketches she had made of him. Did he even know she carried his child? Her faith in the spirit world wavered when she gave this too much thought. But she had work to do here, and so settled herself down against an oak. Opening her book on what she had left of a lap she began:

A. K. BAUMGARD

For My Son

Soon the sun will shine upon your face. God willing, I will look upon it also. (she paused, willing herself to overcome the waves of emotion so common to her in this late stage of pregnancy) *You are Richard Stands Free, named after two wonderful men. Richard H. Pratt, who set the captive Indians free from their chains and restored their humanity while imprisoned at Ft. Marion, Florida in 1875, which is where I met your father, Standing Cloud, one of the "Bravest of the Brave", a Dog Soldier, of the Northern Cheyenne. And you have been born free of Anah Hoffman Moore, that is, an American woman of mixed blood, German, French with some Oneida Indian swirling around in there. Richard Stands Free! Stand Free! So my dear one, if I am not there to raise you I have made the arrangements that you will go to your father's people, so that he will raise and love you, and you will be as fine as he.*

The pen dropped from her lap with the baby's fierce kick. Damn him, did she mean Cloud, the baby, life, what was happening? Not now, she wasn't ready, breathe deeply, calm herself. Look to the clouds, she told herself. Cloud; where is he? Why, oh why isn't he here? One by one, large black shapes silently dropped onto the branches of the oak above her. Not a sound they made landing. Folding their wings, they assembled, until there were just seven. She counted them. One, two, three, ..seven. Seven is a sacred number. Good luck! Crows, black crows! She laid back and relaxed; they stared down at her, not a noise, a few rustled their feathers. Who knew that a murder of crows could be so gentle, like big black songbirds, not harsh, not grating. No caws, no screeching noises. She remembered being a young child running out into a cornfield, and the crows..... She relaxed some more, the pains left her belly, the clouds moved gracefully across the sky. She felt drowsy; perhaps she'd take a little nap right here, as her hand reached down to idly rub the amulet that never left her pocket now. When she woke they were gone. Had she imagined them? No, here was a bright, shiny black feather resting across her book, but her pen; her pen was gone!

As she made her way back to the house, she mused on the months of her confinement. From the panicked, despairing woman that she had been when she first had to confront the possibility, that day when she had fainted and the vision had come to her, to the time of calm acceptance that it was meant to be, she finally saw how her life and Cloud's had been drawn together. If Cloud is unaware that a child exists she must trust that it will be worked out, just as Red Dancing Crane Woman so calmly said to her that wintry night, out on the plains. "There is a child!" mystifying and even angering her at the time. And yet, when the string of half-starved, dirty, bedraggled, ironed and shackled prisoners filed past her in the sweltering heat of that summer day in the old crumbling prison at St. Augustine, as she sat checking off names on a list, one fiercely grabbed her wrist and yanked her to her feet. When their eyes locked, their stars spun into predestined orbits and the story began.

Arriving home, she sat on her bed and bent over to remove her shoes. The child kicked then. "Yes dear," she thought. She talked to him constantly now. "Stand Free, soon. Soon you will be free upon this earth." She lay back upon the bed and put her swollen feet up. Cloud, Anah thought, where are you? If this were one of the fairy tales of my world you would arrive now. Now, now!! She felt that undeniable tightening, like a headache, except it was across her pelvis, not her forehead. They were all looking for him, but no one had heard or seen him. He was alive, she just knew that.

There was a large brass bell with a wooden handle by her night table, placed in every room to summon help. Perhaps it was time, but first she laid the amulet out, and carefully unwound his Dog Rope from her taut mound of a belly. Folding it neatly, she placed it in the drawer next to her Commonplace Book. A hard, clenching cramp gripped her. She bit down and bore it, thinking only, "Oh my darling, when will I ever see you again? Oh Cloud!" and reached for the bell.

He Arrives

Chagrined that it may be yet another false alarm, when Anah woke to the intensely gripping pain that wrested her from her sleep, she determined not to summon the midwives again. As the wave of pain rolled from her body she managed to rise from her bed, needing to pace. "Pacing will help," she thought. Sweeping back the heavy drapes she was thrilled to see a clear, moonlit night with small clouds scudding fiercely through the sky. When the next pang caught her she almost brought the curtain down from from the rod, she gripped it so hard. "Perhaps I should pull that rocker over." As she struggled toward it her waters broke forth, to race across the bare boards of the oak floors. All the rugs were taken up from the rooms of those mothers who were expected to be delivered shortly for just this reason. Much as she wished to be alone with the strong feelings that were surrounding her right now, and pressing in, she knew she had to get to that bell.

Once the bell rang forth the young Irish chambermaid that slept, unbeknownst to Anah on a small pallet outside her door, sprang up, hastily straightened both her garments and deep red curls and set in motion the well-ordered machinery of what was, in essence, a labor and delivery ward. A chain of command began, the culmination, of course, was the child's arrival, hopefully prefaced by the good doctor's. That it was the middle of the night did not bother this crew in the least, and they set about their ordained tasks with good cheer and saucy speculations.

The labor was going smoothly, so smoothly that those in attendance certainly could voice no complaints. That would come later. They thought that they had heard and seen it all. Of course they had been sworn to discretion in order to work here. This woman was well-liked, and certainly undemanding; not like many of the others with their particular wants and requests. As both the night and the labor progressed, their opinions changed. How odd it was that not a whimper escaped her lips. They listened intently for the midwife's comments. No, the labor had not stopped. She was coming along nicely. They began to bicker amongst themselves. "She was full term." "No, she wasn't." "It's breech, a stillborn." "They've given her that new stuff, "flowerform"; it knocked her out." "No, she won't take a drop." "She's dying, or dead!" "But now, oh my! The large windows had to be opened to the chill night air, so that the heavy curtains are now billowing and slapping, it's positively eerie." "No, not the doctor. She demanded that. And yes, the midwife let her!"

"Then there's the birds! They began to arrive, one by one; so silent. Just seven of them, large black ones. Bridget, who was bringing in the hot water, says they're just common field crows. They just sit there in the trees." "I says they are here to snatch the wee babe," the little chambermaid cries out, pulling a well-worn scapula from her chemise. "That woman, in between her pangs that is, says, "Oh, no, they're here for me; they're good." Good she says. They all get more than a bit teetched in the head when delivering. I say go wake up the gardener. He'll shoot them out of the trees for you, Miss, and she gets all frantic, and by then the doctor has arrived and he shoos me out and says The lady says them birds stay. Black, black as that babies hair will be, I bet, and hers as gold as the sunrise! Now Mary Margaret has set to weeping, and they have to send her to the kitchen with the other help. She's no good here, for she's saying that the fine lady is a witch. But it is eerie, not a sound from her as she's laboring, and some of them have got to pacing outside the door themselves. Then Tilly draws aside the heavy drapes and softly summons us to look out, and sure enough there are dozens of them lousy field crows now, heavy in the branches outside her window. Any minute now I expect to see ghosts to come drifting across the lawns. "Ladies," I say, "a few Hail Mary's might be in order." That's when we hear it loud and clear, the babe's cry. Like magic, black magic, I say, them infernal birds rise up as one into the sky and just, poof, disappear like that! The only words from the lady's lips, I think she shouted, "I'm done now, it's finished!" and then babbled away in some strange heathen tongue that she speaks, too."

"I must say we all expected him, (she had insisted it would be a boy, on that she was indeed right) to have cloven hoofs, or at least little nubbins of developing horns, but when I first laid eyes on him he was thrashing his strong, little legs away in a patch of sunlight on the bed without a stitch of clothing on his body, his skin the color of one of

Colonel DuPont's bronzes, and his hair as black as a crow's wing. There was so much of it I couldn't see if it hid any little nubbins or not. I averted my eyes, you can be sure of that, and her just lying there as white as a sheet, with hair the color of golden wheat, just looking so pleased with herself!"

By the time her child was born their was no question of their parting. They were one. It was all she had left of Cloud now. She had worn her part of the Dog Rope wound around her constantly expanding belly under her chemise, and kept the beaded amulet close by, wondering just how she would explain to the midwife how the umbilical cord must not be discarded. That it must be placed in the beaded bag!

She worried it would be a girl child, and thought incessantly of the child she had lost, with vague thoughts that she could not love another as well. She wanted to talk to another woman about this, but feared to violate the others' unspoken privacy, and felt remorse; she wanted most of all Cloud. Then it was upon her. It was time, and she could no longer think, but when she saw the crowning black thatch of hair she practically howled in animalistic joy as the blood-smeared, copper-skinned body slid out. She lay there, as spent as she had ever been in her life, yet quivering with raw pride for having birthed a male child. Vindicated! So this is what it feels like, she thought, as she reached for the beaded amulet tucked beneath her, to hand to the midwife, before she fell to sleep for hours. She woke to the child rooting lustfully at her breast. Richard Stands Free, she named him. Our son!

A Breaking Dam

Carlisle, Pa. 1880

Late fall rain coursed idly down the windowpane, causing her to focus on the convergence of the tracks as they diverted themselves into unforeseen routes that fascinated her. She should have been paying attention to the saucepan of jam bubbling furiously away on the stove. There was the faint sound of it hissing and plopping as it bubbled away. Just then a thunderous, booming rumble shook the earth beneath her feet. Amazingly she found herself mesmerized, wooden spoon clutched in hand, staring down into the concentric circles of the ruby surface of the pot. Quickly removing it from the fire, she undid her apron....

To wake in a cold sweat! She ran to Stands Free's room, frantically checking his forehead, which was cool to the touch, her heart beating wildly. The screened window above his little trundle bed was wide open, letting in the sweet scent of the apple blossoms from the nearby orchard. The calico curtains she had helped the Pawnee girls fashion in Miss Ely's class were luffing slightly in a warm breeze. Utterly confused, she sat down heavily in the cane rocker by his bedside and pulled the old shawl she kept there over her shoulders, to pull herself back into full consciousness.

"That was a dream, wasn't it?" she asked herself. Why had it scared her into full wakefulness? Her child slept peacefully on into the quiet night. Her thoughts turned to Cloud. Where could he be? She let those thoughts slowly gather around her core, then by necessary habit, she tore herself from that worry, for what could such concerns do? Matches, yes, if he were here he would tell me that it was just a dream. The visage of Turn Foot then rose in her mind, bent over a dry clump of withered sage, cutting sign. Isn't that a bit absurd, she thought to herself, superstitious? Wasn't she safely secured here with the boy, a teaching position, a roof over their heads? Soon her head lolled to the side and she slept once more, lulled by the comforting sound of her child's undisturbed sleep.

Later that week, Mrs. Platt, whose surname bore an uncanny

resemblance to her mentors, The Pratts, came by her classroom. This gracious Quaker lady, who had been forty years working with the Pawnees, was now in charge of the dining hall and kitchen here at The Carlisle School. She had faithfully served in the mission field for the Society of Friends as a teacher out on the plains, and was now in service here. Mrs. Platt had developed a special fondness for Anah and her son, and often dropped by to visit them of an evening. "I have brought thee something," and reaching into her voluminous bag, she extracted a small jar of elderberry jam and set it on the table. "It's the last of it. My favorite. I almost burned the batch. Funny thing," as she sat back and began to recount the tale, Anah received a strong premonition that she had heard this story before. "It was late fall, the rains went on unmercifully, and the little bridge across the creek was about to go. So there I was, just staring out the window, mesmerized," At that word, the small hairs on Anah's arms began to rise, "when I should have been tending to my preserves. There's a reason they call it that, preserves, don't you think, my dear? Well, then it all gave away, and before I could escape, the damn burst!"

Providence, was this it? Anah thought of what this little woman now spoke of so easily. Eerie, like her dream of but a few nights ago, Anah thought. She had spoken to no one, and yet here Mrs. Platt was speaking of something so terribly similar to hers, and she knew not what it meant. "Anah, Anah, my dear, I feel thou art troubled." Mrs. Platt had carefully set down her sassafras tea to lean forward and place a thin-skinned, blue-veined hand over hers. "Is it well with your soul?" It was all she could do not to burst into tears; she had no way to explain the upwelling within her. She simply rose to offer more tea, and to rouse Stands Free from his nap.

The child's presence was an expected delight to the old woman. And to Anah; the closest relationship to a grandparent that Stands Free would have while they were in residence at Carlisle. Though Anah's father and his wife knew of the boy's existence, he was treated as an adopted child by them. They had not, in any way, tendered any acceptance towards him, nor did Anah expect any. Stands Free was a beautiful child to look at. His dark eyes gleamed with trust and intelligence, and curiosity in his surroundings was a delight to all that were in his presence. To hear his joyful laughter was to feel blessed. Both women had a tacit understanding that they did not have to refrain from speaking in a native tongue in his presence, either, although the students themselves were forbidden to speak their own languages while at Carlisle. Mrs. Platt had never questioned Anah as to why she was teaching Stands Free Cheyenne. The heart has its own reasons; these women understood that well enough.

The next day in the dining room Anah had the occasion to query Mrs. Platt about her story. She realized that she had not been truly attentive to the telling of it, for some of the similarities to her dream disturbed her, so she hadn't paid the proper attention.

"It was a beaver dam that broke, my dear, just a beaver dam, but the flooding it caused made it untenable for us to stay, and we had to move on!"

Red Thunder Arrives

"Kill the Indian, save the man!"

There had been an inauspicious beginning to the school when the frightened and confused children arrived from their various reservations, to what had been a deserted military base, expecting to be housed and fed, only to find no provisions. No bedding, food, nor clothing had arrived in time from the contracted suppliers. Those Indian children, on their first night away from homes and families, huddled on the bare floor, wrapped in only thin blankets, long braids drawn down over their impassive, guarded faces.

The teaching staff that had been hired had arrived ahead of time, along with many volunteers, eager to participate in Pratt's grand experiment to "kill the Indian and save the man". He had lobbied Washington and those benefactors whose wealth could assist his cause without cease, for them to understand and come to his way of thinking, that by removing the children from their homes and tribal ways, and steep them in the white civilization, would bring about a grand transformation, as it had at Ft. Marion. Thus the Carlisle Indian School was born, and in October of 1879 those first pupils began to arrive from the Spotted Tail and Pine Ridge Agencies.

Within months such transformation occurred: the enrollments had swelled to over 160, comprised of boys and girls from many nations. The boys were dressed smartly in uniforms fashioned from cloth left from the Civil War, girls in Victorian style dress. They all wore hard-soled shoes. Gone was any resemblance to tribal affiliation. They attended classes in reading, writing and arithmetic in the morning, and trades in the afternoon. The boys learned carpentry, tinsmithing and blacksmithing. The girls had domestic training in cooking, sewing, and laundry. Every effort was being made to see that the school had all that was needed to provide a complete education.

Anah, who had never been very sociable, found herself enjoying the few times when her services were requested as a storyteller, as she had earned a favorable reputation as such while at Ft. Marion in St. Augustine. Of course, she could not entertain the students in a native tongue, as that was forbidden to them. She quite frequently recast stories out of *Der Marchen der Bruders Grimm;* she found that the older students especially liked the dark themes that ran through these Germanic tales.

One evening, not long after the evening meal in the dining hall, she was summoned to the infirmary. A young Cheyenne boy had just been brought in from the Spotted Tail agency, and now was the sole occupant of the isolation ward. Miss Soules, one of the nurses, hurried to her side, looking quite distraught. Anguished cries were amplified in a most disturbing way throughout the empty wards. Before Anah could voice any concerns, Miss Soules succinctly addressed them, explaining that though the child was in isolation, she did not believe that he was in any way contagious, but was running a slight fever. Perhaps it was his appendix. In any case the doctor had been summoned from the town, she had been told, but first he had to see to his usual rounds. "And just look at the weather!" as she gestured towards the rain clouds amassed outside, then continued. "We can't get a word out of him!" "He speaks English?" Anah asked her. "No, no, that's why you were summoned," but then she went on telling her that Miss Elly and Lt. Pratt had yet to return from their trip to Philadelphia. "Furthermore, when the barber went to cut his braids, he had to be held down, forcibly restrained, kicking and biting, and had to be removed from the others, and has not ceased that wailing. They summoned me when he refused to eat, and appeared ill. We thought, well, we thought, perhaps you could comfort him, calm him enough, till the doctor arrives, so that he can then be examined." Anah could tell that the nurse was more than anxious to discharge her duties. The tall, uncurtained windows with their wavering glass panes, looked out onto the small graveyard where but a few small headstones poked up like baby's eyeteeth, not a pleasant sight. Anah averted her glance. "His name? Do you know his name?" "It's Thunder, aah, Red? Red Thunder, that's it. Yes, a big name for a small boy!" Anah wanted to tell the nurse that the names were passed down through the families and had great significance apart from physical attributes, but she let it pass. So often lately she had been grieved to see how casually a child's name and identity was stripped from them because a teacher could not pronounce it. True, Cheyenne was hard on the tongue, but French could be also!

Standing quietly at the child's bedside, she could not be sure that he was even aware of her presence, for he was shrouded in the white sheet and sobbing and wailing rhythmically in a way that she recognized as a lament for the dead. How sad, but chances were his appendix was not going to burst. More than likely he was terrorized and bereft at being torn from his home and thrust among what were savages, to him.

Focusing on the potent image of Turn Foot, she began to intone sonorously a simple prayer, one she had often heard him say while she was still in her bedroll, while camped on the tall-grass prairie, traveling to Winter Camp. Soon the boy made an effort and poked his head out from where he had been cocooned, only to grimace in extreme distaste and major disappointment when he saw her pale face next to his bed. "*Wasichu,*" he muttered, betrayal written large over his tear-streaked face.

Anah was prepared for his dismay, and quickly rattled off such a string of his native tongue that he was disarmed. She had been summoned here to give what comfort she could, and offering him his language, which he hadn't heard for days, and was normally forbidden to the students, was what she would do until help arrived.

"They call me The Sweet Grass Woman," she continued without much pause, she did not think more of an introduction was necessary. The storm had descended with moderate force, lashing the branches outside the windows.

"Red Thunder," she began, "when you were barely up to your *tunkashila's* knee, my husband Standing Cloud, was just a young herd boy." Good, she could see she had his attention. Oh my, they really had chopped his hair up; bare patches of his scalp showed through. "It was in the time when blackbirds begin to gather, but the first snowfall was yet to come." The sky continued to darken outside and the wind rattled the loose panes of the near empty ward as she told the tale of

Ghost Buffalo. Just when she hoped that he had drifted off he turned towards her to say, "hurts less."

She left to report to the nurse, who checked his temperature and asked her to stay, if she could, till the doctor arrived. He had been delayed due to the storm.

As the shadows lengthened in the ward, the small white bundle in the bed looked so forlorn, overwhelming her with thoughts of how he must feel to be separated from his family, shorn not only of his hair, clothes, medicine bag, but of his very words, his language.

"Please," came with a slight tug to her skirt, and so she went on with her story, bringing them back to the wintry, high plains of his home, as the spring rains lashed the window panes. " Do you know the story of Mary Standing Soldier?" she now asked him, but he was, at last, asleep. "Good, that's so good, as my voice is almost gone." Before she went to find the nurse she gently tucked a short piece of his crow black hair back from his damp forehead. *"wakan tanka kici un!"*

That night she fell into an exhausted sleep and dreamt that Mary Standing Soldier stood at the edge of a beaver dam, Red Thunder and Stands Free at her side. With a slight smile on her beautiful young face she was beckoning to Anah. The birch, aspen and cottonwood in the dam were starting to shake and tremble as though they might give way with the pent up force behind them. A few rivulets of water were snaking down the front of the bulging dam, and a barely perceptible throbbing beat, like a heart, or was it a far off drum, could be heard.

A. K. BAUMGARD

O'xeve'ho'e, Half-Breed

"Is he yours?"

Visceral, she couldn't really call it that except for that time when the fine hair on her arms rose as Mrs. Platt told the story of her elderberry jam, such similarities to her dream, surely it wasn't about that! Then it came to her, in an intuitive rush, like a flash flood. Of course, the dam, the breaking dam. But that thought left her puzzled, for there was no such danger here, not on these twenty-seven acres that the school inhabited. Just a small pond and a few streams, creeks as they called them here. No dams, and certainly no beavers. She remained baffled. Yet the vision of Mary Standing Soldier, clasping the hands of both Red Thunder and Stands Free, her boy, her own child, would not leave her. Surely an omen, but a warning? Feeling that she could parse no more meaning from these portents, but vowing to be ever alert, careful, and considerate, she put down her boar bristle brush and rose to dress for the day. In the back of her mind, though, the phrase, "life and death were mingled in the spillway of her soul", pressed against her spirit as much as pent up waters against an overburdened dam.

Before leaving the room she caught sight of the penny postcard that had arrived from O-he-wo-toh, Buffalo Meat, one of the Cheyenne prisoners from Ft. Marion who had been repatriated to his agency. He had written her to say that he was planning to bring his children to "the white man's school" here at Carlisle. Holding the frail card in her hand, she did not feel cheered, and that disturbed her.

Was this because of Stands Free? She had to remember to consistently call him Richard among the staff, as the native names were not only discouraged, but simply not tolerated. Increasingly, she found her own inclinations at raising him compromised. Just the other day she had been called from her regular duties to introduce a substitute teacher who had been hired when an arithmetic instructor had been felled suddenly by an attack of appendicitis. The substitute, a Miss Kelly, hailed from Brooklyn. Anah was to spend the day guiding her around, and planned to bring Stands Free along.

Miss Kelly was quite young and attractive, and Stands Free eagerly reached for her hand. "What a sweet child," the young woman replied, grasping his hand easily. "Is he an Apache? Navajo? Delaware?" Anah could tell that this young woman was eager to show that she had studied up a bit on native tribes, but before she could respond Miss Kelly then said easily, "Is he yours?" That query went right to her heart. A question that she had answered many, many times before by saying that she had adopted him while out west, answered it with no hesitation, and received admiring looks for her charity and goodness. But today that question was a flaming arrow. "Yes," she found herself responding, then, noticing the look upon her companion's face, she added, "that is, he's my adopted son." At that Miss Kelly's eyebrows arched up into her lovely face. "He has such lovely skin, rather light, don't you think? Is he what they call a half-breed, or is that half-blood? I do so want to get the terminology right."

Anah could feel the blood rising to her face. How bold, how unmannerly, how intrusive. At that moment they were on the path in front of the woodworking shop and class had just let out. The women had to pause to let the orderly rank and file of the students pass in their neat uniforms. Red Thunder was among them. He made sure to catch Anah's eye, and in doing so he swiftly signed, "Ghost Buffalo", a most welcome shine in his eye. They stood and watched the disciplined line pass away.

"Kill the Indian, save the man!" Miss Kelly exhaled with smug satisfaction. This was more than Anah could bear. "Please, please, do not," Anah said, trying very, very hard to control her displeasure, "use that expression around me, ever again!" Perhaps it was delivered with more than a touch of venom, but quite a bit of color drained from Miss Kelly's robust Irish cheeks. Perhaps she feared for the status of her employ, not knowing exactly who this woman was, who was giving her the tour of the school, but tears now rose to Miss Kelly's eyes. "Oh, Ma'am", a different attitude appeared, one that once served in some household in servitude. " Beg pardon, Ma'am. I didn't mean to offend thee, or those noble savages. Are you a Quaker? I know the Friends have been involved with the school. I was raised in a convent, you see. I'm an orphan, I..." She was close to tears and talking so rapidly, twisting a scrap of hankie in her hands. Anah could see that this young woman had, indeed, spoken out of line. The poor child was beginning to tremble; she feared for her job. Anah reached out to comfort her, though she didn't much feel like it. "Your name, your given name, my dear?" "Emily." "Well Emily, we will have some tea. My name is Anah. I'm not a Quaker, but I will be your friend here. There are over a hundred Indian students here, and you can have them as friends also, if you wish.

Stands Free, who did not understand much of this conversation, nonetheless understood the feelings conveyed, and knew when to extend his hands up between the two women, who willingly held his as they walked along. It did not escape Anah's attention, walking under the large beech trees, as the dappled light struck his hair, that there were gleaming chestnut streaks among the dark brown mat covering his crown, and yes, his skin was several shades lighter than deep copper.

Anah knew that she was going to have to come to terms with her son's true status; how foolish she had been to think otherwise. Of mixed blood, here in this society he would be treated as Indian, but not accepted as one by the full-bloods. Oh, how very naive she had been.

The International Money Order

Crossing to the Administration building, something caught Anah's eye from among the dark glossy leaves of the rhododendron thicket that grew in the rarely used short-cut she had taken. Pushing amongst the stout branches to investigate she discovered, deep in the shady interior, a quiet, almost hallow place. What was disturbing to her was the few scraps of faded cloth hung in the interior, high in the limbs, where it was most unlikely that they would be spotted. These were traditional prayer flags! She touched some with care, then exited, making sure that she hadn't been seen.

Forbidding the practice of the old ways did not cause them to cease; sometimes it produced the opposite. She had been in the girl's dormitory the other evening when a girl from the Brule agency, who had received news that her beloved younger brother had passed from consumption, was having her legs bandaged. Long gashes marked her calves. Crying, she told the nurse that she had fallen into some brambles, but undoubtedly had cut herself, the traditional means of mourning. Anah mulled these things over as she continued on her way.

"But Mr. Arbuckle, surely there is some mistake here," Anah said politely, as she received the very official, extensively stamped, foreign document into her outstretched hand. She had examined it, but briefly, before returning it. "No, no, this has found you at last, though it has been redirected, that is, forwarded, a few times. You must sign for it, though," and with that he reached behind him for a large leather-bound ledger. She did not like this. Immediately thought of her dreams. Opening the ledger, Mr. Arbuckle indicated a place for her signature, and extended the pen, "Here," then flipping a page, "Now here." She hastily scrawled her signature, only too glad to exit. What could this be? Glancing at the lovely stamps as she left, she found a seat on a marble bench outside the building, curiosity having gotten the best of her.

" Schleswig-Holstein, hmm, the office of a Von Houten and Tindel."

She had no more patience and simply ripped it open, disregarding her nails, quickly perused the legal wording it contained and returned to confront Mr. Arbuckle once more.

"What is this? Can you explain this to me? How can this be?" She was much overwrought, he could see that, waving both the letter and some document around but, of course, how could he explain unless she let him examine it? "Mrs. Moore, please, please, may I examine said document? I surely cannot offer my assistance without the possibility of examining it." No sooner had these words left his mouth than Anah became contrite and handed over the entire contents, from which he extracted an interesting document, which caused him to pale considerably. "This," he declared, "Is an International Money Order from a Baron Von Westenhagen, that is, it's from his estate, in your name, for the amount of," here he drew a deep breath and turned the paper toward her, holding both ends rigid, "Pounds Sterling, that is, English pounds!"

They stared at one another as if contemplating what to do next. Then Anah raised her hand for the draft. "Not a word of this." He nodded. "It's a fraud, it must be a fraud, another scheme, since the war, those carpetbaggers. No end to their tricks. It can't be real. Did you see the amount?" "No, no," he immediately responded, "see this watermark?" and he snatched it back from her hand to hold it to the light, at which she pulled his hand back down, looking around as though others might be in the office. "Miss Anah, in '72 the Mail Fraud Act was passed for just such protection as this. This is real, look here." He had gone to look in one of his law books, but turned back to find she was already gone. Things were moving too fast for her now.

Much as she had hated to hear Miss Kelly spout "To save the man, we must kill the Indian," she had heard another slogan of Capt Pratt which was, "To civilize the Indian, get him into civilization, keep him civilized, let him stay." She walked off in a daze, thinking now with this money she could help!

When Anah had a chance to digest her good fortune it came with the bitter sweet realization that her dear friend the Baron Von Westenhagen, Count-One-Two-Three as she had called him so affectionately, was no longer on this good earth. She had never expected to be so generously remembered in his will. How ever did the executors of his estate find her, she wondered? She picked up the letter that had accompanied the bequest to read it carefully once more. As she went to bed that evening her mind naturally drifted back to the wonderful introduction to the western plains that travel with her father and the Baron had provided. The glorious scenes of the Cheyenne summer celebration danced in her head, drum beats pulsed in her blood, and intricate threads that had been woven ceaselessly into her life as she slept began to exert a pull towards the westering sun once again.

Pretty Feet's Deception

Anah had kept up a fairly regular correspondence with Red Dancing Crane Woman since the birth of Stands Free. She also corresponded with Matches. Naturally she was hoping to hear news of Cloud. With the unexpected windfall that the Baron's largesse had brought her, Anah realized that she could be a woman of independent means and was no longer dependent on her employment here. She needed counsel, but had no where to turn. At first she had thought to generously bequeath funds to the school, for The Society of Friends had paid for much of the equipment in use here, right down to the printing press.

An idea was slowly beginning to germinate in her mind, that perhaps she could return to the west, to the high plains, the Powder River country that Cloud loved so well. She could teach the children out there just as well as here, could she not? The idea scared her, and she immediately dispelled it. Well, I'd need a sign. How could I do it on my own? The doubts flew at her like *nacht vogels*, those dark night birds from Grimm. They have missionary schools out there, and the Black Robes have long been among them, too! So she put the funds into an account and dismissed those thoughts, and waited.

There was always an influx of new students pouring into the school from the reservations spread out over the country. They arrived disoriented, confused, travel weary and distraught. They were treated with kindness and consideration; such needs as food and shelter were met, but no one spoke a language that was understood by them. Nothing assuaged the sickness for home. Arriving bone-tired, wrapped in familiar garments, whose patterns and colors signified a tribal affiliation that were soon to be stripped from them, and replaced with dull gray, woolen cloth uniforms and metal buttons. Buttons! Hard, unconforming shoe leather on feet that knew only soft moccasins or the bare earth. Restrictions abounded, not only in tight clothing, but in rules. Conformity. Their identity was so easily taken from them, as easy as removing the colorful and sacred amulet bags from their necks. For the boys long braids were shorn by the resident barber, and the girls had their long, lustrous hair tightly wound and pinned to their scalps. Finally, they were told that their tongues must speak only English, the white-man's tongue. It was what they were sent here to learn. Had not the families given permission? Some had never been in a place with hard wood floors, or glass windows, or to sit on a chair, or walk up stairs, or....the list went on and on.

So here they were in a new land, surrounded by the *wasichus.* They must be brave! The final shock was to discover that the very trees, birds and plants of these new surroundings were strange to them. Anah often found a new student staring up at the open sky, as if in hope something would appear in that space that was familiar to them; seemingly comforted by a cloud, the sun, even the vast blue depth.

Late at night, as she crossed by the dormitories, she sometimes heard soft chants in forbidden tongues. Taking short cuts through little groves she saw incising in the bark on certain trees, or circles of stones in out-of-the-way places, that indicated to her that hidden needs of the heart were being met. She kept this to herself.

She continued in her practice of reading stories, myths and legends the children so liked, resisting telling a tale or two in a native tongue. Occasionally she dared a tale of Rabbit Boy or The Man Who Was Afraid of Nothing, but in English. She hoped none of this would get back to her supervisors. Increasingly, she became lax in guarding her speech, barely noticing when she greeted Red Thunder with *Hau, kola,* hello, friend. He had brought his distant cousin, Pretty Feet, a Brule Sioux girl of eleven years, who had arrived recently after the death of her parents. The girl was rather tall for her age, with dark, haunted looking eyes. Anah was prepared to tell her to take a seat, but then the child began to speak in rapid Lakota. Did she not know about the restriction? Before Anah could chide her, the girl said, "I have a message from Ft. Marion." With her heart in her mouth, thinking it might pertain to Cloud, Anah said not a word, and Pretty Feet continued, "Medicine Water wants you to know that they had a big, very big welcome for him when he arrived home from the prison. A big crowd.

His ankles will forever bear the scars from being ironed. He showed us all. His ankles will bear the scars forever, but his heart will also bear your kindness. That is all." "Wait!" Anah said. Pretty Feet was walking away, then in Lakota Anah repeated, "wait." Pretty Feet turned. "Who is Medicine Water to you?" "He is my uncle." So even though it was against the practice, Anah found herself exchanging small words of greeting surreptitiously with these children to their mutual satisfaction, hoping it would go unnoticed.

Anah was always pleased to hear from Matches, and she was debating seeking his counsel regarding her inheritance. Both he and Cloud had been instrumental in developing her admiration for Sitting Bull, though for different aspects of his character. Matches was doing well with his studies, hoping to take his knowledge of the white-man's medical practice, as he now referred to it, back to the reservations, to combat the ever increasing concerns with the lung sickness and malaria. She knew that he would alert her of any news regarding Cloud. He had sent her something attributed to Sitting Bull that she had copied out and kept pinned above her desk.

"If the Great Spirit had desired me to be a white-man he would have made me so in the first place. He put in your heart certain wishes and plans; in my heart he put other and different desires. Each man is good in the sight of the Great Spirit. It is not necessary that eagles should be crows"

She pondered it. It intrigued her. The Bull was a great statesman; she wished she knew who he had addressed this to and why, and why Matches had sent this to her. Was this another sign? She loved crows! Always had. Eagles! Crows, since she had been a mere child, and eagles? Why, the symbol of the U.S. government is...No, no. And the crows that had arrived at his birth? Well, yes, but... "One more sign, I need one more sign!" Expectant that such would arrive, she slept soundly, but woke dreamless, night after night, baffled.

She could not easily dismiss that the spirit world was speaking to her, trying to get a message through, to break into a realm not controlled by her rational mind. Increasingly her duties and obligations were coming into dire conflict.

Anah picked up her sunbonnet and went to work in the small patch of garden where she was tending some raspberry bushes and rhubarb plants, apart from the school's large plots. By an abandoned tool shed she halted, hearing voices within, low and furtive. She thought she recognized them. She turned and went the way she came, much disturbed. She knew that something was troubling these students for them to be meeting secretly. Red Thunder and Pretty Feet. She was under an obligation to report them. Both would be punished, though not severely.

Arriving back home, she discovered three large steamer trunks on her porch. It was all she could manage to drag them within. They were from Philadelphia. Opening them, she discovered they contained the bulk of her father's treasured Indian artifacts, with a succinct letter from her step-mother stating only that they had purchased a new domicile and, having no longer room, "nor desire", as she stated, for the contents, they were being sent along to her. She went on to add "Your father feels that you might appreciate them. Best, Pollyanna." She did not know whether to weep or shred the letter, but instead drew a soft, pale doeskin garment to herself from the trunk, and sat down on the rug with it, oddly pleased..

"Yes," she thought, so it begins. A vision; was it possible that she had a vision of a little schoolroom, and saw a beautifully painted parfleche and mountain lion quiver adorning well-chinked log walls, a pot-belly stove with a steaming kettle on it?

In the dimly lit recess sat the old scout, Turn Foot, with his beaver wrapped braids, Stands Free nestled on his lap. She scanned the room: boys and girls of mixed ages. She gasped, for there stood Pretty Feet, bent over her desk, correcting papers in English, and yet, tears burned her eyes, this was a vision, was it not? No, no, just her over-active imagination, and then she heard it, the scratching sound; a desperate, frantic, scratching sound, and the call, "Miss Anah, Miss Anah."

The young Brule Sioux girl, now renamed Mary, Mary Pretty

Feet, stood shivering before her, mightily disheveled, her grey dress muddied and torn, her face tear-streaked. Sobbing incoherently in both Lakota and bits of ragged English what sounded like a plea to be hid. Without thinking Anah drew her inside, gently closed the door and drew the curtains fast. The poor child appeared soaked. Whatever had happened to her, each step she took squelched. "Water, that element came to mind, but first I must take care of her, take no thought of my "signs", Anah thought. Pretty Feet, feeling somewhat sheltered, now gave in to a keening, rocking to and fro on the couch where Anah had led her, to hastily throw an afghan over her shoulder while she went to find some dry clothing.

The wailing only increased, but Anah knew instinctively that this was the child's way of comforting herself; that she felt that it was safe to do so here in Anah's presence. When she felt somewhat spent, she would make her some tea and try to find out what had happened. Speaking in her own tongue, which was a great comfort to her, she began to tell not only of all the sorrows that burdened her at Carlisle, but those that had accompanied her here, much like the little foxes that nip at the heels of the wolves at a kill, ever present, ever worrisome. Anah listened patiently; there was naught she could do but listen. Now, Pretty Feet felt, so very, very far from home, one of her last close ties, the only one to help her blind uncle, O-huit-tau, was taken by the lung sickness. She had to go home. He needed her. He needed her eyes, not for her to be an Englisher! They wouldn't let her go home; she tried to run away, she hid in a barrel, but it was wet. Anah couldn't help it, she laughed; a rain barrel. "They save the rain?" Pretty Feet asked in astonishment, "These white man!" To laugh was good! Now they were both laughing.

"My dear," Anah began in Cheyenne, "let me see if I understand why your heart has fallen down." As soon as Anah used this phrase, the girl's face relaxed. "Your uncle, O-huit-tau, who is blind, has lost the only one on the reservation to help him, and you want to go be his eyes now, yes?" Pretty Feet simply threw her arms around Anah's waist and sobbed into her lap.

Ask, Seek, Find

Once Pretty Feet was asleep, Anah left to tell them at the girl's dormitory that she had been found, and to request that she be allowed to spend the night as she was safe, but exhausted, and now sleeping undisturbed. Miss Burgess came for her in the morning, nothing further was said as the girl appeared contrite, just as Anah had instructed her.

Anah folded the bedding and stood looking at the large trunks, only now fully realizing what they contained. The thought again bubbled up in her mind, why did the Indian students have to give up their ways in order to learn to read and and write? She had learned to speak not just Cheyenne, but several other native tongues, and to sign. Many others had done so without going "native". Now, providentially, she had ample funding to open her own small school. She could seek a place, could she not? Well, she had to hurry now, or she would be late for the classes she taught. She was brimming with excitement; she longed to share it.

It was now generally accepted that Pretty Feet was under a special tutelage by Anah. What was not known, and what would certainly not have met with approval if it had been known, was how much they conversed in her native tongue, and spoke of traditional ways. They both missed the High Plains. It was not long before the items in the trunks were being brought out in the privacy of Anah's home, and Pretty Feet, Red Thunder and Stands Free passed many a wonderful evening going through the contents therein. She was gratified and delighted with his interest and, even if it was just a childish pleasure, in the colors and design. The significance of restoring these items to the tribes began to weigh on her; to excite her imagination.

Anah was truly amazed at the extent of Pretty Feet's memory, for she was able to recount the names of up to ten warriors who were killed in 1864, at the Sand Creek Massacre, and their histories. She was not even born then, of course. As a teacher Anah realized the value of oral tradition among the tribes, and was truly amazed. More and more she looked forward to these evenings. She was saddened by the practice here at the school of assigning Christian names to the children, which robbed them of valuable lineage and identity. One boy here, a Cheyenne, O-ne-ah-tah, which translated as Wolf/Mule, named for one lost at Sand Creek, but the teachers found no acceptable equivalent, so he became John One Wolf. And as for Ah-Kah, skunk, a worthy opponent in battle, for all give way in his presence, that boy was simply named Peter Miles. Unfortunate!

Such a simple thing finally determined Anah's move. Mr. Durham, one of the barbers who came regularly to see to the needs of the young men, had most pleasantly volunteered to give young master Richard, as he referred to him, a nice shearing, and he politely pointed out that his "locks" were getting a mite long, he'd just neaten him up a bit! She demurred, begging off, some other time, giving a lame excuse, running her fingers through his hair that was, indeed, down to his collar. As she led him away she realized, like an electric bolt to her brain, that she didn't want his hair cut, ever! "Kill the Indian, my foot,!" she muttered, grabbing his hand rather fiercely and ignoring his protest as she hurried him away. She didn't need another sign. She was leaving. How long would it be before her child would ask her what a half-breed was, What *o'xeve'ho'e* meant? Am I adopted? Who his father was? Where his father was? The full-blooded Indians in residence here couldn't be expected to accept him, now could they? Oh, what had she been thinking?

Within the hour of her momentous decision, Pretty Feet was at her doorstep. "I'm going with you!" she blurted out, and then fled. How did she know? There was no way she could come with her, or could she?

In the ensuing weeks of preparation for departure, the usual channels were breached, citing the need of Pretty Feet's blind uncle, O-huit-tau, Crow, but to no avail. If they made an exception for her, then there would be no end to exceptions being made. Trickster-Changer, Iktomi, Wily Coyote was a tale told across the continent for good reason by the old ones, to rapt children gathered at their knees on many a wintry night, when there were many hours to listen well, and learn.

One night a lean, wan, shivering girl, eyes burning with fever, racked by cough, showed up late at Anah's door, begging entrance. She hardly recognized Pretty Feet as she staggered to the couch. "Where have you been?" The girl was hacking wildly, waving a dirty rag clutched in her hand, a paroxysm threatening to rip her in two. Anah rushed to her side, attempting to steady her, only to be pushed back when, with one last violent cough, Pretty Feet hacked up a huge bloody gob into the rag, only to stand, laughing, laughing, and thrust it open at Anah. "Look! Go ahead, look."

Anah propelled herself backwards, repulsed, whatever had she done to deserve such treatment? "It's not my blood, it's a vole's!" "What?" Anah collapsed in a chair. This was all a bit much for her, but then she knew that somehow she had been tricked by this clever daughter of a high plains medicine man. Clever girl; Good! Good!

She then sat back to enjoy the tale of how Pretty Feet and Red Thunder had been trapping voles and mice, and how the blood was used to simulate the lung sickness. Berry stains utilized for flushed cheeks. Certain herbs could cause the eyes to sparkle, all the symptoms of advanced consumption were so easily fabricated by those who had grown up surrounded by loved ones who had succumbed to this wasting disease; it consumed them and their loved ones. Such a clever girl, she had even arranged to trade desserts with girls in exchange for larger size clothing, to look as though she was, indeed, losing weight. The best treatment, here in this low lying, moist valley was a high, dry altitude. The Northern Plains, just what the doctor ordered!

Anah was once more amazed at the courage of this child, for this was the disease that had decimated her family and recently taken her brother. But could she be a party to this deception? Pretty Feet knew what she was thinking, for she said, "If you do not take me, I shall die here. I'm not an eagle!" The hair rose on Anah's arms. Had she seen Sitting Bull's words posted above her desk? "I will help you." "We will help one another then," and reaching up her sleeve, Pretty Feet withdrew a lustrous black feather and placed it on the desk, then quietly left.

Together they orchestrated a plan. Anah went to Miss Soules, asking to speak to her privately, about her concern regarding a certain student. Divulging those aspects of consumption, but not letting on that she knew of what she spoke, she waited to hear the nurse's assumptions. She then withdrew the bloody rag, which she had wrapped in thick butcher paper. "Do they all spit blood, and cough incessantly? With flushed cheeks?" "Oh dear," answered Miss Soules, very concerned, and wanted this student to come see her immediately. "Oh, I don't think she will. I will try to talk to her, though." They both knew of whom she spoke. "You mustn't breathe a word of this."

The school could certainly not afford to have a contagion spread throughout the girls dormitory, especially when Chief Spotted Tail was due to visit soon. So it was not surprising that Miss Mary Pretty Feet's request to accompany Mrs. Moore out west to her uncle's reservation was soon approved.

Felicitous House

St. Louis 1881, Southern Hotel

Drawing back the hem of her skirt to expose a hint of her quilted "turkey red" petticoat, a parting gift from the Pratt's, and pulling the pale yellow, Chinese embroidered silk shawl, lined in pink over her shoulders, also a gift, Anah took these minutes for sartorial indulgences. Lord knows that where she was heading, the likes of the latest fashions, and the means with which to purchase them would not be hers again! But for now, while the children were still asleep, she would also take a chance to pen this one last correspondence back east.

Pushing her chair back, she gazed off across the mists that rose from the river, where boats were plying incessantly. She found no lasting interest watching and soon lost herself in recall of that very afternoon when it came upon her that she was carrying Cloud's child. Opening her Commonplace Book, she began to write of that time of her deliverance. "The Felicitous House", who could have imagined that such a refuge had even existed!

Stunned and desperate at finding myself pregnant, I had nowhere to turn and no one to go to. In fact, I had been trying to locate Cloud at the various Indian agencies throughout the west, but to no avail. He had been a renegade, deemed a hostile, never registered to a reservation, therefore not required, when released from imprisonment, to return to one. I had also, through Red Crane Woman, been trying to locate Turn Foot, whom I thought might assist me in my search, still hoping to lure him back to the Carlisle School, and myself. Surely now that there was a child coming he would return. All attempts to locate him had been fruitless so far. In fact I had been planning to accompany the Pratts on one of their recruitment tours out to the reservations in hopes of locating him, but now that would not be possible. I needed to stay in one place, not go traveling about, bouncing in a buckboard, as I had heard of Miss Mather's experiences and many discomforts traveling to the reservations. My father? Never! Forbid that thought. I'd be disgraced, even if I did not feel as such. Then a fortuitous event occurred. I'd been invited to a tea here in St. Augustine to increase awareness for the education of the Indian children and the new school up in Carlisle. I was sitting there when suddenly, much to my horror, I had to bolt from the room, to heave the remains of the dainty luncheon into one of the fine linen serviettes. Discretion was observed, of course, but later Mrs. Pratt, who knew of my liaison with Standing Cloud, queried me. What wasn't known was just how deeply involved that liaison had been.

That afternoon in the maid's kitchen, Mrs. Pratt drew me aside. I had gone so many, many years without a mother's love and concern to guide me, but now found myself unburdening my cares and fears to her. Though feeling unimaginable degradation and shame as I spilled out the details of my plight, several names appeared like lighthouses in a storm, and The Felicitous House was one of them.

"Do you remember Miss Harriette Dillaye?" she asked me. I certainly did, for this Quaker woman was most remarkable, dignified, elegant, refined and, one would say, shy. I quickly replied, grateful for a change of subject. "She was the one who said, "I tell my ladies, aim at the moon, and you will hit the steeple, but if you aim at the steeple, you'll hit the ground." Of course I remember her, as she was most enthusiastic about the rights of the Indians here, and interested in the works that you have been doing with them." I replied. Mrs. Pratt went on to tell of how Miss Dillaye and Mary Lucinda Bonney, who ran a ladies seminary in Philadelphia, were advocates of the Indians, but much of what she said washed over my head that night, as all I could think of is that perhaps I would not be driven out into the streets to suffer. I found myself suddenly breaking down into tears, a grown woman, sobbing there on Mrs. Pratt's bosom. I heard comforting snatches, We love you, you'll be cared for, the child can go to the school, can be adopted. You were attacked, yes. "But, that was years ago!" I sobbed. "My dear, we must bend the truth, there is no other way."

Telling Mrs. Pratt had not been as hard as I envisioned. An army base was a small social circle and gossip had laid a firm base already. My good character and sweet, generous disposition to all classes was attested to and opened doors for me, but especially with two ladies who came to my aid. A day trip was made up to Harriet Beecher Stowe's winter home on the St. John's river, in the little town of Mandarin, a pleasant farming community. We went by steamship. Orange and grapefruit groves and lovely oaks festooned with Spanish moss lined the river. While there they spoke of Mary Lucinda Bonney's interests in education for Indians and protection of their lands and wanting to form an association, especially for the native women. It was a lovely visit and through certain connections that powerful women can have, I had these wondrous arrangements fall into place. The Felicitous House, a mansion actually, was on secluded acreage outside Philadelphia, set aside for gentlewomen in difficult circumstances, such as those I now found myself in. They gave excellent care, with discretion provided. Some women left with their newborn. Some did not. Some were visited by husbands, lovers, brothers, or sisters. Some had no visitors at all. The house was well staffed. There were doctors and midwives. It could be arranged to travel into the city accompanied, but not unchaperoned.

Nothing was done to call attention to the house, though. There were a few dogs; they were a comfort. I was surprised to see how very young some of the expectant mothers were. All rooms were private, but you could request a roommate. You could frequently hear weeping. It was not a happy place. One night a gunshot rang out, and heavy footfalls echoed down the halls amid much shouting. The dogs bayed. The heavy wrought iron gates were to be locked ever after that, and one had to ring for entrance.

I had received much counseling, but was adamant on keeping the child, of course. He is my son. I will acknowledge him as such, I calmly said. They could not reason with me as to how I would support him. I know they agreed that I was severely delusional, and as my time approached they thought best not to disturb me, until one day I appraised them of my plan. "I know that the child will be a boy, with dark skin
 and hair. Since I have no intention of giving him away, I will say that I have adopted him. I am an Army widow, with a pension, and I will teach at Capt. Pratt's school in Carlisle. I have made those arrangements."

I remember arriving at a lovely brick colonial mansion, set far back among towering chestnut trees along a branch of the Schuylkill River, with lovely green lawns and well kept paths. When I arrived at the Bryn Mawr station I was met by a solicitous manservant and ushered to a private *room. The place was a philanthropic miracle, the women there of all ages, many free thinkers, who called one another by first names only; some quite young, many surprisingly old. A few of were of color, emancipated slaves, she presumed.*

Cries were sometimes heard in the night. Cries from broken hearts, cries of deliverance, babies being brought into life, or death; a rare stillbirth. The care provided was excellent. Once the babies were born they left, and the mothers, also. This seemed to be the only rule, if there was a rule. No one seemed to be in charge, but the household ran seamlessly. Men were a presence: as groundskeepers, doctors, and undoubtedly, lovers and fathers. They came and went, but none could stay. Midwives were in residence, as were cooks, who were all female. There were no small children; none at all!

The grounds were amply supplied with plantings of colorful flowers. The common rooms were gaily decorated. While there was no attempt to bring the women into any planned gathering at certain times other than meals, there was no discouragement from such. Several benches and gazebos were placed attractively around the grounds, and women could often be seen in solitary thought upon them. Three large Irish wolfhounds of gentle nature roamed the house and grounds, a solace in themselves just to look at.

Anah capped her pen and closed her book, satisfied with what she had written, knowing full well that she had closed another chapter in her life. There was a great satisfaction in knowing that she was once again heading west.

VII

Destiny Manifests

"One must have hope"

Saiciye, The Power of Personal Adornment

1882 St. Louis

A self-styled ethnologist of dubious origins, Mr. Bierman had been holding forth for what seemed like hours on what he referred to as the "Arts of Self Adornment" as practiced by the Plains Indians. Anah held no disagreement with his eye for appreciation of their often exquisite style when faced with such a dearth of materials, but he was getting her dander up at his attributions that it was being done just as a form of grandiose and sheer vanity! In fact, he had attributed nothing spiritual to their practices whatsoever. She wondered if he had given any passing judgment to the vast display of ornate fashion at the table of their hostess!

She was just a dinner guest here, just passing through on her way up north; had no professional affiliations such as he held to bring light to the matter herself, nor did she wish to comment, but the way her foot was beginning to do a small jotter under the table was telling her that she would not tolerate this man's pompous assumptions much longer. Besides, he was wrong, and she felt an obligation to right his allegations. "Whole heads of dried coyotes, skein upon skein of colorful beads, the most fanciful and bizarre..." all heads were turned towards him, their repast practically forgotten, when she interrupted.

"Pardon my rudeness, Mr. Bierman but have you heard of the concept of *Saiciye?* It is the idea held in common by the Nations of the Plains that they adorn themselves appropriately in ceremonial regalia to be in proper relationship to their gods. It is in fact, quite the opposite of how we approach adornment. We adorn "ourselves" to please ourselves or others. They adorn themselves to please their gods."

Before Anah could expostulate further Bierman pushed himself importantly up from his plate, displaying his plump ringed hand upon his ornate gold watch fob. "Poppycock, Mrs. Moore. One just has to have one glimpse at all that fanciful..." But she did not allow him to finish. Coolly staying seated, she exclaimed, "Fanciful? And what do you call the Egret plumes so in fashion these days? Did you know they come from the nests of breeding birds in the Everglades, and that the chicks are then left to starve upon the nest ? How about the top hats of you gentlemen? Beaver, I presume, hard to get these days, decimated by the over trapping of the industry. Those traps are set underwater and drown the animals, leaving the kits, that's the babies, to starve in the lodge." By now Anah was aware that Mrs. Van Houten, her hostess, was giving her horrified looks and that her presence here as a guest would never be accepted again. Anah sped up her delivery, bending down to retrieve her napkin where it had fallen, pushing back her chair to indicate that she would be leaving the table, leaving the assembly, but she wasn't quite finished. "We have indeed proven ourselves the real savages here on this land!" There, she'd delivered the *coup de grace,* if the collective gasp that arose from the dinner guests was any indication, but she wasn't through quite yet. "We have so damaged our relationship with our surroundings. The Indians, those we call "savages", name everything that surrounds them *wakan,* sacred. *Taku, skan skan*, hard to translate, the Everywhere Spirit, like our concept of God, you see!"

The upraised faces reflected incredulity and some, boredom. Aaah! "Heathens, savages? Have any of you given a thought as to where your fine opera gloves come from, that fine leather, unborn calf! Or the caracul lamb coats; that's unborn lamb....not even "those savages" take the unborn for it's fur, Or rip up the earth for gold. Don't get me started on the travesty of "treaties and The Black Hills".

"Oh, please stop!" said Captain Moorehead, as his young fiancee went into a swoon. In a desperate bid to change the direction of Anah's attack, he announced what he thought of as a harmless aside. "Did you all know that Mrs. Moore has a Cheyenne child that she is escorting back north?" Then Nigel Bierman, the erstwhile ethnologist, a bit disconcerted by having lost the focused attention of the dinner party to this upstart, this woman, saw an opportunity, however slim, to redeem his position; to save face. After all, who was she, anyway? He began busily looking for an appropriate entry back into the discussion that would be to his advantage. Meanwhile Mrs. Van Houten, quickly ascertaining that her dinner party was getting out of hand, decided to take the evening into her very practiced hands.

Relying on her best Brahmin accent she turned to Mr. Bierman and literally gave the floor to Anah by saying "I do believe that Mrs. Moore is quite the authority on the Indians, having *actually* lived with them, Nigel, my dear. Moreover, she comes to us from having served as Colonel Richard H. Pratt's personal assistant for the past three years helping with the hostiles taken from the Indian Wars and kept in the dungeons at Ft. Marion in St. Augustine."

Well, now not a demitasse spoon could be heard, all ears were tuned to what was shaping up here. Anah was a bit aghast at how Mrs. Van Houten had come to her defense, but also mollified. Now that all present were informed correctly by their hostess that she now favored this young woman, they were all ears to follow the developments. "So, my dear," their hostess continued, feeling that she had gained proper control once again of her dinner party, " do tell us how you came to adopt the boy. It is a young lad, is it not?"

It was known that this young woman, an officer's widow who had lived with the Indians, and had helped with their schooling, was returning west to start her own school, bringing this Indian child with her. She was eccentric, a known Bluestocking who fraternized with the oddest people, quite liberal, and had lost both her officer husband and their young child under tragic circumstances, which gave her a certain allure. Rumors abounded regarding her and the Pratt family. That she was quite beautiful both helped and hindered her cause in this city. It was known that she was hoping to raise support for her school while here in St. Louis. "Adopted?" An embarrassed silence now gripped the diners, for a most strange look had appeared on Anah's face. She looked quite stricken, taken back, startled, at a loss for words! The servants melted back into the recesses of the room; they understood such dramatic tensions well. It appeared as though the candles on the tables had dimmed perceptibly. Slowly, just as a candle will dim and appear to falter, then flare into a brighter flame, sparks now blazed from Anah's eyes. "Adopted?" She spoke it once more, this time instinctively, catching Nigel Bierman's eye. He sensed something was about to happen to his advantage, at last. He was a born opportunist.

All other eyes were discreetly lowered, an aura of impending shame seemed to be hovering in the wings, for here we were dealing with a widow, and a child whose parentage was perhaps in question. All eyes lowered except for a young serving lad who was simply smitten by his first encounter with a firebrand; awestruck as she began to heat up like a pile of tinder. He saw that spark in her eye when she had said "adopted" the second time, those orange flecks in her eyes glowed in such a fashion that evermore he would search for a girl with such eyes. Whereas the Widow Gallagher had surreptitiously raised her hearing horn, the better to hear the blast of what she assumed would be the vituperative, withering words soon to be aimed at that pompous ass Bierman. Such fun! "Adopted!" and this time Anah turned, beatifically, to the room. Ah, who could resist this woman, unadorned, in Grecian simplicity, sans feathers, furs, jewels; her glorious thick hair all the colors of a ripened wheat field, simply styled upon her finely shaped head, her only adornment the wide Cheyenne armband of worn German silver, and unseen, the remnants of the Dog Rope, wound upon her faithful loins. This unseen badge of honor would give her the courage to stand up to this matronly *doyenne* of St. Louis society, and deliberately offend her and her guests, to honor the man she held dear in her heart! "No," she continued, with just a slight pause. Anah had learned much about oratory from living with some of the greatest orators that ever delivered speeches from their hearts before congress, presidents, generals and their own pipe bearers and shirt wearers, "I did not adopt him!" Making intimate eye contact with all those eager faces now turned to hers, pausing to stare with focused intent at just one, the self-styled expert. "Mr. Bierman, I birthed him," and for added emphasis, as though she needed any, for all eyes were upon her, she moved her lovely, well-formed hands with the sky-blue turquoise ring down to rest upon her well-formed, but slim hips, "from my loins. I am his mother!"

To his great advantage, his diplomatic skills kicked into place, for he assumed, could only assume rape. He half rose to extend a commiserating hand. This exchange was strictly meant for the two of them, as he intended it. Solicitous. He could yet win his audience back, and hopefully, funding for future ethnographic travels, of course. The audience was held spellbound as he muttered, but purposely, loud enough to be overheard, while nodding his head "Those savages!" He reached out his hand for hers solicitously, which was not there. As heads swiveled back and forth, from Anah to Mr. Bierman, confusion reigned, small twitterings rose and fell like gossip birds. Anah most importantly had let Nigel Bierman's hand hang empty! She, too, understood all too well how to work a crowd. Drawing herself a step back from the table, as though preparing to leave, smoothing her skirt on her admirably slim figure, she again commanded her audience. "My husband, and giving a slight, but knowing look to Mrs. Van Houten, whom she knew would repay her social circle in delightful, salacious gossip for years to come, she continued, "I go to join my Cheyenne husband, did I not mention that?"

    Anah sensed that many at the table now were looking at her with new eyes, taking in this new information. Married to one of "them", an Indian. Hmmn! Some women looked aghast, some looked hostile. The men, disgusted or lustful. A few golden strands of her thick, loosely bound hair had come undone in the heat of her passionate exchange. She could feel the men looking here and there at her. No armor would suffice right now. She felt vulnerable, but she would withstand. A feeling rose up in her. Her father, when he was in his cups, quite tipsy, would say "Might as well be hung for a sheep as a lamb!" So she stood there, not knowing how very luminous she looked; defending something with the passion of her ripe womanhood had aroused her. She was an Amazon, an Athena, a warrior maiden. All eyes were still upon her with this new revelation. Especially the men. Some would give anything to avoid her now, at any cost. Some would like to teach her a thing or too, in bed or out, and some would simply like to surround her, make her feel their power, for they thought it not right for her to be so bold and outspoken, but all there would remember her, her flashing eyes, her impassioned speech, and how she defended what she loved. "Savages, those wild men, wild indeed, have many advantages in the marital bed." A gasp rose up from the table. "Those Indians are the finest horsemen ever, and if you think they are adept at riding a horse, well," and she bit her tongue, stifling a giggle. At that she took her exit, noticing only that Mr. Bierman had lowered his head to the table.

Saiciye, Part II

Leaving the stately Greek revival mansion with its glorious Doric columns and stained glass windows behind her, Anah realized that she was likely to never set foot in the likes of such a domicile again. Not that she was uncomfortable in such a setting, she had, after all, been well brought up and educated. Her French was more than passable; her elocution and manners impeccable, but where she was going she would have no use for Limoges soup tureens or the servants to pass them to her!

Knowing that she was now a *persona non grata* among the social elite here gave her enough of a self-righteous head of steam to carry her at a rapid pace down Jefferson Avenue toward lovely Lafayette Park, with its homes and gardens largely unnoticed by her, and into the Soulard area with its modest brick row houses of narrow frontage, to where her lodgings were. A few storefronts in the area were still lit at this hour.

Determined now to cut short her stay and leave at first light, she began to hastily pack. Realizing that she was carelessly grabbing at whatever came to hand, books, garments, brushes; just launching them pell-mell into the trunks with utter disregard of the sleeping children, she came to a sudden stop. "I'm distraught," she thought, raising her hand to her cheek, realized it was wet, "I'm crying my heart out!" Fleeing to the small porch and the relief of the night air, damp and muggy as it felt leaning on the railing, she then began to laugh hysterically. 'Why, if one were to observe me now it would only confirm any, in fact, all, rumors ever attributed to my character," she thought. Removing herself to a nearby wicker rocker, placed there for a guest's enjoyment of the wide expanse of the river, she then rose to fetch a light wrap against the night air, thought to be malarial. Then went to check on the children. Satisfied that both Stands Free, who was deeply content in his slumber, and the Brule Sioux girl Pretty Feet, that she was accompanying back north to her uncle was also sleeping soundly, she retired to the porch.

What an evening! Quite sure now that she had ruined any chances that she had of soliciting support from Mrs. Van Houten and her friends for her school, Anah felt not only discouraged, but humiliated. She had only to glance through the French windows that looked back into the bedroom to see true beauty and innocence in the faces of those children, now her responsibility. How odd, she thought, even though I now have another dearly beloved child of my very own, I carry the loss of Orianna, and like the fabled seventh wave, the one that catches the swimmer unawares and sweeps him away, the sweet, pink-cheeked, dimpled, smiling face of her lost toddler rose up before her, arms outstretched with a yearning look upon her face, tears glistening in her eyes that were as blue as forget-me-nots (she could not turn away) then memory, as that onrush, that onslaught of a monstrous wave brought the tall, erect, handsome form of First Lt. William Byron Moore, in his full dress uniform, brass buttons sparkling as the sun, eyes only for her, only for her, his white gloved hand extended, asking for this dance, Oh, she could not bear it, and buried her face deep in her shawl to give in to horrid, racking sobs.

Yes, she was indeed now crying her heart out, but weeping eventually comes to its own end and when it did, Anah felt oddly refreshed, and remembered a certain day back at the fort in St. Augustine when Matches, dear Matches, had accosted her. Oh, how he had trusted her like no other to advise him on just the precise interpretation of the English language. Her heart gave a sweet, sharp twist; she so hoped that he was doing well, for he was one of the ones who had chosen to stay behind, to follow the White Man's Road, and receive further education, a decision that she never would have guessed when she had first glimpsed the half-starved, gangly Northern Cheyenne warrior with the near unpronounceable name, Chi-i-se-duh, nor would she have been able to predict that he would offer her his friendship.

He had come to her not long after their little group by the fire had had such a good discussion about the pericardium, and one's heart. As he approached he had a very solemn look upon his trusting face, as was often his fashion when seeking knowledge, though he was one of the most fun loving of the younger men, one of the first to try eating oysters, and hunting "water buffalo", as they called the abundant sharks of the bay.

"Mrs. Moore," he addressed her, "our English teacher lady, Miss Kutcher said that she "cried her heart out" when she lost her brother at

Gettysburg. What did she mean?" She explained then that "lost" meant "died". Matches responded, "we say over a sad thing that "Our hearts fell down". This "cry your heart out" is an idiot expression, no?" She couldn't help but laugh. His face perceptively darkened, "No, no, I'm not laughing at you. It's called an idiomatic expression, or an idiom, but what it's called doesn't matter, English is difficult; just go on, please," and she smiled encouragingly, placing a hand on his forearm.

Cheyenne were very prideful, but also very honest. "Well, you said of white man and red man that their hearts are alike," and he paused, awaiting her acknowledgment. Which she gave with a direct and respectful nod, to restore the expected seriousness to his inquiry, and to restore his pride. After all, she had taught him that the only ignorant person is the one who doesn't ask the question, for as soon as the answer is received, one is no longer ignorant. He liked that, but she had just borrowed that from a little book of a Chinese scholar. Now that he had her full and proper attention he proceeded, " How can you cry your heart out through your eyes? Are white men's hearts also in their eyes?"

Anah weighed his question carefully, as carefully as though she were sitting in a circle of elders with a pipe poised in her hands. She studied his face, seeking to know exactly what he was asking her. She knew that he often served as a go-between to the very tall Cheyenne she fancied, though no message of any sort that she could decipher had ever been brought to her. However, they were speaking of the heart, were they not? Hmmn! Was he playing with her? No, she didn't think so. Matches was naive, but anything but simple. He had been brought here as a ringleader.

Warily she guided his hand to her upper chest, well above her collar-bone. Even more warily, he allowed it. She took her other hand, and with two fingers indicated that he look her in the eye directly. He did so. Then with just the tips of his long lean fingers on her chest and looking into one another's eyes she told him, "*kola*, there is no difference, in here, between us," and she then placed her fingertips properly on his chest above his heart, "but there are many, many differences here," and she touched her tongue. Still looking into his dark, glistening eyes, she repeated herself, hoping for the correct words in both Lakota and her limited Cheyenne. Expecting him to laugh at her faulty delivery, she was quite touched when he repeated her words in almost perfect English, made the sign for peace, and wiped the single tear from her cheek with a smiling nod. God, she missed him!

Laughing a bit had done her some good. She couldn't help but wonder just what she was doing heading back west. Here she was at the confluence of the Mississippi and the Missouri. Had it been just over a decade ago, when hundreds of steam driven paddlewheelers plied these waterways and she had been a fresh-faced girl so eager and excited for the adventure of heading west? The sound of a bell tolling the late hour reached her through the rising fog. Stirring her stiffened limbs, she gave a small start as a tiny Saw-Whet owl sprang silently, as they as wont to do, from the railing. In spite of holding no superstitions regarding dire omens of an owl's appearance, she gave an involuntary shudder, finding herself once again hovering on what seemed to be an abyss of amorphous, dark feelings.

Looking to the sky, hoping for some sparkling major constellation there, she found only dull cloud cover, and a heavy one at that, as low as her spirit felt now. Without meaning to she began again a cross-examination of the night's events. The Pratts had so generously provided her an introduction to Mrs. Cornelius Van Houten's circle, ensuring her of their sympathetic stance toward the re-education of the Red Man, the preferred term in their circles. She had been told that as generously as the wine and cordials flowed at their gatherings, so did the contributions from their pockets!

While Anah had amassed enough funds from her modes of inheritance to start her special school, she certainly would need assistance to keep it on it's feet. But now, before she had even collected a small coterie of adherents to what was, admittedly, an unusual methodology, teaching Indians to read and write by using their own culture and history, she had shot herself in the foot, so to speak. She had damn well made a right proper ass of herself in the best circle of St. Louis society! Well done, milady! There was nothing left to do but, as she had heard the boys say in a poker game, "Cut your losses and run!"

Holding back a sob, she thought, "Well, at least the shame was hers, and in no way reflected on the children. Tomorrow was another day." Her Scottish nanny Ethel used to say that in the most dour, downcast way, but tonight she liked the ring of it.

The moon had slunk out briefly from the cloud bank that had obscured it, revealing a few packet steamers docked up and down it's length. By squinting her eyes she could imagine a few bull boats being handled swiftly across its width in the shimmering light. Melancholy, self-pity's cousin, now gripped her as firmly as a vagrant mother cat her lost kitten. Did she even regret what she was leaving behind? Did thoughts that she may never see faces and places again once she crossed these mighty rivers that divide this vast continent disturb her? She was too tired; it was too late. Tomorrow she must finish packing and they must find another passage and head northwest!

Heading Northwest

The sun was barely above the horizon when Anah had the children up, dressed, and in Patience's able care for a few hours while she headed out to find for them the first available decent passage up the Missouri. Patience was perhaps the only good thing that might result from her introduction into Mrs. Van Houten's circle. A lovely young woman of Quaker parentage who had been hired as a governess for an acquaintance of the Van Houten's and had met all the most stringent requirements for the position. Shortly after her arrival in St. Louis from Philadelphia, an unusual problem presented itself. Anah had seen the slim young woman with her young charges, a tow-haired boy of eleven and a red-haired girl around eight, riding tricycles on the elaborate garden paths and noticed nothing amiss. Not given to gossip herself however, it slowly came to Anah's attention what the problem alluded to might be when Mrs Van Houten inquired if perhaps she might be looking for some help with her "wards" as she called Stands Free and Pretty Feet on the long trip up river.

It turned out that Miss Tatum, the governess in question, had a small speech impediment which was quite under her control, however the Van Houten children, ("children being children" Mrs. Van Houten said with an indulgent laugh) had discovered her weak spot. Continuing she added, "My Edvard is quite the bright little devil, gets it from his father, you know. Well, whenever the lad was given a directive by Miss Tatum that he did not want to carry out he simply found that he could goad her, by his disobedience, into a paroxysm of stuttering, poor soul!" And she, to Anah's horror began twittering, a type of suppressed laughter. Poor Miss Tatum, indeed! While Anah had certainly not considered hiring any help, certainly not a governess, servant, or maid, she went away thinking of the young woman, and thought of all she had yet to accomplish. Also a companion might be enjoyable. Besides, all she knew of those of the Quaker persuasion she had high regard for. By that evening she had come up with a plan; the children could teach Miss Tatum to sign, surely that would help with her speech impediment! So the next day Patience joined them as a welcome part of their family.

Now she needed to hurry off to the docks to negotiate a fair price, not only for the supplies, but for the safe passage of the irreplaceable artifacts that she had redeemed from her father's estate, and was now seeking to return to the tribes. Valuable now, both as a gift, and a teaching tool. It was also imperative that a certain amount of secrecy as to the contents of her goods be maintained, as St. Louis and this whole area now abounded with a different sort of fortune seeker from those days when it was voyageurs and mountain men selling their furs, hunters after buffalo, then the gold rush, then the horrible War. Men were after whatever they could lay their hands upon, with whatever means they could manage even after the hides and pelts were long gone. Their very bones gleaned from the face of the earth; ground into fertilizer! Now that the buffalo were most assuredly gone, a new breed arose to exploit the plains, and in new numbers! The magnificent way of life of Horse Warriors, people were hungry for those "artifacts", remnants of that culture. Where once the likes of Prince Maximilian of Wied and the Swiss artist Karl Bodmer came, now people just wanted to simply go to a museum and stare through the glass of a diorama and safely use their imagination, not venture out on an expedition. Large sums were being paid for shields, medicine bundles, war shirts, no matter what their condition, even scalps. She shuddered to think of how they may have been obtained, for she heard it rumored that even the drunks and wastrels were most careful where they lay down to sleep it off these days! Painful to recall how she herself had seen large pyres of such valuables being consigned to flames at Ft. Sill just a few years ago, but then they had been destroyed for a nefarious purpose ; to force the Indians into surrendering.

 Just at Eads Bridge as she paused to watch the steamboats plying the waters, a Mr. Naylor Nesbit of the Peabody Museum, an acquaintance of Mrs. Van Houten's, scurried by, head down, a small bundle wrapped in his arms. She, too, wished not to acknowledge him, but then, social graces being the habit they are, forced Mr. Nesbit to break stride, turn back, and doff his hat to greet her. Having done so, he apparently felt guilty. A bit of a mouse of a man, in fact he looked more like a shrew. Small. Timid, nervous of habit, with pince-nez, that kept sliding down his rather large, but thin nose. He was constantly reaching one spidery, bony finger, quite twisted by arthritis, to push it back up, at which point it only slid back, much to his agitation. His nervousness made him impossible to tolerate for very long, but coupled with his excitability over his imagined greatness of intellect at times made him intolerable. However, at other times he could be quite droll. This morning, as she was in a hurry to obtain passage, but did not wish to have her plans known to Mrs. Van Houten's crowd, she returned his greetings as amiably as possible, hoping against hope not to encourage him in a lengthy spiel of his nonsensical accomplishments.

Shifting his bundle about in his arms quite noticeably, then digging about in his person for his pocket watch, which he finally pulled forth and examined with great satisfaction, then snapped shut, he reminded her so very much of the White Rabbit from Alice In Wonderland. Oh, how she wished he could just pop in some hole and let her get on with her business! Rocking back on his tiny heels, she now noticed that he affected spats. He began to expostulate. He then leaned forward, the better to confide in her, ignoring the morning traffic that was bustling past them. "Mrs. Moore," he now twirled the small bundle, almost thrusting it in her face. "As you may recall, I have been entrusted (she could imagine him puffing out his chest like one of those courting pigeons that twirl themselves in aimless circles, unaware that their intended has wandered off, the ones she had seen down in the square) by the ethnographers at The Peabody to gather such..." Anah lifted her hand; she sensed something unpleasant, just as he sensed that he might lose his captive audience. Rising a bit on his tiptoes, and raising his voice as if to gain importance, he informed her of the contents as he began swiftly unwrapping it. "I have here, in its entirety, the complete skeleton of a ten year old Absaroka child. Complete!" He was wildly gleeful. Anah had seen such expressions on the faces of her father's companions when they had hauled a fine brook trout out after a difficult struggle. She fled!

Walking into their rooms, relieving a composed and smiling Patience of the children, she placed Stands Free down for his nap. Drawing Pretty Feet to her by the shoulder, she just held her hands, but loosely; gently.

There was still not much trust in the child towards her. Anah had been in a boarding school; she understood. It was one of the reasons that she was leaving the East; not just moving west, but leaving the White Man's Road, perhaps never to tread it again. What road she was taking she did not quite know; the road that Pretty Feet's people once walked, that Cloud, Turn Foot, Matches trod no longer existed, but she could not go back east and live in the society as it existed now. The debacle that had occurred at Mrs. Van Houten's last night showed her that.

Time seemed to be standing still for her now, in some strange way, as she stood holding Pretty Feet's hands in hers. Out of the corner of her eye she could see Patience calmly folding freshly laundered clothes into a portmanteau. Stands Free was already asleep, it appeared, and yet her mind was racing across a vast prairie of thought. *Taku skan skan*, the Lakota way of describing what she would call the great mystery of life, she could not understand completely, but it seemed like everything was in constant motion. They had ways of crossing the boundaries between conscious and unconscious experience and thoughts, and to them all life was constantly changing; had power, energy, mystery. Even rocks! That was good enough for her, an incomprehensible something that was bigger than her! Suddenly she realized that she had been thinking all this while holding the girl's hands. How calm and patient she was. What a lovely child.

She began taking the tortoise shell pins and clips from the girl's hair and gently brushing it. What wonderful, thick, raven black hair. Strong too. Orianna's hair had been fine as corn silk, she had loved to wear it in braids, even though it was so silky that it just slid right from the ribbons within a few minutes of play. At school the Indian girls had been taught to keep their hair tightly bound and pinned up in the same confining fashions as their white counterparts, and not to wear it braided, ever. Of course the boys had their hair cut immediately on arrival, feet confined in hard leather shoes with laces that were so difficult to tie. Anah now parted Pretty Feet's hair down the middle and began to braid it. This so alarmed the child that it caused her to exclaim in her native tongue, "Don't!" to which Anah laughingly replied in her excellent Lakota, "My little Pretty Feet, you are going home, you must practice your Lakota." Anah switched back to English, hoping to reassure her, "When you meet your uncle again you will want to be able to show off your English, but you do not," and now she switched back to Lakota, "want his heart to fall down because you have forgotten how to speak the language of your heart. Come, let me finish braiding your lovely hair," and she did. "Now let me tell you of our plans. We will travel up the Big Muddy, the Missouri, on a fire-boat, a steamboat called the "Josephine". Oh, you and Stands Free will have so much fun, and I will, too. Patience will be with us, also. Come now, daughter of the plains, sit here." She patted a place on the rug by the foot of the bed. "Sit here by me," and she began an old tale that Turn Foot had once taught her. The child gazed at her with a look of mingled awe and confusion. Worn out by mid-day, the peaceful weavings of the sounds in the room blended with the rising heat lulled the child to sleep, as well it was meant to.

Upsetting News

Down here on a small fork of the Clearwater, near its confluence with The Snake, he had found a peaceful life. The river was rife with Steelhead and Sockeye salmon. There was a small hot spring nearby, and plentiful game up in the hills. The Bitterroots were to the East, the rolling hills of the Palouse to the west . He could ride up and out onto the Camas Prairie, the traditional gathering place of the Nez Perce, whenever he felt too hemmed in.

Slowly, carefully, he was building a fine herd of Appaloosas; breeding for beauty, strength and endurance. He traded his skills in the nearby towns for the bare necessities that he could not provide otherwise. He had an old brood mare that he'd found out on the prairie; she had that white sclera around her iris and the striped hooves that proved her bloodlines, although not much spotting in her coat. She must have been left behind when Joseph and his band fled the army. But quite a few had been left behind in the Wallowas. Some had escaped or been abandoned. Cloud and his helpers had been busy rounding up what they could and getting word out that he'd provide room and board for those who were able-bodied and willing to help him. He had a buckskin gelding that he rode, and a lamed Appaloosa stallion that he had traded for two mustang pintos he had broken to the saddle from a farmer down in Colfax. Now the old mare was ready to foal again. Yellow Elk had been a boy of less than fifteen winters when he showed up. He came from the big fight, he said, where his grandmother died of cold in the mountains. The Absaroka captured him, but he escaped. Cloud had no reason to doubt his story. The boy was starved looking, but rode into Cloud's camp on a fine spotted mare. Perhaps we can help one another, he thought, as he signed to him to dismount. He pointed to the pot bubbling away on the fire, redolent of stewing elk. It was a good beginning; *mitakuye oyasin*.

"My sister's looking for you," Yellow Elk signed to him from across the corral, where they were working some new mustangs they had brought down from the Camas Prairie. Elk had grown into a fine hand, and put on much needed weight. He paused to nod his assent; she'd know where to find him. Blue Quail came up frequently from the nearby settlements where she worked in the household of a white family, bearing supplies for the camp and, on occasion, mail. She often sought Cloud out, gifting him shyly with camas bulbs, or a small packet of dried sockeye she had pounded with the flavorful but scarce thimbleberries. A handsome girl who sat well on an equally handsome horse, a spotted rump Appaloosa mare so favored by her people.

Here at his camp they were rather isolated, which is how he liked it, but content, he thought. The little herd was growing, and well-managed. It took hard work, but when had life not been hard for him? Looking around at those working the horses, he knew just how hard life had been for them since their Chief's failed outbreak in the summer of '77.

Blue Quail found him locked in reverie, picking at a mare's hoof, and was somewhat affronted when he barely acknowledged her presence. Lately, the more she tried to assert herself, it seemed, the more he withdrew. Finally she just thrust the envelope, ragged from its long journey, at him. "This has come for you!" He was embarrassed for his rudeness and lack of skill at reading the English language, when he spoke it so well. It wasn't like such a missive arrived here every day, and the exchange had already alerted an audience, some of whom were beginning to converge, their curiosity aroused. Blue Quail held her place with the importance conveyed upon her both by being the messenger and by her youth and beauty. Women were a novelty here, and had a mesmerizing effect of importance to all in their immediate vicinity. Cloud was interested regarding the letter, although from its bedraggled appearance, the news it contained had surely lost its immediacy. He wanted nothing other than to shove it into his deepest pocket, make it disappear, and return to the job at hand. He could parse its contents out later, especially since Yellow Elk had wandered over by now, leaving the mustang to buck and snort riotously around the far reaches of the enclosure. Blue Quail held out the letter. He could see now from the markings that it had been sent from Dancing Crane. Elk arrived, more than glad to offer his assistance. Having been taught by missionaries, he loved to exhibit his reading skills! They both looked to him expectantly. At that Cloud quickly took it, meaning to make a quick show of the thing, and be done with it. Handing it over to Yellow Elk, who drew himself up onto the top rail of the nearby corral. He looked to Cloud, who nodded, then slit the seal. Folded inside the letter was a bedraggled, yellowed piece of paper that looked much like a telegram. Holding that separately, he began to read the letter to himself. Cloud said simply, "Elk, read to me!" with such urgency and force that the shy Blue Quail sensed something was amiss, and drew back. As soon as the contents of the brief note divulged that the telegram, most likely once containing an urgent message, had passed through many hands and many places in an effort to find him, Elk paused, looking to Cloud for direction. Blue Quail had melted away, much to Cloud's relief. He again nodded his assent.

As Yellow Elk read the curt, truncated language common to a telegram, Cloud struggled to understand. His people were the masters of pictographs, conveying whole years of a tribes passage upon a buffalo robe in simple drawings. His mind now struggled to take in the terse wording..**Anah**.... as soon as he heard her name his heart soared.. stop -**delivered**- stop- **son**- stop -**Richard**- stop -**Stands**- stop- **Free** -stop,

His mind reeled, this English he did not understand. "Stop?" no, "You stop, Yellow Elk!" Confusion reigned. Elk had stopped. "No, no, keep reading, but why are you saying, stop?" Elk held out the somewhat tattered form, pointing to the much interspersed words. "Go, go on," Cloud practically shouted in a desperate manner. He then began once more. **Carlisle**- "Yes, yes, I know, "stop," now go,"... **School**- stop **Lt Pratt**... At that Cloud snatched the paper from Elk's hands, took but a second to peer at it, then before his eyes the words rose in flames, burned into his brain, singed his heart. Those words, coal black, burnt embers, turning to blackest charcoal, then rising, resurrected, like burning embers do, came dancing through a red mist rising before his eyes; he tried to hold that paper still; it seemed to burn his fingers as he tried to decipher those words, those words:

Carlisle, that school back east she chose over him, Lt. Pratt, his jailer.

His mind no longer worked for him. Something vile rose up from the depths of his gut to blind and confuse him. Anah, the woman he loved, and the lieutenant? A child? Delivered? She's at the Indian School with him!

He crushed the offensive paper, shoving it into his shirt. Tossing the long length of the lariat to the boy next to him, he just stepped away from the corral and made for the stables. Within minutes he mounted his gelding with no explanation given, not that any dared to ask, seeing the look upon his face. Thoughts stung him sharp, fierce and piercing, as though he had stepped upon a downed hornet's nest. How to outrun them? A pounding drummed in his head, a rhythm that the hooves tattooed along the narrow, rocky path to the falls.

He broke into a gallop, trusting his mount's sure-footedness, but the harder he rode, the more insistent the burning accusations rained down upon his head. He found it increasingly hard to breathe, as though the air were growing thick, moist and heated. She's betrayed me. He felt his heart beating, clamoring to break forth from the confines of his chest, needing, no demanding escape. Freedom. Demanding release. Well, he could give it that. Anah, Anah, a white woman. Not like our people, our faithful women. Oh Anah, Oh why, oh why could you not wait, my sweet grass woman, a baby, a boy, no, no, Carlisle, that place, that school. He could hear the pounding of the falls upon the sharp, jagged rocks now, imagined the cooling mist, soon upon his burning face. So easy, so free to just fly off.

How did he hear it over the pounding of the hooves, the thunder of the falls, the turmoil of his soul? He didn't. The wind had picked up, a small but sharp blast drove dust into his face so precisely that he had to dismount and clear his eyes, for how could such a warrior as he stumble to his death. Did it not have to be a leap of grace? He was going to plunge off the cliff edge, but because he couldn't see to do so properly, he reined his mount to clear his vision, and when he did he heard the clear call of the water ouzel, the wren-like bird that walks unafraid, in and out of the fiercest cascade. And then the strangest peace fell upon him, just like that. He sat down at the falls' edge and watched a little grey bird, no bigger than a mountain wren, dip in and out of the frothing torrent. He grew calm as he watched it dive beneath the currents, then resurface to bob and dip on a nearby rock. He spied its moss covered nest tucked close behind a ledge in the fall. Pulled out the rumpled yellow paper, now soaked with sweat. This time the words he saw were "**son**" and "**Stands Free**" and just as he was trying to figure out when their child had been born the wind lifted it from his hand and carried it out onto the roaring cascade. The last words, **-join me,** were swept away, covered in a lacy foam, to be swiftly borne away.

The Chinese Shawl

Ostensibly she had left the cabin to check once more that their belongings were properly secured. Now that they were underway, past the confluence where the two mighty rivers met, and the roustabouts satisfied that they were in the proper channel, most of the passengers had gone to their cabins for the night. Leaning over the railing, she savored the gathering darkness, the mystery of the lights that sparkled the shoreline as they drew steadily along the bluffs. The various sounds, to her, were enchanting, the boatmen marking twain, the "woodhawks" tramping importantly past with their incessant loads of wood to feed the constant hunger of the mighty boilers. All this was exciting to her at the start of what was to be a very long voyage, two to three months in duration at least, heading constantly north by northwest! The excitement she felt, she had no intention of containing.

Oddly free of nostalgia. She had disembarked from this very port, St. Louis, with her father after they had rendezvoused with the Baron, so many years ago. Another lifetime ago, it seemed; she was but a girl then, full of the wonder of an adventure. Now she was filled with a different sense, a passion, a yearning, but banked like the embers of a fire, and the responsibility of young lives that were now entrusted to her.

Somewhere out there, glancing out into the vast swirl of waters, she thought, Cloud is out there. He lived. She knew it. She could not dwell on it, like proud flesh; she could not discuss it with anyone. Too painful. All avenues had been explored. How could she explain to anyone? Perhaps Turn Foot. If he's still alive, well she would find him, or he would find her. The child believed, too. They were his family. She clung to that. She could not let doubt interfere with her purpose. She was strong. He wasn't jailed; he was not rotting away in some jail. He wouldn't let that happen to him again. Not bound, except to one another, and her gaze went up to the inky blackness that had begun to manifest its glory in the gathering darkness above her. Captured her with its beauty; the pinpricks of the stars and constellations so clear that her mind quieted and settled. She found herself simply leaning on the railing, lost in the beauty, the blackness that the night now provided for her to shelter in.

Growing chill, Anah realized that she had been out on the deck for quite some time, content to just gaze into the swiftly moving waters. Thinking back to the enchanted time that she had spent with Cloud in what she called Gullah Land, she idly traced the faint rope burns, now scars, left from being lashed to their make-shift raft. These she would carry upon her wrist throughout her life. She thought of them as a talisman, a memento of their incredible journey through the hurricane seas to the island. "Yes, we are bound together, and not by Hawa, that witch," recalling how she had overheard the women gossiping outside the laundry shed one day, and how she had been able to patch together from the bits of patois the spell that the old woman had tried to place upon them. She failed, Anah thought, we were already bound. *"What no man can put asunder... Oh, God, let that be true. Can I have a sign, just one little sign; I have such a full heart, such empty hands,"* and she felt despair, like a damp, moldy rag coming close to her nose. *No charm, no sage, no way to encourage other than my fervent wishes, no wonder the ancients so loved blood sacrifices,* the thought momentarily crossed her mind, *I'd cheerfully offer up a fat bull or ox right now*, laughing to herself, as two very drunk deck hands quizzically ambled past her. Embarrassed, she pulled her shawl up to her face, reluctant to give up this night, feeling a small rise of ambient power; a twinge, just a twinge of excitement, knowing that this river, this mighty river marked a crossing over, like Moses leaving Egypt. *Oh Anah, aren't you giving yourself such airs! Separating east from west...* And she felt, in her heart, that she would never go back, no matter what was ahead. Her hand went to the German silver armband reflexively.

Like a child she leaned over the railing and spit, satisfied to watch it drop down into the oily blackness of the water. To seal her pledge, she straightened up, loosened her abundant hair, drew it into one long braid, then carefully removed her elegant, embroidered, yellow Chinese silk shawl, lined with pink. It had so delighted her when she had first purchased it on a shopping trip, after delivering Stands Free. She ran the luxurious length of it through her hands, thinking, *"I'm never going east of the Mississippi again!"* leaned over the side and released it.

Caught up in an errant zephyr of a breeze, it rose high and fanned out, as though startled into life. As it settled, like an elegant butterfly, upon the dark billows of the waves, the man above in the Pilot House looked down, mightily intrigued!

At The Captain's Table

"Turn Foot? You know him?" "But of course, a most venerable creature," before he could say more she was out of her seat and impulsively hugging him, knowing instantly that in his judgment of the scout that the Captain had afforded him full measure of his own worth. Before he could get over the shock of being so pleasantly accosted, she was questioning him as to the scout's whereabouts, of which, unfortunately, he did not know at present. She was crestfallen, and while she recovered herself, further adding to the mystery of her person, the Captain knew that any hopes of a liaison with this woman would never come to fruition, for that embrace which she had so swiftly tendered him was strictly avuncular, one reserved for a family friend. Well, good, he thought, good, now we can get on with being friends. And they did just that!

Dinner having been cleared and another round of coffee poured, Captain Grant Marsh offered his hand to Anah, suggesting a stroll around the upper deck. When the Captain had responded so openly to her questions regarding how he had come to the river, they discovered a mutual tie in their backgrounds. As soon as he mentioned having his start as a cabin boy on the Allegheny, she laughingly chimed in a sweet sing-song, "Allegheny, Monongahela and Susquehanna," firmly establishing herself as a child of the Appalachian foothills herself, and not a city girl at all.

He rued the day that the golden era of steamboats upon the Missouri had ended, that was the decade of 1850 to the 60's; the railroads brought an end to that. Then too, he said, the upper reaches are all trapped out of beaver, and the gold rush, thank God, is over. "Well, that is," she said, " till the next one, don't you think? Isn't there always a next one, if not for gold, then some other get-rich-quick-scheme?" He reached into his vest, ostensibly for his pipe fixings, thinking what an astute one she is. Who let her get away? "There's always acolytes willing to kneel at Greed's shiny altar!" she expostulated. "I hadn't pegged you for a mackerel snapper, my dear." It was out of his mouth before he could restrain the crudeness of the expression. Seeming to either take no offense, nor notice, she replied simply, "I was convent schooled, partially, that is," and with a dismissive wave of her hand indicated that she wished him to continue.

"At one time there were as many as forty steamers going between Ft. Benton and the mouth of the Yellowstone alone. I can barely count how many blew up, burst their boilers, sank by striking snags, ice, or caught fire." "Fire?" " Oh, yes, the firemen are to have short working shifts, to keep ever vigilant. I keep mine well paid and well slept for just those reasons. And the wood hawks.." "Wood hawks?" "The lads who chop the fuel, mostly the cottonwood; a lot of competition for that timber. There've been times when we've had to pull up and roust the passengers off in the middle of the night, hand out axes, and order them to chop away, just to keep up the steam." He hesitated to mention attacks by the natives at times when they had run aground.

Anah began to look forward to these evenings once the children were bedded down. This was going to be a long voyage, uneventful in so many ways. Nostalgic too. She kept busy during the days with lessons, helping Pretty Feet and Patience with Lakota, and learning to sign. Pretty Feet in turn was busy instructing Patience in the rudiments of sewing moccasins for them all. But the nights were long. After she left the Captain's table, and she left early, making sure to give no cause for talk, she was often overcome with a certain remorse. Small pox had been brought up this very river to the Mandan, Arikara, Assiniboine, decimating their cultures. The artist George Caitlin preserved them in paintings, as did Karl Bodmer, when he traveled with Prince Maximilian. John James Audubon came up on the steamer *Omega*. So much is gone. She looked out into the darkness on the banks slipping along as though she might see Cloud standing there. Desire and longing can do that to one. Finally worn out with longing, unwarranted, and unrequited, she grew weary enough to retire.

The Drums

Unmistakable but faint, the sound of drums pulsed with insistence that pulled her alert from a dreamless sleep. To her amazement the boy had already struggled from his deep nest of covers to stand at the cabin door, his face now turned to hers, awash in the faint light of the waxing moon, glowing with a strange excitement, his small hand extended toward her, ready to be led out onto the deck. "Oh God, he expects to find his father out there" she thought. "I've groomed him for this, that we've come to seek him; that his father will find us!" She hastily grabbed a shawl and, in consideration of the child's faith and eagerness, they hasted out into the cool night air. A wondrously eerie scene greeted them. *The Josephine* was passing through a large stretch of swamp-like marshes and reeds that lined the banks of a channel kept zealously clean of snags and rills, to guarantee a continuous clear passage. An almost full moon rode shining through the vaporous night airs, illuminating the rising mists as they swirled about the passing boat in undulating skeins and various rope-like thicknesses. Dead cottonwoods stretched their fingers into the sky, upon whose branches large roosting birds of indeterminate species were perched. Far upstream a few pirogues appeared to be aimlessly drifting. Were they occupied? Strange, small lights drifted hither and yon over the marsh. All the while the beat and pulse of the drums sounded, but from where it emanated, she could not tell. The child moved immediately to the railing and seated himself easily into a cross-legged position, staring out into the darkness. Soon he began to sway along to the rhythm of the incessant drums. As she watched him, she knew by his response that he was feeling them, too. She stood transfixed by all this, for while the scene was a spectacle right out of a Gothic novel, it was one which had no such effect of horror upon her soul, but one of a converse effect. One in which the drumming appealed to a natural pulse within her own being, for she found herself relaxing. This was a sound familiar to her from the camps and firesides of the plains. They were entering Indian country, where, at least at night, it seemed to be so! The boat moved, as it should, upriver. The firemen and the roustabouts all worked expediently, while the normal nighttime sounds were muffled by the dampness in the air, creating an all together dream-like quality. She found it enchanting, otherworldly. She could hear someone marking twain and thought, "What a haunting, but lovely sound. I may miss that when I'm off this boat; fancy that!" She had almost forgotten her son when he came to put his head in her lap. She had noted that he, too, had no fear out here; not once did he cower or clutch at her skirts. She realized with a start that he had been awake before her. He had heard the drums first calling out to him. The air was almost luminous now, so filled with faint moonlight and moisture, the hum of the paddle wheel and the drums like a heartbeat bringing them steadily west by northwest, closer to the land Cloud so loved, the land of his people. "Oh Stands Free," she thought, "we are going home. I may not find your father, but I will take you to your people. And Turn Foot, you're alive, I just know it." A long series of yips and howls of the little wolves erupted into the night, as Stands Free laughed in a delighted childish response.

Real Good Coffee
"everything that means home is taken away..."

"My God, woman, you've carried this treasure aboard and managed to keep it secured from thieves!" he expounded merrily, wiping his mustache exorbitantly in pleasure, grinning heartily, lowering his favorite cracked stoneware mug from his lips, but only partway, poised; ready to take another gulp. "This is damn fine! Excuse my French, none of that ersatz stuff, and I've had it all, every matter of ground up root, especially during the war. Wherever, no however did you manage to procure it?" As he paused only to imbibe more, Anah raised her hand, laughing, and leaned over to refill his now drained cup. "My dear Captain, I too have good contacts." Assuming a playful, somewhat supercilious air, he leaned forward and in a teasing manner replied, "Do tell my dear, do tell," and so she did.

She told him how the coffee came right from the docks in New Orleans, along with sugar, and lots of it, knowing how much the Indians value both. He appraised her carefully yet again. She delighted him so; he could never seem to get the full measure of this woman. He lowered his voice in a conspiratorial manner, though at this late hour no one could overhear them, "Whiskey too? Tell me there's not whiskey in the hold," his face growing serious, thinking it to be a dangerous cargo for many reasons. Looking him square in the eye, apparently not offended in the least, and obviously truthful, she simply replied, "No, just coffee and sugar. I plan to run a proper school, and I understand all too well the destructive effects of alcohol. The coffee and sugar are my gifts. They are not for trade. I love these people, you see." He did not, but he was beginning to.

In the first few weeks of the journey these two, the seasoned steamboat captain and the beautiful but strange lady, for this is how the crew, the roustabouts, firemen, and wood hawks saw them, forged the basis of a mutual respect, a respect that during the course of the long voyage up the river became a lifelong friendship.

The Captain, attracted to her, as so many were by her singular beauty and bearing, was not repulsed by her intelligence, or rather by her unwitting habit of engaging in controversial subjects much more appropriate for masculine contemplation, but then she had grown up without a mother. Eavesdropping on her father's affairs is how she developed a taste for engaging in spirited conversations; domestic affairs did not much suit her. The Captain was quite pleased to discover her fine and educated mind and, to be honest, gratified that he was not to be burdened with courtship in any manner. The Captain was married to the River!

Anah was more than curious regarding his concern over her cargo. "I provided a manifest. You just now mentioned contraband. What were your concerns as to my personal belongings?" She delivered this as lightly as she could manage, but was actually concerned. Marsh was equally concerned, especially as he had not quite ascertained her true connections with the tribes to which she was heading. "My dear, I have to be sure that you are not bringing undeclared guns nor ammunition to the reservations." There, he had said it. "But I am quite curious as to why you are bringing drums, and parfleches, war bonnets, peace pipes and the like, old ones; they look authentic, too." "Well they are!" she immediately snapped, then hung her head in an odd state of seeming despair.

Grant was now at odds, not sure at how to proceed. Just what sort of mystery had he uncovered here? Finally she gathered herself up and seemed to speak as from a great distance and in a controlled manner, as though she were speaking of something too intimate or personal to be revealed to another.

Years later, when he thought back on this "Incident of the Crated Artifacts", as he recalled it, he never did quite comprehend it. He just held an image of a lovely, distraught young woman controlling her passions through slightly clenched teeth, tears seated in her green eyes, making them appear like rare Brazilian emeralds. His heart again felt tightly constrained by his age as she spoke, thinking, Oh to be young once again... "Turn backward, turn backward, Oh Time in thy flight, and make me a child again, just for tonight!" He knew so very little about her. Her point of debarkation was St. Louis, the artifacts could have come from, well, anywhere, but where was she taking them, and why?

"Grant, at the Carlisle Indian School," Anah suddenly spoke up, "everything is geared to purge all vestiges of their heritage from the children. ALL! First their clothing, made by their parents, is exchanged, stripped from their bodies. They are then given what the whites wear, unfamiliar and stiff cloth, with buttons. Buttons and holes to fit them through. Soft moccasins are taken off their feet and hard shoe leather forced upon them. Then the final insult, their hair is cut, which, in their culture is a sign of mourning, a death observance. Their language is taken from them, not only can they not speak their native tongue, they are punished if they do, even to one another.

When the men and women, their parents, grandparents, uncles, aunts and cousins, those that survived the massacres, wars, and diseases of the white men arrived at the reservations, when they "surrendered", they had only their weapons and the clothes on their backs. Whatever they had was taken from them and destroyed; their horse herds decimated. Of course, the buffalo were long gone. But the artifacts, as we call them, the war shirts, the bonnets, the drums, the little amulets that their children's umbilical cords are kept in, everything that is familiar is taken away, and, and..." she began to falter in her speech, holding back a sob, it seemed to him.

He could see that her emotions were getting the best of her. He wanted her to stop, but she needed to go on. He understood this, at least. Pouring out a shot of brandy, he pushed it across towards her, which she gulped down unhesitatingly and continued.

"Everything, everything! Elaborately beaded cradle boards, quivers, saddles, buffalo robes with winter counts, irreplaceable items, gone up in smoke. Post after Army post, these goods received the same treatment. Some items were snatched and saved out by greedy scouts as souvenirs, or for trade. A few items, like jewelry, were secreted on one's person, but most went up in flames. So many sacred bundles, gone." He could see that she was confusing episodes of the school with something she must have witnessed.

"So you may ask, how did I come by my artifacts?" Spoken as a challenge, chin up, keeping those sparkling tears, glittering like prisms in those green eyes, so they wouldn't spill. Such pride, though he said not a word, just refilled her glass. "My dear father was an avid collector, began his collection back when we lived in Pennsylvania. That was his impetus for our coming west; the Civil War so disturbed him. He came out to Ft. Laramie as a contract surgeon..." She was winding down, poor child. He could see the young girl who had first arrived here, in love with the ideal of Pocahontas and Leatherstocking tales, only to discover the carnage and reality of the Indian Wars. What could he say?

She held out that shot glass, and began to idly toy with the Cheyenne armband on her thin wrist that he never saw her without, as her lovely blond head sunk slowly down to the table. The Captain took a clean serviette and slid it gently under her cheek. Summoning a cabin boy to let the others know she'd be back to her cabin a bit later on, he withdrew to the Pilot House to gaze out on the moving water.

Some Picnic

Fine weather was upon the prairie, and Anah was determined to take them out for a proper picnic, as *The Josephine* was moored to replenish firewood from the thick stands of cottonwoods that prospered along the banks here. Captain Marsh didn't tie up on those nights when he could keep moving, but the spring run-off had guaranteed a good flow to occasion this stop. Before Anah set off he had insisted that each of the women holster a loaded Army Colt, in spite of Miss Tatum's pacifist conflict that she could in no way fire it. "My dear," he encouraged her, ever so kindly, insisting, as he placed it in her resisting hand, "all I'm asking you to do is carry it upon you person. Concealed, if you must. You do know which end to point, if necessity should occasion, do you not?" "Yes, sir," she managed to stammer, her eyes downcast as she was wont to do in the face of any authority, however slight. Anah wondered if the young woman would ever overcome her shyness and the impediment to her speech, although she had grown quite adept in the use of sign under Pretty Feet's cheerful and patient tutelage.

Puffs of cloud-like cotton bolls drifted high in a tender blue sky. The air, though crisp, was ameliorated by the slight warmth of the returning sun, which it seemed all the surrounding life chose to celebrate in its fashion. Beneath their feet the various grasses were already thrusting up their green shoots, that in a month would obscure a clear vision of the river banks. The tips of the willows were red osiers, and the others bright, chrome yellow. Meadowlarks soared and dipped; small wren-like birds darted to and fro from the protection of the sage they disturbed, releasing an intoxicating, fresh scent.

Spreading out the afghans each had brought from the deck chairs of the steamer, the picnic was laid out, and quite a repast the cook had prepared. Anah had included a few treats for them from her own private stores, some English toffees, horehound drops, and a small tin of biscuits that so intrigued Pretty Feet. Anah had seen that Stands Free would be in the good care of the cook; besides, a fawn had been brought aboard by one of the men when he had taken a deer. The boy was much captivated with the idea of feeding and taming the creature. Captain

Marsh had agreed to let him try. The sound of the woodhawks chopping away, bird calls, the scree of a falcon hunting from the adjacent bluffs, not to mention the effects of a delightful repast and the warm sun had lulled the women into napping, curled upon one another like puppies.

A sharp toe to her hip brought Anah awake. "Well, what do we have here? Three little ladies!" She jerked awake to see, leering above her, a grizzled old man, roughly shod, one hand on the reins of a thin-ribbed mount and the other hooked into his belt, over which hung his paunch. Jumping to her feet, grabbing Patience into an alert wakefulness as well, they both stood shakily before him. Directly behind this aggressive man was a skinny, half-starved, poorly clad youth who didn't seem to have all his wits about him, astride a lop-eared mule, panniers strung with battered equipment. Prospectors? Miners? Vagabonds of some ill-begotten sort! Her mind raced. She immediately knew they were compromised, three women alone out here on the prairie without horses, and that this older man meant them no good. Pretty Feet by now had silently risen beside her. Instinctively, she had her hand to the large, well-sharpened Bowie knife on her hip that her uncle, White Horse, had gifted her with. She was never without it; slept with it beneath her pillow now that they were heading back west. Good girl! Reaching out for her hand, Anah signed to her to tell Patience what to do. The man was looking at the young Sioux girl in a most disgusting manner now, and dropped the reins of his horse, which was most pleased to begin cropping the new grass. Its ribs showed worse than the boy's, who sat statue-like on the mule. "Doesn't he talk?" Anah thought. "Well, I can't just stand here and let this happen!" Then the man grinned, an evil smirk revealing rotten and missing teeth, as he adjusted his pants. She quailed, realizing the intentions that she knew were his from the moment he found them. I can't let this happen to me again. He turned to the boy "Willy, thar's two for me and one for you," beginning to advance on them slowly, knowing they were trapped, thinking they were helpless. "What're missionary ladies doing off the rez, huh?" not really expecting any response as they stood stock still. There was a rifle jutting up from its scabbard on the mule, and he wore a gun on a hip holster, but if his wretched appearance gave any indication, she was the better shot. She was ready; her fingertips grazed the Dog Rope that never left her body.

Then with her heart quaking she stepped boldly forward to challenge him, flinging the shawl back that had covered the holster. "I'm no god damned missionary, you sonuvabitch scum. Draw down!" and she whipped out the walnut handled, well-oiled Army Colt with all the flourish she could muster and aimed it right at his crotch. "Back off, you flea-laden, lice-ridden son-of-a bitch. I'm no lady and I"ll not blow your brains out because I'd rather shoot your goddamn balls off if you don't get on that two-bit nag and get the hell out of here now!" She had remembered to put the safety off and to pull the hammer back. Now, how would this man meet this challenge? Oh God, Grant, I pray you loaded this thing; why hadn't I checked it?

Just then the unmistakable, shrill sound of an eagle bone whistle sounded. Pretty Feet leapt forward toward the boy, brandishing the Bowie knife, a most formidable weapon. The poor lad just hung his head, spurred the mule with a most vicious kick to turn him, a dark stain already beginning to form upon his pant leg. Apparently the rifle was not his to wield, so he trotted off, equipment rattling. The man was still there, to her utter amazement. She then noticed Patience, so calm, holding her Colt steady on, right behind his left ear, with both hands, too. Then she spoke up without a hint of a stammer, "Should I pull the trigger now, Miss Anah? I've already taken the safety off, just like I was taught, and cocked the hammer. I think I would like to pull the trigger now."

Safely back on the boat, they finally managed to laugh. Some picnic, they agreed! How the eagle bone whistle that Pretty Feet had upon her person and had managed to blow that day had so startled the young boy; how the sun's rays had hit her large knife that she had so lovingly honed just that morning made it a terrifying sight. "You may wonder at my most unladylike speech, but I spent many years on an Army post. I heard everything. Cussing may have saved our bacon, as I've heard the old trappers say. And I do know how to shoot."

Anah turned to Patience, who once again had difficulty with her speech, "However did you manage to be so bold, my dear?" "I had no fear," she stammered out, growing quite pale, as though recalling the actual event; standing next to that dirty, smelly, evil-intentioned man, "the Lord was with me," then she fainted dead away. Pretty Feet rushed to her side, pulling her head onto her lap, crooning to her in her language while Anah hurried off for smelling salts.

Captain Grant, receiving the Colts back into his possession again, turned to Anah and cast an appraising eye. "Would you have shot him?" "Without hesitation," she responded, "if I had to. Do you think I could have come to some sort of a gentleman's agreement out there? Said, 'If I allow you to violate us, will you let us live?'" He could tell that she was getting her dander up, so he quickly interjected, "Well, what about the boy? You said he was some sort of a half-wit." "Oh, Grant, I couldn't have shot that poor, half-starved boy. What do you take me for? Neither he nor that ladder-backed mule he was astride had seen a square meal in a month of Sundays. I bet he beat both of them. Why I'd have...." "Brought him back to my boat," he finished for her, laughing, to lighten what had been indeed an ordeal well handled.

By the time she got back to the cabin, Patience was well asleep under the quilts, but Pretty Feet came shyly to her. A spring storm was brewing up over the Big Horn mountains, with ominous rumblings of thunder and slashes of lightning that illuminated their mooring on the river, and the cliffs behind them. "Miss Anah?" She could not get Pretty Feet to just call her by her Christian name. "Yes?"

"That was some picnic!" She turned to head to her own bed, but before she did she remarked "You have good medicine, Miss Anah, and much *woohitika!*" *Woohitika*, what was that? Bravery, no, no, oh yes, courage. Well actually, she thought, more like plain old guts. She turned to go out on the deck, for she loved nothing more than to watch an oncoming storm, when from under the quilts she heard a small laugh, "Some picnic, Miss Anah, some picnic!"

The Old Trappers Cabin

As much as Anah enjoyed this seemingly easy trip up the river, schooling the children and accustoming Patience to her ways, in the evenings, she had to admit, she looked forward to the time with Grant. They had long abandoned the formalities of titles and were on a first name basis. Often, late nights in the Pilot House, a few off duty firemen could also be found quietly occupying a corner, keen to hear one of her "storytales", as they called them. Once they heard her excellent rendition of "the Wendigo", not a tale suitable for a bedtime story. The many years the Captain had plied the vast rivers of the continent, and the many tales he had been privy to gave him an inimitable arsenal, and he outdid himself with one masterful legend after another. The Captain was most surprised to learn that Daniel Boone was a Quaker, but Anah avowed that he was indeed born of a devout Quaker woman. Well, that led to an abundance of stories about the man. It wasn't too long before such tall tales as "The Valley of Headless Men" was parlayed, which led, of course, to a most reticent fireman coming forward after his watch one night, being prodded by his fellows. "G'wan Abe, you tell it, its a good un!" and with the further encouragement of some malt liquor he told the story of "The Headless Horseman of The Mother Lode". But the night she heard "The Great White Stallion of the West" she retired, not to her cabin, but to the upper deck, to watch the storm clouds eat the moon, thinking, "that's my heart, I miss him so. I miss him so!" and she stood until her limbs, brain, and heart grew numb enough for her to shuffle off to a deadened sleep.

When she awoke she knew the time had come to finally get right down to selecting a good place for the school. She had no intention of competing with the Jesuit missions and Catholic schools that had already been established in this vast area. She knew she would need access to good grazing land, for she envisioned horses, and for that she needed water. Marsh had already agreed to bring supplies up river to her as needed. Today they would pour over the maps, and then there were the agencies to consider; she couldn't afford to affront them. "Oh Cloud," she thought, "if only you were here. So very much to consider.

I must avoid battlegrounds, sacred grounds," her head began to swim with the responsibility of it all. Then she thought, "Pretty Feet, perhaps she could help me in some way."

When she found the land she wanted, it was between the Tongue and Powder Rivers, where the Big Horn Mountains bordered the Missouri off to the west and the Black Hills to the east. The area was called the Little Horse Creek Valley, and there stood an old, abandoned trapper's cabin on a small bluff above what was euphemistically called Horse Creek Canyon. It wasn't really much of a canyon at all, but pretty, filled with red willow, cottonwood, and alive with birds dropping down to the creek to drink. There was easy access to a landing on the river. With a small buckboard she could manage. She could not believe her good fortune, for there were several small encampments of northern Cheyenne in this area, an indication that game could be found. She had no idea of how to approach them, or how they would react to her presence here, but she was determined to establish her school. Patience, with her soft-spoken ways, simply walked around smiling, gathering wildflowers, content. A good and godly sign in itself.

Patience Hopes

The slight vermillion stripe on her center part gleamed softly in the sunlight where Patience bent over her beading. Anah, now finished in the classroom for the day, seated herself in the bent cane rocker on the porch and contentedly resumed her mending. Pretty Feet had taken Stands Free into the village to play with the other children. Anah no longer thought of Patience as her companion, or assistant, but as a trusted friend. She noted that, as of late, Patience had taken to wearing her light brown hair in plaits, and that it was quite becoming to her. The red pigment on her pale scalp did not go unnoticed, it was a traditional sign of one who is greatly beloved. Anah sighed, and laid aside Stands Free's shirt. She was eager to ask Patience with whom she had found favor. Was it Wolf Tooth or Strong Right Hand? It was Anah's sincerest hope that this shy young woman would marry. Her gaze wandered out to the meadow, now in full bloom; bear-tongue and paintbrush were scattered amongst the lush greenness. As always, she allowed herself but the briefest moment to dwell on Cloud's return.

"Miss Anah." Oh, could she ever induce Patience to call her by her given name? "You are such a faithful wife; you're certain he will return are you not? I'm sure he will." Just as she was ready to respond, for Patience had dipped her head back to the intricacies of her bead-work, a pair of large men's moccasins, she had noted, Patience continued, "God will see to it!" She did not know how to respond to that. In many ways she wished she held such faith; she certainly had her hopes. In fact, perhaps, that was all she had! Here they were, nestled in this beautiful canyon, well established now. Blessed, as Patience would quietly affirm, attributing it to her God, but it certainly took a lot of negotiating, cooperation, hard work, money, and luck. They had thirteen students now, although that number fluctuated. So many, many factors were involved. Nine northern Cheyenne and two Sioux had been brought from the area near the Standing Rock Reservation, sent by Dancing Crane, and a Kiowa boy from parts unknown. It didn't matter to her where they came from; all were welcome here. The parents or relatives were made welcome, to live nearby and come to the schoolroom itself, to study, to learn, to teach. Some wanted to learn to read, and some to write, also. Both she and Patience wrote letters and translated deeds and documents for the benefit of all. She was learning exactly what *"mitakuye oyasin"*, we are all related, meant, and it both humbled and thrilled her. The giving part, now that she had ample funds, was a delight, but it was with much consternation she found that she did not know how to handle the receiving part. There had been so much work to renovate and prepare the old trapper's cabin for habitation; to build an adequate shelter for the winter for herself, Stands Free, and Patience, and make sure that there would be supplies laid in. All these arrangements kept her busy and, yes, glowing with satisfaction. She arranged to have an extra room added to the small cabin that was being built for her so that Pretty Foot and her blind uncle, O-Huit Tau could live with them. Then certain responses to her largesse appeared: several cords of wood were stacked neatly in a lean-to, enough to last for several months. A small but serviceable hand cart appeared, and on it four stuffed parfleches full of delicious smoked brook trout. Three most precious winter buffalo robes, neatly folded, were found upon the schoolroom floor for their use. Never a day went by that some gift did not appear. She had contracted for ranch-hands to help with the building, but was pleasantly surprised when some of the older Cheyenne men appeared, to tell her that they had learned carpentry skills, and did not wish to be paid. As the months went pleasantly by Anah and Patience were bartering and trading such things as chicken and eggs for game, as Anah was nonetheless uncomfortable accepting something for nothing. She was especially proud of the little orchard she had started with the saplings she had secured with Captain Grant's collusion. He had brought them up the Missouri on *The Josephine.* Grant had also seen that she received a crate of Rhode Island Reds and a pair of Bantams, brought to her by some trappers passing along this route, more than happy to pause here for a good, home-cooked meal. Students brought squirrels and rabbits already dressed out. In the winter months the wood stove had a stew pot bubbling away, with fricassee for the lunch she served up to her students, along with the coffee kept on for the parents. Serendipitous! Nonetheless, her heart, with almost every beat, knew what it missed!

She was no longer thought of as an Army widow, nor spoken to as Mrs. Moore, for Standing Cloud was revered here in this country as the Dog Soldier, a warrior who had stood and fought for his people. She had brought his son back to his land. She had her own battle to fight to see herself as a woman not alone, though. She dared not think of herself as such. She was no Penelope. Did she not have a son, a trusted companion, Pretty Feet, her students, and these people, were they not her people now? Yes, *mitakuye oyasin*. All this she mused on while gazing out into the broad meadow that faced towards the west. She had no regrets at leaving Carlisle, although the Pratts were saddened, and feared that she might never be reunited with Standing Cloud. It was inconceivable to them that he had not been in contact with her.

Since their arrival here she often wondered about Patience's upbringing. She only knew that she was a most devout Quaker. What could have occurred to have separated her from the other like-minded Society of Friends and into Mrs. Van Houten's employ? That of itself was most unusual, surely it could not have been simply due to her speech impediment. Patience never spoke a word of her background though, and answered most inquiries with scripture references that she deemed most applicable. The one most often quoted by her was the apostle Paul's, from the Book of Philippians, and Anah soon learned that whatever unpleasantries had occurred to that young woman, she had no intention whatsoever of repeating that story or dwelling on it! Whatsoever! It sounded like a good policy to Anah. She never saw Patience with a bible; she assumed that she had these scriptures in her heart. Yes, Anah smiled ruefully, imagining Patience as the mother of triplets, named Faith, Hope and Charity! She rose laughing to go indoors.

A.K. BAUMGARD

Mitakuye Oyasin, We are All Related

Spotted Horse Creek Canyon

Lessons were almost over for the day. The afternoon heat was upon them, windows were open, and the door stood ajar to let what little breeze there was enter. The unaccustomed, harsh, jangling sound of spurs upon the wooden floor announced the entrance of a stocky man who dusted his Stetson on his thigh as he strode purposefully toward Anah. His rudeness bore an air of authority!

Anah was not pleased at this interruption, and gave the stranger a steely look, which he returned with a leering, tight smile. By the appearance of his clothing, which was quite trail-worn, he had been traveling long and hard. The few children in today's class had settled right down in curiosity, so that she could clearly hear the stamping, jangling noises of several horses that were outside the classroom. Apparently he wasn't alone. What do they want? Why are they here? Before she had a chance to assess the situation further he sidled up next to her, taking her firmly by the elbow so that she could smell his rankness. Horse thieves? Bank robbers? Outlaws, definitely!

Quietly, he leaned in, "Send those brats home now and be quick about it. My men are posted outside. No funny business." She felt the unmistakable nudge of a pistol in her side. At that he turned to the the rapt audience. "Me and your teach here are going have a private lesson. Go, skedaddle!"

Her mind raced; she was utterly defenseless here. Did he and his men plan to hole up here? Were they being followed? She had no idea. At least the children, the precious children, were to be set free. She turned to Slow Running Fox, one of the older boys, composing her demeanor, to say, "School is dismissed for the day. You may all go to your homes. I will see you tomorrow." She began to give the same instructions in Cheyenne when the man grabbed her wrist painfully, "None of that, speak English," and he snatched at little White Pine's braids as the girl slipped past. It was all Anah could do to calmly respond, "You must let this child go, for her father will be here in an instant if she does not arrive with the others." "Huh," was all he grunted, reluctantly releasing her. "Let me help them with their normal routines. Keep that damn gun on me if you must." At that she boldly spun away to move around the classroom, putting away chalkboards, finding a shawl, moving swiftly until the last child exited the classroom, and went on their way.

As she stood in the doorway, she could feel the gun pointed at her back, and the hovering air of malevolence behind the arrival of the gang, for tied up discreetly outside were several horses. She cursed herself for the first time for the selection of such a site for the school, chosen for it's beauty, nestled deep among the lodge pole pines and aspens. One could hear the creek and look across the wide meadow, beautiful but removed; so isolated from the village. It was not too far for the children to traverse, but who would see these strangers tied up here, and the menace they presented?

"Get back in here, and shut that damn door!" She most reluctantly complied. What choice did she have? Now she would find out what he wanted and expected of her. Seated at her desk, his booted feet were arrogantly up on its surface, the army colt flagrantly lying within his grasp. He had closed the shutters in back and bolted them, she saw with a chill, and was busy now peeling off his sweat-stained gloves. "You saw my men posted outside. We've been riding through the night. We're going to need...."

Thud!.....Thud!.....Thud!.....Thud!....Thud!

"What the hell!" he shouted, leaping to his feet and scrabbling for the Colt, pushing her aside, throwing open the door, which to his utter amazement, and to hers, was studded with five large, fearsomely decorated Cheyenne War Arrows, still quivering!

He looked to her, now secure in his grasp, raised the Colt ready to strike, perhaps to pistol whip her, as though this was her doing, then confusion wiped the fierce scowl from his face as a thought occurred to him. He quickly looked around. "Where are the horses? Where are my damn men?" There were no longer any horses hitched up anywhere. Anah, too, was mystified, but pleasantly. "Oh God," she thought, "please keep a smile from off my lips. I shall remember the look on this man's face forever, Lord, forever. I shall remember it all my life." Just as he tightened his grip on her arm, as though she might provide a hostage, a hair raising, spine-chilling noise that none but a Cheyenne warrior would call a song began issuing from the woods, a War Song.

Out stepped five young men, braves indeed, in various stages of dress, as they had been hastily summoned by Slow Running Fox. Quick to respond to his call they had nonetheless applied dashes of war paint to their faces and persons. Bare chested to be sure, with bows strung and arrows nocked and blood running hot to protect and avenge, for indeed, *mitakuye oyasin,* we are all related.

They stepped forward, a most fearsome sight, and behind them came a more chilling sound, the ululation of some of the mothers, aunts and older sisters of the children who slowly advanced with whatever formidable weapons they could put their hands to at such short notice, to face these hostile strangers. Not a word was said as they drew closer. What was there to say when one's children are at threat?

He re-holstered his gun. Spat on the ground. Mounted his horse. Oh yes, his horse was there; they did not wish him to stay a minute longer than he had to.

After the dust had settled Anah had many questions; not many answers. She never did know who those men were or what they wanted. That they were bad men was all she needed to know. The outcome was that the visit did more good than harm. "Why did you not attack them?" she had asked, and was told that without causing them harm the village would not have to fear any reprisals. She did not have to ask how aid had come to her, because Slow Running Fox was an intuitive child and had immediately sensed danger. They told her "You are family because we are all related," and they laughed at her when she could not contain her sobs. "White women, prairie hens, cry when they are happy, cry when they are sad, cry when they are angry. So strange!"

The Palouse

"In the Spirit of the Horse-catcher"

Cloud lay in his bedroll almost savoring the hard, cold ground beneath him, forcing himself to keep his eyes closed as he awaited daybreak. He could hear his horse quietly grazing on the sparse grass nearby. He had spent the night on top of a solitary granite outcropping that rose over 3,000 ft above the surrounding prairie. As this butte gently swelled unimpeded, stark and dramatic, utterly devoid of trees and human habitation, one could see for hundreds of miles in all directions with nothing to block the view.

He had traveled here before in the company of Lean Deer and Yellow Dog. They had slowly moved north, hunting and fishing the north fork of the Snake. Leisurely camping, they moved out of the coolness of the woods and up out onto the rolling land of the Camas Prairie. The vastness of the land up here reminded him of the high plains of his birth. But this time he came alone!

The day Blue Quail had brought that letter, with the news from back east that he had a son, it seemed almost like being caught up in the throes of an unseen hurricane once more. The very words, as they were being read to him, and the struggle he had to understand, lashed and hurled him around like a storm-driven object: *Richard, delivered, Carlisle, school, Lt. Pratt,!* His mind and heart were buffeted; he could not think clearly. Then he entered briefly what felt just like the eye of the storm, for he heard: *free, join me, stands.* Then something burning began again in his gut, rising up his throat, threatening to destroy. No, he would not believe a lie! They were bound together, were they not? They had a child, she wanted him to join her. He had a son, Stands Free!

Well, that is why he had to leave and come here, away from the others, come out from the pines and his work with the herd and rise up closer to the heavens. Here where the rolling land reminded him of his beloved *Paha Sapha*, he came to pray and plan!

Drawing out his medicine bundle, the one he had made of items he had accrued since his release from Ft. Marion, he spread the contents on the ground beside him. From his vantage point high upon the butte he could see far over the surrounding countryside that so reminded him of his beloved homelands. He had come here to reflect on the stunning news that had arrived on a piece of faded paper, what the *ve'ho'es* call a telegram. A son! Lifting the pale hank of Anah's hair that had been cut from her sleeping form the night he had left St. Augustine, he placed it to his lips and laid it reverently down upon the deerskin cover next to the little western bluebird feathers.

His *hotam'tsit*, dog rope, was still precious to him, but no longer a bittersweet reminder of the warrior he once was. Did she still have the other half in her possession, he wondered?

He had set for himself a journey of remembrance, for now he knew he was soon to embark on another journey in his life, and the Great Mystery had deemed it so, for he was now a father. When he was but nine winters he had sought to prove himself ready to enter the path of a *wicasa wakan*, and sought to capture the eagles. At Sand Creek Silver Spotted Owl left the earth and he, Cottonwood Boy, sought to serve The People by walking The Red Path as a warrior. As Medicine Horse he earned the Dog Rope; he did his utmost, that is, until his picket pin was pulled at Sappa River, and he took the name of Standing Cloud upon himself.

Darkness was settling upon the land surrounding the butte in a magnificent way; the sunset underscoring the layers of the clouds above the western horizon in such harmonious colors that Cloud felt encouraged. He needed this, for as the night approached and the earth cooled around him, his recollections centered on his capture, and the enemies he would face now were not of flesh but of spirit.

Cloud was one of The Bravest of the Brave Dog Soldiers and of a humble demeanor, but to be chained hand and foot brought a new experience: humiliation. For five weeks the irons were upon his body! Scars from sacred ceremonies and war honors were borne with pride, but not the scars left by these irons! As the full darkness fell upon him up on the butte and the wind began to probe, the full sad memories of his time in the Ice House at Ft. Sill returned, and he knew not to fight it. His hand reached toward his medicine bundle, then withdrew. Just as he felt sleep begin to overcome him, he felt an icy weight upon his shoulder; heard a labored breath. His eyes sprang open, Walks Lightly? His stomach knotted in the cruel cramps of deprivation, but how could that be? He had eaten elk steak at the ranch before leaving for the Palouse. The night seemed endless and anything but quiet. He heard the big buffalo guns, the agonized cries of gut shot horses, the pitiful cries of children, then came a long period of silence that seemed oddly agonizing. When the booming of the Howitzers began he sang songs of courage, and, amazingly, heard women ululating. He did not know if he was awake or dreaming, but he saw nothing, for which he was grateful. Then he heard it, an unmistakable noise coming closer, the Iron Monster, with its square prison boxes on its iron rails that divided the plains in two and separated his People and drove the buffalo away. The journey into exile took 24 days, and took him far, far from his homeland. He traveled in chains, eight days by wagon, then by train, steamboat, and once again by wagon, to the fortress by the sea.

Just as Sweet Medicine had prophesied, the white's appetite for the land was huge, no natural barriers had held them back, no treaties or codes restrained them from taking what they wanted. He was their prisoner. Cloud had lived by a warrior's code of honor, and the three years he spent incarcerated at Ft. Marion was quite a revelation to him in so many ways. Within weeks the prisoners were freed from their shackles, given better living conditions and improved lodging. They were allowed to govern and supervise themselves. They were given an opportunity to learn the English language and to earn small amounts of personal income. It was through the humane treatment received in St. Augustine that he was able to realize that not all whites thought of Indians as the enemy. Though he did not hold an idea in his mind of a land called "the United States", there was, for him, a homeland. Anah had come into his life on the whirlwind, as in his first vision up on Bear Butte, and he felt he would soon be joining her once again.

Before the first false light of dawn came he heard a faint sound of drumming, and the fine shrill call of eagle bone whistles, and all too briefly remembered being painted for his first Sun-Gazing Dance. How very strong and bold he felt. Excited and eager, standing there, naked but for the long red loincloth down to his ankles, as the cool stroke of the brush swept across his shoulders, streaking them cobalt. His head had been crowned with a thick wreath of cottonwood leaves. He fought back tears; such ceremonies, he knew, were now forbidden!

As the sky began to slowly lighten with pale pastel streaks, he remembered how it had been, the journey traveling back west from the furthermost realm of the south, St. Augustine. His first taste of freedom. As the elevation rose gradually and the humidity lifted, his skin had felt smooth and dry. It seemed to belong to him once more. He was glad that there was no one that he had to express this thought to, though; how could they understand that! Nonetheless. he was extremely grateful for it. Matches had carefully explained to him that the damp, wet, hot climate was very bad for his people's health, but Cloud privately thought, "and for our spirits, neh!" As he filled his lungs with the clear, dry air it seemed to him that his spirit was lifted up. Weeks passed and his hair grew longer. One day the breeze lifted the hair from his scalp; that, too, felt like freedom. He fashioned a strip of buckskin to wear around his wrist. Tied a small shell he had kept from The Gullah lands, and placed it on a thong around his neck.

He kept making his way, north by northwest. The land he passed was cultivated, inhabited, owned. It wasn't until he crossed back over the big rivers, Missouri and Mississippi, where the sky really opened wide above him, that he felt certain strictures, like scar tissue, soften, relax, and give way, like old moccasin stitches. He had, perhaps naively, thought that he would be able to sit at a council fire once more, and to seek out a holy man, but in his gut he knew what he would find in and around the mandated reservations, for the world he had grown up in, the one he had fought to keep, had been destroyed. He did not know if he could bear to witness the remnants, or observe what it had cost those remaining to survive.

The sun shone bright in his eyes now as he began to line up small bits of quartz, one for each fallen or defeated warrior who had given his all. Roman Nose, and as he did so he briefly gave thanks. Crazy Horse, Sitting Bull; soon there was quite a shining pile. So many had left the good earth and taken the Shining Trail, gone on to the Land of Many Lodges. He idly swept the pile aside, thinking to himself, best to dwell on the living. Little Wolf and Morning Star, would he see them upon his return to eastern Montana, he wondered? Sitting Bull was in Canada. Joseph, well, here I am, raising up some of his fine horses! Soon he found himself sweating profusely. There was no shade up here.

The clear clarion call of a red-tailed hawk cut through the air. He scanned the sky, but did not spot it, then realized that it was a message to look up, and to the future. Ah, yes, and thought of the little bird, the water ouzel that lived at the falls near his ranch. Yes, if not for a speck of dust whirled into his eye that day, he would have, in his head strong way, hurled himself into the falls.

Though Cloud did not know who his mother and father were, he was profoundly aware of his People. Now that he knew that he had a son, he let his thoughts turn in that direction. When the word of the child's birth had finally reached him, in the form of those truncated words on a worn piece of paper, he was at first stunned. He remembered dropping the long braided lariat from his hands, absently passing it off to someone's hand, and exiting the corral. The sun was close to its zenith, sweat poured down his back. He ripped his shirt off, tossed his braids back. Dazed, he crumpled the letter in his hands, hastily shoving it into his pant's pocket, headed out towards the stable and his horse, Blue.

The hot breeze whipped across his face and bare chest until he drew up level to an escarpment and pulled the worn piece of paper out, to carefully discern it once more. A puzzled look had crossed his face. He could only recognize some of the words, and remembered only some of the contents. He realized that he had no idea when the boy had been born, exactly. The name stood out starkly, Richard...Stands Free. Surely she had not named him after the army man who had taken them into captivity? He heard the cicadas begin to buzz loud, then louder still. He remembered a feeling as though the Trickster was beginning to prowl near him. He tried to remember Anah's father's name, but could not. Her dead husband was not named Richard. The cicadas whirred louder yet. Why didn't she let him know of this child coming? Why didn't she come to him? Why didn't she go to Dancing Crane? He recalled now all the bad thoughts that had begun to torment him, to drive him much as one would drive the buffalo to their doom. That word, Carlisle, oh, yes, that very word, well such bitter words had been in their mouths between them. A heat rose upon him, a remembered one; humiliation! It was at that word that he had urged Blue to gallop toward the waterfall, sure that she had been unfaithful! She had named him Stands Free too, spoke a sly grinning Coyote! She will make a little white man of him; she doesn't need you!

And what saved him that day? A speck of dust in his eye, a little bird. The tiny bird that braves the mighty fall of water, that has vision somehow to hunt under the force of it's might.... a little dipper, a wren-like bird. Oh Anah, Ve'keseheso, you are my mighty wren! We are bound together! At that he lay back to rest his head upon a small round rock, which moved! A tortoise! Oh, yes, remembering that Anah's people were linked to the Iroquois, Oneida's, the Turtle Clan, yes, *Mitakuye Oyasin*. We are all related in many, many ways. I doubted her in my weakness, he thought, as undoubtedly she did of me. How could she have come to me? She did not know of my whereabouts.

Cloud was like most Cheyennes in that he could be obstinate and headstrong, but it also meant he could stand firm to follow his goal. He needed many fine horses, appaloosas, roans, palominos, too. Some pintos. A fine breeding herd, brood mares and stallions, with good husky colts. He called on the Spirit of The Horse-catcher; he remembered when he had been gifted with the name Medicine Horse, and was filled with gratitude, for though his days of raiding to build a horse herd were in the past, he knew how to build up a herd by breeding. He would once again excel. He knew how to keep that wily, dark, sly figure from whispering discouragement. His son, his beautiful son, his blood mixed with hers, their blood flowing together like the great rivers flowed together. He would await a summons now. His heart was ready.

He stood. The view was magnificent. Sunlight in clearly delineated spears fell upon the land below that rolled away in undulating humps and hollows that caught innumerable lights and shadows. Each area struck by sun in sharp contrast to the one next to it in deep velvety shade, where all detail was obliterated. The air up here on this vast plateau was so dry that the colors were pure. The sky above seemed an infinite blue. Exhilarating! The values were extreme. A strong breeze moved the clouds rapidly across the land, causing a shifting, ever-changing variety of detail in the colors and pattern of the landscape below. Yet the effect was utterly serene and harmonious.

It was a landscape of endless contrasts, and yet it exuded peace. Cloud lost all sense of time as he stood there and soon felt utterly calm and peaceful.

It was time. He knew now. The herd was large enough. Soon the mountain passes would be open. Lean Deer and Yellow Dog, and perhaps even Blue Quail, would wish to accompany him.

Traveling down the Lewiston Grade, he thought of all he had to do now; the practical aspects of leaving. That night, when he made camp, he thought of the two Nez Perce boys who had managed to escape from the carnage of the battle at Little Big Hole, and how they had made their way back to the Clearwater River. The flight of Chief Joseph, Yellow Wolf, Looking Glass and those that had accompanied him did not end well, though they fought valiantly to reach Grandmother's land in Canada. When Lean Deer and Yellow Dog heard that those Nez Perce who had stayed behind on the reservation and had not tried to escape with the others were nonetheless sent on to Fort Leavenworth, they showed up at Cloud's horse camp. They were just 13 and 16 years old at the time. Cloud was glad to shelter them. He well understood their plight, and in turn their knowledge of breeding Appaloosas was invaluable. Now he could not imagine leaving them behind. Now he would eagerly engage in a different sort of communication with Red Crane Woman and Turn Foot. It was time to begin making those plans for heading back!

A Gift Returned

Today she had chosen to tell her students the story of Dull Knife's heroic flight from Ft. Robinson, an epic journey of over 400 miles. She hoped that this would hold their interest as she explained the complicated use of tenses in the English language. With her back to the class she wrote, "The temperature will drop to freezing. The temperature had dropped," and was poised with the chalk in her hand when a young woman appeared in the open doorway. By all appearances she was an Arapaho, Anah surmised, bemused that she held a large bouquet of lupines in her arms, for the Arapaho are known as The Blue People. Dusting her hands on her skirt, she bade her enter, but the young woman only shyly signed her to step outside, and opened her palm to reveal a red flannel wrapped package.

Once outside the woman handed both the flowers and the small package to her and was swiftly gone with no further utterance, disappearing into the dappled light of the trees. Quickly unwrapping the twine that lightly bound it, she was amazed to see her cameo brooch nestled inside, the very same one she had placed in Turn Foot's hand before she had boarded the train to Ft. Marion years ago. Scanning the horizon, heart palpitating, she stood, expectant, as long as she dared, till the rising noise of the classroom once again became audible. She fully expected the old scout to come forth from the surrounding trees.

By nightfall, with no sign of him, she had become so very fretful that she had to tell Patience. Withdrawing the small red flannel package from her pocket, she knew full-well the consequences that would follow. "Oh, Miss Anah, what have I been telling thee?" Anah sat herself down in a nearby rocker for the duration. "One must have hope," Patience continued in her positive onslaught, but she also allayed her fears that he was deceased, saying that it did not appear to her like a proper way of bequeathing a mere token. At that Anah bridled, "A mere token? Why that was a, a," and she had to fight back angry tears, for she didn't quite know what it represented to her. But Patience had risen and come to her, uncharacteristically suggesting her own opinion outside "The Book". "Perhaps you were hoping to see him again. You wanted him to have a talisman." She then suggested that Anah wear the brooch on her person, and then, of course, to have hope, and faith for things unseen.

Ample light from the full moon allowed the man to satisfy his curiosity fully, as he stood over the large oak desk pushed against the timbered wall of the classroom. A bleached beaver skull used as a paperweight caught his attention, and he marveled at the great design that allowed those large yellow teeth to last a lifetime of gnawing. A fine china cup bore a slight ring of coffee residue. Next to it was a container full of pens decorated with fine quill-work. Idly twirling a red hawk primary that dangled above him by a red cord, he leaned forward to stare at a small daguerreotype in an ornate frame, almost obscured by a pile of braided twists of sweet grass. While he did not believe that one's soul could be captured this way, he thought perhaps a slice of time could. Bringing the frame close to his face, he saw a small, yellow-haired child, a large white bow perched on her curls like a butterfly, her slight, thin form seemingly lost in the puffy billows of her dress, skinny legs emerging to cross at her black booted ankles. Her face was lit with a grin of such satisfaction that he recognized her. Clutched firmly in her arms was a big red hen. He carefully replaced it.

Finding a tin cup from the many stacked at the foot of the stove, he poured himself something from the dregs in the coffeepot, and went out into the night. He stood listening to the soughing of the pines, then fetched his bedroll. The dog followed him inside, to settle down for the night. It had been a long journey, and he was an old man.

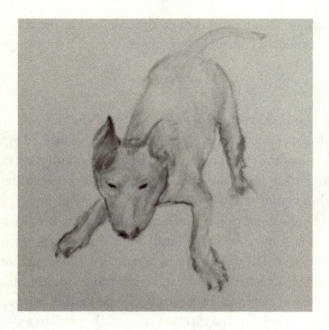

The Old Scout

Turn Foot had always been in an enviable way as a courier, for he had been trusted by both his people and the U.S. military, for whom he had served so many years. To all appearances he was just an old "blanket Indian" plodding along on his lanky mule, but he had not survived all these years without a keen understanding of appearances; how best to use them to his advantage, and how to "cut sign" when needed, to disappear. He traveled openly at will when he wanted to, between many worlds, freely using many languages, offending none, but his external appearance always signaled his age and Northern Cheyenne origin. He frequently availed himself of such conveniences as the telegraph, telegram, mail, and even used the rail to convey himself and messages across the country.

Unbeknownst to Anah, he and Red Dancing Crane Woman had been kept appraised of her doings all these years. While they had not foreseen the events that had drawn Standing Cloud and Anah together, they were quite satisfied that it had been foreseen, and were pleased to welcome Stands Free, in their own way, to the world.

Thus, when Turn Foot determined that it was time to head to the Powder River country, he sent the young Arapaho woman with the lupines and the cameo. This would inform Anah that he would be arriving soon; a nostalgic and symbolic gesture that she would understand. Since she did not speak Arapaho, he assumed that she would get little response from pestering his messenger. He knew that anticipation was the best preparation for his subsequent arrival.

Now that the snow was melting off of the Bitterroots, and the passes to the Nez Perce country would soon open, he could send the most important message of all, the one that would bring Standing Cloud home to his wife and child.

Just as he expected, his reunion with Anah was exceedingly joyful. Vo-ke-cha, White Hat, the densely muscled small dog that he had brought as a gift for Stands Free, raced around yipping in such excitement at their meeting that they could not hear themselves speak, until she bent down and swept the animal into her arms. "Why, she looks like Miss Naughty," then quickly let her down, as she squirmed so. He could tell that Anah was just brim full of questions, as ready to pelt him with them as a heavy cloud full of hail stones. "Sit, child, sit, I have much good news, but first," and he extended an empty coffee mug. With great pleasure he surveyed the classroom where he had slept the night, its walls decorated with a mountain lion quiver, a deerskin shield, a ledger drawing from Ft. Marion, two beautiful parfleches, beaded moccasins. A Blackfoot buckskin beaded shirt with human hair; at that he spoke up. "Anah, where did you," She interrupted him, "My father was a collector. I brought these from my father's home," then easily laughed. Oh my daughter, he thought, Oh Great Spirit, you know how to make choices for us, you know how to ordain our lives. He had to turn his head away. On her desk were the lupines in a China vase. "May I have my Lady pin back now?" he asked. "Only if you teach me how to use a bow and arrow. No, no, that's selfish of me, teach my son. Have you met him? Patience or Pretty Feet will be bringing him into the classroom any minute now."

In the few weeks Turn Foot had been here in the village at Spotted Horse Creek Canyon, he thought how pleased Mahpiya Luta, Red Cloud of the Lakota, would be with the way Anah was schooling the children. Not only was she teaching them to read and write in the manner of the wasichus, but she was seeing that their own traditions and ceremonial ways were being preserved. Red Cloud himself had traveled to Washington to ask, not for money, but for the Black Robes, the Jesuits, to teach his children, but it had yet to be granted. The Carlisle School is not at all what Red Cloud had in mind. Many of the parents who sent their children out east were unhappy, as were the children. When Anah and Turn Foot discussed this she had said that any returning student may come to her village, but they must do so quietly. "I do not want trouble." Turn Foot assured her that she did not need to say more; both of them had seen enough of the "trouble" that could occur when intentions between Indians and whites were misunderstood.

Turn Foot had placed his lodge near the little orchard that she had started from the saplings that had been brought down from the Missouri, at her request, from Captain Marsh. He saw not only a school, but a way of life here, unsupervised by government regulations. There was balance and harmony and a striving towards self-governance. Though the buffalo were gone, game was still plentiful. There were small opportunities available, such as making jam from the incredible harvest of berries that climbed the canyons, and selling them to the tourist lodges that were springing up at the new Yellowstone Park. Young men who became proficient in the English language were making themselves available as hunting and fishing guides. While there was much to miss in the way of horse raiding, there were still celebrations here. Hides were being tanned, moccasins made. Young girls learned beading. None were starving. Fires dotted the night, drums rang out, and yes, courtships began, as ever.

Turn Foot sat with the boy at his knee and began yet another story of Sweet Medicine, feeling the age in his bones, but light in his spirit. Spring was in the air. Mayflies were hatching out on the trout streams. Anah said there would be a picnic tomorrow. Life was good!

A Warrior Returns

As they came down through the Douglas fir and ponderosa of the final pass, and assembled their Appaloosas into a remuda for the night, they saw their first prairie falcon launch itself from the nearby sandstone cliffs. Yellow Elk and the other young Nez Perce, *Hemene*, Wolf, *Peopeo*, Bird, and *Kiyiyah*, Howling Wolf quickly set about preparing their final camp before arriving at Anah's village.

Blue Quail, Elk's younger sister, led her Appaloosa mare over to the nearby stream, its foal following closely. She called out to Cloud in a teasing fashion as she passed, "Would you like me to hobble you for the night?" "Hobble me?" he replied, incomprehension on his face. "Yes, I think you might just drift away otherwise. Tomorrow is the grand encounter, is it not?" When the meaning of her teasing dawned on him, he reached for something to lob at her, but she had already darted away. Matches would like such a one. Ho, in fact, Matches would deserve such a one, Cloud thought, as he turned back to the task which he had set to occupy his mind.

With his fine herd of brood mares and studs and the young Nez Perce people that were now his friends, he felt that his return to the land of his birth would be done with honor, his head held high; a Cut Finger, a true Northern Cheyenne. Laughing to himself, he did indeed feel a need for a tether, so light was his spirit within him. As he stood running his long tapered hands over Running Wind's spotted flanks, he was unaware of the wondrous change that time had wrought in his appearance, for he was as matching in beauty as the mounts that he had chosen for Anah and his son.

Come first light, just as the mists were burning off, found him giving thanks to his creator. Mountain bluebirds flew from bush to bush as the cold water from the stream dried on his body. He began to adorn himself in the traditional fashion of a Northern Cheyenne Dog Soldier, stripped down to a long red breechcloth. His muscles well-developed from his labors, his hair braided and glistening with oil, he began to paint his face carefully with the use of a hand mirror. He knew how to use *saiciye,* the power of personal adornment well.

The mare he had selected and trained for Anah bore one of the beautiful saddles the Nez Perce were famous for, and its saddle blanket had long flowing fringes. Her colt was trained especially for his son, Stands Free. Blue Quail had personally supervised the making of the doe-skin dress that would be draped over the haunches of the mare. Of course, the yoke of the dress was laden with elk teeth. He was mulling all this over when he heard the unmistakable call of a mustang from the ledge high above him.

Silhouetted there was a stallion, rearing up. Not too unusual, since he was driving a herd with more than a few fine mares in it. He was stunned though, for as the light shifted he stared in disbelief, for this was no ordinary horse. There was no denying its unusual markings. It was *wakan,* a rare Medicine Hat Stallion. So very rare, many men had never seen one in their lifetimes. In fact they were hard to describe. This one was mainly white, with a large, shield-like blotch on his chest the color of dried blood, a dark cloud on its head, and one eye that was an amazing blue. The wasichus called them Spanish Mustangs, but those with such markings on their heads were called Medicine Hat. That they were special was agreed. Big medicine, great power to keep its owner safe in battle, even protect you from dying, it was said. Man and horse looked at one another in a moment frozen in time. Then a thought occurred to the man, capture it!

Run back to camp, alert the others, it would only add to his prestige upon his arrival.

Then a darkness winged swiftly down across his heart. "A restriction, a check", those were white-men's words that Anah had taught him when they had been discussing intuition one day, shortly after leaving the Sea Isles, upon their return to Ft. Marion. Medicine words, he recognized them as such. He wanted that beautiful creature so badly. He would give an oath that it had not moved one muscle in its flank. Was it spirit, perhaps? They had not broken their gaze. He rubbed his ankles and wrists, recalling the shackles that had once been placed on his freedom.

"Go," he mouthed, and the beautiful creature thundered off, as

MY HEART GROWS WIDE WITHIN ME

if on Cloud's command, though he would swear he did not give the command utterance.

To be "ironed", in a leg-chained, shuffling gait causes one to stumble, every awkward step a restriction, a painful reminder accompanied by its own clanking, discordant noise, that your freedom has been captured. Chains are there to subdue the prisoner bodily, but they do so much more: they are a violation. They bring shame! Their real weight falls upon the spirit. When Standing Cloud saw the Medicine Horse atop the butte, his first impulse was to capture it, for he could imagine himself astride it, riding in to claim his woman, his herd of Appaloosas churning up the dust behind him. Yet when he looked into the stallion's eye he realized how wrong that notion was! As he walked slowly back to the others in his simple but fine regalia, two eagles sailed out into the open expanse of the blue sky above him, beginning to ride the dihedrals that were now forming as the earth warmed. Yes, as a young boy, when he thought to trod a very different path, he once vowed to never take freedom from another. He watched the two circle slowly upwards above his head, his feet light upon the earth.

A.K. BAUMGARD

The Dog Soldier and The Lady In Green

Spotted Horse Canyon School

This is the first chance I've had in days, since Turn Foot's arrival in Ft. Benton, and I fear that if I don't write now I may be so caught up in coming events that this book will sit on some shelf for an eternity. Now that Turn Foot is here, my heart is at rest as to Cloud's whereabouts. Oh, foolish woman that I am, how can I say that? I am anything but at peace. My excitement grows by the day, the hour, the minute. A contagious feeling I'm sure, for though I've conveyed none of what I know of his impending arrival to Stands Free, I find him sensing his father's return. I find him staring off towards the western passes with an expectant look upon his face each evening, as though he senses that is the direction in which his father will appear.

Though I had not seen my old friend since leaving for Ft. Marion, we greeted one another as though it had been just yesterday. He seemed to know all the details of my relationship to Standing Cloud. When he met Stands Free for the first time he simply smiled and turned to me saying, "It is very good!" an accolade of the highest regard. Those two are seldom seen one without the other these days, which is greatly pleasing to me. Of course, not wanting to brag about all that has been accomplished here at the school, not just by my efforts alone, I have had him shown around by my students and others who have been an integral part of the progress of this community.

The day after this entry we will head up into the mountains to enjoy a high country picnic. As much as I once regretted that I had no brother to guide me in certain refinements when I was growing up as a woman, I will now have a chance to learn, at Turn Foot's hand, of fly-fishing. I am not without hope of bringing some of the fine-fleshed

Turn Foot seems to be pleased with the ways in which we have respected all that Chief Red Cloud had asked of us. He knows, and understands why The Carlisle School fell short of his expectations. Together Turn Foot and I have dreamed up a special winter project. We're calling it "The Leaves Falling Story Catcher Project". Once every tribe kept a winter count upon a buffalo robe to record it's history. Now both those robes and the men who kept them are as rare as a white buffalo. We intend to preserve what history, legends, stories and myths are collectively held by the people of this small village. This will be done by translating it into English, recording it into ledger books, then sealing these books away into the ammunition cans that are surplus from the U.S. Government. I have made arrangements for these supplies with Captain Marsh. We have a genuine Storycatcher, Na-ko-yo-sus, Wounded Bear, living here. There are also quite a few who have survived many battles. The students, who are growing daily in their command of English, can translate and record. We even have a few talented artists to illustrate for us. It's necessary, for now, that we hide these accounts away for safe keeping, as the Indians that were at the Greasy Grass fear reprisal. Pretty Feet's uncle, Crow, is especially excited about this. Turn Foot teases me, saying we must be sure to include the legend of "The Dog Soldier and the Lady in Green". Am I to be part of this history? It was only then that I remembered the legend from Ft. Laramie about a ghost that supposedly appeared on nights of the full moon, and could be seen haunting the area. She was called The Lady In Green, for on the night she disappeared, she rode out dressed in a dark green velveteen riding habit, never to be seen again. She had been the headstrong daughter of an American Fur Agent. Many men, even the officers, claimed to have seen her ghost! A lean Cheyenne scout had been appointed by Lt. Moore to escort me every time I left the post because of this legend. When Turn Foot appeared for the first time, I bridled. He had on a worn serge uniform blouse open to the waist, with a sharp-shooters medal pinned to his thin shoulders, an immaculate, long red breech cloth, silver beaver-wrapped braids and deep black eyes. I don't believe in ghosts, I told him. An escort is unnecessary. But your husband does, he told me, and sat down on the porch, withdrew his pipe bag, and settled in to wait. I could tell that if I wanted to go on visiting the Indian camps that lay beyond Deer Creek, I would have to be escorted. Of course, being headstrong, I did not change out of my green riding habit that day!

How fate weaves our lives together.

"Momma, Momma." Stands Free, a loving projectile running into her skirts, had arrived to tell her the horses were saddled and they were ready to leave for their picnic.

My Heart Grows Wide Within Me

When she rose this morning it was to don the new calico dress; serenely unfazed at knowing that today was the day, she just knew. She edged the piece of foolscap that had born the painfully executed example of his penmanship from her Commonplace Book, N*ESTAVAHOSEVOOMATSE*. "Soon," she muttered, and pressed it to her lips.

An expectant air filled the classroom upon her arrival there. All eyes carefully, secretly scrutinized her. Of course, the whole village was anxiously awaiting Cloud's return. He belonged to them also, as she did by now. She maintained as much decorum as she could manage, but her eyes never left the visage the open door presented of the far meadow. It did not go unnoticed that she had on a new calico dress today, or that when Bear Paw presented his ledger book to her for correction she was holding it upside down. Just when Mo-ke-kah had been persuaded to ask her for an early dismissal, since the whole village was eager to celebrate, she turned abruptly from him. The unmistakable clear call of an eagle bone whistle had reached Anah's ears, and brought her swiftly out the classroom door.

The scene that opened before her eyes was like a stage setting; the meadow lushly green, the sky cerulean blue. She scanned the far horizon, her heart near to bursting with expectation, so much so that it wasn't until her hands touched the reins loosely knotted on the railing that she looked down. Tethered there was a magnificent Appaloosa mare, replete with the gorgeous trappings the Nez Perce were so famous for. Thrown over the haunches was an exquisite garment, its yoke festooned with many elk teeth. Next to the mare was a lovely colt. All was preternaturally quiet.

Her eyes flew once again to the broad open expanse of the meadow. Nothing was there. She again scanned the far horizon. All was still. By this time her students had poured out to crowd around expectantly. Turn Foot appeared quietly at her side, lifting Stands Free high, to gain a better vantage point. All were assembled, watching. Dragonflies skimmed the expanse, though not a bee buzzed.

Then the call came once again, and the hairs on her arm rose . That shrill clarion call of an eagle bone whistle, she felt, called only to her. By now all had exited the classroom, tumbling and shoving their way out, spilling down the steps. She might as well have been on some isolated Widow"s Walk on the Newfoundland coast, spyglass in her hand, searching out a Whaler's return through a heavy gale, so piercing and focused was her gaze, so intent was she for the first far off speck to materialize, till it became a rising plume of dust racing in her direction.

There, that speck began to grow. Approaching at a thunderous gallop was a tall horseman astride an Appaloosa stallion, whooping and hollering as he gracefully flew from one side to the other with all the artistry of a tight-rope walker. Who was this riding at break-neck speed towards the schoolhouse? Her heart began to race. Cloud! Oh, Cloud!

An appreciative noise, many, many *hous* of approval emanated from those who now settled in to watch. The show had begun!

Standing fully upright on the charging back of his appaloosa stallion, long, lean arms raised to the heavens, his red breechcloth rippled between his well-muscled legs, the eagle bone whistle clenched between his teeth. Black braids shone in the glorious sun. The pounding of the hooves rose such a scrim of dust that he appeared elevated above the earth. All this was for her! This was how she was meant to see him, no longer borne by his enemy in chains of defeat.

He gave out exultant whoops and victorious cries. Back-lit by the blazing sun, he stood upright on Wind's fine back, then bent to grasp a handful of his mane. Dropping nimbly to one side as they galloped forward to briefly touch one moccasin foot to the ground, he then vaulted up and over to do so on the other, back and forth, still charging forward to demonstrate those remarkable skills that had made the Plains Indian Horse Warriors the undisputed Kings of the High Plains. Standing for one moment upon the back of his mount, Cloud then leaped nimbly from one foot to traverse from the still galloping horse's moving course to changing over to land on the other, only to repeat, such acrobatics on bareback! He even slid daringly under his horse somehow.

Following him came his young men, mounted up with thundering, pounding, and the whole beautiful herd of Appaloosas. His herd! By now the whole village had been alerted. Look how many horses he had brought home to her.

The village knew what to do. There would be a celebration tonight. Standing Cloud of the Cut Fingers is home from the Pierced Nose People. There will be feasting. Our hearts are high within us today. He has brought us many fine horses today. His Horse Medicine is strong. Wood will be gathered for the bonfires. Men will go out to hunt. But hurry, hurry now; come to the meadow!

It was too much for Anah; she had waited too long. She was transfixed. Hiking up her turkey red petticoat she mounted up, pausing only long enough for Turn Foot to hand over Stands Free to her, then mounted up to head out.

She approached him through the swirling mass of excitement. They encircled one another more than once. Cloud pulled his horse to a dead stop as only a well-trained Buffalo Runner can do. He lifted his son, his *an,* into his arms from where he had been riding on his mother's horse. The boy quickly and deftly sat behind him as the milling throng of horses and men swirled around them. Cloud made no move to dismount, but simply and fixedly looked into the beauty of his wife smiling up at him. "Anah," he had never asked what her name meant, nor had he told her how he liked the sound of it upon his lips. "Anah," She had not broken her gaze from his, "My heart grows wide within me." The smile he so treasured broke then upon her freckled face.

Epilogue

As she was undressing in their fine buffalo skin lodge, her hands went to the much washed, well-worn length of his Dog Rope worn, not upon her waist, where it would be noticeable, but around her hips, where her voluminous skirts would cover it.

He did not have to say a word, his expression said it all as he came forward to place his hands upon it, upon her.

"Now *kola,* my husband," she spoke softly, "You can set me free, free from the battleground that I have staked myself to, waiting for this day, and your return."

When first morning light entered the lodge, it shone upon a conjoined Dog Rope, hanging above their sleeping heads.

Author's Note

Deep in the coastal everglades of south Florida I was given a book on the Plains Indian warriors who were deemed to be the primary leaders during the Red River War of 1875, and were incarcerated at Ft. Marion in St. Augustine, Fl. I had no idea at the time that it would lead to the book you now hold in your hand, or the long journey that it would take me on.

In 2004 I took up residence in Washington, D.C. to obtain a minor teaching degree. Since I would not have the usual familial obligations I decided to try my hand at writing a historical biography of a Cheyenne warrior who had been one of those 73 men imprisoned at Ft. Marion. Washington has some of the best historical research facilities available in the country and the National Museum of The American Indian was just opening, of which I was a charter member.

I love doing research, and I soon had accumulated satchels full of notebooks which I was hauling from one archive to another. As I delved deeper and deeper into the vast array of information that told a vastly different story of what I had learned in any classroom; examining recorded oral accounts scrupulously, "battles" that often translated as "massacres",such as Col Chivington's conversations to fellow officers that preceeded the attack of Nov 29,1864 I became increasingly despondent(and sidetracked from my original intentions of a biography)................

Growing up troubled I kept Kafka's quote "Books are an axe for the frozen sea within" above my writing desk; truly I thought of many books as my friends. Now in my upstairs study hangs this, "Our first teacher is our own heart", a Cheyenne saying.

Disturbed by where my research was taking me,in a despondencyover the nation's past I now had to listen to my heart. I had pieced together a much different story of a turbulent time in a post-civil war. A nation struggling with rapid expansionism, recovering from Depression, dealing with an indigenous culture that they were both trying to re-educate and assimilate by sequestering them on arid reservations, after a policy of warring against them. An extremely complex situation.

Sitting there in the carrels of the Library of Congress I realized a biography was not able to contain my expression. I had researched the relevant facts of an era, but I wanted to illuminate them.(My main objective was to achieve emotional truths that would transcend place and time. I was exceeding my grasp here!) My intention was to write about the tragic demise of a culture and intending to involve the reader emotionally,without expressing bitterness and unresolved sadness. An inveterate reader, I knew my era well, the passing of the magnificent Plains Indian Horse Culture as it met Manifest Destiny, but I wanted to provide much more than I was finding in these dusty tragic annals of historical documents. I realized that I could not continue with a biography; I did not wish to add more negativity to the world by my efforts at documentation.

I had already written a few historical vignettes, character sketches, and retold some native american myths during this timewhile working on the biography. I struggled with the idea do abandoning months of my creative work: Do I give it up? I thought of those Native American traits of character I so admired, one in particular, *woohitika*,Lakota for courage. I had just received permission to march in The Native Nations Procession for the celebration of the new National Museum of The American Indian, my application had been approved and I could walk with the Oneida nation. (I was but one of 25,000 Native Americans that day. (One of my ancestors , Agwrondougwas , was the first white sachem of the Iroquois nation.) More than 80,000 people filled the Mall that day and it gave me the necessary *woohitika* to continue writing. Just what I wasn't sure of!

One evening after that as I sat surrounded by my voluminous notes, gazing at the visual aids I had hung around me as encouragements, still perplexed as how to go forward, I felt two very distinct voices emerge from my imagination. What joy! I opened my heart to them, and began to write the story of Anah and Standing Cloud...a task that occupied and delighted me.

I could not have written this novel without first assembling all the research for a non-fiction account of the period. Once I had the picture, as it is said, I could step outside theframe and let these characters speak for themselves, and to you in my profound belief that some truths can only be told through the emotive power of fiction.

....

The Native American culture of the Plains Indians that was overwhelmed by the rapid expansionism of the dominant culture is slowly recovering, but not without significant difficulties, largely unaddressed. The following are reputable charitable and educational organizations that I have known for over a decade. If you would wish to be better informed please feel free to contact them:

St. Labre Indian School-@stlabre.org
St. Bonaventure Indian Mission &School - @stbonaventuremission.org
Cheyenne River Indian Outreach -@CRIOutreach.org
Red Cloud Indian School- @redcloudschool.org
SoaringEagle-@soaringeagle.org
St. Joseph's Indian School - @stjo.org

If you would so desire to pursue investigating further the historical events mentioned here I would guide you to two excellent books:

Bury My Heart At Wounded Knee, an *Indian History of The American West*, Dee Brown, the illustrated version.
Battlefield & Classroom,*an autobiography by R.H. Pratt,*ed. Robert M. Utley

Mitakuye Oyasin, We are all related
AKB

About the Author

A.K Baumgard holds an MFA in Writing from Vermont College, and has degrees in Anthropology and English, with a life-long interest in Native American Studies. She grew up in the foothills of the Alleghenies, not far from the Warrior Trail. Of mixed blood ancestry, (German and Oneida on her father's side, French and English on her mother's) she is a direct descendant of Agwrondougwas, Good Peter of the Iroquois Nation. She lived and worked in Europe for a decade, resided in the Sangre de Christos, and now lives on the Gulf Coast of Florida with her family. Her main objective in her writings is to achieve emotional truths that transcend place and time.

Printed in the USA
CPSIA information can be obtained
at www.ICGtesting.com
LVHW042354241124
797341LV00001B/15